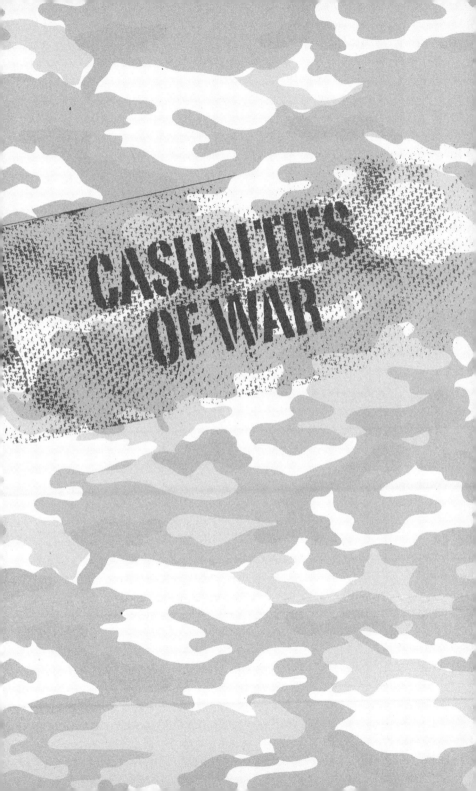

CASUALTIES OF WAR

VIETNAM

BOOK FOUR

CASUALTIES OF WAR

CHRIS LYNCH

SCHOLASTIC PRESS ★ NEW YORK

All rights reserved. Published by Scholastic Press, an imprint of Scholastic Inc., *Publishers since 1920.* SCHOLASTIC, SCHOLASTIC PRESS, and associated logos are trademarks and/or registered trademarks of Scholastic Inc.

Library of Congress
Cataloging-in-Publication Data
Available

ISBN 978-0-545-27023-6
10 9 8 7 6 5 4 3 2 1   13 14 15 16 17
Printed in the U.S.A.   23
First edition, April 2013

The text type was set in Sabon MT.
Book design by Christopher Stengel

CHAPTER ONE

The View from Here

Rudi doesn't write. Ivan doesn't write. Morris writes, but two of the three guys I saw practically every day of my life since I was nine have disappeared from my sight and sound. Despite the fact that we all four have flown to the opposite side of the world to be in this together. We haven't dispersed to the four corners of the earth. We have all dispersed to this same sweaty corner. We stood up to everything together when the biggest threat we faced was having some tough guy look at somebody sideways. Now that the threat is having a tough guy fixing you in the crosshairs of his assault rifle or laying a booby trap to blow all your limbs off, we can't manage to keep in regular contact.

Rudi said all along he wouldn't write to me. Said he was afraid of how I would judge his letter writing. *Afraid.* The numbskull was preparing to slog his way with the US Marine Corp through some of the bloodiest fighting the world has ever seen, and he was afraid of my editorial eye.

But then, he broke down and he wrote. Which was good.

But then, he just stopped. Which was very bad. Better if he just never started than if he started and stopped again. Makes me worry.

Ivan. He never said he wouldn't write. Never said he would, either. I'm not surprised, I guess. Nothing would surprise me about Ivan.

You would think Ivan and I are about as opposite as friends can get, and you'd be essentially correct. But there's more to us than that. If you cut us open and counted our rings you'd find there's a lot more alike about us than different. Like most people, I fear and respect Ivan, which is pretty much exactly what he would like to hear. But I also *know* him, which he might find a little less welcome of an idea.

He is, more than anybody I have ever met, the true sensitive brute. He's the only person I know who could, and would — and has — beat the daylights out of a guy for hurting his *feelings*. I would strongly suggest to the North Vietnamese that they not hurt Ivan's feelings.

It's hard to explain Rudi and me. Hard for me, that is — Rudi'd never be able to manage it. Probably the thing that says the most with the least about us is that, when Rudi was threatened with getting kept back —

for a second time — toward the end of seventh grade, he didn't tell his hero, Ivan, or his unofficial nanny, Morris. He came to me. He had to get respectable grades for the final two months of the year, homework and exams, in science and math. Not only did we work side by side like the Wright brothers hammering thoughts into that head of his. Not only did I basically do approximately seventy percent of the homework assignments just to ensure he made the minimum. Not only did I give countless hours of time that could have been spent thinking about Evelyn DelValle.

On top of all that, I did C-level work. I hated myself for two months.

And we are the only two people who know about it, to this day. By mutual agreement.

And then there is Morris.

Morris is at the other end of the communication scale. He is a Navy man, radioman, and self-appointed guardian angel for our group. Morris is the guy who holds the four of us together. It was his idea to make the one-for-all-and-all-for-one pact that if one of us was going to Vietnam then we all were. And it was his stated aim right from the start of this great and awful experiment that he was going to watch over the rest of us. First from his ship, the USS *Boston* stationed off the coast. And now, in a different way, over the airwaves and from a much smaller boat, a river monitor. He's the friend monitor, on the river.

The reality, though, is somewhat different. We all know that, if anybody's watching over anybody else here, it's the Air Force. And that's me. I'm flying over everybody, and watching.

And I don't much like what I see. Because what I see is danger and destruction in all its variety and in every direction. This country is gorgeous — I mean, *gorgeous* — to the point where I spend half my time thinking I could come back here and live once the war is over.

If there's anything left of it, when the war is over.

What I would like to see is the four of us. Together again. Morris — of course, Morris — has a grand plan to make this happen. Not just eventually, when we get home. But soon, here in Vietnam.

It's a long shot, but if it is possible to get something accomplished by pure will and goodness, then Morris is the guy to get it done.

Meanwhile, the rest of us will proceed with fighting this thing.

———————— ★ ————————

Maybe part of the problem is that they make war *sound* so cool.

I was delivered by Hercules to Phu Cat.

That is a true factual statement, and every time I say it, it gives me a small flutter of thrill because I've never said anything that sounded so slick in my life. It sounds far cooler than "a plane dropped me off in South Vietnam," which would be civilian-speak for the same operation. *I was delivered by Hercules to Phu Cat.* The guy who can say that about himself gets style points just for living, and I can say it.

There is a lot of that kind of thing, in the military generally, and in the United States Air Force specifically.

Operation Rolling Thunder. How does that not grab you? It grabs me, and I don't even want to be here. How about Operation Arc Light? Steel Tiger? Barrel Roll, Eagle Thrust, Bolo, Flaming Dart? A guy's got to feel charged up knowing he is flying as part of something that sounds so sure of itself and potent, doesn't he? Especially if he goes riding in on, say, an F-4 Phantom, a Super Sabre, or a Thunderchief. If you're dropping tonnage on people from a B-52 Stratofortress it's a wonder those people don't just surrender out of sheer awe and intimidation before the bombs even hit the ground.

But, they don't.

It's almost the scariest part of the whole war. And that is saying something, with all the scary, scary parts of this war. Nobody over on their side appears to be quitting or even thinking about quitting, no matter how much we shoot and blast and bomb and torch their coast, their highlands, their riverbanks, their open plains, and their jungles.

I know this, because I'm seeing it. Because I'm doing it.

I'm fighting my portion of the war from the sky, aboard a C-123 "Provider" aircraft, which right away defies the notion that the military doesn't have a sense of humor. What the Provider *provides* is Agent Orange, one of a range of defoliants we use to burn the life out of the vegetation of this dense and lush place. Without the vegetation, the enemy cannot hide out there and move supplies around and kill our guys at will. I understand the aim. The aim, anyway, I understand.

We always get shot at. Always. Operation Ranch Hand involves flying big aircraft, slowly, at low altitude, into areas that are by definition hot with enemy combatants. I know, where can I get some of that, right?

My father and my mother and my sisters all thought I was an idiot for giving up my student deferment to volunteer to fight in Vietnam. We are a university-proud family. I think my dad graduated from Tufts when he was about twelve or something. I have one cousin who went to a technical college back in Boston and the family only speaks of him in hushed tones, like he went to the Walpole State Prison rather than the Wentworth Institute of Technology.

"We're not better than anybody else, Hans," I said when explaining my enlistment to my father. He's always been Hans to me. He, like most everybody, calls me by my last name, Beck.

"Hnnn," he said.

"What does that mean? Hnnn?"

"It means don't do it. Don't be a foolish kid, Beck, because you are not a foolish kid. It is nice that you have friends, and that you are loyal to those friends . . ."

Hans is not the type of father who leaves spaces in his speech casually.

"But . . . ?"

"The universe has better plans for you, Beck."

"Better than it has for the other guys, is that it?"

The bigger the pause, the less the casual.

"Hans? Honest, now. Please."

"Fine, maybe it has other plans for Morris. But war has *always* been the plan for Ivan. If war didn't exist, it would have to be invented to give him something to do. As for Rudi . . ." He sighed, exhaling long enough for three lungs. "He's a good boy."

"He's a good boy, right. They're all good boys. I'm a good boy."

"You are," he said, and there was a slight crack in his normal certainty about everything, always. "You are a good boy, my boy."

"And we good boys made a pledge to one another and good boys keep their word to one another, don't they, Hans?"

What occurred then was not a pause. It was a stop. My dad leaned forward, looked at the floor, clasped his hands together with his index fingers upright like he was going to do *Here is the church, and here is the steeple, open the doors and see all the people.*

"I am not antiwar, son," he said as if he was having his blood drained off at the same time. "I am anti-*you* in *this* war."

I had no strong comeback to that.

"We are a family of logic," he went on. "Sense is what we believe in, and this makes no rational sense. This . . . is kids' stuff. I'm sorry, but this — pledges and promises and bad decisions, it's all boyhood dreaming and nothing to do with the real world."

We are a family of logic. It is one of the things I am proudest of. Which is why, again, I had no comeback here that would explain this well enough.

"I know," I said. "I understand. Still, I have to go."

"I know," he said. "I understand. Still, I had to try."

We shook hands. My father is a hugger. It was the saddest moment of my life when I had to trade that in for a handshake. Then we agreed that we were both too cowardly to tell my mom and sisters so weeks went by before suspicious-looking mail came for me and my mother stood there in my bedroom doorway, the letter in one hand and her other hand pointing determinedly up through the ceiling and the roof and the sky, to the sky beyond that sky.

"You should not be over there fighting. You should be up there, on Apollo missions to the moon."

I came very close to pointing out that all those astronauts started out just where I was starting out. But my mother has sharp debating skills and I didn't want to hear about how the Vietnam War was not the Korean War. The quickest way to get killed would probably be to doubt your mission before you start it.

Instead, I went for optimism, and my University of Wisconsin–Madison scholarship which was being held for me while I served.

"Madison will still be there when I come back, Ma," I said.

Which did not turn out to be the comfort I had intended, since it hinted at things being or not being, people coming back or not. Which set off all kinds of everything.

That is how I still see her all the time. Frozen there, wheezing, weeping, her fears spilling onto my rug, her finger pointing to her hopes in the sky.

CHAPTER TWO

Only You Can Prevent Forests

I am in the sky.

But just barely. It is early morning and we are low, barely above the treetops. We have to spray the stuff before the murderous Southeast Asian sun really heats up. Because then the ground cooks and what we get is our own potent herbicide rising right back up to us on a cloud of misty Agent Orange nastiness.

It's not actually orange. The name refers to the canister it comes in. To differentiate it from its pals Agents White, Purple, and Blue. They are all fine, effective products as these things go, but there is no question, Orange is the star.

Despite our best efforts, we get some of it back anyway. It's unavoidable that some of it wafts back up to us. If we empty our entire one-thousand gallon tank of the stuff and a little bit comes back to us, well, what's a few gallons of poison among USAF comrades?

But we all agree we would like to defoliate ourselves as little as possible.

This crew and I flew our first sorties out of Phu Cat farther north before they moved us down deeper into the south of the country, where we could help out the poor saps fighting on and around the rivers. The Mekong Delta had become a kind of shooting gallery where Vietcong guerillas would unload day and night on the thousands of smaller craft we had working the waterways. There was just too much heavy leafy cover there. And with the 315th Special Operations Wing operating out of both Phan Rang and Phu Cat, it was easy enough to call on my squad, the 12th Special Operations Squadron — we're all in the same SOS family — to come on down and lend a hand.

So here we are. Ranch Hands, lending a hand.

And I still can't believe what I'm seeing, and doing.

We are a four-man crew on the 123, the pilot and copilot up front and the other two of us rattling around the spacious accommodation of the aircraft sometimes lovingly referred to as "Thunder Pig." It's a fat plane, and the two junior crewmen, myself and a guy named McGuire — who everyone just calls "Fingers" because his thumbs look like extra fingers — do a variety of jobs. We are loadmasters, making sure whatever is on board is placed and balanced so that the plane can fly right. We are mechanics, making small-to-medium repairs and adjustments to the gear. Above all, we see to it that our payload gets squirted where and when it's supposed to be.

We tend to have more work to do on the ground before we take off and after we land than we do when it's spray time. So what happens a lot of the time is, we watch.

"Whenever we're up here I feel it a little bit more," I say to Fingers as we watch the white streamings of Orange spread over the canopy from our five rear jets.

"Please, Beck, no," he says, staring off. "This job is hard enough without you narrating everything we do while we're doing it."

"But look at it, Fingers," I say.

"I'm looking at it. Doesn't it look like I'm looking at it?"

"It's just so gorgeous," I say. It's not even like I am seeing it for the first time every time. It's like I've been here for a thousand years. Second time up, I felt like I knew this countryside like I knew my backyard.

We are practically skimming the tops of the trees we're killing. I can just about feel it, like a dog getting his belly rubbed.

I can just about forget what we're doing . . . except I can't.

Ping! P-p-p-p-p-p-p-p-ping-bang-crack.

We are hit. We are hit lots, and it keeps coming. Machine-gun fire, mostly, though now and then a surface-to-air missile whizzes past close enough to whistle in my ear.

This is routine. This is standard. This is my life.

Bu-hooom!

That one was deadly close, and reminds me of another of the 123's nicknames: "Mortar Magnet."

The jets are off now, and we are banking hard to get out of the area as quickly as the big bird can manage. We have one A-1 Skyraider for escort, and I watch from the side as he pours fire down on one of the positions hitting us. But it's just a diversion to buy us time, to get us up and out because, really, it sometimes seems the 123 is nothing but target practice for these guys.

Once we have climbed to a safe height and are headed back to base, I steal another minute to just peer down at the country once again.

From a great height it takes on still another level of beauty. The foliage is so dense and lush, right up to the banks of thousands of miles of rivers, it looks like a green nature jigsaw puzzle down there.

But it's starting to show, too. As we return to areas we have showered before, I can see the difference, the effect we are having. There's a brown patch, and a black patch where it was green a few weeks ago. There is a bald patch where before it was full, overgrown.

Courtesy of the Providers.

On the ground, the four of us take a small tour of the aircraft, inside and out. Some of those rounds have torn clear through one side of the fuselage and out the other.

"Huh," Captain Avery says, sounding both surprised and matter-of-fact. He has three fingers stuck in a hole in the plane's underbelly. "This job is dangerous after all."

Lieutenant Hall, the copilot, chimes in, "Good thing we've got the seamstresses on duty."

He means Fingers and me. Because we spend so much of our time doing "patches." Our plane already has so many sheet-metal Band-Aids — without them, we'd sound like a giant clarinet flying through the air.

"Yes, sir," I say to the indirect order. The pilots are already headed back to quarters by the time I answer.

"You know," Fingers says to me as we sit together in the cockpit, "if I was as smart as you, I sure would have figured out a way to be somewhere else at this point in time."

I am replacing a gauge on the pilot's side of the instrument panel. A bullet appears to have come right up through the floor between the two seats and shattered the thing without the captain even saying boo about it. Capt. Avery has been flying since Korea, and he acts like his job is nothing more complicated than being a milkman.

I have the new dial snapped into place but I pause before securing it with the screws. I am in the captain's seat. I look over the scores of dials and switches, miles of wires, and bunches of buttons and levers. Then I look past all that, through the glass and out over the airfield ahead and the wild countryside beyond that.

"What is *smart* even supposed to mean in this situation anyway?" I ask him. "I mean, really, I've been hearing forever about how clever I am. I shipped over here as part of a deal with three other guys who have spent their whole lives acting as if I was the answer man to every question they ever had or ever would have. My pal Rudi hated it when I knew the answer to every history or math or English question without looking it up. Drove him demented. We were halfway through high school before he decided I wasn't cheating, like book smarts were some kind of card trick.

"How can you not love a guy who asks you questions, then gets mad at you for knowing the answers? And then keeps on asking?

"And so what happens? I get over here and I get sucked in. All the way in, and instantly. Into this," I say, and grip the controls of the plane like I have just been handed the keys to the universe itself.

Fingers laughs, taking the copilot's controllers. "You do get a weird look whenever you get in the big chair."

"I know. How did this happen? How did a guy like me wind up getting swept away by choppers and jets and things that go boom just like some four-year-old boy?"

He keeps smiling, gripping the controls and staring straight ahead as if he were really flying.

"'Cause it's so cool?" he says with a shrug.

That is the kind of thing I should have a bright and sophisticated answer for. Back in Boston I am sure I would have. I hope that some day, in Madison, I will.

It is basically never quiet here at the base at Phan Rang. No matter what routine maintenance job you might be doing on a given day, you are never allowed to let yourself pretend you're just working on your car in your own driveway. If the big Huey helicopters aren't dropping in and jumping off then it's the fairly awesome F-100 Super Sabre screeching down the runway. It was the first supersonic jet the USAF flew, and as the term implies, it is a sonic assault to be around when one lands or takes off. AC-47 and AC-119 aircraft add to the fun, but there probably isn't a more awesome spectacle for my money than watching the big beast B-57 bombers lift off with their massive payloads — then return sometime later with it all gone, having delivered their gifts to the communists.

It is with no empty pride whatsoever that I say I know all these machines intimately, because I have become a fan. I watch whenever I don't have to be doing something, and I visit each aircraft when it is similarly unengaged. I stare, and I poke and I probe the instrument panels, the wiring, the radar gear, and the weapon systems, the way a medical intern studies the bones and muscles and cardiovascular systems of the human body.

Doctors study bodies to better serve those bodies, to keep them running fit, to help them live better, longer, more effective lives. Which is more or less what I am doing. The big difference, of course, is that doctors are helping flesh-and-blood human beings.

So why am I slavishly devoting myself to the apparatus of war? For what purpose?

I have an answer to that. I do. It's because I know what is *not* my purpose here. I have decided: I am not killing anybody.

I am aware that spraying chemicals by the thousands of gallons is kind of a funny way of not killing people. But, short of mutiny, it is the best I can do. I have made a decision to fulfill my duty without deliberately and consciously taking one person's life. My goal when I leave Vietnam will be to have learned everything possible about the machinery of organized killing, without actually killing.

That's my pledge to myself, to keep me right. It was a pledge that got me into this thing, and it's a pledge that's going to get me out.

As we approach our target destination, we cruise at an altitude of about three thousand feet. As usual, I spend whatever time I can just watching, taking in the wonder of the land before me. From this height it is all shapes and colors, green fields and snaking waterways, and you could imagine yourself working on a commercial airliner ferrying people to the holiday of a lifetime in Hawaii, or Bali, or India.

Until we begin the drop.

At a rate of twenty-five hundred feet a minute, we scream down out of the sky, the force of the atmospheric change feeling like it might pop your head right off. We plummet until we hit about five hundred feet then we level off, then get to three hundred, two hundred, and we open up the jets and start pouring the Agent Orange on the head of this triple-canopy jungle. We lay out a spray two hundred and forty feet wide, and we keep laying it down for a strip nearly nine miles long. The canopies, at fifty, one hundred, and one hundred and fifty feet high, need to be hit repeatedly to get full penetration so sometimes, like today, we return, as if to a favorite old holiday spot. This is the second go-round for this strip, and already I am shocked at the difference from just a couple of weeks ago.

It's as if the jungle's head has a great nasty scab all over it. That top layer of foliage has been gradually dying since we last visited, the green fading to brown and gray and black. Big wide leaves, clearly visible from this low altitude, are all curled in on themselves and rotting like toast dunked for too long in a cup of cocoa.

And I keep remembering, this is *South* Vietnam. We are burning the life out of the country we are here to fight for. I am watching from my prime window seat as we personally take the most vivid Technicolor landscape I have ever seen, and singe it beyond recognition.

But I'm doing it for Morris. He is down there on his Zippo boat, on that brown Mekong, and he is trying to look out for Ivan — who probably doesn't need it — and Rudi — who almost certainly does. And Morris is in a lot of danger from fighters on those banks under heavy cover. And if I can help out Morris, a guy who would never hurt a soul except to defend his friends, then my work is good work.

Even if the Vietcong don't see it that way and the North Vietnamese don't see it that way.

And if the South Vietnamese don't see it that way?

We go into our sharply banked turn, our climb back up the sky, meaning we are headed back to base. I watch, listening to the machine-gun fire once again shredding the air to ribbons all along the length of the aircraft. Even though we only have fairly small windows on the sides of the 123, with the top-mounted wings we still have pretty good visibility. What comes into view now is one of our two escort A-1 Skyraiders. It is a single-seat propeller-driven plane that does a whole lot more dirty work than you'd think possible, what with all the more sophisticated stuff in the sky around here. Mostly, these guys identify where the anti-aircraft fire is coming from and harass and antagonize those ground forces enough to let us get in and out relatively unharmed.

The gunfire is becoming fainter and less frequent as we turn for home, and the Skyraider pilot actually drifts close enough to us that I can see him there in his glass bubble of a cockpit. And he can obviously see me, because as I throw up a two-handed thumbs-up thank-you for a job well done, he answers me with a big one-thumb salute back. Presumably he needs the other hand for piloting.

And then:

Schoooommm! Pu-powwww.

My forehead bounces hard off the window in front of me and not for the first time around here I cannot believe what I see.

A surface-to-air missile has come screeching out of nowhere, and I watch with an unobstructed view as it approaches, reaches, then annihilates the A-1. And its pilot.

The guy is practically frozen — is, in my mind, frozen forever — in the thumbs-up when the missile shreds right through the fuselage and the cockpit, exiting out the top of the glass bubble and spraying fire and shrapnel and fifty million pieces of USAF personnel into the hot Vietnamese atmosphere.

I remain attached to that window. I see the wreckage spinning and smoking toward the ground, the whole scene shrinking rapidly as we continue our flight path home.

On board the Provider, there is the spookiest stillness you could imagine. I listen, smell, *feel* for any sign, any sensation that indicates we have registered the horror that has just occurred.

Nothing. The Thunder Pig engines rumble on, but that's it.

CHAPTER THREE

Eyes of the World

It's just a job. That's what I keep hearing. That's what Capt. Avery says, every day, with his words and even more so with his actions. It is not so much that he has become accustomed to the brutality of war. It's more like he chooses not to acknowledge it.

Which is something you can do, I suppose, from up above it all. It's kind of like stepping to the edge of a cliff or a really high building. They always tell you: Just don't look down, and it's like you're standing in your own backyard. We are the only branch of the service that really even has a chance of flying high and pretending we don't see a thing.

Only, I can't do that.

I see it. I see everything.

Right now I am seeing my team, and my beautiful Thunder Pig, getting ready to do it all over again. The engines are thumping, and Fingers is doing all the external safety checks, along with another mechanic I know from sight but nothing else.

That is how it is with everybody here, to be honest. I am friendly enough with all the guys stationed here, as if Phan Rang Air Base is one of those pleasant small towns where everybody recognizes everybody else enough to say hi, even if they don't know each other's names.

I don't want to know anybody I don't have to know. I am not going to kill anybody, and I am not going to lose anybody. If you don't know them then you don't lose them no matter what happens to them. I told this to Fingers about twenty minutes ago as we were suiting up, since, really, there is no way around me knowing him and so he is my complete and sole confidant. A guy certainly should have one of those.

"You're kinda mental already, Beck," he said when I informed him of my plan to know nobody. I kept the *no killing* bit to myself for the time being. "A guy's not supposed to go mental until he's been in-country a few months longer than this. But I suppose maybe because you're a brainbox type you'll be ahead of schedule on pretty much everything, huh?"

"I'm not mental, Fingers," I told him. "I am totally, one hundred percent rational."

"See, now there you go. If you are totally, one hundred percent rational, or even think you are, in the middle of all we're in the middle of . . . then you are nuts, my friend."

That made me laugh, which I couldn't possibly come up with enough money to properly pay him for.

"Thanks," I said. He was suited up already, striding out of the barracks.

"Is this about that guy, the A-1 pilot from the other day?" he asked as he paused in the doorway.

"It's about all the guys," I said, "from all the days."

He nodded, and nodded again. "Okay. Fair enough."

I finished getting myself together and made my way across the base to the Provider, where I stand about thirty yards short of the plane. I think I am only watching for a very brief period of time, but then I put it all together in my head and I realize that I have seen, with my eyes, Fingers and the other no-name — no offense — guy do the whole safety check, which takes the better part of a half hour. And I have also seen with those same eyes Capt. Avery make his way across the tarmac, growing in my vision, growing as he is striding, until he is standing in front of me, my eyes reflecting big in his aviator glasses.

"Beck," he says.

"Captain," I say.

"Did you purchase a ticket for this air show today?"

"Sorry, sir," I say. "I was just . . . I still find the aircraft, all of them, just mesmerizing. The time just got away from me. I'll be right —"

I move to walk past him and get to my job, but he stops me short with a flat palm on my chest.

"Sir?" I say, looking down at his hand.

"Take some time for yourself, Beck."

"Oh, no, sir," I say, feeling suddenly wrong. Weak and embarrassing and exposed and beneath myself. I go to walk past him toward my assignment again.

He flat-palms me again.

"That's two," he says, still friendly enough, but a little edgier. "Once more and we'll call it insubordination. Now, I would like you to sit this one out, kid. We've got it covered. We ain't doin' nothing but crop dusting anyhow, right?"

"Right, sir."

"That, airman, is my favorite phrase, so could you kindly repeat it for me?"

"Right, sir."

"Great. Have a good afternoon, Beck. Cleanse your emotional palette, and come back to me tomorrow ready to take on the world again."

Again? Was I really ready to take on the world before?

I watch the captain strut back to his aircraft and then disappear inside it. Fingers gives me a wave before he and my temporary replacement also board and the door snaps shut behind them. The big beast starts rolling immediately, creeping then crawling then muscling itself down the runway, and from this perspective I think it is a wonder we ever get airborne in that chunky piece of machinery. But there it goes, fast enough, off the ground, and up, up, and gone.

I stand, staring, still with my helmet and flak jacket on.

"All dressed up and nowhere to go?" a voice shouts from right behind me, and I jump.

"What?" I say, turning quickly to see another airman about a foot shorter than me, about a foot behind me. "Ah, yeah, something like that."

"Carney," he says, extending a hand.

I weigh the worth of bothering to explain my *no buddies* policy versus the relative ease of just going with the flow.

"Beck," I say, shaking his hand. *Acquiesce* has always been a favorite word of mine.

"What did you do to get yourself grounded?" he asks.

"Saw a guy get blasted into an infinite number of pieces while he was in the process of giving me a thumbs-up." I look up into the sky where the tail of my plane is still visible. "I'm half expecting the thumb to still come down here someplace."

He puts a hand on my shoulder, which I don't like much, but I understand the impulse so I look back down at him once I stop staring at his hand on my shoulder.

"And it bothered you," he says.

"Yeah. I suppose it did."

He shakes his head sadly, but I don't actually think he's all that sad.

"You're one of them hopeless *humanity* types," he says.

"Unfortunately, yes," I say. "A sad waste of good government funds, that's me. And you? What's your story? *Carney* an actual name or are you a circus freak of some kind?"

He pauses for noise as an F-100 screams down the runway and into the sky.

"Carney is my actual name, but I *am* a two-digit midget if that's any consolation."

He is quite small, which is why he's giving me a raised *go ahead, I dare you* eyebrow right now. But really I'm feeling more jealous than provocative. A two-digit midget is somebody who has fewer than a hundred days left in-country.

"Jerk," I say, which is the reasonable response to somebody flaunting that.

"Thanks," he says with a big smile, which is a reasonable response as well.

"When do you ship out?"

"Three weeks."

"Keeping your head down now, I imagine."

"Don't you know it. Let's get off this runway, huh?"

"Yeah I was just going to —"

"Right, you got a day off. You could hang around with me if you like."

We are walking back in the direction of the barracks. Like with most everyone around here, I have seen Carney around without ever learning the first thing about him. I pull my helmet off.

"No offense," I say, "but why would I want to do that?"

"Because I'm smart, like you."

Okay, this is not going where I expected it to.

I stop there on the path to my quarters, and I turn on him. "What are you talking about? You don't even know me."

"Come on, pal," he says, slapping me on the arm, "this is Phan Rang Air Base, the greatest little American town in Vietnam. Everybody in PRAB knows everybody."

He's actually spooking me. It is the height of the workday here, and planes are coming and going quicker than trains at South Station back home in Boston. The noise is deafening. I shout to be sure he hears, and understands.

"Then how come I don't know you?" I holler.

"You do!" he shouts back, grinning nuttily.

"I don't!"

"Ah, sure ya do," he yells again.

"Right," I say, waving. "See ya around, Carney."

He really is a carnival freak, I'm thinking as I march away from him and the planes and choppers and noise and into my free day of solitude.

"The library," Carney says, rushing to keep up.

"The barracks," I say, pointing in a *land-ho!* fashion toward my destination.

"No," he says. "The library. Where you know me from."

The base has a particularly good library, with about ten thousand titles in it. I spend a good bit of time there and have seen almost nobody else making use of the place.

"I don't."

"You do. And the education center."

Another fine facility, which is so underused you go there basically to avoid people. You can even sign up to take classes there through the University of Maryland, which I briefly considered doing except that my father said enlisting was bad enough but *U. Maryland* was just more than he could bear.

Carney has accompanied me into the barracks now. It's not even his barracks.

"What's wrong with you?" I ask him, confident that he will have an answer for me, confident he has been asked this before.

"Nothing, man. I'm just thinking we should stick together, guys like you and me."

"I don't know about guys like me, but I'm pretty certain there are no other guys like you."

I get to my bunk, start stripping off the flight gear and stowing it away. When I turn, he's standing there looking both a little nutty and, surprisingly, wise.

"Come on, Beck. In my waning weeks I think it might be refreshing to spend time with guys who spend time in libraries. Know what I mean?"

I have to admit that I do know what he means. I have no great desire to do a lot of socializing, but if

I have to talk to somebody it might as well be somebody who wants to talk about something besides war.

"Okay," I say, and start walking back out into the sunshine.

"Excellent," he says, clapping once loudly and following hot on my heels.

"However," I add, "you might want to stop saying that so much, about being a short timer. Don't you watch movies at all? Every time a soldier starts on that *almost home* stuff . . ."

"He gets his head shot off?"

"Something like that, yeah."

"I'm surprised at you, Beck. I mean, the other guys have been telling me to cool it for just that reason, but I didn't figure you to be the superstitious type. Or a fan of corny Hollywood films, for that matter. Maybe you're just jealous because . . . I'm going home! Home! Very soon!"

Carney is having himself a good time as we walk across the compound, side by side until I give him a good shove.

"Keep that up, and I might kill you myself," I tell him. "Anyway, I like those movies okay, and I am not at all superstitious, and could you please just not walk too close? When the time comes, I don't want to get your brain splattered all over me."

He finds this funny. Can't blame him. I imagine everything sounds like a great laugh when you're going home.

Airman Carney, it turns out, is a bomb dump and flight line worker. It sounds to me like his job is fairly self-explanatory, but I am going to explain it anyway. Because I realize now that I've lost some of my regular civilian understanding of things like language. Just when I start thinking that the Air Force has actually improved on the clarity and directness of English as I previously knew it, something like this comes along:

Remember that you are a guest in this country. The Vietnamese have a sensitivity and pride just as you, and simply because their customs are different from yours in certain respects doesn't mean that they are any less correct. The people feel precisely the same emotions that you feel, so always keep in mind that you are here to help them.

— SHELDON B. THOMPSON,
Colonel, USAF
Commander

That is from the welcome letter I received on my arrival at Phan Rang. They are fine words, and I have no reason to doubt the colonel's sincerity in writing them.

But if I am a guest, then I am about the rudest and most horrifying guest anybody ever invited in anywhere. Every day I get in my aircraft and set about laying waste to my host's beautiful home. And every day I get my orders to do it again. I mean, we are trying here, we really are. But it seems like we're trying to exterminate the rats under somebody's porch by burning his house down.

Words. Funny things.

So, Airman Carney is a bomb dump and flight line worker, which means he is responsible for getting some of the most dangerous items in the history of the world from one point to another. Phan Rang, in addition to having a lot of other advantages, has a small mountain plunked right into the middle of it. Okay, the mountain wasn't *plunked* so much as we built ourselves around it, but the *plunked* version is closer to the way the military likes to see things. The mountain is a helpful thing to us in that it allows us to have one side for the flight line — where all the aircraft take off and land — along with most other functions of the base. Then, on the other, is the bomb dump. *Dump* is a bit too blunt sounding, since much more sensitive stuff happens there. For instance, the lugs, booster, and fins are all attached to the bombs over at the dump, turning them from simple explosives into precision-deadly weapons. The bombs are then loaded onto trucks and she-be-comin'-round-the-mountained to the holding area beside the flight line.

"Feel like freelancing?" Carney asks me as I stare up and down a row of freshly assembled M-118 3000-pound GP bombs. He has taken me on the ten minute trek to the dump site and it is the first time I have had a good look at the place, from the ground.

I continue staring, dumbfounded yet again by the machinery of warfare. I am sure that my mouth is hanging open in wonder, and if any of my sisters were here they would slap it shut with a *pop*. But up close, this stuff is awesome, weirdly beautiful with its sleekness, its quiet ferocity like a pride of dozing lions.

"Hey-hey," Carney yells, trying to snap me out of it. And he certainly achieves that when he runs a few steps and actually leaps onto one of the bombs, like a cowboy mounting a horse.

"Are you *nuts*?" I say, running backward, as if ten

feet of distance will in any way protect my body parts if that big beast explodes.

"See?" he says, laughing, bouncing up and down a little in the saddle. "Nothing to worry about. That stuff's all backward in the movies. Stick with me, genius, two-digit midgets are invincible, I tell ya!"

"Fine," I say, "tell me all about it. But tell me from off that thing, okay?"

"Okay," he says, hopping down and coming to meet me a safe distance from the bombs. "But I need to be delivering some of these blue meanies now. Wanna come on my rounds? It'll be fun. We're like lethal milkmen."

I look again to the line of M-118s. I could swear I hear them growl lowly.

"Who's getting these, then?" I ask.

"F-100s, baby. We supply the Super Sabres. Ever been in one?"

"Nope."

"Cool. Let's go."

We go. I ride shotgun in the ammo truck, which is more like a tractor with an open back lined with bombs. The trip — from the relative quiet of the bomb dump, around the mountain into the hive of activity that is the base proper — takes only five minutes, but I'm jumpy as a cat the whole time. Every little bump — and there are about a billion of them — makes me suck breath loudly through my teeth and look back over my shoulder at the load. As if I will be able to see one or more of the things giving off some kind of sign that it's about to blow.

"Relax, will ya?" Carney says, laughing. "Even if one of 'em is gonna pop — which it isn't because, remember, I'm invincible — but even if it is, by the time it does there's not gonna be enough of you left to do anything about it. Right? Get it?"

"Yeah, Carney, I get it. Good job relaxing me."

"Ha," he says, making the last turn and coming to a stop in front of the flight tower. "That's what buddies are for."

Buddies.

He hops out of the truck and goes into the flight tower. All munitions deliveries have to be registered there so they can keep track of where everything is at all times. There are several trucks ahead of us and several behind all doing the same thing, delivering different types of explosives to different types of aircraft. It's a lot to keep straight.

Carney is back a minute later, and in another minute we are pulling up to the revetment, basically the walled-in parking area reserved for the F-100s. There are more than sixty of the big birds stationed here, and they come and go constantly. One passes us on its way out to the flight line, and Carney waves, like a trucker waving at another trucker. Though I have no idea whether anybody on the plane waves back.

We slowly make our way along a line of about a dozen Sabres, until we steer into the slot where the bombs are to be left for the ground crews to do their thing, attaching them to the underbellies of the planes. There are three guys who appear to be waiting for us. They stand hands-on-hips, watching as we approach. One of them theatrically checks his watch.

As we pull to a stop, the three approach us with big swagger (you see a lot of that around here). Suddenly, they all recognize the driver and go into a wild frenzy of mock panic.

"Holy moly, it's the midget!" the first guy yells, and they run in the opposite direction, covering their heads and rear ends as if being attacked from both above and below. They scream loud enough to almost drown out the shriek of a departing AC-119 gunship.

While the ground crew makes a scene, Carney turns calmly to address my probably stunned face.

"You see, they are very afraid of me. Because of the curse of the short-timer. I saw these same guys play touch football with a rocket-propelled grenade one time. And they act like they're deeply unsettled by my presence."

We both laugh as we hop down from the truck. The three wiseguys come back and greet Carney in a more friendly fashion, punching him in the arms hard enough to surely leave bruises.

"This is my pal, Beck," Carney says.

I'm not sure whether *pal* is a promotion or a demotion from *buddy*, but it doesn't matter. I get punched mercilessly up and down my arms. These guys are like really dangerous, muscular puppies. They are instantly frightening and likeable and they do not offer or seem to recognize names. Makes them even more likeable.

The shipment of bombs lies there on the rack like a bunch of steely dolphins as the lead wiseguy surveys them up and down. He seems pleased enough after doing a full circuit, clapping approval and waving the others over.

"Gentlemen, tools!" he calls with some enthusiasm.

From their many fatigue pockets, the other guys produce cans of spray paint and bright markers and two-inch brushes and several pots of paint the size of soda cans.

"Would you care to join in?" one of them asks, holding a brush and a tin of banana-yellow paint in my direction.

"Join in what?" I ask as all the others, including Carney, approach the bombs.

"Decorating, of course. I mean, we are warriors, but not barbarians."

I receive my tools and stand there like a numbskull while the others take to the task as if this were possibly the most important job in the entire war and certainly the most pleasurable. In short order, the explosives have mustaches below their nose cones and eyebrows arched above them. Some have teeth, some have gills, others wings. There are flowers, and skull and crossbones, and one impressive red rendition of the New York Yankees' logo.

I just stare, as if this is all so foreign, and not at all similar to a hundred primary school art classes I've participated in. Aside from an urge to deface the Yankees thing, I don't feel anything like inspiration.

Until they start with the text.

I get up closer to inspect the bombs individually and read the words as the guys write them. There is a lot of laughter as one idea after another takes shape.

Who cut the cheese?

Are we there yet?

Don't make me take my belt off, Charlie.

I swear, it was like this when I got here.

Without having painted a stroke, I have been swept up in the spirit, in a way I have not felt since I arrived in-country. There is something about the goofiness, the lack of anger in the glowing words and pictures, that catches me by surprise and bizarrely makes me feel good about these guys and even the Air Force itself, stupid as that sounds.

"What are you, anti-beauty?" one of the guys says to me as I stand there mutely staring. They have left one bomb untouched, but I know if I hesitate any longer that will not be the case.

And somehow, a big opportunity will be missed.

It feels like the pressure is on now because I waited and now everybody is watching me. The first thing that pops in my mind is:

I apologize.

I get as far as the *I* before I freeze. How many different ways can that be taken? Probably as many ways as there are eyes to read it. I feel like a guest — there's that word again — only now a guest at this party that seems to have a good enough heart in spite of its mission.

I can't apologize. But I can pick up at that *I.*

So in big foot-tall banana letters I color that bomb along its side with:

I PLEDGE ALLEGIANCE.

There is silence, at least among the crew. Jet engines continue scorching the air coming and going around us.

I step back and admire my work, feeling like the guys behind me are doing the same.

"Your friend's kind of a drag," one of them says to Carney.

I slump a little.

"No, he's not," Carney says, coming up behind me and putting a grip on both of my shoulders, which I don't complain about. This time. "He's just an intellectual."

"I am neither," I insist, though in this group I probably do qualify as both. I walk to the unblemished side of my bomb — *my bomb?* — and with great flourishes of paint I inscribe:

Truth, Justice, and Evelyn DelValle.

I straighten up and step back from my handiwork once more, certain I have scored a direct hit this time.

Gradually they all walk around to see what I've come up with.

There is something less than a rousing response.

"Is she *really* pretty?" one of the guys asks.

"Profoundly so," I say triumphantly.

"Okay, then," another one says, before they all start unloading the bombs from the truck with the help of the mini-crane.

Carney comes and stands beside me, looking at the words, then at the guys, then at the words again.

"It's not really funny, though," he says.

"Does it have to be?"

He sighs, like there are just some things a guy should know, which I don't know. "I'm sorry, I really should have befriended you earlier. I'm not sure how much I can help you in the time I have left."

"What?" I say, leaving him behind to go help with the unloading. "Should I have drawn Bugs Bunny or something instead?"

"That would have been perfect," he says, catching up. "Just like one of the guys."

Then I'm glad I didn't do it. I don't want to be one of the guys. No offense, guys.

But I'm also glad I didn't write the *sorry* bit.

As we are finishing up, getting the last of the bombs off the truck and onto racks, I could swear the guys get ever more reckless and rambunctious, pushing the things so they swing and sway before clunking into place.

"Does everybody here on the ground crew have a death wish?" I ask. "Or is it just you guys?"

"Ah no," the lead guy says happily, "you got us all wrong. What we got is a lust for life, and playing like this just proves it. Anyways, it's not the guys who jerk around who are in harm's way, it's the wallflowers. Once you start creeping along the baseboards, looking to dodge every little thing that'll kill ya . . . that's when they'll kill ya. Ya kill your own self, really, is what you do."

Should I be surprised that this place is so versed in death? That everybody seems to have an expert opinion on where it comes from and how to cheat it? No, I shouldn't be surprised, but it does keep surprising me.

"Except when it comes to this midget here," another guy says, and the three of them once again rush Carney and tattoo him with arm punches that must be killing him by now though he just laughs. "Get outta town, ya bad-luck two-digit midget, ya," one yells and they finish punching and kicking him in the direction of his truck.

Like a numbskull, I again stand there spectating until they realize I could use some persuading too and start on me.

"Midget germs, midget germs," they holler and laugh, and I am not too big a man to scream out in pain as I dive back into the shotgun seat and Carney peels away to safety.

Whatever that is.

We drive for about two hundred yards. "Hey," he says as we approach an F-100 that has just pulled into the revetment, back from some mission. "Did you say you wanted to have a look around in there?"

"Well, whether I said so or not, I do."

"Come on, then."

He stops the truck on the edge of the flight line and salutes as the Super Sabre's two-man crew disembarks and files past us.

The maintenance guys are descending upon the plane to give it the once over. One of them, my equivalent on the F-100, is up the ladder already, checking the components, gauges, and wirings while Carney and I hover around his bottom rung like a couple of kids waiting for our turn on the slide.

He senses we are there.

"Can I help you boys?" he says while still going about his business.

"We were wondering if we might just have a quick look around," Carney says. He talks pretty easily to everybody, it seems.

"You might," the engineer says.

Then, nothing.

"How do we get up?" Carney asks.

"That would be by ladder," the guy says.

Then, nothing.

"Well, this is awkward," I say to Carney.

"Don't you speak maintenance?" he says.

I decide to give it a shot. "Hey, ah, airman, hey. Name's Beck. Hi. I work over in the C-123 neighborhood. Same job as you, basically. Do you think maybe out of professional courtesy . . . ?"

It does not at all seem like courtesy of any kind when the guy takes one of his feet off the ladder and sticks his leg straight out sideways about as far as he can into the baked airbase air. Like a dog relieving himself.

"Aw, come on, Carney," I say, "if he's just going to be like —"

Carney cuts me off. Laughing, he takes my face in

his hands and points my eyes in the same direction as the guy's toes are pointing.

"Oh," I say, seeing the second ladder being silently called to our attention.

A few minutes later we have wheeled the thing over to the other side of the Super Sabre. Being by far the more excited of the two of us, I scramble up first.

"Hey, thanks," I say to the engineer who is now directly across the cockpit from me, taking down details on a chart.

"No problem, airman. Can't get enough of the birds myself. You a collector?"

"Huh?"

"A collector. You know, bagging as many different aircraft as you can while you are here and still alive?"

"Well, I hadn't really thought about it."

"Well, think about it now, and get your rear end in that cockpit, because you ain't officially collected until you have sat at the controls in the big boss seat."

"Hey," Carney calls, and I can only just hear him because the whole base sounds like it has turned up its volume.

"Yeah," I call back.

"Lemme up."

"I was just going," I call, and with that clamber up and over and there ya go.

"Congratulations, my man," the engineer says. "You have just bagged yourself the North American Aviation, United States Air Force F-100D Super Sabre." He puts his pen in his mouth like a long, thin blue cigar, reaches out and shakes my hand, grinning cartoonishly. "How d'ya feel now, son?"

Insane. I'm supposed to be above this, aren't I? In my mind I am already flying.

"Pretty good, I must say."

"I hear ya," he says. On the panel in front of me, there are twenty clocks, dials, gauges, what have you. My legs straddle the control stick, which has some kind of magic spell that turns me into a five-year-old. I am using it to steer through clouds and Russian MiGs. There are two big pedal controls at my feet, they're like waffle irons, and more switches and buttons in a bank at my left hand. It's a lot more complicated than up/down, left/right, stop/go. One lever says *Drag Chute*. There's also *Emergency Up*, and *Fuel Purge*. The controls themselves tell you about the adventures involved.

I really like when I get a chance to sit in the pilot's seat of the Thunder Pig, but the Super Sabre is a whole different ball game. It was the Force's first ever supersonic fighter. And it is a *fighter*. A fighter-bomber, in fact, with a two-man crew in a clear hierarchy of pilot ahead and copilot behind and nothing but glass bubble between them and the sky.

I personally have no desire to fight or bomb anybody.

I personally have a desire to take this thing up into the air and make it do everything it is capable of doing.

And yes, I do recognize the slight conflict there.

"We airborne yet?" Carney says, his face popping over the side.

"Gib," I say, pointing with my thumb over my shoulder. In Air Forcish that stands for "Guy In Back." Carney happily takes the copilot's seat.

It's getting really busy outside, more than even the usual midday traffic, so I'm sure we won't be allowed to loiter here too long.

"Can we close it up for a minute?" I ask the guy, gesturing toward the glass hatch above us, which stands straight up from its rear hinge.

The sounds outside resemble a crashing surf of air traffic, coming and going. He checks his watch.

"I can give ya two," he says, and within seconds Carney and I are closed up inside the Sabre and inside a world we are in complete control of.

Just like a kid. Just like a kid would do, I am simulating flight and fire, moving the stick around, pretending to launch rockets and shoot guns as I swerve the thing this way and that. I look straight up into the sky and watch one of our own aircraft, an F-4 Phantom, tearing through the sky northward, probably on its way back to Cam Rahn Bay after a raid.

I am maneuvering right along with him, listening to Carney growling engine noises behind me, when I hear the distinctive whistle sound of a projectile being dropped from the sky.

It lasts no more than a few seconds, then it ends when I hear the most almighty explosion of my life.

Pu-booooom!

It's an explosion that sets off a bunch of other explosions, and I am still looking up as dust and debris come raining down on the glass of my F-100. The engineer, still on the ladder, has flattened himself against the bubble, covering his head with his hands. For probably twenty seconds, bits of rock and shrapnel and whatnot bounce off our plane and probably every other plane at this end of the flight line. There is screaming all over, sirens, squealing tires, chaos.

The hatch opens at last, and the engineer is hollering at us.

"Out you get, men!"

"What's going on?" I scream, my heart thudding in my ears.

"We under attack?" Carney yells as he scrambles down the ladder.

"No," the guy says, rushing down the other ladder. "It's friendly. Bomb dropped off that Phantom. Get back where you need to be, now!"

We race down the ladder and run toward Carney's truck, looking back over our shoulders toward the damage. The smoke reminds me of those nuclear test sites we used to see on the news. Fire crews are already working frantically. It looks like half the base is fighting to get everything under control before more ammo gets set off.

"Come on!" Carney yells as I lag behind.

I run as fast as a guy can while looking behind him. Because I cannot stop looking behind me.

I am hyperventilating as I jump in the seat and talk at Carney while he motors away. "That was the revetment we just —"

"I know," he says flatly.

"Those were the bombs we —"

"I know," he says, same voice.

I pause for breath.

"Those were the guys we just —"

"They were," he says.

We don't talk again until he pulls the truck up to near my barracks. Where he wouldn't leave me earlier but he's leaving me now. Probably should have left me earlier.

"Thanks, Carney," I say, hopping out.

"I guess we established that I'm not so unlucky, huh?" he says, smiling joylessly.

"Um, yeah," I say. "I suppose."

"You, on the other hand, it must be said, seem to be leaving a trail of bodies behind you."

Wow. I guess I'll have to think about that now.

"Thanks for that, Carney."

"Don't mention it. You goin' to the movies tonight?"

"What?" I say, stunned in pretty much every way you can be stunned. "Ah, I hadn't thought about it, actually."

"Ok, well, maybe I'll see you there, then. See, I don't mind hanging around with you, in spite of everything."

"You're a hero, Carney."

He drops even the forced smile now.

"No I'm not, Beck. I'm a survivor. And that is it."

I nod. What else is there? Planes continue screaming overhead, sirens continue screaming down here, and already the base is probably pretty much exactly as dangerous as it was an hour ago. I nod.

"See ya later, then."

"See ya later."

It's called the Happy Valley Drive-in. Honestly.

It's not a bad facility, either. Pretty much like it sounds, it's a big open-air theater with bench seating for maybe six hundred. Concerts come in sometimes. I saw a surf group here a while back, even though I don't much care for surf music, but I had heard of a couple of their songs so that passed for famous and famous passed for a big event here. The Surfaris. I stayed until they'd played both of the songs I knew, "Surfer Joe" and "Wipe Out," and then I went to bed. "Wipe Out" was actually pretty good.

Tonight, a beautiful clear night without too much heat and only a small plague of insects, is a good night for outdoor movies. Despite this, it's not exactly a full house. It is maybe a one-quarter-full house. I wouldn't be here myself except for the fact that the night is so perfect for it, and they have scheduled a double bill of *Billy the Kid vs. Dracula* starring John Carradine and *Jesse James Meets Frankenstein's Daughter.*

Maybe in the military's opinion these films represent the battle of West against East.

Really, the mystery is why there are any empty seats at all.

And okay, maybe it feels like a good moment to be sitting in front of a stupid movie, and beside a friend.

Something's not right, though. The movie is not coming on, and the friend is nowhere I can see him. Instead, they are screening an episode of the TV show *Combat!* It's about American GIs fighting in France during WWII. Pretty much the opposite of what I want to see.

I spend the whole episode scanning the seats between me and the screen, then the seats behind me, for Carney. Nobody appears to be him.

Then the episode ends and an entirely different type of show begins. An AC-47 Spooky gunship passes overhead. It does a big loop of the base, spraying down the area around the perimeter with machine-gun fire, including brilliant tracer rounds that act very much like a laser light show.

It's a weirdly beautiful thing, and a clear upgrade on *Combat!*

The next program begins with Carney still nowhere to be seen, and I am very hopeful that it will involve Billy the Kid and Dracula.

My hope is snuffed out when neither of them appears on-screen. Instead, we get an episode of *Rat Patrol.* It's another TV program about World War II, only this time the soldiers are in North Africa.

I am just about to leave my seat and walk back to my barracks, when a voice speaks right in my ear.

"Which one's Dracula?" Carney asks.

"He's the blond guy in the pointy helmet," I say.

"And Billy the Kid?"

"Well, obviously, he's the one operating the machine gun off the back of the Jeep as it flops wildly over the sand dunes."

"Oh, well, yeah, of course," he says, handing me a cold can over my shoulder. Then he points at the empty rows and rows spread out before me. "These two hundred seats taken?"

"Ah, well, I am expecting company . . . but I suppose."

He hops over the back of the bench and sits right next to me. I look at the bright orange can with the demented doctor-guy logo on it.

"*Moxie?!*" I say, making a *blech* sound and laughing at the same time.

"I see you've met the good doctor before. It is an acquired taste. You want something else instead?"

He reaches for the can, but I hold it away from him. "I got a friend who's nuts for this junk."

"Well, that is a wise friend indeed," he says, popping the top on his Moxie.

"Indeed," I say, popping the top on my Moxie.

"To wise friends," Carney says, bumping his drink against mine.

"To wise friends," I say, miraculously feeling a smile opening up.

CHAPTER FOUR

Death's Own Bubble Gum Card

Beck,

Yes, okay, I will thank you. Thanks for flying overhead and keeping an eye on me while I keep an eye on the other two knuckleheads. And thanks for removing the brush along the banks of the Mekong, too. I know it doesn't make you happy. I know how beautiful the countryside is. You are not killing the place, all right? You're un-killing guys like me. It'll grow back. I won't.

We have to get together. I am working on it and I think it can happen. I have heard from both Ivan and Rudi and, yeah, we have to make it happen. Ivan isn't loving his war nearly as much as he should be, and Rudi is loving his way too much, as far as I can tell. Seems like only you and me are sticking to the script. Ha. I'm sure if we can see them we can get things right again. You know how it works — there's nothing like the old gang to remind you who you are and get you back to that. Am I right?

Tell me I'm right, Beck.

I'm coordinating everybody's locations the best I can, and when I see a place and time when we are anywhere close to being able to catch a couple hours together, I'm going to contact you. You're the mobile one, fly guy, so be on the alert. With Rudi up in Chu Lai and Ivan stocking prey in the Central Highlands someplace, I think if you and I can accommodate them a little bit this could work. It could.

It's a good thing I have the radio, huh? I will use it, so be ready. I will make this happen.

I hope they're going to be all right, man. You're all right, anyway, I know that. Stay smart.

Write. I will call.

Morris

"I'm goin' up, cap," I say when I see Capt. Avery leading what seems to be a full crew across the asphalt to the C-123. I have been here for an hour already, waiting for them, waiting to get back up and back to work.

He stops when he comes face-to-face with me. He's got Lt. Hall, Fingers, and that other guy I don't know and don't want to know right behind him. It looks a little like a schoolyard fight, the type that Ivan would have from time to time, where he'd take on four guys. Only, even with the helmet and flak jacket, I wouldn't stand an Ivan of a chance.

The captain waves the others toward the plane to begin preflight.

"You sure you're ready, Beck?" he asks me.

It is time for me to question this question. I mean, I appreciate my boss's concern and all, but death, frankly, is part of the setup here. Everybody has to deal with it, daily, so why should I not be sure about getting back to work?

"This is my job, sir. Everybody else is doing his job, so why shouldn't I? I want to pull my weight, and I want to back up my team, and I want to serve my country —"

"And you want to go home, and go to college, and achieve great things with the rest of your life, preferably starting the day before yesterday."

"W-well," I stammer, "yes, I do. Wouldn't it be stupid to feel otherwise, with all due respect, sir?"

He laughs at that, which gives me a small shiver.

"Some might say it's stupid to say a thing like that to a career military officer, airman."

It's good I am not armed. If I had a gun I would shoot myself right now, for felony ignorance.

"I'm very sorry, Captain Avery."

"That's okay. We'll chalk it up to stress."

"I'm not under stress, sir."

I'm also not done saying stupid things, apparently.

"Then I should go back to being insulted," he says.

"No, I didn't mean . . . sorry. Okay, maybe a little stress."

"Listen," he says, placing his hand flat on my chest in a way that is both fatherly and intimidating. "You're a different sort. I understand that. In my opinion, the Air Force has the smartest guys anyway. Then there are the smart ones among the smart ones. But all kinds can succeed in this operation, so fortunately *brains* is not too crippling an impediment."

He pauses, so this must be where I thank him.

"Thank you."

"Shush. The thing is, which applies here, is that now and then we get a guy who's very smart, and who is also very sensitive —"

"I'm not —"

"I believe I said shush. So the smart, plus sensitive, plus rampant death, plus, well, let's call it *mission ambivalence* . . . all that can sometimes combine to equal an airman who winds up being not only useless, but dangerous to those around him. So, while I like you, Beck, and I do believe you have a bright future, I didn't ground you for you. I did it for me. And for them," he waves his hand generally over the guys, "and for her." He points at the fat plane getting prepped for flight.

I stare at everything he's gestured at, and at the thoughts he's left floating in the air around our heads.

"See, you're doing it right now," he says, laughing.

I shake my head violently, like a cartoon character trying to unscramble his brain after a collision.

"No, sir. I am a member of this team, this Air Force, this military action, and this country. Well, y'know, *that* country. I am not a liability. To anybody. I have never been a liability on any level and I am not going to start now. I am here for a reason, and I believe in that reason."

Even if my reason isn't the same as his reason. Even if my reason has more to do with three bozos from Boston than it does with Ho Chi Minh and his trail.

My buddies are out fighting in those jungles, and those jungles are sheltering my buddies' enemies.

He just nods at me.

"Only we can prevent forests, captain," I say.

And with that, I march in step behind my captain as we approach the Provider, the Thunder Pig, the Ranch Hand, Mortar Magnet, or whatever the beauty is calling herself today, and we ready for action. Capt. Avery informs my temporary replacement that his services will no longer be required, and the guy gives me a camaraderie chuck on the upper arm as he heads off. I smile at him, until he's passed.

Then I wince with pain.

The three stooges and the punches they gave me. The pain feels bone deep.

"You okay?" Fingers asks as we finish the safety checks on the outside of the plane. The engines splutter, cough, and kick into life. Black smoke wafts past us and the propellers rev faster and faster.

"Why does everybody keep asking me that?" I yell.

"Because you have the *spooked* look these days," he yells back.

I smile and yell slowly like I am explaining things to a simple child.

"No, I don't have any *spooked* look."

He shrugs, laughs, and waves me to follow him into the plane.

━━━━━ ★ ━━━━━

As the C-123 makes its slow, rumbly ascent, Fingers and I make sure that the tanks are primed and ready to saturate the world. Hoses, valves, switches, wiring, everything is checked and checked again, all systems go. It feels so different, primitive almost, being inside the Thunder Pig compared to the Super Sabre. The space age is happening there, in the F-100, and even that bird is on the verge of being replaced by something newer.

This Ranch Hand business, by comparison, feels like the rear end of fighting. Like if the jets are the fist-fighters, we're the guys who just hang back and stick a foot out to trip guys running past.

But this business is my business, and I know why I'm here.

"You had a close call," Fingers says, plunking down on the jump seat next to me. I am, as I usually am, watching the lushness of Vietnam out the window while it's still there.

"Meaning?" I say without looking, I ask without wondering.

"You know, the three ground crew guys. Heard you were there with them just a few minutes before they got smithereened."

"Yeah," I say, "that's about accurate."

"Well, I'm glad you're okay," he says, slapping my knee. "If I were you . . . well, I'm not sure how I would handle it, myself."

If I were being honest I'd say I'm not sure how I'm handling it, myself. But who wants honesty around here anyhow? And what, really, are one's options for *handling*? You just *do*.

"What's to handle, right?" I say.

"Well, there's the transference, for starters."

Okay, now I need to look away from the window. The Provider is rumbling extra-hard today anyway, rendering my view all shaky-blurry.

"Transference?" I ask.

"Yeah, you know, guys talk about it like it's a big deal. But it probably wouldn't bother you anyway, since I don't suppose there's anything superstitious about you at all."

"Well, no, I don't suppose there is. But stranger things have happened to a guy's beliefs in wartime. You know the old saying: There are no atheists in foxholes."

Fingers stares at me blankly. "Is that a Marines joke?"

I stare at him blankly. "Transference, Fingers?"

"Right, it's just a thing, I've heard it around. People say death does a transference with guys who are always close by death but never dying. The death essence gets on the guy and stays there. Like, when you get a pack of baseball cards? The cards always smell like the bubble gum, and that slate of bubble gum always tastes like a baseball card?"

The Provider is working really hard, like it's going to shake itself to pieces before we reach our destination.

"And that's me?" I shout above the rattle and roar.

"Death's own bubble gum card," he shouts back with such goofy good humor that I have to smile no matter how unsettling the words might be.

We get the word from the captain to man the tanks, because it's just about Agent Orange time. I turn to the window to steal one last look, and I once again cannot believe the lushness of the shiny green and blue of that triple-canopy jungle, all snaked through with rivers leading to a great white scythe of sandy beach in the distance, where Vietnam bumps the South China Sea.

Rat-arat-arat-arat-arat-arat-arat-arat-arat . . . !

We are hit by so much, so heavy, so varied gunfire I could swear the shooters were clinging to the side of our plane. A rocket of some kind comes up and *buubh!* clips the starboard wing right at the armpit, sending the plane wavering through the sky and me and Fingers tumbling all over the belly of the craft.

I hear Capt. Avery and Lt. Hall yelling into the radio and at the enemy and at each other as I try and get my feet under me and hang on to something stable.

But it's no good. The machine-gun fire is more relentless than anything we have ever faced. I can actually see bullet holes opening up all over the place as rounds rip right through the walls. Another rocket slams us, tearing into the tail, and I can't even attempt to get upright now as the plane twirls like a huge oak leaf falling from a tree. Fingers slams right down on my ribs, then he's gone again, bouncing, just like myself, off everything else.

We are not far from the ground. We are never really far from the ground on Ranch Hand.

Lt. Hall is screaming Capt. Avery's name and getting nothing in response when, with one elongated thunder crunch —

Everything stops.

CHAPTER FIVE

Transference

There are nothing but horror stories about being a POW in Vietnam.

And among those stories there are no stories more horrifying than those about how captured airmen are treated. The Air Force is seen as inflicting the heaviest losses on the North and the Vietcong, and back home in the States most of the high-profile heroes are fighter pilots. However accurate this portrayal is, the thing that is undeniable right here right now is that there is a bloodlust for an airman shot down in a plane whether that airman was firing sidewinder missiles at Hanoi or just pushing a snack trolley up and down the aisles for the crew. Some airmen get taken up to the North, regardless of where they're found. They're paraded through villages where mobs go crazy and attack them. The capture can be reenacted two or three times, for different newspapers and for TV, in different provinces, so everybody gets to have their time at you. After all that, solitary confinement is pretty common for an airman, being left in a cell for years with no company but the rats.

I really don't like rats.

They claim they mistreat and execute our guys because we mistreat and execute their guys, or at least that we hand them over to the ARVN for the nasty stuff. All violations of the Geneva Convention.

There's lots of talk on both sides about war crimes.

What is a war crime, anyway?

What isn't?

The plane is in two completely separated halves as I sit on the ground wondering what happened to me. There is thick smoke from small fires, and a distinct acrid chemical smell mixing with the foresty wet green smell of the jungle.

"What happened?" I ask Fingers, who is about ten feet away and looking right at me. He is at the base of a tree and folded right in half at the waist.

Backward.

His eyes are facing me, and the soles of his boots are facing me, both feet up by his left ear, with his pelvis behind him just about embedded in the tree.

"Where is your sidearm?"

I look up, and Lt. Hall is standing over me. He is wearing two pistols on his hips, he's got a sheathed knife in his belt, and he's carrying an M-16 rifle.

I am dazed as I look up at him. I can't seem to get my mind working at regular speed.

"Are you injured?" he asks me.

I look at myself, at my component parts. Nothing's moving except my head. But I don't think I'm actually trying, either.

I look back up at him, silently staring into his eyes beneath the visor.

He crouches down, lifts his visor, stares into my eyes. My own helmet is still on, though probably a little sideways. There is enough open space for him to reach in and slap me, one-two, forehand-backhand across the face.

"Do you want to live, Beck?"

"Yes I do, lieutenant."

"Then start *thinking*. Right now. Are you hurt anywhere?"

I do a proper inventory this time, wiggling fingers and toes. I swivel my head around, bend forward at the hips.

My ribs groan. They hurt like somebody is spearing me with a hockey stick. But knowing that I just fell out of the sky, knowing what's happened to my man Fingers over there, it seems I am doing very, very well indeed.

"I think I'm okay," I say, wincing as Hall gives me a hand up.

"Great. Well, if you have any hopes of remaining okay, you'll get yourself armed right this minute."

Ten seconds of standing also fills me in on the state of my head. It hurts. It swims. I have had my bell rung pretty good, but even with the pain and the wobbly, I don't think this rates as much of a plane crash injury. The brain, inside the bone, inside the skin — it all feels like it's sloshing around a little, but the helmet should hold everything together for now.

I don't know when it started raining. Was it like this when we took off? It is hot, and it is raining. Soup. Medium thick. I look in all directions at the density of this jungle, which must be unique to this part of the world. Even in geography books and *National Geographic* I never got the feeling there was anything like this, where you inhale and the taste of green is all up inside you.

This is what I have been trying to eradicate. This very patch right here was my target for today.

"We were trying to wipe this all out," I say to Lt. Hall, as if I know something he doesn't know. "This very jungle right here."

"Yes," he says, coming right up close, helmet-to-helmet, whisper growling. "You know what that means?"

I pause, until he shakes me.

"Well," I say at last, "among other things, it means we failed."

"And why did we fail?"

"We got shot down."

"We got shot down," he says, all teeth and grrr, "from right *here*." He points in all directions into the trees surrounding us. "This area is *hot*, Beck. We survived so far, but it's going to take some doing to keep it up."

Information like that will bring clarity back to a ringing head. And it'll bring questions along with it.

"Captain Avery?" I ask hopelessly.

"Was a very good man," he says, dragging my body toward dead Fingers. He shoves me in that direction, where I know what I have to do.

I manage to work the holster off him and strap the gun to myself. I never bothered wearing mine because, honestly, I never really thought of myself as a soldier. My gear was in the plane somewhere and is now in the jungle somewhere, perhaps soon to join the enemy in hunting me down. I get Fingers's knife as well, and Hall pulls me away just as I am saying my thank-you to the poor guy.

"Your manners are touching," Hall says as he pulls me away from my expired teammate. I am thinking about how insanely random it is, this death. Same guys, same jobs, same place, same equipment, same *crash*. Same trees, same ground. Yet Fingers is snapped in half and wholly gone, while I have a bruised rib or two.

Hall tows me toward the front half of the plane, about thirty yards away. The rain falls fat and unhelpful. There is a brand-new clearing between the two parts of the aircraft, created by our crashing, but other than that there is solid-wall foliage everywhere.

The two of us scour every bit of fuselage and eventually come up with one more rifle, two small backpacks of ammo and C-rations, and a machete.

There is air traffic in the far distance. There is a haunting nothingness all around close. That is terrifying. I am shaking. I look at my hands shake and the funny feeling in my head vibrating at the back of my eyes magnifies the effect so I look even more cowardly to myself than I must to Hall.

I see the remaining part of the captain's skull as Hall drags me away. It's the rear half. He looks like a big open pomegranate.

"How bad are you hurt?" I ask Hall as I follow behind his pronounced limp.

"Not as bad as we're both gonna be if we make any more noise than necessary out here."

"Where are we headed?" I whisper as quietly as I can.

"When I figure that out, I'll let you know," he says helpfully.

"Okay," I say, and for quite some time that's that. As of that moment, Hall is my commanding officer. He is my guide, my North Star, my hobbling protector. The rain washes us relentlessly, but never clean. Hall is fierce and determined. He never asks me any questions, never tells me where we are going, never slows down. When he walks upright, slashing a path for us with the machete, I walk upright in his footsteps. When he crouches to make his way hunch-backed through a weeping tunnel of giant leaves, I go hunchback, too. That becomes tough going after only a few minutes and we get back upright for as long as we can, then before I know it we are down, all the way down onto our bellies, crawling our way through the mud below us and the spongy broad leaves above.

Lt. Hall stops, silent, and I lie there, stupid and soaked, behind him waiting for information, enlightenment, or possibly death.

"Lieutenant?" I finally ask.

He shushes me by kicking at me with the toe of one boot.

I lie flat and still in the mud. I listen, and hear the slightest sounds of movement, of something working through the brush about thirty yards ahead. The sounds are barely louder than the raindrops, but they are there. Lt. Hall draws one of his pistols, and so I do the same. He lays the machete down and eases the M-16 rifle into place like a sniper.

I can hear my heart much more than I can hear any enemy. What am I doing here? I am not an infantryman. I am not a soldier. I am sure as shootin' not a sniper. Ivan is a sniper, and I am the anti-Ivan of this war. I am not trained for this.

We are soaked now, and as the rain pulverizes the ground, the hard earth softens and the water pools around us. We are getting closer to bathtub conditions. The water is already that warm, and soon will be that deep if this keeps up.

The enemy soldiers are closer. Twenty yards? I cannot breathe, which is probably good. I can't tell how many, but certainly there are enough of them to kill off the two of us several times over. I see Hall poised behind the rifle in his left grip, the pistol hanging at a weird angle in his right, like a small sailboat tacking hard into the wind.

They are thirteen yards away. I think there are about eight or ten of them.

They know we are out here. They are looking for the undead crew of the Provider.

We are not breathing. There is no air coming into my lungs, none going out, and if Lt. Hall were any stiller he'd be a plant.

The rain lets up, a lot. It feels like a shower that somebody is gradually turning off, slow for a shower, but really, really unhelpfully quick for a couple of airmen who are out of air and in need of whatever diversions nature can provide for them.

While I may or may not have just wet myself in terror, these guys pad through the mucky ground easy and sure and slick, like they were born to it.

Funnily enough.

And fortunately enough, they pad through and past, and keep on going.

It would have been nearly impossible for them to have come any closer without stumbling right onto us.

When enough time has passed for the patrol to be out of reach, I tug on Lt. Hall's trouser leg. I get nothing. So I wait. Wait for him to tell me it is okay to move again, lying in the increasingly uncomfortable jungle muck, listening to the unlimited wildlife of Vietnam coming to life the way it does when the rain relents. I don't know what sounds snakes make, but in my mind I hear the killer bamboo vipers out there, chasing the rats for now, the rats carrying the insects carrying the diseases that are surely going to get us now that the Vietcong didn't.

"Hey," I whisper, pulling on his leg again. Then, not waiting any longer, I belly crawl up alongside him to find why he was so good at staying still. He is unconscious.

I pat lightly on the side of his face, careful not to startle him into doing anything rash like shooting me. His eyes open halfway. He smiles a little bit and whispers, "I wish I could machete my leg off."

I look at the back half of him and there is something off about the way his left leg won't lie straight like the right one.

"What is it?" I whisper.

"Knee's all shredded. Can't believe I played running back for four years in a no-pass offense, never missed a down, and now a tiny little plane crash blows out my ligaments. Cracked the patella, too, I think."

I can see in the rollback of his eyes that the pain is sucking the energy right out of him, and when he closes his eyes again I leave him. We'll lie low, catch our breath, and start moving again later. I take advantage of the moment myself, and as I rest my weary helmeted head on the ground I have a vision of the least fun three-legged race ever.

I don't know how long we are resting. I don't know if I fall asleep or pass out or ever completely lose consciousness myself — which I believe would be bad if I have the concussion my head wants to tell me I have. But the ground heats up quite quickly, as a Vietnam ground will do in the aftermath of rain. It is surprising how comfy even a mucky ground can be when you are tired and scared and battle-beat and the earth around you seems to want to warm and shrink and just pull you in safe and sound.

"Lieutenant," I say when my eyes open to a brighter day than when I closed them.

He is slow to respond, but I feel him stir, bumped right up against me as we lie aligned on the ground.

"Lieutenant," I say more firmly. There is no real need to whisper now.

Standing over us — and pointing AK-47 rifles at us — are two Vietcong in the famous black pajamas. If I survive this ordeal I promise to make a point of telling Rudi that in one day I doubled the number of times he wet himself over the Vietnam War. These two guys, in fact, don't look a whole world away from, say, Rudi and Morris, in age, in innocence, in fear.

I have my hands up in an awkward sort of mini-surrender sign, at my sides like a startled penguin, but clearly away from my firearms. Which is the important thing.

I realize how close I am to death. Still, what is crashing through my sorry skull right now is a storm of every horror story I have heard about captured airmen, tales of torture in the infamous "Hanoi Hilton" prison, flyers kept in rat cages too small to stand up or lie down, whole villages of locals called out to take turns poking the naked and blindfolded prisoners with Punji sticks like a big ol' primitive boar hunt.

"Lt. Hall," I say, bumping him with my elbow, inviting him to the party.

Lt. Hall is a more natural fighting man than I am.

I see one eye roll half-open, then the other, as he

comes to something like realization of what we've got here, and he —

Brrrraatatatatatatatatatatatatata . . . ! Brrraaa . . . Braaaaa! Braaaa-at-at-at . . .

And on it goes, and on, and on. The AK-47 fire, from both of these kids' guns, goes nonstop for twenty seconds, then sporadically, on, off, on, off, punctuating the oily smoky air with intermittent blasts until they have shredded and pulverized Lt. Hall almost into two or three distinct pulpy segments. Through it all, my body convulses, as I wriggle and roll away from the shots and the results but never so far away that I can avoid getting completely drenched, yet again, this time in a comrade's blood.

I still have my penguin surrender hands out to my sides, though. Don't know where I learned that discipline but I am pretty sure it is the reason I am still here to wonder.

The three of us now stare at each other, and if our six lungs could be hooked up we could power a space shot from Cape Canaveral. We are all breathing fast and loud and it may even wind up being some kind of competition because their staring and breathing is only making my heart scream and jump all the more and if I do win this hyperventilation contest it is fairly certain to be the only thing I beat them at today.

The guy closer to me — maybe he's the older one by a week and so he's the leader — snaps bossiness at the other guy, who goes about the business of relieving Lt. Hall's pieces of all the weaponry he no longer needs. Won't do him any good now. Surely didn't do him any good before.

Now the boss comes to me. I flinch, out of terror, which makes him raise the rifle menacingly as he snaps some kind of order at me.

I keep my hands out and shrug, shaking my head slowly. The brim of my helmet is halfway between up and down, and dripping with blood. Angrily the guy reaches down and half pulls–half slaps the thing sideways off my head.

My brain screams with the pain. It feels like it's reverberating off the inner skull walls.

He looks at me, kind of surprised. When he dislodged the helmet, my hair flopped out and matted itself across my eyes. I have let it grow pretty long for active military, but the way things are at this point in the war, nobody's getting too serious about that kind of regulation. I can see the guy okay through the hair without being altogether seen.

Until he reaches out and brushes the hair out of my eyes.

We have almost the same hair, I realize.

The other VC has gathered the weapons on a canvas on the ground. It's like a small parachute or a flattened tent with straps they will use to wrap themselves a nice package of goodies. The boss snaps again, and the junior guy begins relieving me of my weapons, which I am frankly happy to be relieved of just now.

The boss takes up the machete.

He orders the other guy once more, and the guy starts securing the bundle for transport while my friend here admires the machete. Then suddenly, he looks down hard at me.

He takes two steps in my direction, where now I am just sitting in the mud, my legs crossed in front of me and my hands on my thighs.

I close my eyes. I think about my dad. Hans said I was stupid to do this. Still never been wrong once, Hans.

The point of the machete burns as it pokes into the small U bend that curves into the top of the chest bones at the base of my throat.

This awfulness holds for several centuries of seconds of silence. I'd be crying and peeing if I had any body fluids to spare.

He says some words, right into my chin. He says them fairly quietly.

I open my eyes to see the guy looking not at my face, but at my collar.

He is fingering my scapular, which I cannot even believe I have on. My little cloth postage stamp with the face of Christ on it that I received from Ivan's mom. I thought I'd ditched it long ago.

I just look straight ahead, waiting. While waiting I see, dangling from my captor, a silver crucifix. He quickly tucks it back into his black pajama shirt.

The other guy says something that sounds like impatience.

My guy says something back that sounds like impatience repellent.

Then he says something to me.

I have no idea what it is.

So now he is impatient. He reaches out and pulls me to my feet. Calmly, but in an *I'm only gonna tell you this once* voice, he speaks, thumps his own chest, and points over my head, roughly west, I think. Then he points at me, then in the opposite direction, roughly toward Phan Rang in the east.

Sure, I could crawl home, and maybe get there in time for the next war. Which sounds pretty all right to me.

The two stand there as I tentatively walk a few steps toward what might be freedom. I watch them for a couple of steps, then I don't. I half wait for the sounds of gunfire.

"Hey," he snaps, which sounds like *hey* but probably isn't but makes me jump six feet into the air either way.

I freeze, then turn to find him standing in front of me. He reaches over, slips the scapular up over my head, and puts it on himself.

It definitely blends in better with his outfit — which he probably appreciates.

He nods, I go, and our long relationship is over. I'm betting he doesn't care to be thanked.

I think it's an hour.

It's probably an hour.

I think it's east. It's probably east.

I am doing what the man told me to do, making my way back vaguely toward something homelike. But with every step I believe in what I am doing just a little bit less. I can hear the war, off in the distance, which is never the war you worry about, the distant one, the noisy one. I am petrified that each step is going to be my last. I know a bamboo viper is going to get me. I know some unchristian enemy combatant with short hair and an old leathery face is going to take an unliking to me and a big knife to my guts. By now I certainly must have done all the transferring I can and death is so pleased with my work he's ready to call me back to the home office.

I am unarmed. I have no food or water other than what I am able to slurp off the foliage that is everywhere and probably tainted by my own Agent Orange. I have no machete to cut through that insane density of greenery, so not only is it taking me a caterpillar's time to cross this expanse of jungle, but the jungle is chopping me a lot more than I am it.

The only thing missing is the thunder.

It comes in so heavy right over my throbbing head that I squat down like a monkey in the bush as it passes. Holding my ears, holding my head together from bursting with my palms pressed as hard as possible to my skull, I look up and see the nutty-looking skeletal helicopter, the skelicopter, the thing actually known in the USAF as a Sky Crane, zooming in the same direction as me. I stand dumb, watching as it tows its load, hanging from a wire below it, to some point yonder.

Then I recognize the load. Holy smokes, it's a big fat bomb. What they call the Daisy Cutter. The Daisy

Cutter has a very specific purpose, and I watch as the crane carries it about another twenty seconds beyond my vision and . . .

Bu-hoooom!

It has cut the daisies. Meaning, it has blasted the daylights out of an area of trees large enough to create a landing zone where there was previously no landing zone.

To provide space for . . .

Thyup-thup-thup-thup-thup . . .

Immediately, a big beautiful UH-1 Huey helicopter, a troop carrier, comes pounding along to go and make use of that very landing zone. To fill it with United States Army personnel.

The Sky Crane is already zooming back over my head as I thrash and crash and slash my way through the brush toward that glorious, wonderful collection of friendly killers.

PART
TWO

CHAPTER SIX

Tour of Many Duties

Who ever would have thought you'd be leaving here before me?" Carney says as we stand together by the flight line for what will be the last time.

"Now you'll have the whole library to yourself," I say.

"And the education center," he says.

"And the University of Maryland," I say.

"Are you calling me a terrapin?"

We laugh, awkward and a little sad, as he walks me toward the C-130 Hercules transport idling in the few minutes before it launches me on the first leg of my journey. I am headed home, sort of. First I'm off to Langley, Virginia, for some retraining before they allow me a thirty-six-hour dogleg to Boston before I'm headed back here for more fun. My ribs and my head still ache, but they say that should clear up by the time I see American soil.

"Thanks," I say over the engines to Carney, because there isn't anything else left to say.

"For what?" He laughs.

He's been good about not mentioning the transference thing again. I guess it's a pretty good gag after you see one guy killed, and maybe after two. Then it becomes something else.

Don't know what I would do if he did mention it, though. It almost feels more eerie to have it just hang there, unacknowledged.

"Thanks for not dropping dead in front of me, maybe?" I say, shrugging.

"Don't mention it. Happy to oblige. I like not dying. It's one of my favorite things."

I nod at him, smile. A helpful airman takes my kit bag from me and throws it on board, waving for me to follow it.

"Take care of yourself, Carney," I say, pointing a commanding finger at him.

He pushes my hand quickly aside, acting all scared. "Hey, do you mind not pointing that thing at me? It's kinda lethal."

"Midget jerk," I say, shaking his hand.

"Safe home," he says, shaking back.

I have a letter to read on the plane. It's from Rudi. I still have not heard anything from Ivan in some time, but I did talk to Morris on a radio hookup during my short stay in the base hospital. I will say this for ol' mother hen Morris: He said he was going to make it his business to watch over everybody and keep everybody connected, and he does indeed seem to be making our business his business.

"Why didn't you call me?" he demanded when they handed me the phone. This was not three hours after I got into my hospital bed.

Instead of answering him with words, I burst out in probably the biggest laugh I have had in months. Which is good, because the laugh covered up that I had started, at that very same moment, to cry. And I wouldn't want to share that with Morris . . . especially with me in the comfy bed and him clearly in the vicinity of gunfire and low-flying aircraft.

"How in the world did you find out about this?" I said.

"What, you think you can keep things from me? Do you even know who you are talking to? I tell ya, if my boat were not basically under attack right now, I would come right over and slap you silly."

My goodness, I had never laughed like this. Never mind the last several months. I had never *in my life* laughed like this, and no, I do not care to examine the psycho depths of it.

"Ha-ha," he said, as something apparently exploded in the water near him.

"Are you all right?" I asked.

"Yeah," he said, "it sounds worse than it is. My guys have it under control."

I have to believe him, as false bravery was never a part of Morris's arsenal. The real kind was rare enough.

"So how are *you*?" he said, getting a whole lot more serious.

"I have a headache," I said.

"They told me that much. They told me a few other things, too, so now I'm gonna ask you again, but gently, how are ya, Beck?"

I pause for a comfortable long while.

"I'm good, Morris. I am, really. Now that I'm hearing you . . . getting home for a bit . . . talking to you, talking to my dad . . . I'll be good."

"When you come back, we are getting together. For real. I just about have the last pieces together. You are going to be stationed farther north, right? A lot closer to where Rudi is. He says if we can meet anywhere within striking distance of Chu Lai, he's there. He's dying to see everybody, show us the *sights and sounds* of Rudiworld East. Meanwhile, I am licking every boot I can around here to make sure I have enough brownie points that I can get away at short notice when the time comes. I make long-distance phone calls magically come true for everybody, and you'd be surprised how valuable that can be."

"Hnnn," I said, the hole in the conversation becoming obvious. "So, you been magically able to talk to Ivan lately?"

"No," he said crisply. "But by the time you're back in-country, I'm gonna have this thing together. That's my quest."

"I like your quest."

"It's a fine quest."

"Still wish you'd managed to talk to Ivan, though."

Pause. The action around him seemed to have subsided.

"Yeah. Me, too. And I half wish I *hadn't* talked to Rudi."

That would seem to be about as provocative a thing as Morris could possibly say.

And yet I was not provoked. And yet, we somehow both knew what he meant.

"We really do need to get in the same place, Morris. Even for just a little while."

"Yes, we do, Beck. Even for a minute."

So as I settle into my journey, it is with a mix of good-buddy anticipation and dread that I take out my Rudi letter, with its second-grade lettering, and finger open the envelope.

Hello Beck,

HERE'S something. HERE'S something I know you never expected. I never expected it, nobody anywhere ever expected it. It turns out there is a place on planet Earth where you and me are equal. Or even, possibly, where I am more equal than you.

Place is called Vietnam.

I don't want to brag — yes I do — but I am an amazing soldier. I am better at this every day. Are you better at this every day? Bet you're not.

This is me now, I am a Marine. You're probably counting your days to DEROS, am I right or am

I wrong? Don't get me wrong, I'm not looking down on you or nothing, just sayin it like it is and isn't. I miss my old pals and that is a fact, no matter what has happened and will happen we will always be us, won't we? Well, except for me. I won't be me anymore, but don't worry about that because I'll be a lot better than that. The three of you guys should still be you, I would like that, so stay being you.

Morris is getting us together can you believe that guy? If he gets it done it will probably be up here in my neighborhood someplace which makes me thrilled with thrills because I want to show you around and show you stuff. No offense, but especially Ivan. I want to show Ivan stuff the most. I'm a man now, Beck. Wait til you all see, you just won't believe it. I want Ivan to see what kind of a man I am now and I want him to be proud of me like if I had a dad.

And hey if you come up and you're good maybe I'll kill somebody for ya. HA!

CAN'T WAIT TO SEE YOU guys. STAY SAFE AND don't fix my gRAMMAR. HA!

Rudi MAN

His spelling is fine. He has even clearly spent an inordinate amount of time on his penmanship.

That's great. Good for Rudi.

CHAPTER SEVEN

You Can Go Home Again. Briefly.

Retraining.

What did I learn during my retraining at Langley Air Force Base? I learned mostly the same stuff I learned when I went through advanced training after basic training the first time around. I learned a little bit more about the workings of a few aircraft I had not worked on before. And I learned more about shooting from those aircraft than I have ever learned before or than I am ever likely to need as a mechanic.

Mostly I learned how to be watched. More Air Force officers inquired about my health and welfare in two weeks at Langley than in the whole time in Vietnam, when my health and welfare were decidedly more in question. In the end I believe the whole operation was a combination holiday and psychological assessment to be sure I was worth sending back into combat.

I enjoyed the holiday part, moderate Virginia

weather and not one person dying and all. As for the assessment, well, I guess I passed.

"Thirty-six hours, airman," my supervisory trainer says at 0600 on the morning of my fourteenth day on American soil. "You are free as a bird to do what you like until tomorrow chow time, at which point you are to be here and ready to fly out the following morning. Back to home."

"Which does not mean Boston, Massachusetts, USA," I say.

"Which means Phu Cat, Binh Dinh Province, Vietnam."

I had actually been informed yesterday, but this acts as a sort of starter gun for my whirlwind trip home. It does serve a cool purpose in that it has me excited to run out of here and squeeze the most out of every minute, like I'm seven or eight years old and about to go on one of our beach holidays in Marshfield. I am packed and ready and, knowing my father's punctuality, I am expecting to see his big Buick Electra bub-bubbing right outside the gate.

I am trotting with my bag over my shoulder when I approach the gate and there it is, the gold four-door hardtop boat waiting faithfully. I am as excited to see Hans as when he came home from work twelve years ago.

So it's a bit of a shock when my sisters pile out instead.

Ingrid comes bounding out of the driver's seat, while Elkie comes around from the passenger side. I am stunned, but hardly less happy as the two of them actually lift me off the ground with their kisses and hugs.

"So," I say, playing the spoiled returning hero while they'll still let me, "where's Greta?"

They drop me.

"She's in college," Ingid says. "Where you should be, ya dope."

"Yeah," Elkie says, "ya dope." She cuffs me lightly across the back of the head.

Shortest honeymoon ever, I'd have to think.

Ingrid and Elkie graduated one and two years ago and now are working nurses at Mass General and Children's hospitals. Greta is a sophomore at Berkeley, so I suppose it may have been a bit presumptuous of me to be expecting her here.

I am in the back seat, stretched out, when Ingrid guns the Electra in the direction of Massachusetts.

"I thought Hans was coming to get me," I say.

Elkie turns around in her seat. "Is that really what you thought? Did you really expect a sixty-three-year-old man to drive through the night, pick you up, then turn around and drive you back again?"

I did. You know, I did. Funny, no matter what the Air Force and war and all have done to make a man out of me, I still came home in some ways a little boy. Expecting the world from his almighty dad.

"Sorry," I say. "Can we just chalk it up to shell shock or battle fatigue or whatever they're calling it these days?"

"Post-Vietnam Syndrome," the driver says in a low near-growl that suggests to me she has professional experience of it at Mass General.

I don't want to talk about that.

"Okay, call it that, and I'm sorry. I'm thrilled, of course, that you two drove all this way for me. What's the trip, seven hours, eight hours?"

"Depends on if we angle through Vermont or upstate New York."

"What?" I say. "What about Massachusetts?"

"What about Quebec?" Elkie says.

The tone is playful-dangerous, like wrestling around with adolescent lionesses like they did in the movie *Born Free*. Very much the *love you to shreds* lionesses, my sisters.

"I'm not going to Canada, girls. I'm going back to Vietnam."

"Well, we had a lot of time to talk about this on the drive down," Elkie says.

"And I'm afraid we decided we can't allow that, Beck. Sorry, man."

As a military man I have been trained to suss out situations like this, and I conclude that my options here are few.

"Ah, girls, come on. I don't have a lot of time. Can't we just leave this? Huh?"

"He's right," Ingrid says, turning to Elkie.

"He is," Elkie says in response. "He's always been a bright boy."

"Well, once upon a time, anyway."

"But now he's more of a killing machine, so maybe we shouldn't rile him."

"Fine," I say. "I'm going to sleep."

A very clever move on my part. Like that was ever going to stop them.

"How many, Beck?" Ingrid says, loud enough that I know if I were really trying to get some sleep that that would not be permitted just yet.

"How many, what?" I say with dread.

"Confirmed kills?"

Oh. Oh. Ouch. Oh. My sisters famously take no prisoners, but I didn't see this coming. Really, the government would have done better sending these guys over rather than me.

"Seven," I answer, serious as death. They wouldn't care to hear about transference any more than I care to tell them. Doesn't matter. Those are kills, and I personally confirmed them.

I open my eyes to see exactly what I expect to see. Four wide blue eyes trained on me.

"Eyes on the road there, Ingrid."

She turns with a snap back toward the pavement ahead, while Elkie continues gawping at me.

"You've never really been one to lie to us, have you, Beck?"

"I never have."

"So right now, we are left to decide whether the Air Force has turned you into a liar, or a killer?"

She stares at me. I stare at her. In the rearview, Ingrid makes the triangle complete.

I actually am very tired. I was so excited for this that I didn't get more than two hours' sleep last night.

"Can I nap now?" I ask.

Elkie nods, then turns around in her seat.

I tip over sideways as soon as the girls let me, and the reassuring thrum of the Buick's engine on the highway is my companion for a good long while. I waft in and out of consciousness, sometimes rousing because of my sisters' low murmuring sadnesses over me, sometimes because of unwelcome dreams of flight.

And another thing. How could it happen that any dreams of flight are unwelcome?

But each time I am just about awoken, I am almost as quickly put back down again with the familiarity of this car, this position, this safety. We have always been a Buick family, and right now we are more than ever a Buick family.

I only fully come out of it when the car comes to a stop. I emerge from a deep unconscious, the kind that leaves the back of my hand laminated in drool.

"Where are we?" I say, straightening up, drying my hand on my leg.

"Connecticut," Ingrid says, putting the car in park and cutting the engine.

I look out the window and see a vast village green, swarming with people. There is chanting and pacing back and forth, people carrying signs.

"Ingrid?" I say as she opens her door.

"It'll be good for you," she says, slamming it shut.

Elkie stares at me, sweetly sad and militantly pacifist. I take some pride in thinking my family are the only people who can make such a face.

"You should join us," she says, less aggressive than Ingrid but surely no less convinced.

I read signs out the window that say normal stuff like *U.S. Out of Vietnam Now!* And *Stop the War!* And I think, fair enough. Then I see the creative stuff, the *Baby Killers!* And especially this . . .

Hey Monsanto! Hey Dow!

Chemical warfare is not war fair!

And the chanting comes floating over like a personalized invitation:

"You can run, but you can't hide,
from war crimes and herbicide!"

I look back at Elkie, then over to the crowd where my beloved oldest sister has joined in. Everybody seems to be on the same side. That side.

"We just want no more killing," Elkie says sadly.

I look into her eyes, trying to find our common place again in there.

"Everybody dead I know is American," I say. I feel

like that explains something. Something of me, to her. Though really, I know it doesn't.

"Come on," she says, reaching over and gently holding my hand.

"I can't," I say.

She nods, gets out of the car, and joins the demonstration.

I stare, with my head against the side window glass, for forty-five minutes while these people all do what they feel they need to do. I have no idea what the focus is, possibly somebody from Dow Chemical or Monsanto — makers of many agents, including Orange — is in the area. But I am glad when the time passes and the operation breaks up.

My sisters are walking back to the car, wrangling over the car keys. It is exactly zero surprise when Ingrid fails to relinquish them.

They are inside now, and the engine comes on like some combination of a favorite song and my mother's embrace.

"I understand why you had to do it," I say.

Elkie turns to me. "I understand why you couldn't."

Ingrid opts for neither of these. "We do it for you, you know," she says.

"I was just about to say the same thing to you," I say.

My parents are on the lawn when we pull up and I am giddy at the sight of them. There is a slight Mr. and Mrs. Claus to their look now. They were always a bit older than everybody else's parents. But I can see before the car even stops that they are more than six months older than they were six months ago.

Which may be a contributing factor to why I do not wait for the car to come to a stop before I jump out and run to them.

"Muti," I say, bending low to bury my face in her salty-peppered perm.

I get no words out of my mother. There is a kind of warbling cry, a mix of nightingale and turkey noises trying to be words.

I look at Hans over her shoulder, and he is beaming and straining like he might not even wait his turn but instead barrel right in and start a parental pigpile.

But then my mother releases me into the bear care of my father.

"Hey, Hans," I say, standing in front of him.

"Hey, Beck," he says, and he gathers me up in his arms, where I fall in and disappear back into 1955.

"So, you'll tell me everything," he says softly in my ear.

"So, I'll do no such thing," I say.

Precious as my few hours home are, I make some modest use of them. I spend that first hour or so hugging my dad. Then I fill the family in on everything I have been doing, which is to say, I fly planes and go to the movies and go to the library and fly planes and fix planes and eat and see the country of Vietnam which is by some distance the most beautiful place I have seen, in or out of the *National Geographic* magazines that decorate one whole wall of my father's study with their smart yellow spines. Death does not feature in my beautiful Vietnam, and while nobody in the room truly buys this I tell the pictures pretty enough that nobody is moved to challenge me, either.

But soon, sooner than I would have imagined, I am needing to get out and be by myself. Nobody anywhere loves his family or is loved by them more than me, but after a couple of hours I am feeling a need to get away from them so extreme I fear I might say something nasty and hurtful to make it happen.

And they haven't done a single thing wrong. They could not be nicer or more understanding, or more intolerable.

I walk. This feeling will pass, whatever it is. I walk. And I walk and walk.

I go all around the neighborhood, past my primary school and the shops and the baseball fields and all the other tiny, tiny, tiny little elements that made up my life. I say I walk, but it only starts that way. I walk, then I hot-step, then I trot, then, by the time I reach the aboretum and climb Peters Hill, I am sprinting, nearly out of breath when I stop to look out over the hazy skyline of Boston.

Even Boston looks tiny. I can't believe that's the first thing that comes to mind, looking out over my hometown. My handsome, smart, special city. Then I realize I am thinking about Boston in the same terms my parents use on me, but I sure hope they feel it more than I do. It's not that I feel negative about the place. It's that I don't feel much of *anything*.

I ride the trolley into town, walk around the Common. I get myself a mocha frappe, which, finally, has me feeling something. I love mocha frappes.

I take the green line back out to Brookline Village, take the long way home, walking along the muddy river, then across Daisey Field and up past Jamaica Pond. These are *the* places of my life, and I can see in the mothers and children feeding the ducks and geese, the young guys throwing rocks into the water and at boats, the bike riders circling the Pond and getting drinks from the boathouse, that these are good places. Great places. I understand that.

Understand, as opposed to *feel*.

When I figure I have checked all the boxes, seen all the sights, touched the touchstones, I make my way slowly back to home, where the main event of the visit awaits. The big dinner with my folks, Ivan's folks, Morris's and Rudi's moms.

"I'll be driving you back tomorrow," Hans says to me as we set the table. The girls are both working tonight and have already left.

"I'll get a bus, Hans, don't worry about it."

"Don't be a fool, Beck. This is the kind of thing a father should be able to do for his son. You're over there busting a gut to make the world a better place and it's too much for your old man to do a few hours of driving?"

The latest in a series of surprising reactions comes over me. I am suddenly in a panic at this thought.

"Ah, around fifteen hours. You're hardly going to be up to that. What about your back?"

"Back's fine."

"And your knee?"

"Knee's fine."

"Okay, well, you got fat."

We are on opposite sides of the table. I am folding and placing cloth napkins at each setting. Hans was distributing silverware up to now. Before he dropped the whole bunch in a clattering heap on the table. He stares at me across the table.

I stare back. I am determined not to laugh first. That becomes a lot easier when he throws me the curve.

"I love you," he says, his eyes all watery.

Right, a fine time for me to start feeling things.

"Jeez, old man," I say, walking over to his side and reaching around him to collect up the silverware. "Look at you, ya big fat baby. Helpless, you are." I get busy with knives and forks and avoidance.

"Yeah," he says, standing in that same spot like a game of freeze tag.

As I go around and get each place setting down, the statue of my father speaks.

"You can tell me, Beck."

"Hnn," I say, cleverly failing to ask him to clarify what needs no clarification.

"You don't need to protect me. I'm supposed to protect *you*, remember. That's my job. Has been my job for all of time."

I wish my mother would come in and break this up, though somehow I know she will not be doing that. He wouldn't say there is no need to protect her, that's for sure, but I'm pretty sure she is out there protecting herself, with a turkey baster and a gravy whisk.

"Why would I ever think I had to protect you, Hans? There's nothing to say. Really. My tour's been pretty boring. Everything's great. I'm great."

Now, he moves, puts his hands flat on the dining room table, and leans way over across to where I have to meet his face.

"No," he says. "You're not."

I am finished delivering cutlery. I assume his mirror image on my side of the table, palms flat, nose to his nose.

The doorbell rings. I run for it with such gusto you'd think there was an honorable discharge waiting for me on the other side.

"Heyyy —" I say, and that's as far as I get before Morris's mom gets a two-arm crunch around my waist tight enough to squeeze out any wordmaking capability. Rudi's mom reaches over her to offer me a pat on both cheeks. Beyond her I see Ivan's parents, The Captain and Mrs. Bucyk, pulling up in their car.

I am still being patted and squeezed by the time the Bucyks make their way up the path, and I am thinking that with all the effort the Air Force has put into preparing me, there simply isn't any training for this.

My mom is a fantastic cook. What kind of a rat of a returning-vet son doesn't say that about his mom?

Fact is, she is an unfussy, decent cook, and that is the unaltered truth.

That is also where the unaltered truth ends this evening.

"You'd be surprised," I say to the second or third query about the dangers of VC antiaircraft artillery. I receive these questions as they are lobbed like grenades across the chicken and biscuits and gravy and green beans amandine and powdery dry oven-roasted potatoes. The bird is perfectly moist, which is strategically helpful as it allows for more of the gravy to be deployed to help revive the potatoes. "The news, I guess, makes everything look horrific, but probably they embellish just for the ratings. It's all about ratings these days, viewer numbers and advertising. Vietnam horror stories pull in the viewers. The reality is . . . really less chaotic than that."

I do not want to be sexist about this, so maybe what I will say is that I am being *motherist* about how I read the reactions around the table. The more I talk, the more the mothers invest in my talk. The more I talk, the more the fathers retreat into hooded-eye quiet. They are very polite, they don't challenge one syllable of my fantastic fables, but The Captain and Hans sink deeper into *I know better* postures and sad faces that hurt me even as I persist in provoking them.

The mothers want me to be true. They want this version to be true.

"I keep wondering about that as I watch the TV," Rudi's mom says. "I keep saying, right out loud, that they have to be exaggerating. How could it be the nightmare that they are portraying every night and not have every single one of you showing up home in a box? I mean, there's never been anything like it. World War II was nothing like what we're seeing, was it, Captain?"

"No," he says somberly, "it wasn't."

"And let's face it, if it really was that bad, my Rudi would have been the first silly sausage shipped home in a bag. I think the first words that boy knew were 'Don't put your eye out,' because I said it so many times. 'Don't do that, Rudi. You'll put your eye out. Don't put your eye out.' He was always *this* close to putting his eye out, so I don't see how he could manage over there at all if it was anything like how they're playing it to be."

There is an uneven mix of nervous laughter and the real kind as Rudi's mom goes on. There is, however, nobody rushing to tell her that her assessment of her son is off the mark.

"Actually," I say, "from what I can gather, Rudi is doing really quite well. He's the model Marine."

She is beaming and denying simultaneously. "I wouldn't know, of course, since we don't write or anything. I told him the only writing I was doing the minute he went out that door for boot camp was writing him *off*. Because I was convinced he was already a goner, and so I would just start getting used to the idea. And that way, if he did come home it would be just a wonderful surprise which we could then celebrate."

This time there is only the nervous laughter.

"Morris tells me you're all going to be meeting up," Morris's mom says hopefully.

"That's the plan," I say. "And no surprise it's your boy who's making it all happen."

A joyful small ripple rolls around the table as one after another of them echoes, "Nope," "Nah," "No surprise there," "Not surprised in the least," all to the sweet soundtrack of laughs of admiration.

"He said he was going to watch out for all of us," I say, "and boy, ol' Morris is as good as his word."

It is with great satisfaction that I note the comfort this little nugget brings to every member of the dinner party. Even without being here, Morris has the ability to reassure people more than I do in the flesh.

"Tell Rudi not to put his eye out," Rudi's mom says, with such grim seriousness there is no laughter of any kind anywhere.

"I will," I say.

"Is there Moxie there?" The Captain blurts.

Ivan's beverage of choice. His passion, his mania. Moxie is Ivan, Ivan is Moxie.

The Captain looks so sad. This is not his war. I mean, he is The Captain, so all wars are his wars, but I know the messages he is receiving are not helping him to feel good. He is order, The Captain. He is good and bad and the righteous fight, and he is might making right when everybody can identify wrong. But this war, and the way it is coming home to people, is not providing him any of that. And he needs order and sense and control to hang his helmet on. He'd be over in Southeast Asia right now sorting things out himself if this were his time. But it is not his time now, it is Ivan's.

"I mean," he adds when maybe I sit there staring mutely at him for a few tics too long, "can he get it? Is it readily available, Moxie, or maybe should we try and get some shipped over there to him?"

Ivan and Moxie together make sense. It's a little bit of life being exactly the way it's supposed to be.

"Not as available as Coke," I say finally, "but it's definitely there. I have seen it. And if it is possible . . ."

"Ivan will find a way," The Captain says proudly, clearly his evening's high watermark.

Though I should not be, I am quickly wearying of all this talk and I keep trying to pull back from the conversation at every opportunity. Those opportunities are almost nonexistent. When I try and turn the conversation to my mother's food, Morris's mom asks for a detailed rundown of the state of military food provision. When I try and brag a little on how nicely my folks have kept up the garden, Rudi's mom asks me to put into vivid terms just how jungly the infamous Vietnamese jungle really is, and don't leave out one little detail about the tigers and snakes and killer insects and aquatic rats and leeches.

I hang in as best I can but do find myself thinking uncharitable thoughts about how when my parents start clearing away dishes that they could likewise scrape away these lovely and concerned people with all their reasonable questions and fears and good wishes.

It is coffee and dessert time and I tear a bit impolitely through a small pile of penuche fudge and oatmeal-raisin-maple cookies in, I suppose, an unconscious attempt to influence the whole crowd to eat too fast and be done with the evening. I feel like I am almost succeeding when Mrs. Bucyk cuts through with one of her few interjections of the evening.

"You are still wearing your scapular, aren't you, Beck?"

Oh. Oh. I didn't even think. I somehow thought . . . well, of course she would ask, stupid. It was one of the last things, before we all left. She put them on each of us, like garlic necklaces to ward off the evil vampiric hordes of Vietcong. Of course she would want to know.

I am about to rev up for one final push, one last charge of the nonsense brigade of my safe-and-happy sunshine stories that will probably unravel as soon as I leave, even among the moms who will want so much to believe.

But, looking into her serious and fair and questioning eyes, I can't do it. I cannot work up the energy this time to lie, to create the sentences that will create the fantasy that will create the feeling that will let me tell myself I did it for the good of everybody.

She deserves something else. They all deserve something better.

"Funny story," I say, stretching the definition of the word funny like some hybrid of taffy and Silly Putty.

Always leave 'em wanting more, right, is one of the rules of storytelling. I achieve that with my story of the scapular in Vietnam. I leave them wanting more of the feel-good stuff that is there in abundance. I leave them wanting more of what can only be provided when the four of us are home and safe and spinning our various tales of daring all around this very table or perhaps around a bigger one at a nice restaurant celebration.

My plane crash becomes, in my telling, not a crash but a ditching due to mechanical failure. The heroic Capt. Avery not only gets us onto the ground safely but is probably telling his own version in a hotel in Bangkok right now. The rest of the crew and I were ordered to bail out, and we parachuted to the ground but got separated in the process. There is no machete, but the AK-47 survives the telling. It's got a lot of rust on it, though. The very exciting Daisy Cutter/Huey rescue bit has to make the final cut, and when the four of us leave the ground on that chopper there isn't a dry eye in the house.

But of course, it's all about the scapular.

"I knew there was a Christian presence in that country," Mrs. Bucyk says with wide-eyed wonder, "but I thought they were persecuted. I never thought you'd find a *Catholic in the Vietcong*!"

I have to laugh at her amazement at this fact among all the facts. Happy, I am, to laugh at whatever funny presents itself.

"Well," I say, "from what I understand, yeah, they're not all that popular. But the VC go around conscripting all kinds, persuading, convincing, forcing some guys to fight. So I suppose a Catholic kid in his position maybe feels a little . . . isolated? Lonely?"

"Human?" Morris's mom pipes up.

"Yeah," I say, happy to hear it. "And so I suppose it just triggered something in him, right time right place, and he cuts me the break of a lifetime."

Maybe I shouldn't be surprised that this turns out, even with the edits, to be a *bring the house down* kind of a story. I'd figured it was enough that my version of events involved my being spared *capture*, without nasty old death sticking its parched leather face in anywhere. However, I realize that my mom, who at a critical juncture excused herself to go to the bathroom, has completely forgotten to return to her own party.

Hans now seems to share my enthusiasm for wrapping up proceedings, and the other guests appear to have noticed the missing hostess and a general air of *turn out the lights, the party's over.*

"I have every faith in you, Beck," Morris's mom says as she recreates the spine-snapping hug that began the evening. "In all of you boys. Men. Look out for yourselves. Look out for each other."

Spoken like a true Morris Mom.

"Absolutely," I say. "That's what we do."

Rudi's mom hugs me in an entirely different way. It's a handshake of a hug, and that's okay for me — though I'm thinking it's one of those disappointments Rudi has always known.

"Tell that boy of mine not to put his eye out, Beck. Will you promise to tell him that for me?"

"I promise," I say.

The Captain absolutely crushes my bones in a handshake that is not meant so much as a test or a challenge as, I think, an encouragement. I have no doubt The Captain, a real man o' war, saw through just about every one of my un-bellishments this evening. He might not know the specifics of what each of us is going through over there, but he knows there's more to it than I've revealed.

At least his wife seems to have come away with something uplifting.

"So then, if it were not for that scapular, you wouldn't be here today," she says, poking me gently and playfully right about the spot where the scapular would be.

The Captain, finally finishing off my hand bones, adds slyly, "There ya go, Beck. It's true, Jesus saves."

I don't know whether he is going for sincerity or blasphemy, but I know what he does achieve.

"That's just what Ivan would say," I say, laughing.

Hans and I stand wearily in the doorway, waving as they drive off, waving back crazy fast like they're trying to rub something awful off the cars' windows.

And then it is done. And then there are two.

"Nice story," he says, as we shift the last of the mess from the dining room table to the kitchen sink and the surrounding countertops. Calling it *nice* is, of course, a big fat lie.

"I thought you'd like it," I respond with my own big fat lie.

"Why don't you tell me the rest now?"

Because I would rather cut out my own tongue than see the heavy pain I have already put in your basset hound eyes, and there is no power on earth or elsewhere that could make me do anything to make it worse.

"I think we're both too tired at this point for any more big talking tonight, eh, Hans? And anyway, I think you need to be looking after Muti, no?"

He inhales for about ninety seconds, then blows it all back out in about three.

"We'll have a good talk, son. On the trip. We'll have plenty of time. It'll be good."

I say nothing, but smile at him, intense and effortless smiling that must tell him the important stuff that the words just wouldn't help.

We hug as if we will never hug again. But that's not true. It's just not true.

It's also not true that we will have a good talk on the trip, that we will have plenty of time, that it will be good.

I wake up with the sun. I spend a very inadequate forty-five minutes composing a letter to Hans and Muti and Ingrid and Elkie and Greta trying to explain myself. I read along with fascination as I write because, honestly, I feel like I need to explain myself to myself at the same time.

My letter will defuse approximately none of the fury at my leaving like this, but that is almost not the point. I have to go. I have to go now and alone and this way. They have to have my words, on paper, at least trying to explain, because we are people of words and logic and all that. If it takes a year or a lifetime to understand things, well, at least the words are there to work with.

I am massively sad and empty and correct when I pull the door quietly behind me and walk down the road that has always been my home and head back to the place that is likely to define who I am every bit as much.

It takes a total of seven lifts to hitchhike from Boston to Virginia. With stops in Providence, Rhode Island, and Hartford, Connecticut, and tiny towns in New Jersey and Maryland, I travel down the east coast of my country with a fair cross section of the American population. I travel by big-rig truck and a Volkswagen Beetle where you can see the road speeding past below, through the rotted floorboards. It's hypnotic. I travel in one pickup truck, one Lincoln Continental, and on the back of one Triumph motorcycle. The strangers upon whose kindness I rely are men and women and black and white and brown and in their twenties and thirties and fifties. I don't believe anybody in their forties ever stopped for me, whatever that means.

Without exception these people are kind and polite, but I suppose the kinds of people who pick up traveling vagabonds are either killers or nice, so I have to feel I have done all right on that score. But also, without exception I do not speak unless I am asked to and even then I give the kind of clipped answers that don't encourage a great deal of follow-up.

What I do tell each and every one of these folks is that I am a student, returning to my classes at Virginia Commonwealth University.

I allow myself a small laugh at the thought that I'm not sure what will rile my father more, that I bugged out on him, or that I told seven people that I go to Virginia Commonwealth.

Though actually it's only six people. I can't very well get away with telling that to the last gentleman, who drives me across the Virginia state line and who very graciously swerves a few miles out of his way to deposit me right at the gate of Langley Air Force Base.

I thank him as I grab my bag and step outside.

He looks across the bench seat of his car, over me, at the gate of the base, and back to me again.

"*Vaya con Dios*, man," he says. "God help you."

I search my brain for an appropriate response, the way you search the jumbled floor of your closet for that other shoe.

"Yeah" is what I come up with.

CHAPTER EIGHT

Back to Cat

For the second time I get to say one of the coolest sounding sentences imaginable:

I was delivered by Hercules to Phu Cat.

Only this time, with these months and miles behind me, it doesn't seem to possess quite the coolness it did the first time.

I have my new orders, and as I report to the captain I am to be flying with I can't avoid certain thoughts. And one of the things that I notice has changed about me is that thought thoughts can become spoken thoughts whether I want them to or not, depending on the situation.

"Captain Gilroy," I say, handing him my orders.

"Ah, Beck, there you are," he says, looking over the paperwork. We are in the hangar where my new office is sitting. It is an AC-47 gunship. Affectionately known as a Spooky.

"Yes, everything looks fine. Just go and get yourself settled and fed and whatnot then report back here this afternoon so you can get acclimated to the Spookster."

The Spookster. This is already starting badly.

"Can I ask you a question, sir?" I ask.

"Of course you can," he says.

"Am I here for a reason?"

He gives me a most quizzical look, full-on tilted-head, one-eye-squinted confusion.

"Most airmen don't start right off with existential questions, Beck. That usually takes a couple of weeks and several near-death happenings."

"I mean, regarding my transfer."

"What about it?"

"Was there anything about it, any special circumstance, that prompted me to be sent from Phan Rang?"

He sighs an impatient sigh. The hangar is a hive of activity, but as with the business of Phan Rang there is a casual routineness about it that suggests nobody's really rushing anywhere important. Still, the captain seems unenthusiastic about coddling me or anybody else.

"Well, Beck, from what I understand, you had neither an aircraft nor a crew to return to, so you had to go someplace, right?"

His bluntness is almost a relief. Not quite, but better than awkwardness, avoidance, or superstition. And helpfully, it invites bluntness in return.

"What I'm getting at, Captain Gilroy, is that I wonder if I was considered something like bad luck back at Phan Rang, and if maybe I was cleared out because of the whole death transference thing."

He strokes his chin in a way that's supposed to indicate deep thought about a subject, which nobody ever really does when they're thinking deeply. And so I am being mocked.

"A transference transfer, you say? Hmmm, I don't believe I've come across that in United States Air Force protocol before, son. Tell me, how many actual American service casualties have you been witness to now?"

"Seven," I say.

"*Seven?*" he says, all shock-horror-surprise. "Well, boy you're just getting started, then. I saw seven guys die before chow on my second day in-country. If we transferred guys every time they saw seven people get killed, man, we wouldn't even have time to kill anybody because everybody would be in the sky transferring their transferences from one lucky base to the next one."

"Right, sir," I say, already growing quite agitated at being so obviously mocked by a man I have already concluded is an ignoramus. A hardheaded half-wit who's now going to be ordering me around on a daily basis. "I just thought it was worth mentioning because —"

"Transference," he practically spits, cutting me off. "Get over yourself, Beck. We are *all* transferring death, all over this sorry little country, just as fast as we can. That is what we do. Now, go get yourself sorted out, get your head screwed on right, and be ready to be useful. Is that clear, kid?"

"Clear, sir."

So I have gone from "Provider" to "Spooky" so far in my military career, and that strikes me as appropriate. It's about how I feel.

I wonder all the time whether, if Morris, Ivan, and Rudi were not here, I would have come back. I wondered it through most of the night before I took off, and through the whole of the journey back to Langley from Boston, and still I don't have a definitive answer.

Not that it matters anyway. Because they are here.

There is a crew of eight on the AC-47, and it is my intention not to really get to know a single one of them. Pilot/Copilot/Navigator/Loadmaster/Gunner 1/Gunner 2/and South Vietnamese Air Force Observer. Hi, guys. Nice to meet ya.

And then there is me. Flight engineer. I keep things running more or less the way they are supposed to run. Truth is, that's my specialty, but probably everybody on board has the ability to do what I do. Most of us are interchangeable, with a certain amount of overlapping training to ensure that all systems will remain go in the event of something unexpected such as the brutal, untimely death of one or more members of the crew.

But flight engineer is the job that suits me, and even more than my backroom job on Operation Ranch Hand, this assignment leaves me my comfortable fantasy life where I really don't do any specific harm to anybody.

I have developed this thing, where in my mind, this aircraft is a mail carrier.

A very, very loud mail carrier.

The sound is deafening. The three 7.62-mm machine guns hammer away while I play my game of maintenance and repair in the middle of it all. Two of the guns are manned — one at a side window and one at the cargo door — with the third operated by the copilot remotely.

The Spooky is one of the primary ships called in for close air support when our troops on the ground get into a hairy situation. What we then do is fly to the location and suppress enemy activity so ferociously from the sky that our guys can push on and proceed to finish the job, take the ground, win the fight — or lose it and scram out of there — or whatever it is we are supposed to be achieving on the given day.

Our method is simple but no less impressive for that. We get our coordinates and then bank into our pylon turn, flying in a fifty-two-yard diameter elliptical lefthand pattern — all our guns are mounted on the left — and just pour holy mayhem down on the target until we're called off. We can spend four hours just like that, circling and shooting, shooting and circling, and it is some kind of magic that we don't all spend half the time puking and then step off the plane and into a spin like a bunch of human tops afterward.

We are doing our thing, ruthlessly and efficiently as ever, when the forward window gun fails.

"Beck!" the captain shouts from the cockpit.

"Yes, sir," I shout back.

"Get that gun functioning."

"Yes, sir," I say, thinking about how I am going to fool myself this time, to work this gun repair job into my postal plane fantasy.

The other two gunners continue their relentless assault on the ground below. I marvel at their trance-like focus.

The thing is burning hot to the touch but with the right gloves, enough oil, and persistence, I find the problem and unjam it.

"All set, cap," I call.

Immediately the copilot calls back to me. "Negative. I'm getting nothing."

Unfortunately the jam itself has caused some kind of problem with the remote mechanism.

"Man the gun, Beck," Capt. Gilroy commands.

"I'm not a gunner, sir," I say, thinking this is somehow a reasonable thing to say to my commanding officer in wartime. "It's not my job."

I can practically hear his eyeballs bounce off the windshield. "Your *job*, Beck, is to do what I tell you to do, when I tell you to do it. Now man that station and fire that weapon!"

"Yes, sir," I call, and approach the gun without any idea how I am going to explain this one to myself.

It's the same. I see it right down there, below me. This is the canopy, the jungle, the lushlands that I tried to destroy the first time around, with my Thunder Pig and my chemicals. It is just the same, exactly the same, just as beautiful, possibly more beautiful than when I first saw it. From this angle, it sure looks like I failed at that project, to strip and burn the land of its natural wondrous cover.

"Beck!" the captain shouts. "Fire that weapon!"

It is dusky, the light just starting to go. Below, the muzzle flashes tell us where the enemy fire is coming from, and where I am supposed to aim my own rounds. In case it is not all clear enough for me, suddenly one or more of my colleagues fires a number of flares down into the zone, lighting up the area and turning the muzzle flashes into people for me to shoot.

How did we get into this? How did I get into this?

I would love to live my whole life having never shot at anybody. As of this moment I would very much like for that to be one of my life goals.

And as of this moment that is absolutely, unequivocally, not a possibility.

"Beck!" Capt. Gilroy screams.

But it's not because of that.

It's because, just as quick as my mail carrier became a gunship, and as quick as my mechanic job became shooter, as quick as those trees and bushes became muzzle flashes that became, under bright phosphorescent flares, *people* . . . those people became people shooting at my people.

How did we get here? How did I get here?

That could be Ivan down there. It could.

My whole body quakes with the *ratatat-atatatatatatata* of the machine-gun fire.

This is why I am here.

Ratatatatatatatata! As soon as I start firing the gun, firing the gun becomes the most natural thing in the world.

Raaaaaaatatatatatatatatatat!

Firing the gun becomes the rightest thing there could be. Firing the gun at those humans down there is my function. If I wasn't prepared to do this then I should have just deserted like Ingrid told me to. Like I thought about through the long night in my childhood bed.

Ceasing to fire now would feel unnatural.

I watch, going deeper into the trance I recognized in the other gunners, as my eyes follow the glowing red tracer rounds through the air and all the way down to their intended targets.

———————— ★ ————————

As I lay in my bunk, my hands and my arms almost up to my elbows are still numb with the reverberations from the gun. I keep wondering whether I killed anybody, and if I did, how do I feel about that.

I find myself, deep into the night, staring at my hands as I turn them over and around and I examine every angle possible.

Am I any different?

If somebody died, or if I missed every time, with every last one of the thousands and thousands of rounds I delivered, am I somehow different from who I was before?

Yes.

I decide yes, I am different. *If* I killed somebody down there I am a different person from who I was the very second before that. The question is, did I?

I'm glad I don't know the answer.

Except, there's one gigantic difference right there. I was never before glad not to know the answer, to anything.

I am going over the aircraft along with the loadmaster, whose name is Manion. I have finished with all my checks, repairs, and adjustments, and everything is ready for the next flight in a few hours' time.

"What are you doing?" Manion asks as he hops down from the cargo door and I don't follow. I stand in the doorway, looking out into the perfect day, the clear sunny sky. Then I turn back into the plane.

"Just hanging around," I say.

"Suit yourself," he says.

I walk around inside the plane, just looking, touching stuff. I sit in the pilot's seat, imagine myself flying. It is still a stunning thing, this thing, this flying, killing machine. I think about this a lot now, how much magnificence goes into this. The planes, the helicopters, the missiles, all stunningly beautiful and sophisticated and magical things that are the result of how many years, how many million man hours, how many brains, how many bright guys waking up in the middle of the night and realizing, *Wait; I have it, I know how to make this work* and then writing down the final note on the bedside notebook that clicks in the final piece that becomes an atomic bomb or an armor-piercing bullet.

All that brilliance. In service of what?

"Democracy?" comes a voice that makes me jump like a thief out of the captain's seat.

"Oh man," I say, practically falling over with the fright of the surprise. I stumble out of the seat and away from the controls. I rub my temples to massage out a stab of pain. Since the crash I am finding myself more prone to headaches than I ever was before.

"Hey," I say, walking back through the airplane. I look all around, and there's nobody here. "Who said that?"

Nothing.

I go back to the cargo door, stand there looking all around, and see nobody in the vicinity.

I rub my temples some more, squint from the strong sunshine.

"Tricks," I say. It's a place that plays tricks, no doubt about that.

I stand there in the doorway, looking out across the airfield, scanning the array of airpower lined up out there.

We have three AC-47s stationed here, and usually at least one is on the ground standing by for the call at all times. The others will be in the air, cruising for trouble, waiting for some desperate groundhogs to call for help. I see at the far end of the runway a brother Spooky sitting ready, and on either side of that a couple of F-100 Super Sabres. There are a few Huey helicopters pausing for breath before the next rescue, and a whole slew of awesome F-4 Phantom jets.

It still chokes me up, to see the specialness of all this gear, the brilliance and wonderment that went into the concepts and details of each bit.

But it will never again feel like it did when I first saw it all. It couldn't. It'll be different tomorrow, and again the day after.

I have no idea how much of that wonder will come home with me. I wonder if there will be any left at all.

When we go up that evening for a bit of night action, I am all antsy and agitated. Something's gotten into me and I cannot wait to get up there, and when we do I do something that even I think is strange, even as I'm doing it.

I man the unmanned machine gun without being asked.

Rattattattatta . . . Rarattatatatatatatatata.

I watch the poetry of the red tracers flowing down like molten deadly candy drops pouring out of the sky in search of my enemy. An enemy I would not have but for the fact that my brother's enemy is my enemy, and these guys are trying to kill my brothers.

A guy has got to have a sense of purpose here. He has to have a focus, or he could well go altogether mad.

"Beck!" I hear someplace out there as I follow the tracers. Then one of the other guys starts pumping out the flares from the open cargo bay door, and the night becomes better than day down there in the target zone and we fire away like nobody's business.

Ratatatatatatatataa . . .

"Beck!"

"What?" I call back to the captain, as if he is an irritant in the way of my doing my very important thing.

"I am having issues here with hydraulic fluid. What the devil are you doing?"

"Doing my job, cap. Making that spot there on the ground safe for democracy."

"Well how 'bout you make this particular plane safe for flying and landing before we all get killed? Unless it is part of your master plan to *transfer* you and me and this entire crew to the Promised Land."

"Right, sir," I say, but the truth is I spend a good bunch of seconds and hundreds more rounds before I can break the spell and pull myself away from the shooting.

It turns out that the fluid problem is a symptom of something much more extensive with the hydraulics all over the Spooky. I go into a minor panic as I scramble to both stabilize the situation and not appear to be frantically working to stabilize the situation. Especially since the monitoring of the fluids is close to one hundred percent my responsibility and my taking my eye off the ball is largely responsible for the fix we're in.

"Captain Gilroy," I say to him when I have the thing as stable as I can get it for now. I know for sure that the landing gear is going to sound like a rusty robot giant waking from a hundred-year sleep when we go to put it down, and I don't need the crew to tell me that they are feeling the stiffness in the controls already.

"I have done what I can on the fly, captain. We're going to have to cut this sortie short 'til I can get a better look at the source of the problem."

"Yeah," he says, pulling on the stick, test-flapping the flaps. "Right, we're calling it a day. Home, gentlemen."

I am doing the once-over with the chief mechanic when I get called to the communications office to take a radio call.

There is hardly any great mystery to who it might be. I don't get a lot of calls.

"What's happening, Morris, man?"

"It. *It* is happening, Beck. Time to roll out, because the boys are meeting up."

"Really? When? How?" My dormant heart is pumping alive at the sound of this, and for no good reason or for very good reason I feel like this is the thing that will do it for me. Seeing my guys will be the tonic for my soul.

And just the fact that I am talking in terms of heart and soul rather than mind is hint enough that I need something.

"Now, man. We're on our way right now."

"We? Who's we?"

He gets a bit laughy, can't seem to contain himself.

"Well, me and Ivan, for starters."

"Ivan? You've been talking to Ivan?"

"Talking to him? Boy, I'm looking at him. Right this minute."

"Get outta here. You're not."

"I am."

"I want to talk to him. Put him on, now."

"Ivan," he says. "Beck says you have to talk to him. Right now."

There is some muffled, growly voicing off in the background, followed by Morris laughing some more.

"Beck?" Morris says. "Yeah, okay I have a direct quote for you: 'I don't have to do nothin'. Go sit on a live claymore, brainbox.'"

I pause, smiling broadly and silently for a few seconds.

"Well, okay, so you do have Ivan there. Right, tell me, tell me, what's the plan?"

"Right, we are in Pleiku right now."

"*Pleiku?* I thought you were on a *boat*?"

"You want to give me geography lessons right now, Beck, or you want to coordinate?"

"Coordinate."

"Okay, so Pleiku's where Ivan's been prowling the highlands big game hunting. And with me working with all those Army guys on the Riverine Assault Force, I made connections, made arrangements, and anyway, I'm here. Now Ivan and I have got us a hitch on a transport flying out to Da Nang in a couple of hours. I talked to Rudi and that's a doable trip for him, so he's on his way north to meet us there later today."

"I can get to Da Nang!" I blurt.

"Of course you can. This is our moment, man."

"No, I mean, I know exactly *how* I can get there. But I have to rush. Listen, I will get there. We meet at the base, dinnertime. See you at the chow line."

"Ha!" He laughs, a real joy of a laugh. "That's just what Rudi said."

I run hard back to the spot just outside the hangar where the chief mechanic is doing his assessment. We have a repair shop here on base, but it has its limits and so do we. Whenever a plane needs real repairs, it's sent up to Da Nang.

"How's the patient, doc?" I say as I run up to him. He's staring up into the guts of the landing gear. The landing itself was something sinister, with worse noise than I had anticipated, as if a great big can opener was ripping into the belly of the plane. There was real concern all around that we were going to come in on our belly.

The chief mechanic is an older guy, probably thirty, and one of the most tired-looking people I have seen here. He moves slowly and gives the impression he would like to just hand his job off to the next sap who comes along.

"Seen worse," he says. "But I would be surprised if this landing gear ever gets back up inside the bird again under its own power."

"Oh," I say, matching his weary tone. "Shame. Too much for us to handle here, I suppose."

"Well, nah. It'll take a while that's for sure, but we can probably manage it. What with all the other dings and dangs on this machine it's probably not a bad idea to ground her for a week or so anyway, get her truly airworthy. Somebody has *not* been properly looking after this gal."

I feel bad. I do. But it wasn't only me. I just got here.

He sighs a big sigh, places a hand kindly on the frozen strut of the landing gear, and shakes his head.

"Wouldn't Da Nang do a better job?" I say hopefully.

He looks away from the stricken bird, and right into me.

"I suppose," he says. Then, "Looking to go to Da Nang, I reckon?"

"Ah," I say, thinking about time, and my friends, and time. "Just thinking about the aircraft. Oh, and the Air Force, of course."

"Uh-huh," he says. "And possibly the ladies?" His eyebrows right now show more life than his whole body has otherwise.

"What ladies? I don't know anything about any ladies."

"The WAFs," he says.

"What's a WAF?"

"Women's Air Force."

"*Everything* gets abbreviated in the military," I say.

"Except the misery," he says in a voice and with eyes that convince me he has been in every war since the Revolution. "I'll send your plane to the hospital for a couple of days," he says, walking past me toward the administration buildings. "They'll get it done quicker and righter up there, anyways."

Capt. Gilroy is happy to let both me and the plane go for two days. It's like a short vacation for him and the crew, and the plane they get back will be deadlier than ever. The landing gear will have to stay down for the whole flight, but other than that it shouldn't be noticeably compromised.

In short order I am airborne. I have thrown a few things in a bag, personally greased up every moving part in that plane, showered, and taken my seat alongside one of the first four enlisted WAFs to serve in Vietnam. There have been a few female officers serving in-country, but this is the first of the regulars to get here. I think the Air Force is making a mini-tour of them, to get some positive press by making each base stop a good-news event. Those have been thin on the ground lately. Or in the air, for that matter.

"Halfway through," I say in answer to the question about my tour of duty.

Seating on the Spooky is not ideal, despite it being converted from a DC-3 passenger plane. I am sitting at one of the gun stations, while my new friend, Airwoman First Class Shirley Brown, sits at another.

"And you?" I ask. "You're just getting started, right?"

"Yeah. Mostly it's been public relations. I'd like to do some fighting, though."

"Really?"

"Of course. Why else would I be here? I don't have to be here."

"Good point," I say and look out my little window over the gun, at the country below. You can barely even tell how much we've shot it up from here. How much I have shot it up.

"You don't sound like you like the fighting. So I guess you were drafted, then."

"No," I say, surprised even now to remember that I wasn't.

"Why'd you join up?"

I think about where I'm going, and where I'm coming from. I think about who I'm seeing in a very short while. Boston and Rudi and Phan Rang and Ingrid and

Elkie and Canada and Madison, Wisconsin, all play across the Happy Valley Drive-In of my mind.

"It's kind of complicated," I say.

"Well, for me," Shirley Brown says, "I'm a big fan of keeping it uncomplicated. I'm fighting for my brothers and sisters. Remember that and I'll be strong. Forget it even a little, and it could get sticky."

I turn away now from my beloved countryside to take in the fresh and smart and focused face of WAF A1C Shirley Brown.

"I'm really glad they finally wised up and sent you over here, Sister WAF."

She looks just a bit of the right kind of bashful as she looks away from me and out the window at the country I am completely certain she is going to love very soon.

"You and me both, airman," she says generous and kind, as a sister would.

CHAPTER NINE

Da Nang

The air base at Da Nang is large, like a big-city airport with only a small city attached to it. Once we land there is business to sort out, and once all the business is sorted out it is nearly dinnertime and I am on the fly to the mess. It takes me fifteen minutes to find it, but I find it.

How do I describe my feelings as I approach the building? Like that first day of freshman year of high school, headed to lunch in the big cafeteria for the first time? Yeah, there's that bigness, uncertainty, nervousness. Like crossing to the girls' side of the auditorium to ask for a dance at the first dance of that same freshman year? Yeah, there's that, too.

Why? How and why did I wind up back in freshman year? In Vietnam of all places?

And why, oh why, am I feeling this strangeness over the oldest and most important friends I have in the world?

It makes no sense. It makes no sense and I have no idea why it is.

I am lying, of course.

I do know the why of it. The fear, uncertainty, strangeness, trepidation? Because I don't know what I am going to find here. Because if these people are somehow not the people I know them to be and need them to be, then what does that do to my world?

And I fear this fear because, if after this much time in Vietnam I don't know if I even know myself, how will I know them?

Which is why what happens next is the best thing that could ever happen to me at the best moment it could ever happen.

"Beck!" Morris calls, almost embarrassingly unselfconsciously. He jumps out of his seat at the closest table to the mess hall door like he's a spring-loaded Sidewinder missile. Before I can even react he is standing right in front of me with one hand holding on to each of my shoulders, squeezing as tight as he can. Fortunately he is Morris. If Ivan decides to do the same thing — which is, ah, unlikely — I won't be able to raise my arms for weeks.

But more than the grip, it's the look. Morris, with his big round open eyes, looks at me, looks into me in his singular Morris way, bringing that way with him across months and miles and oceans and deaths and all that, to this spot right here.

And just like that, I am me. I remember to be me, and how to do it.

He doesn't say anything right off, aware that smiling and squeezing and knowing is enough for now. Then, as he is about ready to talk, Ivan runs out of patience and bumps him away like they are playing roller derby.

"How are ya, man?" Ivan says, going the more traditional manly handshake route.

"I'm great, Ivan, great," I say as we pump each other's hands for a good long time. His face, always less readable than most, has actually lost some expressiveness since I saw him last. Though maybe I'm just imagining that. "How have you been? You're up in the Central Highlands now. I hear that is stunning country up there."

Ivan releases my hand like he's trying to throw it on the floor, but he laughs at the same time.

"Leave it to you, Beck, to talk about this death trap like it's one big holiday."

I follow the two of them back to the table, where we plunk down. Morris is beside me, Ivan across.

"So, Rudi?" I ask, palms upturned.

"He's not here," Ivan says.

"He'll be here soon," Morris says. "He's not late yet."

The big dining hall is heavy with hungry traffic. I am too worked up to think about food.

"I'm getting something to eat," Ivan says, standing. "Anybody coming?"

"I'll wait for Rudi," Morris says.

"Yeah," I add. "Me, too."

As soon as Ivan is gone, Morris says, "I don't know about that guy."

"Did you ever?" I ask.

"Hah," he says, elbowing me.

"Ivan's fine," I say. "Ivan'll always be fine. Tell me a story, pal."

"Okay," he says, "I'll tell you a story."

Morris then goes into great detail about his time on the USS *Boston*, and how they were attacked by friendly fire. I know the story of course, but that's the thing about war stories. There's the story, and the *story*, which you can only ever get for real from a guy who was there. Morris tells a good story.

And I can't believe this is even us. Sitting here telling *war stories*. Like a bunch of old geezers.

"We already know that story." Ivan snarls as he takes his seat again. He's got two cheeseburgers and a full helmet of coleslaw on his plate. He heaps a big plop of slaw onto one of the burgers, puts its hat back on, then points at me with his fork. "You tell us a story, flyboy." He takes a sloppy bite.

"Oh," I say, getting my bearings. Okay. I can tell a story. To these guys, I can tell a story.

Probably *only* to these guys — including Rudi, that is, but lateness has its price, pal. I'll tell him that. Then I'll tell him whatever he's missed.

So while Ivan eats and Morris leans close, I tell them a story about an escort pilot in a Skyraider making the last gesture he will ever make. A thumbs-up to me.

One burger has departed by the time I finish that one.

"That's an okay story," Ivan says, slawing the other burger mercilessly. "Tell us another one."

"Maybe there isn't another one," I say.

Ivan gets very serious, leans across the table, and looks into my eyes in a way that makes me edgy. I try not to but I look away, first down, then up.

"Oh, there's another one," he says. "And another one. And another one after that, I bet."

I sigh as he stares me down while biting into that disgusting creamy milky mess of a slawburger of his.

I tell them about the three ground crew workers and the stray bomb.

He is still chewing, smiling and giving me the *come on, come on, cough it up* gesture with his free hand. Not as pretty a sight as it sounds, but to me it's beautiful because it is all thoroughly Ivan.

"All right," I say, but first, you have to pay admission to this one. "Let's see the scapulars, gentlemen."

Without hesitation, they produce the little cloth Christ likenesses they have been wearing since Mrs. Bucyk laid them on us.

"Very good," I say. "I'm impressed."

"Show us yours, then," Morris says.

I smile a sheepish smile and just shake my head. Ivan points that fork at me again.

"I am telling my mother on you," he says.

"Don't bother," I say. "I already told her myself."

And with that, I tell my two friends every true detail about what transpired that day in the air, in the jungle, and in my head. I tell them what happened to my crew, what happened to me, and what didn't happen to me. I leave nothing out. When I finish, finally, telling the biggest story of my life, which I will probably never repeat in such detail again, I feel almost as drained as the day it all went down.

And when I look up — because much of it was told with me looking at my hands, at Ivan's plate, at a blurry middle distance between here and Boston — I take in my pals' expressions.

"Beck . . . ," Morris says, squeezing his own head with his hands like he's trying to get juice out of it. "You're a . . . you're a *war veteran*, man."

I chuckle. "I know, right? How did *that* happen?"

"And Ivan's mom saved your life, so you owe him big time now."

"Well, according to The Captain, Jesus Saves is the story, so I will pay the proper debt when my time comes."

I look across to Ivan. There is not a trace of anything in his expression. It's like a dehumanized collection of Ivanesque features that don't add up to Ivan.

"You maybe got the transference, then," he says flatly, spooking me right out of my socks.

"You've heard of it, too?" I ask.

"People talk about it. Mostly fools. Not smart guys like yourself."

"Yeah, *only* fools," Morris adds. "That leaves Beck out. That leaves you out, doesn't it, Beck?"

He has grabbed me by the shirt, like he's going to get tough with me.

All at once the three of us burst out laughing at this, and man oh man oh man is this the best thing right now.

"So, Ivan," I say, "tell us a story."

The laughter subsides and something like unreality in this unreal place takes hold once more.

"I decline," says Ivan.

"Come on," Morris says.

Then, in a calm tone that is not angry or fierce but carries with it the promise of anger and ferocity as only Ivan Bucyk's voice can, he expands and contracts his statement all at once.

"My story is the most boring story of war," he says. "You know what I do. I know what I do. That's it."

And *it*, that certainly is. He's a sniper. Even in his language, he's a sniper, lean and lethal.

It's also been an hour and a half already since I walked through the door.

"Rudi?" I say again, palms up again. It occurs to me that that should probably be the international sign language gesture for Rudi.

"Come on," Morris says, getting up, grabbing his backpack, and storming toward the door. "Let's go make a call."

We hop up and follow behind our newly fearless leader, into a gorgeous Vietnam sunset. I carry my small backpack, half empty, and Ivan carries a long bag, more like something a hockey player would lug around, with his tools of the trade. We are all red, gold, orange glowing as we make our way across the compound to find the communications center. Something about it puts a lump in my throat.

Then I feel another thing entirely. Ivan comes up close and claps me on the back. Then he squeezes the back of my neck so hard I hear vertebrae crackle.

"But you don't kill anybody," he says to me.

I try to look over at him but my neck seems to be immobilized, and this seems to be deliberate.

"I don't think I do, no," I say, and the steady squeeze becomes more of a pulsating thing.

"That's good, pal. That's really good. You're gonna be all right then. You're gonna be all right."

"Thanks, Ivan man," I say, and though the pain is kind of crippling, I'd rather have my neck snap in two than ask him to stop.

One of the most useful and impressive things about this current version of Morris is how he is one of those guys who simply gets things done. Mostly through his radio-man skills, he has learned to talk everybody's language, how to ask the right questions, find the right person, pull the operative levers of power. He's become one of those guys who, if he doesn't know the right guy, then he finds the guy who knows the guy who knows the right guy.

I won't say that the war has been good for Morris. But man, he's a man now.

"Right, numbskull, so where are you?" he snaps into the phone after only about twenty minutes tracking down the guy and the guy and finally, the numbskull. "I'll call you whatever I want. We have been here for over two hours already, and you were the one who had the shortest distance to travel. . . . What? So, what, are you sensitive all of a sudden? I'm not yelling. And no, you won't hang up. You know how difficult it is to make one of these —"

I snatch the phone out of his hand.

"Rudi, man, how are you?"

He goes all quiet. "Beck? It's you. It's . . . this is amazing."

"Okay, well, we don't want you to get so amazed you can't speak. What's going on? How come you're not here, man? We're a wheel short."

"Ah, I know. Listen. This is the Marines, y'know, the backbone of the whole war. I can't just take a day off just 'cause I want one."

"You mean, you're on duty?"

"I go out every day, man. Every, single, day, I do a patrol. Sometimes more than one."

"Jeez, man, they're really slave driving down there in Chu Lai."

"But I want to go out. I get funny, in the head, any day I can't get out there."

This is not the thing I want to hear. This is almost precisely the thing I do not want to hear.

"Are you saying that's where you have been while we've been waiting? Out on a patrol? On a *voluntary* patrol?"

Morris starts flapping his arms and flailing all over the office while Ivan, sitting on a desk with his long bag across his lap, just stares at the phone coldly.

"Had to do it, Beck. I'm busy making the world safe for lazy so-and-sos like you three bums. But I'll be there. I really want to see you guys. I'll get there."

"How?" I say. "How will you get here, and when?"

Morris starts shaking his head emphatically and pacing back and forth in front of me. "No," he says. "This isn't working. After everything . . . all the effort, all the coordination and planning it took, and the simpleton, the guy who could have got here the easiest . . . THANKS FOR NOTHING, PAL!"

It would almost be comical. If it weren't so wrong. I have never in memory seen Morris so angry. I bet he wasn't this angry when our own guys attacked his ship.

Ivan reaches across and coolly grabs the receiver out of my hand.

"Yeah, it's me," Ivan says. "You stay right where you are. We're coming to you."

There is a little Rudi voice audible on the other end, motormouthing away, and I can even detect his voice getting higher and higher with nervous excitement as he talks at Ivan.

Ivan listens unresponsively for about five seconds before hanging the handset up with the voice still chattering at speed.

"So how do we get to Chu Lai?" Ivan asks both of us.

CHAPTER TEN

I's of the World

It is approximately fifty-six miles from Da Nang to Chu Lai, and by the time we finish talking our way through the bumpy ride in the back of a cargo truck, I just about feel like the three of us added up would pretty much constitute one complete tour-of-*tours* of Vietnam. Morris has gone from floating off the coast to drifting along all the veins and arteries that constitute the Mekong mouth, delta, river, and tributaries. I started briefly in Phu Cat, transferred down to Phan Rang, then came back up coast to the Cat again. Ivan's stalked everywhere from the lowlands to the plains to the highlands, doing that thing he does. Really, if you look at a map, we have been there, covered it, done it. The only one who's been able to more or less stay put the whole time has been Rudi, and you know, he's doing it again right now.

It's dark, and well into the night when we enter the base at Chu Lai. The place houses mostly Marines but is also host to the Army's Americal Division and it has a small air base full of USMC fighter jets, so for a small place it seems to about hold a little bit of everything the United States military has brought to this party.

One of the duty guards looks at a list and locates where Rudi's quarters are, and after a short walk I believe we have found it.

"This place is pretty slack," Ivan says, looking all around like a burglar casing a bank job.

"It does have a less military kind of feel than what I'm used to," I say.

It's almost like a local village, the way it's set up with hooches that sleep four or five guys. And we don't seem to have a great deal of trouble moving around freely in the middle of the night.

Morris walks straight into the hooch identified as Rudi's. I follow. Ivan stands outside, still looking all around.

"Can I help you?" comes a low voice from the one occupied bunk.

"Yeah," Morris says. "We were told we could find our pal here. Rudi?"

The guy doesn't move, not even to prop himself up on his elbow.

"He's out."

"Out where?"

"Who are you people again?"

"We're his friends," I say, "from back home. He's expecting us."

"Then I guess he's *expecting* you to wait. 'Cause he's out. Like I said."

"Out where?" Ivan snaps from outside the door.

Now the guy props up, and it feels tense.

"We just want to know if you can point out, if he's on the base, where we might go and find him," Morris says.

"No. Because he ain't on the base. He's out. Like patrolling."

"Now?" I say. "He was sent out on night patrol, after being on patrol just this afternoon?"

"Nobody sent him," the guy says. "He sent himself. Like he does."

We are all speechless for several seconds, until Morris blurts, "Are you telling me —"

"I ain't tellin' you nothin'. He's out. No idea when he'll be back."

I hesitate, then ask, "Mind if we wait here for him?"

"I mind very much. If you want to just set up camp in the mess hall I will send him that way as soon as he gets in. Good night, gentlemen."

With our options being extraordinarily limited, we go and find the mess hall. It is open but deserted, and immediately Morris stretches out across a table and I do likewise across a row of chairs. Ivan sits up at the next table over, looking like he's expecting waitress service.

"Why don't you try and get some rest, Ivan, man," I say, sitting up to look at his tired face.

He doesn't bother with words, just waves me back down.

And like some puppet controlled by his hand, I lower right back down and might even be nodding off by the time I get all the way horizontal.

However long later, I wake up to a tap tap tapping on the sole of my boot. I blink myself awake to find I'm looking up at an atomic GI Joe version of my old simple friend, Rudi. He is armed to the gills, with an M-16 with bayonet attached, bandoliers of bullets crisscrossing his chest, a knife on one hip and a pistol on the other. He has on camouflage fatigues and helmet, and his face is smoke-soot smeared.

I remain lying there and take him in. His pose says *don't mess with me*, but I am happy to report that now that I see him I wouldn't consider him dangerous if he had a lit fuse sticking out of his skull.

"Come here, ya dope," I say, leaping up and embracing him.

He is bigger, for sure. He's put on some muscle pounds here while I am pretty sure the other three of us have lost weight.

"Don't put your eye out," I say into his ear, because I gave my word.

He says, "Huh?"

"Your mom told me to tell you, don't put your eye out."

I can feel, against my head, he's shaking his own head. "Good t'see ya, Beck," he says, his embrace equal parts hug and backslap. "I believe you might have met my good pal Sunshine here."

It's only then I notice the guy from the hooch is here, too.

"Sunshine," I say, taking his firm handshake. He nods at me, wordless, not unfriendly. I turn to the other guys, one spread out on a table and doing a fair imitation of a cadaver on a slab, the other slumped, seated, no less unconscious. "Hey," I snap at them. "Hey, look what we got here."

Morris is the first up. "There he is," Morris says, hopping up just like I did, getting and giving the same hugs. Meeting Sunshine.

The main event, though, we all know what it is. Ivan is different.

Ivan looks up from his seat, as clear-eyed as if he'd had a full eight hours of sleep, or as if he hadn't needed any at all.

"How are ya, Rudi Rude boy?" Ivan says, standing very slowly, then extending a hand.

Rudi's face is so full of excitement and confusion as he looks at Ivan, about to jump into his arms, but not, like a puppy that's been left alone too long but still knows not to jump all over the master when he comes home.

They shake hands, firm and long, until it seems like they may have forgotten everything else. Guys are already rolling in looking for breakfast, which the kitchen boys are already slapping together up at the long counter. The place smells institutional-food good.

"You will be Ivan, then," Sunshine says.

"I will be for as long as I can," Ivan says, over one more handshake to complete the set.

"I have heard a *lot* about you, sir. Rudi here says you are the man who made the man, and my hat is off to you for that. This boy's a beast. America's finest."

Rudi finally can't hold back anymore, and the burst he was holding back can be held no more.

"My hat's off to you too, Ivan!" he says, and whips his helmet off, plops it down on the table, then quickly works open his shirt.

Oh. Oh my.

"Oh, my," Morris says.

In a Baltic-cold voice that lowers the temperature all around us, Ivan says, "What in the world is that?"

"It's my I," Rudi answers with a nutty kind of glee.

It is a tattoo, of a capital letter I, right in the middle of his chest. Amateurish. Almost looks like he could have done it himself.

"Why?" Ivan says, barely audible.

Rudi looks all around like this is some kind of joke.

"It's for *you*, Ivan man. 'Cause of all you done for me. 'Cause I wouldn't be here, a million times over, if it wasn't for you. And I sure wouldn't be the Marine I am."

"And he is one remarkable fighting man, Ivan. Not like most of what we're left with in I Corps at this stage. Things here are dire, and if it wasn't for this man here, I don't know what-all I'd do."

Ivan's face is drained of color. He stares with glassy cat eyes at Sunshine.

"Could you . . . would you mind . . . go?"

"Nothing personal," I say when I see Sunshine bristle. "It's just that we haven't seen each other in a long while. And we only have a limited amount of time. . . ."

"Appreciate it," Morris says. "Thanks. Nice meeting you. We're normally really friendly, but . . . yeah, thanks."

Rudi just keeps staring bright-eyed at Ivan as if he is unaware what else might be happening all around him. Sunshine turns and goes without a nod or a wink or a word.

"For *me*?" Ivan asks.

"Yeah. It's my IOU to you, for everything," Rudi chirps, as if he's been rehearsing this for some time. "Because *I*," he points at the chest, "*owe*," he makes an OK circle with his thumb and index finger, "*you*," he takes that index finger and pokes his hero sharply in his own chest.

Ivan smacks that hand away with a crack loud enough that the kitchen guys at the far end of the hall look our way.

"Who's hungry?" Morris says, trying to apply his special Morris powers of unity to a situation that, frankly, badly needs them.

"You have to get that thing removed, Rudi," Ivan

says, looking completely haunted as he stares at the awfulness of the thing.

The mess hall is maybe one-third full now, and guys are starting to sit down near us.

"I'm going to go get a plate of food," Morris says, "and when I come back I am expecting us to be all the way back to normal and having the laughs we came here for, right?"

"Right, I'll come with you," I say.

He goes a few steps in the direction of the kitchen, then turns to meet me. "Don't you think maybe we should take turns so there's always one of us to keep an eye on them?"

"No," I say. "They are surrounded by jarheads already, I am starving, and you know what? That's Ivan and Rudi over there. No matter what else has happened to the world, that is Ivan and Rudi and if we just step back the universe will tilt back where it belongs."

We do, however, fairly sprint through the process of heaping our plates with several varieties of pork products, eggs, toast, and grits. We can see, at least, that they are sitting and talking as we approach.

"You're a murderer, Rudi" is the first thing we hear, so talk isn't always good.

You know when somebody says something about you, calls you something, accuses you of something that is supposed to be terrible and *is* terrible and you argue with it but you can't fight off a smile that is all wrong for the situation anyway? That is Rudi's stupid little face now, and I wish I could slap it from here all the way back to the school playground.

"So are you," Rudi says back. "So is everybody here. Don't give me that stuff, man, 'cause you know better. *You* know. We're all murderers in this job, only difference is some of us are good at it and some aren't. You and I are the best, while I'm pretty sure these two stink."

We are all speechless. Which Rudi takes as encouragement.

"Right?" he says, pointing at each of us one at a time.

"Could you at least button your shirt?" Morris says, squinting while trying to eat.

"Got any tattoos yourself, Morris?" Rudi asks.

"No," he says, acting now like eating is a task that takes full concentration.

"Beck?"

"Don't be stupid, Rudi," I say.

"Hah!" he says, clapping his hands. "I was wondering who was gonna be the first one to say that. I was thinking Ivan, but you were my second choice. What about you, my-man-I-van, I bet you got tattoos. Probably loads of 'em. Right? Bet you got a big R for me someplace, huh?"

Silently, Ivan rolls up his sleeve, and flexes his Moxie tonic logo on his inner biceps. The mad scientist guy in the artwork looks more reasonable than Rudi by about a factor of twelve.

"Moxie!" Rudi says. "I always knew you'd bring the Moxie to Vietnam, man, I knew it. Come on, pal, let's go get some chow."

Ivan shakes his head slowly. "Not hungry," he says.

"Fine," Rudi says. "Be right back. Save me a seat, like the good old days."

Holy smokes. Were there good old days? Where are we? Who are we?

"Holy smokes," I say.

"Holy smokes," Morris says.

I stare at Ivan, who stares at our old pal up there, fueling up for the next assault.

"Maybe we can help him," Morris says. Of course Morris says that.

Ivan turns his laser stare on Morris, until Rudi is back with us.

This is how we sit, the four of us, in a configuration not unlike in the high school cafeteria. Rudi to my right, across from Morris, who is next to Ivan. Three of the four of us are eating, and for a couple of minutes that is all that happens. I feel a little bit better, then a little bit more. That's what food does, and why people should eat together. Rudi's plate is all meat and one piece of toast. Ivan's plate does not, unfortunately, exist.

"Here," I say, offering a sausage link across the table. "You have to have something. So have something. You'll feel better."

"How many?" Ivan asks Rudi.

Rudi stops eating, smiles. They know what they're talking about.

"You know as well as anybody," Rudi says, "that I'm lousy at counting."

"Gimme a ballpark," Ivan says. .

"*Don't* give him a ballpark," Morris says, slamming down his knife and fork.

"Who can tell, at this point," Rudi says, "with the free-fire zones and all. You go into a village . . . they are *all* enemy combatants, by the way, and don't let any-body tell you any different. All of them."

"Not all of them, pal," I say right up against the side of his fair-haired head. "You can't be believing that."

"Grow up, Beck," he says, breathing smoky bacon right into me. "You might be smart, but that don't mean you know nothin', all right? Back in Boston, maybe . . . not here. Not here. This is where *I* know stuff. Right? And the Marines is where *I* am the smart guy."

"You know," Morris says, and even he has to strain to sound levelheaded, "this doesn't have to be —"

"It does," Rudi says, actually bringing it all down a notch himself. "No offense, but for the first time, prob-ably ever, I am right and you guys are wrong. I'm not here to tell you how to run your war, so have some respect and don't come into my place and think you're gonna tell me how to run mine."

Ivan is nothing if not focused. "How many, Rudi?"

If that question just wouldn't make him smile, I think we could get somewhere. There is a weird and impossible and awful thing happening here in addition to the obvious awful. Ivan is shrinking. Right before our eyes, he is ebbing back from the all-mighty man he has always been, since way before he was ever a man. And it is directly proportional to how much Rudi is growing right in front of us, not as a man, so much as a *thing*, some kind of thing that is just getting bigger and stronger, and the balance of it is so wrong as to rival the other many horrors war has brought us already.

"I can tell you this much," Rudi says, chewing the last of his pork steak gristle, "whatever's mine is yours."

"No," Ivan says. "No."

"Yes," Rudi says. "I owe you. We're a two-for-one, body-count-wise."

"No!" Ivan snaps. People start staring at us for real now. Mostly Marines, too, so it would not be unlike getting in a fight in a Vietcong bar. "You owe me nothing, Rudi. You got that? You don't owe me anything."

Rudi just smiles, not like a wiseguy but like somebody who is absolutely convinced that when the smoke clears you are going to get his point and agree. It's chilling, really.

"I brought something for you," he says, and while this does not sound promising at all, it happens too quickly. He reaches into his breast pocket and pulls out a photograph which he flips into the middle of the table like a card shark.

Morris lunges to grab it but not quick enough to beat Ivan.

Ivan's eyes, already bloody red around the edges, push out so far they look like they will just spill out of the sockets. Morris looks over his shoulder, and actually covers his mouth in shock.

Since nobody seems able to speak, I have to rip the photo out of Ivan's hands.

The photo is of a dead young VC, in the black pajamas and all. Shirtless Rudi is posed with the guy, propping him up. Rudi's got his knife in one hand and the dead guy's forehead is freshly cut and dripping.

With a big capital I.

Rudi in the picture is talking into the dead ear, just like right now he is talking into mine, but he's talking loud enough for all of us to hear.

"That's what I do, see? I leave our brand. And here's the best part: You know what I'm sayin' to him there? I say, 'Hey Charlie, I got my I on you.' Right? Get it?"

He looks around now for reaction, sees . . . I don't know what he sees, to be honest.

"I'm going to get a pancake," Rudi says, pushing off from the table and going back toward the kitchen.

"He is insane," Morris says, his mouth hanging open when he's done.

"Of course he is," I say.

Ivan is watching our boy, our fair-haired fool for-ever, walk away with so much confidence toward the pancakes.

"No, he's not," he says sadder than grieving. "At least, no more than he ever was. My father, he has a saying. He says, *War doesn't create monsters, it just explains them.*"

It feels like we have been in the firefight of our lives, with bodies now strewn about all over the place.

"What are we gonna do?" Morris says.

Ivan stands up, pulls his long bag up over his shoul-der. He sticks his hand out across the table and we shake.

"I don't know what you guys are gonna do. But I'm going home."

"Home?" Morris says, standing and dissolving into a rough hug. "What home?"

"Yeah, what home?" Rudi says, standing there sud-denly with a plate dripping syrup off the side.

Ivan grabs the plate and practically Frisbees it onto the table. Then he takes Rudi into a hug that is massive, it is volcanic. It would be embarrassing if it were not so wondrous.

"I gotta go, pal," Ivan says breathlessly, almost voicelessly.

The hug lasts a long time. I choke up watching it, gasping for breath like it was mine being squeezed out. Ivan looks like he's inhaling him.

And then he's off.

"Hey," I call, "come back with us. We'll go together."

"Work on your geography, brainbox," he calls, rushing, pointing into the distance. "Pleiku's *that* way."

And there, after all that and everything, he goes.

CHAPTER ELEVEN

Allegiance

So," Rudi says, meat in his belly and a bounce in his boots, "what's your schedule?"

"I have to be back with my plane in Da Nang by tomorrow," I say.

We are walking back from the mess hall to the hooch.

"And I'll hitch a ride with him," Morris says, "then finagle something from Phu Cat."

"Great," Rudi says, "let's get some rest, and then later we can go have some fun. There's not a million things to do here, but we could find something. Nice beach. Village is okay."

"Maybe you'll be more yourself then," Morris says, giving me a hopeful wink as I hold the hooch door for him.

Rudi starts immediately disarming. "If you're looking for the old self from Boston, ol' Rudy-Judy, you might be disappointed," he says. He strips down to his boxer shorts and big I.

There is nobody else currently in the hooch, and Morris and I flop on a couple of bunks across the room. We look at each other, hard but lost as we lie down. I pat his arm, telling him it'll be all right though I have no such information.

Sleep, like food, often does wonders. We can hope.

I startle awake, though it is very quiet. It's midafternoon, sunny and still and warm, and there is nothing to disturb an all-kinds-of-tired airman from a well-deserved sleep.

"Hey," I say, meaning Morris but getting Sunshine.

"What?" Sunshine asks from his bunk and a comic book. Morris pops up, too.

"Where's Rudi?" I say.

"Patrol," Sunshine says, like he's pointing out nothing more than the sunshine.

"No," I say, jumping up and grabbing my shirt. "Not again, not already, not now."

"Ah, come on, Rudi," Morris says, getting up as well. "We've only got one day."

"You guys get upset pretty easy," Sunshine says. "He just left five minutes ago."

"Argghh!" I say. "Would you know where he went?"

"Probably," he says, then sighs, then gets up and waves us to follow.

We jog together, across the compound, between buildings, out through the big old Chu Lai gate.

"It is really VC hot around here now," Sunshine says, gesturing to the surrounding countryside. "We're losing more and more. Takes more and more patrolling to root it out. Most guys don't want it, some others . . ."

"Are more than ready," Morris says.

We get to a well-worn narrow path that leads into a lightly wooded patch. Sunshine stops. "He kind of thinks of this as his mile, his beat. He watches over —"

Crrraaaak!

Echoing through the trees is the all-too-familiar snap of a sniper's round, followed by a wounded wolf-like holler, about a hundred yards straight up.

The three of us break into a run, and before all the thoughts that want to and don't want to come have a chance to surface, we arrive at Rudi.

I knock past Sunshine and drop to the ground. Blood is shooting straight out of his temple just below his helmet. "No!" I scream, using both hands to stop the blood, to hold him together, to get our boy back in there. "No, no!" I scream.

Morris is pressing, howling, compressing Rudi's chest, pumping as hard as he can, pumping too hard trying to get the life back in there, and still, even more, the blood streams out of poor stupid Rudi's stupid head, all over my hands.

Morris collapses, sobbing like a baby, crying too loud for it not to be real, collapses listening to nothing in Rudi's ribs, beneath that awful, evil I.

He is lying across Rudi's chest, and I put my face right to my old pal's stupid face and the blood is seeping now, rather than gushing, all over my hands, his nose, his eyes, and now it's in my eyes and on my cheek as I lean on him, talk to him, reason with him.

"Don't put your eye out, Rudi," I say, right into him. "Don't put your eye out, stupid. . . ." He put his eye out, though. He put everybody's eyes out.

"Don't . . ." I say, even when I can't see him anymore, can't hear him anymore.

But there is no reasoning here.

About the Author

Chris Lynch is the author of numerous acclaimed books for middle-grade and teen readers, including the Cyberia series and the National Book Award finalist *Inexcusable.* He teaches in the Lesley University creative writing MFA program, and divides his time between Massachusetts and Scotland.

gentle, but also to the harsh. 19For this *is*
[u]commendable, if because of conscience
toward God one endures grief, suffering
wrongfully. 20For [v]what credit *is it* if, when
you are beaten for your faults, you take
it patiently? But when you do good and
suffer, if you take it patiently, this *is* commendable before God. 21For [w]to this you
were called, because Christ also suffered
for us,* [x]leaving us* an example, that you
should follow His steps:

22 *"Who [y]committed no sin,*
*Nor was deceit found in His mouth";**

23[z]who, when He was reviled, did not revile in return; when He suffered, He did
not threaten, but [a]committed *Himself*
to Him who judges righteously; 24[b]who
Himself bore our sins in His own body
on the tree, [c]that we, having died to sins,
might live for righteousness—[d]by whose
stripes you were healed. 25For [e]you were
like sheep going astray, but have now returned [f]to the Shepherd and Overseer* of
your souls.

Submission to Husbands

3 Wives, likewise, *be* [a]submissive to your
own husbands, that even if some do
not obey the word, [b]they, without a word,
may [c]be won by the conduct of their wives,
2[d]when they observe your chaste conduct
accompanied by fear. 3[e]Do not let your
adornment be *merely* outward—arranging
the hair, wearing gold, or putting on *fine*
apparel— 4rather *let it be* [f]the hidden person of the heart, with the incorruptible
beauty of a gentle and quiet spirit, which
is very precious in the sight of God. 5For
in this manner, in former times, the holy
women who trusted in God also adorned
themselves, being submissive to their own
husbands, 6as Sarah obeyed Abraham,
[g]calling him lord, whose daughters you
are if you do good and are not afraid with
any terror.

A Word to Husbands

7[h]Husbands, likewise, dwell with *them*
with understanding, giving honor to the
wife, [i]as to the weaker vessel, and as *being*
heirs together of the grace of life, [j]that your
prayers may not be hindered.

Called to Blessing

8Finally, all *of you be* of one mind, having compassion for one another; love as
brothers, *be* tenderhearted, *be* courteous;*
9[k]not returning evil for evil or reviling for
reviling, but on the contrary [l]blessing,
knowing that you were called to this, [m]that
you may inherit a blessing. 10For

[n]*"He who would love life*
And see good days,
[o]*Let him refrain his tongue from evil,*
And his lips from speaking deceit.
11 *Let him [p]turn away from evil and do*
good;
[q]*Let him seek peace and pursue it.*
12 *For the eyes of the* LORD *are on the*
righteous,
[r]*And His ears are open to their prayers;*
But the face of the LORD *is against*
*those who do evil."**

* **2:21** NU-Text reads *you.* • NU-Text and M-Text read *you.* * **2:22** Isaiah 53:9 * **2:25** Greek *Episkopos* * **3:8** NU-Text reads *humble.* * **3:12** Psalm 34:12–16

2:20 *For what credit.* There is no advantage to believers for successfully enduring a deserved punishment for wrongdoing, yet there is great value when we honor God with our actions when we are unfairly condemned by others (3:17). ***take it patiently.*** Patience and perseverance in the face of suffering please God.
2:24 *who Himself bore our sins.* The Greek wording emphasizes Jesus' personal involvement in the act of paying the price for our sins. ***having died to sins, might live for righteousness.*** The purpose of Christ's bearing our sins is that we might live to please Him.
2:25 *Overseer.* No one else is qualified to be the one Shepherd and Overseer of our souls—only Christ is. For this reason the New Testament regularly describes the church and its congregations as having more than one leader (Titus 1:5).
3:1 *without a word.* A godly wife does not preach to her non-Christian husband with words but with the Christlike beauty of her daily life. The goal is to see that husband become a Christian.
3:3 *merely outward.* Christians are to spend more time developing their inner character than attempting to make themselves look beautiful on the outside (1 Sam. 16). Peter is not condemning women who wear jewelry. He is emphasizing the importance of a woman's character.
3:4 *gentle and quiet spirit.* Peter encourages Christian wives to exhibit attitudes that do not demand personal rights, attitudes that are not harsh and grating but are soothing and tranquil.
3:6 *calling him lord.* Sarah was not worshiping Abraham; she was showing him respect.
3:7 *dwell with them with understanding.* A Christian husband should be intimately aware of his wife's needs, her strengths and weaknesses, and her goals and desires. He should know as much about her as possible in order to respond in the best way to her.
3:9 *evil for evil.* Peter encourages Christians to act like the Lord Jesus. He endured suffering and ridicule in silence, entrusting His just cause to the ultimate Judge.
3:12 *eyes . . . ears.* Peter uses this imagery to remind his readers that God knows everything about believers, especially their suffering, and that He listens and responds to their cries for help (Heb. 4:12–16).

2:19 [u] Matt. 5:10 **2:20** [v] Luke 6:32–34 **2:21** [w] Matt. 16:24 [x] [1 John 2:6] **2:22** [y] Is. 53:9 **2:23** [z] Is. 53:7 [a] Luke 23:46 **2:24** [b] [Heb. 9:28] [c] Rom. 7:6 [d] Is. 53:5 **2:25** [e] Is. 53:5, 6 [f] [Ezek. 34:23] **3:1** [a] Eph. 5:22 [b] 1 Cor. 7:16 [c] Matt. 18:15 **3:2** [d] 1 Pet. 2:12; 3:6 **3:3** [e] 1 Tim. 2:9 **3:4** [f] Rom. 2:29 **3:6** [g] Gen. 18:12 **3:7** [h] [Eph. 5:25] [i] 1 Cor. 12:23 [j] Job 42:8 **3:9** [k] [Prov. 17:13] [l] Matt. 5:44 [m] Matt. 25:34 **3:10** [n] Ps. 34:12–16 [o] James 1:26 **3:11** [p] Ps. 37:27 [q] Rom. 12:18 **3:12** [r] John 9:31

Suffering for Right and Wrong

[13s]And who *is* he who will harm you if you become followers of what is good? [14t]But even if you should suffer for righteousness' sake, *you are* blessed. [u]"*And do not be afraid of their threats, nor be troubled.*"* [15]But sanctify the Lord God* in your hearts, and always [v]be ready to *give* a defense to everyone who asks you a reason for the [w]hope that is in you, with meekness and fear; [16x]having a good conscience, that when they defame you as evildoers, those who revile your good conduct in Christ may be ashamed. [17]For *it is* better, if it is the will of God, to suffer for doing good than for doing evil.

Christ's Suffering and Ours

[18]For Christ also suffered once for sins, the just for the unjust, that He might bring us* to God, being put to death in the flesh but made alive by the Spirit, [19]by whom also He went and preached to the spirits in prison, [20]who formerly were disobedient, when once the Divine longsuffering waited* in the days of Noah, while *the* ark was being prepared, in which a few, that is, eight souls, were saved through water. [21y]There is also an antitype which now saves us—baptism [z](not the removal of the filth of the flesh, [a]but the answer of a good conscience toward God), through the resurrection of Jesus Christ, [22]who has gone

into heaven and [b]is at the right hand of God, [c]angels and authorities and powers having been made subject to Him.

4 Therefore, since Christ suffered for us* in the flesh, arm yourselves also with the same mind, for he who has suffered in the flesh has ceased from sin, [2]that he no longer should live the rest of *his* time in the flesh for the lusts of men, [a]but for the will of God. [3]For we *have* spent enough of our past lifetime* in doing the will of the Gentiles—when we walked in lewdness, lusts, drunkenness, revelries, drinking parties, and abominable idolatries. [4]In regard to these, they think it strange that you do not run with *them* in the same flood of dissipation, speaking evil of you. [5]They will give an account to Him who is ready [b]to judge the living and the dead. [6]For this reason [c]the gospel was preached also to those who are dead, that they might be judged according to men in the flesh, but [d]live according to God in the spirit.

Serving for God's Glory

[7]But [e]the end of all things is at hand; therefore be serious and watchful in your prayers. [8]And above all things have fervent

* 3:14 Isaiah 8:12   * 3:15 NU-Text reads *Christ as Lord.*   * 3:18 NU-Text and M-Text read *you.*
* 3:20 NU-Text and M-Text read *when the long-suffering of God waited patiently.*   * 4:1 NU-Text omits *for us.*   * 4:3 NU-Text reads *time.*

3:15 sanctify the Lord God in your hearts. Believers should acknowledge the eternal holiness of Christ by revering Him as the Lord of the universe who is in control of all things. **to give a defense.** Peter assumes that the Christian faith will be falsely accused. He therefore encourages Christians to have rational answers to respond to those false accusations.

3:17 For it is better. Peter is not encouraging believers to seek out situations in which they will experience suffering. Instead, he is saying that believers should make certain that when they suffer, it is the result of having been faithful to God rather than because they have done evil (2:19).

3:19–20 spirits in prison. The Greek term translated *spirits* can refer to human spirits, angels, or demons. There are three main interpretations: (1) Some interpret these verses as describing Jesus as going to the place where fallen angels are incarcerated and declaring His final victory over evil in His work on the cross; (2) others hold that *spirits* refers to human spirits; thus Christ preached to human beings who had died in Noah's day and were in the realm of the dead (hell or hades); and (3) another major interpretation understands this passage as describing Christ preaching through Noah to the unbelievers of his day. **4:1 has ceased from sin.** Those who serve God faithfully in the midst of suffering take on a different attitude toward sin than what they previously held. Sin no longer holds the same grip on them.

4:3 abominable idolatries. The idea here is that some forms of idolatry may have been detestable even to the civil authorities. Of course, all types of idolatry are hateful to God.

4:5 will give an account. Although unbelievers think

they are free to do as they please, they are greatly mistaken. There are consequences to what they do. One day they will stand defenseless before God and give an account of all of their wickedness (Rev. 20:11–15).

4:6 to those who are dead. There are four main interpretations of Peter's meaning here: (1) Some see a connection between the gospel preached in this verse and the proclamation of Christ in 3:19–20; accordingly, they understand this verse to be about Christ offering salvation to those who lived in pre-Christian times; (2) another group of commentators also connects this preaching to 3:19–20, but holds that this verse is speaking of Christ preaching the gospel only to the righteous people of Old Testament times; (3) Peter was speaking of the gospel which was preached to believers who are now dead; and (4) Peter is referring to the spiritually dead; the gospel was being preached to them so that they could come alive spiritually.

4:8 love will cover a multitude of sins. Peter is not suggesting that one Christian's love atones for another Christian's sins. Rather, by introducing this proverb from the Old Testament (Prov. 10:12), he is reminding us that love does not stir up sins. We can demonstrate our love for our fellow believers by truly forgiving them and not talking openly about their past sins.

3:13 [s]Prov. 16:7   **3:14** [t]James 1:12 [u]Is. 8:12   **3:15** [v]Ps. 119:46 [w][Titus 3:7]   **3:16** [x]Heb. 13:18   **3:21** [y]Eph. 5:26 [z][Titus 3:5] [a][Rom. 10:10]   **3:22** [b]Ps. 110:1 [c]Rom. 8:38 **4:2** [a]John 1:13   **4:5** [b]Acts 10:42   **4:6** [c]1 Pet. 1:12; 3:19 [d][Rom. 8:9, 13]   **4:7** [e]Rom. 13:11

love for one another, for *f"love will cover a multitude of sins."** **9g**Be hospitable to one another *h*without grumbling. **10i**As each one has received a gift, minister it to one another, *j*as good stewards of *k*the manifold grace of God. **11l**If anyone speaks, *let him speak* as the oracles of God. If anyone ministers, *let him do it* as with the ability which God supplies, that *m*in all things God may be glorified through Jesus Christ, to whom belong the glory and the dominion forever and ever. Amen.

Suffering for God's Glory

12Beloved, do not think it strange concerning the fiery trial which is to try you, as though some strange thing happened to you; **13**but rejoice *n*to the extent that you partake of Christ's sufferings, that *o*when His glory is revealed, you may also be glad with exceeding joy. **14**If you are reproached for the name of Christ, *p*blessed *are you*, for the Spirit of glory and of God rests upon you.* On their part He is blasphemed, *q*but on your part He is glorified. **15**But let none of you suffer as a murderer, a thief, an evildoer, or as a busybody in other people's matters. **16**Yet if *anyone suffers* as a Christian, let him not be ashamed, but let him glorify God in this matter.*

17For the time *has come f*for judgment to begin at the house of God; and if *it begins* with us first, *s*what will *be* the end of those who do not obey the gospel of God? **18**Now

t"If the righteous one is scarcely saved,
Where will the ungodly and the sinner
*appear?"**

19Therefore let those who suffer according to the will of God *u*commit their souls

to Him in doing good, as to a faithful Creator.

Shepherd the Flock

5 The elders who are among you I exhort, I who am a fellow elder and a *a*witness of the sufferings of Christ, and also a partaker of the *b*glory that will be revealed: **2c**Shepherd the flock of God which is among you, serving as overseers, *d*not by compulsion but willingly,* *e*not for dishonest gain but eagerly; **3**nor as *f*being lords over *g*those entrusted to you, but *h*being examples to the flock; **4**and when *i*the Chief Shepherd appears, you will receive *j*the crown of glory that does not fade away.

Submit to God, Resist the Devil

5Likewise you younger people, submit yourselves to *your* elders. Yes, *k*all of *you* be submissive to one another, and be clothed with humility, for

l"God resists the proud,
*But m*gives grace to the humble."**

6Therefore humble yourselves under the mighty hand of God, that He may exalt you in due time, **7**casting all your care upon Him, for He cares for you.

8Be sober, be vigilant; because* your adversary the devil walks about like a roaring lion, seeking whom he may devour. **9**Resist him, steadfast in the faith, knowing that the same sufferings are experienced

* 4:8 Proverbs 10:12   * 4:14 NU-Text omits the rest of this verse.   * 4:16 NU-Text reads *name*.
* 4:18 Proverbs 11:31   * 5:2 NU-Text adds *according to God*.   * 5:5 Proverbs 3:34   * 5:8 NU-Text and M-Text omit *because*.

4:9 Be hospitable. In New Testament times, hospitality typically meant housing and feeding travelers for two to three days with no expectation of payment in return.

4:10 As each one has received a gift. Every believer is gifted to serve. **stewards.** These are managers or trustees who will be held accountable for using their gift in the best interest of the One who gave it to them.

4:12 do not think it strange. Apparently Peter's readers were astonished that they had to suffer as Christians, especially to the extent that they were suffering. **fiery trial.** The Greek word translated here was also used to speak of the intense fire that burned away impurities in metals.

4:17 for judgment to begin. Judgment does not always imply condemnation in Scripture. When used in relation to Christians, it consistently refers to the evaluation of a believer's works for the purpose of reward (1 Cor. 3:10–15).

5:1 partaker. This terms speaks of sharing in Christ's reign in the coming kingdom (Rom. 8:17; Rev. 2:26–28; 5:9–10). Peter considers himself to be already participating partly in the glory that one day he will experience fully.

5:2 Shepherd the flock of God. An ancient Israelite shepherd would go before his sheep to lead them;

he would not drive the sheep in front of him. Church leaders should lead the people of God in the same way; feeding, protecting, and guiding them (John 21:15–17). Christian leaders should also remember that they have been given responsibility for tending a flock that belongs to God, not to themselves. **not for dishonest gain.** Christian leaders need to make certain that their work is not motivated by money, but by a passion for the good of those believers put in their charge (1 Tim. 3:3,8; Titus 1:11).

5:3 nor as being lords over. Echoing a command that Peter heard directly from Jesus during His earthly ministry, Peter reminds all Christian leaders that they need to perform the role of servants, not masters, to those whom God has assigned to their care (Matt. 20:25–28; Mark 10:42–45).

5:8 your adversary. Satan is our avowed enemy. He never ceases from being hostile toward us; he is

4:8 *f* [Prov. 10:12]   4:9 *g* Heb. 13:2 *h* 2 Cor. 9:7
4:10 *i* Rom. 12:6–8 *j* 1 Cor. 4:1, 2 *k* [1 Cor. 12:4]   4:11 *l* Eph. 4:29 *m* [1 Cor. 10:31]   4:13 *n* James 1:2 *o* 2 Tim. 2:12
4:14 *p* Matt. 5:11 *q* Matt. 5:16   4:17 *r* Is. 10:12 *s* Luke 10:12
4:18 *t* Prov. 11:31   4:19 *u* 2 Tim. 1:12   5:1 *a* Matt. 26:37
b Rom. 8:17, 18   5:2 *c* Acts 20:28 *d* 1 Cor. 9:17 *e* 1 Tim. 3:3
5:3 *f* Ezek. 34:4 *g* Ps. 33:12 *h* Phil. 3:17   5:4 *i* Heb. 13:20
j 2 Tim. 4:8   5:5 *k* Eph. 5:21 *l* Prov. 3:34 *m* Is. 57:15

by your brotherhood in the world. [10]But may* the God of all grace, [n]who called us* to His eternal glory by Christ Jesus, after you have suffered a while, perfect, establish, strengthen, and settle you. [11][o]To Him be the glory and the dominion forever and ever. Amen.

Farewell and Peace

[12]By [p]Silvanus, our faithful brother as I consider him, I have written to you briefly, exhorting and testifying [q]that this is the true grace of God in which you stand.

[13]She who is in Babylon, elect together with you, greets you; and so does [r]Mark my son. [14]Greet one another with a kiss of love.

Peace to you all who are in Christ Jesus. Amen.

*5:10 NU-Text reads But the God of all grace ... will perfect, establish, strengthen, and settle you. • NU-Text and M-Text read you.

constantly accusing us before God (Job 1:9—2:7; Zech. 3:1; Luke 22:31; Rev. 12:10). **like a roaring lion.** Satan is both cunning and cruel. He attacks when least expected and desires to destroy completely those whom he attacks.
5:10 establish...you. As a consequence of our facing the attacks of our enemy, God will build in us a firm foundation that makes us steadfast and immovable.

5:11 dominion forever and ever. God is in control of all things both in this world and throughout eternity.

5:10 [n] 1 Cor. 1:9   **5:11** [o] Rev. 1:6   **5:12** [p] 2 Cor. 1:19   [q] Acts 20:24   **5:13** [r] Acts 12:12, 25; 15:37, 39

THE SECOND EPISTLE OF
PETER

▶ **AUTHOR:** No other book in the New Testament poses as many problems of authenticity as does 2 Peter. But in spite of the external and internal problems, the traditional position of Petrine authorship overcomes more difficulties than any other option. This epistle was written just before the apostle's death (1:14), probably from Rome.

▶ **TIME:** c. A.D. 64–66   ▶ **KEY VERSES:** 2 Pet. 1:20–21

▶ **THEME:** While 1 Peter deals with suffering and persecution caused by people outside the church, 2 Peter deals more with the need for the true spiritual knowledge and maturity in the face of false teachers who would distort the faith from inside the church. He gives his readers insight into the thinking of the false teachers and encourages opposition to them. He also urges watchfulness for Christ's return through all the events at the end of the age.

Greeting the Faithful

1 Simon Peter, a bondservant and ªapostle of Jesus Christ,

To those who have obtained ᵇlike precious faith with us by the righteousness of our God and Savior Jesus Christ:

²ᶜGrace and peace be multiplied to you in the knowledge of God and of Jesus our Lord, ³as His ᵈdivine power has given to us all things that *pertain* to life and godliness, through the knowledge of Him ᵉwho called us by glory and virtue, ⁴ᶠby which have been given to us exceedingly great and precious promises, that through these you may be ᵍpartakers of the divine nature, having escaped the corruption *that is* in the world through lust.

Fruitful Growth in the Faith

⁵But also for this very reason, ʰgiving all diligence, add to your faith virtue, to virtue ⁱknowledge, ⁶to knowledge self-control, to self-control perseverance, to perseverance godliness, ⁷to godliness brotherly kindness, and ʲto brotherly kindness love. ⁸For if these things are yours and abound, *you* will be neither barren ᵏnor unfruitful in the knowledge of our Lord Jesus Christ. ⁹For he who lacks these things is ˡshortsighted,

---

1:1 apostle. With this term Peter identifies himself as an authorized spokesman for the truth that Christ proclaimed. In verses 1–4 Peter describes the resources his readers have that will make growth in grace and knowledge possible. His apostleship is the first of these resources. **like precious faith.** Anyone who has faith in Jesus has the same access to God as any other believer. This access is the second great resource that Peter's readers possess.

1:2 the knowledge of God. The Greek word translated *knowledge* is a key word in this letter. It describes a special kind of knowledge, a kind that is complete. Since our knowledge of Jesus grows as we mature in the faith, we will experience His grace and peace on many different occasions in our Christian walk.

1:3 divine power. This power is identified as the "power of resurrection" (Phil. 3:10; 4:13). This power is the third resource for godly living that Peter lists in this letter. **by glory and virtue.** These words suggest the qualities of Jesus that attract believers to Him. The glory that John saw in Jesus (John 1:14) was His authority and power.

1:4 exceedingly great and precious promises. This phrase refers to the numerous offers of divine provision found in Scripture. These promises offer us the glory and virtue of Christ as the basis for our growing participation in the divine nature. We have Christ within us, as He promised (John 14:23), to enable us to become increasingly Christlike (2 Cor. 3:18).

1:5 virtue. This term is the same word used in verse 3 in reference to Christ's character. We cannot produce virtue ourselves; but we can choose to obey the promptings of the Holy Spirit who lives in us.

1:6 perseverance. A person who exercises self-control will not easily succumb to discouragement or the temptation to quit. Viewing all circumstances as coming from the hand of a loving Father who is in control of all things is the secret of perseverance.

1:9 blindness. This kind of person is one who looks only at earthly and material values—what is close at hand—and does not see the eternal spiritual realities. Concerned only with this present life, such a person becomes blind to the things of God, forgetting

---

1:1 ª Gal. 2:8 ᵇ Eph. 4:5 **1:2** ᶜ Dan. 4:1 **1:3** ᵈ 1 Pet. 1:5 ᵉ 1 Thess. 2:12 **1:4** ᶠ 2 Cor. 1:20; 7:1 ᵍ [2 Cor. 3:18] **1:5** ʰ 2 Pet. 3:18 ⁱ 2 Pet. 1:2 **1:7** ʲ Gal. 6:10 **1:8** ᵏ [John 15:2] **1:9** ˡ 1 John 2:9–11

even to blindness, and has forgotten that he was cleansed from his old sins.

[10]Therefore, brethren, be even more diligent [m]to make your call and election sure, for if you do these things you will never stumble; [11]for so an entrance will be supplied to you abundantly into the everlasting kingdom of our Lord and Savior Jesus Christ.

Peter's Approaching Death

[12]For this reason [n]I will not be negligent to remind you always of these things, [o]though you know and are established in the present truth. [13]Yes, I think it is right, [p]as long as I am in this tent, [q]to stir you up by reminding you, [14]rknowing that shortly I *must* put off my tent, just as [s]our Lord Jesus Christ showed me. [15]Moreover I will be careful to ensure that you always have a reminder of these things after my decease.

The Trustworthy Prophetic Word

[16]For we did not follow [t]cunningly devised fables when we made known to you the [u]power and [v]coming of our Lord Jesus Christ, but were [w]eyewitnesses of His majesty. [17]For He received from God the Father honor and glory when such a voice came to Him from the Excellent Glory: [x]"This is My beloved Son, in whom I am well pleased." [18]And we heard this voice which came from heaven when we were with Him on [y]the holy mountain.

[19]And so we have the prophetic word confirmed,* which you do well to heed as a [z]light that shines in a dark place, [a]until [b]the day dawns and the morning star rises in your [c]hearts; [20]knowing this first, that [d]no prophecy of Scripture is of any private interpretation,* [21]for [e]prophecy never came by the will of man, [f]but holy men of God* spoke *as they were* moved by the Holy Spirit.

Destructive Doctrines

2 But there were also false prophets among the people, even as there will be [a]false teachers among you, who will secretly bring in destructive heresies, even denying the Lord who bought them, *and* bring on themselves swift destruction. [2]And many will follow their destructive ways, because of whom the way of truth will be blasphemed. [3]By covetousness they will exploit you with deceptive words; for a long time their judgment has not been idle, and their destruction does* not slumber.

Doom of False Teachers

[4]For if God did not spare the angels who sinned, but cast *them* down to hell and delivered *them* into chains of darkness, to be

* **1:19** Or *We also have the more sure prophetic word.*   * **1:20** Or *origin*   * **1:21** NU-Text reads *but men spoke from God.*   * **2:3** M-Text reads *will not.*

---

the wonderful sense of cleansing that comes from turning oneself over to Christ.

1:11 entrance . . . abundantly. Peter distinguishes between a just-barely-made-it entrance into the eternal kingdom and a richly abundant one. The Scripture indicates that fruitful and faithful living here will be rewarded by greater privileges and rewards in glory (Rev. 22:12).

1:15 a reminder . . . after my decease. Several early church fathers took these words to be Peter's promise to leave behind a testimony of the truth for his readers, which they considered to be the Gospel of Mark.

1:16 cunningly devised fables. Peter countered the false teacher's faith claims with an eyewitness account. Peter himself had actually seen the power and the coming of the Lord Jesus Christ. These are the twin themes of this letter; the power of Jesus available for holy living and the coming of Jesus as the glorious hope of each believer.

1:19 the prophetic word confirmed. As strong as an eyewitness account (vv. 16–18) may be, there is an even stronger confirmation that Jesus is who He said He was. The written Scriptures are even more trustworthy than the personal experience of the apostle Peter.

1:20 of any private interpretation. Although some have taken this phrase to mean that no individual Christian has the right to interpret prophecy for himself or herself, the context and the Greek word for *interpretation* indicates another meaning for the verse. The Greek word for *interpretation* can also mean "origin." In the context of verse 21, it is clear that Peter is speaking of Scripture's "origin" from

God Himself and not the credentials of the one who interprets it. There is no private source for the Bible; the prophets did not supply their own solutions or explanations to the mysteries of life. Rather, God spoke through them; He alone is responsible for what is written in Scripture.

2:1 destructive heresies. Peter is addressing here the ethical implication of false teaching. The Greek word translated *destructive* means "shameful" or "deliberately immoral." The false teachers gloried in the privileges of Christianity but treated its moral demands with indifference.

2:3 judgment . . . destruction. Peter turns from the description of the false teachers to a description of their fate. Verses 4–8 provide examples of judgment of false teachers of the past.

2:4 angels who sinned. There are two main interpretations of this passage, depending on one's understanding of Genesis 6:1–6. Some think that Peter is referring to "sons of God" in Genesis 6:2. According to this interpretation, the "sons of God" were angels who rebelled against God and their role in creation. They began to engage in forbidden practices with the daughters of men. Their conduct was met with immediate judgment. A second group of commentators

1:10 [m] 1 John 3:19   **1:12** [n] Phil. 3:1   [o] 1 Pet. 5:12   **1:13** [p] [2 Cor. 5:1, 4]   [q] 2 Pet. 3:1   **1:14** [r] [2 Tim. 4:6]   [s] John 13:36; 21:18, 19   **1:16** [t] 1 Cor. 1:17   [u] [Eph. 1:19–22]   [v] [1 Pet. 5:4]   [w] Matt. 17:1–5   **1:17** [x] Matt. 17:5   **1:18** [y] Matt. 17:1   **1:19** [z] [John 1:4, 5, 9]   [a] Prov. 4:18   [b] Rev. 2:28; 22:16   [c] [2 Cor. 4:5–7]   **1:20** [d] [Rom. 12:6]   **1:21** [e] [2 Tim. 3:16]   [f] 2 Sam. 23:2   **2:1** [a] 1 Tim. 4:1, 2

reserved for judgment; [5]and did not spare the ancient world, but saved Noah, *one of eight people*, a preacher of righteousness, bringing in the flood on the world of the ungodly; [6]and turning the cities of [b]Sodom and Gomorrah into ashes, condemned *them* to destruction, making *them* an example to those who afterward would live ungodly; [7]and [c]delivered righteous Lot, *who was* oppressed by the filthy conduct of the wicked [8](for that righteous man, dwelling among them, [d]tormented *his* righteous soul from day to day by seeing and hearing *their* lawless deeds)— [9]*then* [e]the Lord knows how to deliver the godly out of temptations and to reserve the unjust under punishment for the day of judgment, [10]and especially [f]those who walk according to the flesh in the lust of uncleanness and despise authority. [g]*They are* presumptuous, self-willed. They are not afraid to speak evil of dignitaries, [11]whereas [h]angels, who are greater in power and might, do not bring a reviling accusation against them before the Lord.

Depravity of False Teachers

[12]But these, [i]like natural brute beasts made to be caught and destroyed, speak evil of the things they do not understand, and will utterly perish in their own corruption, [13]*and* will receive the wages of unrighteousness, *as* those who count it pleasure [k]to carouse in the daytime. [l]*They are* spots and blemishes, carousing in their own deceptions while [m]they feast with you, [14]having eyes full of adultery and that cannot cease from sin, enticing unstable souls. [n]They have a heart trained in covetous practices, *and are* accursed children. [15]They have forsaken the right way and gone astray, following the way of [o]Balaam the *son* of Beor, who loved the wages of unrighteousness; [16]but he was rebuked for his iniquity: a dumb donkey speaking with a man's voice restrained the madness of the prophet.

[17b]These are wells without water, clouds* carried by a tempest, for whom is reserved the blackness of darkness forever.*

Deceptions of False Teachers

[18]For when they speak great swelling *words* of emptiness, they allure through the lusts of the flesh, through lewdness, the ones who have actually escaped* from those who live in error. [19]While they promise them liberty, they themselves are slaves of corruption; [q]for by whom a person is overcome, by him also he is brought into bondage. [20]For if, after they [r]have escaped the pollutions of the world through the knowledge of the Lord and Savior Jesus Christ, they are [s]again entangled in them and overcome, the latter end is worse for them than the beginning. [21]For [t]it would have been better for them not to have known the way of righteousness,

---

* **2:17** NU-Text reads *and mists*. • NU-Text omits *forever*. * **2:18** NU-Text reads *are barely escaping*.

---

balk at the suggestion of sexual relations between angels and women. They consider this verse to simply be a reference to those angels who fell with Satan.
2:5 did not spare the ancient world. Peter's second example of God's judgment is the flood (3:6). **preacher of righteousness.** This is a reference to Noah because his righteous life put to shame the immoral lives of his neighbors. Noah's building of the ark would certainly have given him the opportunity to explain the coming judgment and to invite people to repent and believe in God. But the entreaties fell on deaf ears, just as the truth of Christ's atonement fell on the deaf ears of the false teachers of Peter's day. Such indifference and unbelief brought the ungodly of Noah's world to certain destruction.
2:6 Sodom and Gomorrah. These cities are Peter's third example of God's judgment. Genesis 19 makes it clear that sexual perversion was the primary cause of their destruction.
2:9–10 presumptuous, self-willed. These words describe the character and methods of false teachers. Their actions are characterized by boldness; they recklessly defy both God and man. Behind their presumption is a commitment to their own desires.
2:12 like natural brute beasts. False teachers are compared to animals in their behavior because they act in ignorance of the realities of death and judgment. Like animals they also react only to present circumstances, without giving thought to the consequences of their actions.
2:13 carouse in the daytime. Even pagan societies

thought it strange and unnatural to hold drunken riots in the daylight. However, the false teachers had no qualms about practicing their erroneous concept of Christian liberty in clear daylight.
2:14 eyes full of adultery. They could not cease from sin because their fantasizing had become habitual. As a consequence, they convinced unstable souls in the church that adultery was acceptable Christian behavior and lured them into sexual immorality.
2:15–16 following the way of Balaam. The account of Balaam in Numbers 22–24 is used here, as well as in Jude 11 and Revelation 2:14, to depict the danger of forsaking the right way and going astray.
2:17 wells . . . clouds. Peter accuses the heretical teachers of awakening false expectations, like wells that contain no water or storm clouds that darken but produce no rain.
2:20 they have escaped. The subject of this phrase is the heretical teachers who are called "servants of corruption" in verse 19. This verse seems to indicate that the teachers had formerly turned from the pollution of the world through a full and experiential knowledge of Christ. Now, however, they have fallen again into immorality, even becoming teachers of sinful

---

2:6 [b] Gen. 19:1–26   **2:7** [c] Gen. 19:16, 29   **2:8** [d] Ps. 119:139   **2:9** [e] Ps. 34:15–19   **2:10** [f] Jude 4, 7, 8 [g] Jude 8   **2:11** [h] Jude 9   **2:12** [i] Jude 10   **2:13** [j] Phil. 3:19 [k] Rom. 13:13 [l] Jude 12 [m] 1 Cor. 11:20, 21   **2:14** [n] Jude 11   **2:15** [o] Num. 22:5, 7   **2:17** [p] Jude 12, 13   **2:19** [q] John 8:34   **2:20** [r] Matt. 12:45 [s] [Heb. 6:4–6]   **2:21** [t] Luke 12:47

than having known *it*, to turn from the holy commandment delivered to them. 22But it has happened to them according to the true proverb: u"A *dog returns to his own vomit*,"* and, "a sow, having washed, to her wallowing in the mire."

God's Promise Is Not Slack

3 Beloved, I now write to you this second epistle (in *both of* which ᵃI stir up your pure minds by way of reminder), 2that you may be mindful of the words ᵇwhich were spoken before by the holy prophets, ᶜand of the commandment of us,* the apostles of the Lord and Savior, 3knowing this first: that scoffers will come in the last days, ᵈwalking according to their own lusts, 4and saying, "Where is the promise of His coming? For since the fathers fell asleep, all things continue as *they were* from the beginning of ᵉcreation." 5For this they willfully forget: that ᶠby the word of God the heavens were of old, and the earth ᵍstanding out of water and in the water, 6ʰby which the world *that* then existed perished, being flooded with water. 7But ⁱthe heavens and the earth *which* are now preserved by the same word, are reserved for ʲfire until the day of judgment and perdition of ungodly men.

8But, beloved, do not forget this one thing, that with the Lord one day *is* as a thousand years, and ᵏa thousand years as one day. 9ˡThe Lord is not slack concerning *His* promise, as some count slackness, but ᵐis longsuffering toward us,* ⁿnot willing that any should perish but ᵒthat all should come to repentance.

The Day of the Lord

10But ᵖthe day of the Lord will come as a thief in the night, in which ᑫthe heavens will pass away with a great noise, and the elements will melt with fervent heat; both the earth and the works that are in it will be burned up.* 11Therefore, since all these things will be dissolved, what manner *of persons* ought you to be ʳin holy conduct and godliness, 12ˢlooking for and hastening the coming of the day of God, because of which the heavens will ᵗbe dissolved, being on fire, and the elements will ᵘmelt with fervent heat? 13Nevertheless we, according to His promise, look for ᵛnew heavens and a ʷnew earth in which righteousness dwells.

Be Steadfast

14Therefore, beloved, looking forward to these things, be diligent ˣto be found by Him in peace, without spot and blameless; 15and consider *that* ʸthe longsuffering of our Lord *is* salvation—as also our beloved brother Paul, according to the wisdom given to him, has written to you, 16as also in all his ᶻepistles, speaking in them of these things, in which are some things hard to understand, which untaught and unstable *people* twist to their own destruction, as *they do* also the ᵃrest of the Scriptures.

17You therefore, beloved, ᵇsince you know *this* beforehand, ᶜbeware lest you also fall from your own steadfastness, being led away with the error of the wicked; 18ᵈbut grow in the grace and knowledge of our Lord and Savior Jesus Christ.

ᵉTo Him *be* the glory both now and forever. Amen.

---

*2:22 Proverbs 26:11 *3:2 NU-Text and M-Text read *commandment of the apostles of your Lord and Savior* or *commandment of your apostles of the Lord and Savior.* *3:9 NU-Text reads *you.* *3:10 NU-Text reads *laid bare* (literally *found*).

---

lifestyles. **the latter end is worse for them than the beginning.** This phrase is almost certainly taken from Jesus' words in Matthew 12:45 and probably reflects Peter's memory of that occasion.

2:22 *according to the true proverb.* Jews considered dogs and pigs among the lowest of animals, so Peter chooses these animals to describe people who have known the truth but have turned away from it.

3:2 *words which were spoken before.* The only way Peter's readers could recognize the errors of the heretical teachers was to compare their teaching with the teaching of the holy prophets and apostles. As Peter had already reminded his readers in 1:21, "holy men" spoke words given to them by the Holy Spirit, which were therefore utterly reliable.

3:4 *fathers fell asleep.* This refers to the Old Testament patriarchs. **all things continue.** The basis for denying the supernatural reappearance of Jesus is that nothing of that nature has occurred in the past.

3:8 *a thousand years.* God will surely accomplish His purposes and promises, even though it may appear that He is slow in doing so. His timing is always perfect.

3:10 *day of the Lord.* This phrase describes the end-time events, the second coming (Dan. 9:24–27; 1 Thess. 5:2; 2 Thess. 2:1–12). Peter's description requires the unlimited power of God in dissolving the very elements of the universe, from which He will create a new heaven and a new earth (v. 13; Rev. 21:22).

3:11 *what manner of persons.* The primary purpose of prophetic teaching is not to satisfy our curiosity but to motivate us to change our lives. Rather than work for things that will ultimately be destroyed, we should work for things that are eternal.

3:16 *untaught and unstable people twist.* Untaught refers to one whose mind is untrained and undisciplined in habits of thought. *Unstable* refers to one whose conduct is not properly established.

2:22 ᵘProv. 26:11 **3:1** ᵃ2 Pet. 1:13 **3:2** ᵇ2 Pet. 1:21 ᶜJude 17 **3:3** ᵈ2 Pet. 2:10 **3:4** ᵉGen. 6:1–7 **3:5** ᶠGen. 1:6, 9 ᵍPs. 24:2; 136:6 **3:6** ʰGen. 7:11, 12, 21–23 **3:7** ⁱ2 Pet. 3:10, 12 ʲ[2 Thess. 1:8] **3:8** ᵏPs. 90:4 **3:9** ˡHab. 2:3 ᵐIs. 30:18 ⁿEzek. 33:11 ᵒ[Rom. 2:4] **3:10** ᵖRev. 3:3; 16:15 ᑫPs. 102:25, 26 **3:11** ʳ1 Pet. 1:15 **3:12** ˢ1 Cor. 1:7, 8 ᵗPs. 50:3 ᵘMic. 1:4 **3:13** ᵛIs. 65:17; 66:22 ʷRev. 21:1 ˣ1 Cor. 1:8; 15:58 **3:15** ʸRom. 2:4 **3:16** ᶻ1 Cor. 15:24 ᵃ2 Tim. 3:16 **3:17** ᵇMark 13:23 ᶜEph. 4:14 **3:18** ᵈEph. 4:15 ᵉ2 Tim. 4:18

THE FIRST EPISTLE OF
JOHN

▶ **AUTHOR:** First John was universally accepted without dispute as authoritative by the early church. The internal evidence supports this tradition because the "we" (apostles), "you" (readers), and "they" (false teachers) phraseology places the writer in the sphere of apostolic eyewitness (1:1–3; 4:14). John's name was well known to the readers, and it was unnecessary for him to mention it. The style and vocabulary of 1 John are so similar to those of the fourth Gospel that most scholars acknowledge these books to be by the same hand. First John was probably written in Ephesus after the Gospel of John, but the date cannot be fixed with certainty.

▶ **TIME:** c. A.D. 89–95   ▶ **KEY VERSES:** 1 John 1:3–4

▶ **THEME:** Shortly after the church began, people like the Gnostics continually tried to recast the gospel in their own terms. Gnosticism made a distinction between the material or carnal, which was evil to them, and the spiritual, which was pure. John writes as one who was acquainted with Jesus personally, physically, and spiritually. He wants the reader to take the Christ he knew at face value. John wants his readers to believe the truth of his experience of Jesus and not the philosophical speculation of the Gnostics. In these letters we see the same themes as in John's Gospel—light and darkness, truth and falsehood, life and death, love and hate. John weaves these themes together with a straightforward skill and fatherly care.

What Was Heard, Seen, and Touched

1 That *a*which was from the beginning, which we have heard, which we have *b*seen with our eyes, *c*which we have looked upon, and *d*our hands have handled, concerning the *e*Word of life— 2*f*the life *g*was manifested, and we have seen, *h*and bear witness, and declare to you that eternal life which was *i*with the Father and was manifested to us— 3that which we have seen and heard we declare to you, that you also may have fellowship with us; and truly our

fellowship *is* *i*with the Father and with His Son Jesus Christ. 4And these things we write to you *k*that your* joy may be full.

Fellowship with Him and One Another

5*l*This is the message which we have heard from Him and declare to you, that *m*God is light and in Him is no darkness at all. 6*n*If we say that we have fellowship with Him, and walk in darkness, we lie and do

---

* **1:4** NU-Text and M-Text read *our.*

1:1–4 the Word of life. These verses emphasize the personal experience of the apostles with the incarnate Word. The memory of Jesus Christ burned in the mind of John as he reflected on the three and one-half years that he and the other disciples were with the Lord. Now he wanted to be sure that the churches under his care enjoyed fellowship with the resurrected Lord and other disciples.
1:2 life was manifested. The life was not hidden or obscured so that few, if any, could find it. Rather, this life was made known openly and had its origin in God the Father. God had provided truth about Himself in nature and through the prophets of old, but the revelation in His Son (Heb. 1:1–2) is God's finest and clearest presentation of Himself.
1:3 have fellowship. The idea of this word carries both the thought of a positive relationship that people share and participation in a common interest or goal.

1:5 God is light. This is God's nature, in His essential being, just as He is Spirit (John 4:24) and love (4:8). Light refers to God's moral character. *no darkness at all.* God is holy, untouched by any evil or sin. Because God is light, those who desire fellowship with Him must also be pure.
1:6 fellowship with Him, and walk in darkness. To walk in darkness means to live contrary to the moral character of God, to live a sinful life. To claim fellowship with God without living a moral life or practicing the truth is to live a lie, since God cannot compromise His holiness to accommodate sin.

1:1 *a* [John 1:1] *b* John 1:14 *c* 2 Pet. 1:16 *d* Luke 24:39 *e* [John 1:1, 4, 14] **1:2** *f* John 1:4 *g* Rom. 16:26 *h* John 21:24 *i* [John 1:1, 18; 16:28] **1:3** *j* 1 Cor. 1:9 **1:4** *k* John 15:11; 16:24 **1:5** *l* 1 John 3:11 *m* [1 Tim. 6:16] **1:6** *n* [1 John 2:9–11]

not practice the truth. 7But if we [o]walk in
the light as He is in the light, we have fellowship with one another, and [p]the blood
of Jesus Christ His Son cleanses us from
all sin.
8If we say that we have no sin, we deceive ourselves, and the truth is not in us.
9If we [q]confess our sins, He is [r]faithful and
just to forgive us *our* sins and to [s]cleanse us
from all unrighteousness. 10If we say that
we have not sinned, we [t]make Him a liar,
and His word is not in us.

2 My little children, these things I write
to you, so that you may not sin. And if
anyone sins, [a]we have an Advocate with
the Father, Jesus Christ the righteous.
2And [b]He Himself is the propitiation for
our sins, and not for ours only but [c]also for
the whole world.

The Test of Knowing Him

3Now by this we know that we know
Him, if we keep His commandments.
4He who says, "I know Him," and does
not keep His commandments, is a [d]liar,
and the truth is not in him. 5But [e]whoev-
er keeps His word, truly the love of God
is perfected [f]in him. By this we know that
we are in Him. 6[g]He who says he abides in
Him [h]ought himself also to walk just as He
walked.
7Brethren,* I write no new commandment
to you, but an old commandment which
you have had [i]from the beginning. The
old commandment is the word which you
heard from the beginning.* 8Again, [j]a new
commandment I write to you, which thing
is true in Him and in you, [k]because the
darkness is passing away, and [l]the true
light is already shining.
9[m]He who says he is in the light, and
hates his brother, is in darkness until now.
10[n]He who loves his brother abides in the
light, and [o]there is no cause for stumbling
in him. 11But he who [p]hates his brother is
in darkness and [q]walks in darkness, and
does not know where he is going, because
the darkness has blinded his eyes.

Their Spiritual State

12 I write to you, little children,
Because [r]your sins are forgiven you
for His name's sake.
13 I write to you, fathers,
Because you have known Him *who is*
[s]from the beginning.
I write to you, young men,
Because you have overcome the
wicked one.
I write to you, little children,
Because you have [t]known the Father.

* 2:7 NU-Text reads *Beloved.* • NU-Text omits *from the beginning.*

1:8–9 *If we confess.* To confess is to agree with God, to admit that we are sinners in need of His mercy. If a believer confesses his or her specific sins to God, He will cleanse all unrighteousness from that person. Forgiveness and cleansing are guaranteed because God is faithful to His promises. Those promises are legitimated because God is just. God can maintain His perfect character and yet forgive us because of the perfect and righteous sacrifice of Jesus, His own Son (2:2).

1:10 *His word is not in us.* A person who denies committing sinful acts does not have the Word of God changing his or her life.

2:1 *My little children . . . that you may not sin.* John's statements about sin (1:8–10) were designed to make believers aware of sin's ever-present danger and to put them on guard against it. According to Greek grammar, the *if* before *anyone sins* carries the added sense of "and it is assumed that we all do." This statement is not an encouragement to sin but a warning to all Christians to be on guard against sinful tendencies.

2:2 *propitiation.* This act brings about the merciful removal of guilt through divine forgiveness. In the Greek Old Testament, the Greek term for propitiation was used for the sacrificial mercy seat on which the high priest placed the blood of the Israelites' sacrifices (Ex. 25:17–22). This practice indicates that God's righteous wrath had to be appeased somehow. God sent His Son and satisfied His own wrath with Jesus' sacrifice on the cross. Our sins made it necessary for Jesus to suffer the agonies of the crucifixion; but God demonstrated His love and justice by providing His own Son.

2:3 *we know Him.* The New Testament speaks of knowing God in two senses. One who has trusted Christ knows Him (John 17:3), that is to say, has met Him. One who has previously met the Lord can also come to know Him intimately (Phil. 3:10). In this verse John is talking about knowing the Lord intimately.

2:6 *abides in Him.* Abiding is habitual obedience. It has the idea of settling down in Christ or resting in Him. It is evidenced by a life modeled after Christ. ***ought himself also to walk.*** The admonition to live by the teaching of Jesus reveals that this conformity comes from us. The Christian, as a child of God, ought to obey God because of a sincere desire to do so. It should be a joy to follow in the footsteps of the One who died for us.

2:8 *new commandment.* This refers to love (v. 10). It may be that John is simply repeating the statement of Christ in John 13:34. The command to love reached its truest and fullest expression in the life of Christ. He demonstrated what true love is by coming into our world and giving His life for us.

2:11 *he who hates his brother.* Hating one's brother opposes the teaching of Christ to love one another. The idea that one could hate a brother and yet claim fellowship with God shows the utter darkness that has blinded the Christian to the truth.

1:7 [o] Is. 2:5 [p] [1 Cor. 6:11] **1:9** [q] Prov. 28:13 [r] [Rom. 3:24–26] [s] Ps. 51:2 **1:10** [t] 1 John 5:10 **2:1** [a] Heb. 7:25; 9:24 **2:2** [b] [Rom. 3:25] [c] John 1:29 **2:4** [d] Rom. 3:4 **2:5** [e] John 14:21, 23 [f] [1 John 4:12] **2:6** [g] John 15:4 [h] 1 Pet. 2:21 **2:7** [i] 1 John 3:11, 23; 4:21 **2:8** [j] John 13:34; 15:12 [k] Rom. 13:12 [l] [John 1:9; 8:12; 12:35] **2:9** [m] [1 Cor. 13:2] **2:10** [n] [1 John 3:14] [o] 2 Pet. 1:10 **2:11** [p] [1 John 2:9; 3:15; 4:20] [q] John 12:35 **2:12** [r] [1 Cor. 6:11] **2:13** [s] John 1:1 [t] [Rom. 8:15–17]

14 I have written to you, fathers,
Because you have known Him *who is*
from the beginning.
I have written to you, young men,
Because *u*you are strong, and the
word of God abides in you,
And you have overcome the wicked
one.

Do Not Love the World

15*v*Do not love the world or the things in
the world. *w*If anyone loves the world, the
love of the Father is not in him. 16For all
that *is* in the world—the lust of the flesh,
*x*the lust of the eyes, and the pride of life—
is not of the Father but is of the world.
17And *y*the world is passing away, and the
lust of it; but he who does the will of God
abides forever.

Deceptions of the Last Hour

18*z*Little children, *a*it is the last hour; and
as you have heard that *b*the* Antichrist is
coming, *c*even now many antichrists have
come, by which we know *d*that it is the last
hour. 19*e*They went out from us, but they
were not of us; for *f*if they had been of us,
they would have continued with us; but
they went out *g*that they might be made
manifest, that none of them were of us.
20But *h*you have an anointing *i*from the
Holy One, and *j*you know all things.* 21I
have not written to you because you do not
know the truth, but because you know it,
and that no lie is of the truth.
22*k*Who is a liar but he who denies that
*l*Jesus is the Christ? He is antichrist who

denies the Father and the Son. 23*m*Whoever
denies the Son does not have the *n*Father
either; *o*he who acknowledges the Son has
the Father also.

Let Truth Abide in You

24Therefore let that abide in you *p*which
you heard from the beginning. If what you
heard from the beginning abides in you,
*q*you also will abide in the Son and in the
Father. 25*r*And this is the promise that He
has promised us—eternal life.
26These things I have written to you
concerning those who *try to* deceive you.
27But the *s*anointing which you have received from Him abides in you, and *t*you do
not need that anyone teach you; but as the
same anointing *u*teaches you concerning all
things, and is true, and is not a lie, and just
as it has taught you, you will* abide in Him.

The Children of God

28And now, little children, abide in Him,
that when* He appears, we may have *v*confidence and not be ashamed before Him
at His coming. 29*w*If you know that He is
righteous, you know that *x*everyone who
practices righteousness is born of Him.

3 Behold *a*what manner of love the Father
has bestowed on us, that *b*we should
be called children of God!* Therefore the
world does not know us,* *c*because it did

---

* **2:18** NU-Text omits *the.* * **2:20** NU-Text reads
you all know. * **2:27** NU-Text reads *you abide.*
* **2:28** NU-Text reads *if.* * **3:1** NU-Text adds *And
we are.* • M-Text reads *you.*

2:15 *Do not love the world.* These words may be
rephrased as "stop loving the world." John's readers
were acting in a way that was inconsistent with the
relationship with Christ. "World" here is the morally
evil system opposed to all that God is and holds dear.
In this sense, the "world" is the satanic system opposing Christ's kingdom on this earth (v. 16; 3:1; 4:4; 5:19;
John 12:31; Eph. 6:11–12; James 4:4).
**2:16 *lust of the flesh . . . lust of the eyes . . . pride of
life.*** The world is characterized by these three lusts,
which have been interpreted as corresponding to the
three different ways Eve was tempted in the garden
(Gen. 3:6), or the three different temptations Jesus
experienced (Luke 4:1–12). However, the correspon-
dences are not close enough to make it certain that
John was alluding to either of these. Instead, John
was probably making a short list of the different ways
believers could be lured away from a loving God. *Lust
of the flesh* refers to desires of sinful sensual pleasure.
The lust of the eyes refers to covetousness or material-
ism. *The pride of life* refers to being proud about one's
position in this world.
2:17 *passing away.* John highlights the brevity of
life. To be consumed with this life is to be unprepared
for the next.
2:18 *antichrists.* This word is a combination of two
Greek words: *anti*, meaning "instead of" or "against";
and *christos*, meaning "anointed one." *Antichrists*
most likely means those who seek to take the place
of Christ.

2:20 *anointing.* This is a reference to either the Holy
Spirit or to Scripture. This unction, or anointing, is the
protection that believers have against the false teachers. The true Anointed One, Jesus, also has representatives who are anointed. One of the main heresies the
first century church faced was Gnosticism, whose followers claimed to have secret knowledge of the truth
that led to salvation. Here John was opposing this
teaching by asserting that all believers knew the truth.
2:22–23 *that Jesus is the Christ.* In John's epistles,
denying that Jesus came in the flesh is to deny His
status as the Anointed One. A person cannot worship
God while denying Jesus' full deity and full humanity.
2:28 *ashamed before Him at His coming.* The
shame is the result of not having had a lifestyle of
obedience when Christ returns.
3:1 *what manner of love.* John stands in amazement
of God's love. But the greater amazement and appre-
ciation is for the fact that God's love is expressed to

2:14 *u* Eph. 6:10   **2:15** *v* [Rom. 12:2] *w* James 4:4
2:16 *x* [Eccl. 5:10, 11]   **2:17** *y* 1 Cor. 7:31   **2:18** *z* John
21:5 *a* 1 Pet. 4:7 *b* 2 Thess. 2:3 *c* 2 John 7 *d* 1 Tim.
4:1   **2:19** *e* Deut. 13:13 *f* Matt. 24:24 *g* 1 John
11:19   **2:20** *h* 2 Cor. 1:21 *i* Acts 3:14 *j* [John 16:13]
2:22 *k* 2 John 7 *l* 1 John 4:3   **2:23** *m* John 15:23 *n* John
5:23 *o* 1 John 5:1   **2:24** *p* 2 John 5, 6 *q* John
14:23   **2:25** *r* John 3:14–16; 6:40; 17:2, 3   **2:27** *s* [John
14:16; 16:13] *t* [Jer. 31:33] *u* [John 14:16]   **2:28** *v* 1 John
3:21; 4:17; 5:14   **2:29** *w* Acts 22:14 *x* 1 John 3:7, 10
3:1 *a* [1 John 4:10] *b* [John 1:12] *c* John 15:18, 21; 16:3

not know Him. 2Beloved, [d]now we are children of God; and [e]it has not yet been revealed what we shall be, but we know that
when He is revealed, [f]we shall be like Him,
for [g]we shall see Him as He is. 3[h]And everyone who has this hope in Him purifies himself, just as He is pure.

Sin and the Child of God

4Whoever commits sin also commits
lawlessness, and [i]sin is lawlessness. 5And
you know [j]that He was manifested [k]to
take away our sins, and [l]in Him there is no
sin. 6Whoever abides in Him does not sin.
Whoever sins has neither seen Him nor
known Him.
7Little children, let no one deceive you.
He who practices righteousness is righteous, just as He is righteous. 8[m]He who
sins is of the devil, for the devil has sinned
from the beginning. For this purpose the
Son of God was manifested, [n]that He might
destroy the works of the devil. 9Whoever
has been [o]born of God does not sin, for [p]His
seed remains in him; and he cannot sin, because he has been born of God.

The Imperative of Love

10In this the children of God and the
children of the devil are manifest: Whoever does not practice righteousness is
not of God, nor *is* he who does not love his
brother. 11For this is the message that you
heard from the beginning, [q]that we should
love one another, 12not as [r]Cain *who* was
of the wicked one and murdered his brother. And why did he murder him? Because
his works were evil and his brother's righteous.
13Do not marvel, my brethren, if [s]the
world hates you. 14We know that we have
passed from death to life, because we love
the brethren. He who does not love *his*
*brother** abides in death. 15[t]Whoever hates
his brother is a murderer, and you know
that [u]no murderer has eternal life abiding
in him.

The Outworking of Love

16[v]By this we know love, [w]because He
laid down His life for us. And we also ought
to lay down *our* lives for the brethren. 17But
[x]whoever has this world's goods, and sees
his brother in need, and shuts up his heart
from him, how does the love of God abide
in him?
18My little children, [y]let us not love in
word or in tongue, but in deed and in truth.
19And by this we know* [z]that we are of the
truth, and shall assure our hearts before
Him. 20[a]For if our heart condemns us, God

* **3:14** NU-Text omits *his brother.* * **3:19** NU-Text reads *we shall know.*

---

human beings and that Christians are included in His family.

3:2 We Have a New Family—One of the primary benefits of becoming a Christian is that we also become part of Christ's family. The Bible refers to this change as being *born again* (John 3:3). When an individual places his faith in Christ as Savior, he is born again into a new, spiritual, familial relationship with God (Gal. 3:26). He gains God as Father (Eph. 4:6) and other Christians as brothers and sisters (Heb. 3:1). God also adopts us when we become His children (Eph. 1:5). This image implies a dramatic transformation of status from slave to son (Gal. 4:1–5). One is no longer in bondage to the master but becomes a free son possessing all the rights and privileges of sonship. One of these benefits is the right to call God *Abba*, an affectionate term meaning "Father" (Rom. 8:15). A marvelous relationship is possible when one becomes a part of the family of God. As in any family, there are also responsibilities. The Christian must exhibit the family character and grow into spiritual maturity.

3:3 *everyone who has this hope.* Knowing that Christ is morally pure helps a person pursue purity even more.

3:4 *commits sin.* This verse is not referring to occasional sin but a consistent lifestyle of sin. ***lawlessness.*** This is active rebellion against the law.

3:5–6 *Whosoever abides in Him does not sin.* Habitually sinful conduct indicates an absence of fellowship with Christ. Thus, if we claim to be a Christian but sin is our way of life, our status as children of God can legitimately be questioned.

3:8 *destroy the works of the devil.* A person who sins is of the devil in the sense that he is participating in the devil's activity (2:19). Thus John is indicating that it is possible for believers to do that which is of the devil (Mark 8:31–33; James 3:6).

3:10 *children of the devil.* Believers who sin are not expressing their nature as children of God; instead, they are following the devil's pattern.

3:14 *have passed from death to life.* The tense of the verb "have passed" indicates that something experienced in the past has continuing and abiding results in the present. Thus John is saying that Christians, who have experienced Christ's salvation in the past, should demonstrate their salvation by loving their fellow believers in the present.

3:18 *love in word or in tongue.* This phrase means to speak loving words but to stop short of doing anything to prove that love. The opposite of loving in word is loving *in deed and in truth.*

3:20 *our heart condemns us.* This will happen when we recognize that we do not measure up to the standard of love and feel insecure in approaching God. Our conscience may not acknowledge the loving deeds we have done in the power of the Holy Spirit, but God does, and He is superior to our heart. Unlike our conscience, God takes everything into account, including Christ's atoning work for us. God is more compassionate and understanding toward us than we sometimes are toward ourselves.

3:2 [d] [Rom. 8:15, 16] [e] [Rom. 8:18, 19, 23] [f] Rom. 8:29 [g] [Ps. 16:11] **3:3** [h] 1 John 4:17 **3:4** [i] Rom. 4:15 **3:5** [j] 1 John 1:2; 3:8 [k] John 1:29 [l] [2 Cor. 5:21] **3:8** [m] Matt. 13:38 [n] Luke 10:18 **3:9** [o] John 1:3; 3:3 [p] 1 Pet. 1:23 **3:11** [q] [John 13:34; 15:12] **3:12** [r] Gen. 4:4, 8 **3:13** [s] [John 15:18; 17:14] **3:15** [t] Matt. 5:21 [u] [Gal. 5:20, 21] **3:16** [v] [John 3:16] [w] John 10:11; 15:13 **3:17** [x] Deut. 15:7 **3:18** [y] Ezek. 33:31 **3:19** [z] John 18:37 **3:20** [a] [1 Cor. 4:4, 5]

is greater than our heart, and knows all things. [21]Beloved, if our heart does not condemn us, [b]we have confidence toward God. [22]And [c]whatever we ask we receive from Him, because we keep His commandments [d]and do those things that are pleasing in His sight. [23]And this is His commandment: that we should believe on the name of His Son Jesus Christ [e]and love one another, as He gave us* commandment.

The Spirit of Truth and the Spirit of Error

[24]Now [f]he who keeps His commandments [g]abides in Him, and He in him. And [h]by this we know that He abides in us, by the Spirit whom He has given us.

4 Beloved, do not believe every spirit, but [a]test the spirits, whether they are of God; because [b]many false prophets have gone out into the world. [2]By this you know the Spirit of God: [c]Every spirit that confesses that Jesus Christ has come in the flesh is of God, [3]and every spirit that does not confess that* Jesus Christ has come in the flesh is not of God. And this is the *spirit* of the Antichrist, which you have heard was coming, and is now already in the world.

[4]You are of God, little children, and have overcome them, because He who is in you is greater than [d]he who is in the world. [5e]They are of the world. Therefore they speak *as* of the world, and [f]the world hears them. [6]We are of God. He who knows God hears us; he who is not of God does not hear us. [g]By this we know the spirit of truth and the spirit of error.

Knowing God Through Love

[7h]Beloved, let us love one another, for love is of God; and everyone who [i]loves is born of God and knows God. [8]He who does not love does not know God, for God is love. [9j]In this the love of God was manifested toward us, that God has sent His only begotten [k]Son into the world, that we might live through Him. [10]In this is love, [l]not that we loved God, but that He loved us and sent His Son [m]to be the propitiation for our sins. [11]Beloved, [n]if God so loved us, we also ought to love one another.

Seeing God Through Love

[12]oNo one has seen God at any time. If we love one another, God abides in us, and His love has been perfected in us. [13p]By this we know that we abide in Him, and He in us, because He has given us of His Spirit. [14]And [q]we have seen and testify that [r]the Father has sent the Son *as* Savior of the world. [15s]Whoever confesses that Jesus is the Son of God, God abides in him, and he in God. [16]And we have known and believed the love that God has for us. God is love, and [t]he who abides in love abides in God, and God [u]in him.

The Consummation of Love

[17]Love has been perfected among us in this: that [v]we may have boldness in the day of judgment; because as He is, so are we in

---

* **3:23** M-Text omits *us*.   * **4:3** NU-Text omits *that and Christ has come in the flesh.*

3:24 We Have a Witness—Some of the benefits of being a believer are best described as being spiritual or even mystical. The whole idea of abiding in Christ while He abides in us is one of those concepts. Abide is best understood as "remain with." God doesn't come and go in our lives. He carries on a permanent relationship with us because He is always there for us and in us. We sense His presence primarily through the work of the Holy Spirit, whose role it is to stand beside us and comfort us. It happens in our hearts and minds and is largely invisible. Yet, it is also what most accurately describes the most important aspect of our day-to-day life as Christians. As we abide in Christ, He nourishes us spiritually the same way a vine gives nourishment to its branches (John 15:16).

4:1 false prophets. These persons obey evil spirits. A true prophet is one who receives direct revelation from God. A false prophet claims to have received direct revelation from God but in fact promotes erroneous ideas.

4:2 Christ has come in the flesh. This test seems to be aimed at Docetists. They taught that Christ did not have a physical body. The test may also be aimed at the followers of Cerinthus who claimed that Jesus and "the Christ" were two separate beings, one physical and the other spiritual. In this letter, John is careful to use the name and the title of Jesus Christ together to clearly express the complete union of the two titles in one person.

4:4 he who is in the world. This phrase refers to the devil.

4:8 does not know God. The knowledge of God here refers to an intimate, experiential knowledge (v. 6; 2:3) of God, rather than just information about God. John never says that those who do not love are not born of God (v. 7). Yet it is impossible to know God intimately without loving others, for God is love. Anyone in whom God dwells reflects His character. To claim to know God while failing to love others is to make a false claim (1:6).

4:13 that we abide in Him, and He in us. Mutual abiding refers to the fellowship we have with God as a result of our salvation. The evidence that God abides in us and we in Him is the experience of the Holy Spirit dwelling in us. In the remainder of this passage, John explains how a believer can know that the Spirit is working in his or her life.

4:15 Whoever confesses. To be a Christian, a person must believe that Jesus is the Son of God.

3:21 [b] [1 John 2:28; 5:14]   **3:22** [c] Ps. 34:15 [d] John 8:29   **3:23** [e] Matt. 22:39   **3:24** [f] John 14:23 [g] John 14:21; 17:21 [h] Rom. 8:9, 14, 16   **4:1** [a] 1 Cor. 14:29 [b] Matt. 24:5   **4:2** [c] 1 Cor. 12:3   **4:4** [d] John 14:30; 16:11   **4:5** [e] John 3:31 [f] John 15:19; 17:14   **4:6** [g] [1 Cor. 2:12–16]   **4:7** [h] 1 John 3:10, 11, 23 [i] 1 Thess. 4:9   **4:9** [j] Rom. 5:8 [k] John 3:16   **4:10** [l] Titus 3:5 [m] 1 John 2:2   **4:11** [n] Matt. 18:33   **4:12** [o] John 1:18   **4:13** [p] John 14:20   **4:14** [q] John 1:14 [r] John 3:17; 4:42   **4:15** [s] [Rom. 10:9]   **4:16** [t] [1 John 3:24] [u] [John 14:23]   **4:17** [v] 1 John 2:28

this world. [18]There is no fear in love; but perfect love casts out fear, because fear involves torment. But he who fears has not been made perfect in love. [19w]We love Him* because He first loved us.

Obedience by Faith

[20x]If someone says, "I love God," and hates his brother, he is a liar; for he who does not love his brother whom he has seen, how can* he love God [y]whom he has not seen? [21]And [z]this commandment we have from Him: that he who loves God *must* love his brother also.

5 Whoever believes that [a]Jesus is the Christ is [b]born of God, and everyone who loves Him who begot also loves him who is begotten of Him. [2]By this we know that we love the children of God, when we love God and [c]keep His commandments. [3d]For this is the love of God, that we keep His commandments. And [e]His commandments are not burdensome. [4]For [f]whatever is born of God overcomes the world. And this is the victory that [g]has overcome the world—our* faith. [5]Who is he who overcomes the world, but [h]he who believes that Jesus is the Son of God?

The Certainty of God's Witness

[6]This is He who came [i]by water and blood—Jesus Christ; not only by water, but by water and blood. [j]And it is the Spirit who bears witness, because the Spirit is truth. [7]For there are three that bear witness in heaven: the Father, [k]the Word, and the Holy Spirit; [l]and these three are one. [8]And there are three that bear witness on earth:* [m]the Spirit, the water, and the blood; and these three agree as one.

[9]If we receive [n]the witness of men, the witness of God is greater; [o]for this is the witness of God which* He has testified of His Son. [10]He who believes in the Son of

God [p]has the witness in himself; he who does not believe God [q]has made Him a liar, because he has not believed the testimony that God has given of His Son. [11]And this is the testimony: that God has given us eternal life, and this life is in His Son. [12r]He who has the Son has life; he who does not have the Son of God does not have life. [13]These things I have written to you who believe in the name of the Son of God, that you may know that you have eternal life,* and that you may *continue to* believe in the name of the Son of God.

Confidence and Compassion in Prayer

[14]Now this is the confidence that we have in Him, that [s]if we ask anything according to His will, He hears us. [15]And if we know that He hears us, whatever we ask, we know that we have the petitions that we have asked of Him.

[16]If anyone sees his brother sinning a sin *which does* not *lead* to death, he will ask, and [t]He will give him life for those who commit sin not *leading* to death. [u]There is sin *leading* to death. [v]I do not say that he should pray about that. [17w]All unrighteousness is sin, and there is sin not *leading* to death.

Knowing the True—Rejecting the False

[18]We know that [x]whoever is born of God does not sin; but he who has been born of

* **4:19** NU-Text omits *Him*.   * **4:20** NU-Text reads *he cannot*.   * **5:4** M-Text reads *your*.   * **5:8** NU-Text and M-Text omit the words from *in heaven* (verse 7) through *on earth* (verse 8). Only four or five very late manuscripts contain these words in Greek.   * **5:9** NU-Text reads *God, that*.   * **5:13** NU-Text omits the rest of this verse.

5:1 born of God. This condition happens when one believes or trusts in Jesus Christ. Only correct, sincere belief produces spiritual birth. This birth is reflected in love for others who also have been born into the family of God (2:3–11).

5:6 by water and blood. This phrase has been interpreted at least four ways: (1) as Jesus' baptism and death; (2) as His incarnation; (3) as the water and blood that flowed from His side on the cross; and (4) as the baptism of the believer and the Lord's Supper. Most scholars favor the first interpretation. John is correcting the false teacher, Cerinthus, who claimed that the Spirit came on Jesus at His baptism but left Him before His death (4:2–3).

5:11 this is the testimony. God's witness or testimony is that He has given us eternal life in His Son. Eternal life is not a wage to be earned, but a gift to be received from God (Rom. 6:23).

5:14–15 according to His will. The key to knowing that God hears is to pray this way.

5:16–17 There is sin leading to death. This phrase may refer to blaspheming the Holy Spirit, rejecting

Christ as Savior, rejecting the humanity or deity of Jesus, a specific sin such as murder (3:12,15), or a life of habitual sin. Whatever it is, the sin seems to be a flagrant violation of the sanctity of the Christian community (Acts 5:1–11; 1 Cor. 5:5; 11:30). In other words, John is encouraging us to help fellow believers who are straying; we can be the tools God uses to restore an erring brother or sister to the true fellowship.

5:18–20 We know. This phrase introduces three concluding absolute truths. The general idea of this concluding section is that a proper relationship with God

4:19 [w] 1 John 4:10   **4:20** [x] [1 John 2:4]   [y] 1 John 4:12   **4:21** [z] [Matt. 5:43, 44; 22:39]   **5:1** [a] 1 John 2:22; 4:2, 15   [b] John 1:13   **5:2** [c] John 15:10   **5:3** [d] John 14:15   [e] Matt. 11:30; 23:4   **5:4** [f] John 16:33   [g] 1 John 2:13; 4:4   **5:5** [h] 1 Cor. 15:57   **5:6** [i] John 1:31–34   [j] [John 14:17]   **5:7** [k] [John 1:1]   [l] John 10:30   **5:8** [m] John 15:26   **5:9** [n] John 5:34, 37; 8:17, 18   [o] [Matt. 3:16, 17]   **5:10** [p] [Rom. 8:16]   [q] John 3:18, 33   **5:12** [r] [John 3:15, 36; 6:47; 17:2, 3]   **5:14** [s] [1 John 2:28; 3:21, 22]   **5:16** [t] Job 42:8   [u] [Matt. 12:31]   [v] Jer. 7:16; 14:11   **5:17** [w] 1 John 3:4   **5:18** [x] [1 Pet. 1:23]

God ʸkeeps himself,* and the wicked one does not touch him.

¹⁹We know that we are of God, and ᶻthe whole world lies *under the sway of the* wicked one.

²⁰And we know that the ᵃSon of God has come and ᵇhas given us an understanding, ᶜthat we may know Him who is true; and we are in Him who is true, in His Son Jesus Christ. ᵈThis is the true God ᵉand eternal life.

²¹Little children, keep yourselves from idols. Amen.

---

* **5:18** NU-Text reads *him.*

---

results in confidence of our position in Christ with a hostile world.

5:21 idols. This term may refer to literal idols, foods sacrificed to idols, false ideas in contrast to God's truth, or doctrines of false teachers. John has just reminded his readers of the true God (v. 20). It is appropriate that he closes by exhorting them to stay away from false gods.

5:18 ʸ James 1:27   **5:19** ᶻ Gal. 1:4   **5:20** ᵃ 1 John 4:2
ᵇ Luke 24:45 ᶜ John 17:3 ᵈ Is. 9:6 ᵉ 1 John 5:11, 12

THE SECOND EPISTLE OF
JOHN

▶ **AUTHOR:** Second John was not widely circulated at first because of its brevity and subject matter. Its strong resemblance to the tone and style of 1 John and the Fourth Gospel support the early tradition that John was the author of this epistle sometime after A.D. 90.

▶ **TIME:** C. A.D. 90–95   ▶ **KEY VERSES:** 2 John 9–10

▶ **THEME:** The addressee of 2 John is a woman in a local church that apparently had a strong friendship with John. The apostle writes to warn her about showing hospitality to false teachers. He cautions her against unwittingly aiding these teachers who were sowing seeds of heresy and hurting the church.

Greeting the Elect Lady

The Elder,

To the elect lady and her children, whom I love in truth, and not only I, but also all those who have known ᵃthe truth, ²because of the truth which abides in us and will be with us forever:

³ᵇGrace, mercy, *and* peace will be with you* from God the Father and from the Lord Jesus Christ, the Son of the Father, in truth and love.

Walk in Christ's Commandments

⁴I ᶜrejoiced greatly that I have found *some* of your children walking in truth, as we received commandment from the Father. ⁵And now I plead with you, lady, not as though I wrote a new commandment to you, but that which we have had from the beginning: ᵈthat we love one another. ⁶ᵉThis is love, that we walk according to His commandments. This is the commandment, that ᶠas you have heard from the beginning, you should walk in it.

Beware of Antichrist Deceivers

⁷For ᵍmany deceivers have gone out into the world ʰwho do not confess Jesus Christ *as* coming in the flesh. ⁱThis is a deceiver and an antichrist. ⁸ʲLook to yourselves, ᵏthat we* do not lose those things we worked for, but *that* we* may receive a full reward.

⁹ˡWhoever transgresses* and does not abide in the doctrine of Christ does

* 3 NU-Text and M-Text read *us.*   * 8 NU-Text reads *you.* • NU-Text reads *you.*   * 9 NU-Text reads *goes ahead.*

---

1 *The Elder.* This is probably the apostle John. The title can refer either to an old man, an older person deserving respect, or a church leader. ***the elect lady.*** This may be a specific person, or the phrase may be a figurative description of the local church.

4 *walking in truth.* This phrase means having an authentic relationship with God. Our walk with the Lord, if genuine, must be based upon His word.

6 *His commandments.* God's love is the basis of His desire for our obedience, and it is the reason He has revealed His will in His word. We prove our obedience to Christ by demonstrating love toward one another. Love is an unlimited resource readily available to us, and it is tremendously effective in furthering the work of Christ.

7 *coming in the flesh.* These words refer to the Incarnation, the fact that Jesus is the God-man. The humanity of Jesus provides a test by which false teachers can be identified. The Gnostic heresy, against which John wrote in 1 and 2 John, included a denial of the physical body of Christ. People who deny the physical reality of Jesus are not Christians, but antichrists.

8 *Look to yourselves.* Being seduced by false teachers is one way that Christians can lose their reward at the judgment. With this in mind, John writes that the reason to guard against deceivers is our own desire not to lose our reward at the judgment seat of Christ.

9 *transgresses.* This phrase has the strong sense of running too far ahead. Departure from Christ into doctrinal error indicates that a person does not have God.

1 ᵃCol. 1:5   3 ᵇ1 Tim. 1:2   4 ᶜ3 John 3, 4   5 ᵈ[John 13:34, 35; 15:12, 17]   6 ᵉ1 John 2:5; 5:3   ᶠ1 John 2:24   7 ᵍ1 John 2:19; 4:1   ʰ1 John 4:2   ⁱ1 John 2:22   8 ʲMark 13:9   ᵏGal. 3:4   9 ˡJohn 7:16; 8:31

not have God. He who abides in the doctrine of Christ has both the Father and the Son. [10]If anyone comes to you and [m]does not bring this doctrine, do not receive him into your house nor greet him; [11]for he who greets him shares in his evil deeds.

John's Farewell Greeting

[12][n]Having many things to write to you, I did not wish *to do so* with paper and ink; but I hope to come to you and speak face to face, [o]that our joy may be full.

[13][p]The children of your elect sister greet you. Amen.

---

10 *this doctrine.* Jesus is completely human and completely divine. A Christian should not only refuse to receive false teachers in the sense of supporting them while they visit the community, a Christian should also avoid appearing to endorse their teachings. The proper response to deceivers is to reject them as unbelievers. This shows how seriously we should take the Scriptures and how careful we should be in evaluating the teachings of everyone.

10 [m] Rom. 16:17   **12** [n] 3 John 13, 14   [o] John 17:13
13 [p] 1 Pet. 5:13

THE THIRD EPISTLE OF
JOHN

▶ **AUTHOR:** Much like 2 John, this letter had a very limited circulation in the early church, but was accepted as authoritative on account of its apostolic authorship. Its style and vocabulary strongly resemble that of John's Gospel and other epistles.

▶ **TIME:** c. A.D. 90–95   ▶ **KEY VERSE:** 3 John 11

▶ **THEME:** Third John has two main purposes. The first is to commend Gaius for being hospitable to itinerant missionaries. The second is to advise Gaius about Diotrephes, a man in the church who refuses to help the same kind of missionaries and who even gossips about them.

Greeting to Gaius

The Elder,

To the beloved Gaius, *a*whom I love in truth:

2Beloved, I pray that you may prosper in all things and be in health, just as your soul prospers. 3For I *b*rejoiced greatly when brethren came and testified of the truth *that is* in you, just as you walk in the truth. 4I have no greater *c*joy than to hear that *d*my children walk in truth.*

Gaius Commended for Generosity

5Beloved, you do faithfully whatever you do for the brethren and* for strangers, 6who have borne witness of your love before the church. *If* you send them forward on their journey in a manner worthy of God, you will do well, 7because they went forth for His name's sake, *e*taking nothing from the Gentiles. 8We therefore ought to *f*receive* such, that we may become fellow workers for the truth.

Diotrephes and Demetrius

9I wrote to the church, but Diotrephes, who loves to have the preeminence among them, does not receive us. 10Therefore, if I come, I will call to mind his deeds which he does, *g*prating against us with malicious words. And not content with that, he himself does not receive the brethren, and forbids those who wish to, putting *them* out of the church.

11Beloved, *h*do not imitate what is evil, but what is good. *i*He who does good is of God, but* he who does evil has not seen *j*God.

12Demetrius *k*has a *good* testimony from all, and from the truth itself. And we also bear witness, *l*and you know that our testimony is true.

Farewell Greeting

13*m*I had many things to write, but I do not wish to write to you with pen and ink; 14but I hope to see you shortly, and we shall speak face to face.

Peace to you. Our friends greet you. Greet the friends by name.

---

*4 NU-Text reads *the truth.*   *5 NU-Text adds *especially.*   *8 NU-Text reads *support.*
*11 NU-Text and M-Text omit *but.*

---

2 may prosper . . . and be in health. John's greeting may imply that Gaius was physically weak though spiritually strong. More probably John is simply following the pattern of greetings common to Greek letters.
4 my children. This is a description Paul uses of those he has led to saving faith in Christ (1 Cor. 4:14–17) and may indicate that Gaius was one of John's converts. It may also be a term John uses to describe those under his pastoral care as reflected in 1 John 2:1,12,18; 3:7,18; 4:4; 5:21.
5–12 you do faithfully. In these verses, John affirms Gaius' responsibility to assist Demetrius despite the opposition of Diotrephes and his expulsion of those who receive traveling missionaries.
7 Gentiles. In this case the term refers to unbelievers, not to Gentile Christians. The majority of Christians

in the churches of Asia Minor were Gentile converts rather than Jewish.
11 has not seen God. Our sin is a result of a faulty vision of God. Therefore, the Scriptures encourage us to look at Christ (2 Cor. 3:18; 4:16–18; Heb. 12:2–3), for the day when we see Him perfectly will be the day that we will be like Him (1 John 3:2–3).
12 from the truth itself. Demetrius' life measured up to the teaching of Scripture and Christ's commands. His conduct matched his theology.

---

1 *a* 2 John 1   3 *b* 2 John 4   4 *c* 1 Thess. 2:19, 20 *d* [1 Cor. 4:15]   7 *e* 1 Cor. 9:12, 15   8 *f* Matt. 10:40   10 *g* Prov. 10:8, 10   11 *h* Ps. 34:14; 37:27 *i* [1 John 2:29; 3:10] *j* [1 John 3:10]   12 *k* 1 Tim. 3:7 *l* John 19:35; 21:24   13 *m* 2 John 12

THE EPISTLE OF
JUDE

▶ **AUTHOR:** In spite of its limited subject matter and size, Jude was accepted as authentic and quoted by early church fathers. It is unlikely that the author is the apostle Jude (Luke 6:16), but rather Jude the brother of Jesus and James (called Judas in Matthew 13:55 and Mark 6:3). Because of the silence of the New Testament and tradition concerning Jude's later years, we cannot know where or when this epistle was written.

▶ **TIME:** c. A.D. 66–80   ▶ **KEY VERSE:** Jude 3

▶ **THEME:** Jude's letter is hard-hitting, short, and right to the point. False teachers are on the loose in the church and Jude wants to make sure his readers understand the destructive implications of their teaching. He urges Christians to resist these false teachers and to defend the faith and the body of truth received from the apostles that they have come to know and believe. He finishes by reminding them of the hope they have in knowing Christ is coming again.

Greeting to the Called

Jude, a bondservant of Jesus Christ, and *a*brother of James,

To those who are *b*called, sanctified* by God the Father, and *c*preserved in Jesus Christ:

²Mercy, *d*peace, and love be multiplied to you.

Contend for the Faith

³Beloved, while I was very diligent to write to you *e*concerning our common salvation, I found it necessary to write to you exhorting *f*you to contend earnestly for the faith which was once for all delivered to the saints. ⁴For certain men have crept in unnoticed, who long ago were marked out for this condemnation, ungodly men, who turn the grace of our God into lewdness and deny the only Lord God* and our Lord Jesus Christ.

Old and New Apostates

⁵But I want to remind you, though you once knew this, that *g*the Lord, having saved the people out of the land of Egypt, afterward destroyed those who did not believe. ⁶And the angels who did not keep their proper domain, but left their own abode, He has reserved in everlasting chains under darkness for the judgment of the great day; ⁷as *h*Sodom and Gomorrah, and the cities around them in a similar manner to these, having given themselves over to sexual immorality and gone after strange flesh, are set forth as an example, suffering the vengeance of eternal fire.

⁸*i*Likewise also these dreamers defile the flesh, reject authority, and *j*speak evil

* 1 NU-Text reads *beloved.*   * 4 NU-Text omits *God.*

2 peace. This is the state of a person who rests in God completely for salvation and protection.
3 common salvation. Jude intended to write a more general doctrinal letter, but the present crisis demanded this short, pointed attack on doctrinal error.
4 turn the grace of our God into lewdness. The teaching of grace can be dangerous when perverted by false teachers or carnal people who believe that because they have been saved by grace they may live as they please (Rom. 6:1–2).
5 destroyed those who did not believe. The Israelites of the Exodus had a magnificent beginning in Egypt but a disastrous ending in the wilderness. That we have begun with the Lord does not mean that we will have the glorious conclusion we might have envisioned at the beginning of our salvation journey.

The false believers who had infiltrated God's people would be judged, just like the false believers who rejected God in the wilderness (Num. 25:1–9).
6 angels. These are not holy angels of God. Instead these angels could be those who had previously fallen with Satan. Some think that these angels are "the sons of God" of Genesis 6:2, who took on human form and married women before the flood.
8 reject authority. The false teachers even despised those who were placed in positions of authority in local congregations. They not only preferred error to truth but also demeaned and rejected those who taught the truth.

1 *a* Acts 1:13 *b* Rom. 1:7 *c* John 17:11, 12   2 *d* 1 Pet. 1:2
3 *e* Titus 1:4 *f* Phil. 1:27   5 *g* 1 Cor. 10:5–10   7 *h* Gen.
19:24   8 *i* 2 Pet. 2:10 *j* Ex. 22:28

of dignitaries. [9]Yet Michael the archangel, in contending with the devil, when he disputed about the body of Moses, dared not bring against him a reviling accusation, but said, [k]"The Lord rebuke you!" [10l]But these speak evil of whatever they do not know; and whatever they know naturally, like brute beasts, in these things they corrupt themselves. [11]Woe to them! For they have gone in the way [m]of Cain, [n]have run greedily in the error of Balaam for profit, and perished [o]in the rebellion of Korah.

Apostates Depraved and Doomed

[12]These are spots in your love feasts, while they feast with you without fear, serving *only* themselves. *They are* clouds without water, carried about* by the winds; late autumn trees without fruit, twice dead, pulled up by the roots; [13p]raging waves of the sea, [q]foaming up their own shame; wandering stars [r]for whom is reserved the blackness of darkness forever.

[14]Now Enoch, the seventh from Adam, prophesied about these men also, saying, "Behold, the Lord comes with ten thousands of His saints, [15]to execute judgment on all, to convict all who are ungodly among them of all their ungodly deeds which they have committed in an ungodly way, and of all the [s]harsh things which ungodly sinners have spoken against Him."

Apostates Predicted

[16]These are grumblers, complainers, walking according to their own lusts; and they [t]mouth great swelling *words,* [u]flattering people to gain advantage. [17v]But you, beloved, remember the words which were spoken before by the apostles of our Lord Jesus Christ: [18]how they told you that [w]there would be mockers in the last time who would walk according to their own ungodly lusts. [19]These are sensual persons, who cause divisions, not having the Spirit.

Maintain Your Life with God

[20]But you, beloved, [x]building yourselves up on your most holy faith, [y]praying in the Holy Spirit, [21]keep yourselves in the love of God, [z]looking for the mercy of our Lord Jesus Christ unto eternal life. [22]And on some have compassion, making a distinction;* [23]but [a]others save with fear, [b]pulling *them* out of the fire,* hating even [c]the garment defiled by the flesh.

Glory to God

24 [d]Now to Him who is able to keep you*
 from stumbling,
 And [e]to present *you* faultless
 Before the presence of His glory with
  exceeding joy,
25 To God our Savior,*
 Who alone is wise,*
 Be glory and majesty,
 Dominion and power,*
 Both now and forever.
 Amen.

---

* **12** NU-Text and M-Text read *along.* * **22** NU-Text reads *who are doubting* (or *making distinctions*). * **23** NU-Text adds *and on some have mercy with fear* and omits *with fear* in first clause. * **24** M-Text reads *them.* * **25** NU-Text reads *To the only God our Savior.* • NU-Text omits *Who ... is wise* and adds *Through Jesus Christ our Lord.* • NU-Text adds *Before all time.*

---

9 *disputed about the body of Moses.* Jude's description here is probably taken from an apocryphal book called *The Assumption of Moses,* written in the first century A.D. There is no record in the Bible itself of the archangel's encounter with Satan, or a detailed account of Moses' body.

11 *they have gone in the way of Cain.* The heretics are compared to three Old Testament failures. Cain did not place his faith in the Lord. The "way of Cain" is the way of pride and self-righteousness (Gen. 4:3–8; Heb. 11:4; 1 John 3:12). *Balaam.* He was the epitome of the sin of greed (Num. 31:16). *Korah.* This was the Levite Korah (Num. 16:1–3,31–35) who resented the prominent positions of Moses and Aaron as God's representatives. The Lord brought judgment on him and his followers for rebelling against those He had placed in authority.

13 *raging waves . . . foaming . . . wandering stars.* These godless people put on a great show but lacked any substance. They boasted of liberty but placed the people of God in bondage to sin (2 Pet. 2:19). After they had done their evil deeds and made their profits, they, like wandering stars, moved on to other places to exploit God's people again.

15 *ungodly.* This word is repeated four times, making the verse one of the most striking in the letter. In view of the wicked nature of evil persons, how could the church allow them to stay in their midst?

18 *there would be mockers.* One of the main tactics that the false teachers used to gain credibility was to tear down godly leaders.

22–23 *some have compassion.* We have certain obligations to other believers. First, we need to show compassion to those in any kind of spiritual or physical need. Second, we need to use discernment in helping our brothers and sisters in the church. Some will require tender care and patience to help them grow in Christ. With others we may need to use drastic action to rescue them from the temptations of sin. *hating even the garment defiled by the flesh.* This is a metaphor for staying wary of sin—as Paul says, "considering yourself lest you also be tempted" (Gal. 6:1).

24 *faultless.* This is a Greek word used of sacrificial animals that had no blemish and thus were fit to be offered to God. Only God can save us, cleanse us from our sins, and present us to Himself as faultless, for God is the Author and Finisher of our faith (Heb. 12:2).

9 [k]Zech. 3:2   **10** [l]2 Pet. 2:12   **11** [m]Gen. 4:3–8 [n]2 Pet. 2:15 [o]Num. 16:1–3, 31–35   **13** [p]Is. 57:20 [q][Phil. 3:19] [r]2 Pet. 2:17   **15** [s]1 Sam. 2:3   **16** [t]2 Pet. 2:18 [u]Prov. 28:21   **17** [v]2 Pet. 3:2   **18** [w][1 Tim. 4:1]   **20** [x]Col. 2:7 [y][Rom. 8:26]   **21** [z]Titus 2:13   **23** [a]Rom. 11:14 [b]Amos 4:11 [c][Zech. 3:4, 5]   **24** [d][Eph. 3:20] [e]Col. 1:22

THE
REVELATION
OF JESUS CHRIST

▶ **AUTHOR:** The style, symmetry, and plan of Revelation show that it was written by one author, four times named "John" (Rev. 1:1,4,9; 22:8). Because of its contents and its address to seven churches, Revelation quickly circulated and became widely known and accepted in the early church. From the beginning, Revelation was considered an authentic work of the apostle John, the same John who wrote the Gospel and Epistles. Revelation was written at a time when Roman hostility to Christianity was erupting into overt persecution. It is likely that John wrote this book in A.D. 95 or 96 when the severe persecution of Christians began under the emperor Domitian.

▶ **TIME:** c. A.D. 95–96   ▶ **KEY VERSES:** Rev. 19:11–15

▶ **THEME:** John wrote this book late in his life while in exile on the island of Patmos off the coast of Asia. It is safe to say that no book of the Bible has generated more theories of interpretation over the last two millennia. In this context probably one of the best approaches to interpreting and understanding Revelation is to concentrate on the major themes such as worship. When the reader does that, one finds great comfort and assurance in the book. Many scholars think the purpose of the book is to provide comfort in the midst of persecution and difficult times, as the form of the book is in the tradition of Jewish apocalyptic literature that is designed to communicate hope through symbolic imagery.

Introduction and Benediction

1 The Revelation of Jesus Christ, *ᵃ*which God gave Him to show His servants— things which must shortly take place. And *ᵇ*He sent and signified *it* by His angel to His servant John, ²*ᶜ*who bore witness to the word of God, and to the testimony of Jesus Christ, to all things *ᵈ*that he saw. ³*ᵉ*Blessed *is* he who reads and those who hear the words of this prophecy, and keep those things which are written in it; for *ᶠ*the time *is* near.

Greeting the Seven Churches

⁴John, to the seven churches which are in Asia:

Grace to you and peace from Him *ᵍ*who is and *ʰ*who was and who is to come, *ⁱ*and from the seven Spirits who are before His throne, ⁵and from Jesus Christ, *ʲ*the faithful *ᵏ*witness, the *ˡ*firstborn from the dead, and *ᵐ*the ruler over the kings of the earth. To Him *ⁿ*who loved us *ᵒ*and washed* us from our sins in His own blood, ⁶and has *ᵖ*made us kings* and priests to His God and Father, *ᵍ*to Him *be* glory and dominion forever and ever. Amen.

⁷Behold, He is coming with *ʳ*clouds, and every eye will see Him, even *ˢ*they who

* **1:5** NU-Text reads *loves us and freed;* M-Text reads *loves us and washed.*   * **1:6** NU-Text and M-Text read *a kingdom.*

1:1 *Revelation.* The word "revelation," which means "unveiling," or "disclosure," indicates that this book is a type of literature known as *apocalyptic literature,* or literature which reveals hidden things. *of Jesus Christ.* This revelation is both from Jesus Christ and about Him. *John.* John is the human writer, and Jesus is the divine Author.
1:3 *Blessed.* The word "blessed" means "spiritually happy." Even though some of the words of this book speak of terrifying and solemn times, it is a blessing to know how thoroughly the Lord holds all time and all times in His hands. Those who take time to read and try to understand this book will find themselves blessed by the hope of heaven and by the nearness of our Lord and Savior.
1:4 *the seven churches.* The seven churches are in

the Roman province of Asia, which today is southwestern Turkey. Their names are given in order going clockwise from the southwest.
1:5 *firstborn from the dead.* This phrase refers to the resurrection of Christ, the first to come back from the dead. This is the basis of the hope of resurrection held by Christians (1 Cor. 15:20–24).
1:7 *coming with clouds . . . every eye.* "Coming with clouds" recalls Daniel's vision of the Son of Man (Dan.

1:1 *ᵃ* John 3:32 *ᵇ* Rev. 22:6   **1:2** *ᶜ* 1 Cor. 1:6 *ᵈ* 1 John 1:1   **1:3** *ᵉ* Luke 11:28 *ᶠ* James 5:8   **1:4** *ᵍ* Ex. 3:14 *ʰ* John 1:1 *ⁱ* [Is. 11:2]   **1:5** *ʲ* John 8:14 *ᵏ* Is. 55:4 *ˡ* [Col. 1:18] *ᵐ* Rev. 17:14 *ⁿ* John 13:34 *ᵒ* Heb. 9:14   **1:6** *ᵖ* 1 Pet. 2:5, 9 *ᵍ* 1 Tim. 6:16   **1:7** *ʳ* Matt. 24:30 *ˢ* Zech. 12:10–14

pierced Him. And all the tribes of the earth will mourn because of Him. Even so, Amen.

8t"I am the Alpha and the Omega, *the* Beginning and *the* End,"* says the Lord,* u"who is and who was and who is to come, the vAlmighty."

Vision of the Son of Man

9I, John, both* your brother and wcompanion in the tribulation and xkingdom and patience of Jesus Christ, was on the island that is called Patmos for the word of God and for the testimony of Jesus Christ. 10yI was in the Spirit on zthe Lord's Day, and I heard behind me qa loud voice, as of a trumpet, 11saying, "I am the Alpha and the Omega, the First and the Last," and,* "What you see, write in a book and send *it* to the seven churches which are in Asia:* to Ephesus, to Smyrna, to Pergamos, to Thyatira, to Sardis, to Philadelphia, and to Laodicea."

12Then I turned to see the voice that spoke with me. And having turned bI saw seven golden lampstands, 13cand in the midst of the seven lampstands dOne like the Son of Man, eclothed with a garment down to the feet and fgirded about the chest with a golden band. 14His head and ghair *were* white like wool, as white as snow, and hHis eyes like a flame of fire; 15iHis feet *were* like fine brass, as if refined in a furnace, and jHis voice as the sound of many waters; 16kHe had in His right hand seven stars, lout of His mouth went a sharp two-edged sword, mand His countenance *was* like the sun shining in its strength. 17And nwhen I saw Him, I fell at His feet as dead. But oHe laid His right hand on me, saying

to me,* "Do not be afraid; pI am the First and the Last. 18qI *am* He who lives, and was dead, and behold, rI am alive forevermore. Amen. And sI have the keys of Hades and of Death. 19Write* the things which you have tseen, uand the things which are, vand the things which will take place after this. 20The mystery of the seven stars which you saw in My right hand, and the seven golden lampstands: The seven stars are wthe angels of the seven churches, and xthe seven lampstands which you saw* are the seven churches.

The Loveless Church

2 "To the angel of the church of Ephesus write,

'These things says aHe who holds the seven stars in His right hand, bwho walks in the midst of the seven golden lampstands: 2c"I know your works, your labor, your patience, and that you cannot bear those who are evil. And dyou have tested those ewho say they are apostles and are not, and have found them liars; 3and you have persevered and have patience, and have labored for My name's sake and have fnot become weary. 4Nevertheless I have *this* against you, that you have left your first love. 5Remember therefore from

---

* **1:8** NU-Text and M-Text omit *the Beginning and the End.* • NU-Text and M-Text add *God.*
* **1:9** NU-Text and M-Text omit *both.*   * **1:11** NU-Text and M-Text omit *I am* through third *and.* • NU-Text and M-Text omit *which are in Asia.*   * **1:17** NU-Text and M-Text omit *to me.*
* **1:19** NU-Text and M-Text read *Therefore, write.*
* **1:20** NU-Text and M-Text omit *which you saw.*

7:13; Matt. 24:30) and the ascension of Christ (Acts 1:11). "Every eye" indicates that Christ will be universally visible at His second coming.
1:8 the Alpha and the Omega. The Lord's description of Himself as the first and last letters of the Greek alphabet means that He is the beginning and the end of all creation.
1:9 tribulation. The apostle Paul said there would be many tribulations (Acts 14:22), and John identifies both the suffering of others and his own exile on Patmos as part of the "troubles." The great tribulation is the time when the wrath of God is poured out on the earth (Mark 13:14–23); that time is explained in greater detail in this book.
1:12 seven golden lampstands. The seven lampstands represent the seven churches.
1:13 One like the Son of Man. The term "Son of Man" echoes Daniel 7:13. Comparisons of these two passages, along with Jesus' common use of the name "Son of Man" for Himself, indicate that Christ is the subject of verses 12–18.
1:14 white. The white appearance is parallel to the description of the "Ancient of Days" in Daniel 7:9, and of Christ on the Mount of Transfiguration (Matt. 17:2). The similarity of descriptions demonstrates the purity and eternality of both God the Father and God the Son. Overcoming believers will also be "clothed in white garments" (3:5; 19:8) in Christ's presence, symbolizing purity.

1:16 sharp two-edged sword. The sword coming out of Christ's mouth is symbolic of the judging power of the Word of God (Is. 49:2; Heb. 4:12).
1:18 keys of Hades and of Death. Christ has authority over those who have died physically and over their present resting place, which will be emptied and destroyed at the time of the great white throne judgment (20:11–15). Hades is the place where the dead rest.
1:20 angels. Angels are created spirit beings who minister to believers (Heb. 1:14).
2:1 Ephesus. Ephesus was the most important city in Asia Minor when Revelation was written. It was the center of the worship of Artemis (or Diana; Acts 19:28), a goddess of fertility. It was a strategic commercial center and a great seaport.
2:5 Remember. A generation earlier the same church was commended for love (Eph. 1:15; 6:24).

1:8 t Is. 41:4 u Rev. 4:8; 11:17 v Is. 9:6   **1:9** w Phil. 1:7
x [2 Tim. 2:12]   **1:10** y Acts 10:10 z Acts 20:7 a Rev. 4:1
1:12 b Ex. 25:37   **1:13** c Rev. 2:1 d Ezek. 1:26 e Dan. 10:5
f Rev. 15:6   **1:14** g Dan. 7:9 h Dan. 10:6   **1:15** i Ezek.
1:7 j Ezek. 1:24; 43:2   **1:16** k Rev. 1:20; 2:1; 3:1 l Is. 49:2
m Matt. 17:2   **1:17** n Ezek. 1:28 o Dan. 8:18; 10:10, 12 p Is.
41:4; 44:6; 48:12   **1:18** q Rom. 6:9 r Rev. 4:9 s Ps. 68:20
1:19 t Rev. 1:9–18 u Rev. 2:1 v Rev. 4:1   **1:20** w Rev. 2:1
x Zech. 4:2   **2:1** a Rev. 1:16 b Rev. 1:13   **2:2** c Ps. 1:6
d 1 John 4:1 e 2 Cor. 11:13   **2:3** f Gal. 6:9

where you have fallen; repent and do the first works, ᵍor else I will come to you quickly and remove your lampstand from its place—unless you repent. ⁶But this you have, that you hate the deeds of the Nicolaitans, which I also hate.

⁷ʰ"He who has an ear, let him hear what the Spirit says to the churches. To him who overcomes I will give ⁱto eat from ʲthe tree of life, which is in the midst of the Paradise of God."'

The Persecuted Church

⁸"And to the angel of the church in Smyrna write,

'These things says ᵏthe First and the Last, who was dead, and came to life: ⁹"I know your works, tribulation, and poverty (but you are ˡrich); and I know the blasphemy of ᵐthose who say they are Jews and are not, ⁿbut are a synagogue of Satan. ¹⁰ₒDo not fear any of those things which you are about to suffer. Indeed, the devil is about to throw some of you into prison, that you may be tested, and you will have tribulation ten days. ᵖBe faithful until death, and I will give you ᑫthe crown of life.

¹¹ʳ"He who has an ear, let him hear what the Spirit says to the churches. He who overcomes shall not be hurt by ˢthe second death."'

The Compromising Church

¹²"And to the angel of the church in Pergamos write,

'These things says ᵗHe who has the sharp two-edged sword: ¹³"I know your works, and where you dwell, where Satan's throne is. And you hold fast to My name, and did not deny My faith even in the days

in which Antipas was My faithful martyr, who was killed among you, where Satan dwells. ¹⁴But I have a few things against you, because you have there those who hold the doctrine of ᵘBalaam, who taught Balak to put a stumbling block before the children of Israel, ᵛto eat things sacrificed to idols, ʷand to commit sexual immorality. ¹⁵Thus you also have those who hold the doctrine of the Nicolaitans, which thing I hate.* ¹⁶Repent, or else I will come to you quickly and ˣwill fight against them with the sword of My mouth.

¹⁷"He who has an ear, let him hear what the Spirit says to the churches. To him who overcomes I will give some of the hidden ʸmanna to eat. And I will give him a white stone, and on the stone ᶻa new name written which no one knows except him who receives it."'

The Corrupt Church

¹⁸"And to the angel of the church in Thyatira write,

'These things says the Son of God, ᵃwho has eyes like a flame of fire, and His feet like fine brass: ¹⁹ᵇ"I know your works, love, service, faith,* and your patience; and as for your works, the last are more than the first. ²⁰Nevertheless I have a few things against you, because you allow* that woman* ᶜJezebel, who calls herself a prophetess, to teach and seduce* My servants ᵈto commit sexual immorality and eat things

---

* 2:15 NU-Text and M-Text read likewise for which thing I hate.　* 2:19 NU-Text and M-Text read faith, service.　* 2:20 NU-Text and M-Text read I have against you that you tolerate. • M-Text reads your wife Jezebel. • NU-Text and M-Text read and teaches and seduces.

2:6 Nicolaitans. The Nicolaitans were a heretical group that troubled the churches at Ephesus and Pergamos (v. 15). Apparently their teaching and practice were immoral, perhaps even idolatrous (v. 14).

2:7 Paradise. Jesus told the believing thief on the cross that he would be with Jesus in paradise (Luke 23:42). Paul uses the term interchangeably with "the third heaven" (2 Cor. 12:2,4).

2:8 Smyrna. Smyrna was an important seaport 35 miles north of Ephesus. The presence of a Roman imperial cult and a large Jewish population made life difficult for believers in Smyrna. However, the churches of Smyrna and Philadelphia are the only two of the seven not rebuked by Christ in some way.

2:10 crown of life. The Greek crown or garland of green leaves was given to winners in athletic events. James 1:12 also promises the crown of life to believers who persevere under trial.

2:11 second death. The second death refers to the experience of eternal death in the lake of fire (20:14–15). No believer will suffer the second death.

2:12 Pergamos. Pergamos was the ancient capital of the province of Asia. It was said to be the place where parchment was first used. Pergamos means "citadel" in Greek. It was located 50 miles north of Smyrna and was situated on a high hill dominating the valley

below. **two-edged sword.** The two-edged sword is the powerful word of the Lord (1:16; Heb. 4:12).

2:13 Satan's throne. This implies that Satan's authority and power were honored either openly or in effect. **Antipas.** Antipas (not Herod Antipas) had already suffered martyrdom, thus receiving the promised "crown of life."

2:14 doctrine of Balaam. The background for this teaching is in the Old Testament (Num. 22:1—25:31). Balak hired Balaam to turn the hearts of Israel away from the Lord. Apparently seduction similar to that which Balaam instigated was taking place at the church at Pergamos, especially in relation to idols and sexual immorality (Acts 15:20).

2:18 Thyatira. Thyatira was a city with a large military detachment about 30 miles southeast of Pergamos. Recognized for its wool and dye industries, the

---

2:5 ᵍ Matt. 21:41　**2:7** ʰ Matt. 11:15　ⁱ [Rev. 22:2, 14]　ʲ [Gen. 2:9; 3:22]　**2:8** ᵏ Rev. 1:8, 17, 18　**2:9** ˡ Luke 12:21　ᵐ Rom. 2:17　ⁿ Rev. 3:9　**2:10** ᵒ Matt. 10:22　ᵖ Matt. 24:13　ᑫ James 1:12　**2:11** ʳ Rev. 13:9　ˢ [Rev. 20:6, 14; 21:8]　**2:12** ᵗ Rev. 1:16; 2:16　**2:14** ᵘ Num. 31:16　ᵛ Acts 15:29　ʷ 1 Cor. 6:13　**2:16** ˣ 2 Thess. 2:8　**2:17** ʸ Ex. 16:33, 34　ᶻ Rev. 3:12　**2:18** ᵃ Rev. 1:14, 15　**2:19** ᵇ Rev. 2:2　**2:20** ᶜ 1 Kin. 16:31; 21:25　ᵈ Ex. 34:15

sacrificed to idols. 21And I gave her time eto repent of her sexual immorality, and she did not repent.* 22Indeed I will cast her into a sickbed, and those who commit adultery with her into great tribulation, unless they repent of their* deeds. 23I will kill her children with death, and all the churches shall know that I am He who fsearches the minds and hearts. And I will give to each one of you according to your works.

24"Now to you I say, and* to the rest in Thyatira, as many as do not have this doctrine, who have not known the gdepths of Satan, as they say, hI will* put on you no other burden. 25But hold fast iwhat you have till I come. 26And he who overcomes, and keeps jMy works until the end, kto him I will give power over the nations—

27 'Hel shall rule them with a rod of iron;
They shall be dashed to pieces like the potter's vessels'*—

as I also have received from My Father; 28and I will give him mthe morning star. 29"He who has an ear, let him hear what the Spirit says to the churches."'

The Dead Church

3 "And to the angel of the church in Sardis write,

'These things says He who ahas the seven Spirits of God and the seven stars: "I know your works, that you have a name that you are alive, but you are dead. 2Be watchful, and strengthen the things which remain, that are ready to die, for I have not found your works perfect before God.* 3bRemember therefore how you have received and heard; hold fast crepent. dTherefore if you will not watch, I will

come upon you eas a thief, and you will not know what hour I will come upon you. 4You* have fa few names even in Sardis who have not gdefiled their garments; and they shall walk with Me hin white, for they are worthy. 5He who overcomes shall be clothed in white garments, and I will not iblot out his name from the kBook of Life; but lI will confess his name before My Father and before His angels.

6m"He who has an ear, let him hear what the Spirit says to the churches."'

The Faithful Church

7"And to the angel of the church in Philadelphia write,

'These things says nHe who is holy, oHe who is true, p"He who has the key of David, qHe who opens and no one shuts, and rshuts and no one opens":* 8s"I know your works. See, I have set before you tan open door, and no one can shut it;* for you have a little strength, have kept My word, and have not denied My name. 9Indeed I will make uthose of the synagogue of Satan, who say they are Jews and are not, but lie—indeed vI will make them come and worship before your feet, and to know that I have loved you. 10Because you have kept My command to persevere, wI also will keep you from the hour of trial which shall

---

* **2:21** NU-Text and M-Text read *time to repent, and she does not want to repent of her sexual immorality.* * **2:22** NU-Text and M-Text read *her.* * **2:24** NU-Text and M-Text omit *and.* • NU-Text and M-Text omit *will.* * **2:27** Psalm 2:9 * **3:2** NU-Text and M-Text read *My God.* * **3:4** NU-Text and M-Text read *Nevertheless you have a few names in Sardis.* * **3:7** Isaiah 22:22 * **3:8** NU-Text and M-Text read *which no one can shut.*

---

city was also noted for its trade guilds. **eyes like a flame . . . feet like fine brass.** This is essentially the same wording as Daniel 10:6.
2:24 depths of Satan. The deep things may be secrets known by those initiated into the things of the devil. When the apostle Paul addressed the subject of walking in the Light (the revelation of Christ), he not only said not to participate in the unfruitful deeds of darkness, but he went on to say that it is disgraceful even to speak of those things done in secret (Eph. 5:11–12).
2:28 the morning star. The morning star is Christ Himself in 22:16. For the believer, Christ's presence is the light in the dark and difficult times. The morning star (the planet Venus, which can be seen in the sky just before sunrise) is the harbinger of day; it is easy to see how the return of Christ could be paralleled with the morning star. When Satan is referred to as the morning star, that is thought to be a description of what Satan was like before he rebelled (Is. 14:12).
3:1 Sardis. Sardis, located 30 miles southeast of Thyatira, had been the capital of Lydia. The worship of the Roman Caesar and Artemis, goddess of fertility, were active here.
3:3 as a thief. Christ's warning that He will come as unexpectedly as a thief echoes His repeated emphasis in Matthew 24:36—25:13 (see also 16:15).

3:5 Book of Life. The Book of Life is the list of the redeemed (20:11–15; Ex. 32:32–33).
3:7 Philadelphia. Philadelphia, which means "brotherly love" in Greek, was a small city located about 40 miles southeast of Sardis. Its location, vineyards, and wine production made it wealthy and commercially important. **key of David.** This key represents the authority of the One who opens and shuts the door in the Davidic kingdom (Is. 22:22), a prerogative that is Christ's as the rightful "son of David" (Matt. 1:1).
3:8 an open door, and no one can shut it. The door, in this context, seems to be entrance into heaven and "the New Jerusalem" (v. 12; chs. 21–22).
3:10 keep you from the hour of trial. Christ's promise to keep the believers from the hour of trial is often considered a promise that He will remove them before the period of unparalleled tribulation

2:21 eRev. 9:20; 16:9, 11 **2:23** fJer. 11:20; 17:10 **2:24** g2 Tim. 3:1–9 hActs 15:28 **2:25** iRev. 3:11 **2:26** j[John 6:29] k[Matt. 19:28] **2:27** lPs. 2:8; 9 **2:28** m2 Pet. 1:19 **3:1** aRev. 1:4, 16 **3:3** b1 Tim. 6:20 cRev. 3:19 dMatt. 24:42, 43 e[Rev. 16:15] **3:4** fActs 1:15 g[Jude 23] hRev. 4:4; 6:11 **3:5** i[Rev. 19:8] jEx. 32:32 kPhil. 4:3 lLuke 12:8 **3:6** mRev. 2:7 **3:7** nActs 3:14 o1 John 5:20 pIs. 9:7; 22:22 q[Matt. 16:19] rJob 12:14 **3:8** sRev. 3:1 t1 Cor. 16:9 **3:9** uRev. 2:9 vIs. 45:14; 49:23; 60:14 **3:10** w2 Pet. 2:9

come upon [x]the whole world, to test those
who dwell [y]on the earth. 11 Behold,* [z]I am
coming quickly! [a]Hold fast what you have,
that no one may take [b]your crown. 12 He
who overcomes, I will make him [c]a pillar
in the temple of My God, and he shall [d]go
out no more. [e]I will write on him the name
of My God and the name of the city of My
God, the [f]New Jerusalem, which [g]comes
down out of heaven from My God. [h]And *I
will write on him* My new name.
13 [i]"He who has an ear, let him hear what
the Spirit says to the churches." '

The Lukewarm Church

14 "And to the angel of the church of the
Laodiceans* write,
[j]'These things says the Amen, [k]the Faithful and True Witness, [l]the Beginning of the
creation of God: 15 [m]"I know your works,
that you are neither cold nor hot. I could
wish you were cold or hot. 16 So then, because you are lukewarm, and neither cold
nor hot,* I will vomit you out of My mouth.
17 Because you say, [n]'I am rich, have become
wealthy, and have need of nothing'—and
do not know that you are wretched, miserable, poor, blind, and naked— 18 I counsel
you [o]to buy from Me gold refined in the fire,
that you may be rich; and [p]white garments,
that you may be clothed, *that* the shame of
your nakedness may not be revealed; and
anoint your eyes with eye salve, that you
may see. 19 [q]As many as I love, I rebuke and
[r]chasten. Therefore be zealous and repent.
20 Behold, [s]I stand at the door and knock. [t]If
anyone hears My voice and opens the door,
[u]I will come in to him and dine with him,
and he with Me. 21 To him who overcomes
[v]I will grant to sit with Me on My throne,
as I also overcame and sat down with My
Father on His throne.
22 [w]"He who has an ear, let him hear what
the Spirit says to the churches." ' "

The Throne Room of Heaven

4 After these things I looked, and behold,
a door *standing* [a]open in heaven. And
the first voice which I heard *was* like a
[b]trumpet speaking with me, saying, "Come
up here, and I will show you things which
must take place after this."
2 Immediately [c]I was in the Spirit; and
behold, [d]a throne set in heaven, and *One*
sat on the throne. 3 And He who sat there
was* [e]like a jasper and a sardius stone in
appearance; [f]and *there was* a rainbow
around the throne, in appearance like
an emerald. 4 [g]Around the throne *were*
twenty-four thrones, and on the thrones
I saw twenty-four elders sitting, [h]clothed
in white robes; and they had crowns* of
gold on their heads. 5 And from the throne
proceeded [i]lightnings, thunderings, and
voices.* [j]Seven lamps of fire *were* burning
before the throne, which are [k]the* seven
Spirits of God.
6 Before the throne *there was** [l]a sea of
glass, like crystal. [m]And in the midst of the
throne, and around the throne, *were* four
living creatures full of eyes in front and in
back. 7 [n]The first living creature *was* like a
lion, the second living creature like a calf,
the third living creature had a face like a
man, and the fourth living creature *was*
like a flying eagle. 8 *The* four living creatures, each having [o]six wings, were full of
eyes around and within. And they do not
rest day or night, saying:

[p]"Holy, holy, holy,*
[q]Lord God Almighty,
[r]Who was and is and is to come!"

9 Whenever the living creatures give glory and honor and thanks to Him who sits
on the throne, [s]who lives forever and ever,

* **3:11** NU-Text and M-Text omit *Behold.*
* **3:14** NU-Text and M-Text read *in Laodicea.*
* **3:16** NU-Text and M-Text read *hot nor cold.*
* **4:3** M-Text omits *And He who sat there was* (which makes the description in verse 3 modify the throne rather than God). * **4:4** NU-Text and M-Text read *robes, with crowns.* * **4:5** NU-Text and M-Text read *voices, and thunderings.* • M-Text omits *the.* * **4:6** NU-Text and M-Text add *something like.* * **4:8** M-Text has *holy* nine times.

(1 Thess. 4:16–18). Others believe that this means that believers will not be removed, but will be protected during the trial. The "hour of trial" is another way of referring to the unparalleled judgment of the "great tribulation" (7:14) predicted in Daniel 12:1 and Matthew 24:21.

3:14 *Laodiceans.* Laodicea was 45 miles southeast of Philadelphia and 90 miles east of Ephesus. It was a wealthy city with thriving banks, a textile industry, and a medical school. The city was also known for its sparse water supply. All of these characteristics are played upon in Christ's message to the church.

4:4 *clothed in white . . . crowns.* The white robes point to those who are confirmed in righteousness. The crowns are for those who possess ruling authority, and possibly also indicate that the elders have already been judged and rewarded.

4:6 *four living creatures.* These creatures are remarkably similar to the cherubim (angels) that Ezekiel saw close to God's throne (Ezek. 1:4–10).

4:7 *lion . . . calf . . . man . . . eagle.* This description recalls the four cherubim in Ezekiel 1:4–10.

3:10 [x]Luke 2:1 [y]Is. 24:17 **3:11** [z]Phil. 4:5 [a]Rev. 2:25 [b][Rev. 2:10] **3:12** [c]1 Kin. 7:21 [d]Ps. 23:6 [e][Rev. 14:1; 22:4] [f][Heb. 12:22] [g]Rev. 21:2 [h][Rev. 2:17; 22:4] **3:13** [i]Rev. 2:7 **3:14** [j]2 Cor. 1:20 [k]Rev. 1:5; 3:7; 19:11 [l][Col. 1:15] **3:15** [m]Rev. 3:1 **3:17** [n]Hos. 12:8 **3:18** [o]Is. 55:1 [p]2 Cor. 5:3 **3:19** [q]Job 5:17 [r]Heb. 12:6 **3:20** [s]Song 5:2 [t]Luke 12:36, 37 [u][John 14:23] **3:21** [v]Matt. 19:28 **3:22** [w]Rev. 2:7 **4:1** [a]Ezek. 1:1 [b]Rev. 1:10 **4:2** [c]Rev. 1:10 [d]Is. 6:1 **4:3** [e]Rev. 21:11 [f]Ezek. 1:28 **4:4** [g]Rev. 11:16 [h]Rev. 3:4, 5 **4:5** [i]Rev. 8:5; 11:19; 16:18 [j]Ex. 37:23 [k][Rev. 1:4] **4:6** [l]Rev. 15:2 [m]Ezek. 1:5 **4:7** [n]Ezek. 1:10; 10:14 **4:8** [o]Is. 6:2 [p]Is. 6:3 [q]Rev. 1:8 [r]Rev. 1:4 **4:9** [s]Rev. 1:18

[10]tthe twenty-four elders fall down before Him who sits on the throne and worship Him who lives forever and ever, and cast their crowns before the throne, saying:

[11] "You[u] are worthy, O Lord,*
To receive glory and honor and power;
[v]For You created all things,
And by [w]Your will they exist* and were created."

The Lamb Takes the Scroll

5 And I saw in the right *hand* of Him who sat on the throne [a]a scroll written inside and on the back, [b]sealed with seven seals. [2]Then I saw a strong angel proclaiming with a loud voice, [c]"Who is worthy to open the scroll and to loose its seals?" [3]And no one in heaven or on the earth or under the earth was able to open the scroll, or to look at it.

[4]So I wept much, because no one was found worthy to open and read* the scroll, or to look at it. [5]But one of the elders said to me, "Do not weep. Behold, [d]the Lion of the tribe of [e]Judah, [f]the Root of David, has [g]prevailed to open the scroll [h]and to loose* its seven seals."

[6]And I looked, and behold,* in the midst of the throne and of the four living creatures, and in the midst of the elders, stood [i]a Lamb as though it had been slain, having seven horns and [j]seven eyes, which are [k]the seven Spirits of God sent out into all the earth. [7]Then He came and took the scroll out of the right hand [l]of Him who sat on the throne.

Worthy Is the Lamb

[8]Now when He had taken the scroll, [m]the four living creatures and the twenty-four elders fell down before the Lamb, each having a harp, and golden bowls full of incense, which are the [n]prayers of the saints. [9]And [o]they sang a new song, saying:

[p]"You are worthy to take the scroll,
And to open its seals;
For You were slain,
And [q]have redeemed us to God [r]by Your blood

Out of every tribe and tongue and people and nation,
[10] And have made us* [s]kings* and [t]priests to our God;
And we* shall reign on the earth."

[11]Then I looked, and I heard the voice of many angels around the throne, and the living creatures, and the elders; and the number of them was ten thousand times ten thousand, and thousands of thousands, [12]saying with a loud voice:

"Worthy is the Lamb who was slain
To receive power and riches and wisdom,
And strength and honor and glory and blessing!"

[13]And [u]every creature which is in heaven and on the earth and under the earth and such as are in the sea, and all that are in them, I heard saying:

[v]"Blessing and honor and glory and power
Be to Him [w]who sits on the throne,
And to the Lamb, forever and ever!"*

[14]Then the four living creatures said, "Amen!" And the twenty-four* elders fell down and worshiped Him who lives forever and ever.*

First Seal: The Conqueror

6 Now [a]I saw when the Lamb opened one of the seals;* and I heard [b]one of the four living creatures saying [b]with a voice like thunder, "Come and see." [2]And I looked, and behold, [c]a white horse. [d]He who sat on it had a bow; [e]and a crown was

---

* **4:11** NU-Text and M-Text read *our Lord and God.* • NU-Text and M-Text read *existed.* * **5:4** NU-Text and M-Text omit *and read.* * **5:5** NU-Text and M-Text omit *to loose.* * **5:6** NU-Text and M-Text read *I saw in the midst ... a Lamb standing.* * **5:10** NU-Text and M-Text read *them.* • NU-Text reads *a kingdom.* • NU-Text and M-Text read *they.* * **5:13** M-Text adds *Amen.* * **5:14** NU-Text and M-Text omit *twenty-four.* • NU-Text and M-Text omit *Him who lives forever and ever.* * **6:1** NU-Text and M-Text read *seven seals.*

4:10 *cast their crowns before the throne.* This act symbolizes the willing surrender of their authority in light of the worthiness of God as Creator. Because no one but God can create, He alone should be worshiped and recognized as sovereign.
5:1 *a scroll.* The scroll apparently contains the judgments and redemption seen in later chapters. It may also be the book that was sealed in Daniel 12:4. There appears to be an allusion to the scroll the Lord handed Ezekiel (Ezek. 2:9–10). *sealed with seven seals.* A scroll cannot be unrolled until the seals have all been opened.
5:5 *Lion of the tribe of Judah, the Root of David.* Both of these titles are messianic titles (Gen. 49:8–10, Is. 11:1,10).
5:7 *took the scroll.* The Lamb taking the scroll from the Father demonstrates that judgment and

authority over the earth is committed to the Son (Dan. 7:13–14). The scroll may be the same one that was sealed in Daniel 12:9.
6:2 *white horse . . . conquering.* Because the first rider is on a white horse and is conquering, some take it to be Christ (19:11). If so, His full conquest is considerably delayed (19:11—20:6). Another view is

---

4:10 [t] Rev. 5:8, 14; 7:11; 11:16; 19:4 **4:11** [u] Rev. 1:6; 5:12 [v] Gen. 1:1 [w] Col. 1:16 **5:1** [a] Ezek. 2:9, 10 [b] Is. 29:11 **5:2** [c] Rev. 4:11; 5:9 **5:5** [d] Gen. 49:9 [e] Heb. 7:14 [f] Is. 11:1, 10 [g] Rev. 3:21 [h] Rev. 6:1 **5:6** [i] [John 1:29] [j] Zech. 3:9; 4:10 [k] Rev. 1:4; 3:1; 4:5 **5:7** [l] Rev. 4:2 **5:8** [m] Rev. 4:8–10; 19:4 [n] Rev. 8:3 **5:9** [o] Rev. 14:3 [p] Rev. 4:11 [q] John 1:29 [r] [Heb. 9:12] **5:10** [s] Ex. 19:6 [t] Is. 61:6 **5:13** [u] Phil. 2:10 [v] 1 Chr. 29:11 [w] Rev. 4:2, 3; 6:16; 20:11 **6:1** [a] [Rev. 5:5–7, 12; 13:8] [b] Rev. 4:7 **6:2** [c] Zech. 1:8; 6:3 [d] Ps. 45:4, 5, LXX [e] Zech. 6:11

given to him, and he went out *f*conquering and to conquer.

Second Seal: Conflict on Earth

3When He opened the second seal, *g*I heard the second living creature saying, "Come and see."* **4**hAnother horse, fiery red, went out. And it was granted to the one who sat on it to *i*take peace from the earth, and that *people* should kill one another; and there was given to him a great sword.

Third Seal: Scarcity on Earth

5When He opened the third seal, *j*I heard the third living creature say, "Come and see." So I looked, and behold, *k*a black horse, and he who sat on it had a pair of *l*scales in his hand. **6**And I heard a voice in the midst of the four living creatures saying, "A quart* of wheat for a denarius,* and three quarts of barley for a denarius; and *m*do not harm the oil and the wine."

Fourth Seal: Widespread Death on Earth

7When He opened the fourth seal, *n*I heard the voice of the fourth living creature saying, "Come and see." **8**oSo I looked, and behold, a pale horse. And the name of him who sat on it was Death, and Hades followed with him. And power was given to them over a fourth of the earth, *p*to kill with sword, with hunger, with death, *q*and by the beasts of the earth.

Fifth Seal: The Cry of the Martyrs

9When He opened the fifth seal, I saw under *r*the altar *s*the souls of those who had been slain *t*for the word of God and for *u*the testimony which they held. **10**And they cried with a loud voice, saying, *v*"How long, O Lord, *w*holy and true, *x*until You judge and avenge our blood on those who dwell on the earth?" **11**Then a *y*white robe was given to each of them; and it was said

to them *z*that they should rest a little while longer, until both *the number of* their fellow servants and their brethren, who would be killed as they *were*, was completed.

Sixth Seal: Cosmic Disturbances

12I looked when He opened the sixth seal, *a*and behold,* there was a great earthquake; and *b*the sun became black as sackcloth of hair, and the moon* became like blood. **13**cAnd the stars of heaven fell to the earth, as a fig tree drops its late figs when it is shaken by a mighty wind. **14**dThen the sky receded as a scroll when it is rolled up, and *e*every mountain and island was moved out of its place. **15**And the *f*kings of the earth, the great men, the rich men, the commanders,* the mighty men, every slave and every free man, *g*hid themselves in the caves and in the rocks of the mountains, **16**hand said to the mountains and rocks, "Fall on us and hide us from the face of Him who *i*sits on the throne and from the wrath of the Lamb! **17**For the great day of His wrath has come, *j*and who is able to stand?"

The Sealed of Israel

7 After these things I saw four angels standing at the four corners of the earth, *a*holding the four winds of the earth, *b*that the wind should not blow on the earth, on the sea, or on any tree. **2**Then I saw another angel ascending from the east, having the seal of the living God. And he cried with a loud voice to the four angels to whom it was granted to harm the earth and the sea, **3**saying, *c*"Do not harm the earth, the sea, or the trees till we have sealed the servants of our God *d*on their foreheads."

---

* **6:3** NU-Text and M-Text omit *and see.*
* **6:6** Greek *choinix;* that is, approximately one quart • This was approximately one day's wage for a worker. * **6:12** NU-Text and M-Text omit *behold.* • NU-Text and M-Text read *the whole moon.* * **6:15** NU-Text and M-Text read *the commanders, the rich men.*

---

that this is a spirit of conquest and delusion (Matt. 23:3–6). The bow suggests that the rider is a warrior. The crown suggests that he is a ruler.
6:8 pale. The color of the pale horse is the color of a corpse. It is fitting that this pale horse is ridden by a figure named "Death." This fourth judgment is the inevitable consequence of the first three. **sword . . . hunger . . . death.** These plagues are the same ones that God used to bring the nation of Israel to repentance (1 Kin. 8:33–39; 1 Chr. 21:12), and in Revelation a godly nucleus does arise as a result of these judgments (7:3–8).
6:9 under the altar. Sacrificial blood was poured beside the base of the altar in the temple (Ex. 29:12).
6:12–13 sun . . . moon . . . stars. The effects of the great earthquake on the sun, moon, and stars are worded similarly to Matthew 24:29, placing these events in proximity to the coming of the Son of Man (Matt. 24:30).
6:14 receded . . . rolled up. When the sky is rolled back, the people on earth can see "Him who sits on the throne" (v. 16). They will suddenly see that God is

not far away or nonexistent and they will have to be accountable to Him.
6:17 who is able to stand. This rhetorical question is answered in the surrounding context. The unbelievers, no matter how strong, cannot stand. Those who are protected by the Lord are enabled to stand, whether on earth (7:1–8) or in God's presence in heaven (7:9–17).
7:3 sealed. The seal was a mark of ownership or authority. In ancient times a seal was fixed to a document by pressing a carved stamp or signet into a

---

6:2 *f*Matt. 24:5 **6:3** *g*Rev. 4:7 **6:4** *h*Zech. 1:8; 6:2 *i*Matt. 24:6, 7 **6:5** *j*Rev. 4:7 *k*Zech. 6:2, 6 *l*Matt. 24:7 **6:6** *m*Rev. 7:3; 9:4 **6:7** *n*Rev. 4:7 **6:8** *o*Zech. 6:3 *p*Ezek. 5:12, 17; 14:21; 29:5 *q*Lev. 26:22 **6:9** *r*Rev. 8:3 *s*[Rev. 20:4] *t*Rev. 1:2, 9 *u*2 Tim. 1:8 **6:10** *v*Zech. 1:12 *w*Rev. 3:7 *x*Rev. 11:18 **6:11** *y*Rev. 3:4, 5; 7:9 *z*Heb. 11:40 **6:12** *a*Matt. 24:7 *b*Joel 2:10, 31; 3:15 **6:13** *c*Rev. 8:10; 9:1 **6:14** *d*Is. 34:4 *e*Rev. 16:20 **6:15** *f*Ps. 2:2–4 *g*Is. 2:10, 19, 21; 24:21 **6:16** *h*Luke 23:29, 30 *i*Rev. 20:11 **6:17** *j*Zeph. 1:14 **7:1** *a*Dan. 7:2 *b*Rev. 7:3; 8:7; 9:4 **7:3** *c*Rev. 6:6 *d*Rev. 22:4

⁴ᵉAnd I heard the number of those who were sealed. ᶠOne hundred *and* forty-four thousand ᵍof all the tribes of the children of Israel *were* sealed:

⁵ of the tribe of Judah twelve thousand *were* sealed;*
of the tribe of Reuben twelve thousand *were* sealed;
of the tribe of Gad twelve thousand *were* sealed;
⁶ of the tribe of Asher twelve thousand *were* sealed;
of the tribe of Naphtali twelve thousand *were* sealed;
of the tribe of Manasseh twelve thousand *were* sealed;
⁷ of the tribe of Simeon twelve thousand *were* sealed;
of the tribe of Levi twelve thousand *were* sealed;
of the tribe of Issachar twelve thousand *were* sealed;
⁸ of the tribe of Zebulun twelve thousand *were* sealed;
of the tribe of Joseph twelve thousand *were* sealed;
of the tribe of Benjamin twelve thousand *were* sealed.

A Multitude from the Great Tribulation

⁹After these things I looked, and behold, ʰa great multitude which no one could number, ⁱof all nations, tribes, peoples, and tongues, standing before the throne and before the Lamb, ʲclothed with white robes, with palm branches in their hands, ¹⁰and crying out with a loud voice, saying, ᵏ"Salvation *belongs* to our God ˡwho sits on the throne, and to the Lamb!" ¹¹ᵐAll the angels stood around the throne and the elders and the four living creatures, and fell on their faces before the throne and ⁿworshiped God, ¹²ᵒsaying:

"Amen! Blessing and glory and wisdom,

Thanksgiving and honor and power and might,
Be to our God forever and ever. Amen."

¹³Then one of the elders answered, saying to me, "Who are these arrayed in ᵖwhite robes, and where did they come from?"

¹⁴And I said to him, "Sir,* you know."

So he said to me, ᑫ"These are the ones who come out of the great tribulation, and ʳwashed their robes and made them white in the blood of the Lamb. ¹⁵Therefore they are before the throne of God, and serve Him day and night in His temple. And He who sits on the throne will ˢdwell among them. ¹⁶ᵗThey shall neither hunger anymore nor thirst anymore; ᵘthe sun shall not strike them, nor any heat; ¹⁷for the Lamb who is in the midst of the throne ᵛwill shepherd them and lead them to living fountains of waters.* ʷAnd God will wipe away every tear from their eyes."

Seventh Seal: Prelude to the Seven Trumpets

8 Whenᵃ He opened the seventh seal, there was silence in heaven for about half an hour. ²ᵇAnd I saw the seven angels who stand before God, ᶜand to them were given seven trumpets. ³Then another angel, having a golden censer, came and stood at the altar. He was given much incense, that he should offer *it* with ᵈthe prayers of all the saints upon ᵉthe golden altar which was before the throne. ⁴And ᶠthe smoke of the incense, with the prayers of the saints, ascended before God from the angel's hand. ⁵Then the angel took the censer, filled it with fire from the altar, and threw *it* to the earth. And ᵍthere were

---

* **7:5** In NU-Text and M-Text *were sealed* is stated only in verses 5a and 8c; the words are understood in the remainder of the passage. * **7:14** NU-Text and M-Text read *My lord*. * **7:17** NU-Text and M-Text read *to fountains of the waters of life*.

---

lump of clay or wax at the point where the document was opened and closed.

7:4 One hundred and forty-four thousand. Those sealed are all the children of Israel, fulfilling the promise that when the "fullness of the Gentiles has come in" all Israel will be saved (Rom. 11:25–27).

7:5–8 Judah. Judah is placed first in this list of the Israelite tribes because Christ, the Messiah, is the "Lion of the tribe of Judah" (5:5; Gen. 49:8–10). **Reuben.** Reuben is next as Jacob's firstborn (Gen. 49:3–4). Dan and Ephraim are omitted, perhaps because of their gross idolatry during the period of the judges, demonstrated by the incident in the territory of Dan (Judg. 18). **Joseph.** Joseph and his son Manasseh are both included, bringing the number of tribes to twelve.

7:14 great tribulation. This vast multitude has come out of the great tribulation, referring to "the hour of trial which shall come upon the whole world" (3:10).

In view of the great loss of life during this time period, martyrdom is most likely the means of their escape. Tribulation was already being experienced by the church in John's day (2:10; Acts 14:22). However, the great tribulation, predicted in Daniel 12:1, will be of an intensity "such as has not been since the beginning of the world until this time, no, nor ever shall be" (Matt. 24:21).

8:1 seventh seal. When the seventh seal is broken, the book can finally be opened.

7:4 ᵉ Rev. 9:16 ᶠ Rev. 14:1, 3 ᵍ Gen. 49:1–27 **7:9** ʰ Rom. 11:25 ⁱ Rev. 5:9 ʲ Rev. 3:5, 18; 4:4; 6:11 **7:10** ᵏ Ps. 3:8 ˡ Rev. 5:13 **7:11** ᵐ Rev. 4:6 ⁿ Rev. 4:11; 5:9, 12, 14; 11:16 **7:12** ᵒ Rev. 5:13, 14 **7:13** ᵖ Rev. 7:9 **7:14** ᑫ Rev. 6:9 ʳ [Heb. 9:14] **7:15** ˢ Is. 4:5, 6 **7:16** ᵗ Is. 49:10 ᵘ Ps. 121:6 **7:17** ᵛ Ps. 23:1 ʷ Rev. 21:4 **8:1** ᵃ Rev. 6:1 **8:2** ᵇ [Matt. 18:10] ᶜ 2 Chr. 29:25–28 **8:3** ᵈ Rev. 5:8 ᵉ Ex. 30:1 **8:4** ᶠ Ps. 141:2 **8:5** ᵍ Rev. 11:19; 16:18

noises, thunderings, [h]lightnings, [i]and an earthquake. [6]So the seven angels who had the seven trumpets prepared themselves to sound.

First Trumpet: Vegetation Struck

[7]The first angel sounded: [j]And hail and fire followed, mingled with blood, and they were thrown [k]to the earth.* And a third [l]of the trees were burned up, and all green grass was burned up.

Second Trumpet: The Seas Struck

[8]Then the second angel sounded: [m]And something like a great mountain burning with fire was thrown into the sea, [n]and a third of the sea [o]became blood. [9p]And a third of the living creatures in the sea died, and a third of the ships were destroyed.

Third Trumpet: The Waters Struck

[10]Then the third angel sounded: [q]And a great star fell from heaven, burning like a torch, [r]and it fell on a third of the rivers and on the springs of water. [11s]The name of the star is Wormwood. [t]A third of the waters became wormwood, and many men died from the water, because it was made bitter.

Fourth Trumpet: The Heavens Struck

[12u]Then the fourth angel sounded: And a third of the sun was struck, a third of the moon, and a third of the stars, so that a third of them were darkened. A third of the day did not shine, and likewise the night.

[13]And I looked, [v]and I heard an angel* flying through the midst of heaven, saying with a loud voice, [w]"Woe, woe, woe to the inhabitants of the earth, because of the remaining blasts of the trumpet of the three angels who are about to sound!"

Fifth Trumpet: The Locusts from the Bottomless Pit

9 Then the fifth angel sounded: [a]And I saw a star fallen from heaven to the earth. To him was given the key to [b]the bottomless pit. [2]And he opened the bottomless pit, and smoke arose out of the pit like the smoke of a great furnace. So the [c]sun and the air were darkened because of the smoke of the pit. [3]Then out of the smoke locusts came upon the earth. And to them was given power, [d]as the scorpions of the earth have power. [4]They were commanded [e]not to harm [f]the grass of the earth, or any green thing, or any tree, but only those men who do not have [g]the seal of God on their foreheads. [5]And they were not given authority to kill them, [h]but to torment them for five months. Their torment was like the torment of a scorpion when it strikes a man. [6]In those days [i]men will seek death and will not find it; they will desire to die, and death will flee from them.

[7i]The shape of the locusts was like horses prepared for battle. [k]On their heads were crowns of something like gold, [l]and their faces were like the faces of men. [8]They had hair like women's hair, and [m]their teeth were like lions' teeth. [9]And they had breastplates like breastplates of iron, and the sound of their wings was [n]like the sound of chariots with many horses running into battle. [10]They had tails like scorpions, and there were stings in their tails. Their power was to hurt men five months. [11]And they had as king over them [o]the angel of the bottomless pit, whose name in Hebrew is Abaddon, but in Greek he has the name Apollyon.

[12p]One woe is past. Behold, still two more woes are coming after these things.

* **8:7** NU-Text and M-Text add and a third of the earth was burned up.　* **8:13** NU-Text and M-Text read eagle.

8:7 hail . . . fire . . . blood. This blend of destruction and horror sounds like a combination of the first and seventh plagues of God upon Egypt (Ex. 7:19–20; 9:22–25).
8:11 Wormwood. Wormwood is a plant found in the Middle East, known for its bitter taste. Here and elsewhere (Lam. 3:19) the term is figurative for bitterness. Normally wormwood is not poisonous, but the plague of the third trumpet involves effects far more potent than the taste of this bitter plant: many men die from the water.
8:13 Woe, woe, woe. The "woes" refer to the impact of the three remaining trumpet judgments on the unbelieving inhabitants of the earth. The first woe is the fifth trumpet (9:12); the second woe is the sixth trumpet (11:14). The third woe comes quickly and may be the same as the seventh trumpet (11:15–19), although that is not stated. If not, the final woe may be focused on Babylon, the great harlot, because of the climactic use of "woe" in 18:10, 16, and 19.
9:1 star fallen from heaven. The star may be a demon (v. 11), Satan himself (12:9), or an angel serving God (20:1). **bottomless pit.** The pit is the interim jail for some demons (Luke 8:31). It is also the place

of origin of the beast (11:7; 17:8). Furthermore, it will be the place where Satan will be imprisoned during Christ's reign (20:2–3).
9:3 locusts. Locusts, or grasshoppers, were greatly feared in agricultural societies because they devoured crops. In Exodus 10:12–15, a plague of locusts wiped out what was left of Egypt's crops. Joel 1:2 tells of an invasion of locusts that the Lord used to judge unrepentant Judah, which was a foreshadowing of the day of the Lord. **scorpions.** Scorpions sting with their tails, causing great pain and even death (v. 10).
9:11 angel of the bottomless pit. The angel is demonic and controls the demonic locusts (3:10). If

8:5 [h]Rev. 4:5 [i]2 Sam. 22:8 **8:7** [j]Ezek. 38:22 [k]Rev. 16:2 [l]Rev. 9:4, 15–18 **8:8** [m]Jer. 51:25 [n]Ex. 7:17 [o]Ezek. 14:19 **8:9** [p]Rev. 16:3 **8:10** [q]Is. 14:12 [r]Rev. 14:7; 16:4 **8:11** [s]Ruth 1:20 [t]Ex. 15:23 **8:12** [u]Is. 13:10 **8:13** [v]Rev. 14:6; 19:17 [w]Rev. 9:12; 11:14; 12:12 **9:1** [a]Rev. 8:10 [b]Luke 8:31 **9:2** [c]Joel 2:2, 10 **9:3** [d]Judg. 7:12 **9:4** [e]Rev. 6:6 [f]Rev. 8:7 [g]Rev. 7:2, 3 **9:5** [h]Rev. 9:10; 11:7] **9:6** [i]Jer. 8:3 **9:7** [j]Joel 2:4 [k]Nah. 3:17 [l]Dan. 7:8 **9:8** [m]Joel 1:6 **9:9** [n]Joel 2:5–7 **9:11** [o]Eph. 2:2 **9:12** [p]Rev. 8:13; 11:14

Sixth Trumpet: The Angels from the Euphrates

13Then the sixth angel sounded: And
I heard a voice from the four horns of the
[q]golden altar which is before God, 14saying
to the sixth angel who had the trumpet, "Release the four angels who are bound [r]at the
great river Euphrates." 15So the four angels,
who had been prepared for the hour and
day and month and year, were released to
kill a [s]third of mankind. 16Now [t]the number
of the army [u]of the horsemen *was* two hundred million; [v]I heard the number of them.
17And thus I saw the horses in the vision:
those who sat on them had breastplates
of fiery red, hyacinth blue, and sulfur yellow; [w]and the heads of the horses *were* like
the heads of lions; and out of their mouths
came fire, smoke, and brimstone. 18By
these three *plagues* a third of mankind was
killed—by the fire and the smoke and the
brimstone which came out of their mouths.
19For their power* is in their mouth and in
their tails; [x]for their tails *are* like serpents,
having heads; and with them they do harm.
20But the rest of mankind, who were not
killed by these plagues, [y]did not repent of
the works of their hands, that they should
not worship [z]demons, [a]and idols of gold,
silver, brass, stone, and wood, which can
neither see nor hear nor walk. 21And they
did not repent of their murders [b]or their
sorceries* or their sexual immorality or
their thefts.

The Mighty Angel with the Little Book

10 I saw still another mighty angel coming down from heaven, clothed with
a cloud. [a]And a rainbow *was* on [b]his head,
his face *was* like the sun, and [c]his feet like
pillars of fire. 2He had a little book open in
his hand. [d]And he set his right foot on the
sea and *his* left *foot* on the land, 3and cried
with a loud voice, as *when* a lion roars.
When he cried out, [e]seven thunders uttered
their voices. 4Now when the seven thunders
uttered their voices,* I was about to write;
but I heard a voice from heaven saying to
me,* [f]"Seal up the things which the seven
thunders uttered, and do not write them."
5The angel whom I saw standing on the
sea and on the land [g]raised up his hand*
to heaven 6and swore by Him who lives
forever and ever, [h]who created heaven and
the things that are in it, the earth and the
things that are in it, and the sea and the
things that are in it, [i]that there should be
delay no longer, 7but [j]in the days of the
sounding of the seventh angel, when he is
about to sound, the mystery of God would
be finished, as He declared to His servants
the prophets.

John Eats the Little Book

8Then the voice which I heard from
heaven spoke to me again and said, "Go,
take the little book which is open in the
hand of the angel who stands on the sea
and on the earth."
9So I went to the angel and said to him,
"Give me the little book."
And he said to me, [k]"Take and eat it; and
it will make your stomach bitter, but it will
be as sweet as honey in your mouth."
10Then I took the little book out of the
angel's hand and ate it, [l]and it was as sweet
as honey in my mouth. But when I had eat-
en it, [m]my stomach became bitter. 11And
he* said to me, "You must prophesy again
about many peoples, nations, tongues, and
kings."

* **9:19** NU-Text and M-Text read *the power of the horses.* * **9:21** NU-Text and M-Text read *drugs.* * **10:4** NU-Text and M-Text read *sounded.* • NU-Text and M-Text omit *to me.* * **10:5** NU-Text and M-Text read *right hand.* * **10:11** NU-Text and M-Text read *they.*

this angel serves God, this is another instance where the activity of Satan or his demons is under the Lord's sovereign control (2 Cor. 12:7,9).

9:14 *great river Euphrates.* This river is the eastern boundary of the land promised to Abraham for his descendants (Gen. 15:18), as well as the geographic area from which powerful enemies like Assyria and Babylon came to invade Israel (Is. 8:5–8). It may represent the seat of Satan's former victory (in the garden of Eden).

9:18 *a third of mankind.* A third of mankind could number in the billions. Coupled with the former destruction of one-fourth of humanity (6:8), over one-half of the world's population will have been killed.

10:1 *mighty angel.* This mighty angel could be the "strong angel" of 5:2 or the angel "having great authority" of 18:1. It is unlikely that this is Michael, who is referred to by name elsewhere (12:7; Dan. 12:1) or Christ, since He is never called an angel in the New Testament. Furthermore, unlike Christ, this angel comes to earth before the time of tribulation is over.

10:2 *little book.* The little book is not the same as the book that was unsealed in 6:1—8:1. It is more like the scroll eaten by Ezekiel (Ezek. 2:9—3:3), although this scroll caused John's stomach to become bitter (vv. 9–10), not just his spirit (Ezek. 3:14).

10:10 *sweet . . . bitter.* The Word of God is always sweet, but the soberness of the judgments and what this will mean to the "peoples, nations, tongues, and kings," to whom John must prophesy is enough to turn John's stomach. It is a terrible thing to contemplate the fate of those who refuse to repent (9:21).

9:13 [q] Rev. 8:3 **9:14** [r] Rev. 16:12 **9:15** [s] Rev. 8:7–9; 9:18 **9:16** [t] Dan. 7:10 [u] Ezek. 38:4 [v] Rev. 7:4 **9:17** [w] Is. 5:28, 29 **9:19** [x] Is. 9:15 **9:20** [y] Deut. 31:29 [z] 1 Cor. 10:20 [a] Dan. 5:23 **9:21** [b] Rev. 21:8; 22:15 **10:1** [a] Rev. 4:3 [b] Rev. 1:16 [c] Rev. 1:15 **10:2** [d] Matt. 28:18 **10:3** [e] Ps. 29:3–9 **10:4** [f] Dan. 8:26; 12:4, 9 **10:5** [g] Dan. 12:7 **10:6** [h] Rev. 4:11 [i] Rev. 16:17 **10:7** [j] Rev. 11:15 **10:9** [k] Jer. 15:16 **10:10** [l] Ezek. 3:3 [m] Ezek. 2:10

The Two Witnesses

11 Then I was given ^aa reed like a measuring rod. And the angel stood,* saying, ^b"Rise and measure the temple of God, the altar, and those who worship there. ²But leave out ^cthe court which is outside the temple, and do not measure it, ^dfor it has been given to the Gentiles. And they will ^etread the holy city underfoot *for* ^fforty-two months. ³And I will give *power* to my two ^gwitnesses, ^hand they will prophesy ⁱone thousand two hundred and sixty days, clothed in sackcloth."

⁴These are the ^jtwo olive trees and the two lampstands standing before the God* of the earth. ⁵And if anyone wants to harm them, ^kfire proceeds from their mouth and devours their enemies. ^lAnd if anyone wants to harm them, he must be killed in this manner. ⁶These ^mhave power to shut heaven, so that no rain falls in the days of their prophecy; and they have power over waters to turn them to blood, and to strike the earth with all plagues, as often as they desire.

The Witnesses Killed

⁷When they ⁿfinish their testimony, ^othe beast that ascends ^pout of the bottomless pit ^qwill make war against them, overcome them, and kill them. ⁸And their dead bodies *will lie* in the street of ^rthe great city which spiritually is called Sodom and Egypt, ^swhere also our* Lord was crucified. ^{9t}Then *those* from the peoples, tribes, tongues, and nations will see their dead bodies three-and-a-half days, ^uand not allow* their dead bodies to be put into graves.

^{10v}And those who dwell on the earth will rejoice over them, make merry, ^wand send gifts to one another, ^xbecause these two prophets tormented those who dwell on the earth.

The Witnesses Resurrected

^{11y}Now after the three-and-a-half days ^zthe breath of life from God entered them, and they stood on their feet, and great fear fell on those who saw them. ¹²And they* heard a loud voice from heaven saying to them, "Come up here." ^aAnd they ascended to heaven ^bin a cloud, ^cand their enemies saw them. ¹³In the same hour ^dthere was a great earthquake, ^eand a tenth of the city fell. In the earthquake seven thousand people were killed, and the rest were afraid ^fand gave glory to the God of heaven.

^{14g}The second woe is past. Behold, the third woe is coming quickly.

Seventh Trumpet: The Kingdom Proclaimed

¹⁵Then ^hthe seventh angel sounded: ⁱAnd there were loud voices in heaven, saying, ^j"The kingdoms* of this world have become *the kingdoms* of our Lord and of His Christ, ^kand He shall reign forever and ever!" ¹⁶And ^lthe twenty-four elders who

* **11:1** NU-Text and M-Text omit *And the angel stood.* * **11:4** NU-Text and M-Text read *Lord.* * **11:8** NU-Text and M-Text read *their.* * **11:9** NU-Text and M-Text read *nations see … and will not allow.* * **11:12** M-Text reads *I.* * **11:15** NU-Text and M-Text read *kingdom … has become.*

11:1 *reed like a measuring rod.* John's measuring rod is much like that used by Ezekiel (Ezek. 40:3–5) in his vision of measuring the temple.
11:3 *two witnesses.* The two unnamed witnesses are strikingly similar to Elijah (vv. 5–6; 1 Kin. 17; Mal. 4:5) and Moses (v. 6; Ex. 7–11), who appeared together with Christ on the Mount of Transfiguration (Luke 9:29–32). *one thousand two hundred and sixty days.* Forty-two months (v. 2) is the same length of time as twelve hundred and sixty days (12:6). Almost certainly "a time and times and half a time" (12:14) is also a period of three and a half years made up of 42 thirty-day months. These expressions draw from the prophecies in Daniel (Dan. 12:6–7,11–12). *sackcloth.* Sackcloth is a sign of mourning.
11:4 *two olive trees . . . two lampstands.* The witnesses are described as olive trees and lampstands, linking them to the vision in Zechariah 4 of "the two anointed ones, who stand beside the Lord of the whole earth" (Zech. 4:14). The passage in Zechariah refers to Zerubbabel and Joshua the priest. But the overarching principle for these and all other witnesses for the Lord is that their testimony to the truth is "Not by might nor by power, but by My Spirit" (Zech. 4:6).
11:6 *no rain . . . waters . . . blood . . . plagues.* The power to prevent rain identifies the witnesses with Elijah (James 5:17), and turning the water into blood and striking the earth with plagues is reminiscent of Moses in Egypt (Ex. 7:11–21).

11:7 *bottomless pit.* The beast, who emerges as the satanically empowered world ruler (chs. 13; 17), comes from the bottomless pit, as did the demonic locust plague of the fifth trumpet (9:1–10).
11:8 *great city.* The great city in Revelation is often Babylon (14:8), which possibly represents Rome (1 Pet. 5:13). But the further description "where also our Lord was crucified" seems to refer to Jerusalem. *Sodom and Egypt.* Sodom is the prototype for the moral degeneration of this great city (Gen. 19) and Egypt was the prototype for its rampant idolatry.
11:14 *second woe.* The second woe includes the sixth trumpet (9:12–21) and a second interlude (10:1—11:13). *third woe.* The third woe is apparently the seventh trumpet (vv. 15–19), since it "is coming quickly" and 8:13 relates the woes to the last three blasts of the trumpet. The final woe may extend further since the word "woe" recurs in 12:12.

11:1 ^aEzek. 40:3—42:20 ^bNum. 23:18 **11:2** ^cEzek. 40:17, 20 ^dPs. 79:1 ^eDan. 8:10 ^fRev. 12:6; 13:5 **11:3** ^gRev. 20:4 ^hRev. 19:10 ⁱRev. 12:6 **11:4** ^jZech. 4:2, 3, 11, 14 **11:5** ^k2 Kin. 1:10–12 ^lNum. 16:29 **11:6** ^m1 Kin. 17:1 **11:7** ⁿLuke 13:32 ^oRev. 13:1, 11; 17:8 ^pRev. 9:1, 2 ^qDan. 7:21 **11:8** ^rRev. 14:8 ^sHeb. 13:12 **11:9** ^tRev. 17:15 ^uPs. 79:2, 3 **11:10** ^vRev. 12:12 ^wEsth. 9:19, 22 ^xRev. 11:6 **11:11** ^yRev. 11:9 ^zEzek. 37:5, 9, 10 **11:12** ^aIs. 14:13 ^bActs 1:9 ^c2 Kin. 2:11, 12 **11:13** ^dRev. 6:12; 8:5; 11:19; 16:18 ^eRev. 16:19 ^fRev. 14:7; 16:9; 19:7 **11:14** ^gRev. 8:13; 9:12 **11:15** ^hRev. 8:2; 10:7 ⁱIs. 27:13 ^jRev. 12:10 ^kEx. 15:18 **11:16** ^lRev. 4:4

sat before God on their thrones fell on their faces and ^mworshiped God, ^17saying:

"We give You thanks, O Lord God Almighty,
The One ^nwho is and who was and who is to come,*
Because You have taken Your great power ^oand reigned.
^18 The nations were ^pangry, and Your wrath has come,
And the time of the ^qdead, that they should be judged,
And that You should reward Your servants the prophets and the saints,
And those who fear Your name, small and great,
And should destroy those who destroy the earth."

^19Then ^rthe temple of God was opened in heaven, and the ark of His covenant* was seen in His temple. And ^sthere were lightnings, noises, thunderings, an earthquake, ^tand great hail.

The Woman, the Child, and the Dragon

12 Now a great sign appeared in heaven: a woman clothed with the sun, with the moon under her feet, and on her head a garland of twelve stars. ^2Then being with child, she cried out ^ain labor and in pain to give birth.

^3And another sign appeared in heaven: behold, ^ba great, fiery red dragon having seven heads and ten horns, and seven diadems on his heads. ^4cHis tail drew a third ^dof the stars of heaven ^eand threw them to the earth. And the dragon stood ^fbefore the woman who was ready to give birth, ^gto devour her Child as soon as it was born. ^5She bore a male Child ^hwho was to rule all nations with a rod of iron. And her Child was ^icaught up to God and His throne. ^6Then ^jthe woman fled into the wilderness, where she has a place prepared by God, that they should feed her there ^kone thousand two hundred and sixty days.

Satan Thrown Out of Heaven

^7And war broke out in heaven: ^lMichael and his angels fought ^mwith the dragon; and the dragon and his angels fought, ^8but they did not prevail, nor was a place found for them* in heaven any longer. ^9So ^nthe great dragon was cast out, ^othat serpent of old, called the Devil and Satan, ^pwho deceives the whole world; ^qhe was cast to the earth, and his angels were cast out with him.

---

* **11:17** NU-Text and M-Text omit *and who is to come.*   * **11:19** M-Text reads *the covenant of the Lord.*   * **12:8** M-Text reads *him.*

11:17–18 We give You thanks. The 24 elders (4:10–11; 5:8–10) praise God's power and wrath, and the corresponding distribution of reward and judgment. This stanza of heavenly thanksgiving seems to reflect on the fulfillment of the great messianic prophecy in Psalm 2.

11:19 ark of His covenant. The ark of the covenant made by Moses disappeared at the time of the Babylonian captivity (2Chr. 36:18–19). The ark represented God's presence, leadership, and protection of Israel (Num. 10:33–36; Josh. 3:3,15–17).

12:1 woman clothed with the sun. The woman is the nation Israel. To Israel belongs the covenant and the promises. If Satan can make even one of those promises fail, he will have "won." This is why the dragon stands over the woman in such a predatory manner (v. 4).

12:3 great, fiery red dragon. The sign of the dragon is interpreted in verse 9 as Satan, who first appeared in Scripture as the serpent in the garden of Eden (Gen. 3). The imagery is in keeping with Old Testament and extrabiblical usage (Is. 27:1). **seven heads . . . ten horns . . . seven diadems.** The dragon with the seven heads and ten horns refers to Satan and the empire over which he rules during the course of time. The seven heads, ten horns, and seven diadems refer to Satan's brilliance, power, and glory as "god of this age" (2 Cor. 4:4). This description is almost identical to that of the beast from the sea in 13:1.

12:4 a third of the stars. This image may refer to the rebellion of a third of the angelic host following Satan. **devour her Child.** The attempt of the dragon to devour the newborn Christ Child reveals that the strategy of Herod to kill the baby Jesus (Matt. 2:3–16) was satanically inspired.

12:5 male Child, who was to rule. The male Child who will rule with a rod of iron is the messianic figure of Psalm 2:8–9; however, there is no earthly rule over all nations at this point. From the perspective of this heavenly scene, the Child-ruler is soon caught up to the throne of God, apparently referring to the ascension of Christ (Acts 1:9).

12:6 one thousand two hundred and sixty days. The detailed way in which this same length of time is expressed ("a time and times and half a time," v. 14), suggests half of a literal seven-year tribulation period (Dan. 9:27).

12:7–8 Michael. Michael is an archangel (Jude 9). According to Daniel 12:1, he is a special guardian angel for the nation of Israel. Apparently he commands an army of angels. Michael and the heavenly forces are victorious, making heaven off-limits to Satan and his demons. (In Job 1 and 1 Kings 22:22 it is clear that at one time Satan did have access to heaven.)

12:9 to the earth. The devil's expulsion from heaven to the earth means that this world becomes his base of operations, and that his anger is vented toward the remaining inhabitants of the earth (v. 12). It is likely that the end times will be the greatest period of spiritual warfare (Eph. 6:10–18) in history.

11:16 ^m Rev. 4:11; 5:9, 12, 14; 7:11   **11:17** ^n Rev. 16:5 ^o Rev. 19:6   **11:18** ^p Ps. 2:1 ^q Dan. 7:10   **11:19** ^r Rev. 4:1; 15:5, 8 ^s Rev. 8:5 ^t Rev. 16:21   **12:2** ^a Is. 26:17; 66:6–9 **12:3** ^b Rev. 13:1; 17:3, 7, 9   **12:4** ^c Rev. 9:10, 19 ^d Rev. 8:7, 12 ^e Dan. 8:10 ^f Rev. 12:2 ^g Matt. 2:16   **12:5** ^h Ps. 2:9 ^i Acts 1:9–11   **12:6** ^j Rev. 12:4, 14 ^k Rev. 11:3; 13:5 **12:7** ^l Dan. 10:13, 21; 12:1 ^m Rev. 20:2   **12:9** ^n John 12:31 ^o Gen. 3:1, 4 ^p Rev. 20:3 ^q Rev. 9:1

10Then I heard a loud voice saying in heaven, r"Now salvation, and strength, and the kingdom of our God, and the power of His Christ have come, for the accuser of our brethren, swho accused them before our God day and night, has been cast down. 11And tthey overcame him by the blood of the Lamb and by the word of their testimony, uand they did not love their lives to the death. 12Therefore vrejoice, O heavens, and you who dwell in them! wWoe to the inhabitants of the earth and the sea! For the devil has come down to you, having great wrath, xbecause he knows that he has a short time."

The Woman Persecuted

13Now when the dragon saw that he had been cast to the earth, he persecuted ythe woman who gave birth to the male Child. 14zBut the woman was given two wings of a great eagle, athat she might fly binto the wilderness to her place, where she is nourished cfor a time and times and half a time, from the presence of the serpent. 15So the serpent dspewed water out of his mouth like a flood after the woman, that he might cause her to be carried away by the flood. 16But the earth helped the woman, and the earth opened its mouth and swallowed up the flood which the dragon had spewed out of his mouth. 17And the dragon was enraged with the woman, and he went to make war with the rest of her offspring, who keep the commandments of God and have the testimony of Jesus Christ.*

The Beast from the Sea

13 Then I* stood on the sand of the sea. And I saw aa beast rising up out of the sea, bhaving seven heads and ten horns,* and on his horns ten crowns, and on his heads cblasphemous name. 2Now the beast which I saw was like a leopard, his feet were like the feet of a bear, and his mouth like the mouth of a lion. The ddragon gave him his power, his throne, and great authority. 3And I saw one of his heads eas if it had been mortally wounded, and his deadly wound was healed. And fall the world marveled and followed the beast. 4So they worshiped the dragon who gave authority to the beast; and they worshiped the beast, saying, g"Who is like the beast? Who is able to make war with him?"

5And he was given ha mouth speaking great things and blasphemies, and he was given authority to continue* for iforty-two months. 6Then he opened his mouth in blasphemy against God, to blaspheme His name, iHis tabernacle, and those who dwell in heaven. 7It was granted to him kto make war with the saints and to overcome them. And lauthority was given him over every tribe,* tongue, and nation. 8All who dwell on the earth will worship him, mwhose names have not been written in the Book of Life of the Lamb slain nfrom the foundation of the world.

9oIf anyone has an ear, let him hear. 10pHe who leads into captivity shall go into captivity; qhe who kills with the sword must be killed with the sword. rHere is the patience and the faith of the saints.

---

* **12:17** NU-Text and M-Text omit *Christ*.
* **13:1** NU-Text reads *he*. • NU-Text and M-Text read *ten horns and seven heads*. * **13:5** M-Text reads *make war*. * **13:7** NU-Text and M-Text add *and people*.

12:11 blood of the Lamb . . . word of their testimony . . . did not love their lives. The heavenly defeat of Satan (vv. 7–9) is followed by reference to his earthly setbacks, including the crucifixion of Christ, the verbal witness of believers, and the martyrdom of some of the believers. The fact that these witnesses were willing to die for their testimony showed that they knew that Christ had defeated death.
12:14 a time. A "time" probably equals one year, so the period of protection here is three and a half years, which corresponds to the length of the two witnesses' testimony in 11:3. It is also equivalent to the period of the beast's authority ("forty-two months" in 13:5), which includes his ability to "make war with the saints and to overcome them" (13:7; Ps. 122:7; Dan. 7:25).
12:17 the rest of her offspring. The rest of the children are believers in Christ.
13:1–2 beast. The parallel to the four beasts (especially the fourth) in Daniel 7, and the explanation of the beast given in 17:8–11 make it seem that the beast symbolizes both a revived Roman Empire, which exercises universal authority, and a specific ruler, whom John calls the antichrist (1 John 2:18).
13:1 a blasphemous name. The blasphemous name may be the common claim of ancient Roman emperors to be divine, or blasphemy against the name of

the true God (vv. 5–6) as Daniel predicted of the willful king during the tribulation period (Dan. 11:36).
13:3 mortally wounded . . . deadly wound. The apparently fatal wound that was healed is a satanic attempt to mimic the wounds of Christ from His crucifixion, which Christ still carries after the resurrection. This is part of the fulfillment of the prophecy of the "power, signs, and lying wonders, and . . . unrighteous deception" that accompany the "lawless one" (2 Thess. 2:8–12).
13:4 worshiped the dragon . . . and . . . the beast. Any false worship or idolatry is ultimately demonic and satanic (1 Cor. 10:20–22).
13:5 forty-two months. Forty-two months is the duration of the beast's worldwide supremacy, in keeping with the prophecy of Daniel 7:25.
13:9 If anyone has an ear, let him hear. This phrase is used frequently in the Bible. It seems to imply that

---

12:10 r Rev. 11:15 s Zech. 3:1 **12:11** t Rom. 16:20 u Luke 14:26 **12:12** v Ps. 96:11 w Rev. 8:13 x Rev. 10:6 **12:13** y Rev. 12:5 **12:14** z Ex. 19:4 a Rev. 12:6 b Rev. 17:3 c Dan. 7:25; 12:7 **12:15** d Is. 59:19 **13:1** a Dan. 7:2, 7 b Rev. 12:3 c Rev. 17:3 **13:2** d Rev. 12:3, 9; 13:4, 12 **13:3** e Rev. 13:12, 14 f Rev. 17:8 **13:4** g Rev. 18:18 **13:5** h Dan. 7:8, 11, 20, 25; 11:36 i Rev. 11:2 **13:6** j [Col. 2:9] **13:7** k Dan. 7:21 l Rev. 11:18 **13:8** m Ex. 32:32 n Rev. 17:8 **13:9** o Rev. 2:7 **13:10** p Is. 33:1 q Gen. 9:6 r Rev. 14:12

The Beast from the Earth

11 Then I saw another beast [s]coming up
out of the earth, and he had two horns like
a lamb and spoke like a dragon. 12 And he
exercises all the authority of the first beast
in his presence, and causes the earth and
those who dwell in it to worship the first
beast, [t]whose deadly wound was healed.
13 [u]He performs great signs, [v]so that he
even makes fire come down from heaven
on the earth in the sight of men. 14 [w]And
he deceives those* who dwell on the earth
[x]by those signs which he was granted to
do in the sight of the beast, telling those
who dwell on the earth to make an image to
the beast who was wounded by the sword
[y]and lived. 15 He was granted *power* to give
breath to the image of the beast, that the
image of the beast should both speak [z]and
cause as many as would not worship the
image of the beast to be killed. 16 He causes all, both small and great, rich and poor,
free and slave, [a]to receive a mark on their
right hand or on their foreheads, 17 and that
no one may buy or sell except one who has
the mark or* [b]the name of the beast, [c]or the
number of his name.

18 [d]Here is wisdom. Let him who has [e]un-
derstanding calculate [f]the number of the
beast, [g]for it is the number of a man: His
number *is* 666.

The Lamb and the 144,000

14 Then I looked, and behold, a* [a]Lamb
standing on Mount Zion, and with
Him [b]one hundred *and* forty-four thousand, having* His Father's name [c]written
on their foreheads. 2 And I heard a voice
from heaven, [d]like the voice of many waters, and like the voice of loud thunder.
And I heard the sound of [e]harpists playing their harps. 3 They sang as it were a
new song before the throne, before the four
living creatures, and the elders; and no
one could learn that song [f]except the hundred *and* forty-four thousand who were
redeemed from the earth. 4 These are the
ones who were not defiled with women,
[g]for they are virgins. These are the ones
[h]who follow the Lamb wherever He goes.
These [i]were redeemed* from *among* men,
[j]*being* firstfruits to God and to the Lamb.
5 And [k]in their mouth was found no deceit,* for [l]they are without fault before the
throne of God.*

The Proclamations of Three Angels

6 Then I saw another angel [m]flying in the
midst of heaven, [n]having the everlasting
gospel to preach to those who dwell on the
earth—[o]to every nation, tribe, tongue, and
people— 7 saying with a loud voice, [p]"Fear
God and give glory to Him, for the hour of
His judgment has come; [q]and worship Him

* **13:14** M-Text reads *my own people.* * **13:17** NU-Text and M-Text omit *or.* * **14:1** NU-Text and M-Text read *the.* • NU-Text and M-Text add *His name and.* * **14:4** M-Text adds *by Jesus.* * **14:5** NU-Text and M-Text read *falsehood.* • NU-Text and M-Text omit *before the throne of God.*

---

what has just been said has a wider context, or a significant present application. The statement is not just for future reference. Therefore, widespread spiritual delusion and blasphemy, as well as persecution and martyrdom, should not surprise believers at any point in history.

13:11 ***another beast.*** This beast's actions described in verses 12–17 make it virtually certain that he is the false prophet spoken of in 16:13; 19:20; 20:10. The two beasts may symbolize the intermingling of religious power and of secular, political power during the Roman period and during the last days. ***lamb.*** This is the only place in Revelation where "lamb" does not refer to Christ. The lamb with two horns is an emblem of Jewish worship and religious authority.

13:12–15 ***great signs.*** Calling fire from heaven and giving speech to the image of the first beast are persuasive signs of power. These signs are similar to those performed by the two witnesses (11:5–6). The performance of great signs and the power of Satan is part of the mass deception prophesied by Paul in 2 Thessalonians 2:8–12.

13:16 ***to receive a mark.*** The mark is some sort of identifiable proof of ownership and loyalty, an evil counterfeit of the seal on the foreheads of the servants of God (7:3; 14:1).

13:18 ***Let him who has understanding calculate . . . 666.*** No one knows exactly what this means. It is the number of the beast, and the number of a man, so the beast is merely a man, not a god. We can be sure that this "man's number" will someday be understood in relation to the number 666, and that when the people who are living at the time of the fulfillment of the prophecies in this book need to understand this clearly, the Lord will make it plain. In the meantime, the warning is enough for all that will hear.

14:5 ***they are without fault.*** This statement is not a reference to sinless perfection, but it is stating that they are considered pure before God. They have been sealed by God because of their belief in Christ (v. 1; 7:4).

14:6–7 ***angel . . . everlasting gospel.*** The angel who preaches the gospel to "every nation, tribe, tongue, and people" helps to fulfill God's promise that the gospel "will be preached in all the world as a witness to all the nations" (Matt. 24:14) before Christ returns. The word "gospel," which literally means "good news," is used in Revelation only once. Even at this late stage in God's judgment He continues to offer everlasting life to the world (John 3:16). The gospel message at this point beseeches unbelievers to fear God and give glory to Him, and to escape the hour of His judgment.

13:11 [s]Rev. 11:7 **13:12** [t]Rev. 13:3, 4 **13:13** [u]Matt. 24:24 [v]1 Kin. 18:38 **13:14** [w]Rev. 12:9 [x]2 Thess. 2:9 [y]2 Kin. 20:7 **13:15** [z]Rev. 16:2 **13:16** [a]Rev. 7:3; 14:9; 20:4 **13:17** [b]Rev. 14:9–11 [c]Rev. 15:2 **13:18** [d]Rev. 17:9 [e][1 Cor. 2:14] [f]Rev. 15:2 [g]Rev. 21:17 **14:1** [a]Rev. 5:6 [b]Rev. 7:4; 14:3 [c]Rev. 7:3; 22:4 **14:2** [d]Rev. 1:15; 19:6 [e]Rev. 5:8 **14:3** [f]Rev. 5:9 **14:4** [g][2 Cor. 11:2] [h]Rev. 3:4; 7:17 [i]Rev. 5:9 [j]James 1:18 **14:5** [k]Ps. 32:2 [l]Eph. 5:27 **14:6** [m]Rev. 8:13 [n]Eph. 3:9 [o]Rev. 13:7 **14:7** [p]Rev. 11:18 [q]Neh. 9:6

who made heaven and earth, the sea and springs of water."

8And another angel followed, saying, r"Babylon* is fallen, is fallen, that great city, because sshe has made all nations drink of the wine of the wrath of her fornication."

9Then a third angel followed them, saying with a loud voice, t"If anyone worships the beast and his image, and receives his umark on his forehead or on his hand, 10he himself vshall also drink of the wine of the wrath of God, which is wpoured out full strength into xthe cup of His indignation. yHe shall be tormented with zfire and brimstone in the presence of the holy angels and in the presence of the Lamb. 11And athe smoke of their torment ascends forever and ever; and they have no rest day or night, who worship the beast and his image, and whoever receives the mark of his name."

12bHere is the patience of the saints; chere are those* who keep the commandments of God and the faith of Jesus.

13Then I heard a voice from heaven saying to me,* "Write: d"Blessed are the dead ewho die in the Lord from now on.'"

"Yes," says the Spirit, f"that they may rest from their labors, and their works follow gthem."

Reaping the Earth's Harvest

14Then I looked, and behold, a white cloud, and on the cloud sat One like the Son of Man, having on His head a golden crown, and in His hand a sharp sickle. 15And another angel hcame out of the temple, crying with a loud voice to Him who sat on the cloud, i"Thrust in Your sickle and reap, for the time has come for You* to reap, for the harvest jof the earth is ripe." 16So He who sat on the cloud thrust in His sickle on the earth, and the earth was reaped.

Reaping the Grapes of Wrath

17Then another angel came out of the temple which is in heaven, he also having a sharp sickle.

18And another angel came out from the altar, kwho had power over fire, and he cried with a loud cry to him who had the sharp sickle, saying, l"Thrust in your sharp sickle and gather the clusters of the vine of the earth, for her grapes are fully ripe." 19So the angel thrust his sickle into the earth and gathered the vine of the earth, and threw it into mthe great winepress of the wrath of God. 20And nthe winepress was trampled ooutside the city, and blood came out of the winepress, pup to the horses' bridles, for one thousand six hundred furlongs.

Prelude to the Bowl Judgments

15 Then aI saw another sign in heaven, great and marvelous: bseven angels having the seven last plagues, cfor in them the wrath of God is complete.

2And I saw something like da sea of glass emingled with fire, and those who have the victory over the beast, fover his image and over his mark* and over the gnumber of his name, standing on the sea of glass, hhaving harps of God. 3They sing ithe song of Moses, the servant of God, and the song of the jLamb, saying:

k"Great and marvelous are Your works,
  Lord God Almighty!
  lJust and true are Your ways,
  O King of the saints!*
4 mWho shall not fear You, O Lord, and
      glorify Your name?
  For You alone are nholy.
  For oall nations shall come and
      worship before You,
  For Your judgments have been
      manifested."

* **14:8** NU-Text reads Babylon the great is fallen, is fallen, which has made; M-Text reads Babylon the great is fallen. She has made. * **14:12** NU-Text and M-Text omit here are those. * **14:13** NU-Text and M-Text omit to me. * **14:15** NU-Text and M-Text omit for You. * **15:2** NU-Text and M-Text omit over his mark. * **15:3** NU-Text and M-Text read nations.

14:8 Babylon. Babylon is first mentioned in Revelation here, and it becomes the focus of God's judgment in the following sections (chs. 16–18).

14:13 Blessed. "Blessed" signals the second of seven beatitudes in Revelation (1:3; 16:15; 19:9; 20:6; 22:7,14). Six of the seven are clustered in the latter third of the book, perhaps as promises to encourage exemplary Christian response in the extremely difficult circumstances of the end times.

14:16 thrust in His sickle. The power of the Son of Man (Jesus Christ) is shown in that, with one swing of His sickle, the harvest of the earth is reaped. This pictures the events of chapters 16–19 as parts of one rapid succession of judgment, which is experienced by the inhabitants of the entire world.

15:1 another sign. The previous sign was about the woman clothed with the sun (12:1). This sign is "great and marvelous" because it deals with the seven last plagues sent by the Lord. The plagues, "the bowls of the wrath of God" (16:1), are much stronger and

more widespread than the trumpet judgments in 8:2—11:19. The wrath of God is complete with the seven last plagues (15:1—19:5). They are immediately followed by the second coming and the marriage supper of the Lamb (19:6–21).

15:3 song of Moses. The song of Moses is a reference to Exodus 15:1–18 in which Israel celebrated its deliverance from Pharaoh's army (Ex. 14). This

14:8 r Is. 21:9 s Jer. 51:7 **14:9** t Rev. 13:14, 15; 14:11 u Rev. 13:16 **14:10** v Ps. 75:8 w Rev. 18:6 x Rev. 16:19 y Rev. 20:10 z 2 Thess. 1:7 **14:11** a Is. 34:8–10 **14:12** b Rev. 13:10 c Rev. 12:17 **14:13** d Eccl. 4:1, 2 e 1 Cor. 15:18 f Heb. 4:9, 10 g [1 Cor. 3:11–15; 15:58] **14:15** h Rev. 16:17 i Joel 3:13 j Jer. 51:33 **14:18** k Rev. 16:8 l Joel 3:13 **14:19** m Rev. 19:15 **14:20** n Is. 63:3 o Heb. 13:12 p Is. 34:3 **15:1** a Rev. 12:1, 3 b Rev. 21:9 c Rev. 14:10 **15:2** d Rev. 4:6 e [Matt. 3:11] f Rev. 13:14, 15 g Rev. 13:17 h Rev. 5:8 **15:3** i Ex. 15:1–21 j Rev. 15:3 k Deut. 32:3, 4 l Ps. 145:17 **15:4** m Ex. 15:14 n Lev. 11:44 o Is. 66:23

5After these things I looked, and be-hold,* pthe temple of the tabernacle of the testimony in heaven was opened. 6And out of the temple came the seven angels having the seven plagues, qclothed in pure bright linen, and having their chests girded with golden bands. 7rThen one of the four living creatures gave to the seven angels seven golden bowls full of the wrath of God swho lives forever and ever. 8tThe temple was filled with smoke ufrom the glory of God and from His power, and no one was able to enter the temple till the seven plagues of the seven angels were completed.

16 Then I heard a loud voice from the temple saying ato the seven angels, "Go and pour out the bowls* bof the wrath of God on the earth."

First Bowl: Loathsome Sores

2So the first went and poured out his bowl cupon the earth, and a foul and dloath-some sore came upon the men ewho had the mark of the beast and those fwho wor-shiped his image.

Second Bowl: The Sea Turns to Blood

3Then the second angel poured out his bowl gon the sea, and hit became blood as of a dead *man;* iand every living creature in the sea died.

Third Bowl: The Waters Turn to Blood

4Then the third angel poured out his bowl jon the rivers and springs of water, kand they became blood. 5And I heard the angel of the waters saying:

l"You are righteous, O Lord,*
  The One mwho is and who was and
    who is to be,*
  Because You have judged these things.

6 For nthey have shed the blood oof
    saints and prophets,
  pAnd You have given them blood to drink.
  For* it is their just due."

7And I heard another from* the altar saying, "Even so, qLord God Almighty, rtrue and righteous *are* Your judgments."

Fourth Bowl: Men Are Scorched

8Then the fourth angel poured out his bowl son the sun, tand power was given to him to scorch men with fire. 9And men were scorched with great heat, and they ublasphemed the name of God who has power over these plagues; vand they did not repent wand give Him glory.

Fifth Bowl: Darkness and Pain

10Then the fifth angel poured out his bowl xon the throne of the beast, yand his kingdom became full of darkness; zand they gnawed their tongues because of the pain. 11They blasphemed the God of heav-en because of their pains and their sores, and did not repent of their deeds.

Sixth Bowl: Euphrates Dried Up

12Then the sixth angel poured out his bowl aon the great river Euphrates, band its water was dried up, cso that the way of the kings from the east might be prepared. 13And I saw three unclean dspirits like frogs *coming* out of the mouth of ethe drag-on, out of the mouth of the beast, and out of the mouth of fthe false prophet. 14For they are spirits of demons, gperforming signs, *which* go out to the kings of the earth and*

---

* 15:5 NU-Text and M-Text omit *behold.*
* 16:1 NU-Text and M-Text read *seven bowls.*
* 16:5 NU-Text and M-Text omit *O Lord.* • NU-Text and M-Text read *who was, the Holy One.*
* 16:6 NU-Text and M-Text omit *For.* * 16:7 NU-Text and M-Text omit *another from.* * 16:14 NU-Text and M-Text omit *of the earth and.*

---

song was sung by Jews in their Sabbath gatherings, as well as by early Christians at Easter. **song of the Lamb.** The song of the Lamb celebrates the finished work of God, when all of His righteous acts have been revealed, from creation to atonement to judgment.
16:6 saints. Saints are those who are set apart because of their relationship with Jesus Christ. **prophets.** The prophets are God's spokesmen. Probably this passage is referring both to the saints and prophets (11:3–18) who have been killed and persecuted during the tribu-lation as well as those from past history. Jesus referred to the pattern of killing prophets (Matt. 23:35) when He spoke to the Pharisees of the coming judgment.
16:8 fourth . . . bowl. The fourth bowl and the fourth trumpet both affect the sun, but in the bowl judgment the sun's heat is intensified instead of diminished.
16:9–10 did not repent. They cannot argue against the existence or power of God, but even so they will not repent and give glory to God. The good news of Christ is still in effect even just before His return (19:11–21), though it is apparently rejected by all unbelievers who are still alive.

16:12 sixth . . . bowl. The sixth bowl involves the Euphrates River, as does the sixth trumpet (9:14). Both judgments deal with demonically inspired military forces. The army of two hundred million (9:16) will kill a third of all humankind (9:18); the army of verses 12–14 will do battle against God (19:19–21).
16:13–14 unclean spirits . . . go out to the kings. The kings of the earth recoil in fear before the judgment of the Lamb (6:15–16), yet because of the deceptive words of the demons, they are willing to wage war

---

15:5 p Num. 1:50 **15:6** q Ex. 28:6 **15:7** r Rev. 4:6 s 1 Thess. 1:9 **15:8** t Ex. 19:18; 40:34 u 2 Thess. 1:9 **16:1** a Rev. 15:1 b Rev. 14:10 **16:2** c Rev. 8:7 d Ex. 9:9–11 e Rev. 13:15–17; 14:9 f Rev. 13:14 **16:3** g Rev. 8:8; 11:6 h Ex. 7:17–21 i Rev. 8:9 **16:4** j Rev. 8:10 k Ex. 7:17–20 **16:5** l Rev. 15:3, 4 m Rev. 1:4, 8 **16:6** n Matt. 23:34 o Rev. 11:18 p Is. 49:26 **16:7** q Rev. 15:3 r Rev. 13:10; 19:2 **16:8** s Rev. 8:12 t Rev. 9:17, 18 **16:9** u Rev. 16:11 v Dan. 5:22 w Rev. 11:13 **16:10** x Rev. 13:2 y Rev. 8:12; 9:2 z Rev. 11:10 **16:12** a Rev. 9:14 b Jer. 50:38 c Is. 41:2, 25; 46:11 **16:13** d 1 John 4:1 e Rev. 12:3, 9 f Rev. 13:11, 14; 19:20; 20:10 **16:14** q 2 Thess. 2:9

of [h]the whole world, to gather them to [i]the battle of that great day of God Almighty. [15j]"Behold, I am coming as a thief. Blessed is he who watches, and keeps his garments, [k]lest he walk naked and they see his shame."

[16l]And they gathered them together to the place called in Hebrew, Armageddon.*

Seventh Bowl: The Earth Utterly Shaken

[17]Then the seventh angel poured out his bowl into the air, and a loud voice came out of the temple of heaven, from the throne, saying, [m]"It is done!" [18]And [n]there were noises and thunderings and lightnings; [o]and there was a great earthquake, such a mighty and great earthquake [p]as had not occurred since men were on the earth. [19]Now [q]the great city was divided into three parts, and the cities of the nations fell. And [r]great Babylon [s]was remembered before God, [t]to give her the cup of the wine of the fierceness of His wrath. [20]Then [u]every island fled away, and the mountains were not found. [21]And great hail from heaven fell upon men, each hailstone about the weight of a talent. Men blasphemed God because of the plague of the hail, since that plague was exceedingly great.

The Scarlet Woman and the Scarlet Beast

17 Then [a]one of the seven angels who had the seven bowls came and talked with me, saying to me,* "Come, [b]I will show you the judgment of [c]the great harlot [d]who sits on many waters, [2e]with whom the kings of the earth committed fornication, and [f]the inhabitants of the earth were made drunk with the wine of her fornication."

[3]So he carried me away in the Spirit [g]into the wilderness. And I saw a woman sitting [h]on a scarlet beast which was full of [i]names of blasphemy, having seven heads and ten horns. [4]The woman [j]was arrayed in purple and scarlet, [k]and adorned with gold and precious stones and pearls, [l]having in her hand a golden cup [m]full of abominations and the filthiness of her fornication.* [5]And on her forehead a name was written:

[n]MYSTERY, BABYLON THE GREAT,
THE MOTHER OF HARLOTS
AND OF THE ABOMINATIONS
OF THE EARTH.

[6]I saw [o]the woman, drunk [p]with the blood of the saints and with the blood of [q]the martyrs of Jesus. And when I saw her, I marveled with great amazement.

The Meaning of the Woman and the Beast

[7]But the angel said to me, "Why did you marvel? I will tell you the mystery of the woman and of the beast that carries her, which has the seven heads and the ten horns. [8]The beast that you saw was, and is not, and [r]will ascend out of the bottomless pit and [s]go to perdition. And those who [t]dwell on the earth [u]will marvel, [v]whose names are not written in the Book of Life from the foundation of the world, when they see the beast that was, and is not, and yet is.*

[9w]"Here is the mind which has wisdom: [x]The seven heads are seven mountains on

---

* **16:16** M-Text reads Megiddo.   * **17:1** NU-Text and M-Text omit to me.   * **17:4** M-Text reads the filthiness of the fornication of the earth.
* **17:8** NU-Text and M-Text read and shall be present.

---

against God. The difference seems to be their confidence in the power of the beast, since they reason, "Who is able to make war with him?" (13:4). **great day of God.** The battle of that great day takes place at Armageddon (Mount of Megiddo) (v. 16; 19:17–21).
16:15 Blessed. This is the third of seven beatitudes in Revelation (see note at 14:13). Jesus warned believers to be vigilant because of the unexpected timing of His return (Matt. 24:43–44). The warning to watch is a reminder of the parable of the ten virgins (Matt. 25:1–13): "Watch therefore, for you know neither the day nor the hour."
16:17 It is done. The seventh bowl is the climax of all of Revelation's judgments. This is God's final act of judgment before Christ comes.
16:19 Babylon. Babylon may refer to the rebuilt ancient city, or it may be a symbolic name for Rome (17:9). It may also be a way of referring to any proud human society that attempts to exist apart from God. Babylon's classic manifestations of rebellion against God are the Tower of Babel (Gen. 11:1–9) and the Babylonian Empire under Nebuchadnezzar (Dan. 4:30).
17:1 judgment of the great harlot. Babylon is called "the harlot" in verses 1,5,16, and 19:2. Her habitual immorality was introduced in 14:8, as was her

imminent and well-deserved judgment. Both the kings of the earth and the inhabitants of the earth are seduced into committing spiritual adultery with Babylon. The indication is that she made them drunk with power, material possessions, false worship, and pride. The wine of Babylon's immorality (14:8) is judged forcefully and finally by God in the "wine of the fierceness of His wrath" (16:19).
17:9 seven mountains. The word that is translated "mountains" can also be translated "hills." Most interpreters understand this as a reference to the seven hills along the Tiber River, a well-known designation of the city of Rome.

16:14 [h] Luke 2:1 [i] Rev. 17:14; 19:19; 20:8   **16:15** [j] Matt. 24:43 [k] 2 Cor. 5:3   **16:16** [l] Rev. 19:19   **16:17** [m] Rev. 10:6; 21:6   **16:18** [n] Rev. 4:5 [o] Rev. 11:13 [p] Dan. 12:1   **16:19** [q] Rev. 14:8 [r] Rev. 17:5, 18 [s] Rev. 14:8; 18:5 [t] Is. 51:17   **16:20** [u] Rev. 6:14; 20:11   **17:1** [a] Rev. 1:1; 21:9 [b] Rev. 16:19 [c] Nah. 3:4 [d] Jer. 51:13   **17:2** [e] Rev. 2:22; 18:3, 9 [f] Jer. 51:7   **17:3** [g] Rev. 12:6, 14; 21:10 [h] Rev. 12:3 [i] Rev. 13:1   **17:4** [j] Rev. 18:12, 16 [k] Dan. 11:38 [l] Jer. 51:7 [m] Rev. 14:8   **17:5** [n] 2 Thess. 2:7   **17:6** [o] Rev. 18:24 [p] Rev. 13:15 [q] Rev. 6:9, 10   **17:8** [r] Rev. 11:7 [s] Rev. 13:10; 17:11 [t] Rev. 3:10 [u] Rev. 13:3 [v] Rev. 13:8   **17:9** [w] Rev. 13:18 [x] Rev. 13:1

which the woman sits. [10]There are also seven kings. Five have fallen, one is, *and* the other has not yet come. And when he comes, he must [y]continue a short time. [11]The [z]beast that was, and is not, is himself also the eighth, and is of the seven, and is going to perdition.

[12a]"The ten horns which you saw are ten kings who have received no kingdom as yet, but they receive authority for one hour as kings with the beast. [13]These are of one mind, and they will give their power and authority to the beast. [14b]These will make war with the Lamb, and the Lamb will [c]overcome them, [d]for He is Lord of lords and King of kings; [e]and those *who are* with Him *are* called, chosen, and faithful."

[15]Then he said to me, [f]"The waters which you saw, where the harlot sits, [g]are peoples, multitudes, nations, and tongues. [16]And the ten horns which you saw on* the beast, [h]these will hate the harlot, make her [i]desolate [j]and naked, eat her flesh and [k]burn her with fire. [17]For God has put it into their hearts to fulfill His purpose, to be of one mind, and to give their kingdom to the beast, [m]until the words of God are fulfilled. [18]And the woman whom you saw [n]is that great city [o]which reigns over the kings of the earth."

The Fall of Babylon the Great

18 After[a] these things I saw another angel coming down from heaven, having great authority, [b]and the earth was illuminated with his glory. [2]And he cried mightily* with a loud voice, saying, [c]"Babylon the great is fallen, is fallen, and [d]has become a dwelling place of demons, a prison for every foul spirit, and [e]a cage for every unclean and hated bird! [3]For all the nations [f]have drunk of the wine of the wrath of her fornication, the kings of the earth have committed fornication with her, [g]and the merchants of the earth have become rich through the abundance of her luxury."

[4]And I heard another voice from heaven saying, [h]"Come out of her, my people, lest you share in her sins, and lest you receive of her plagues. [5i]For her sins have reached* to heaven, and [j]God has remembered her iniquities. [6k]Render to her just as she rendered to you,* and repay her double according to her works; [l]in the cup which she has mixed, [m]mix double for her. [7n]In the measure that she glorified herself and lived luxuriously, in the same measure give her torment and sorrow; for she says in her heart, 'I sit *as* [o]queen, and am no widow, and will not see sorrow.' [8]Therefore her plagues will come [p]in one day—death and mourning and famine. And [q]she will be utterly burned with fire, [r]for strong *is* the Lord God who judges* her.

The World Mourns Babylon's Fall

[9s]"The kings of the earth who committed fornication and lived luxuriously with her [t]will weep and lament for her, [u]when they

---

* **17:16** NU-Text and M-Text read *saw, and the beast.*   * **18:2** NU-Text and M-Text omit *mightily.*
* **18:5** NU-Text and M-Text read *have been heaped up.*   * **18:6** NU-Text and M-Text omit *to you.*
* **18:8** NU-Text and M-Text read *has judged.*

17:10 Five have fallen. The five that have fallen would be past kingdoms, perhaps Egypt, Assyria, Babylon, Medo-Persia, and Greece. **one is.** The Roman Empire was the current power at the time of this writing. **has not yet come.** People speculate that the future kingdom may be a revived Roman Empire. **17:11 the eighth, and is of the seven.** The beast is related to the seventh king, but also has a separate identity. It seems that the eighth world empire may be some form of a revived Roman Empire over which the antichrist establishes the imperial authority of a dictator. He will overcome three horns, or nations (Dan. 7:20), and will claim universal authority. **17:12 one hour.** The time frame for these events may coincide with 16:14, in which the preparations for the battle at Armageddon are described. **17:14 make war with the Lamb.** The Lamb (Christ) will easily overcome the ten kings at His second coming (19:19–21). The beast and his forces are allowed by God to "make war with the saints and to overcome them" (13:7). Many of those whom the beast defeated and even killed are now numbered in the conquering army of the Lamb. The Lord's army is composed of the called, chosen, and faithful, probably the heavenly soldiers of 19:14. **17:16–17 ten horns . . . will hate the harlot.** Since this description is similar to God's judgment on Babylon in 18:8, it seems that the Lord uses the forces of the beast as His instrument of judgment on the kingdom of antichrist (ch. 18) before they themselves are destroyed (19:19–21). With the advent of the beast as a supreme ruler given to self-deification (Dan. 11:36; Matt. 24:15; 2 Thess. 2), Satan has originated an entirely new order. This order is so radically different from the great harlot (vv. 1–6) that the beast, or perhaps the political aspect of Babylon, turns upon and destroys the religious aspect of Babylon. **17:18 that great city.** The woman in John's vision is the great city Babylon (16:19), yet she is also the ancient "mother of harlots" (v. 5). The satanic influence of this city over the world's leaders has continued from Babel through Babylon to Rome (vv. 9–10), its classic manifestation in the first century A.D. **18:4 Come out.** The command echoes Isaiah 52:11 and especially Jeremiah 51:45, prophecies proclaimed at a time when the Babylonian Empire was ripe for judgment. **18:9–19 weep and lament for her.** This section is framed like an ancient lament and is especially similar

---

17:10 [y]Rev. 13:5   **17:11** [z]Rev. 13:3, 12, 14; 17:8
17:12 [a]Dan. 7:20   **17:14** [b]Rev. 16:14; 19:19   [c]Rev. 19:20
[d]1 Tim. 6:15   [e]Jer. 50:44   **17:15** [f]Is. 8:7   [g]Rev. 13:7
17:16 [h]Jer. 50:41   [i]Rev. 18:17, 19   [j]Ezek. 16:37, 39   [k]Rev. 18:8
17:17 [l]2 Thess. 2:11   [m]Rev. 10:7   **17:18** [n]Rev. 11:8; 16:19
[o]Rev. 12:4   **18:1** [a]Rev. 17:1, 7   [b]Ezek. 43:2   **18:2** [c]Is. 13:19;
21:9   [d]Is. 13:21; 34:11, 13–15   [e]Is. 14:23   **18:3** [f]Rev. 14:8
[g]Is. 47:15   **18:4** [h]Is. 48:20   **18:5** [i]Gen. 18:20   [j]Rev. 16:19
18:6 [k]Ps. 137:8   [l]Rev. 14:10   [m]Rev. 16:19   **18:7** [n]Ezek.
28:2–8   [o]Is. 47:7, 8   **18:8** [p]Rev. 18:10   [q]Rev. 17:16   [r]Jer.
50:34   **18:9** [s]Ezek. 26:16; 27:35   [t]Jer. 50:46   [u]Rev. 19:3

see the smoke of her burning, [10]standing at a distance for fear of her torment, saying, v"Alas, alas, that great city Babylon, that mighty city! wFor in one hour your judgment has come.'

[11]"And xthe merchants of the earth will weep and mourn over her, for no one buys their merchandise anymore: [12]ymerchandise of gold and silver, precious stones and pearls, fine linen and purple, silk and scarlet, every kind of citron wood, every kind of object of ivory, every kind of object of most precious wood, bronze, iron, and marble; [13]and cinnamon and incense, fragrant oil and frankincense, wine and oil, fine flour and wheat, cattle and sheep, horses and chariots, and bodies and zsouls of men. [14]The fruit that your soul longed for has gone from you, and all the things which are rich and splendid have gone from you,* and you shall find them no more at all. [15]The merchants of these things, who became rich by her, will stand at a distance for fear of her torment, weeping and wailing, [16]and saying, 'Alas, alas, athat great city bthat was clothed in fine linen, purple, and scarlet, and adorned with gold and precious stones and pearls! [17]cFor in one hour such great riches came to nothing.' dEvery shipmaster, all who travel by ship, sailors, and as many as trade on the sea, stood at a distance [18]eand cried out when they saw the smoke of her burning, saying, f'What is like this great city?'

[19]g"They threw dust on their heads and cried out, weeping and wailing, and saying, 'Alas, alas, that great city, in which all who had ships on the sea became rich by her wealth! hFor in one hour she is made desolate.'

[20]i"Rejoice over her, O heaven, and you holy apostles* and prophets, for jGod has avenged you on her!"

Finality of Babylon's Fall

[21]Then a mighty angel took up a stone like a great millstone and threw it into the sea, saying, k"Thus with violence the great city Babylon shall be thrown down, and lshall not be found anymore. [22]mThe sound of harpists, musicians, flutists, and trumpeters shall not be heard in you anymore.

No craftsman of any craft shall be found in you anymore, and the sound of a millstone shall not be heard in you anymore. [23]nThe light of a lamp shall not shine in you anymore, oand the voice of bridegroom and bride shall not be heard in you anymore. For pyour merchants were the great men of the earth, qfor by your sorcery all the nations were deceived. [24]And rin her was found the blood of prophets and saints, and of all who swere slain on the earth."

Heaven Exults over Babylon

19 After these things aI heard* a loud voice of a great multitude in heaven, saying, "Alleluia! bSalvation and glory and honor and power belong to the Lord* our God! [2]For ctrue and righteous are His judgments, because He has judged the great harlot who corrupted the earth with her fornication; and He dhas avenged on her the blood of His servants shed by her." [3]Again they said, "Alleluia! eHer smoke rises up forever and ever!" [4]And fthe twenty-four elders and the four living creatures fell down and worshiped God who sat on the throne, saying, g"Amen! Alleluia!" [5]Then a voice came from the throne, saying, h"Praise our God, all you His servants and those who fear Him, iboth* small and great!"

[6]jAnd I heard, as it were, the voice of a great multitude, as the sound of many waters and as the sound of mighty thunderings, saying, "Alleluia! For kthe* Lord God Omnipotent reigns! [7]Let us be glad and rejoice and give Him glory, for lthe marriage of the Lamb has come, and His wife has made herself ready." [8]And mto her it was granted to be arrayed in fine linen, clean and bright, nfor the fine linen is the righteous acts of the saints.

[9]Then he said to me, "Write: o'Blessed are those who are called to the marriage supper of the Lamb!'" And he said to me, p"These are the true sayings of God." [10]And

---

* **18:14** NU-Text and M-Text read been lost to you. * **18:20** NU-Text and M-Text read saints and apostles. * **19:1** NU-Text and M-Text add something like. • NU-Text and M-Text omit the Lord. * **19:5** NU-Text and M-Text omit both. * **19:6** NU-Text and M-Text read our.

---

in content to Ezekiel's lament over the destruction of Tyre (Ezek. 27).

18:20 Rejoice . . . heaven, and you holy apostles and prophets. This call to rejoice is a compressed introduction to the longer praise hymn in 19:1–5. Judgment for killing God's prophets is mentioned in 16:6, but this is the only place in Revelation other than 21:14 where Christ's apostles are mentioned. If specific apostles are in mind here, Peter and Paul's deaths at the hands of the state in Rome probably apply. If Babylon is the symbol of all the enemies of God and His people, and not just the Babylonian or Roman manifestations, even the killing of James in Acts 12:1–2 is being avenged here.

19:9 Blessed. This is the fourth of the seven beatitudes in Revelation (see note at 14:13). marriage supper. The

18:10 v Is. 21:9 w Rev. 18.17, 19 **18.11** x Ezek. 27:27 **18:12** y Rev. 17:4 **18:13** z Ezek. 27:13 **18:16** a Rev. 17:18 b Rev. 17:4 **18:18** c Rev. 18:10 d Is. 23:14 **18:18** e Ezek. 27:30 f Rev. 13:4 **18:19** g Josh. 7:6 h Rev. 18:8 **18:20** i Jer. 51:48 j Luke 11:49 **18:21** k Jer. 51:63, 64 l Rev. 12:8; 16:20 **18:22** m Jer. 7:34; 16:9; 25:10 **18:23** n Jer. 25:10 o Jer. 7:34; 16:9 p Is. 23:8 q 2 Kin. 9:22 **18:24** r Rev. 16:6; 17:6 s Jer. 51:49 **19:1** a Rev. 11:15; 19:6 b Rev. 4:11 **19:2** c Rev. 15:3; 16:7 d Deut. 32:43 **19:3** e Is. 34:10 **19:4** f Rev. 4:4, 6, 10 g 1 Chr. 16:36 **19:5** h Ps. 134:1 i Rev. 11:18 **19:6** j Ezek. 1:24 k Rev. 11:15 **19:7** l [Matt. 22:2; 25:10] **19:8** m Ezek. 16:10 n Ps. 132:9 **19:9** o Luke 14:15 p Rev. 22:6

*q*I fell at his feet to worship him. But he said to me, *r*"See *that you do* not *do that!* I am your *s*fellow servant, and of your brethren *t*who have the testimony of Jesus. Worship God! For the *u*testimony of Jesus is the spirit of prophecy."

Christ on a White Horse

11*v*Now I saw heaven opened, and behold, *w*a white horse. And He who sat on him *was* called *x*Faithful and True, and *y*in righteousness He judges and makes war. 12*z*His eyes *were* like a flame of fire, and on His head *were* many crowns. *a*He had* a name written that no one knew except Himself. 13*b*He *was* clothed with a robe dipped in blood, and His name is called *c*The Word of God. 14*d*And the armies in heaven, *e*clothed in fine linen, white and clean,* followed Him on white horses. 15Now *f*out of His mouth goes a sharp* sword, that with it He should strike the nations. And *g*He Himself will rule them with a rod of iron. *h*He Himself treads the winepress of the fierceness and wrath of Almighty God. 16And *i*He has on *His* robe and on His thigh a name written:

*j*KING OF KINGS AND
LORD OF LORDS.

The Beast and His Armies Defeated

17Then I saw an angel standing in the sun; and he cried with a loud voice, saying to all the birds that fly in the midst of heaven, *k*"Come and gather together for the supper of the great God,* 18*l*that you may eat the flesh of kings, the flesh of captains, the flesh of mighty men, the flesh of horses and of those who sit on them, and the flesh of all *people,* free* and slave, both small and great."

19*m*And I saw the beast, the kings of the earth, and their armies, gathered together to make war against Him who sat on the horse and against His army. 20*n*Then the beast was captured, and with him the false prophet who worked signs in his presence, by which he deceived those who received the mark of the beast and *o*those who worshiped his image. *p*These two were cast alive into the lake of fire *q*burning with brimstone. 21And the rest *r*were killed with the sword which proceeded from the mouth of Him who sat on the horse. *s*And all the birds *t*were filled with their flesh.

Satan Bound 1,000 Years

20 Then I saw an angel coming down from heaven, *a*having the key to the bottomless pit and a great chain in his hand. 2He laid hold of *b*the dragon, that serpent of old, who is *the* Devil and Satan, and bound him for a thousand years; 3and he cast him into the bottomless pit, and shut him up, and *c*set a seal on him, *d*so that he should deceive the nations no more till the thousand years were finished. But after these things he must be released for a little while.

The Saints Reign with Christ 1,000 Years

4And I saw *e*thrones, and they sat on them, and *f*judgment was committed to them. Then *I saw* *g*the souls of those who had been beheaded for their witness to Jesus and for the word of God, *h*who had

* **19:12** M-Text adds *names written, and.*
* **19:14** NU-Text and M-Text read *pure white linen.*
* **19:15** M-Text adds *two-edged.* * **19:17** NU-Text and M-Text read *the great supper of God.*
* **19:18** NU-Text and M-Text read *both free.*

---

marriage supper of John's day would begin on the evening of the wedding, but the celebration might continue for days. The marriage supper here is a time of joyous feasting to be enjoyed by the saints.
19:15 *sharp sword.* The sharp sword that comes out of Christ's mouth is the two-edged sword spoken of in 1:16. ***rod of iron.*** Christ will rule with a rod of iron in fulfillment of the messianic prophecies in Psalm 2:8–9 and Isaiah 11:4.
19:20–21 *beast . . . false prophet . . . cast alive into the lake of fire.* The lake of fire is the eternal destiny of all unbelievers (20:10,14–15). They are apparently the first to suffer the torment of the lake. The rest of the beast's allies are killed by the word from the mouth of the victorious Christ. Apparently all those who now suffer death go to hades (Matt. 16:18), to which Jesus has the keys (1:8), until death and hades are emptied and cast into the lake of fire (20:13–15).
20:1 *angel.* The angel here may be the same one who had the key to the bottomless pit in 9:1–2.
20:2–3 *bottomless pit . . . shut him up . . . till the thousand years.* The abyss, or bottomless pit, is presently the place of imprisonment of some demons (Luke 8:31) and will be the place from which the beast ascends (17:8). Thus, it is fitting that the devil will be held there for a thousand years. The dragon of 12:3,9, known as Satan, was in control of the serpent in the garden of Eden (Gen. 3). God has a plan for Satan. He will be shut up in the abyss for a thousand years and then will be briefly released to deceive the nations one final time (vv. 7–9) before being cast into the lake of fire (v. 10). ***must be released.*** This phrase indicates that Satan will not escape from the pit but instead will be allowed to go forth from the pit to fulfill God's plan.
20:4 *thrones . . . reigned.* This may be a partial fulfillment of Daniel 7:18,27. The aspect of judgment in ruling is referred to in 1 Corinthians 6:2–4. At the onset of the kingdom, authority is officially transferred

19:10 *q* Rev. 22:8 *r* Acts 10:26 *s* [Heb. 1:14] *t* 1 John 5:10 *u* Luke 24:27 **19:11** *v* Rev. 15:5 *w* Rev. 6:2; 19:19, 21 *x* Rev. 3:7, 14 *y* Is. 11:4 **19:12** *z* Rev. 1:14 *a* Rev. 2:17; 19:16 **19:13** *b* Is. 63:2, 3 *c* [John 1:1, 14] **19:14** *d* Rev. 14:20 *e* Matt. 28:3 **19:15** *f* Is. 11:4 *g* Ps. 2:8, 9 *h* Is. 63:3–6 **19:16** *i* Rev. 2:17; 19:12 *j* Dan. 2:47 **19:17** *k* Ezek. 39:17 **19:18** *l* Ezek. 39:18–20 **19:19** *m* Rev. 16:13–16 **19:20** *n* Rev. 16:13 *o* Rev. 13:8, 12, 13 *p* Dan. 7:11 *q* Rev. 14:10 **19:21** *r* Rev. 19:15 *s* Rev. 19:17, 18 *t* Rev. 17:16 **20:1** *a* Rev. 1:18; 9:1 **20:2** *b* 2 Pet. 2:4 **20:3** *c* Dan. 6:17 *d* Rev. 12:9; 20:8, 10 **20:4** *e* Dan. 7:9 *f* [1 Cor. 6:2, 3] *g* Rev. 6:9 *h* Rev. 13:12

not worshiped the beast [i]or his image, and
had not received *his* mark on their foreheads or on their hands. And they [j]lived
and [k]reigned with Christ for a* thousand years. 5But the rest of the dead did
not live again until the thousand years
were finished. This *is* the first resurrection. 6Blessed and holy *is* he who has
part in the first resurrection. Over such
[l]the second death has no power, but they
shall be [m]priests of God and of Christ,
[n]and shall reign with Him a thousand
years.

Satanic Rebellion Crushed

7Now when the thousand years have
expired, Satan will be released from his
prison 8and will go out [o]to deceive the
nations which are in the four corners of
the earth, [p]Gog and Magog, [q]to gather
them together to battle, whose number *is*
as the sand of the sea. 9[r]They went up on
the breadth of the earth and surrounded
the camp of the saints and the beloved
city. And fire came down from God out
of heaven and devoured them. 10The
devil, who deceived them, was cast into
the lake of fire and brimstone [s]where* the
beast and the false prophet *are.* And they
[t]will be tormented day and night forever
and ever.

The Great White Throne Judgment

11Then I saw a great white throne and
Him who sat on it, from whose face [u]the
earth and the heaven fled away. [v]And
there was found no place for them. 12And
I saw the dead, [w]small and great, standing before God,* [x]and books were opened.
And another [y]book was opened, which
is *the Book* of Life. And the dead were
judged [z]according to their works, by the
things which were written in the books.
13The sea gave up the dead who were in
it, [a]and Death and Hades delivered up the
dead who were in them. [b]And they were
judged, each one according to his works.
14Then [c]Death and Hades were cast into

*20:4 M-Text reads *the.* *20:10 NU-Text and M-Text add *also.* *20:12 NU-Text and M-Text read *the throne.*

---

from angels to men (Heb. 2:5,8). Christ, as the second Adam, fulfills God's original purpose for the earth. A new world order is established with the overcoming saints of the church age ruling together with Christ in His kingdom (Rom. 8:17). Incredible as it may seem, with a perfect Ruler who is totally just, totally kind, and totally wise, there will still be men who will rebel (vv. 7–9).

20:5 ***did not live again.*** The resurrection of the dead will not encompass all people at the same time (Dan. 12:2; John 5:29). This passage indicates that there will be a first resurrection of dead believers before the thousand years of Christ's reign (1 Cor. 15:23,52) and a final resurrection after the millennium is finished, before the great white throne judgment (vv. 11–13). It is generally considered that this is the time of resurrection of the Old Testament saints as well as those martyred in the great tribulation.

20:6 ***Blessed.*** This is the fifth of the seven beatitudes in Revelation (see note at 14:13). All look forward to life with Christ beyond the first resurrection (v. 5). Resurrection is assured for all believers. But the blessedness mentioned here belongs more precisely to those martyrs who will have a part as rulers with Christ in the first resurrection. ***second death.*** The second death is the everlasting death of torment in the lake of fire for unbelievers who face the great white throne judgment (vv. 11–15). John has previously stated that the one who overcomes will not be hurt by the second death (2:11).

20:8 ***Gog and Magog.*** Gog and Magog was a common rabbinical title for the nations in rebellion against the Lord, and the names recall the prophesied invasion of Israel in Ezekiel 38:39. Some hold that the battle of verses 8–9 is the one spoken of in Ezekiel, but there are major differences as well as similarities in the two passages.

20:9 ***beloved city.*** The beloved city may symbolically refer to the home of God's people. However, the New Jerusalem is commonly called "the city of My God" (3:12) and "the holy city" (21:2). The city here may be the renewed earthly Jerusalem, ready to give way to the everlasting sinless glory of the New Jerusalem (21:1—22:5).

20:11 ***great white throne.*** The great white throne is a picture of God's holy rule and judgment. The One occupying the throne may be God the Father (1 Cor. 15:24–28) or both the Father and the Lamb (Christ), as in the New Jerusalem (22:1–3). ***the earth and the heaven fled away.*** There is no place for this sin-polluted creation in the new heaven and new earth (21:1—22:5). The earth and all of its works will be burned up (2 Pet. 3:10–13).

20:12 ***the dead.*** The dead, called "the rest of the dead" (v. 5), are raised and made to stand before God's throne of judgment. ***books.*** The books are thought to refer to the record of all works done in this life. Since all have sinned and fall short of God's standard (Rom. 3:23), the opening of these books will certainly lead to eternal sentences in the lake of fire. ***Book of Life.*** The Book of Life is God's register of those who have believed in Jesus (17:8). Although no one can be judged acceptable based on works (Eph. 2:8–9) many will be saved by God's grace received by faith in Jesus Christ.

20:14 ***Death and Hades.*** Death and Hades refers not only to dying, but to existence beyond the grave (1:18; 6:8). If one considers "death" as a place, it would be the place where the body lies, and Hades would be the place for the soul. The picture here is of all human bodies being given up to God's judgment. While unbelieving humanity is judged according to its works, Death and Hades, the Lord's final enemy (1 Cor. 15:26), is also destroyed by being cast into the

20:4 [i]Rev. 13:15 [j]John 14:19 [k]Rom. 8:17 **20:6** [l][Rev. 2:11; 20:14] [m]Is. 61:6 [n]Rev. 20:4 **20:8** [o]Rev. 12:9; 20:3, 10 [p]Ezek. 38:2; 39:1, 6 [q]Rev. 16:14 **20:9** [r]Ezek. 38:9, 16 **20:10** [s]Rev. 19:20; 20:14, 15 [t]Rev. 14:10 **20:11** [u]2 Pet. 3:7 [v]Dan. 2:35 **20:12** [w]Rev. 19:5 [x]Dan. 7:10 [y]Ps. 69:28 [z]Matt. 16:27 **20:13** [a]Rev. 1:18; 6:8; 21:4 [b]Rev. 2:23; 20:12 **20:14** [c]1 Cor. 15:26

the lake of fire. dThis is the second death.*
15And anyone not found written in the Book of Life ewas cast into the lake of fire.

All Things Made New

21 Now aI saw a new heaven and a new earth, bfor the first heaven and the first earth had passed away. Also there was no more sea. 2Then I, John,* saw cthe holy city, New Jerusalem, coming down out of heaven from God, prepared das a bride adorned for her husband. 3And I heard a loud voice from heaven saying, "Behold, ethe tabernacle of God is with men, and He will dwell with them, and they shall be His people. God Himself will be with them and be their God. 4fAnd God will wipe away every tear from their eyes; gthere shall be no more death, hnor sorrow, nor crying. There shall be no more pain, for the former things have passed away."

5Then iHe who sat on the throne said, j"Behold, I make all things new." And He said to me,* "Write, for kthese words are true and faithful."

6And He said to me, l"It is done!* mI am the Alpha and the Omega, the Beginning and the End. nI will give of the fountain of the water of life freely to him who thirsts. 7He who overcomes shall inherit all things,* and oI will be his God and he shall be My son. 8pBut the cowardly, unbelieving,* abominable, murderers, sexually immoral, sorcerers, idolaters, and all liars shall have their part in qthe lake which burns with fire and brimstone, which is the second death."

The New Jerusalem

9Then one of rthe seven angels who had the seven bowls filled with the seven last plagues came to me* and talked with me, saying, "Come, I will show you sthe bride, the Lamb's wife."* 10And he carried me away tin the Spirit to a great and high mountain, and showed me uthe great city, the holy* Jerusalem, descending out of heaven from God, 11vhaving the glory of God. Her light was like a most precious stone, like a jasper stone, clear as crystal. 12Also she had a great and high wall with wtwelve gates, and twelve angels at the gates, and names written on them, which are the names of the twelve tribes of the children of Israel: 13xthree gates on the east, three gates on the north, three gates on the south, and three gates on the west.

14Now the wall of the city had twelve foundations, and yon them were the names* of the twelve apostles of the Lamb. 15And he who talked with me zhad a gold reed to measure the city, its gates, and its wall. 16The city is laid out as a square; its length is as great as its breadth. And he measured the city with the reed: twelve thousand furlongs. Its length, breadth, and height are equal. 17Then he measured its

---

* **20:14** NU-Text and M-Text add *the lake of fire.*
* **21:2** NU-Text and M-Text omit *John.*   * **21:5** NU-Text and M-Text omit *to me.*   * **21:6** M-Text omits *It is done.*   * **21:7** M-Text reads *overcomes, I shall give him these things.*   * **21:8** M-Text adds *and sinners.*   * **21:9** NU-Text and M-Text omit *to me.* • M-Text reads *I will show you the woman, the Lamb's bride.*   * **21:10** NU-Text and M-Text omit *the great* and read *the holy city, Jerusalem.*
* **21:14** NU-Text and M-Text read *twelve names.*

---

lake of fire. **second death.** The second death is spiritual and eternal, the just punishment of the wicked. The first death is physical dying. Both are included in the overall meaning of the death that came upon the human race because of Adam and Eve's sin (Gen. 2:16–17; 3:1–19; Rom. 5:12).
20:15 not found written in the Book of Life. Only those who have accepted Jesus Christ as their Savior will be found in the book. The rejection of the eternal gospel results in eternal condemnation (14:6–7).
21:1 new. "New" here suggest freshness, not just a second beginning. This is the fulfillment of the prophecies of Isaiah 65:17; 66:22 and 2 Peter 3:13. Significantly, this eternal renewal has already begun in the life of the believer because, using the same term, Paul says, "if anyone is in Christ, he is a new creation" (2 Cor. 5:17). **passed away . . . no more sea.** The present heaven and earth, including the sea, were burned up in the great white throne judgment (20:11–13). There will be a continuation of some features of the present creation in the new heaven and new earth, yet the drastic difference in the new eternal state is obvious from the fact that there will be no more sea, which was a major part of the original creation (Gen. 1:6–10).
21:2 bride. Christ's bride (v. 9) is the New Jerusalem, the redeemed inhabitants of the holy city (vv. 3–7,24–27).
21:6 It is done. For the third time, it is done. The

first statement of "finishing" was on the cross (John 19:30), the second was at the end of God's wrath (16:17), and the third is when there is no more death, a new heaven and a new earth. **water of life.** The water of life may be recalling Jesus' references to living water in John 4:14 and 7:38, in connection with eternal life and life in the Holy Spirit. This water is further described in 22:1. A similar offer of God's grace to him who spiritually thirsts is repeated in 22:17.
21:12 twelve gates . . . twelve tribes. The description of the high wall and the twelve gates echoes Ezekiel 48:30–35. It is a glorious picture of the place that Israel holds in the New Jerusalem when the new covenant with Israel is at last fulfilled.
21:14 twelve foundations . . . apostles. This picture calls to mind Paul's imagery of the apostles as the foundation of the house of God in Ephesians 2:20.

20:14 dRev. 21:8   **20:15** eRev. 19:20   **21:1** a[2 Pet. 3:13] bRev. 20:11   **21:2** cIs. 52:1   dter 2 Cor. 11:2   **21:3** eLev. 26:11   **21:4** fIs. 25:8   g1 Cor. 15:26   hIs. 35:10; 51:11; 65:19   **21:5** iRev. 4:2, 9; 20:11   jIs. 43:19   kRev. 19:9; 22:6   **21:6** lRev. 10:6; 16:17   mRev. 1:8; 22:13   nJohn 4:10   **21:7** oZech. 8:8   **21:8** p1 Cor. 6:9   qRev. 20:14   **21:9** rRev. 15:1   sRev. 19:7; 21:2   **21:10** tRev. 1:10   uEzek. 48   **21:11** vRev. 15:8; 21:23; 22:5   **21:12** wEzek. 48:31–34   **21:13** xEzek. 48:31–34   **21:14** yEph. 2:20   **21:15** zEzek. 40:3

wall: one hundred *and* forty-four cubits, *according* to the measure of a man, that is, of an angel. ¹⁸The construction of its wall was *of* jasper; and the city *was* pure gold, like clear glass. ¹⁹ᵃThe foundations of the wall of the city *were* adorned with all kinds of precious stones: the first foundation *was* jasper, the second sapphire, the third chalcedony, the fourth emerald, ²⁰the fifth sardonyx, the sixth sardius, the seventh chrysolite, the eighth beryl, the ninth topaz, the tenth chrysoprase, the eleventh jacinth, and the twelfth amethyst. ²¹The twelve gates *were* twelve ᵇpearls: each individual gate was of one pearl. ᶜAnd the street of the city *was* pure gold, like transparent glass.

The Glory of the New Jerusalem

²²ᵈBut I saw no temple in it, for the Lord God Almighty and the Lamb are its temple. ²³ᵉThe city had no need of the sun or of the moon to shine in it,* for the glory* of God illuminated it. The Lamb *is* its light. ²⁴ᶠAnd the nations of those who are saved* shall walk in its light, and the kings of the earth bring their glory and honor into it.* ²⁵ᵍIts gates shall not be shut at all by day ʰ(there shall be no night there). ²⁶ⁱAnd they shall bring the glory and the honor of the nations into it.* ²⁷But ʲthere shall by no means enter it anything that defiles, or causes* an abomination or a lie, but only those who are written in the Lamb's ᵏBook of Life.

The River of Life

22 And he showed me ᵃa pure* river of water of life, clear as crystal, proceeding from the throne of God and of the Lamb. ²ᵇIn the middle of its street, and on either side of the river, *was* ᶜthe tree of life, which bore twelve fruits, each *tree* yielding

its fruit every month. The leaves of the tree *were* ᵈfor the healing of the nations. ³And ᵉthere shall be no more curse, ᶠbut the throne of God and of the Lamb shall be in it, and His ᵍservants shall serve Him. ⁴ʰThey shall see His face, and ⁱHis name *shall be* on their foreheads. ⁵ʲThere shall be no night there: They need no lamp nor ᵏlight of the sun, for ˡthe Lord God gives them light. ᵐAnd they shall reign forever and ever.

The Time Is Near

⁶Then he said to me, ⁿ"These words *are* faithful and true." And the Lord God of the holy* prophets ᵒsent His angel to show His servants the things which must ᵖshortly take place.

⁷ᵃ"Behold, I am coming quickly! ʳBlessed *is* he who keeps the words of the prophecy of this book."

⁸Now I, John, saw and heard* these things. And when I heard and saw, ˢI fell down to worship before the feet of the angel who showed me these things. ⁹Then he said to me, ᵗ"See *that you do* not *do that.* For* I am your fellow servant, and of your brethren the prophets, and of those who keep the words of this book. Worship God." ¹⁰ᵘAnd he said to me, "Do not seal the words of the prophecy of this book, ᵛfor the time is at hand. ¹¹He who is unjust, let him be unjust still; he who is

---

* 21:23 NU-Text and M-Text omit *in it.* • M-Text reads *the very glory.* * 21:24 NU-Text and M-Text omit *of those who are saved.* • M-Text reads *the glory and honor of the nations to Him.* * 21:26 M-Text adds *that they may enter in.* * 21:27 NU-Text and M-Text read *anything profane, nor one who causes.* * 22:1 NU-Text and M-Text omit *pure.* * 22:6 NU-Text and M-Text read *spirits of the prophets.* * 22:8 NU-Text and M-Text read *am the one who heard and saw.* * 22:9 NU-Text and M-Text omit *For.*

21:19–20 all kinds of precious stones. The exact color of some of the stones is uncertain, but it is probable that jasper is colorless, sapphire is blue, chalcedony is green or greenish-blue, emerald is bright green, sardonyx has layers of red and white, sardius is blood red, chrysolite is yellow, beryl is blue or blue-green, topaz is golden, and amethyst is purple or violet.

22:2 tree of life. The tree of life in the original creation was in the middle of the garden of Eden (Gen. 2:9), from which all of humanity was excluded after sin entered the world (Gen. 3:22–24). Ezekiel's apocalyptic vision included trees bearing fruit every month with medicinal leaves (Ezek. 47:12). Since only one tree of life is mentioned here, even though it is on both sides of the river, it is probably meant as a parallel to Genesis 2, implying that a new, better, and everlasting Eden has come.

22:3 no more curse. The affliction of sin, especially on the human race and creation (Gen. 3:14–19), will be erased. As God had fellowship with Adam and Eve before their fall into sin (Gen. 3:8), so the Lord will again be with His servants eternally. In turn, His servants will worship and serve Him (Rom. 12:1).

22:4 see His face. The believer's hope today is to see

the Lord face to face (1 Cor. 13:12), something neither Moses nor any other human was previously allowed to do (Ex. 33:20).

22:7 Blessed. "Blessed" begins the sixth of seven beatitudes in Revelation (see note at 14:13). And indeed, those who pay attention to this book will be blessed. The Lord has shown the things that must come to pass, the things that His servants must pay attention to, the ultimate fate of unbelievers, and a beautiful glimpse of eternity, which leaves all believers with an eagerness for the return of the Lord.

22:11 unjust . . . filthy . . . righteous . . . holy. This verse, on the surface, seems to be a statement that believers and unbelievers will live out their lives true

---

21:19 ᵃ Is. 54:11 **21:21** ᵇ Matt. 13:45, 46 ᶜ Rev. 22:2 **21:22** ᵈ John 4:21, 23 **21:23** ᵉ Is. 24:23; 60:19, 20 **21:24** ᶠ Is. 60:3, 5; 66:12 **21:25** ᵍ Is. 60:11 ʰ Is. 60:20 **21:26** ⁱ Rev. 21:24 **21:27** ʲ Joel 3:17 ᵏ Phil. 4:3 **22:1** ᵃ Ezek. 47:1 **22:2** ᵇ Ezek. 47:12 ᶜ Gen. 2:9 ᵈ Rev. 21:24 **22:3** ᵉ Zech. 14:11 ᶠ Ezek. 48:35 ᵍ Rev. 7:15 **22:4** ʰ [Matt. 5:8] ⁱ Rev. 14:1 **22:5** ʲ Rev. 21:23 ᵏ Rev. 7:15 ˡ Ps. 36:9 ᵐ Dan. 7:18, 27 **22:6** ⁿ Rev. 19:9 ᵒ Rev. 1:1 ᵖ Heb. 10:37 **22:7** ᵠ [Rev. 3:11] ʳ Rev. 1:3 **22:8** ˢ Rev. 19:10 **22:9** ᵗ Rev. 19:10 **22:10** ᵘ Dan. 8:26 ᵛ Rev. 1:3

filthy, let him be filthy still; he who is righteous, let him be righteous* still; he who is holy, let him be holy still."

Jesus Testifies to the Churches

12"And behold, I am coming quickly, and ʷMy reward *is* with Me, ˣto give to every one according to his work. 13ʸI am the Alpha and the Omega, *the* Beginning and *the* End, the First and the Last."*

14ᶻBlessed *are* those who do His commandments,* that they may have the right ᵘto the tree of life, ᵇand may enter through the gates into the city. 15But* ᶜoutside *are* ᵈdogs and sorcerers and sexually immoral and murderers and idolaters, and whoever loves and practices a lie.

16ᵉ"I, Jesus, have sent My angel to testify to you these things in the churches. ᶠI am the Root and the Offspring of David, ᵍthe Bright and Morning Star."

17And the Spirit and ʰthe bride say, "Come!" And let him who hears say, "Come!" ⁱAnd let him who thirsts come. Whoever desires, let him take the water of life freely.

A Warning

18For* I testify to everyone who hears the words of the prophecy of this book: ʲIf anyone adds to these things, God will add* to him the plagues that are written in this book; 19and if anyone takes away from the words of the book of this prophecy, ᵏGod shall take away* his part from the Book* of Life, from the holy city, and *from* the things which are written in this book.

I Am Coming Quickly

20He who testifies to these things says, "Surely I am coming quickly."

Amen. Even so, come, Lord Jesus!

21The grace of our Lord Jesus Christ *be* with you all.* Amen.

* **22:11** NU-Text and M-Text read *do right.*
* **22:13** NU-Text and M-Text read *the First and the Last, the Beginning and the End.* * **22:14** NU-Text reads *wash their robes.* * **22:15** NU-Text and M-Text omit *But.* * **22:18** NU-Text and M-Text omit *For.* • M-Text reads *may God add.*
* **22:19** M-Text reads *may God take away.* • NU-Text and M-Text read *tree of life.* * **22:21** NU-Text reads *with all;* M-Text reads *with all the saints.*

---

to their nature until the final judgment (20:12–15). However, because this book is to be read before the events it foretells take place, it is almost certainly an implied, indirect evangelistic appeal based on the continuing offer of the gospel (v. 7; 14:6–7).

22:12–13 *My reward is with Me.* The rewarding of each believer according to his or her works is taught in 2 Corinthians 5:10. Christ's rewards are meant to provide a powerful incentive for an obedient life. Little wonder that the apostle Paul rigorously disciplined himself so that he would not be disqualified from the prize (1 Cor. 9:24–27; Phil. 3:10–14). The judgment seat of Christ can be a time of great regret (1 Cor. 3:5–10), or it can be an occasion of supreme joy (2 Cor. 5:9–11). After Christ comes again, He will give rewards to His own. This can be counted on because Christ is in control of all history and all eternity.

22:14 *Blessed.* This is the last of the seven beatitudes in Revelation (see note at 14:13). This beatitude is speaking of those justified by faith who express that faith in obedience (Eph. 2:8–10).

22:15 *dogs.* According to the context of Deuteronomy 23:18 a "dog" is a male prostitute.

22:16 *the Root and the Offspring of David.* Jesus is both the Source and Son of David, echoing the words of Isaiah 11:1,10. Jesus is both greater than David and the rightful heir to the throne of David.

22:17 *Come.* This book, so full of the pictures of the

fulfillment of God's righteous judgment, still closes with the sweet and compelling invitation to come to Christ. This is one of the reasons it is "blessed" to read this book.

22:18–19 *add to . . . take away.* The Book of Revelation was intended to be heard and obeyed (v. 7; 1:3), not tampered with. The person who either adds to or takes away from its contents will receive from God the strictest punishment, a punishment with eternal consequences.

22:20 *I am coming quickly.* The fact that Jesus is coming quickly within the scope of God's overall plan for this creation is a repeated theme in Revelation (3:11; 22:7–12). John adds the hope of all believers to the declaration of Christ with his prayer, "come, Lord Jesus."

22:21 *grace.* The grace of our Lord Jesus Christ begins and concludes the Book of Revelation (1:4), implying that the message of grace and the free gift of eternal life in Christ (Eph. 2:8–9), not merely the message of judgment upon unbelievers, can be found in this book.

22:12 ʷ Is. 40:10; 62:11 ˣ Rev. 20:12 **22:13** ʸ Is. 41:4 **22:14** ᶻ Dan. 12:12 ᵃ [Prov. 11:30] ᵇ Rev. 21:27 **22:15** ᶜ 1 Cor. 6:9 ᵈ Phil. 3:2 **22:16** ᵉ Rev. 1:1 ᶠ Rev. 5:5 ᵍ Num. 24:17 **22:17** ʰ [Rev. 21:2, 9] ⁱ Is. 55:1 **22:18** ʲ Deut. 4:2; 12:32 **22:19** ᵏ Ex. 32:33

Theological Notes Index by Location

Theological Notes Index by Title

CONCORDANCE

A

ABASED
I know how to be *a* ....Phil 4:12

ABBA
And He said, "A............. Mark 14:36
whom we cry out, "A....... Rom 8:15

ABIDE
the Most High Shall *a* ....Ps 91:1
Him, "If you *a* ....John 8:31
"If you *a* in Me..................John 15:7
a in My love ....John 15:9

ABIDES
He who *a* in Me.................John 15:5
will of God *a* forever .... 1 John 2:17

ABILITY
to his own *a*......................Matt 25:15
a which God supplies...... 1 Pet 4:11

ABLE
shall give as he is *a*........ Deut 16:17
whom we serve is *a*......... Dan 3:17
God is *a* to raise up..............Matt 3:9
fear Him who is *a*............Matt 10:28
you *a* to drink the............Matt 20:22
that He is *a*.......................2 Tim 1:12
learning and never *a* ....2 Tim 3:7
that God was *a* to............Heb 11:19

ABOLISHED
having *a* in His flesh.........Eph 2:15
Christ, who has *a* ....2 Tim 1:10

ABOMINABLE
deny Him, being *a*............Titus 1:16
unbelieving, *a* ....Rev 21:8

ABOMINATION(S)
Yes, seven are an *a*.........Prov 6:16
the scoffer is an *a*.............Prov 24:9
the *a* of desolation .... Dan 12:11
the '*a* of desolation,' ....Matt 24:15
delights in their *a*...................Is 66:3
a golden cup full of *a*........Rev 17:4

ABOUND
the offense might *a* .... Rom 5:20
sin that grace may *a*.........Rom 6:1
to make all grace *a* ....2 Cor 9:8
and I know how to *a*..........Phil 4:12

ABOUNDED
But where sin *a* .... Rom 5:20

ABOUNDING
immovable, always *a*.... 1 Cor 15:58

ABOVE
that is in heaven *a*............. Ex 20:4
"He who comes from *a*.... John 3:31
I am from *a* ....John 8:23
things which are *a* ....Col 3:1
perfect gift is from *a*......James 1:17

ABSENT
in the body we are *a* ....2 Cor 5:6

ABSTAIN
we write to them to *a* .....Acts 15:20
A from every form...... 1 Thess 5:22

ABUNDANCE
put in out of their *a*....... Mark 12:44
not consist in the *a*.........Luke 12:15

ABUNDANTLY
a satisfied with the................Ps 36:8
may have it more *a*........John 10:10
to do exceedingly *a*............Eph 3:20

ACCEPT
offering, I will not *a* ....Jer 14:12
Should I *a* this from...........Mal 1:13

ACCEPTABLE
a time I have heard................Is 49:8
proclaim the *a* year...............Is 61:2
proclaim the *a* year.........Luke 4:19
is that good and *a* .... Rom 12:2

ACCEPTABLY
we may serve God *a*........Heb 12:28

ACCEPTED
Behold, now is the *a*.........2 Cor 6:2
which He made us *a*...........Eph 1:6

ACCORD
continued with one *a*........Acts 1:14

ACCOUNT
they will give *a* ....Matt 12:36
put that on my *a*............. Philem 18

ACCOUNTED
in the LORD, and He *a* ......Gen 15:6
his faith is *a*.......................Rom 4:5
God, and it was *a* ....Gal 3:6
God, and it was *a* ....James 2:23

ACCURSED
not know the law is *a* ......John 7:49
of God calls Jesus *a*........ 1 Cor 12:3
to you, let him be *a* ....Gal 1:8

ACCUSATION
over His head the *a*.........Matt 27:37
they might find an *a* ....Luke 6:7

ACCUSER
a of our brethren.............Rev 12:10

ACKNOWLEDGE
a my transgressions.............Ps 51:3
In all your ways *a* ....Prov 3:6

ACQUIT
at all *a* the wicked.............. Nah 1:3

ACTIONS
by Him *a* are weighed.....1 Sam 2:3

ACTS
of Your awesome *a*............Ps 145:6

ADD
Do not *a* to His words ......Prov 30:6

ADMONISH
a him as a .... 2 Thess 3:15

ADMONITION
written for our *a*............ 1 Cor 10:11
in the training and *a*...........Eph 6:4

ADOPTION
the Spirit of *a* .... Rom 8:15
waiting for the *a*............... Rom 8:23
to whom pertain the *a*.......Rom 9:4

ADORNED
God also *a* themselves ...... 1 Pet 3:5
prepared as a bride *a* ....Rev 21:2

ADULTERER(S)
The eye of the *a*.................Job 24:15
nor idolaters, nor *a* .... 1 Cor 6:9
a God will judge ....Heb 13:4

ADULTEROUS
a generation ....Matt 12:39

ADULTERY
You shall not commit *a*......Ex 20:14
already committed *a*.........Matt 5:28
is divorced commits *a* ......Matt 5:32
another commits *a*........ Mark 10:11
those who commit *a* ....Rev 2:22

ADVANTAGE
a that I go away...............John 16:7
Satan should take *a*........2 Cor 2:11

ADVERSARIES
and there are many *a* ..... 1 Cor 16:9
terrified by your *a*..............Phil 1:28

ADVERSARY
"Agree with your *a* ....Matt 5:25
opportunity to the *a*........1 Tim 5:14
a the devil walks .... 1 Pet 5:8

ADVERSITY
I shall never be in *a* ....Ps 10:6
the day of *a* consider........ Eccl 7:14

ADVICE
in this I give my *a* ....2 Cor 8:10

ADVOCATE
sins, we have an *A* .... 1 John 2:1

AFAR
and not a God *a*................. Jer 23:23
to you who were *a* ....Eph 2:17
having seen them *a*..........Heb 11:13

AFFECTION
to his wife the *a* .... 1 Cor 7:3

AFFECTIONATE
Be kindly *a* to one.......... Rom 12:10

AFFLICT
a Your heritage ....Ps 94:5
For He does not *a*............Lam 3:33

AFFLICTED
To him who is *a*...................Job 6:14
hears the cry of the *a*......Job 34:28
days of the *a* are evil ..... Prov 15:15
Smitten by God, and *a* ....Is 53:4
"O you *a* one....................Is 54:11
being destitute, *a* ....Heb 11:37

AFFLICTION
is, the bread of *a*.............. Deut 16:3
a take hold of me ....Job 30:16
and it is an evil *a* ....Eccl 6:2
For our light *a*..................2 Cor 4:17
supposing to add *a*............Phil 1:16

AFRAID
garden, and I was *a* ....Gen 3:10
saying, "Do not be *a* ....Gen 15:1
none will make you *a* ...... Lev 26:6
ungodliness made me *a* ....Ps 18:4
Whenever I am *a*................Ps 56:3
one will make them *a*............Is 17:2
do not be *a*........................Matt 14:27
if you do evil, be *a*.......... Rom 13:4
do good and are not *a* ...... 1 Pet 3:6

AFTERWARD
a receive me to glory..........Ps 73:24
you shall follow Me *a*.... John 13:36

AGAIN

'You must be born *a* .... John 3:7
having been born *a* .... 1 Pet 1:23

AGAINST

come to 'set a man *a* .... Matt 10:35
or house divided *a* .... Matt 12:25
Me is *a* Me........................ Matt 12:30
a the Spirit will not........ Matt 12:31
lifted up his heel .... John 13:18
LORD and *a* His Christ...... Acts 9:5
to kick *a* the goads.............. Gal 3:21
a the promises of God........ Gal 3:21
we do not wrestle *a*..........Eph 6:12
I have a few things *a* .... Rev 2:20

AGE

the grave at a full *a*..............Job 5:26
and in the *a* to come ..... Mark 10:30

AGED

one as Paul, the *a*..............Philem 9

AGES

ordained before the *a* .... 1 Cor 2:7

AGONY

And being in *a* ....Luke 22:44

AGREE

that if two of you *a* ....Matt 18:19

AGREEMENT

what *a* has the temple .... 2 Cor 6:16

AIR

the birds of the *a* .... Gen 1:26
of the *a* have nests........Luke 9:58
of the power of the *a* .... Eph 2:2
the Lord in the *a*......... 1 Thess 4:17

ALIENATED

darkened, being *a* .... Eph 4:18
you, who once were *a* .... Col 1:21

ALIENS

A have devoured his........... Hos 7:9
Christ, being *a* .... Eph 2:12

ALIVE

I kill and I make *a*........ Deut 32:39
was dead and is *a*..........Luke 15:24
presented Himself *a*..........Acts 1:3
indeed to sin, but *a* .... Rom 6:11
all shall be made *a*....... 1 Cor 15:22
that we who are *a* .... 1 Thess 4:15
and behold, I am *a* .... Rev 1:18
These two were cast *a*.....Rev 19:20

ALLELUIA

Again they said, "A............Rev 19:3

ALPHA

"I am the *A* and the .... Rev 1:8
"I am the *A* and the ....Rev 22:13

ALTAR(S)

Then Noah built an *a* .... Gen 8:20
'An *a* of earth you ....Ex 20:24
your gift to the *a*..............Matt 5:23
swears by the *a*............Matt 23:18
I even found an *a* ....Acts 17:23
We have an *a* from ....Heb 13:10
Even Your *a*, O LORD..........Ps 84:3
and torn down Your *a*..... Rom 11:3

ALWAYS

delight, Rejoicing *a*..........Prov 8:30
the poor with you *a* ....Matt 26:11
lo, I am with you *a*........Matt 28:20
to them, that men *a*..........Luke 18:1
immovable, *a* .... 1 Cor 15:58
Rejoice in the Lord *a* ....Phil 4:4
thus we shall *a*.............. 1 Thess 4:17
a be ready to give a .... 1 Pet 3:15

AM

to Moses, "I *A* WHO I........Ex 3:14
First and I *a* the Last ....Is 44:6
in My name, I *a* ....Matt 18:20
a the bread of life............John 6:35
a the light of the..............John 8:12
I *a* from above ....John 8:23
Abraham was, I *A*..........John 8:58
"I *a* the door .... John 10:9
a the good shepherd......John 10:11

a the resurrection...........John 11:25
to him, "I *a* the way .... John 14:6
of God I *a* what I *a*........ 1 Cor 15:10

AMBASSADOR(S)

for which I am an *a* ....Eph 6:20
we are *a* for Christ.......... 2 Cor 5:20

AMBITION

Christ from selfish *a*..........Phil 1:16

AMEN

are Yes, and in Him *A*... 2 Cor 1:20
creatures said, "A.............. Rev 5:14

ANCHOR

hope we have as an *a*........Heb 6:19

ANCIENT

Do not remove the *a*...... Prov 23:10
"until the *A* of Days.......... Dan 7:22

ANGEL

"Behold, I send an *A*..........Ex 23:20
Manoah said to the *A* .... Judg 13:17
the *A* of His Presence............Is 63:9
things, behold, an *a*..........Matt 1:20
for an *a* of the Lord ....Matt 28:2
Then an *a* of the Lord ......Luke 1:11
And behold, an *a*..............Luke 2:9
a appeared to Him ....Luke 22:43
For an *a* went down at......John 5:4
a has spoken to Him......John 12:29
But at night an *a*..............Acts 5:19
A who appeared to him ...Acts 7:35
immediately an *a*..........Acts 12:23
himself into an *a* ....2 Cor 11:14
even if we, or an *a* ....Gal 1:8
Then I saw a strong *a*..........Rev 5:2
Jesus, have sent My *a* .....Rev 22:16

ANGELS

If He charges His *a*............Job 4:18
lower than the *a* ....Ps 8:5
He shall give His *a*..............Ps 91:11
He shall give His *a*..............Matt 4:6
not even the *a* ....Matt 24:36
and all the holy *a* ....Matt 25:31
twelve legions of *a* ....Matt 26:53
And she saw two *a* ....John 20:12
and worship of *a* ....Col 2:18
much better than the *a*........Heb 1:4
entertained *a*...................Heb 13:2
things which *a* desire ..... 1 Pet 1:12
did not spare the *a*..........2 Pet 2:4
a who did not keep ....Jude 6

ANGER

For His *a* is but for *a*............Ps 30:5
gracious, Slow to *a* ....Ps 103:8
Nor will He keep His *a*........Ps 103:9
around at them with *a*...... Mark 3:5
bitterness, wrath, *a*............Eph 4:31

ANGRY

Cain. "Why are you *a*..........Gen 4:6
"Let not the Lord be *a* ....Gen 18:30
the Son, lest He be *a*............Ps 2:12
a man stirs up strife....... Prov 29:22
right for you to be *a*...........Jon 4:4
you that whoever is *a*......Matt 5:22
"Be *a*, and do not................Eph 4:26

ANGUISH

remembers the *a* ....John 16:21
tribulation and *a*..................Rom 2:9

ANIMAL(S)

of every clean *a* .... Gen 7:2
of *a* after their kind...........Gen 6:20
of four-footed *a*..............Acts 10:12

ANOINT

a my head with oil ....Ps 23:5
when you fast, ...Matt 6:17
a My body for burial ..... Mark 14:8
a your eyes with eye..........Rev 3:18

ANOINTED

"Surely the LORD's *a*...1 Sam 16:6
destroy the LORD's *a*........1 Sam 26:9
"Do not touch My *a* ...... 1 Chr 16:22
Because He has *a*............Luke 4:18
but this woman has *a* ......Luke 7:46
a the eyes of the ....John 9:6
that Mary who *a*..............John 11:2

Jesus, whom You *a*..........Acts 4:27
and has *a* us is God .... 2 Cor 1:21

ANOINTING

But you have an *a*.........1 John 2:20

ANOTHER

that you love one *a* .... John 13:34

ANSWER

Call, and I will *a*................Job 13:22
How shall I *a* Him............Job 31:14
the day that I call, *a*...........Ps 102:2
In Your faithfulness *a* ....Ps 143:1
a turns away wrath..........Prov 15:1
a a fool according ....Prov 26:4
or what you should *a*......Luke 12:11
you may have an *a* .... 2 Cor 5:12

ANT

Go to the *a*.........................Prov 6:6

ANTICHRIST

heard that the *A* .... 1 John 2:18
a who denies the .... 1 John 2:22
is a deceiver and an *a*.......2 John 7

ANXIETY

A in the heart of man .... Prov 12:25

ANXIOUS

Be *a* for nothing ....Phil 4:6

APOSTLE

called to be an *a* ....Rom 1:1
consider the *A* ....Heb 3:1

APOSTLES

of the twelve *a* ....Matt 10:2
He also named *a*...........Luke 6:13
am the least of the *a* ...... 1 Cor 15:9
none of the other *a*.............Gal 1:19
gave some to be *a* ....Eph 4:11

APPAREL

gold rings, in fine *a*..........James 2:2
or putting on fine *a* .... 1 Pet 3:3

APPEAL

love's sake I rather *a* ....Philem 9

APPEAR

and let the dry land *a* ....Gen 1:9
also outwardly *a*..............Matt 23:28
God would *a*...................Luke 19:11
For we must all *a*........... 2 Cor 5:10

APPEARANCE

Do not look at his *a*.....1 Sam 16:7
judge according to *a*........John 7:24
those who boast in *a*...... 2 Cor 5:12
found in *a* as a man............Phil 2:8

APPEARED

an angel of the Lord *a*.....Luke 1:11
who in glory and............Luke 9:31
brings salvation has *a* ..... Titus 2:11
of the ages, He has *a* ....Heb 9:26

APPEARING

Lord Jesus Christ's *a*......1 Tim 6:14
and the dead at His *a* ....2 Tim 4:1
who have loved His *a*.......2 Tim 4:8

APPEARS

can stand when He *a*.......... Mal 3:2
who is our life *a*..................Col 3:4
the Chief Shepherd *a*....... 1 Pet 5:4
that when He *a* .... 1 John 2:28

APPETITE

are a man given to *a*.........Prov 23:2

APPLES

fitly spoken is like *a* ...... Prov 25:11

APPROACHING

as you see the Day *a*........Heb 10:25

APPROVED

to God and *a* by men..... Rom 14:18
to present yourself *a*.......2 Tim 2:15

ARBITRATOR

Me a judge or an *a*.........Luke 12:14

ARCHANGEL

the voice of an *a* .... 1 Thess 4:16

ARISE

A, shine......................................Is 60:1
But the LORD will a................Is 60:2
you who sleep, A................Eph 5:14

ARK

"Make yourself an a..........Gen 6:14
him, she took an a..................Ex 2:3
Bezalel made the a..............Ex 37:1
in heaven, and the a.......Rev 11:19

ARM

with an outstretched a..........Ex 6:6
Have you an a like God.....Job 40:9
strength with His a..........Luke 1:51
a yourselves also with.....1 Pet 4:1

ARMIES

And he sent out his a.......Matt 22:7
surrounded by a.............Luke 21:20
And the a in heaven........Rev 19:14
the earth, and their a.......Rev 19:19

ARMOR

Put on the whole a.............Eph 6:11

ARMS

are the everlasting a.....Deut 33:27
took Him up in his a........Luke 2:28

AROMA

the one we are the a.......2 Cor 2:16
for a sweet-smelling a........Eph 5:2

AROUSED

LORD was greatly a.......Num 11:10
Then Joseph, being a......Matt 1:24

ARRAYED

his glory was not a..........Matt 6:29
"Who are these a................Rev 7:13

ARROGANCE

Pride and a and the..........Prov 8:13

ARROWS

a pierce me deeply.................Ps 38:2
Like a in the hand of.........Ps 127:4

ASCEND

Who may a into the..............Ps 24:3
If I a into heaven.................Ps 139:8
'I will a into heaven.............Is 14:13
see the Son of Man a.......John 6:62

ASCENDED

You have a on high ....Ps 68:18
"No one has a ....John 3:13
"When He a on high............Eph 4:8

ASCRIBE

A strength to God ....Ps 68:34

ASHAMED

Let me not be a.....................Ps 25:2
And Israel shall be a..........Hos 10:6
For whoever is a..............Mark 8:38
am not a of the gospel.....Rom 1:16
Therefore God is not a.....Heb 11:16

ASHES

become like dust and a....Job 30:19
in sackcloth and a..........Luke 10:13

ASIDE

lay something a...............1 Cor 16:2
lay a all filthiness..........James 1:21
Therefore, laying a ....1 Pet 2:1

ASK

when your children a........Josh 4:6
"A a sign for yourself...........Is 7:11
whatever things
  you a..........................Matt 21:22
a, and it will be.................Luke 11:9
that whatever You a......John 11:22
a anything in My...........John 14:14
in that day you will a.....John 16:23
wisdom, let him a............James 1:5
But let him a in faith.......James 1:6
because you do not a.......James 4:2

ASKS

For everyone who a............Matt 7:8
you who, if his son a ....Matt 7:9
Or if he a for a fish ....Luke 11:11

ASLEEP

But He was a......................Matt 8:24
some have fallen a..........1 Cor 15:6
those who are a...........1 Thess 4:15

ASSEMBLING

not forsaking the a..........Heb 10:25

ASSEMBLY

a I will praise You...............Ps 22:22
fast, Call a sacred a ....Joel 1:14
a I will sing praise..............Heb 2:12
to the general a.................Heb 12:23

ASSURANCE

riches of the full a ....Col 2:2
Spirit and in much a..... 1 Thess 1:5
to the full a of hope............Heb 6:11

ASSURE

a our hearts before ....1 John 3:19

ASTONISHED

Just as many were a............Is 52:14
who heard Him were a ...Luke 2:47

ASTRAY

one of them goes a.........Matt 18:12
like sheep going a............1 Pet 2:25

ATONEMENT

the blood that makes a....Lev 17:11
for it is the Day of A........Lev 23:28
there will be no a ....Is 22:14

ATTAIN

It is high, I cannot a............Ps 139:6
worthy to a that age .....Luke 20:35
by any means, I may a.....Phil 3:11

ATTENTION

My son, give a to my ....Prov 4:20

AUTHOR

For God is not the a...... 1 Cor 14:33
unto Jesus, the a.................Heb 12:2

AUTHORITIES

a that exist are.................. Rom 13:1

AUTHORITY

them as one having a ....Matt 7:29
"All a has been given .....Matt 28:18
a I will give You ....Luke 4:6
and has given Him a ....John 5:27
You have given Him a .....John 17:2
the flesh, reject a....................Jude 8

AVAILS

of a righteous man a......James 5:16

AVENGE

Beloved, do not a .... Rom 12:19
a our blood on those..........Rev 6:10

AVENGER

the Lord is the a............. 1 Thess 4:6

AWAKE

be satisfied when I a...........Ps 17:15
it is high time to a ....Rom 13:11
A to righteousness ....1 Cor 15:34

AWAY

the wind drives a....................Ps 1:4
Do not cast me a ....Ps 51:11
A time to cast a ....Eccl 3:5
fair one, And come a ....Song 2:10
minded to put her a ....Matt 1:19
and earth will pass a ......Matt 24:35
"I am going a ....John 8:21
they cried out, "A ....John 19:15
unless the falling a........ 2 Thess 2:3
in Asia have turned a.....2 Tim 1:15
heard, lest we drift a...........Heb 2:1
if they fall a ....Heb 6:6
can never take a ....Heb 10:11
world is passing a ....1 John 2:17
if anyone takes a..............Rev 22:19

AWESOME

a is this place ....Gen 28:17
God, the great and a ....Deut 7:21
By a deeds in ....Ps 65:5
O God,You are more a.......Ps 68:35
Your great and a name......Ps 99:3

BABE

the b leaped in my ....Luke 1:44
You will find a B ....Luke 2:12
for he is a b ....Heb 5:13

BABES

Out of the mouth of b.............Ps 8:2
revealed them to b ....Matt 11:25
of the mouth of b............Matt 21:16
as to carnal, as to b............1 Cor 3:1
as newborn b .... 1 Pet 2:2

BACK

for the fool's b...................Prov 26:3
I gave My b to those ....Is 50:6
plow, and looking b........Luke 9:62
of those who draw b.......Heb 10:39
someone turns him b.....James 5:19

BACKBITING

b tongue an angry......... Prov 25:23

BACKSLIDER

The b in heart will be .... Prov 14:14

BACKSLIDINGS

And I will heal your b .... Jer 3:22

BAD

b tree bears b fruit ....Matt 7:17

BALANCES

Falsifying the b..................Amos 8:5

BALD

every head shall be b .... Jer 48:37

BALM

no b in Gilead .... Jer 8:22

BANDAGED

and b his wounds..........Luke 10:34

BANKERS

my money with the b......Matt 25:27

BANNERS

we will set up our b ....Ps 20:5
as an army with b ....Song 6:4

BAPTISM(S)

coming to his b....................Matt 3:7
b that I am baptized........Matt 20:22
"But I have a b................Luke 12:50
said, "Into John's b ....Acts 19:3
Lord, one faith, one b........Eph 4:5
buried with Him in b ....Col 2:12
of the doctrine of b ....Heb 6:2

BAPTIZE(D)

"I indeed b you with ....Matt 3:11
Himself did not b................John 4:2
b will be saved............... Mark 16:16
every one of you be b.......Acts 2:38
all his family were b.......Acts 16:33
Arise and be b ....Acts 22:16
were b into Christ ....Rom 6:3
I thank God that I b .... 1 Cor 1:14
Spirit we were all b..........1 Cor 12:13

BAPTIZING

b them in the name of ....Matt 28:19

BARLEY

here who has five b ....John 6:9

BARN(S)

the wheat into my b........Matt 13:30
reap nor gather into b ......Matt 6:26
I will pull down my b ....Luke 12:18

BARREN

But Sarai was b ....Gen 11:30
"Sing, O b ....Is 54:1

BASKET(S)

and put it under a b ....Matt 5:15
I was let down in a b ..... 2 Cor 11:33
they took up twelve b.....Matt 14:20

BATHED

to him, "He who is b ......John 13:10

BATTLE

b is the LORD's...............1 Sam 17:47
the b to the strong............ Eccl 9:11
became valiant in b ....Heb 11:34

BEAR

greater than I can *b* ....Gen 4:13
whom Sarah shall *b*.........Gen 17:21
not *b* false witness ....Ex 20:16
b their iniquities ....Is 53:11
child, and *b* a Son ....Matt 1:23
A good tree cannot *b*........Matt 7:18
how long shall I *b* ....Matt 17:17
by, to *b* His cross............Mark 15:21
whoever does not *b*........Luke 14:27
are strong ought to *b* ....Rom 15:1
B one another's ....Gal 6:2
b the sins of many.............Heb 9:28

BEARD

the edges of your *b* ....Lev 19:27
Running down on the *b* ......Ps 133:2

BEARING

goes forth weeping, *B*.........Ps 126:6
And He, *b* His cross.......John 19:17
b His reproach ....Heb 13:13

BEAST

You preserve man and *b* .....Ps 36:6
And I saw a *b* rising ....Rev 13:1
the mark of the *b*..............Rev 19:20

BEAT

b their swords into...................Is 2:4
spat in His face and *b*.....Matt 26:67

BEATEN

Three times I was *b* ......2 Cor 11:25

BEAUTIFUL

B in elevation.........................Ps 48:2
has made everything *b*..... Eccl 3:11
my love, you are as *b* ....Song 6:4
How *b* upon the.....................Is 52:7
indeed appear *b*............Matt 23:27

BEAUTY

"The *b* of Israel is...........2 Sam 1:19
To behold the *b* ....Ps 27:4
see the King in His *b* ....Is 33:17
no *b* that we should ....Is 53:2

BECAME

b a living being.....................Gen 2:7
to the Jews I *b*.................. 1 Cor 9:20

BED

I remember You on my *b* ....Ps 63:6
if I make my *b* in hell ....Ps 139:8
"Arise; take up your *b* ....Matt 9:6
be two men in one *b*......Luke 17:34
and the *b* undefiled............Heb 13:4

BEFOREHAND

up, do not worry *b* ....Mark 13:11
told you all things *b* ....Mark 13:23
when He testified *b*..........1 Pet 1:11

BEG

b you as sojourners..........1 Pet 2:11

BEGGAR

there was a certain *b*.....Luke 16:20

BEGGARLY

weak and *b* elements............Gal 4:9

BEGINNING

b God created the.................Gen 1:1
In the *b* was the Word.......John 1:1
a murderer from the *b*......John 8:44
True Witness, the *B* ....Rev 3:14
and the Omega, the *B*........Rev 21:6

BEGOTTEN

I have *b* You...........................Ps 2:7
glory as of the only *b*........John 1:14
loves him who is *b* ....1 John 5:1

BEGUILING

b unstable souls................2 Pet 2:14

BEGUN

Having *b* in the Spirit..........Gal 3:3

BEHALF

you on Christ's *b* ....2 Cor 5:20

BEHAVE

does not *b* rudely ....1 Cor 13:5

BEHAVED

blamelessly we *b*......... 1 Thess 2:10

BEHAVIOR

of good *b*, hospitable ....1 Tim 3:2

BEHEADED

and had John *b*..............Matt 14:10

BEHOLD

B, the virgin shall..................Is 7:14
Judah, "*B* your God ....Is 40:9
"*B* the Lamb of God........John 1:36
to them, "*B* the Man........John 19:5
B what manner of ....1 John 3:1

BEHOLDING

with unveiled face, *b* ....2 Cor 3:18

BEING

move and have our *b*......Acts 17:28
who, *b* in the form of...........Phil 2:6

BELIEVE

tears, "Lord, I *b*............... Mark 9:24
have no root, who *b*.........Luke 8:13
slow of heart to *b* ....Luke 24:25
to those who *b* ....John 1:12
this, that they may *b*.......John 11:42
that you may *b*.................John 20:31
the Lord Jesus and *b*....... Rom 10:9
Christ, not only to *b*...........Phil 1:29
comes to God must *b*........Heb 11:6
b that there is one ....James 2:19
Even the demons *b* ....James 2:19

BELIEVED

And he *b* in the LORD ....Gen 15:6
Who has *b* our report............Is 53:1
seen Me, you have *b*.....John 20:29
"Abraham *b* God...............Rom 4:3
whom I have *b*..................2 Tim 1:12

BELIEVERS

example to the *b*...............1 Tim 4:12

BELIEVES

The simple *b* every .... Prov 14:15
that whoever *b* in Him ....John 3:16
"He who *b* in the Son ......John 3:36
with the heart one *b* ......Rom 10:10

BELLY

On your *b* you shall go......Gen 3:14
and Jonah was in the *b*......Jon 1:17
whose god is their *b* ....Phil 3:19

BELOVED

so He gives His *b*................Ps 127:2
My *b* is mine ....Song 2:16
"This is My *b*.....................Matt 3:17
us accepted in the *B*...........Eph 1:6
Luke the *b* physician.........Col 4:14
"This is My *b*.....................2 Pet 1:17

BESEECH

b you therefore .... Rom 12:1

BESIDE

He leads me *b* the ....Ps 23:2
"Paul, you are *b* ....Acts 26:24

BEST

desire the *b*...................... 1 Cor 12:31

BESTOWED

love the Father has *b*...... 1 John 3:1

BETRAY

you, one of you will *b*.....Matt 26:21

BETRAYED

Man is about to be *b*.......Matt 17:22

BETRAYING

"Judas, are you *b*...........Luke 22:48

BETRAYS

who is the one who *b* ....John 21:20

BETROTHED

to a virgin *b* to a man......Luke 1:27

BETTER

b than sacrifice ....1 Sam 15:22
It is *b* to trust in.................Ps 118:8
For it is *b* to marry............1 Cor 7:9
Christ, which is far *b*.........Phil 1:23

b than the angels.................Heb 1:4
b things concerning.............Heb 6:9

BEWARE

"*B* of false prophets ....Matt 7:15

BIND

and whatever you *b*........Matt 16:19
'*B* him hand and foot.....Matt 22:13

BIRD

soul, "Flee as a *b* ....Ps 11:1

BIRDS

b make their nests............Ps 104:17
"Look at the *b*...................Matt 6:26
have holes and *b* ....Matt 8:20

BIRTH

the day of one's *b*................ Eccl 7:1
Now the *b* of Jesus.........Matt 1:18
will rejoice at his *b*..........Luke 1:14
conceived, it gives *b* ......James 1:15

BIRTHRIGHT

Esau despised his *b*.........Gen 25:34

BISHOP

the position of a *b* ....1 Tim 3:1
b must be blameless ....Titus 1:7

BITE

A serpent may *b*...........Eccl 10:11
But if you *b* and..................Gal 5:15

BITTER

b herbs they ....Ex 12:8
and do not be *b*...................Col 3:19
But if you have *b*...........James 3:14

BITTERLY

And Hezekiah wept *b* .....2 Kin 20:3
went out and wept *b*.......Matt 26:75

BITTERNESS

you are poisoned by *b*......Acts 8:23
b springing up cause ....Heb 12:15

BLACK

one hair white or *b* ....Matt 5:36
a *b* horse ....Rev 6:5
and the sun became *b* .....Rev 6:12

BLADE

first the *b* ....Mark 4:28

BLAME

be holy and without *b* ....Eph 1:4

BLAMELESS

and that man was *b* ....Job 1:1
body be preserved *b* ... 1 Thess 5:23

BLASPHEME

b Your name forever.........Ps 74:10
compelled them to *b* ....Acts 26:11
b that noble name ....James 2:7

BLASPHEMED

who passed by *b* Him......Matt 27:39
great heat, and they *b* ....Rev 16:9

BLASPHEMER

I was formerly a *b*...........1 Tim 1:13

BLASPHEMES

b the name of the ....Lev 24:16
"This Man *b*........................Matt 9:3

BLASPHEMIES

is this who speaks *b* ....Luke 5:21

BLASPHEMY

but the *b* against.............Matt 12:31
was full of names of *b*.......Rev 17:3

BLEMISH

be holy and without *b* ....Eph 5:27
as of a lamb without *b*.....1 Pet 1:19

BLEMISHED

to the Lord what is *b* ....Mal 1:14

BLESS

b those who *b* you.............Gen 12:3
You go unless You *b* ....Gen 32:26
"The LORD *b* you and ...... Num 6:24
b the LORD at all...................Ps 34:1
b You while I live ....Ps 63:4

b His holy name ....Ps 103:1
b those who curse ....Luke 6:28
B those who ....Rom 12:14
Being reviled, we *b* ....1 Cor 4:12

BLESSED
B is the man who walks.........Ps 1:1
B is the man to whom ....Ps 32:2
B is the nation whose ....Ps 33:12
B is he who comes ....Ps 118:26
rise up and call her *b*.... Prov 31:28
"*B* are the poor in............Matt 5:3
B are those who mourn...Matt 5:4
B are the meek ....Matt 5:5
B are those who hunger....Matt 5:6
B are the merciful ....Matt 5:7
B are the pure in ....Matt 5:8
B are the peacemakers....Matt 5:9
B are those who are.........Matt 5:10
B is He who comes ....Matt 21:9
'It is more *b* to give ....Acts 20:35
B be the God and ....Eph 1:3
"*B* are the dead who ....Rev 14:13

BLESSING
And you shall be a *b*.........Gen 12:2
before you today a *b*...... Deut 11:26
shall be showers of *b*....Ezek 34:26
and you shall be a *b* ....Zech 8:13
that the *b* of Abraham......Gal 3:14
with every spiritual *b* ....Eph 1:3

BLIND
To open *b* eyes.......................Is 42:7
His watchmen are *b*............Is 56:10
b leads the *b*....................Matt 15:14
to Him, "Are we *b*.........John 9:40
miserable, poor, *b* ....Rev 3:17

BLOOD
of your brother's *b*.............Gen 4:10
b shall be shed.....................Gen 9:6
b that makes ....Lev 17:11
hands are full of *b*.................Is 1:15
And the moon into *b* ....Joel 2:31
For this is My *b* ....Matt 26:28
"His *b* be on us and........Matt 27:25
covenant in My *b* ....Luke 22:20
were born, not of *b* ....John 1:13
b has eternal life..............John 6:54
with His own *b* ....Acts 20:28
propitiation by His *b*......Rom 3:25
justified by His *b*.............Rom 5:9
through His *b*......................Eph 1:7
brought near by the *b*......Eph 2:13
against flesh and *b*...........Eph 6:12
peace through the *b*..........Col 1:20
with the precious *b* ....1 Pet 1:19
b of Jesus Christ His........1 John 1:7
our sins in His own *b* ....Rev 1:5
us to God by Your *b*..........Rev 5:9
them white in the *b*........Rev 7:14
overcame him by the *b* ...Rev 12:11
a robe dipped in *b*...........Rev 19:13

BLOODTHIRSTY
The LORD abhors the *b* ....Ps 5:6

BLOSSOM
and *b* as the rose ....Is 35:1

BLOT
from my sins, and *b*...........Ps 51:9
and I will not *b* ....Rev 3:5

BLOTTED
your sins may be *b*...........Acts 3:19

BOAST
puts on his armor *b* ......1 Kin 20:11
and make your *b* ....Rom 2:17
lest anyone should *b*...........Eph 2:9

BOASTERS
God, violent, proud, *b*...... Rom 1:30

BOASTING
Where is *b* then ....Rom 3:27

BODIES
b a living sacrifice............Rom 12:1
not know that your *b*......1 Cor 6:15
wives as their own *b*........Eph 5:28

BODILY
b form like a dove...........Luke 3:22
of the Godhead *b*..................Col 2:9

BODY
of the *b* is the eye..............Matt 6:22
those who kill the *b* ....Matt 10:28
this is My *b*........................Matt 26:26
of the temple of His *b*......John 2:21
deliver me from this *b* ..... Rom 7:24
redemption of our *b*......... Rom 8:23
members in one *b* .... Rom 12:4
But I discipline my *b*...... 1 Cor 9:27
b which is broken .... 1 Cor 11:24
baptized into one *b* .... 1 Cor 12:13
are the *b* of Christ .... 1 Cor 12:27
though I give my *b*.... 1 Cor 13:3
It is sown a natural *b*.... 1 Cor 15:44
in the *b* of His flesh.............Col 1:22
our sins in His own *b* ...... 1 Pet 2:24

BOILS
Job with painful *b*.................Job 2:7

BOLDLY
therefore come *b* ....Heb 4:16

BOLDNESS
in whom we have *b* ....Eph 3:12
that we may have *b*.... 1 John 4:17

BOND
love, which is the *b*............Col 3:14

BONDAGE
out of the house of *b*...........Ex 13:14
again with a yoke of *b*.........Gal 5:1

BONDSERVANTS
B, be obedient to ....Eph 6:5
Masters, give your *b*............Col 4:1

BONE
b clings to my skin...........Job 19:20

BONES
I can count all My *b*............Ps 22:17
and my *b* waste away.........Ps 31:10
I kept silent, my *b*.............Ps 32:3
the wind, Or how the *b* .... Eccl 11:5
say to them, 'O dry *b*........Ezek 37:4
of dead men's *b* ....Matt 23:27
b shall be broken ....John 19:36

BOOK
are written in the *b*............Gal 3:10
in the Lamb's *B* ....Rev 21:27
the prophecy of this *b* .....Rev 22:18

BORDERS
and enlarge the *b* ....Matt 23:5

BORE
And to Sarah who *b* ....Is 51:2
b the sin of many ....Is 53:12
b our sicknesses ....Matt 8:17
Himself *b* our sins........... 1 Pet 2:24
b a male Child who was ...Rev 12:5

BORN
A time to be *b* ....Eccl 3:2
unto us a Child is *b*..................Is 9:6
b Jesus who is called........Matt 1:16
unless one is *b* again ....John 3:3
"That which is *b* ....John 3:6
having been *b* again .... 1 Pet 1:23
who loves is *b* of God..... 1 John 4:7

BORROWER
b is servant to the............Prov 22:7

BORROWS
The wicked *b* and does ......Ps 37:21

BOSOM
to Abraham's *b*.............Luke 16:22
Son, who is in the *b* ....John 1:18

BOTTOMLESS
ascend out of the *b*...........Rev 17:8
the key to the *b*..................Rev 20:1

BOUGHT
b the threshing floor....2 Sam 24:24
all that he had and *b*......Matt 13:46
For you were *b* at a........ 1 Cor 6:20
denying the Lord who *b* ...2 Pet 2:1

BOUND
on earth will be *b*............Matt 16:19
And see, now I go *b*........Acts 20:22

who has a husband is *b* .....Rom 7:2
Are you *b* to a wife ....1 Cor 7:27
Devil and Satan, and *b*......Rev 20:2

BOW
"You shall not *b*..................Ex 23:24
let us worship and *b* ....Ps 95:6
who sat on it had a *b*..........Rev 6:2

BOWED
stood all around and *b* ......Gen 37:7
And they *b* the knee ....Matt 27:29

BOWL(S)
and poured out his *b*..........Rev 16:2
Go and pour out the *b* ....Rev 16:1

BRANCH
raise to David a *B* ....Jer 23:5
forth My Servant the *B* ....Zech 3:8
b that bears fruit He ....John 15:2

BRANCHES
vine, you are the *b* ....John 15:5

BRASS
become sounding *b*........ 1 Cor 13:1

BRAVE
in the faith, be *b* .... 1 Cor 16:13

BREAD
brought out *b* ....Gen 14:18
shall eat unleavened *b*....... Ex 23:15
not live by *b* alone .... Deut 8:3
b eaten in secret is ....Prov 9:17
B gained by deceit is ...... Prov 20:17
Cast your *b* upon the....... Eccl 11:1
for what is not *b*................Is 55:2
these stones become *b* ....Matt 4:3
not live by *b* alone ....Matt 4:4
this day our daily *b* ....Matt 6:11
eating, Jesus took *b* ....Matt 26:26
"I am the *b* of life ....John 6:48
betrayed took *b* ....1 Cor 11:23

BREAK
covenant I will not *b*...........Ps 89:34
together to *b* bread ....Acts 20:7

BREAKING
in the *b* of bread ....Acts 2:42
b bread from house to......Acts 2:46

BREASTPLATE
righteousness as a *b* ....Is 59:17
having put on the *b*...........Eph 6:14

BREASTS
Your two *b* are like............Song 4:5
b which nursed You ......Luke 11:27

BREATH
nostrils the *b* of life..............Gen 2:7
that there was no *b* .... 1 Kin 17:17
Man is like a *b* ....Ps 144:4
everything that has *b*.........Ps 150:6
"Surely I will cause *b*......Ezek 37:5
gives to all life, *b* ....Acts 17:25
power to give *b*.................Rev 13:15

BRETHREN
and you are all *b* ....Matt 23:8
least of these My *b*..........Matt 25:40
among many *b* .... Rom 8:29
thus sin against the *b* ..... 1 Cor 8:12
over five hundred *b* .... 1 Cor 15:6
perils among false *b* ....2 Cor 11:26
sincere love of the *b*...... 1 Pet 1:22
we love the *b*................... 1 John 3:14
our lives for the *b*........... 1 John 3:16

BRIBE(S)
you shall take no *b* .... Ex 23:8
b blinds the eyes............. Deut 16:19
hand is full of *b* ....Ps 26:10

BRICK(S)
people straw to make *b*.........Ex 5:7
"Come, let us make *b* ....Gen 11:3

BRIDE
I will show you the *b*.........Rev 21:9
the Spirit and the *b*..........Rev 22:17

BRIDEGROOM
And as the *b* rejoices.............Is 62:5
mourn as long as the *b*....Matt 9:15

went out to meet the *b* .....Matt 25:1
the friend of the *b* ....John 3:29

BRIDLE
b the whole body..............James 3:2

BRIGHTER
a light from heaven, *b* ....Acts 26:13

BRIGHTNESS
And kings to the *b* ....Is 60:3
who being the *b*...................Heb 1:3

BRIMSTONE
the lake of fire and *b* ....Rev 20:10

BRING
b back his soul...................Job 33:30
b My righteousness...............Is 46:13
Who shall *b* a charge ....Rom 8:33
b Christ down from .... Rom 10:6
even so God will *b* ...... 1 Thess 4:14

BROAD
b is the way that...............Matt 7:13

BROKE
b them at the foot of........Ex 32:19
He blessed and *b*...............Matt 14:19
b the legs of the..............John 19:32

BROKEN
this stone will be *b*.........Matt 21:44
Scripture cannot be *b*....John 10:35
body which is *b* ....1 Cor 11:24

BROKENHEARTED
He heals the *b* And............Ps 147:3

BRONZE
So Moses made a *b*..........Num 21:9
b walls against the............Jer 1:18
a third kingdom of *b*........ Dan 2:39

BROOD
"B of vipers.......................Matt 12:34
hen gathers her *b*...........Luke 13:34

BROTHER
"Where is Abel your *b*.........Gen 4:9
b offended is harder ..... Prov 18:19
b will deliver up................Matt 10:21
how often shall my *b*.......Matt 18:21
b will rise again..............John 11:23
b goes to law against........ 1 Cor 6:6
Whoever hates his *b*....1 John 3:15

BROTHERHOOD
Love the *b*.........................1 Pet 2:17

BROTHERLY
b love continue ....Heb 13:1

BROTHER'S
Am I my *b* keeper................Gen 4:9
at the speck in your *b*........Matt 7:3

BROTHERS
is My mother, or My *b* ... Mark 3:33
b are these who hear......Luke 8:21

BRUISE
He shall *b* your head ....Gen 3:15
the Lord to *b* Him ....Is 53:10

BRUISED
He was *b* for our ....Is 53:5
b reed He will not...........Matt 12:20

BUCKLER
be your shield and *b*............Ps 91:4

BUILD
b ourselves a city ....Gen 11:4
"Would you *b* a house....2 Sam 7:5
labor in vain who *b*.............Ps 127:1
down, And a time to *b*....... Eccl 3:3
'This man began to *b*....Luke 14:30
What house will you *b* ... Acts 7:49
"For if I *b* again ....Gal 2:18

BUILDER
foundations, whose *b* ......Heb 11:10

BUILT
has *b* her house ....Prov 9:1
to a wise man who *b* ....Matt 7:24
having been *b* on the........Eph 2:20

BUNDLE
man's *b* of money............Gen 42:35

BURDEN(S)
Cast your *b* on the ....Ps 55:22
easy and My *b* is light ....Matt 11:30
we might not be a *b*...... 1 Thess 2:9
on you no other *b*...........Rev 2:24
"For they bind heavy *b*.....Matt 23:4
Bear one another's *b* ....Gal 6:2

BURIAL
she did it for My *b*............Matt 26:12
for the day of My *b* ....John 12:7

BURIED
Therefore we were *b* ....Rom 6:4
and that He was *b*........... 1 Cor 15:4
b with Him in baptism ....Col 2:12

BURN
the bush does not *b*................Ex 3:3
"Did not our heart *b* .....Luke 24:32

BURNED
If anyone's work is *b*...... 1 Cor 3:15
my body to be *b*...............1 Cor 13:3

BURNING
b torch that passed ....Gen 15:17
b fire shut up in my .... Jer 20:9
plucked from the *b*.........Amos 4:11

BURNT
lamb for a *b* offering ....Gen 22:7
delight in *b* offering............Ps 51:16

BUSH
from the midst of a *b*............Ex 3:2

BUSYBODIES
at all, but are *b*............. 2 Thess 3:11

BUTTER
were smoother than *b* ....Ps 55:21

BUY
Yes, come, *b* wine and ....Is 55:1
"I counsel you to *b* ....Rev 3:18
and that no one may *b* ....Rev 13:17

C

CAKE(S)
Ephraim is a *c*.....................Hos 7:8
and love the raisin *c* ....Hos 3:1

CALF
and made a molded *c* ....Ex 32:4
bring the fatted *c*...........Luke 15:23

CALL
C upon Him while He............Is 55:6
c His name Jesus...............Matt 1:21
c the righteous................Matt 9:13
Lord our God will *c* ....Acts 2:39
c them My people .... Rom 9:25
c and election sure...........2 Pet 1:10

CALLED
c the light Day ....Gen 1:5
c his wife's name Eve........Gen 3:20
I have *c* you by your..............Is 43:1
"Out of Egypt I *c* ....Matt 2:15
city *c* Nazareth ....Matt 2:23
For many are *c* ....Matt 20:16
to those who are the *c*...... Rom 8:28
these He also *c*................... Rom 8:30
c children of God .... 1 John 3:1

CALLING
the gifts and the *c* .... Rom 11:29
For you see your *c* .... 1 Cor 1:26
remain in the same *c* ...... 1 Cor 7:20

CAPTIVE(S)
and be led away *c* ....Luke 21:24
He led captivity *c* ....Eph 4:8
and make *c*..........................2 Tim 3:6

CAPTIVITY
every thought into *c*........2 Cor 10:5

CARE
"Lord, do You not *c* ......Luke 10:40
how will he take *c*............1 Tim 3:5

CARELESS
But, he who is *c*............. Prov 19:16

CARES
No one *c* for my soul.........Ps 142:4
for He *c* for you .... 1 Pet 5:7

CARNAL
c mind is enmity.................Rom 8:7

CARPENTER
"Is this not the *c* .... Mark 6:3

CARRY
for you to *c* your bed.......John 5:10
it is certain we can *c*.........1 Tim 6:7

CASSIA
myrrh and aloes and *c* ....Ps 45:8

CAST
Why are you *c* down ....Ps 42:5
whole body to be *c*............Matt 5:30
My name they will *c*..... Mark 16:17
by no means *c* out.............John 6:37
c their crowns before ....Rev 4:10
the great dragon was *c*.....Rev 12:9

CASTING
c down arguments ....2 Cor 10:5
c all your care.................... 1 Pet 5:7

CASTS
perfect love *c* out........... 1 John 4:18

CATCH
c Him in His words.......Mark 12:13
now on you will *c*............Luke 5:10

CATCHES
and the wolf *c* the ....John 10:12
c the wise in their...........1 Cor 3:19

CAUGHT
him was a ram *c*..............Gen 22:13
her Child was *c* up............Rev 12:5

CAUSE
hated Me without a *c*.....John 15:25
For this *c* I was born......John 18:37

CEASE
and night Shall not *c*........Gen 8:22
He makes wars *c*..................Ps 46:9
tongues, they will *c*......... 1 Cor 13:8

CEASING
pray without *c* .... 1 Thess 5:17

CEDAR
dwell in a house of *c*........2 Sam 7:2

CELESTIAL
but the glory of the *c* .... 1 Cor 15:40

CHAFF
be chased like the *c* ....Is 17:13
He will burn up the *c*........Matt 3:12

CHAIN(S)
pit and a great *c* .... Rev 20:1
And his *c* fell off................Acts 12:7
am, except for these *c* ....Acts 26:29

CHAMBERS
brought me into his *c* ....Song 1:4

CHANGE
now and to *c* my tone........Gal 4:20
there is also a *c*..................Heb 7:12

CHANGED
c the glory of the............. Rom 1:23
but we shall all be *c*...... 1 Cor 15:51

CHARIOT(S)
that suddenly a *c* .... 2 Kin 2:11
Some trust in *c* ....Ps 20:7

CHARITABLE
you do not do your *c* ....Matt 6:1
c deeds which she...........Acts 9:36

CHARM
C is deceitful and .... Prov 31:30

CHARMS
who sew magic *c*...........Ezek 13:18

CHASTE
present you as a c .... 2 Cor 11:2

CHASTEN
a father does not c .... Heb 12:7
I love, I rebuke and c .... Rev 3:19

CHASTENED
c us as seemed best .... Heb 12:10

CHASTENING
do not despise the c .... Job 5:17
Now no c seems to be ..... Heb 12:11

CHASTISEMENT
The c for our peace .... Is 53:5

CHATTER
c leads only to .... Prov 14:23

CHEAT
Beware lest anyone c .... Col 2:8

CHEEK(S)
on your right c .... Matt 5:39
His c are like a bed .... Song 5:13

CHEER
"Son, be of good c .... Matt 9:2

CHEERFUL
for God loves a c .... 2 Cor 9:7

CHEERFULNESS
shows mercy, with c .... Rom 12:8

CHERISHES
but nourishes and c .... Eph 5:29

CHERUBIM
above it were the c .... Heb 9:5

CHIEF
of whom I am c .... 1 Tim 1:15
Zion a c cornerstone .... 1 Pet 2:6

CHILD
Train up a c in the .... Prov 22:6
For unto us a C .... Is 9:6
virgin shall be with c ..... Matt 1:23
of God as a little c .... Mark 10:15
So the c grew and .... Luke 1:80
When I was a c .... 1 Cor 13:11
She bore a male C .... Rev 12:5

CHILDBEARING
she will be saved in c ..... 1 Tim 2:15

CHILDBIRTH
pain as a woman in c .... Is 13:8

CHILDLESS
give me, seeing I go c .... Gen 15:2
this man down as c .... Jer 22:30

CHILDREN
c are a heritage .... Ps 127:3
c rise up and call her ..... Prov 31:28
and become as little c ...... Matt 18:3
"Let the little c .... Matt 19:14
the right to become c ...... John 1:12
now we are c of God ...... 1 John 3:2

CHOOSE
therefore c life .... Deut 30:19
"You did not c .... John 15:16

CHOSE
Just as He c us in Him .... Eph 1:4

CHOSEN
servant whom I have c .... Is 43:10
whom I have c .... John 13:18
c the foolish things ...... 1 Cor 1:27
Has God not c the .... James 2:5

CHRIST
Jesus who is called C .... Matt 1:16
"You are the C .... Matt 16:16
a Savior, who is C .... Luke 2:11
It is C who died .... Rom 8:34
to be justified by C .... Gal 2:17
been crucified with C .... Gal 2:20
C is head of the .... Eph 5:23
to me, to live is C .... Phil 1:21
which is C in you .... Col 1:27
C who is our .... Col 3:4
Jesus C is the same .... Heb 13:8

C His Son cleanses us .... 1 John 1:7
that Jesus is the C .... 1 John 5:1

CHRISTIAN(S)
anyone suffers as a C ...... 1 Pet 4:16
were first called C .... Acts 11:26

CHURCH
rock I will build My c ..... Matt 16:18
c daily those who were .... Acts 2:47
Himself a glorious c .... Eph 5:27
as the Lord does the c .... Eph 5:29
body, which is the c .... Col 1:24
assembly and c .... Heb 12:23

CIRCUMCISED
among you shall be c ...... Gen 17:10
who will justify the c .... Rom 3:30
if you become c .... Gal 5:2

CIRCUMCISION
c is that of the heart .... Rom 2:29
C is nothing and .... 1 Cor 7:19
Christ Jesus neither c .... Gal 5:6

CIRCUMSPECTLY
then that you walk c .... Eph 5:15

CITIES
He overthrew those c ...... Gen 19:25
three parts, and the c .... Rev 16:19

CITIZEN(S)
But I was born a c .... Acts 22:28
but fellow c with the .... Eph 2:19

CITIZENSHIP
For our c is in heaven .... Phil 3:20

CITY
shall make glad the c .... Ps 46:4
c has become a harlot .... Is 1:21
How lonely sits the c .... Lam 1:1
c that is set on a .... Matt 5:14
He has prepared a c .... Heb 11:16
have no continuing c ...... Heb 13:14
John, saw the holy c .... Rev 21:2

CLAY
pit, out of the miry c .... Ps 40:2
We are the c .... Is 64:8
blind man with the c .... John 9:6
have power over the c ...... Rom 9:21

CLEAN
He who has c hands and ..... Ps 24:4
make yourselves c .... Is 1:16
c out His threshing .... Matt 3:12
You can make me c .... Matt 8:2
"You are not all c .... John 13:11
"You are already c .... John 15:3

CLEANSE
C me from secret .... Ps 19:12
And c me from my sin .... Ps 51:2
How can a young man c ...... Ps 119:9
might sanctify and c .... Eph 5:26
us our sins and to c .... 1 John 1:9

CLEANSED
"Were there not ten c .... Luke 17:17

CLOAK
let him have your c .... Matt 5:40
using liberty as a c .... 1 Pet 2:16

CLOTHED
of skin, and c them .... Gen 3:21
A man c in soft .... Matt 11:8
naked and you c .... Matt 25:36
legion, sitting and c .... Mark 5:15
desiring to be c .... 2 Cor 5:2
that you may be c .... Rev 3:18

CLOTHES
c became shining .... Mark 9:3
many spread their c .... Luke 19:36
a poor man in filthy c ...... James 2:2

CLOTHING
c they cast lots .... Ps 22:18
do you worry about c .... Matt 6:28
to you in sheep's c .... Matt 7:15
c they cast lots .... John 19:24

CLOTHS
in swaddling c .... Luke 2:12

CLOUD
My rainbow in the c .... Gen 9:13
day in a pillar of c .... Ex 13:21
He led them with the c .... Ps 78:14
behold, a bright c .... Matt 17:5
of Man coming in a c ...... Luke 21:27
c received Him out of .... Acts 1:9
by so great a c .... Heb 12:1

CLOUDS
Man coming on the c ...... Matt 24:30
with them in the c .... 1 Thess 4:17
are c without water .... Jude 12
He is coming with c .... Rev 1:7

CLOVEN
chew the cud or have c ... Deut 14:7

COAL(S)
in his hand a live c .... Is 6:6
doing you will heap c .... Rom 12:20

COBRA
the lion and the c .... Ps 91:13

COFFIN
and he was put in a c ...... Gen 50:26
touched the open c .... Luke 7:14

COIN
if she loses one c .... Luke 15:8

COLD
and harvest, C and .... Gen 8:22
of many will grow c .... Matt 24:12
that you are neither c .... Rev 3:15

COLT
on a donkey, A c .... Zech 9:9
on a donkey, A c .... Matt 21:5

COME
He will c and save you .... Is 35:4
who have no money, C .... Is 55:1
Your kingdom c .... Matt 6:10
"C to Me .... Matt 11:28
I have c in My .... John 5:43
thirsts, let him c .... John 7:37
c as a light into the .... Luke 12:46
O Lord, c .... 1 Cor 16:22
the door, I will c .... Rev 3:20

COMELINESS
He has no form or c .... Is 53:2

COMFORT
and Your staff, they c .... Ps 23:4
yes, c My people .... Is 40:1
c each other .... 1 Thess 5:11

COMFORTED
So Isaac was c after .... Gen 24:67
Refusing to be c .... Jer 31:15

COMFORTS
I, even I, am He who c .... Is 51:12

COMING
see the Son of Man c .... Mark 13:26
mightier than I is c .... Luke 3:16
are Christ's at His c ...... 1 Cor 15:23
Behold, I am c .... Rev 3:11
"Surely I am c .... Rev 22:20

COMMAND
c I have received .... John 10:18
and I know that
His c .... John 12:50
If you do whatever
I c .... John 15:14

COMMANDMENT(S)
c of the LORD is pure .... Ps 19:8
which is the great c .... Matt 22:36
"A new c I give to .... John 13:34
which is the first c .... Eph 6:2
And this is His c .... 1 John 3:23
covenant, the Ten C .... Ex 34:28
as doctrines the c .... Matt 15:9
c hang all the Law .... Matt 22:40
"He who has My c .... John 14:21

COMMANDS
with authority He c .... Mark 1:27

COMMENDABLE
patiently, this is c .... 1 Pet 2:20

COMMENDS
but whom the Lord c....2 Cor 10:18

COMMIT
"You shall not c..................Ex 20:14
into Your hands I c........Luke 23:46

COMMON
c people heard Him ...... Mark 12:37
had all things in c..............Acts 2:44
concerning our c....................Jude 3

COMMUNION
c of the Holy Spirit ....2 Cor 13:14

COMPANION(S)
a man my equal, My c........Ps 55:13
while you became c.........Heb 10:33

COMPANY
Great was the c....................Ps 68:11
to an innumerable c.........Heb 12:22

COMPARE
c ourselves with.............2 Cor 10:12

COMPASSION
are a God full of c ....Ps 86:15
He was moved with c.......Matt 9:36
whomever I will have c... Rom 9:15
He can have c on those......Heb 5:2

COMPASSIONATE
the Lord is very c...........James 5:11

COMPASSIONS
because His c fail not ......Lam 3:22

COMPELS
the love of Christ c..........2 Cor 5:14

COMPLAINED
some of them also c...... 1 Cor 10:10

COMPLAINERS
These are grumblers, c........Jude 16

COMPLAINING
all things without c ....Phil 2:14

COMPLAINT
For the LORD has a c .... Mic 6:2

COMPLETE
work in you will c..............Phil 1:6
and you are c in Him.........Col 2:10
of God may be c.............2 Tim 3:17

COMPLETELY
sanctify you c............... 1 Thess 5:23

COMPREHEND
which we cannot c.............Job 37:5
the darkness did not c....... John 1:5

CONCEALED
Than love carefully c........Prov 27:5

CONCEIT
selfish ambition or c...........Phil 2:3

CONCEITED
Let us not become c...........Gal 5:26

CONCEIVE
the virgin shall c....................Is 7:14
And behold, you will c....Luke 1:31

CONDEMN
world to c the world .... John 3:17

CONDEMNATION
can you escape the c .....Matt 23:33
"And this is the c............... John 3:19
Their c is just ....Rom 3:8
therefore now no c..............Rom 8:1

CONDEMNED
does not believe is c......... John 3:18
c sin in the flesh ....Rom 8:3

CONDEMNS
Who is he who c.............. Rom 8:34

CONDUCT
from your aimless c..........1 Pet 1:8
may be won by the c ....1 Pet 3:1

CONFESS
c my transgressions..............Ps 32:5
that if you c with.............. Rom 10:9

every tongue shall c....... Rom 14:11
If we c our sins .... 1 John 1:9

CONFESSED
c that He was Christ........John 9:22

CONFESSES
c that Jesus is the.......... 1 John 4:15

CONFESSION
with the mouth c............. Rom 10:10
High Priest of our c.........Heb 3:1
let us hold fast our c.........Heb 4:14

CONFIDENCE
c shall be your ....Is 30:15
Jesus, and have no c...........Phil 3:3

CONFIRMED
covenant that was c...........Gal 3:17
c it by an oath....................Heb 6:17

CONFIRMING
c the word through .... Mark 16:20

CONFLICT(S)
to know what a great c........Col 2:1
Outside were c...................2 Cor 7:5

CONFORMED
predestined to be c........... Rom 8:29
And do not be c .... Rom 12:2

CONFUSE
c their language.................Gen 11:7

CONFUSED
the assembly was c.........Acts 19:32

CONGREGATION
Nor sinners in the c ....Ps 1:5
God stands in the c ....Ps 82:1

CONQUER
conquering and to c.............Rev 6:2

CONQUERORS
we are more than c.......... Rom 8:37

CONSCIENCE
convicted by their c .... John 8:9
strive to have a c ....Acts 24:16

CONSECRATED
c this house which you..... 1 Kin 9:3

CONSIDER
When I c Your heavens ....Ps 8:3
My people do not c ....Is 1:3
C the lilies of the ....Matt 6:28
"C the ravens ....Luke 12:24
c Him who endured ....Heb 12:3

CONSIST
in Him all things c..............Col 1:17

CONSOLATION
if there is any c.....................Phil 2:1
us everlasting c............ 2 Thess 2:16

CONSOLE
c those who mourn ....Is 61:3

CONSUMED
but the bush was not c..........Ex 3:2
mercies we are not c.........Lam 3:22
beware lest you be c...........Gal 5:15

CONSUMING
our God is a c fire ....Heb 12:29

CONTAIN
of heavens cannot c...........2 Chr 6:2
c the books that.............John 21:25

CONTEMPTIBLE
and his speech c............2 Cor 10:10

CONTEND
c earnestly for the.................Jude 3

CONTENT
state I am, to be c..............Phil 4:11
covetousness: be c.............Heb 13:5

CONTENTIOUS
anyone seems to be c ... 1 Cor 11:16

CONTENTMENT
c is great gain ....1 Tim 6:6

CONTINUAL
a merry heart has a c .... Prov 15:15
c coming she weary........Luke 18:5

CONTINUALLY
heart was only evil c ....Gen 6:5
will give ourselves c ....Acts 6:4
remains a priest c.................Heb 7:3

CONTINUE
Shall we c in sin that.........Rom 6:1
C earnestly in prayer...........Col 4:2
Let brotherly love c ....Heb 13:1

CONTRARY
to worship God c.............Acts 18:13

CONTRITE
A broken and a c.................Ps 51:17
poor and of a c spirit ....Is 66:2

CONVERSION
describing the c ....Acts 15:3

CONVERTED
unless you are c................Matt 18:3

CONVICT
He has come, He will c ... John 16:8

CONVINCED
Let each be fully c............ Rom 14:5

COOL
and c my tongue.............Luke 16:24

COPPER
sold for two c coins..........Luke 12:6

COPPERSMITH
c did me much harm.......2 Tim 4:14

CORD
this line of scarlet c...........Josh 2:18

CORDS
had made a whip of c...... John 2:15

CORNERSTONE
become the chief c ....Matt 21:42
in Zion A chief c................ 1 Pet 2:6

CORRECT
C your son .... Prov 29:17

CORRECTED
human fathers who c........Heb 12:9

CORRECTION
Do not withhold c .... Prov 23:13
for reproof, for c.............2 Tim 3:16

CORRECTS
the LORD loves He c.........Prov 3:12

CORRUPT
in these things they c ....Jude 10

CORRUPTED
for all flesh had c ....Gen 6:12
Your riches are c.............James 5:2

CORRUPTIBLE
redeemed with c............... 1 Pet 1:18

CORRUPTION
Your Holy One to see c......Ps 16:10
c inherit incorruption ... 1 Cor 15:50
having escaped the c ....2 Pet 1:4

COST
and count the c...............Luke 14:28

COULD
c remove mountains....... 1 Cor 13:2
which no one c number ...... Rev 7:9

COUNSEL
Who walks not in the c..........Ps 1:1
We took sweet c..................Ps 55:14
guide me with Your c.........Ps 73:24
according to the c ....Eph 1:11
immutability of His c........Heb 6:17
"I c you to buy from...........Rev 3:18

COUNSELOR
be called Wonderful, C ....Is 9:6

COUNSELORS
c there is safety .... Prov 11:14

COUNTED
Even a fool is c .... Prov 17:28
who rule well be c .... 1 Tim 5:17

COUNTENANCE
The LORD lift up His c ..... Num 6:26
with a sad c .... Matt 6:16
His c was like.................... Matt 28:3
of the glory of his c .... 2 Cor 3:7

COUNTRY
"Get out of your c.............. Gen 12:1
that is, a heavenly c......... Heb 11:16

COURAGE
strong and of good c........ Deut 31:6

COURTEOUS
be tenderhearted, be c....... 1 Pet 3:8

COURTS
and into His c...................... Ps 100:4

COVENANT
I will establish My c.......... Gen 6:18
the LORD made a c.......... Gen 15:18
will show them His c.......... Ps 25:14
sons will keep My c.......... Ps 132:12
I will make a new c............ Jer 31:31
the Messenger of the c........ Mal 3:1
cup is the new c.............. Luke 22:20
He says, "A new c.............. Heb 8:13
Mediator of the new c....... Heb 12:24
of the everlasting c .... Heb 13:20

COVENANTS
the glory, the c.................... Rom 9:4

COVER
He shall c you with.............. Ps 91:4
c a multitude of sins ...... James 5:20

COVERED
Whose sin is c.................... Ps 32:1
c all their sin .... Ps 85:2
For there is nothing c ..... Matt 10:26

COVERINGS
and made themselves c....... Gen 3:7

COVET
"You shall not c .... Ex 20:17

COVETED
c no one's silver.............. Acts 20:33

COVETOUS
nor thieves, nor c .... 1 Cor 6:10

COVETOUSNESS
heed and beware of c....Luke 12:15

COWARDLY
the c, unbelieving.............. Rev 21:8

CRAFTILY
His people, to deal c .... Ps 105:25

CRAFTINESS
deceived Eve by his c ..... 2 Cor 11:3
in the cunning c.................. Eph 4:14

CRAFTY
the devices of the c .... Job 5:12
Nevertheless, being c ... 2 Cor 12:16

CREATED
So God c man in His .... Gen 1:27
Has not one God c .... Mal 2:10
c in Christ Jesus................ Eph 2:10
new man which was c......... Eph 4:24

CREATION
know that the whole c..... Rom 8:22
Christ, he is a new c .... 2 Cor 5:17
anything, but a new c......... Gal 6:15

CREATOR
Remember now your C.... Eccl 12:1
God, the LORD, The C...... Is 40:28
rather than the C............. Rom 1:25

CREATURE
the gospel to every c..... Mark 16:15

CREDITOR
There was a certain c......Luke 7:41

CREEP
sort are those who c .... 2 Tim 3:6

CREEPING
c thing and beast of.......... Gen 1:24

CRIED
the poor who c out............ Job 29:12
of the depths I have c......... Ps 130:1

CRIMES
land is filled with c .... Ezek 7:23

CRIMINALS
also two others, c .... Luke 23:32

CROOKED
c places shall be made .... Is 40:4
in the midst of a c .... Phil 2:15

CROSS
does not take his c .... Matt 10:38
to bear His c...................... Matt 27:32
down from the c............... Matt 27:40
lest the c of Christ........... 1 Cor 1:17
boast except in the c........... Gal 6:14
the enemies of the c.......... Phil 3:18
Him endured the c........... Heb 12:2
shall not follow a c............ Ex 23:2

CROWN
c the year with Your.......... Ps 65:11
they had twisted a c........ Matt 27:29
obtain a perishable c...... 1 Cor 9:25
laid up for me the c........... 2 Tim 4:8
on his head a golden c.... Rev 14:14

CROWNED
angels, And You have c......... Ps 8:5
athletics, he is not c .... 2 Tim 2:5

CROWNS
His head were many c..... Rev 19:12

CRUCIFIED
"Let Him be c................... Matt 27:22
Calvary, there they c.....Luke 23:33
lawless hands, have c....... Acts 2:23
that our old man was c ..... Rom 6:6
Jesus Christ and
Him c.............................. 1 Cor 2:2
"I have been c .... Gal 2:20

CRUCIFY
out again, "C Him .... Mark 15:13

CRUEL
hate me with c hatred .... Ps 25:19

CRUELTY
the haunts of c .... Ps 74:20

CRUSH
of peace will c................ Rom 16:20

CRUSHED
every side, yet not c......... 2 Cor 4:8

CRY
and their c came up to .... Ex 2:23
Does not wisdom c .... Prov 8:1
at midnight a c................... Matt 25:6
His own elect who c .... Luke 18:7

CRYING
nor sorrow, nor c .... Rev 21:4

CRYSTAL
a sea of glass, like c............ Rev 4:6

CUNNING
the serpent was more c....... Gen 3:1
c craftiness of deceitful ..... Eph 4:14

CUP
My c runs over .... Ps 23:5
Then He took the c .... Matt 26:27
c is the new covenant.....Luke 22:20
cannot drink the c........... 1 Cor 10:21
c is the new .... 1 Cor 11:25

CURE
and to c diseases .... Luke 9:1

CURES
and perform c .... Luke 13:32

CURSE
c the ground for man's......Gen 8:21
C God and die........................ Job 2:9

"I will send a c .... Mal 2:2
law are under the c............ Gal 3:10

CURSED
c more than all cattle........ Gen 3:14
from Me, you c .... Matt 25:41

CURSES
I will curse him who c........ Gen 12:3

CUT
evildoers shall be c .... Ps 37:9
the wicked will be c.......... Prov 2:22

CYMBAL
or a clanging c................. 1 Cor 13:1

D

DAILY
Give us this day our d .... Matt 6:11
take up his cross d .... Luke 9:23
the Scriptures d .... Acts 17:11

DANCE
mourn, And a time to d...... Eccl 3:4
And you did not d .... Matt 11:17

DANCED
Then David d before......2 Sam 6:14

DANCING
saw the calf and the d .... Ex 32:19
he heard music and d....Luke 15:25

DARK
I tell you in the d .... Matt 10:27
shines in a d place............ 2 Pet 1:19

DARKENED
their understanding d........ Eph 4:18

DARKNESS
d He called Night .... Gen 1:5
Those who sat in d............ Ps 107:10
d Have seen a............................ Is 9:2
And deep d the people .... Is 60:2
body will be full of d........ Matt 6:23
cast out into outer d........... Matt 8:12
d rather than light............ John 3:19
For you were once d............ Eph 5:8
called you out of d .... 1 Pet 2:9
d is reserved...................... 2 Pet 2:17
and in Him is no d .... 1 John 1:5
d is passing away............ 1 John 2:8

DASH
You shall d them to .... Ps 2:9
Lest you d your foot .... Matt 4:6

DAUGHTER
"Rejoice greatly, O d.......... Zech 9:9
"Fear not, d of Zion......... John 12:15
the son of Pharaoh's d.....Heb 11:24

DAUGHTERS
of God saw the d .... Gen 6:2
d shall prophesy .... Acts 2:17

DAY
God called the light D .... Gen 1:5
And d and night .... Gen 8:22
the Sabbath d........................ Ex 20:8
For a d in Your courts........ Ps 84:10
d the LORD has .... Ps 118:24
not strike you by d............. Ps 121:6
For the d of the LORD........ Joel 2:11
who can endure the d........... Mal 3:2
d our daily bread............... Matt 6:11
sent Me while it is d........... John 9:4
person esteems one d...... Rom 14:5
D will declare it .... 1 Cor 3:13
again the third d .... 1 Cor 15:4
with the Lord one d .... 2 Pet 3:8

DAYS
d are swifter than a............... Job 7:6
of woman is of few d.......... Job 14:1
The d of our lives are .... Ps 90:10
Before the difficult d........ Eccl 12:1
shortened those d.......... Mark 13:20
raise it up in three d......... John 2:20

DAYSPRING
With which the D...........Luke 1:78

DEACONS
with the bishops and *d*........Phil 1:1
d must be reverent............1 Tim 3:8
d be the husbands...........1 Tim 3:12

DEAD
But the *d* know nothing.....Eccl 9:5
d bury their own *d*............Matt 8:22
not the God of the *d*.......Matt 22:32
this my son was a ....Luke 15:24
d will hear the voice........John 5:25
was raised from the *d*........Rom 6:4
yourselves to be *d* .... Rom 6:11
be Lord of both the *d*...... Rom 14:9
resurrection of the *d* ....1 Cor 15:12
And the *d* in Christ .... 1 Thess 4:16
without works is *d*.........James 2:26
And the *d* were judged....Rev 20:12

DEADLY
drink anything *d*............Mark 16:18
evil, full of *d* poison ....James 3:8

DEAF
d shall be unstopped..............Is 35:5
are cleansed and the *d* .....Matt 11:5

DEATH
d parts you and me .... Ruth 1:17
and the shadow of *d*........Job 10:21
I sleep the sleep of *d*...........Ps 13:3
of the shadow of *d*...........Ps 23:4
house leads down to *d*......Prov 2:18
who hate me love *d*..........Prov 8:36
swallow up *d* forever...........Is 25:8
no pleasure in the *d* ......Ezek 18:32
who shall not taste *d* ......Matt 16:28
but has passed from *d*....John 5:24
Nevertheless *d* reigned....Rom 5:14
D no longer has.................Rom 6:9
the wages of sin is *d* ...... Rom 6:23
the Lord's *d* .... 1 Cor 11:26
since by man came *d*....1 Cor 15:21
D is swallowed up in ....1 Cor 15:54
The sting of *d* is sin.......1 Cor 15:56
is sin leading to *d*.........1 John 5:16
Be faithful until *d* ....Rev 2:10
shall be no more *d* ....Rev 21:4
which is the second *d*......Rev 21:8

DEBTOR
I am a *d* both to .... Rom 1:14
that he is a *d* to keep ....Gal 5:3

DEBTORS
as we forgive our *d* ....Matt 6:12
of his master's *d* ....Luke 16:5
brethren, we are *d* .... Rom 8:12

DECEIT
Nor was any *d* in His.............Is 53:9
philosophy and empty *d* .....Col 2:8
no sin, nor was *d*............ 1 Pet 2:22
mouth was found no *d* ......Rev 14:5

DECEITFUL
deliver me from the *d*..........Ps 43:1
"The heart is *d* ....Jer 17:9
are false apostles, *d* ......2 Cor 11:13

DECEITFULLY
an idol, Nor sworn *d*..........Ps 24:4
the word of God *d*.............2 Cor 4:2

DECEITFULNESS
this world and the *d*........Matt 13:22

DECEIVE
rise up and *d* many ....Matt 24:11
Let no one *d* you with ....Eph 5:6
we have no sin, we ....1 John 1:8

DECEIVED
"The serpent *d* ....Gen 3:13
the commandment, *d*.......Rom 7:11
deceiving and being *d* ....2 Tim 3:13

DECEIVER
how that *d* said...............Matt 27:63
This is a *d* and an..............2 John 7

DECEIVES
heed that no one *d* ....Matt 24:4

DECEPTIVE
you with *d* words ....2 Pet 2:3

DECLARE
The heavens *d* the.................Ps 19:1
d Your name to My............Ps 22:22
seen and heard we *d*...... 1 John 1:3

DECREE
"I will declare the *d*.................Ps 2:7
in those days that a *d* ....Luke 2:1

DEDICATION
it was the Feast of *D*......John 10:22

DEED(S)
you do in word or *d* ....Col 3:17
because their *d* ....John 3:19
"You do the *d*....................John 8:41
one according to his *d*........Rom 8:13
you put to death the *d* .....Rom 8:13

DEEP
LORD God caused a *d* ....Gen 2:21
d uttered its voice............. Hab 3:10
"Launch out into the *d*......Luke 5:4
I have been in the *d* ......2 Cor 11.25

DEER
As the *d* pants for the...........Ps 42:1
shall leap like a *d*...................Is 35:6

DEFEND
D the fatherless ....Is 1:17

DEFENSE
For wisdom is a *d*............. Eccl 7:12
am appointed for the *d*......Phil 1:17
be ready to give a *d* .... 1 Pet 3:15

DEFILED
lest they should be *d*.......John 18:28
and conscience are *d*.......Titus 1:15

DEFILES
mouth, this a *d* a man.......Matt 15:11
it anything that *d*.............Rev 21:27

DEFRAUD
d his brother in this ...... 1 Thess 4:6

DELICACIES
of the king's *d* ....Dan 1:5

DELICATE
a lovely and *d* woman...........Jer 6:2

DELIGHT
But his *d* is in the ....Ps 1:2
I *d* to do Your will.................Ps 40:8
And I was daily His *d*.........Prov 8:30
And let your soul *d*...............Is 55:2
call the Sabbath a *d*............Is 58:13
For I *d* in the law of ....Rom 7:22

DELIGHTS
For the LORD *d* in you ....Is 62:4

DELIVER
Let Him *d* Him.......................Ps 22:8
I will *d* him and honor........Ps 91:15
into temptation, But *d*........Matt 6:13
let Him *d* Him now if.........Matt 27:43
And the Lord will *d* ....2 Tim 4:18
d the godly out of...............2 Pet 2:9

DELIVERED
who was *d* up because ....Rom 4:25
was once for all *d*..................Jude 3

DELIVERER
D will come out of.........Rom 11:26

DELIVERS
even Jesus who *d* .... 1 Thess 1:10

DEMON
Jesus rebuked the *d*.......Matt 17:18
and have a *d*......................John 8:48

DEMONIC
is earthly, sensual, *d*......James 3:15

DEMONS
authority over all *d*.........Luke 9:1
the *d* are subject.............Luke 10:17
Even the *d* believe.........James 2:19

DEMONSTRATE
faith, to *d* His .... Rom 3:25

DEMONSTRATES
d His own love toward.......Rom 5:8

DEN
cast him into the *d* .... Dan 6:16
it a '*d* of thieves..............Matt 21:13

DENARIUS
the laborers for a *d* ....Matt 20:2

DENIED
before men will be *d*.......Luke 12:9
Peter then *d* again..........John 18:27
d the Holy One and the....Acts 3:14
things cannot be *d*...........Acts 19:36
household, he has *d*.........1 Tim 5:8

DENIES
But whoever *d* ....Matt 10:33
d that Jesus is the.......... 1 John 2:22

DENY
let him *d* himself..............Matt 16:24
He cannot *d* Himself.......2 Tim 2:13

DENYING
but *d* its power..................2 Tim 3:5
d the Lord who bought .....2 Pet 2:1

DEPART
scepter shall not *d*...........Gen 49:10
on the left hand, '*D*.......Matt 25:41
will *d* from the faith.........1 Tim 4:1

DEPARTING
heart of unbelief in *d*........Heb 3:12

DEPRESSION
of man causes *d*............. Prov 12:25

DEPTH
nor height nor *d* .... Rom 8:39
Oh, the *d* of the.............. Rom 11:33

DEPTHS
our sins Into the *d*.............. Mic 7:19

DESCEND
d now from the cross....Mark 15:32
Lord Himself will *d*..... 1 Thess 4:16

DESCENDANTS
"We are Abraham's *d*......John 8:33

DESCENDING
God ascending and *d*.......John 1:51
the holy Jerusalem, *d* ......Rev 21:10

DESERT
d shall rejoice.........................Is 35:1
'Look, He is in the *d* ......Matt 24:26

DESERTED
d place by Himself ....Matt 14:13

DESERTS
They wandered in *d*.........Heb 11:38

DESIGN
with an artistic *d* .... Ex 26:31

DESIRABLE
the eyes, and a tree *d*...........Gen 3:6

DESIRE
d shall be for your..............Gen 3:16
Behold, You *d* truth in...........Ps 51:6
"Father, I *d* that ....John 17:24
all manner of evil *d*............Rom 7:8
Brethren, my heart's *d* ....Rom 10:1
d the best gifts .... 1 Cor 12:31
the two, having a *d*...........Phil 1:23

DESIRED
d are they than gold............Ps 19:10
One thing I have *d* ....Ps 27:4

DESIRES
shall give you the *d*..............Ps 37:4
the devil, and the *d* ....John 8:44
not come from your *d*......James 4:1

DESOLATE
any more be termed *D* ....Is 62:4
house is left to you *d* .....Matt 23:38

DESOLATION
the 'abomination of *d* .....Matt 24:15

DESPAIRED
strength, so that we *d*.......2 Cor 1:8

DESPISE
one and *d* the other..........Matt 6:24
d the riches of His.............Rom 2:4

DESPISED
He is *d* and rejected..............Is 53:3
the things which are *d*.... 1 Cor 1:28

DESPISES
d his neighbor sins......... Prov 14:21

DESPISING
the cross, *d* the shame......Heb 12:2

DESTROY
Why should you *d*............. Eccl 7:16
shall not hurt nor *d*...............Is 11:9
I did not come to *d*............Matt 5:17
Him who is able to *d*......Matt 10:28
Barabbas and Jesus.....Matt 27:20
to save life or to *d* ....Luke 6:9
d men's lives but to.........Luke 9:56
d the wisdom of the .... 1 Cor 1:19
able to save and to *d*......James 4:12

DESTROYED
d all living things................Gen 7:23
house, this tent, is *d*.........2 Cor 5:1

DESTRUCTION
You turn man to *d*................Ps 90:3
d that lays waste ....Ps 91:6
your life from *d*................Ps 103:4
Pride goes before *d*........ Prov 16:18
whose end is *d* ....Phil 3:19
with everlasting *d*........ 2 Thess 1:9

DESTRUCTIVE
bring in *d* heresies ....2 Pet 2:1

DETERMINED
d their preappointed ....Acts 17:26
For I *d* not to know .... 1 Cor 2:2

DEVICES
not ignorant of his *d* ....2 Cor 2:11

DEVIL
to be tempted by the *d*........Matt 4:1
prepared for the *d*.........Matt 25:41
of your father the *d*.........John 8:44
give place to the *d*.............Eph 4:27
the snare of the *d* ....2 Tim 2:26
the works of the *d*........... 1 John 3:8

DEVIOUS
And who are *d*...................Prov 2:15

DEVISES
d wickedness on his..............Ps 36:4
But a generous man *d*..........Is 32:8

DEVOID
who is *d* of wisdom........ Prov 11:12

DEVOUR
For you *d* widows'..........Matt 23:14
bite and *d* one another ......Gal 5:15
whom he may *d*.................1 Pet 5:8
d her Child as ....Rev 12:4

DEVOURED
wild beast has *d*...............Gen 37:20
birds came and *d* them....Matt 13:4
of heaven and *d* them......Rev 20:9

DEVOUT
man was just and *d*.........Luke 2:25
d soldier from among.......Acts 10:7

DIAMOND
d it is engraved .... Jer 17:1

DIE
it you shall surely *d* ....Gen 2:17
but a person shall *d* ....2 Chr 25:4
I shall not *d* ....Ps 118:17
born, And a time to *d* .... Eccl 3:2
eat of it and not *d*...........John 6:50
to you that you will *d* ......John 8:24
though he may *d* ....John 11:25
one man should *d*...........John 11:50
the flesh you will *d*........... Rom 8:13
For as in Adam all *d* ..... 1 Cor 15:22

and to *d* is gain ....Phil 1:21
for men to *d* once ....Heb 9:27
are the dead who *d* ....Rev 14:13

DIED
And all flesh *d* ....Gen 7:21
in due time Christ *d* ....Rom 5:6
Christ *d* for us.....................Rom 5:8
Now if we *d* with.................Rom 6:8
and He *d* for all....................2 Cor 5:15
for if we *d* with Him ....2 Tim 2:11

DILIGENCE
d it produced in you........2 Cor 7:11

DILIGENT
d makes rich ....Prov 10:4

DILIGENTLY
d lest anyone fall.............Heb 12:15

DIMLY
we see in a mirror, *d*..... 1 Cor 13:12

DINE
come in to him and *d*.........Rev 3:20

DINNER
invites you to *d*............. 1 Cor 10:27

DIRECT
Now may the Lord *d* .... 2 Thess 3:5

DISARMED
d principalities....................Col 2:15

DISASTER
will end with *d*.................Acts 27:10

DISCERN
d the face of the sky ....Matt 16:3
senses exercised to *d*.........Heb 5:14

DISCERNED
they are spiritually *d* ...... 1 Cor 2:14

DISCERNER
d of the thoughts ....Heb 4:12

DISCERNS
a wise man's heart *d*........... Eccl 8:5

DISCIPLE(S)
he cannot be My *d* ....Luke 14:26
d whom Jesus loved ......John 21:7
word, you are My *d* ....John 8:31
but we are Moses' *d* ....John 9:28

DISCIPLINES
he who loves him *d*........ Prov 13:24

DISCORD
And one who sows *d* ....Prov 6:19

DISCOURAGED
lest they became *d* ....Col 3:21
become weary and *d* ....Heb 12:3

DISCRETION
d will preserve you ....Prov 2:11

DISHONOR
Father, and you *d* Me .....John 8:49
d their bodies among....... Rom 1:24
It is sown in *d* .... 1 Cor 15:43

DISHONORED
But you have *d* the...........James 2:6

DISHONORS
For son *d* father................... Mic 7:6

DISOBEDIENT
out My hands To a *d*...... Rom 10:21

DISORDERLY
for this *d* gathering.........Acts 19:40

DISPERSION
the pilgrims of the *D*.......... 1 Pet 1:1

DISPLEASE(D)
LORD see it, and it *d*...... Prov 24:18
they were greatly *d*........Matt 20:24
it, He was greatly *d*........ Mark 10:14

DISPUTES
But avoid foolish *d*............ Titus 3:9

DISQUALIFIED
should become *d* .... 1 Cor 9:27

DISSENSION
had no small *d* and ....Acts 15:2

DISSOLVED
the heavens will be *d*.......2 Pet 3:12

DISTRESS
d them in His deep.................Ps 2:5
tribulation, or *d*................. Rom 8:35

DISTRESSED
and deeply *d*................... Mark 14:33

DISTRESSES
Bring me out of my *d* ....Ps 25:17

DISTRIBUTED
and they *d* to each as........Acts 4:35

DISTRIBUTING
d to the needs of the ...... Rom 12:13

DIVERSITIES
There are *d*....................... 1 Cor 12:4

DIVIDE
d the spoil with the .... Prov 16:19
"Take this and *d* ....Luke 22:17

DIVIDED
and the waters were *d*......Ex 14:21
they were not *d*...............2 Sam 1:23
"Every kingdom *d* ....Matt 12:25
Is Christ *d* .... 1 Cor 1:13

DIVIDES
at home *d* the spoil ....Ps 68:12

DIVIDING
rightly *d* the word of.......2 Tim 2:15

DIVINATION
shall you practice *d*......... Lev 19:26
a spirit of *d* met us ....Acts 16:16

DIVINE
d service and the ....Heb 9:1

DIVISION(S)
So there was a *d*..............John 7:43
those who cause *d*.......... Rom 16:17
persons, who cause *d* ....Jude 19

DIVISIVE
Reject a *d* man after ....Titus 3:10

DIVORCE
her a certificate of *d*......... Deut 24:1
a certificate of *d*............... Mark 10:4

DO
men to *d* to you, *d* ....Matt 7:12
He sees the Father *d* ....John 5:19
without Me you can *d*...... John 15:5
"Sirs, what must I *d* ....Acts 16:30
d evil that good may...........Rom 3:8
or whatever you *d*, *d*.... 1 Cor 10:31

DOCTRINE
What new *d* is this .... Mark 1:27
"My *d* is not Mine.............John 7:16
with every wind of *d*.........Eph 4:14
is contrary to sound *d* ...1 Tim 1:10
is profitable for *d*.............2 Tim 3:16
not endure sound *d*..........2 Tim 4:3

DOCTRINES
commandments and *d*.......Col 2:22
various and strange *d*........Heb 13:9

DOERS
But be *d* of the word......James 1:22

DOG
d is better than a .... Eccl 9:4
d returns to his own.........2 Pet 2:22

DOGS
what is holy to the *d*..........Matt 7:6
d eat the crumbs..............Matt 15:27
But outside are *d* ....Rev 22:15

DOMINION
let them have *d*..................Gen 1:26
d is an everlasting............. Dan 4:34
sin shall not have *d*......... Rom 6:14
glory and majesty, *D* ....Jude 25

DONKEY
d its master's crib .... Is 1:3
and riding on a *d* .... Zech 9:9
colt, the foal of a *d* .... Matt 21:5
d speaking with a .... 2 Pet 2:16

DOOM
for the day of *d* .... Prov 16:4

DOOR
stone against the *d* .... Matt 27:60
to you, I am the *d* .... John 10:7
before you an open *d* .... Rev 3:8
I stand at the *d* .... Rev 3:20

DOORPOSTS
write them on the *d* .... Deut 6:9

DOUBLE
from the LORD's hand *D* .... Is 40:2
worthy of *d* honor .... 1 Tim 5:17

DOUBLE-MINDED
he is a *d* man .... James 1:8

DOUBT
faith, why did you *d* .... Matt 14:31

DOUBTING
in faith, with no *d* .... James 1:6

DOUBTS
why do *d* arise in .... Luke 24:38
for I have *d* about you .... Gal 4:20

DOVE
d found no resting .... Gen 8:9
descending like a *d* .... Matt 3:16

DOVES
and harmless as *d* .... Matt 10:16

DOWNCAST
who comforts the *d* .... 2 Cor 7:6

DRAGON
they worshiped the *d* .... Rev 13:4
He laid hold of the *d* .... Rev 20:2

DRAW
d honey from the .... Deut 32:13
me to *d* near to God .... Ps 73:28
And the years *d* .... Eccl 12:1
will *d* all peoples .... John 12:32
D near to God and He ..... James 4:8

DREAM
Now Joseph had a *d* .... Gen 37:5
Your old men shall *d* .... Joel 2:28
to Joseph in a *d* .... Matt 2:13
things today in a *d* .... Matt 27:19

DREAMERS
d defile the flesh .... Jude 8

DREAMS
Nebuchadnezzar had *d* ...... Dan 2:1

DRIED
of her blood was *d* .... Mark 5:29
saw the fig tree *d* .... Mark 11:20

DRINK
gave me vinegar to *d* .... Ps 69:21
Lest they *d* and forget ...... Prov 31:5
follow intoxicating *d* .... Is 5:11
d the milk of the .... Is 60:16
bosom, That you may *d* ..... Is 66:11
"Bring wine, let us *d* .... Amos 4:1
that day when I *d* .... Matt 26:29
mingled with gall to *d* .... Matt 27:34
with myrrh to *d* .... Mark 15:23
to her, "Give Me a *d* .... John 4:7
him come to Me and *d* ... John 7:37
do, as often as you *d* ... 1 Cor 11:25
No longer *d* only .... 1 Tim 5:23

DRINKS
to her, "Whoever *d* ...... John 4:13
d My blood has .... John 6:54
he who eats and *d* .... 1 Cor 11:29

DROSS
purge away your *d* .... Is 1:25

DROUGHT
in the year of *d* .... Jer 17:8
"For I called for a *d* .... Hag 1:11

DROVE
So He *d* out the man .... Gen 3:24
temple of God and *d* .... Matt 21:12

DROWN
Nor can the floods *d* .... Song 8:7
harmful lusts which *d* .... 1 Tim 6:9

DRUNK
of the wine and was *d* ...... Gen 9:21
the guests have well *d* ..... John 2:10
"For these are not *d* .... Acts 2:15
and another is *d* .... 1 Cor 11:21
I saw the woman, *d* ...... Rev 17:6

DRUNKARD
to and fro like a *d* .... Is 24:20
or a reviler, or a *d* .... 1 Cor 5:11

DRUNKENNESS
will be filled with *d* .... Ezek 23:33
not in revelry and *d* .... Rom 13:13
envy, murders, *d* .... Gal 5:21

DRY
place, and let the *d* .... Gen 1:9
made the sea into *d* .... Ex 14:21
It was *d* on the fleece .... Judg 6:40
will be done in the *d* .... Luke 23:31

DUE
pay all that was *d* .... Matt 18:34
d time Christ died .... Rom 5:6
d season we shall .... Gal 6:9
exalt you in *d* time .... 1 Pet 5:6

DULL
heart of this people *d* .... Is 6:10
people have grown *d* ...... Matt 13:15

DUMB
the tongue of the *d* .... Is 35:6

DUST
formed man of the *d* .... Gen 2:7
d you shall return .... Gen 3:19
And repent in *d* .... Job 42:6
that we are *d* .... Ps 103:14
counted as the small *d* .... Is 40:15
city, shake off the *d* .... Matt 10:14
of the man of *d* .... 1 Cor 15:49

DUTY
done what was our *d* ..... Luke 17:10

DWELL
Who may *d* in Your holy .... Ps 15:1
"I *d* in the high and .... Is 57:15
"I will *d* in them .... 2 Cor 6:16
that Christ may *d* .... Eph 3:17
men, and He will *d* .... Rev 21:3

DWELLING
built together for a *d* .... Eph 2:22
a foreign country, *d* .... Heb 11:9

DWELLS
He who *d* in the secret .... Ps 91:1
but the Father who *d* ..... John 14:10
d all the fullness .... Col 2:9
which righteousness *d* .... 2 Pet 3:13
you, where Satan *d* .... Rev 2:13

DWELT
became flesh and *d* .... John 1:14
By faith he *d* in the .... Heb 11:9

DYING
in the body the *d* .... 2 Cor 4:10

E

EAGLE
fly away like an *e* .... Prov 23:5
The way of an *e* .... Prov 30:19
like a flying *e* .... Rev 4:7

EAGLES
up with wings like *e* .... Is 40:31
e will be gathered .... Matt 24:28

EAR
shall pierce his *e* .... Ex 21:6
And the *e* of the wise ...... Prov 18:15
e is uncircumcised .... Jer 6:10
you hear in the *e* .... Matt 10:27
cut off his right *e* .... John 18:10

not seen, nor *e* heard .... 1 Cor 2:9
"He who has an *e* .... Rev 2:7

EARLY
Very *e* in the morning .... Mark 16:2
arrived at the tomb *e* .... Luke 24:22

EARNESTLY
He prayed more *e* .... Luke 22:44
e that it would not .... James 5:17
you to contend *e* .... Jude 3

EARS
And hear with their *e* .... Is 6:10
"He who has *e* .... Matt 11:15
they have itching *e* .... 2 Tim 4:3

EARTH
to judge the *e* .... 1 Chr 16:33
foundations of the *e* .... Job 38:4
e is the LORD's .... Ps 24:1
You had formed the *e* .... Ps 90:2
there was ever an *e* .... Prov 8:23
e abides forever .... Eccl 1:4
for the meek of the *e* .... Is 11:4
e is My footstool .... Is 66:1
I will darken the *e* .... Amos 8:9
shall inherit the *e* .... Matt 5:5
heaven and *e* pass .... Matt 5:18
e as it is in heaven .... Matt 6:10
treasures on *e* .... Matt 6:19
then shook the *e* .... Heb 12:26
heaven and a new *e* .... Rev 21:1

EARTHLY
"If I have told you *e* .... John 3:12
that if our *e* house .... 2 Cor 5:1
their mind on *e* things .... Phil 3:19
from above, but is *e* ...... James 3:15

EARTHQUAKE(S)
after the wind an *e* .... 1 Kin 19:11
there was a great *e* .... Matt 28:2
And there will be *e* .... Mark 13:8

EASIER
"Which is *e*, to say .... Mark 2:9
"It is *e* for a camel .... Mark 10:25

EAST
goes toward the *e* .... Gen 2:14
wise men from the *E* .... Matt 2:1
many will come from *e* .... Matt 8:11
will come from the *e* ...... Luke 13:29

EAT
you may freely *e* .... Gen 2:16
'You shall not *e* .... Gen 3:17
e this scroll .... Ezek 3:1
life, what you will *e* .... Matt 6:25
give us His flesh to *e* ..... John 6:52
one believes he may *e* .... Rom 14:2
e meat nor drink wine .... Rom 14:21
I will never again *e* .... 1 Cor 8:13
neither shall he *e* .... 2 Thess 3:10

EATEN
Have you *e* from the .... Gen 3:11
he was *e* by worms .... Acts 12:23

EATS
receives sinners and *e* .... Luke 15:2
"Whoever *e* My flesh ...... John 6:54
e this bread will live .... John 6:58
He who *e*, *e* to the .... Rom 14:6
unworthy manner *e* ...... 1 Cor 11:29

EDIFICATION
has given me for *e* .... 2 Cor 13:10
rather than godly *e* .... 1 Tim 1:4

EDIFIES
puffs up, but love *e* .... 1 Cor 8:1

EDIFY
but not all things *e* .... 1 Cor 10:23

EDIFYING
of the body for the *e* .... Eph 4:16

ELDERS
the tradition of the *e* .... Matt 15:2
be rejected by the *e* ...... Luke 9:22
they had appointed *e* ..... Acts 14:23
e who rule well be .... 1 Tim 5:17
lacking, and appoint *e* ...... Titus 1:5
e obtained a good .... Heb 11:2

e who are among you I ..... 1 Pet 5:1
I saw twenty-four *e* .... Rev 4:4

ELDERSHIP
of the hands of the *e* .... 1 Tim 4:14

ELECT
gather together His .....Matt 24:31
e have obtained it............. Rom 11:7
e according to the .... 1 Pet 1:2
A chief cornerstone, *e* .... 1 Pet 2:6

ELECTION
call and *e* sure.................. 2 Pet 1:10

ELEMENTS
weak and beggarly *e* ....Gal 4:9
e will melt with................. 2 Pet 3:10

ELOQUENT
an *e* man and mighty ..... Acts 18:24

EMBALM
to *e* his father.....................Gen 50:2

ENCOURAGED
is, that I may be *e*............ Rom 1:12
and all may be *e*........... 1 Cor 14:31

END
make me to know my *e*........Ps 39:4
shall keep it to the *e* ....Ps 119:33
e is the way of death...... Prov 14:12
Declaring the *e* ....Is 46:10
what shall be the *e* .... Dan 12:8
the harvest is the *e*.........Matt 13:39
always, even to the *e* .....Matt 28:20
He loved them to the .... John 13:1
For Christ is the *e*............. Rom 10:4
But the *e* of all .... 1 Pet 4:7
the latter *e* is worse .... 2 Pet 2:20
My works until the *e* ....Rev 2:26
Beginning and the *E*........Rev 22:13

ENDLESS
and *e* genealogies.............1 Tim 1:4
to the power of an *e*...........Heb 7:16

ENDURANCE
e the race that ....Heb 12:1

ENDURE
as the sun and moon *e*........Ps 72:5
His name shall *e*.................Ps 72:17
persecuted, we *e*.............. 1 Cor 4:12

ENDURED
he had patiently *e* ....Heb 6:15
e as seeing Him who ....Heb 11:27
consider Him who *e*...........Heb 12:3

ENDURES
And His truth *e*..................Ps 100:5
For His mercy *e* ....Ps 136:1
But he who *e* to the........Matt 10:22
e only for a while ....Matt 13:21
for the food which *e* ....John 6:27
he has built on it *e* .... 1 Cor 3:14
hopes all things, *e* .... 1 Cor 13:7
word of the LORD *e* .... 1 Pet 1:25

ENEMIES
the presence of my *e* ....Ps 23:5
e will lick the dust.............Ps 72:9
to you, love your *e* ....Matt 5:44
e will be those.................Matt 10:36
e we were reconciled....... Rom 5:10
till He has put all *e* .... 1 Cor 15:25
were alienated and *e* ....Col 1:21
His *e* are made His..........Heb 10:13

ENEMY
If your *e* is hungry .... Prov 25:21
rejoice over me, my *e* .... Mic 7:8
and hate your *e*.................Matt 5:43
last *e* that will be .... 1 Cor 15:26
become your *e* because.......Gal 4:16
count him as an *e* .... 2 Thess 3:15
makes himself an *e* ....James 4:4

ENJOY
richly all things to *e*.......1 Tim 6:17
than to *e* the passing ......Heb 11:25

ENLIGHTEN
E my eyes ....Ps 13:3

ENLIGHTENED
those who were once *e*........Heb 6:4

ENMITY
And I will put *e*..................Gen 3:15
the carnal mind is *e* ....Rom 8:7
in His flesh the *e* ....Eph 2:15

ENSNARES
sin which so easily *e*..........Heb 12:1

ENTER
E into His gates ....Ps 100:4
you will by no means *e* ....Matt 5:20
"*E* by the narrow...............Matt 7:13
e the kingdom of God....Matt 19:24
E into the joy of your......Matt 25:21
and pray, lest you *e* ....Matt 26:41
"Strive to *e* through ....Luke 13:24
who have believed do *e*......Heb 4:3
e the temple till the ....Rev 15:8

ENTERED
Then Satan *e* Judas ....Luke 22:3
through one man sin *e* .... Rom 5:12
ear heard, Nor have *e*...... 1 Cor 2:9
the forerunner has *e* ....Heb 6:20
e the Most Holy Place ......Heb 9:12

ENTERS
If anyone *e* by Me .... John 10:9

ENVY
e slays a simple ....Job 5:2
e is rottenness................ Prov 14:30
not let your heart *e* .... Prov 23:17
full of *e* .... Rom 1:29
not in strife and *e* .... Rom 13:13
love does not *e* .... 1 Cor 13:4
e, murders ....Gal 5:21
living in malice and *e* ....Titus 3:3

EPISTLE
You are our *e* written .... 2 Cor 3:2

ERROR(S)
a sinner from the *e*........James 5:20
led away with the *e*....... 2 Pet 3:17
run greedily in the *e* ....Jude 11
can understand his *e* ....Ps 19:12

ESCAPE
e all these things ....Luke 21:36
same, that you will *e*.......Rom 2:3
make the way of *e*......... 1 Cor 10:13
how shall we *e* if we ....Heb 2:3

ESTABLISH
seeking to *e* their own..... Rom 10:3
faithful, who will *e* .... 2 Thess 3:3
E your hearts ....James 5:8
a while, perfect, *e*............ 1 Pet 5:10

ESTABLISHED
Your throne is *e*.................Ps 93:2
built up in Him and *e*..........Col 2:7
covenant, which was *e*.......Heb 8:6

ESTEEM
and we did not *e*...................Is 53:3
e others better than............. Phil 2:3

ESTEEMED
For what is highly *e* ......Luke 16:15

ETERNAL
e God is your refuge ...... Deut 33:27
For man goes to his *e* .... Eccl 12:5
and inherit *e* life.............Matt 19:29
in the age to come, *e*....Mark 10:30
not perish but have *e* ....John 3:15
you think you have *e* ....John 5:39
I give them *e* life............John 10:28
"And this is *e* life..............John 17:3
the gift of God is *e*...........Rom 6:23
are not seen are *e* .... 2 Cor 4:18
lay hold on *e* life............1 Tim 6:12
e life which was.............. 1 John 1:2

ETERNITY
Also He has put *e* .... Eccl 3:11
One who inhabits *e* ....Is 57:15

EUNUCH(S)
of Ethiopia, a *e* ....Acts 8:27
made themselves *e* ....Matt 19:12

EVANGELIST(S)
of Philip the *e*....................Acts 21:8
do the work of an *e*..........2 Tim 4:5
some prophets, some *e*......Eph 4:11

EVERLASTING
from *E* is Your name..........Is 63:16
awake, Some to *e* life .... Dan 12:2
not perish but have *e*...... John 3:16
who sent Me has *e* .... John 5:24
endures to *e* life................ John 6:27
in Him may have *e*........... John 6:40
believes in Me has *e* .... John 6:47
e destruction from........ 2 Thess 1:9

EVIDENCE
e of things not seen...........Heb 11:1

EVIL
of good and *e* ....Gen 2:9
knowing good and *e*...........Gen 3:5
his heart was only *e*............Gen 6:5
I will fear no *e*.....................Ps 23:4
e more than good................Ps 52:3
To do *e* is like sport .... Prov 10:23
e will bow before the...... Prov 14:19
Keeping watch on the *e* ...Prov 15:3
e All the days of her ...... Prov 31:12
to those who call *e*...............Is 5:20
of peace and not of *e* .... Jer 29:11
Seek good and not *e*........Amos 5:14
deliver us from the *e*........Matt 6:13
"If you then, being *e* ....Matt 7:11
e treasure brings ....Matt 12:35
everyone practicing *e* ...... John 3:20
done any good or *e* .... Rom 9:11
Repay no one *e* for......... Rom 12:17
provoked, thinks no *e* ..... 1 Cor 13:5

EVILDOER
"If He were not an *e*....... John 18:30
suffer trouble as an *e*........2 Tim 2:9

EVILDOERS
e shall be cut off...................Ps 37:9
from me, you *e*...............Ps 119:115
iniquity, A brood of *e*............Is 1:4
against you as *e*............... 1 Pet 2:12

EXALT
e His name together ....Ps 34:3
E the humble...................Ezek 21:26
And he shall *e* himself ..... Dan 8:25

EXALTATION
who rejoice in My *e* ....Is 13:3
brother glory in his *e*.......James 1:9

EXALTED
Let God be *e*................2 Sam 22:47
I will be *e* among the...........Ps 46:10
You are far above ....Ps 97:9
His name alone is *e*.........Ps 148:13
valley shall be *e* ....Is 40:4
"Him God has *e* ....Acts 5:31
And lest I should be *e*..... 2 Cor 12:7
also his highly *e* ....Phil 2:9

EXALTS
Righteousness *e*....... Prov 14:34
high thing that *e*........ 2 Cor 10:5
e himself above all .... 2 Thess 2:4

EXAMINE
But let a man *e* .... 1 Cor 11:28
But let each one *e*................Gal 6:4

EXAMPLE
to make her a public *e*......Matt 1:19
I have given you an *e* ....John 13:15
youth, but be an *e* .... 1 Tim 4:12
us, leaving us an *e*........... 1 Pet 2:21
are set forth as an *e*...........Jude 7

EXAMPLES
to them as *e*.................. 1 Cor 10:11
to you, but being *e* .... 1 Pet 5:3

EXCHANGED
Nor can it be *e* ....Job 28:17
e the truth of God for ...... Rom 1:25

EXCUSE(S)
now they have no *e*........ John 15:22
they are without *e* .... Rom 1:20
began to make *e*.............Luke 14:18

EXECUTE(S)
e judgment also .... John 5:27
e wrath on him who .... Rom 13:4
e justice for me .... Mic 7:9

EXHORT
e him as a father .... 1 Tim 5:1
Speak these things, *e* ...... Titus 2:15
e one another .... Heb 3:13

EXHORTATION
he who exhorts, in *e* .... Rom 12:8
to reading, to *e* .... 1 Tim 4:13

EXPECTATION
the people were in *e* .... Luke 3:15
a certain fearful *e* .... Heb 10:27

EXPLAIN
no one who could *e* .... Gen 41:24
"*E* this parable to us ...... Matt 15:15
to say, and hard to *e* .... Heb 5:11

EXTORTION
they are full of *e* .... Matt 23:25

EXTORTIONERS
e will inherit .... 1 Cor 6:10

EYE
the ear, But now my *e* .... Job 42:5
guide you with My *e* .... Ps 32:8
e is not satisfied .... Eccl 1:8
the apple of His *e* .... Zech 2:8
if your right *e* .... Matt 5:29
it was said, 'An *e* .... Matt 5:38
plank in your own *e* .... Matt 7:3
e causes you to sin .... Matt 18:9
Or is your *e* evil .... Matt 20:15
the *e* of a needle .... Luke 18:25
the twinkling of an *e* ...... 1 Cor 15:52
every *e* will see Him .... Rev 1:7
your eyes with *e* salve .... Rev 3:18

EYES
e will be opened .... Gen 3:5
And my *e* shall behold ..... Job 19:27
e are ever toward the .... Ps 25:15
The *e* of the Lord are .... Ps 34:15
I will lift up my *e* .... Ps 121:1
but the *e* of a fool .... Prov 17:24
be wise in his own *e* ...... Prov 26:5
You have dove's *e* .... Song 1:15
e have seen the King .... Is 6:5
Who have *e* and see .... Jer 5:21
rims were full of *e* .... Ezek 1:18
You are of purer *e* .... Hab 1:13
blessed are your *e* .... Matt 13:16
"He put clay on my *e* .... John 9:15
e they have closed .... Acts 28:27
E that they should not ..... Rom 11:8
have seen with our *e* ..... 1 John 1:1
the lust of the *e* .... 1 John 2:16
as snow, and His *e* .... Rev 1:14
creatures full of *e* .... Rev 4:6
horns and seven *e* .... Rev 5:6

EYESERVICE
not with *e* .... Eph 6:6

EYEWITNESSES
the beginning were *e* .... Luke 1:2
e of His majesty .... 2 Pet 1:16

F

FABLES
nor give heed to *f* .... 1 Tim 1:4
cunningly devised *f* .... 2 Pet 1:16

FACE
"For I have seen God *f* .... Gen 32:30
f shone while he .... Ex 34:29
sins have hidden His *f* ...... Is 59:2
f shone like the sun .... Matt 17:2
dimly, but then *f* .... 1 Cor 13:12
with unveiled *f* .... 2 Cor 3:18
withstood him to his *f* ...... Gal 2:11
They shall see His *f* .... Rev 22:4

FAIL
tittle of the law to *f* .... Luke 16:17
faith should not *f* .... Luke 22:32
they will *f* .... 1 Cor 13:8
Your years will not *f* .... Heb 1:12

FAILS
Love never *f* .... 1 Cor 13:8

FAINTS
My soul *f* for Your .... Ps 119:81
And the whole heart *f* .... Is 1:5
the earth, Neither *f* .... Is 40:28

FAITH
shall live by his *f* .... Hab 2:4
you, O you of little *f* .... Matt 6:30
not found such great *f* ..... Matt 8:10
that you have no *f* .... Mark 4:40
"Increase our *f* .... Luke 17:5
will He really find *f* .... Luke 18:8
are sanctified by *f* .... Acts 26:18
God is revealed from *f* ..... Rom 1:17
f apart from the deeds ..... Rom 3:28
his *f* is accounted for .... Rom 4:5
those who are of the *f* ..... Rom 4:16
f which we preach .... Rom 10:8
f comes by hearing .... Rom 10:17
and you stand by *f* .... Rom 11:20
in proportion to our *f* ..... Rom 12:6
Do you have *f* .... Rom 14:22
though I have all *f* .... 1 Cor 13:2
And now abide *f* .... 1 Cor 13:13
For we walk by *f* .... 2 Cor 5:7
the flesh I live by *f* .... Gal 2:20
f are sons of Abraham .... Gal 3:7
But after *f* has come .... Gal 3:25
of the household of *f* .... Gal 6:10
been saved through *f* .... Eph 2:8
one Lord, one *f* .... Eph 4:5
taking the shield of *f* .... Eph 6:16
your work of *f* .... 1 Thess 1:3
for not all have *f* .... 2 Thess 3:2
the mystery of the *f* .... 1 Tim 3:9
I have kept the *f* .... 2 Tim 4:7
in our common *f* .... Titus 1:4
not being mixed with *f* .... Heb 4:2
f is the substance .... Heb 11:1
without *f* it is .... Heb 11:6
says he has *f* .... James 2:14
Show me your *f* .... James 2:18
and not by *f* only .... James 2:24
f will save the sick .... James 5:15
add to your *f* virtue .... 2 Pet 1:5
the patience and the *f* ..... Rev 13:10

FAITHFUL
God, He is God, the *f* .... Deut 7:9
Lord preserves the *f* .... Ps 31:23
eyes shall be on the *f* ...... Ps 101:6
But who can find a *f* .... Prov 20:6
the Holy One who is *f* ..... Hos 11:12
"Who then is a *f* .... Matt 24:45
good and *f* servant .... Matt 25:23
"He who is *f* in what .... Luke 16:10
Judged me to be *f* .... Acts 16:15
God is *f* .... 1 Cor 1:9
is my beloved and *f* .... 1 Cor 4:17
But as God is *f* .... 2 Cor 1:18
f brethren in Christ .... Col 1:2
who calls you is *f* .... 1 Thess 5:24
This is a *f* saying and ..... 1 Tim 1:15
f High Priest in .... Heb 2:17
He who promised is *f* .... Heb 10:23
He is *f* and just to .... 1 John 1:9
Be *f* until death .... Rev 2:10
words are true and *f* .... Rev 21:5

FAITHFULNESS
I have declared Your *f* ...... Ps 40:10
Your *f* also surrounds .... Ps 89:8
f endures to all .... Ps 119:90
Great is Your *f* .... Lam 3:23
unbelief make the *f* .... Rom 3:3

FAITHLESS
"O *f* generation .... Mark 9:19
If we are *f* .... 2 Tim 2:13

FALL
a deep sleep to *f* .... Gen 2:21
Let them *f* by their .... Ps 5:10
righteous man may *f* ...... Prov 24:16
But the wicked shall *f* ..... Prov 24:16
the blind, both will *f* .... Matt 15:14
the stars will *f* .... Matt 24:29
"I saw Satan .... Luke 10:18
take heed lest he *f* .... 1 Cor 10:12
if they *f* away .... Heb 6:6

lest anyone *f* short of ...... Heb 12:15
and rocks, "*F* on us .... Rev 6:16

FALSE
"You shall not bear *f* .... Ex 20:16
I hate every *f* way .... Ps 119:104
f witness shall perish ..... Prov 21:28
"Beware of *f* prophets .... Matt 7:15
f christs and *f* .... Matt 24:24
and we are found *f* .... 1 Cor 15:15
of *f* brethren .... Gal 2:4
f prophets have gone ...... 1 John 4:1
mouth of the *f* prophet .... Rev 16:13

FAMILIES
in you all the *f* .... Gen 12:3
the God of all the *f* .... Jer 31:1
in your seed all the *f* ...... Acts 3:25

FAMINES
And there will be *f* .... Matt 24:7

FAR
Your judgments are *f* .... Ps 10:5
Be not *f* from Me .... Ps 22:11
The Lord is *f* from .... Prov 15:29
their heart is *f* from .... Matt 15:8
going to a *f* country .... Mark 13:34
though He is not *f* .... Acts 17:27
you who once were *f* .... Eph 2:13

FARMER
The hard-working *f* .... 2 Tim 2:6
See how the *f* waits .... James 5:7

FAST
f as you do this day .... Is 58:4
f that I have chosen .... Is 58:5
"Moreover, when you *f* .... Matt 6:16
disciples do not *f* .... Matt 9:14
'I *f* twice a week .... Luke 18:12

FASTED
'When you *f* and .... Zech 7:5
And when He had *f* .... Matt 4:2

FASTING
by prayer and *f* .... Matt 17:21
give yourselves to *f* .... 1 Cor 7:5

FATHER
man shall leave his *f* .... Gen 2:24
and you shall be a *f* .... Gen 17:4
I was a *f* to the poor .... Job 29:16
A *f* of the fatherless .... Ps 68:5
f pities his children .... Ps 103:13
God, Everlasting *F* .... Is 9:6
You, O Lord, are our *F* ...... Is 63:16
time cry to Me, 'My *F* .... Jer 3:4
For I am a *F* to Israel .... Jer 31:9
"A son honors his *f* .... Mal 1:6
Have we not all one *F* .... Mal 2:10
Our *F* in heaven .... Matt 6:9
"He who loves *f* .... Matt 10:37
know the *F* .... Matt 11:27
'He who curses *f* .... Matt 15:4
for One is your *F* .... Matt 23:9
"*F* will be divided .... Luke 12:53
F loves the Son .... John 3:35
F raises the dead .... John 5:21
F judges no one .... John 5:22
He has seen the *F* .... John 6:46
F who sent Me bears .... John 8:18
we have one *F* .... John 8:41
of your *f* the devil .... John 8:44
"I and My *F* are one .... John 10:30
'I am going to the *F* .... John 14:28
came forth from the *F* .... John 16:28
that he might be the *f* ..... Rom 4:11
one God and *F* of all .... Eph 4:6
"I will be to Him a *F* .... Heb 1:5
down from the *F* .... James 1:17
if you call on the *F* .... 1 Pet 1:17
and testify that the *F* .... 1 John 4:14

FATHERLESS
the helper of the *f* .... Ps 10:14
He relieves the *f* .... Ps 146:9
do not defend the *f* .... Is 1:23
they may rob the *f* .... Is 10:2
You the *f* finds mercy .... Hos 14:3

FATHER'S
you in My *F* kingdom ..... Matt 26:29
I must be about My *F* ...... Luke 2:49

F house are many .... John 14:2
that a man has his *f* .... 1 Cor 5:1

FATHERS

the LORD God of our *f* .....Ezra 7:27
f trusted in You......................Ps 22:4
our ears, O God, our *f*........Ps 44:1
f ate the manna...................John 6:31
of whom are the *f*..............Rom 9:5
unaware that all our *f*..... 1 Cor 10:1

FAULT

I have found no *f*...........Luke 23:14
does He still find *f*........... Rom 9:19
of God without *f* ....Phil 2:15

FAULTLESS

covenant had been *f* ....Heb 8:7
to present you *f*....................Jude 24

FAULTS

"I remember my *f*..............Gen 41:9
me from secret *f* ....Ps 19:12

FAVOR

granted me life and *f* ....Job 10:12
His *f* is for life ....Ps 30:5
A good man obtains *f*.......Prov 12:2
and stature, and in *f*........Luke 2:52
God and having *f*..............Acts 2:47

FAVORED

"Rejoice, highly *f*.............Luke 1:28

FAVORITISM

not show personal *f*.......Luke 20:21
God shows personal *f*..........Gal 2:6

FEAR

live, for I *f* God.................Gen 42:18
to put the dread and *f*......Deut 2:25
said, "Does Job *f*................Job 1:9
Yes, you cast off *f*..............Job 15:4
The *f* of the LORD is ....Ps 19:9
of death, I will *f* ....Ps 23:4
Whom shall I *f* ....Ps 27:1
Oh, *f* the LORD ....Ps 34:9
There is no *f* of God............Ps 36:1
The *f* of the LORD is...........Ps 111:10
The *f* of man brings a ...... Prov 29:25
F God and keep His........ Eccl 12:13
Let Him be your *f*.................Is 8:13
"Be strong, do not *f* ....Is 35:4
who would not *f* .... Jer 10:7
f Him who is able ....Matt 10:28
"Do not *f* ....Luke 12:32
"Do you not even *f* ....Luke 23:40
And walking in the *f*....... Acts 9:31
given us a spirit of *f*........2 Tim 1:7
those who through *f*..........Heb 2:15
because of His godly *f*.......Heb 5:7
F God................................. 1 Pet 2:17
love casts out *f*............... 1 John 4:18

FEARED

He is also to be *f*............ 1 Chr 16:25
f God more than ....Neh 7:2
Yourself, are to be *f*............Ps 76:7
Then those who *f*...............Mal 3:16

FEARFULLY

f and wonderfully..............Ps 139:14

FEARS

upright man, one who *f*......Job 1:8
me from all my *f*................Ps 34:4
nation whoever *f* ....Acts 10:35
f has not been made ..... 1 John 4:18

FEAST

and you shall keep a *f* ... Num 29:12
hate, I despise your *f*......Amos 5:21
every year at the *F*..........Luke 2:41
when you give a *f*...........Luke 14:13
Now the Passover, a *f*....... John 6:4
great day of the *f*...........John 7:37

FEASTS

the best places at *f* ....Luke 20:46
spots in your love *f* ....Jude 12

FEEBLE

strengthened the *f* ....Job 4:4
And there was none *f* ....Ps 105:37
And my flesh is *f* ....Ps 109:24
hang down, and the *f*.......Heb 12:12

FEED

ravens to *f* you there....... 1 Kin 17:4
and *f* your flocks ....Is 61:5
to him, "*F* My lambs ......John 21:15
your enemy
  hungers, *f* .... Rom 12:20
goods to *f* the poor.......... 1 Cor 13:3

FEEDS

your heavenly Father *f*.....Matt 6:26

FEET

all things under his *f*...............Ps 8:6
He makes my *f* like the ......Ps 18:33
You have set my *f* ....Ps 31:8
For their *f* run to................Prov 1:16
Her *f* go down to death .....Prov 5:5
mountains Are the *f*.............Is 52:7
place of My *f* glorious..........Is 60:13
in that day His *f* ....Zech 14:4
two hands or two *f* ....Matt 18:8
began to wash His *f*.........Luke 7:38
wash the disciples' *f*.........John 13:5
f are swift to shed............. Rom 3:15
beautiful are the *f*............ Rom 10:15
things under His *f* .... 1 Cor 15:27
and having shod your *f*.....Eph 6:15
fell at His *f* as dead ....Rev 1:17

FELLOWSHIP

doctrine and *f*...................Acts 2:42
were called into the *f*....... 1 Cor 1:9
f has righteousness ....2 Cor 6:14
the right hand of *f* ....Gal 2:9
And have no *f* with the......Eph 5:11
of love, if any *f*......................Phil 2:1
and the *f* of His ....Phil 3:10
we say that we have *f*..... 1 John 1:6
the light, we have *f*.......... 1 John 1:7

FERVENT

f prayer of a....................James 5:16
will melt with *f*..................2 Pet 3:10

FEW

let your words be *f*............. Eccl 5:2
and there are *f*...................Matt 7:14
but the laborers are *f*........Matt 9:37
called, but *f* chosen ....Matt 20:16
"Lord, are there *f*............Luke 13:23

FIELD

Let the *f* be joyful ....Ps 96:12
"The *f* is the world............Matt 13:38
and buys that *f*................Matt 13:44
you are God's *f* .... 1 Cor 3:9

FIERY

LORD sent *f* serpents........ Num 21:6
shall make them as a *f* ....Ps 7:13
burning *f* furnace .... Dan 3:6
concerning the *f*................. 1 Pet 4:12

FIG

f leaves together ....Gen 3:7
"Look at the *f*..................Luke 21:29
'I saw you under the *f*......John 1:50

FIGHT

"The LORD will *f* ....Ex 14:14
Our God will *f* for us........Neh 4:20
My servants would *f*........John 18:36
to him, let us not *f* .... Acts 23:9
F the good *f* ....1 Tim 6:12
have fought the good *f*....2 Tim 4:7

FIGHTS

your God is He who *f* .....Josh 23:10
because my lord *f*.........1 Sam 25:28
f come from among.........James 4:1

FILL

f the earth and subdue ......Gen 1:28
"Do I not *f* heaven............ Jer 23:24
f this temple with ....Hag 2:7
"*F* the waterpots ....John 2:7
that He might *f*...................Eph 4:10

FILLED

the whole earth be *f*...........Ps 72:19
For they shall be *f* ....Matt 5:6
"Let the children be *f*.......Mark 7:27
would gladly have *f* ....Luke 15:16
being *f* with all.................. Rom 1:29

but be *f* with the ....Eph 5:18
be warmed and *f* ....James 12:16

FILTHY

with *f* garments .... Zech 3:3
poor man in *f* clothes......James 2:2
oppressed by the *f*.............2 Pet 2:7
let him be *f* ....Rev 22:11

FIND

sure your sin will *f*........ Num 32:23
waters, For you will *f* .... Eccl 11:1
seek, and you will *f*............Matt 7:7
f a Babe wrapped ....Luke 2:12
f no fault in this Man ......Luke 23:4
f grace to help in ....Heb 4:16

FINDS

f me *f* life.............................Prov 8:35
f a wife *f* a good............. Prov 18:22
and he who seeks *f* ....Matt 7:8
f his life will lose ....Matt 10:39
and he who seeks *f* ....Luke 11:10

FINGER

written with the *f*............... Ex 31:18
dip the tip of his *f*..........Luke 16:24
"Reach your *f*.................John 20:27

FINISHED

f the work which You...... John 17:4
He said, "It is *f* ....John 19:30
I have *f* the race................2 Tim 4:7

FIRE

rained brimstone and *f*....Gen 19:24
to him in a flame of *f* .... Ex 3:2
who answers by *f*.......... 1 Kin 18:24
LORD was not in the *f* ... 1 Kin 19:12
We went through *f*..........Ps 66:12
f goes before Him................Ps 97:3
burns as the *f* ....Is 9:18
you walk through the *f*.........Is 43:2
f that burns all the...............Is 65:5
He break out like *f*...........Amos 5:6
for conflict by *f*................Amos 7:4
like a refiner's *f* ....Mal 3:2
the Holy Spirit and *f*........Matt 3:11
f is not quenched ....Mark 9:44
"I came to send *f*............Luke 12:49
tongues, as of *f*.................. Acts 2:3
f taking vengeance........ 2 Thess 1:8
and that burned with *f* ....Heb 12:18
And the tongue is a *f* ....James 3:6
vengeance of eternal *f*..........Jude 7
into the lake of *f* ....Rev 20:14

FIRMAMENT

Thus God made the *f*..........Gen 1:7
f shows His handiwork ....Ps 19:1

FIRST

f father sinned.......................Is 43:27
desires to be *f*..................Matt 20:27
f shall be slave .... Mark 10:44
the gospel must *f* ....Mark 13:10
evil, of the Jew *f* ....Rom 2:9
f man Adam became .... 1 Cor 15:45
that we who *f* trusted.........Eph 1:12
Him because He *f*........... 1 John 4:19
I am the *F* and the ....Rev 1:17
you have left your *f*............Rev 2:4
is the *f* resurrection............Rev 20:5

FIRSTBORN

LORD struck all the *f*.......... Ex 12:29
brought forth her *f*............Matt 1:25
that He might be the *f*.... Rom 8:29
invisible God, the *f*............Col 1:15
the beginning, the *f*...........Col 1:18
witness, the *f* from ....Rev 1:5

FIRSTFRUITS

also who have the *f*........ Rom 8:23
and has become the *f*.... 1 Cor 15:20
Christ the *f*...................... 1 Cor 15:23

FISH

had prepared a great *f*........Jon 1:17
belly of the great *f*..........Matt 12:40
five loaves and two *f*.......Matt 14:17
and likewise the *f*..........John 21:13

FISHERS

and I will make you *f*........Matt 4:19

FIVE
f smooth stones............1 Sam 17:40
about *f* thousand men.....Matt 14:21
and *f* were foolish ....Matt 25:2

FLAME
appeared to him in a *f* .... Ex 3:2
tormented in this *f*.........Luke 16:24
and His ministers a *f*............Heb 1:7
and His eyes like a *f* .... Rev 1:14

FLATTERING
f speech deceive .... Rom 16:18
swelling words, *f* ....Jude 16

FLEE
Or where can I *f* ....Ps 139:7
And the shadows *f*..........Song 2:17
who are in Judea *f*..........Matt 24:16
F sexual immorality....... 1 Cor 6:18
f these things and...........1 Tim 6:11
devil and he will *f*............James 4:7

FLESH
bone of my bones And *f*....Gen 2:23
shall become one *f* ....Gen 2:24
f had corrupted their.........Gen 6:12
f I shall see God.................Job 19:26
My *f* also will rest in ....Ps 16:9
is wearisome to the *f* ..... Eccl 12:12
And all *f* shall see it ....Is 40:5
"All *f* is grass............................Is 40:6
out My Spirit on all *f*.........Joel 2:28
two shall become one *f* ....Matt 19:5
were shortened, no *f*.....Matt 24:22
shall become one *f* .... Mark 10:8
the Word became *f* .... John 1:14
I shall give is My *f*........... John 6:51
f profits nothing................John 6:63
of God, but with the *f* ..... Rom 7:25
on the things of the *f* ....Rom 8:5
to the *f* you will die .... Rom 8:13
f should glory in His ...... 1 Cor 1:29
"shall become one *f*........ 1 Cor 6:16
For the *f* lusts ....Gal 5:17
have crucified the *f*............Gal 5:24
may boast in your *f*............Gal 6:13
the lust of the *f*.............. 1 John 2:16
has come in the *f*............. 1 John 4:2

FLESHLY
f wisdom but by the .... 2 Cor 1:12
f lusts which ....1 Pet 2:11

FLOAT
and he made the iron *f*..... 2 Kin 6:6

FLOCK
lead Joseph like a *f*.............Ps 80:1
He will feed His *f*.................Is 40:11
you do not feed the *f*......Ezek 34:3
my God, "Feed the *f*........Zech 11:4
sheep of the *f*..................Matt 26:31
"Do not fear, little *f*.......Luke 12:32
there will be one *f* .... John 10:16
Shepherd the *f* of God .... 1 Pet 5:2
examples to the *f* .... 1 Pet 5:3

FLOOD
the waters of the *f*.............Gen 7:10
them away like a *f*..............Ps 90:5
the days before the *f*......Matt 24:38
bringing in the *f*................ 2 Pet 2:5
of his mouth like a *f*........Rev 12:15

FLOODS
me, And the *f* of..................Ps 18:4
f on the dry ground...........Is 44:3
rain descended, the *f*.......Matt 7:25

FLOWER
As a *f* of the field.............Ps 103:15
beauty is a fading *f* ....Is 28:4
grass withers, the *f*..............Is 40:7
of man as the *f* .... 1 Pet 1:24

FLOWING
'a land *f* with milk.............. Deut 6:3
the Gentiles like a *f*.............Is 66:12

FLUTE(S)
play the harp and *f*.............Gen 4:21
instruments and *f* ....Ps 150:4

FOLLOW
f You wherever You go....Matt 8:19
He said to him, "*F* ....Matt 9:9
up his cross, and *f* ....Mark 8:34
will by no means *f*............John 10:5
serves Me, let him *f* .... John 12:26
that you should *f* .... 1 Pet 2:21
f the Lamb wherever ....Rev 14:4
and their works *f*..............Rev 14:13

FOLLOWED
f the Lord my God ....Josh 14:8
we have left all and *f* .... Mark 10:28

FOLLY
taken much notice of *f*.....Job 35:15
not turn back to *f* ....Ps 85:8
F is joy to him who is.... Prov 15:21
F is set in great .... Eccl 10:6

FOOD
you it shall be for *f*............Gen 1:29
that lives shall be *f* ....Gen 9:3
f which you eat shall ......Ezek 4:10
the fields yield no *f* .... Hab 3:17
That there may be *f* .... Mal 3:10
to give them *f* ....Matt 24:45
and you gave Me *f* ....Matt 25:35
and he who has *f*..............Luke 3:11
have you any *f* ....John 21:5
they ate their *f* ....Acts 2:46
our hearts with *f*...............Acts 14:17
destroy with your *f* .... Rom 14:15
f makes my brother .... 1 Cor 8:13
the same spiritual *f* .... 1 Cor 10:3
sower, and bread for *f*.... 2 Cor 9:10
And having *f* and ....1 Tim 6:8
and not solid *f* ....Heb 5:12
But solid *f* belongs to........Heb 5:14
of *f* sold his ....Heb 12:16
destitute of daily *f* ....James 2:15

FOOL
f has said in his......................Ps 14:1
is like sport to a *f*........... Prov 10:23
f is right in his own....... Prov 12:15
is too lofty for a *f*...........Prov 24:7
whoever says, 'You *f*........Matt 5:22
I have become a *f* .... 2 Cor 12:11

FOOLISH
I was so *f* and.....................Ps 73:22
f pulls it down with..........Prov 14:1
f man squanders it .... Prov 21:20
Has not God made *f*........ 1 Cor 1:20
O *f* Galatians.............................Gal 3:1
were also once *f*..................Titus 3:3
But avoid *f* disputes ....Titus 3:9

FOOLISHNESS
F is bound up in the....... Prov 22:15
devising of *f* is sin ....Prov 24:9
of the cross is *f*................ 1 Cor 1:18
Because the *f* of God....... 1 Cor 1:25

FOOLS
f despise wisdom ....Prov 1:7
folly of *f* is deceit..............Prov 14:8
F mock at sin ....Prov 14:9
We are *f* for Christ's .... 1 Cor 4:10

FOOT
will not allow your *f* ....Ps 121:3
f will not stumble ....Prov 3:23
From the sole of the *f* ....Is 1:6
f causes you to sin...........Matt 18:8
you dash your *f*.................Luke 4:11
If the *f* should say.......... 1 Cor 12:15

FORBID
said, "Do not *f* .... Mark 9:39
"Can anyone *f*..................Acts 10:47
f that I should boast ....Gal 6:14

FOREHEADS
put a mark on the *f* ....Ezek 9:4
seal of God on their *f* .... Rev 9:4
his mark on their *f* ....Rev 20:4

FOREIGNER
"I am a *f* and a ....Gen 23:4
of me, since I am a *f*........ Ruth 2:10
to God except this *f*........Luke 17:18

FOREIGNERS
f who were there ....Acts 17:21
longer strangers and *f*......Eph 2:19

FOREKNEW
For whom He *f*.................. Rom 8:29
His people whom He *f*..... Rom 11:2

FOREKNOWLEDGE
purpose and *f* of God........Acts 2:23

FOREVER
and eat, and live *f*..............Gen 3:22
to our children *f*.............. Deut 29:29
Lord sits as King *f*............Ps 29:10
Do not cast us off *f*............Ps 44:23
throne, O God, is *f*..............Ps 45:6
"You are a priest *f*............Ps 110:4
His mercy endures *f*.........Ps 136:1
of our God stands *f*............Is 40:8
My salvation will be *f*...........Is 51:6
will not cast off *f*...............Lam 3:31
Like the stars *f*..................Dan 12:3
and the glory *f*....................Matt 6:13
the Christ remains *f*......John 12:34
who is blessed *f*............. 2 Cor 11:31
to whom be glory *f*.............Gal 1:5
generation, *f* and ever ....Eph 3:21
and Father be glory *f*........Phil 4:20
throne, O God, is *f*..............Heb 1:8
lives and abides *f*............. 1 Pet 1:23
of darkness *f*.........................Jude 13
power, Both now and *f*.......Jude 25
And they shall reign *f*......Rev 22:5

FOREVERMORE
Blessed be the Lord *f*......Ps 89:52
this time forth and *f*...........Ps 113:2
behold, I am alive *f*...........Rev 1:18

FORGAVE
to repay, he freely *f*.........Luke 7:42
God in Christ *f*...................Eph 4:32
even as Christ *f*...................Col 3:13

FORGET
f the Lord who .... Deut 6:12
I will not *f* Your word.......Ps 119:16
If I *f* you.............................Ps 137:5
My son, do not *f* ....Prov 3:1
f the Lord your Maker.......Is 51:13
f your work and labor ....Heb 6:10

FORGETTING
f those things which...........Phil 3:13

FORGIVE
f their sin and heal.........2 Chr 7:14
good, and ready to *f*.............Ps 86:5
And *f* us our debts............Matt 6:12
Father will also *f*..............Matt 6:14
his heart, does not *f* ....Matt 18:35
Who can *f* sins but
  God .... Mark 2:7
f the sins of any ....John 20:23
you ought rather to *f*........ 2 Cor 2:7
F me this wrong .... 2 Cor 12:13
f us our sins and to .... 1 John 1:9

FORGIVEN
sins be *f* them................... Mark 4:12
to whom little is *f*.............Luke 7:47
f you all trespasses..............Col 2:13
your sins are *f*................ 1 John 2:12

FORGIVENESS
But there is *f* with...............Ps 130:4
preached to you the *f*.....Acts 13:38
they may receive *f*...........Acts 26:18
His blood, the *f*....................Eph 1:7

FORGIVES
f all your iniquities.............Ps 103:3
is this who even *f* ....Luke 7:49

FORGIVING
tenderhearted, *f*..................Eph 4:32
and *f* one another................Col 3:13

FORGOTTEN
f the God who .... Deut 32:18
not one of them is *f*.........Luke 12:6
f the exhortation................Heb 12:5
f that he was.......................2 Pet 1:9

FORM

earth was without f ....Gen 1:2
Who would f a god or..........Is 44:10
f the light and create..............Is 45:7
descended in bodily f.......Luke 3:22
time, nor seen His f........John 5:37
For the f of this .... 1 Cor 7:31
who, being in the f..............Phil 2:6
having a f of ....2 Tim 3:5

FORMED

And the LORD God f ....Gen 2:7
f my inward parts................Ps 139:13
say of him who f....................Is 29:16
"Before I f you in ....Jer 1:5
Will the thing f.................. Rom 9:20
until Christ is f.....................Gal 4:19

FORNICATION

"We were not born of f.... John 8:41
of the wrath of her f...........Rev 14:8

FORNICATOR(S)

you know, that no f..............Eph 5:5
lest there be any f.............Heb 12:16
but f and adulterers ....Heb 13:4

FORSAKE

But I did not f.....................Ps 119:87
father, And do not f...........Prov 1:8
of you does not f............Luke 14:33
never leave you nor f...........Heb 13:5

FORSAKEN

My God, why have You f....Ps 22:1
seen the righteous f...........Ps 37:25
a mere moment I have f........Is 54:7
God, why have You f.....Matt 27:46
persecuted, but not f..........2 Cor 4:9
for Demas has f ....2 Tim 4:10

FORSAKING

f the assembling ....Heb 10:25

FORTRESS

is my rock, my f.............2 Sam 22:2
my rock of refuge, a f...........Ps 31:2

FOUND

f a helper comparable ....Gen 2:20
a thousand I have f ....Eccl 7:28
LORD while He may be f.......Is 55:6
fruit on it and f none.......Luke 13:6
he was lost and is f ....Luke 15:24
f the Messiah" (which...... John 1:41
and be f in Him....................Phil 3:9

FOUNDATION

Of old You laid the f........Ps 102:25
the earth without a f............Luke 6:49
loved Me before the f.....John 17:24
I have laid the f................ 1 Cor 3:10
f can anyone lay than..... 1 Cor 3:11
us in Him before the f.........Eph 1:4
not laying again the f............Heb 6:1
Lamb slain from the f........Rev 13:8

FOUNDATIONS

when I laid the f ....Job 38:4
And the f of the wall........Rev 21:19

FOUNTAIN(S)

will become in him a f.....John 4:14
on that day all the f...........Gen 7:11
lead them to living f............Rev 7:17

FRAGRANCE

was filled with the f........John 12:3
we are to God the f ....2 Cor 2:15

FREE

'You will be made f.........John 8:33
And having been set f ...... Rom 6:18
Jesus has made me f...........Rom 8:2
is neither slave nor f...........Gal 3:28
Christ has made us f,...   Gal 5:1
he is a slave or f ....Eph 6:8

FREELY

the garden you may f ....Gen 2:16
F you have received..........Matt 10:8
f give us all .... Rom 8:32
the water of life f..............Rev 22:17

FRIEND

of Abraham Your f ....2 Chr 20:7
f who sticks closer .... Prov 18:24

a f of tax collectors ....Matt 11:19
of you shall have a f ....Luke 11:5
f Lazarus sleeps..............John 11:11
he was called the f ....James 2:23
wants to be a f ....James 4:4

FRIENDS

My f scorn me....................Job 16:20
the rich has many f........ Prov 14:20
one's life for his f...........John 15:13
I have called you f..........John 15:15
to forbid any of his f......Acts 24:23

FROGS

your territory with f................ Ex 8:2
f coming out of the..........Rev 16:13

FRUIT

showed them the f..........Num 13:26
brings forth its f.....................Ps 1:3
f is better than gold..........Prov 8:19
with good by the f..........Prov 12:14
like the first f.......................Is 28:4
does not bear good f.........Matt 3:10
good tree bears good f......Matt 7:17
not drink of this f ....Matt 26:29
and blessed is the f...........Luke 1:42
life, and bring no f ....Luke 8:14
and he came seeking f.....Luke 13:6
'And if it bears f...............Luke 13:9
branch that bears f.............John 15:2
that you bear much f ....John 15:8
should go and bear f......John 15:16
God, you have your f ...... Rom 6:22
that we should bear f..........Rom 7:4
But the f of the....................Gal 5:22
yields the peaceable f.....Heb 12:11
Now the f of ....James 3:18
autumn trees without f........Jude 12
tree yielding its f................ Rev 22:2

FRUITFUL

them, saying, "Be f.............Gen 1:22
wife shall be like a f...........Ps 128:3
pleasing Him, being f ....Col 1:10

FRUITS

Therefore bear f ....Matt 3:8
know them by their f.......Matt 7:16
of mercy and good f......James 3:17
which bore twelve f ....Rev 22:2

FULFILL

for us to f all.......................Matt 3:15
f the law of Christ ....Gal 6:2
f my joy by being ....Phil 2:2
and f all the good .... 2 Thess 1:11
If you really f ....James 2:8

FULFILLED

the law till all is f...............Matt 5:18
of the Gentiles are f........Luke 21:24
all things must be f ....Luke 24:44
of the law might be f..........Rom 8:4
loves another has f........... Rom 13:8
For all the law is f ....Gal 5:14

FULLNESS

f we have all received.... John 1:16
But when the f of the............Gal 4:4
filled with all the f............Eph 3:19
Him dwells all the f..............Col 2:9

FURNACE

you out of the iron f............Deut 4:20
of a burning fiery f.............. Dan 3:6
cast them into the f.........Matt 13:42
the smoke of a great f...........Rev 9:2

G

GAIN

and to die is g ....Phil 1:21
rubbish, that I may g..........Phil 3:8
is a means of g....................1 Tim 6:5
contentment is great g.....1 Tim 6:6
for dishonest g..................... 1 Pet 5:2

GALL

They also gave me g...........Ps 69:21
wine mingled with g.......Matt 27:34

GARDEN

LORD God planted a g.........Gen 2:8
g enclosed Is my...........Song 4:12

Eden, the g of God ....Ezek 28:13
where there was a g ....John 18:1
g a new tomb in..............John 19:41

GARMENT

the hem of His g..............Matt 9:20
on a wedding g ....Matt 22:11
cloth on an old g ....Mark 2:21
all grow old like a g..........Heb 1:11
hating even the g..................Jude 23

GARMENTS

g did not wear out on .... Deut 8:4
They divide My g..................Ps 22:18
from Edom, With dyed g......Is 63:1
"Take away the filthy g....Zech 3:4
man clothed in soft g.........Matt 11:8
spread their g on the ....Matt 21:8
and divided His g...........Matt 27:35
by them in shining g........Luke 24:4
g are moth-eaten ....James 5:2
be clothed in white g ....Rev 3:5

GATE

by the narrow g ....Matt 7:13
by the Sheep G a pool......John 5:2
laid daily at the g ....Acts 3:2
suffered outside the g......Heb 13:12

GATES

up your heads, O you g........Ps 24:7
The LORD loves the g...........Ps 87:2
is known in the g............. Prov 31:23
Go through the g.................Is 62:10
and the g of Hades........Matt 16:18
wall with twelve g...........Rev 21:12
g were twelve pearls.........Rev 21:21
g shall not be shut...........Rev 21:25

GATHER(S)

And a time to g stones .... Eccl 3:5
g the lambs with His............Is 40:11
g His wheat into the ....Matt 3:12
sow nor reap nor g.........Matt 6:26
Do men g grapes from .....Matt 7:16
g where I have not ....Matt 25:26
g together His .... Mark 13:27
The Lord GOD, who g..........Is 56:8
together, as a hen g ....Matt 23:37

GAVE

to be with me, she g...........Gen 3:12
g You this authority........Matt 21:23
that He g His only...........John 3:16
Those whom You g..........John 17:12
but God g the increase ..... 1 Cor 3:6
g Himself for our sins.........Gal 1:4
g Himself for me ....Gal 2:20
g Himself for it ....Eph 5:25

GENERATION(S)

One g passes away .... Eccl 1:4
who will declare His g..........Is 53:8
and adulterous g.............Matt 12:39
this g will by no..............Matt 24:34
from this perverse g........Acts 2:40
But you are a chosen g..... 1 Pet 2:9
be remembered in all g......Ps 45:17
g will call me blessed......Luke 1:48

GENTILES

G were separated..............Gen 10:5
As a light to the G.................Is 42:6
G shall come to your.............Is 60:3
all these things the G......Matt 6:32
into the way of the G.......Matt 10:5
revelation to the G ....Luke 2:32
G are fulfilled..................Luke 21:24
My name before G.............Acts 9:15
poured out on the G.......Acts 10:45
a light to the G.................Acts 13:47
also the God of the G.... Rom 3:29
mystery among the G........Col 1:27
a teacher of the G..............1 Tim 2:7

GENTLE

from Me, for I am g ....Matt 11:29
we were g among............ 1 Thess 2:7
to be peaceable, g..............Titus 3:2
only to the good and g .... 1 Pet 2:18
ornament of a g .... 1 Pet 3:4

GENTLENESS

love and a spirit of g....... 1 Cor 4:21
g, self-control ....Gal 5:23

all lowliness and *g* ....Eph 4:2
Let your *g* be known to......Phil 4:5
love, patience, *g*..............1 Tim 6:11

GHOST
supposed it was a *g*........ Mark 6:49

GIFT
it is the *g* of God............... Eccl 3:13
"If you knew the *g*........... John 4:10
but the *g* of God is .... Rom 6:23
each one has his own *g*.... 1 Cor 7:7
though I have the *g*....... 1 Cor 13:2
it is the *g* of God..................Eph 2:8
Do not neglect the *g* ....1 Tim 4:14
you to stir up the *g*...........2 Tim 1:6
tasted the heavenly ....Heb 6:4
Every good *g* and..........James 1:17

GIFTS
You have received *g*.........Ps 68:18
and Seba Will offer *g* ....Ps 72:10
how to give good *g*...........Matt 7:11
rich putting their *g*...........Luke 21:1
g differing.......................... Rom 12:6
are diversities of *g*.......... 1 Cor 12:4
and desire spiritual *g*...... 1 Cor 14:1
captive, And gave *g*...........Eph 4:8

GIVE
g you the desires ....Ps 37:4
G me understanding.........Ps 119:34
"*G* to him who asks".........Matt 5:42
G us this day our...............Matt 6:11
authority *I* will *g*................Luke 4:6
g them eternal life..........John 10:28
commandment *I g*..........John 13:34
g us all things................... Rom 8:32
g him who has need ....Eph 4:28
g thanks to God.......... 2 Thess 2:13
g yourself entirely...........1 Tim 4:15

GIVEN
to him more will be *g* .....Matt 13:12
has, more will be *g*.........Matt 25:29

GIVES
g life to the world............. John 6:33
"All that the Father *g*....... John 6:37
The good shepherd *g*.......John 10:11
not as the world *g* .... John 14:27
g us richly all things.......1 Tim 6:17
who *g* to all liberally.......James 1:5
g grace to the humble........James 4:6

GLAD
streams shall make *g*............Ps 46:4
I was *g* when they said ......Ps 122:1
make merry and be *g*.....Luke 15:32
he saw it and was *g*...........John 8:56

GLADNESS
me hear joy and *g*.................Ps 51:8
Serve the LORD with *g* ....Ps 100:2

GLORIFIED
and they *g* the God of....Matt 15:31
Jesus was not yet *g*...........John 7:39
when Jesus was *g*..........John 12:16
this My Father is *g*............John 15:8
"I have *g* You on the.........John 17:4
g His Servant Jesus ....Acts 3:13
these He also *g* .... Rom 8:30
things God may be *g* ....1 Pet 4:11

GLORIFY
g your Father in.................Matt 5:16
"Father, *g* Your name......John 12:28
"He will *g* Me ....John 16:14
"And now, O Father, *g* ...John 17:5
death he would *g*.............John 21:19
therefore *g* God in........... 1 Cor 6:20
also Christ did not *g* ....Heb 5:5
ashamed, but let him *g* ....1 Pet 4:16

GLORIOUS
G things are spoken..............Ps 87:3
g splendor of Your...............Ps 145:5
habitation, holy and *g*..........Is 63:15
it to Himself a *g*..................Eph 5:27
be conformed to His *g*.......Phil 3:21
g appearing of our ....Titus 2:13

GLORY
show me Your *g*.................Ex 33:18
g has departed from ......1 Sam 4:21

Who is this King of *g*...........Ps 24:8
Your power and Your *g*......Ps 63:2
wise shall inherit *g*...........Prov 3:35
It is the *g* of God to ....Prov 25:2
g I will not give...................Is 42:8
that they may have *g*.......Matt 6:2
the power and the *g*...........Matt 6:13
g was not arrayed ....Matt 6:29
will come in the *g*..........Matt 16:27
power and great *g*..........Matt 24:30
"*G* to God in the ....Luke 2:14
and we beheld His *g*........John 1:14
and manifested His *g*........John 2:11
not seek My own *g* ....John 8:50
"Give God the *g*...............John 9:24
g which I had with ....John 17:5
g which You gave Me.... John 17:22
he did not give *g*............Acts 12:23
doing good seek for *g*........Rom 2:7
fall short of the *g*............. Rom 3:23
in faith, giving *g* .... Rom 4:20
the adoption, the *g*............Rom 9:4
the riches of His *g* .... Rom 9:23
God, alone wise, be *g* ... Rom 16:27
who glories, let him *g*..... 1 Cor 1:31
to His riches in *g* ....Phil 4:19
appear with Him in *g* .... Col 3:4
For you are our *g* .... 1 Thess 2:20
many sons to *g* ....Heb 2:10
grass, And all the *g*.......... 1 Pet 1:24
to whom belong the *g*...... 1 Pet 4:11
for the Spirit of *g*............. 1 Pet 4:14
the presence of His *g*.........Jude 24
O Lord, to receive *g*..........Rev 4:11
g of God illuminated......... Rev 21:23

GLUTTON(S)
g shames his ....Prov 28:7
you say, 'Look, a *g*...........Luke 7:34
evil beasts, lazy *g*.............Titus 1:12

GO
'Let My people *g*....................Ex 5:1
Where can I *g* from.............Ps 139:7
to whom shall we *g* .... John 6:68
g you cannot come........... John 8:21
I *g* to prepare a place...... John 14:2

GOAL
I press toward the *g*...........Phil 3:14

GOD
G created the heavens.........Gen 1:1
Abram of *G* Most ....Gen 14:19
and I will be their *G*.........Deut 4:24
"I am the LORD your *G*........ Ex 20:2
G is a consuming fire ..... Deut 4:24
If the LORD is *G*............... 1 Kin 18:21
G is greater than all..........2 Chr 2:5
You have been My *G*.......Ps 22:10
G is our refuge....................Ps 46:1
G in the midst of................Ps 46:5
me a clean heart, O *G*.......Ps 51:10
Our *G* is the *G*..................Ps 68:20
Who is so great a *G* ....Ps 77:13
Restore us, O *G* ....Ps 80:7
You alone are *G* ....Ps 86:10
Exalt the LORD our *G*...........Ps 99:9
Yes, our *G* is merciful ....Ps 116:5
For *G* is in heaven................ Eccl 5:2
Counselor, Mighty *G*..............Is 9:6
G is my salvation ....Is 12:2
stricken, Smitten by *G* ....Is 53:4
"*G* with us......................Matt 1:23
in *G* my Savior ....Luke 1:47
"For *G* so loved the ....John 3:16
"*G* is Spirit.......................John 4:24
"My Lord and my *G*......John 20:28
Christ is the Son of *G*......Acts 8:37
Indeed, let *G* be true.........Rom 3:4
If *G* is for us .... Rom 8:31
G is faithful .... 1 Cor 1:9
G shall supply all ....Phil 4:19
and *I* will be their *G*..........Heb 8:10
G is a consuming fire ......Heb 12:29
for *G* is love..................... 1 John 4:8
No one has seen *G*..... 1 John 4:12
G Himself will be ....Rev 21:3
and I will be his *G*...............Rev 21:7

GODDESS
after Ashtoreth the *g*...... 1 Kin 11:5
of the great *g* Diana........Acts 19:35

GODHEAD
eternal power and *G*........ Rom 1:20
the fullness of the *G*...........Col 2:9

GODLINESS
is the mystery of *g* ....1 Tim 3:16
g with contentment..........1 Tim 6:6
having a form of *g* ....2 Tim 3:5
to perseverance *g*.............2 Pet 1:6

GODLY
who desire to live *g*........2 Tim 3:12
reverence and *g* fear......Heb 12:28
to deliver the *g*...................2 Pet 2:9

GOLD
g I do not have....................Acts 3:6
with braided hair or *g* ....1 Tim 2:9
a man with *g* rings.........James 2:2
Your *g* and silver are....James 5:3
more precious than *g*....... 1 Pet 1:7
like silver or *g*.................. 1 Pet 1:18
of the city was pure *g*.... Rev 21:21

GOOD
God saw that it was *g*.......Gen 1:10
but God meant it for *g*....Gen 50:20
indeed accept *g*..................Job 2:10
is none who does *g* ....Ps 14:1
Truly God is *g* to ....Ps 73:1
g word makes it glad.... Prov 12:25
on the evil and the *g*........Prov 15:3
A merry heart does *g* ... Prov 17:22
Learn to do *g* ....Is 1:17
talked to me, with *g*........Zech 1:13
they may see your *g*......Matt 5:16
"A *g* man out of the ....Matt 12:35
No one is *g* but One........Matt 19:17
For she has done a *g*......Matt 26:10
g works I have shown ....John 10:32
went about doing *g* ....Acts 10:38
g man someone would ....Rom 5:7
in my flesh) nothing *g* ..... Rom 7:18
overcome evil with *g* ..... Rom 12:21
Jesus for *g* works ....Eph 2:10
fruitful in every *g* ....Col 1:10
know that the law is *g*.....1 Tim 1:8
For this is *g* and...............1 Tim 2:3
bishop, he desires a *g*......1 Tim 3:1
for this is *g* and...............1 Tim 5:4
prepared for every *g*.......2 Tim 2:21
Every *g* gift and..............James 1:17

GOODNESS
"I will make all My *g* ..... Ex 33:19
and abounding in *g*........... Ex 34:6
"You are my Lord, My *g*......Ps 16:2
Surely *g* and mercy ....Ps 23:6
That I would see the *g*......Ps 27:13
the riches of His *g* ....Rom 2:4
consider the *g* and .... Rom 11:22
kindness, *g* ....Gal 5:22

GOSPEL
The beginning of the *g* .... Mark 1:1
and believe in the *g*......... Mark 1:15
g must first be................. Mark 13:10
separated to the *g*..............Rom 1:1
not ashamed of the *g* .... Rom 1:16
to a different *g* ....Gal 1:6
the everlasting *g* ....Rev 14:6

GRACE
But Noah found *g*................Gen 6:8
G is poured upon Your ....Ps 45:2
The LORD will give *g*..........Ps 84:11
the Spirit of *g*...................Zech 12:10
and the *g* of God was ......Luke 2:40
g and truth came ....John 1:17
And great *g* was upon.....Acts 4:33
receive abundance of *g*... Rom 5:17
g is no longer *g* .... Rom 11:6
For you know the *g*.........2 Cor 8:9
g is sufficient...................2 Cor 12:9
The *g* of the Lord ....2 Cor 13:14
you have fallen from *g*........Gal 5:4
to the riches of His *g* ....Eph 1:7
g you have been ....Eph 2:8
g was given according ......Eph 4:7
G be with all those............Eph 6:24
shaken, let us have *g* ....Heb 12:28
But He gives more *g*.......James 4:6
but grow in the *g*..............2 Pet 3:18

GRACIOUS
he said, "God be *g*............Gen 43:29
I will be *g* to whom I.........Ex 33:19
at the *g* words which.......Luke 4:22
that the Lord is *g*.............. 1 Pet 2:3

GRAIN
it treads out the *g*............ Deut 25:4
be revived like *g*.................Hos 14:7
to pluck heads of *g*.............Matt 12:1
unless a *g* of wheat........ John 12:24

GRAPES
brought forth wild *g* ....Is 5:2
have eaten sour *g*.............Ezek 18:2
Do men gather *g* ....Matt 7:16
g are fully ripe.................Rev 14:18

GRASS
The *g* withers..........................Is 40:7
so clothes the *g*.................Matt 6:30
"All flesh is as *g*................ 1 Pet 1:24

GRAVE(S)
my soul up from the *g*..........Ps 30:3
And they made His *g*.............Is 53:9
the power of the *g*...........Hos 13:14
g were opened................Matt 27:52
g which are not..............Luke 11:44
g will hear His voice........ John 5:28

GREAT
and make your name *g*.....Gen 12:2
For the Lord is *g*........ 1 Chr 16:25
Who does *g* things................Job 5:9
g is the Holy One ....Is 12:6
G is Your faithfulness.....Lam 3:23
he shall be called *g*...........Matt 5:19
one pearl of *g* price.........Matt 13:46
desires to become *g*........Matt 20:26
g drops of blood ....Luke 22:44
appearing of our *g* ....Titus 2:13
Mystery, Babylon the *G*....Rev 17:5

GREATER
of heaven is *g*...................Matt 11:11
place there is One *g*..........Matt 12:6
a servant is not *g*...........John 13:16
"*G* love has no one.........John 15:13
'A servant is not *g*.........John 15:20
who prophesies is *g*........ 1 Cor 14:5
God is *g*............................ 1 John 3:20
witness of God is *g*......... 1 John 5:9

GREATEST
little child is the *g*..............Matt 18:4
but the *g* of these is...... 1 Cor 13:13

GREEDINESS
all uncleanness with *g*.......Eph 4:19

GREEDY
of everyone who is *g* ....Prov 1:19
not violent, not *g* ....1 Tim 3:3

GREEK
written in Hebrew, *G*....John 19:20
and also for the *G* .... Rom 1:16
is neither Jew nor *G* ....Gal 3:28

GRIEF
and acquainted with *g*...........Is 53:3
joy and not with *g*...........Heb 13:17

GRIEVE(D)
g the Holy Spirit.................Eph 4:30
earth, and He was *g*...........Gen 6:6
g His Holy Spirit ....Is 63:10
with anger, being .... Mark 3:5

GROANING(S)
I am weary with my *g*...........Ps 6:6
Then Jesus, again *g*.......John 11:38
g which cannot................. Rom 8:26

GROUND
"Cursed is the *g*................Gen 3:17
you stand is holy *g*.................Ex 3:5
up your fallow *g* ....Jer 4:3
others fell on good *g*........Matt 13:8
bought a piece of *g* ....Luke 14:18
God, the pillar and *g*.......1 Tim 3:15

GROW
truth in love, may *g* ....Eph 4:15
but *g* in the grace and .....2 Pet 3:18

GUARANTEE
in our hearts as a *g*........ 2 Cor 1:22
us the Spirit as a *g* .... 2 Cor 5:5
who is the *g* of our.............Eph 1:14

GUIDE
He will be our *g*...................Ps 48:14
g our feet into the...........Luke 1:79
has come, He will *g* ....John 16:13

GUILTLESS
g who takes His name........Ex 20:7
have condemned the *g*.....Matt 12:7

GUILTY
"We are truly *g*.................Gen 42:21
world may become *g*...... Rom 3:19
in one point, he is *g*.......James 2:10

H

HADES
be brought down to *H*....Matt 11:23
H shall not.........................Matt 16:18
in torments in *H*..............Luke 16:23
not leave my soul in *H*.....Acts 2:27
I have the keys of *H*...........Rev 1:18
H were cast into the.........Rev 20:14

HAIR(S)
you cannot make
one *h*..............................Matt 5:36
"But not a *h* of your.......Luke 21:18
not with braided *h*..............1 Tim 2:9
h like women's *h* ....Rev 9:8
"But the very *h*.................Matt 10:30

HALLOWED
the Sabbath day and *h*......Ex 20:11
who is holy shall be *h*.............Is 5:16
heaven, *H* be Your
name..................................Matt 6:9

HAND
the *h* of God was............1 Sam 5:11
My times are in Your *h*....Ps 31:15
"Sit at My right *h* ....Ps 110:1
heart is in the *h*.................Prov 21:1
Whatever your *h* ....Eccl 9:10
is at his right *h*..................Eccl 10:2
do not withhold your *h* .... Eccl 11:6
My *h* has laid the................Is 48:13
Behold, the Lord's *h* ....Is 59:1
are the work of Your *h* ....Is 64:8
"Am I a God near at *h*......Jer 23:23
of heaven is at *h*................Matt 3:2
if your right *h*....................Matt 5:30
do not let your left *h*........Matt 6:3
h causes you to sin..........Mark 9:43
sitting at the right *h*...... Mark 14:62
at the right *h* of God ....Acts 7:55
The Lord is at *h*...................Phil 4:5
"Sit at My right *h* ....Heb 1:13
down at the right *h*..........Heb 10:12

HANDIWORK
firmament shows His *h*........Ps 19:1

HANDLE
H Me and see.................Luke 24:39
do not taste, do not *h*..........Col 2:21

HANDS
took his life in his *h*.......1 Sam 19:5
but His *h* make whole........Job 5:18
They pierced My *h*.............Ps 22:16
h formed the dry land ....Ps 95:5
than having two *h*............Matt 18:8
"Behold My *h* and.........Luke 24:39
h the print of the ....John 20:25
his *h* what is good.............Eph 4:28
the laying on of the *h* .....1 Tim 4:14
to fall into the *h*................Heb 10:31

HANGED
went and *h* himself ....Matt 27:5

HAPPY
H is the man who has........Ps 127:5

HARDENED
But Pharaoh *h* his ....Ex 8:32
their heart was *h* ....Mark 6:52
and *h* their hearts..........John 12:40
lest any of you be *h* ....Heb 3:13

HARLOT
of a *h* named Rahab ....Josh 2:1
h is one body with........... 1 Cor 6:16
of the great *h* who.............Rev 17:1

HARLOTRY
are the children of *h* ....Hos 2:4
For the spirit of *h* ....Hos 5:4

HARLOTS
h enter the ....Matt 21:31
Great, The Mother of *H* ....Rev 17:5

HARP(S)
Lamb, each having a *h*........Rev 5:8
We hung our *h* Upon the...Ps 137:2

HARVEST
Seedtime and *h*.................Gen 8:22
"The *h* is past ....Jer 8:20
h truly is plentiful.............Matt 9:37
sickle, because the *h*....... Mark 4:29
already white for *h* ....John 4:35

HATE
love the Lord, *h* evil...........Ps 97:10
h every false way ....Ps 119:104
h the double-minded.......Ps 119:113
I *h* and abhor lying ....Ps 119:163
love, And a time to *h* .... Eccl 3:8
You who *h* good and .... Mic 3:2
either he will *h*...................Matt 6:24

HATED
But Esau I have *h*............... Mal 1:3
"And you will be *h*............Matt 10:22
have seen and also *h* ...... John 15:24
but Esau I have *h* .... Rom 9:13
For no one ever *h* ....Eph 5:29

HATEFUL
h woman when she is.... Prov 30:23
in malice and envy, *h* ....Titus 3:3

HATES
six things the Lord *h* ....Prov 6:16
lose it, and he who *h*......John 12:25
"If the world *h*..................John 15:18
h his brother is .... 1 John 2:11

HAUGHTY
bring down *h* looks............Ps 18:27
my heart is not *h* ....Ps 131:1
h spirit before a fall .... Prov 16:18

HEAD
He shall bruise your *h*.......Gen 3:15
and gave Him to be *h*........Eph 1:22
For the husband is *h*.........Eph 5:23

HEAL
O Lord, *h* me..........................Ps 6:2
h your backslidings .... Jer 3:22
torn, but He will *h*.................Hos 6:1
"*H* the sick..........................Matt 10:8
So that I should *h*...........Matt 13:15
sent Me to the...................Luke 4:18
Physician, *h* yourself.......Luke 4:23

HEALED
And return and be *h*..............Is 6:10
His stripes we are *h*...............Is 53:5
"When I would have *h*........Hos 7:1
and He *h* them....................Matt 4:24
that you may be *h*...........James 5:16
his deadly wound was *h* ... Rev 13:3

HEALING(S)
shall arise With *h*................ Mal 4:2
and *h* all kinds of ....Matt 4:23
tree were for the *h* ....Rev 22:2
to another gifts of *h* .... 1 Cor 12:9

HEALS
h all your diseases ....Ps 103:3
Jesus the Christ *h*.............Acts 9:34

HEAR
"*H*, O Israel...........................Deut 6:4
Him you shall *h*............. Deut 18:15
H me when I call...................Ps 4:1
O You who *h* prayer............Ps 65:2
ear, shall He not *h*.............Ps 94:9
h rather than to give........... Eccl 5:1
'Hearing you will *h*........Matt 13:14
heed what you *h*.............. Mark 4:24

that God does not *h* .... John 9:31
And how shall they *h* .... Rom 10:14
man be swift to *h*............James 1:19
h what the Spirit says..........Rev 2:7

HEARD

h their cry because of ....Ex 3:7
that they will be *h* ....Matt 6:7
h the word believed ....Acts 4:4
not seen, nor ear *h* .... 1 Cor 2:9
things that you have *h*.......2 Tim 2:2
the word which they *h* ....Heb 4:2
which we have *h* .... 1 John 1:1
Lord's Day, and I *h* ....Rev 1:10

HEARERS

for not the *h* of the ....Rom 2:13
the word, and not *h* ....James 1:22

HEARING

'Keep on *h* ....Is 6:9
h they do not....................Matt 13:13
h they may hear .... Mark 4:12
or by the *h* of faith ....Gal 3:2

HEARS

out, and the Lord *h* ....Ps 34:17
of God *h* God's words......John 8:47
"And if anyone *h* ....John 12:47
who is of the truth *h* .....John 18:37
He who knows God *h*.... 1 John 4:6
And let him who *h* ....Rev 22:17

HEART

h was only evil....................Gen 6:5
h rejoices in the Lord ....1 Sam 2:1
gave him another *h*........1 Sam 10:9
Lord looks at the *h* ....1 Sam 16:7
his wives turned his *h* .... 1 Kin 11:4
He pierces my *h*................Job 16:13
My *h* also instructs me........Ps 16:7
h is overflowing....................Ps 45:1
h shall depart from me.......Ps 101:4
look and a proud *h*............Ps 101:5
with my whole *h*...............Ps 111:1
as he thinks in his *h*........Prov 23:7
h reveals the man........... Prov 27:19
trusts in his own *h* .... Prov 28:26
The *h* of the wise is .... Eccl 7:4
And a wise man's *h* .... Eccl 8:5
h yearned for him ....Song 5:4
And the whole *h*...................Is 1:5
The yearning of Your *h* ......Is 63:15
h is deceitful above .... Jer 17:9
I will give them a *h* .... Jer 24:7
and take the stony *h*......Ezek 11:19
yourselves a new *h* ......Ezek 18:31
are the pure in *h* ....Matt 5:8
is, there your *h*..................Matt 6:21
of the *h* proceed evil........Matt 15:19
h will flow rivers ....John 7:38
"Let not your *h* ....John 14:1
Satan filled your *h* ....Acts 5:3
h that God has raised ...... Rom 10:9
refresh my *h* in the ....Philem 20
and shuts up his *h* ....1 John 3:17

HEARTILY

you do, do it *h* ....Col 3:23

HEARTS

God tests the *h*......................Ps 7:9
And he will turn The *h*........ Mal 4:6
h failing them from.......Luke 21:26
will guard your *h*..................Phil 4:7
of God rule in your *h*.........Col 3:15

HEAVEN

called the firmament *H* ....Gen 1:8
Lord looks down
    from *h*....................................Ps 14:2
word is settled in *h*.........Ps 119:89
For God is in *h* .... Eccl 5:2
"*H* is My throne......................Is 66:1
for the kingdom of *h*...........Matt 3:2
your Father in *h*...............Matt 5:16
On earth as it is in *h*...........Matt 6:10
"*H* and earth will ....Matt 24:35
Him a sign from *h* ....Mark 8:11
have sinned against *h*....Luke 15:18
you shall see *h* ....John 1:51
one has ascended to *h* .....John 3:13
the true bread from *h* ......John 6:32
a voice came from *h* ......John 12:28

sheet, let down from *h* .....Acts 11:5
laid up for you in *h* ....Col 1:5
there was silence in *h*..........Rev 8:1
Now I saw a new *h* ....Rev 21:1

HEAVENLY

your *h* Father will ....Matt 6:14
h host praising God ....Luke 2:13
if I tell you *h* things...........John 3:12
blessing in the *h* ....Eph 1:3
a better, that is, a *h*..........Heb 11:16
the living God, the *h*........Heb 12:22

HEAVENS

and the highest *h*............ Deut 10:14
h cannot contain............. 1 Kin 8:27
h declare the glory ....Ps 19:1
For as the *h* are high ....Ps 103:11
behold, I create new *h*.........Is 65:17
and behold, the *h* ....Matt 3:16
h will be shaken ....Matt 24:29
h are the work of Your .....Ps 102:25
h will pass away................2 Pet 3:10

HEEL

you shall bruise His *h*........Gen 3:15
has lifted up his *h*..................Ps 41:9
Me has lifted up his *h*.... John 13:18

HEIGHT

nor *h* nor depth................. Rom 8:39
length and depth and *h*.....Eph 3:18

HEIR(S)

He has appointed *h*...............Heb 1:2
world and became *h*..........Heb 11:7
if children, then *h*............. Rom 8:17
should be fellow *h*...............Eph 3:6

HELL

shall be turned into *h* ....Ps 9:17
go down alive into *h* ....Ps 55:15
H and Destruction are... Prov 27:20
be in danger of *h* fire........Matt 5:22
to be cast into *h* ....Matt 18:9
condemnation of *h*.........Matt 23:33
power to cast into *h*........Luke 12:5

HELP

May He send you *h*..............Ps 20:2
A very present *h* ....Ps 46:1
He is their *h* and..................Ps 115:9
Our *h* is in the name.........Ps 124:8
h my unbelief................Mark 9:24
and find grace to *h*............Heb 4:16

HELPER

I will make him a *h*...........Gen 2:18
Behold, God is my *h* ....Ps 54:4
give you another *H*.........John 14:16
"But when the *H*.............John 15:26
"The Lord is my *h* ....Heb 13:6

HELPFUL

all things are not *h* .... 1 Cor 6:12

HERESIES

dissensions, *h*........................Gal 5:20

HERITAGE

for that is his *h*.................. Eccl 3:22
This is the *h* of the ....Is 54:17
of My people, My *h*..........Joel 3:2
The flock of Your *h* .... Mic 7:14

HIDDEN

And my sins are not *h*..........Ps 69:5
Your word I have *h*..........Ps 119:11
h that will not...................Matt 10:26
the *h* wisdom which .... 1 Cor 2:7
bring to light the *h*........... 1 Cor 4:5
have renounced the *h*.......2 Cor 4:2
rather let it be the *h* .... 1 Pet 3:4
give some of the *h*.............Rev 2:17

HIDE

H me under the shadow.......Ps 17:8
You shall *h* them in ....Ps 31:20
You *h* Your face ....Ps 104:29
darkness shall not *h* ....Ps 139:12
You are God, who *h* ....Is 45:15
"Fall on us and *h* ....Rev 6:16

HIDING

You are my *h* place..............Ps 32:7

HIGH

priest of God Most *H*......Gen 14:18
For the Lord Most *H*...........Ps 47:2
"I dwell in the *h*...................Is 57:15
know That the Most *H*..... Dan 4:17
up on a *h* mountain by....Matt 17:1
your mind on *h* things.... Rom 12:16
h thing that exalts..........2 Cor 10:5
and faithful *H* Priest.........Heb 2:17

HILL

My King on My holy *h*..........Ps 2:6
h cannot be hidden............Matt 5:14
and *h* brought low.............Luke 3:5

HINDERED

Who *h* you from obeying.....Gal 5:7
prayers may not be *h* .... 1 Pet 3:7

HOLINESS

You, glorious in *h*...............Ex 15:11
I have sworn by My *h* ....Ps 89:35
the Highway of *H*..................Is 35:8
to the Spirit of *h* ....Rom 1:4
spirit, perfecting *h*............2 Cor 7:1
uncleanness, but in *h*.... 1 Thess 4:7
be partakers of His *h*........Heb 12:10

HOLY

where you stand is *h* .... Ex 3:5
day, to keep it *h*................Ex 20:8
Lord your God am *h*........ Lev 19:2
h seed is mixed..................Ezra 9:2
God sits on His *h*.................Ps 47:8
God, in His *h* mountain........Ps 48:1
"*H, h, h*,...............................Is 6:3
child of the *H* Spirit .... Mark 1:18
baptize you with the *H*.... Mark 1:8
who speak, but the *H* ... Mark 13:11
H Spirit will come ....Luke 1:35
H Spirit descended..........Luke 3:22
Father give the *H* ....Luke 11:3
H Spirit will teach..........Luke 12:12
H Spirit was not .... John 7:39
H Spirit has come ....Acts 1:8
all filled with the *H*............. Acts 2:4
receive the *H* Spirit...........Acts 19:2
joy in the *H*.......................Rom 14:17
H Spirit teaches............. 1 Cor 2:13
that we should be *h* ....Eph 1:4
were sealed with the *H* .....Eph 1:13
partakers of the *H*.............Heb 6:4
H Spirit sent from .... 1 Pet 1:12
it is written, "Be *h* .... 1 Pet 1:16
moved by the *H* Spirit .....2 Pet 1:21
anointing from the *H*... 1 John 2:20
says He who is *h* ....Rev 3:7
For You alone are *h*..........Rev 15:4
is *h*, let him be *h* ....Rev 22:11

HOME

sparrow has found a *h* ....Ps 84:3
to his eternal *h*...............Eccl 12:5
that while we are at *h*......2 Cor 5:6
to show piety at *h*..............1 Tim 5:4

HOMEMAKERS

be discreet, chaste, *h* ....Titus 2:5

HONEY

and with *h* from the...........Ps 81:16
was locusts and wild *h*.......Matt 3:4

HONEYCOMB

than honey and the *h* ....Ps 19:10
fish and some *h* ....Luke 24:42

HONOR

"*H* your father and your ...Ex 20:12
will deliver him and ....Ps 91:15
H and majesty are................Ps 96:6
H the Lord with your ....Prov 3:9
before *h* is humility........ Prov 15:33
spirit will retain *h*.......... Prov 29:23
Father, where is My *h* ....Mal 1:6
is not without *h*...............Matt 13:57
'*H* your father and ....Matt 15:4
h the Son just as they ......John 5:23
"I do not receive *h*...........John 5:41
but I *h* My Father ....John 8:49
"If I *h* Myself ....John 8:54
him My Father will .....John 12:26
to whom fear, *h*................ Rom 13:7
sanctification and *h* ...... 1 Thess 4:4

alone is wise, be *h*...........1 Tim 1:17
and clay, some for *h* ....2 Tim 2:20
no man takes this *h* ....Heb 5:4
from God the Father *h*....2 Pet 1:17
give glory and *h* ....Rev 4:9

HONORABLE
His work is *h* and................Ps 111:3
holy day of the LORD *h* ....Is 58:13
providing *h* things...........2 Cor 8:21
Marriage is *h* among........Heb 13:4
having your conduct *h* .... 1 Pet 2:12

HOPE
h He has uprooted.............Job 19:10
also will rest in *h*..................Ps 16:9
My *h* is in You ....Ps 39:7
For You are my *h* ....Ps 71:5
I *h* in Your word.............Ps 119:147
good that one should *h*....Lam 3:26
to *h*, in *h* believed............. Rom 4:18
h does not disappoint......Rom 5:5
were saved in this *h*......... Rom 8:24
now abide faith, *h*......... 1 Cor 13:13
life only we have *h*........ 1 Cor 15:19
may know what is the *h*....Eph 1:18
were called in one *h*...........Eph 4:4
Christ in you, the *h* ....Col 1:27
Jesus Christ, our *h* ....1 Tim 1:1
for the blessed *h*..............Titus 2:13
to lay hold of the *h*............Heb 6:18
in of a better *h* ....Heb 7:19
who has this *h* in Him.... 1 John 3:3

HOSANNA
H in the highest.................Matt 21:9

HOSPITABLE
Be *h* to one another .... 1 Pet 4:9

HOUR
is coming at an *h*............Matt 24:44
"But the *h* is coming ....John 4:23
save Me from this *h* ......John 12:27
keep you from the *h* ....Rev 3:10

HOUSE
as for me and my *h*........Josh 24:15
Through wisdom a *h* ....Prov 24:3
better to go to the *h* ....Eccl 7:2
h was filled with.....................Is 6:4
h divided against............Matt 12:25
h shall be called a ....Matt 21:13
make My Father's *h*.........John 2:16
h are many mansions......John 14:2
publicly and from *h* ....Acts 20:20
who rules his own *h*..........1 Tim 3:4
the church in your *h*..........Philem 2
For every *h* is built.............Heb 3:4
His own *h*, whose *h* ....Heb 3:6

HOUSEHOLD
the ways of her *h*........... Prov 31:27
be those of his own *h* .....Matt 10:36
h were baptized..............Acts 16:15
saved, you and your *h*....Acts 16:31
who are of Caesar's *h*......Phil 4:22

HOUSES
H and riches are an .... Prov 19:14
who has left *h* or ....Matt 19:29
you devour widows' *h*....Matt 23:14

HUMBLE
man Moses was very *h*.... Num 12:3
the cry of the *h* ....Ps 9:12
h shall hear of it and ....Ps 34:2
contrite and *h* spirit ....Is 57:15
A meek and *h* people....Zeph 3:12
associate with the *h*....... Rom 12:16
gives grace to the *h*........James 4:6
H yourselves in the....... James 4:10
gives grace to the *h*........ 1 Pet 5:5
h yourselves under the..... 1 Pet 5:6

HUMBLED
as a man, He *h* Himself......Phil 2:8

HUMILITY
the Lord with all *h* ....Acts 20:19
delight in false *h*................Col 2:18
mercies, kindness, *h*.........Col 3:12
h correcting those ....2 Tim 2:25
gentle, showing all *h*........ Titus 3:2
and be clothed with *h*...... 1 Pet 5:5

HUNGER
They shall neither *h*.............Is 49:10
are those who *h*..................Matt 5:6
for you shall *h*...................Luke 6:25
to Me shall never *h* ....John 6:35
hour we both *h* ....1 Cor 4:11
"They shall neither *h*.........Rev 7:16

HUNGRY
and fills the *h* ....Ps 107:9
gives food to the *h*.............Ps 146:7
'for I was *h* and you.......Matt 25:35
did we see You *h*.............Matt 25:37
to be full and to be *h*..........Phil 4:12

HURT
h a woman with child........Ex 21:22
but *I* was not *h*................ Prov 23:35
another to his own *h*............Eccl 8:9
They shall not *h*.......................Is 11:9
it will by no means *h*....Mark 16:18
shall not be *h* by the ....Rev 2:11

HUSBAND(S)
h safely trusts her .... Prov 31:11
your Maker is your *h*...........Is 54:5
now have is not your *h* ... John 4:18
you will save your *h*...... 1 Cor 7:16
the *h* of one wife...............1 Tim 3:2
H, love your wives ....Eph 5:25
Let deacons be the *h*.....1 Tim 3:12

HYMN(S)
they had sung a *h*...........Matt 26:30
praying and singing *h* ....Acts 16:25
in psalms and *h* ....Eph 5:19

HYPOCRISY
you are full of *h*.............Matt 23:28
Pharisees, which is *h*.......Luke 12:1
Let love be without *h*.......Rom 12:9
away with their *h*...............Gal 2:13
and without *h*..................James 3:17
malice, all deceit, *h* .... 1 Pet 2:1

HYPOCRITE
and the joy of the *h*.............Job 20:5
For everyone is a *h* ....Is 9:17
also played the *h*..................Gal 2:13

HYPOCRITES
not be like the *h*.................Matt 6:5
do you test Me, you *h*.....Matt 22:18
and Pharisees, *h* ....Matt 23:13

I

IDLE
i person will suffer .... Prov 19:15
i word men may ....Matt 12:36
saw others standing *i* ....Matt 20:3
they learn to be *i* ....1 Tim 5:13

IDOL
thing offered to an *i* .... 1 Cor 8:7
That an *i* is anything .... 1 Cor 10:19

IDOLATER(S)
or covetous, or an *i* .... 1 Cor 5:11
fornicators, nor *i*................ 1 Cor 6:9
and murderers and *i*........Rev 22:15

IDOLATRIES
and abominable *i*................ 1 Pet 4:3

IDOLATRY
beloved, flee from *i*........ 1 Cor 10:14
i, sorcery ....Gal 5:20

IDOLS
land is also full of *i*...................Is 2:8
in the room of his *i*........Ezek 8:12
who regard worthless *i* ....Jon 2:8
You who abhor *i* .... Rom 2:22
yourselves from *i*........... 1 John 5:21
worship demons, and *i*.....Rev 9:20

IGNORANCE
that you did it in *i*............Acts 3:17
i God overlooked.............Acts 17:30
sins committed in *i*.............Heb 9:7

ILLUMINATED
after you were *i*...............Heb 10:32
and the earth was *i*...........Rev 18:1
for the glory of God *i*.......Rev 21:23

IMAGE
Us make man in Our *i*........Gen 1:26
since he is the *i*................ 1 Cor 11:7
He is the *i* of the ....Col 1:15
and not the very *i*..............Heb 10:1
the beast and his *i*............Rev 14:9

IMMANUEL
shall call His name *I*..............Is 7:14
shall call His name *I*........Matt 1:23

IMMORAL
murderers, sexually *i*.........Rev 21:8

IMMORALITY
except sexual *i*...................Matt 5:32
abstain from sexual *i*... 1 Thess 4:3

IMMORTAL
to the King eternal, *i*.......1 Tim 1:17

IMMORTALITY
mortal must put on *i*..... 1 Cor 15:53
who alone has *i* ....1 Tim 6:16

IMPOSSIBLE
God nothing will be *i*......Luke 1:37
without faith it is *i*.............Heb 11:6

IMPUTED
might be *i* to them............ Rom 4:11
but sin is not *i* .... Rom 5:13

IMPUTES
i righteousness apart ....Rom 4:6

INCORRUPTIBLE
the glory of the *i*............... Rom 1:23
dead will be raised *i*.... 1 Cor 15:52
to an inheritance *i*............. 1 Pet 1:4

INCREASE
Of the *i* of His...........................Is 9:7
Lord "I our faith ....Luke 17:5
"He must *i*...................... John 3:30
but God gave the *i*............ 1 Cor 3:6

INDIGNATION
i which will devour ....Heb 10:27
into the cup of His *i* ....Rev 14:10

INEXPRESSIBLE
Paradise and heard *i*......2 Cor 12:4
you rejoice with joy *i*......... 1 Pet 1:8

INFIRMITIES
"He Himself took our *i* .....Matt 8:17

INHERIT
love me to *i* wealth...........Prov 8:21
i the kingdom..................Matt 25:34
unrighteous will not *i* ...... 1 Cor 6:9
who overcomes shall *i*......Rev 21:7

INHERITANCE
"You shall have no *i* ......Num 18:20
is the place of His *i* ....Deut 32:9
the portion of my *i* ....Ps 16:5
i shall be forever................Ps 37:18
He will choose our *i*...........Ps 47:4
will arise to your *i*........Dan 12:13
God gave him no *i*..............Acts 7:5
and give you an *i*...........Acts 20:32
For if the *i* is of the..........Gal 3:18
we have obtained an *i*.......Eph 1:11
be partakers of the *i*..........Col 1:12
receive as an *i*..................Heb 11:8
i incorruptible .... 1 Pet 1:4

INIQUITIES
i have overtaken me ....Ps 40:12
forgives all your *i*.............Ps 103:3
LORD, should mark *i*..........Ps 130:3
was bruised for our *i*.........Is 53:5
He shall bear their *i*.........Is 53:11
i have separated you.........Is 59:2

INIQUITY
God, visiting the *i* of the....Ex 20:5
was brought forth in *i*.......Ps 51:5
If I regard *i* in my............Ps 66:18
i have dominion.............Ps 119:133
i will reap sorrow........Prov 22:8
A people laden with *i* ....Is 1:4
i is taken away......................Is 6:7
has laid on Him the *i*.........Is 53:6
will remember their *i*.........Hos 9:9

to those who devise *i*........... Mic 2:1
like You, Pardoning *i* .... Mic 7:18
all you workers of *i*.......Luke 13:27
a fire, a world of *i*.............James 3:6

INN
room for them in the *i* ....Luke 2:7
brought him to an *i*......Luke 10:34

INNOCENT
because I was found *i*...... Dan 6:22
saying, "I am *i*..................Matt 27:24
this day that I am *i*.........Acts 20:26

INSPIRATION
is given by *i* of God........2 Tim 3:16

INSTRUCT
I will *i* you and teach...........Ps 32:8
Lord that he may *i*......... 1 Cor 2:16

INSTRUCTED
This man had been *i*.......Acts 18:25
are excellent, being *i* ...... Rom 2:18
Moses was divinely *i* ....Heb 8:5

INSTRUCTION
seeing you hate *i* ....Ps 50:17
Hear *i* and be wise ....Prov 8:33
Give *i* to a wise man ....Prov 9:9
for correction, for *i*.........2 Tim 3:16

INSTRUMENTS
your members as *i* .... Rom 6:13

INSUBORDINATE
for the lawless and *i* ....1 Tim 1:9

INSULTED
will be mocked and *i* ....Luke 18:32
i the Spirit of grace ....Heb 10:29

INTEGRITY
In the *i* of my heart ....Gen 20:5
in doctrine showing *i*........Titus 2:7

INTERCEDE
the Lord, who will *i* ...1 Sam 2:25

INTERCESSION
of many, And made *i*...........Is 53:12
Spirit Himself makes *i*..... Rom 8:26
always lives to make *i*......Heb 7:25

INTERPRET
Do all *i* ?.......................... 1 Cor 12:30
pray that he may *i* .... 1 Cor 14:13

INTERPRETATION(S)
to another the *i* .... 1 Cor 12:10
of any private *i* ....2 Pet 1:20
"Do not *i* belong to............Gen 40:8

INVISIBLE
of the world His *i* .... Rom 1:20
is the image of the *i*..........Col 1:15
eternal, immortal, *i*.........1 Tim 1:17
as seeing Him who
is *i*..................................Heb 11:27

INWARD
You have formed my *i*......Ps 139:13
God according to the *i*..... Rom 7:22
i man is being ....2 Cor 4:16

INWARDLY
i they are...........................Matt 7:15
is a Jew who is one *i*........ Rom 2:29

IRON
i sharpens *i*.....................Prov 27:17
its feet partly of *i*.............. Dan 2:33

ISRAEL
"Hear, O *I* ....Deut 6:4
For they are not all *I*.........Rom 9:6
and upon the *I* of God ....Gal 6:16

ITCHING
they have *i* ears ....2 Tim 4:3

J

JEALOUS
God, am a *j* God ....Ex 20:5
a consuming fire, a *j*........ Deut 4:24
For I am *j* for you ....2 Cor 11:2

JEALOUSY
provoked Him to *j*..........Deut 32:16
as strong as death, *j*..........Song 8:6
for you with godly *j*........2 Cor 11:2

JESUS
J Christ was as...................Matt 1:18
shall call His name *J*.........Matt 1:21
J was led up by the ....Matt 4:1
and laid hands on *J*........Matt 26:50
and destroy *J*...................Matt 27:20
J withdrew with His......... Mark 3:7
J went into.....................Mark 11:11
they were eating, *J*.......Mark 14:22
and he delivered *J*........ Mark 15:15
truth came through *J*........John 1:17
J lifted up His eyes............John 6:5
J wept...............................John 11:35
J was crucified.................John 19:20
"This *J* God has raised .....Acts 2:32
of Your holy Servant *J*.....Acts 4:30
believed on the Lord *J*....Acts 11:17
your mouth the Lord *J*..... Rom 10:9
among you except *J*........ 1 Cor 2:2
perfect in Christ *J*.............Col 1:28
But we see *J* ....Heb 2:9
looking unto *J* ....Heb 12:2
Revelation of *J* Christ..........Rev 1:1
so, come, Lord *J* ....Rev 22:20

JOINED
and mother and be *j* ....Gen 2:24
what God has *j*..................Matt 19:6
the whole body, *j*................Eph 4:16

JOINT
j as He wrestled...............Gen 32:25
My bones are out of *j*..........Ps 22:14
j heirs with Christ .... Rom 8:17

JOINTS
and knit together by *j*........Col 2:19
and spirit, and of *j*.............Heb 4:12

JOT
one *j* or one tittle ....Matt 5:18

JOY
is fullness of *j*.....................Ps 16:11
j comes in the morning ....Ps 30:5
j you will draw....................Is 12:3
ashes, The oil of *j* ....Is 61:3
shall sing for *j*...................Is 65:14
receives it with *j* ....Matt 13:20
Enter into the *j*.................Matt 25:21
in my womb for *j*...............Luke 1:44
there will be more *j*............Luke 15:7
did not believe for *j*.........Luke 24:41
My *j* may remain in.........John 15:11
they may have My *j*..........John 17:13
the Spirit is love, *j*............Gal 5:22
are our glory and *j* ...... 1 Thess 2:20
j that was set before..........Heb 12:2
count it all *j*.......................James 1:2
with exceeding *j* .... 1 Pet 4:13

JOYFUL
Make a *j* shout to the..........Ps 100:1
And make them *j*....................Is 56:7

JUDGE
The Lord *j* between...........Gen 16:5
coming to *j* the earth .... 1 Chr 16:33
sword The Lord will *j*........Is 66:16
deliver you to the *j*..........Matt 5:25
"*J* not ....Matt 7:1
who made Me a *j*..........Luke 12:14
j who did not fear God ....Luke 18:2
As I hear, I *j*..................John 5:30
"Do not *j* according..........John 7:24
I *j* no one........................John 8:15
j the world but to...........John 12:47
this, O man, you who *j*......Rom 2:3
Therefore let us not *j*....... Rom 14:13
Christ, who will *j*..............2 Tim 4:1
But if you *j* the law........James 4:11

JUDGES
He makes the *j* of the ....Is 40:23
For the Father *j*.................John 5:22
he who is spiritual *j* ....1 Cor 2:15
j me is the Lord .... 1 Cor 4:4
Him who *j* righteously.... 1 Pet 2:23

JUDGMENT
Teach me good *j*.................Ps 119:66
from prison and from *j*..........Is 53:8
be in danger of the *j*........Matt 5:21
shall not come into *j* ....John 5:24
and My *j* is righteous........John 5:30
if I do judge, My *j*...........John 8:16
"Now is the *j*....................John 12:31
the righteous .... Rom 1:32
j which came from one.... Rom 5:16
appear before the *j*...........2 Cor 5:10
after this the *j*....................Heb 9:27
time has come for *j* .... 1 Pet 4:17
a long time their *j*..............2 Pet 2:3
darkness for the *j* ....Jude 6

JUDGMENTS
The *j* of the Lord are ....Ps 19:9
unsearchable are
His *j*.............................. Rom 11:33

JUST
Noah was a *j* man ....Gen 6:9
j man who perishes.............Eccl 7:15
j shall live by his ....Hab 2:4
her husband, being a *j*......Matt 1:19
resurrection of the *j*.........Luke 14:14
j persons who need no ....Luke 15:7
the Holy One and the *J* ....Acts 3:14
dead, both of the *j* ....Acts 24:15
j shall live by faith .... Rom 1:17
that He might be *j* .... Rom 3:26
j men made perfect............Heb 12:23
have murdered the *j*.........James 5:6
He is faithful and *j* .... 1 John 1:9

JUSTICE
j as the noonday ....Ps 37:6
And Your poor with *j*...........Ps 72:2
j the measuring line ....Is 28:17
the Lord is a God of *j* ....Is 30:18
He will bring forth *j*...........Is 42:1
J is turned back ....Is 59:14
I, the Lord, love *j* ....Is 61:8
truth, and His ways *j* ......Dan 4:37
'Execute true *j*...................Zech 7:9
"Where is the God of *j*......Mal 2:17
And He will declare *j*........Matt 12:18
His humiliation His *j*......Acts 8:33

JUSTIFICATION
because of our *j* .... Rom 4:25
offenses resulted in *j*........ Rom 5:16

JUSTIFIED
Me that you may be *j*.........Job 40:8
words you will be *j*..........Matt 12:37
"But wisdom is *j* ....Luke 7:35
j rather than the.............Luke 18:14
who believes is *j* ....Acts 13:39
"That You may be *j*...........Rom 3:4
law no flesh will be *j*...... Rom 3:20
j freely by His grace ...... Rom 3:24
having been *j* by................Rom 5:1
these He also *j* .... Rom 8:30
that we might be *j* ....Gal 2:16
no flesh shall be *j* ....Gal 2:16
the harlot also *j*.............James 2:25

K

KEEP
k you wherever you........Gen 28:15
day, to *k* it holy................Ex 20:8
Let all the earth *k*............. Hab 2:20
k the commandments....Matt 19:17
"If you love Me, *k*..........John 14:15
k through Your name....John 17:11
orderly and *k* the law......Acts 21:24
k the unity of the.................Eph 4:3
k His commandments .... 1 John 2:3

KEEPER
Am I my brother's *k* ....Gen 4:9
The Lord is your *k* ....Ps 121:5

KEY
taken away the *k*...........Luke 11:52
"He who has the *k*................Rev 3:7

KILL
k the Passover ....Ex 12:21
I *k* and I make alive....... Deut 32:39
"Am I God, to *k* .... 2 Kin 5:7

A time to *k*............................Eccl 3:3
of them they will *k*.........Luke 11:49
afraid of those who *k* .....Luke 12:4
Why do you seek to *k* ......John 7:19
k and eat............................Acts 10:13

KILLED
Abel his brother and *k*........Gen 4:8
k the Prince of life.............Acts 3:15
Your sake we are *k*......... Rom 8:36
k both the Lord........... 1 Thess 2:15

KIND
animals after their *k*.........Gen 6:20
k can come out by........... Mark 9:29
suffers long and is *k* .... 1 Cor 13:4
And be *k* to one.................Eph 4:32

KINDNESS
For His merciful *k*...............Ps 117:2
k shall not depart................Is 54:10
I remember you, The *k*.........Jer 2:2
by longsuffering, by *k*...... 2 Cor 6:6
longsuffering, *k* ....Gal 5:22
and to brotherly *k* .... 2 Pet 1:7

KING
"Yet I have set My *K* ....Ps 2:6
The LORD is *K* forever........Ps 10:16
And the *K* of glory.............Ps 24:7
For God is my *K*..................Ps 74:12
when your *k* is a child..... Eccl 10:16
and the everlasting *K* ...... Jer 10:10
the LORD shall be *K*........ Zech 14:9
who has been born *K*...........Matt 2:2
This Is Jesus The *K*........Matt 27:37
"Behold your *K*.............John 19:14
Now to the *K* eternal......1 Tim 1:17
only Potentate, the *K*......1 Tim 6:15
this Melchizedek, *k*............Heb 7:1
K of Kings and Lord........Rev 19:16

KINGDOM
Yours is the *k*...................1 Chr 29:11
k is the LORD's.....................Ps 22:28
the scepter of Your *k*..........Ps 45:6
is an everlasting *k*..........Ps 145:13
k which shall never be ..... Dan 2:44
High rules in the *k* .... Dan 4:17
"Repent, for the *k*...............Matt 3:2
for Yours is the *k* ....Matt 6:13
"But seek first the *k*........Matt 6:33
the mysteries of the *k*....Matt 13:11
are the sons of the *k*......Matt 13:38
of such is the *k*................Matt 19:14
back, is fit for the *k*.........Luke 9:62
against nation, and *k*....Luke 21:10
he cannot see the *k*.........John 3:3
he cannot enter the *k*..... John 3:5
If My *k* were of this ....John 18:36
for the *k* of God is .... Rom 14:17
will not inherit the *k*.........Gal 5:21
the scepter of Your *k*.........Heb 1:8
we are receiving a *k* ....Heb 12:28

KINGDOMS
the *k* were moved.................Ps 46:6
showed Him all the *k* ....Matt 4:8
have become the *k*...........Rev 11:15

KINGS
The *k* of the earth set ....Ps 2:2
By me *k* reign ....Prov 8:15
governors and *k* ....Matt 10:18
k have desired to see.....Luke 10:24
You have reigned as *k* ..... 1 Cor 4:8
and has made us *k* ....Rev 1:6
that the way of the *k*.......Rev 16:12

KISS
K the Son...............................Ps 2:12
"You gave Me no *k*.....Luke 7:45
one another with a *k* ..... 1 Pet 5:14

KISSED
they *k* one another.......1 Sam 20:41
and *k* Him.....................Matt 26:49
and she *k* His feet
    and....................................Luke 7:38

KNEE
That to Me every *k*...........Is 45:23
have not bowed the *k*...... Rom 11:4
of Jesus every *k*.................Phil 2:10

KNEW
in the womb I *k* ....Jer 1:5
to them, 'I never *k*.............Matt 7:23
k what was in man .... John 2:25
He made Him who *k*.......2 Cor 5:21

KNOCK
k, and it will be...................Matt 7:7
at the door and *k*...............Rev 3:20

KNOW
k good and evil...................Gen 3:22
k that I am the LORD ....Ex 6:7
k that my Redeemer.........Job 19:25
make me to *k* wisdom...........Ps 51:6
Who can *k* it.......................Jer 17:9
saying, 'K the LORD ....Jer 31:34
k what hour your ....Matt 24:42
an oath, "I do not *k* ....Matt 26:72
the world did not *k* .... John 1:10
We speak what We *k* ...... John 3:11
k that You are...................John 6:69
My voice, and I *k*...........John 10:27
If you *k* these things ......John 13:17
k whom I have................John 13:18
are sure that You *k*.......John 16:30
k that I love You.............John 21:15
k times or seasons................ Acts 1:7
and said, "Jesus I *k* ....Acts 19:15
wisdom did not *k* .... 1 Cor 1:21
nor can he *k* them............ 1 Cor 2:14
For we *k* in part and...... 1 Cor 13:9
k the love of Christ ....Eph 3:19
k whom I have .... 2 Tim 1:12
we *k* that we *k* Him .... 1 John 2:3
and you *k* all things........ 1 John 2:20
By this we *k* love........... 1 John 3:16
k that He abides .... 1 John 3:24
k that we are of God..... 1 John 5:19
"I *k* your works.....................Rev 2:2

KNOWLEDGE
and the tree of the *k* ....Gen 2:9
unto night reveals *k*..............Ps 19:2
k is too wonderful..............Ps 139:6
people store up *k*............ Prov 10:14
k spares his words .... Prov 17:27
and he who
    increases *k*.......................Eccl 1:18
k is that wisdom .... Eccl 7:12
k shall increase................. Dan 12:4
more accurate *k*................Acts 24:22
having the form of *k*...... Rom 2:20
law is the *k* of sin............ Rom 3:20
whether there is *k* .... 1 Cor 13:8
Christ which passes *k* ......Eph 3:19
is falsely called *k*..........1 Tim 6:20
in the grace and *k* ....2 Pet 3:18

KNOWN
If you had *k* Me................John 8:19
My sheep, and am *k* ......John 10:14
The world has not *k* ......John 17:25
peace they have not *k* .... Rom 3:17
"For who has *k* ....Rom 11:34
after you have *k* ....Gal 4:9
requests be made *k*..............Phil 4:6
k the Holy Scriptures .....2 Tim 3:15

KNOWS
"For God *k* that in ....Gen 3:5
k what is in the .... Dan 2:22
k the things you have ......Matt 6:8
and hour no one *k*..........Matt 24:36
God *k* your hearts..........Luke 16:15
searches the hearts *k*....... Rom 8:27
k the things of God .... 1 Cor 2:11
k those who are His........2 Tim 2:19
to him who *k* to do........James 4:17
and *k* all things............... 1 John 3:20

L

LABOR
Six days you shall *l*..........Ex 20:9
things are full of *l*............. Eccl 1:8
has man for all his *l*........ Eccl 2:22
He shall see the *l*............. Is 53:11
to Me, all you who *l*........Matt 11:28
"Do not *l* for the............. John 6:27
knowing that your *l*.... 1 Cor 15:58
but rather let him *l*...........Eph 4:28
mean fruit from my *l*.......Phil 1:22

your work of faith, *l*...... 1 Thess 1:3
forget your work and *l*......Heb 6:10
your works, your *l* ....Rev 2:2

LABORERS
but the *l* are few ....Matt 9:37

LACK
What do I still *l*................Matt 19:20
"One thing you *l* .... Mark 10:21

LADDER
and behold, a *l*.................Gen 28:12

LAKE
cast alive into the *l*..........Rev 19:20

LAMB
but where is the *l*...............Gen 22:7
He was led as a *l* ....Is 53:7
The *L* of God who ....John 1:29
the elders, stood a *L* ....Rev 5:6
"Worthy is the *L*...............Rev 5:12
by the blood of the *L* ....Rev 12:11

LAME
l shall leap like a ....Is 35:6
blind see and the *l*............Matt 11:5
And a certain man *l*...........Acts 3:2

LAMP
Your word is a *l*............Ps 119:105
the *l* of the wicked............Prov 13:9
his *l* will be put out .... Prov 20:20
"Nor do they light a *l*........Matt 5:15
"The *l* of the body...........Matt 6:22
when he has lit a *l*..........Luke 8:16
l gives you light ....Luke 11:36
does not light a *l*.............Luke 15:8
burning and shining *l*...... John 5:35

LAMPSTAND
branches of the *l*................Ex 25:32
a basket, but on a *l*..........Matt 5:15
and remove your *l*................Rev 2:5

LAND
l that I will show you.........Gen 12:1
l flowing with milk.................Ex 3:8
They will see the *l*.............Is 33:17
Bethlehem, in the *l*.............Matt 2:6

LANGUAGE
whole earth had one *l*........Gen 11:1
speak in his own *l* .... Acts 2:6
blasphemy, filthy *l* ....Col 3:8

LAST
He shall stand at *l* ....Job 19:25
First and I am the *L* ....Is 44:6
l will be first.....................Matt 20:16
the First and the *L*..............Rev 1:11

LAUGH
"Why did Sarah *l*............Gen 18:13
Woe to you who *l*............Luke 6:25

LAW
stones a copy of the *l*........Josh 8:32
The *l* of the LORD is ....Ps 19:7
I delight in Your *l*............Ps 119:70
Oh, how I love Your *l*......Ps 119:97
And Your *l* is truth.........Ps 119:142
l will proceed from Me........Is 51:4
in whose heart is My *l*...........Is 51:7
The *L* is no more ....Lam 2:9
The *l* of truth was in .... Mal 2:6
to destroy the *L* ....Matt 5:17
for this is the *L* ....Matt 7:12
hang all the *L* and
    the..................................Matt 22:40
"The *l* and the ....Luke 16:16
l was given through......... John 1:17
"Does our *l* judge a .... John 7:51
l is the knowledge........... Rom 3:20
because the *l* brings........ Rom 4:15
when there is no *l*............ Rom 5:13
you are not under *l* .... Rom 6:14
For what the *l* could......Rom 8:3
l that I might live.............Gal 2:19
under guard by the *l*....... Gal 3:23
born under the *l*...................Gal 4:4
l is fulfilled in one .... Gal 5:14
into the perfect *l* ....James 1:25
fulfill the royal *l*.................James 2:8

LAWFUL
Is it *l* to pay taxes............Matt 22:17
All things are *l*................ 1 Cor 6:12

LAWLESSNESS
Me, you who practice *l*.....Matt 7:23
l is already at work....... 2 Thess 2:7

LAZY
l man will be put to........ Prov 12:24
wicked and *l* servant .....Matt 25:26
liars, evil beasts, *l*............Titus 1:12

LEAD
L me in Your truth and........Ps 25:5
And do not *l* us into..........Matt 6:13
"Can the blind *l*................Luke 6:39

LEADS
He *l* me in the paths..............Ps 23:3
And if the blind *l*............Matt 15:14

LEAN
all your heart, And *l*..........Prov 3:5

LEARN
L to do good............................Is 1:17
yoke upon you and *l*......Matt 11:29

LEARNED
Me The tongue of the *l*..........Is 50:4
have not so *l* Christ............Eph 4:20
in all things I have *l*..........Phil 4:12

LEAST
so, shall be called *l*............Matt 5:19

LEAVE
a man shall *l* his ....Gen 2:24
For You will not *l* ....Ps 16:10
"I will never *l*.......................Heb 13:5

LEAVEN
of heaven is like *l*...........Matt 13:33
l leavens the whole ....Gal 5:9

LEAVES
and they sewed fig *l*............Gen 3:7
The *l* of the tree ....Rev 22:2

LENDER
is servant to the *l*..............Prov 22:7

LEPERS
"And many *l* were in ....Luke 4:27

LETTER
for the *l* kills.......................2 Cor 3:6
or by word or by *l* ....2 Thess 2:2

LEVIATHAN
"Can you draw out *L* ....Job 41:1

LEVITE
"Likewise a *L* ....Luke 10:32

LEWDNESS
wickedness, deceit, *l*.......Mark 7:22

LIAR
for he is a *l* and the..........John 8:44
but every man a *l* ....Rom 3:4
we make Him a *l* ....1 John 1:10
his brother, he is a *l* ......1 John 4:20

LIARS
"All men are *l*.....................Ps 116:11
l shall have their................Rev 21:8

LIBERALLY
who gives to all *l*.............James 1:5

LIBERTY
year, and proclaim *l*.......Lev 25:10
'To proclaim *l* to the ....Luke 4:18
into the glorious *l*............ Rom 8:21
Lord is, there is *l* ....2 Cor 3:17
therefore is the *l*....................Gal 5:1

LIE
Do not *l* to one.......................Col 3:9
God, who cannot *l*..............Titus 1:2
an abomination or a *l*.......Rev 21:27

LIED
You have not *l* to men......Acts 5:4

LIES
sin *l* at the door....................Gen 4:7
speaking *l* in.......................1 Tim 4:2

LIFE
the breath of *l* ....Gen 2:7
'For the *l* of the ....Lev 17:11
before you today *l*..........Deut 30:15
He will redeem their *l*.........Ps 72:14
word has given me *l* ....Ps 119:50
She is a tree of *l*.................Prov 3:18
finds me finds *l*..................Prov 8:35
L is more than..................Luke 12:23
l was the light ....John 1:4
so the Son gives *l* ....John 5:21
spirit, and they are *l*.........John 6:63
have the light of *l* ....John 8:12
and I lay down My *l*.........John 10:15
resurrection and the *l*....John 11:25
you lay down your *l*.........John 13:38
l which I now live...............Gal 2:20
l is hidden with.....................Col 3:3
For what is your *l*.........James 4:14
l was manifested............... 1 John 1:2
and the pride of *l*............ 1 John 2:16
has given us eternal *l*.... 1 John 5:11
the Lamb's Book of *L*.....Rev 21:27
right to the tree of *l*.........Rev 22:14
the water of *l* freely ....Rev 22:17
from the Book of *L* ....Rev 22:19

LIFT
I will *l* up my eyes to ....Ps 121:1
Lord, and He will *l*.........James 4:10

LIFTED
your heart is *l*...................Ezek 28:2
in Hades, he *l* up his......Luke 16:23
the Son of Man be *l* ....John 3:14
"And I, if I am *l*.............John 12:32

LIGHT
"Let there be *l* ....Gen 1:3
The LORD is my *l*...................Ps 27:1
and a *l* to my path...........Ps 119:105
The *l* of the righteous ....Prov 13:9
The LORD gives *l* ....Prov 29:13
Truly the *l* is sweet............ Eccl 11:7
let us walk in the *l*...................Is 2:5
l shall break forth.................Is 58:8
"You are the *l*....................Matt 5:14
"Let your *l* so shine.........Matt 5:16
than the sons of *l*.............Luke 16:8
and the life was the *l*........John 1:4
darkness rather than *l*.....John 3:19
saying, "I am the *l*............John 8:12
God who commanded *l*...2 Cor 4:6
Walk as children of *l*.........Eph 5:8
You are all sons of *l*...... 1 Thess 5:5
into His marvelous *l*.......... 1 Pet 2:9
to you, that God is *l* .... 1 John 1:5
l as He is in the................ 1 John 1:7
says he is in the *l*............ 1 John 2:9
The Lamb is its *l*.............Rev 21:23

LIGHTNING
"For as the *l*.....................Matt 24:27
countenance was like *l*....Matt 28:3

LIGHTS
"Let there be *l* ....Gen 1:14
whom you shine as *l*..........Phil 2:15

LIKENESS
according to Our *l*.............Gen 1:26
carved image—any *l*........ Ex 20:4
when I awake in Your *l* .....Ps 17:15
and coming in the *l*............Phil 2:7

LINEN
wrapped Him in the *l* .... Mark 15:46

LIPS
off all flattering *l* ....Ps 12:3
The *l* of the righteous .... Prov 10:21
But the *l* of................... Prov 20:15
am a man of unclean *l*...........Is 6:5
other *l* I will speak .... 1 Cor 14:21
from evil, And his *l* .... 1 Pet 3:10

LISTEN(S)
you are not able to *l*........John 8:43
you who fear God, *l*........Acts 13:16
But whoever *l* to me ....Prov 1:33

LITTLE
Though you are *l*.................. Mic 5:2
l ones only a cup ....Matt 10:42
"O you of *l* faith................Matt 14:31
to whom *l* is forgiven......Luke 7:47
faithful in a very *l*..........Luke 19:17

LIVE
eat, and *l* forever ....Gen 3:22
a man does, he shall *l*...... Lev 18:5
"Seek Me and I ....Amos 5:4
But the just shall *l* ....Hab 2:4
l by bread alone...................Matt 4:4
"for in Him we *l*..............Acts 17:28
l peaceably with all....... Rom 12:18
the life which I now *l*.......Gal 2:20
If we *l* in the Spirit ....Gal 5:25
to me, to *l* is Christ............Phil 1:21

LIVES
but man *l* by every............ Deut 8:3
but Christ *l* in me ....Gal 2:20
to lay down our *l*.......... 1 John 3:16
"I am He who *l*...................Rev 1:18

LIVING
and man became a *l*............Gen 2:7
in the light of the *l*...........Ps 56:13
the dead, but of the *l*....Matt 22:32
do you seek the *l*..............Luke 24:5
the word of God is *l*........Heb 4:12
l creature was like a ....Rev 4:7

LOAVES
have here only five *l*.......Matt 14:17
you ate of the *l*.................. John 6:26

LOCUST(S)
What the chewing *l*..............Joel 1:4
and his food was *l*..............Matt 3:4

LOFTY
Wisdom is too *l*.................Prov 24:7

LONG
your days may be *l* .... Deut 5:16
Who *l* for death ....Job 3:21
I *l* for Your salvation......Ps 119:174
go around in *l* robes...... Mark 12:38

LONGSUFFERING
is love, joy, peace, *l*...........Gal 5:22
and gentleness, with *l*..........Eph 4:2
for all patience and *l*........Col 1:11
might show all *l*..............1 Tim 1:16
once the Divine *l* .... 1 Pet 3:20
and consider that the *l* ....2 Pet 3:15

LOOK
A proud *l*............................Prov 6:17
"*L* to Me .... Is 45:22
l on Me whom they........Zech 12:10
say to you, '*L* here............Luke 17:23
while we do not *l* ....2 Cor 4:18

LOOKING
the plow, and *l* back ....Luke 9:62
l for the blessed hope ......Titus 2:13
l unto Jesus..........................Heb 12:2
l carefully lest ....Heb 12:15
l for the mercy of............Jude 21

LOOSE
and whatever you *l*.........Matt 16:19
said to them, "*L* him ......John 11:44

LORD
L is my strength ....Ex 15:2
L our God, the *L*............ Deut 6:4
You alone are the *L*...........Neh 9:6
The *L* of hosts ....Ps 24:10
Gracious is the *L* ....Ps 116:5
L surrounds His people......Ps 125:2
The *L* is righteous ....Ps 129:4
L is near to all who...........Ps 145:18
L is a God of justice...........Is 30:18
L Our Righteousness ....Jer 23:6
"The *L* is one.....................Zech 14:9
shall not tempt the *L* ....Matt 4:7
shall worship the *L*...........Matt 4:10
Son of Man is also *L*.......Mark 2:28
who is Christ the *L* ....Luke 2:11
L is risen indeed..............Luke 24:34
Me Teacher and *L*..........John 13:13
He is *L* of all.....................Acts 10:36

with your mouth the L .... Rom 10:9
say that Jesus is L .... 1 Cor 12:3
second Man is the L ...... 1 Cor 15:47
the Spirit of the L .... 2 Cor 3:17
that Jesus Christ is L .... Phil 2:11
and deny the only L .... Jude 4
L God Omnipotent .... Rev 19:6

LORDS
for He is Lord of l .... Rev 17:14

LOSES
but if the salt l .... Matt 5:13
and l his own soul .... Matt 16:26

LOST
save that which was l ..... Matt 18:11
and none of them is l ...... John 17:12
You gave Me I have l ...... John 18:9

LOTS
garments, casting l .... Mark 15:24
And they cast their l .... Acts 1:26

LOVE
l your neighbor as .... Lev 19:18
l the LORD your God .... Deut 6:5
Oh, l the LORD .... Ps 31:23
he has set his l .... Ps 91:14
Oh, how I l Your law .... Ps 119:97
l covers all sins .... Prov 10:12
A time to l .... Eccl 3:8
banner over me was l ...... Song 2:4
l is as strong as .... Song 8:6
do justly, To l mercy .... Mic 6:8
to you, l your enemies ...... Matt 5:44
which of them will l .... Luke 7:42
you do not have the l .... John 5:42
If you have l for one ...... John 13:35
"If you l Me .... John 14:15
and My Father will l ...... John 14:23
l one another as I .... John 15:12
l has no one than this ..... John 15:13
because the l of God .... Rom 5:5
to l one another .... Rom 13:8
L suffers long and is .... 1 Cor 13:4
L never fails .... 1 Cor 13:8
greatest of these is l ...... 1 Cor 13:13
For the l of Christ .... 2 Cor 5:14
of the Spirit is l .... Gal 5:22
Husbands, l your wives ..... Eph 5:25
the commandment is l ..... 1 Tim 1:5
For the l of money is ...... 1 Tim 6:10
Let brotherly l .... Heb 13:1
having not seen you l ...... 1 Pet 1:8
for "l will cover a .... 1 Pet 4:8
brotherly kindness l .... 2 Pet 1:7
By this we know l .... 1 John 3:16
Beloved, let us l .... 1 John 4:7
for God is l .... 1 John 4:8
There is no fear in l ...... 1 John 4:18
l Him because He .... 1 John 4:19
loves God must l .... 1 John 4:21
For this is the l .... 1 John 5:3
have left your first l .... Rev 2:4

LOVED
L one and friend You .... Ps 88:18
Yet Jacob I have l .... Mal 1:2
forgiven, for she l .... Luke 7:47
so l the world that .... John 3:16
whom Jesus l .... John 13:23
"As the Father l .... John 15:9
l them as You have .... John 17:23
the Son of God, who l .... Gal 2:20
l the church and gave .... Eph 5:25
Beloved, if God so l .... 1 John 4:11
To Him who l us and .... Rev 1:5

LOVELY
he is altogether l .... Song 5:16
whatever things are l .... Phil 4:8

LOVES
"He who l father or .... Matt 10:37
l his life will lose .... John 12:25
l Me will be loved .... John 14:21
l a cheerful giver .... 2 Cor 9:7
If anyone l the world ..... 1 John 2:15
l God must love his .... 1 John 4:21

LOWER
made him a little l .... Heb 2:7

LOWLY
for I am gentle and l .... Matt 11:29
in presence am l .... 2 Cor 10:1
l brother glory .... James 1:9

LUKEWARM
because you are l .... Rev 3:16

LUST
looks at a woman to l .... Matt 5:28
not fulfill the l .... Gal 5:16
You l and do not
have .... James 4:2
the l of the flesh .... 1 John 2:16

LUSTS
to fulfill its l .... Rom 13:14
also youthful l .... 2 Tim 2:22
and worldly l .... Titus 2:12
to the former l .... 1 Pet 1:14
abstain from fleshly l ...... 1 Pet 2:11
to their own ungodly l .... Jude 18

LUXURY
in pleasure and l .... James 5:5
the abundance of her l ...... Rev 18:3

LYING
I hate and abhor l .... Ps 119:163
righteous man hates l ...... Prov 13:5
not trust in these l .... Jer 7:4
signs, and l wonders ..... 2 Thess 2:9

M

MADE
m the stars also .... Gen 1:16
things My hand has m .... Is 66:2
All things were m .... John 1:3

MAGIC
m brought their books ... Acts 19:19

MAGNIFIED
let Your name be m .... 2 Sam 7:26
the Lord Jesus was m ..... Acts 19:17
also Christ will be m .... Phil 1:20

MAGNIFIES
"My soul m the Lord .... Luke 1:46

MAGNIFY
m the LORD with me .... Ps 34:3

MAJESTY
right hand of the M .... Heb 1:3
eyewitnesses of His m ..... 2 Pet 1:16
wise, Be glory and l .... Jude 25

MAKE
"Let Us m man in Our ...... Gen 1:26
m you a great nation .... Gen 12:2
"You shall not m .... Ex 20:4
m Our home with .... John 14:23

MAKER
M is your husband .... Is 54:5
has forgotten his M .... Hos 8:14
builder and m is God ...... Heb 11:10

MALICE
in m be babes .... 1 Cor 14:20
laying aside all m .... 1 Pet 2:1

MAN
"Let Us make m .... Gen 1:26
m that You are mindful .... Ps 8:4
of the Son of M .... Matt 24:27
"Behold the M .... John 19:5
by m came death .... 1 Cor 15:21
our outward m .... 2 Cor 4:16
the m of God may .... 2 Tim 3:17
is the number of a m ...... Rev 13:18

MANGER
and laid Him in a m .... Luke 2:7

MANIFESTED
"I have m Your name ...... John 17:6
God was m in the .... 1 Tim 3:16
the life was m .... 1 John 1:2

MANNA
of Israel ate m .... Ex 16:35
"Our fathers ate the m ..... John 6:31

MANNER
Is this the m of man .... 2 Sam 7:19
in an unworthy m .... 1 Cor 11:27
what m of love .... 1 John 3:1

MANSIONS
house are many m .... John 14:2

MARK
And the LORD set a m ...... Gen 4:15
receives the m .... Rev 14:11

MARRIAGE
M is honorable among ..... Heb 13:4

MARRIED
But he who is m .... 1 Cor 7:33

MARRY
they neither m nor .... Matt 22:30
forbidding to m .... 1 Tim 4:3

MARTYRS
the blood of the m .... Rev 17:6

MARVELED
Jesus heard it, He m .... Matt 8:10
so that Pilate m .... Mark 15:5

MARVELOUS
It is m in our eyes .... Ps 118:23
of darkness into His m ...... 1 Pet 2:9

MASTER
a servant like his m .... Matt 10:25
greater than his m .... John 13:16
and useful for the M .... 2 Tim 2:21

MASTERS
can serve two m .... Luke 16:13
who have believing m ...... 1 Tim 6:2

MATURE
understanding be m ...... 1 Cor 14:20
us, as many as are m .... Phil 3:15

MEASURE
a perfect and just m .... Deut 25:15
give the Spirit by m .... John 3:34
to each one a m .... Rom 12:3

MEASURED
m the waters in the .... Is 40:12
you use, it will be m .... Matt 7:2

MEASURING
behold, a man with a m .... Zech 2:1
m themselves by .... 2 Cor 10:12

MEAT
will never again eat m .... 1 Cor 8:13

MEDIATOR
by the hand of a m .... Gal 3:19
is one God and one M ..... 1 Tim 2:5
to Jesus the M of the .... Heb 12:24

MEDICINE
does good, like m .... Prov 17:22

MEDITATE
but you shall m .... Josh 1:8
M within your heart on .... Ps 4:4
I will m on Your .... Ps 119:15
m beforehand on .... Luke 21:14
m on these things .... Phil 4:8

MEDITATES
in His law he m .... Ps 1:2

MEDITATION
of my mouth and the m ..... Ps 19:14
It is my m all the day .... Ps 119:97

MEDIUM(S)
a woman who is a m .... Lev 20:27
"Seek those who are m .... Is 8:19

MEEK
with equity for the m .... Is 11:4
Blessed are the m .... Matt 5:5

MEEKNESS
are done in the m .... James 3:13

MELODY
singing and making m ..... Eph 5:19

MEMBER
body is not one *m*.......... 1 Cor 12:14

MEMBERS
you that one of your *m*.....Matt 5:29
do not present your *m*..... Rom 6:13
neighbor, for we are *m*......Eph 4:25

MEMORIAL
and this is My *m*...................Ex 3:15
also be told as a *m*.........Matt 26:13

MEN
m began to call on the.......Gen 4:26
make you fishers of *m*......Matt 4:19
goodwill toward *m*...........Luke 2:14
heaven or from *m*.........Luke 20:4
Likewise also the *m*......... Rom 1:27
the Lord, and not to *m*........Eph 5:8
between God and *m*.........1 Tim 2:5

MERCIFUL
Lord, the Lord God, *m*......Ex 34:6
He is ever *m*.........................Ps 37:26
Blessed are the *m*................Matt 5:7
saying, 'God be *m*.........Luke 18:13
"For I will be *m*.........Heb 8:12

MERCY
but showing *m* to ....Ex 20:6
and abundant in *m*........Num 14:18
m endures forever.......1 Chr 16:34
M and truth have met.....Ps 85:10
m is everlasting..................Ps 100:5
Let not *m* and truth.........Prov 3:3
For I desire *m* and not........Hos 6:6
do justly, To love *m*...........Mic 6:8
'I desire *m* and not...........Matt 9:13
And His *m* is on those....Luke 1:50
"I will have *m*................... Rom 9:15
that He might have *m*.... Rom 11:32
m has made..................... 1 Cor 7:25
as we have received *m*.....2 Cor 4:1
God, who is rich in *m*.........Eph 2:4
but I obtained *m*..............1 Tim 1:13
that he may find *m*.........2 Tim 1:18
to His *m* He saved us......Titus 3:5
that we may obtain *m* ....Heb 4:16

MERRY
m heart makes a............. Prov 15:13
we should make *m*.........Luke 15:32

MESSIAH
Until *M* the Prince............. Dan 9:25
"We have found the *M*....John 1:41

MIDST
God is in the *m*......................Ps 46:5
I am there in the *m* ....Matt 18:20

MIGHT
'My power and the *m* ...... Deut 8:17
'Not by *m* nor by .... Zech 4:6
in the power of His *m*.......Eph 6:10
honor and power and *m* ...Rev 7:12

MIGHTIER
coming after me is *m*......Matt 3:11

MIGHTY
He was a *m* hunter............Gen 10:9
m have fallen ....2 Sam 1:19
The Lord *m* in battle............Ps 24:8
their Redeemer is *m* ...... Prov 23:11
m has done great.............Luke 1:49
the flesh, not many *m*..... 1 Cor 1:26
the working of His *m*.........Eph 1:19

MILK
come, buy wine and *m*..........Is 55:1
shall flow with *m* ....Joel 3:18
have come to need *m*.........Heb 5:12
desire the pure *m* .... 1 Pet 2:2

MIND
put wisdom in the *m*...........Job 38:36
perfect peace, Whose *m*........Is 26:3
have an anxious *m*.........Luke 12:29
m I myself serve the ...... Rom 7:25
who has known the *m*... Rom 11:34
Be of the same *m*........... Rom 12:16
in his own *m* .... Rom 14:5
has known the *m*........... 1 Cor 2:16
are out of your *m* .... 1 Cor 14:23

Let this *m* be in you.............Phil 2:5
love and of a sound *m*......2 Tim 1:7

MINDFUL
is man that You are *m*............Ps 8:4
for you are not *m* ....Matt 16:23
is man that You are *m*.........Heb 2:6

MINDS
put My law in their *m*....... Jer 31:33
I stir up your pure *m* ....2 Pet 3:1

MINISTER
For he is God's *m*............. Rom 13:4
you will be a good *m*........1 Tim 4:6

MINISTERS
for they are God's *m*........ Rom 13:6
If anyone *m*........................1 Pet 4:11

MINISTRIES
are differences of *m*........ 1 Cor 12:5

MINISTRY
But if the *m* of death........2 Cor 3:7
since we have this *m* ....2 Cor 4:1
has given us the *m* ....2 Cor 5:18
for the work of *m* ....Eph 4:12
fulfill your *m*.....................2 Tim 4:5
a more excellent *m* ....Heb 8:6

MIRACLE(S)
one who works a *m* .... Mark 9:39
worked unusual *m*...........Acts 19:11
the working of *m*........... 1 Cor 12:10

MOCK
Fools *m* at sin.....................Prov 14:9
to the Gentiles to *m* ....Matt 20:19

MOCKED
noon, that Elijah *m*....... 1 Kin 18:27
deceived, God is not *m*.........Gal 6:7

MOCKER
Wine is a *m*........................Prov 20:1

MOCKS
He who *m* the poor..........Prov 17:5

MODERATION
with propriety and *m*........1 Tim 2:9

MOMENT
in a *m* they die...................Job 34:20
in a *m*, in the................... 1 Cor 15:52

MONEY
be redeemed without *m* ....Is 52:3
And you who have no *m* ......Is 55:1
and hid his lord's *m*........Matt 25:18
to give him *m*.................. Mark 14:11
"Carry neither *m*..............Luke 10:4
I sent you without *m*.......Luke 22:35
be purchased with *m*........Acts 8:20
not greedy for *m*...............1 Tim 3:3
m is a root of all ....1 Tim 6:10

MONEY CHANGERS
the tables of the *m* ....Matt 21:12

MOON
until the *m* is no more.........Ps 72:7
m will not give its.......... Mark 13:24

MORNING
Evening and *m* and at........Ps 55:17
Lucifer, son of the *m* ....Is 14:12
very early in the *m*.........Luke 24:1
the Bright and *M* Star .....Rev 22:16

MORTAL
sin reign in your *m* .... Rom 6:12
and this *m* must put...... 1 Cor 15:53

MOTH
where *m* and rust ....Matt 6:19

MOTHER
because she was the *m*......Gen 3:20
leave his father and *m*......Matt 19:5
"Behold your *m* ....John 19:27
The *M* of Harlots...............Rev 17:5

MOUNT
come up to *M* Sinai............Ex 19:23
They shall *m* up with..........Is 40:31

MOUNTAIN
to Horeb, the *m*....................Ex 3:1
let us go up to the *m*................Is 2:3
became a great *m*............. Dan 2:35
are you, O great *m*............Zech 4:7
you will say to this *m* .....Matt 17:20
Him on the holy *m*...........2 Pet 1:18

MOUNTAINS
m were brought forth...........Ps 90:2
m shall depart And the ....Is 54:10
in Judea flee to the *m*.....Matt 24:16
that I could remove *m* .... 1 Cor 13:2

MOURN
A time to *m* .... Eccl 3:4
are those who *m*...................Matt 5:4
of the earth will *m*................ Rev 1:7

MOURNING
shall be a great *m*...........Zech 12:11
be turned to *m* and ....James 4:9

MOUTH
"Who has made man's *m*.... Ex 4:11
Out of the *m* of babes............Ps 8:2
knowledge, But the *m* ... Prov 10:14
The *m* of an immoral..... Prov 22:14
And a flattering *m* .... Prov 26:28
m speaking pompous .... Dan 7:8
m defiles a man................Matt 15:11
m I will judge you ....Luke 19:22
I will give you a *m* ....Luke 21:15
m confession is made.... Rom 10:10
m great swelling words......Jude 16
vomit you out of My *m*.... Rev 3:16

MOVED
she shall not be *m*.................Ps 46:5
spoke as they were *m*......2 Pet 1:21

MUCH
m study is .... Eccl 12:12
to whom *m* is given ....Luke 12:48

MULTIPLIED
of the disciples *m* ....Acts 6:7
of God grew and *m*.........Acts 12:24

MULTIPLY
"Be fruitful and *m* ....Gen 1:22
m the descendants .... Jer 33:22

MULTITUDE
stars of heaven in *m* .... Deut 1:10
In the *m* of words sin .... Prov 10:19
compassion on the *m* .....Matt 15:32
with the angel a *m* ....Luke 2:13
"love will cover a *m* .... 1 Pet 4:8
and behold, a great *m* .... Rev 7:9

MURDER
"You shall not *m* .... Ex 20:13
'You shall not *m* ....Matt 5:21
You *m* and covet and ......James 4:2

MURDERED
up Jesus whom you *m*......Acts 5:30

MURDERER
He was a *m* from the .... John 8:44
his brother is a *m*........... 1 John 3:15

MURDERERS
and profane, for *m*...........1 Tim 1:9
abominable, *m*...................Rev 21:8

MURDERS
evil thoughts, *m*...............Matt 15:19

MYSTERIES
to you to know the *m* .....Matt 13:11
and understand all *m* ..... 1 Cor 13:2

MYSTERY
given to know the *m*....... Mark 4:11
wisdom of God in a *m*...... 1 Cor 2:7
I tell you a *m*.................. 1 Cor 15:51
made known to us the *m* ....Eph 1:9
the *m* of godliness...........1 Tim 3:16

N

NAILED
n it to the cross ....Col 2:14

o their understanding....Luke 24:45
Now I saw heaven *o* ....Rev 19:11

OPPORTUNITY
But sin, taking *o* ....Rom 7:8
as we have *o* ....Gal 6:10
but you lacked *o* ....Phil 4:10

OPPRESS
he loves to *o* ....Hos 12:7
o the widow or the..........Zech 7:10
Do not the rich *o* ....James 2:6

OPPRESSED
for all who are *o* ....Ps 103:6
The tears of the *o* .... Eccl 4:1
He was *o* and He was...........Is 53:7
all who were *o* ....Acts 10:38

OPPRESSION
have surely seen the *o*...........Ex 3:7
their life from *o* ....Ps 72:14
brought low through *o* .....Ps 107:39
me from the *o* ....Ps 119:134
considered all the *o*............ Eccl 4:1
o destroys a wise................ Eccl 7:7
justice, but behold, *o*..............Is 5:7
surely seen the *o* ....Acts 7:34

ORACLES
received the living *o* ....Acts 7:38
were committed the *o*........Rom 3:2
principles of the *o* ....Heb 5:12

ORDAINED
o you a prophet ....Jer 1:5
whom He has *o*................Acts 17:31

ORPHANS
will not leave you *o*........John 14:18
to visit *o* and widows.....James 1:27

OUTSIDE
and dish, that the *o* ....Matt 23:26
Pharisees make the *o*....Luke 11:39
toward those who
are *o*.....................................Col 4:5
to Him, *o* the camp ....Heb 13:13
But *o* are dogs and..........Rev 22:15

OUTWARD
at the *o* appearance ....1 Sam 16:7
adornment be merely *o*..... 1 Pet 3:3

OVERCOME
good cheer, I have ......John 16:33
and the Lamb will *o*.........Rev 17:14

OVERCOMES
of God *o* the world......... 1 John 5:4
o I will give to eat................Rev 2:7
o shall not be hurt...............Rev 2:11
o shall inherit all ....Rev 21:7

OVERSEER
to the Shepherd and *O*....1 Pet 2:25

OVERSEERS
you, serving as *o* .... 1 Pet 5:2

OVERSHADOW
of the Highest will *o* ....Luke 1:35

OVERTHROWS
And *o* the mighty ....Job 12:19
o them in the night...........Job 34:25
o the words of the ....Prov 22:12

OVERWHELMED
and my spirit was *o* ....Ps 77:3
my spirit is *o* within..........Ps 143:4

OVERWORK
Do not *o* to be rich...........Prov 23:4

OWE
O no one anything ....Rom 13:8

OWN
He came to His *o*.............John 1:11
having loved His *o*..........John 13:1
would love its *o*...............John 15:19
you are not your *o* ....1 Cor 6:19
But each one has his *o* ....1 Cor 7:7
For all seek their *o* ....Phil 2:21
from our sins in His *o*..........Rev 1:5

OX
shall not muzzle an *o* ...... Deut 25:4
o knows its owner...................Is 1:3
Sabbath loose his *o*......Luke 13:15
shall not muzzle an *o* ...... 1 Cor 9:9

P

PAIN
p you shall bring ....Gen 3:16
p as a woman in.....................Is 13:8
Why is my *p* perpetual..... Jer 15:18
shall be no more *p* ....Rev 21:4

PAINED
My heart is severely *p*..........Ps 55:4
I am *p* in my very................ Jer 4:19

PAINS
The *p* of death.....................Ps 116:3
having loosed the *p*...........Acts 2:24

PALACE(S)
enter the King's *p*..............Ps 45:15
guards his own *p*............Luke 11:21
evident to the whole *p*.......Phil 1:13
Out of the ivory *p*................Ps 45:8

PALM
p branches in their..............Rev 7:9

PALMS
struck Him with the *p* ....Matt 26:67

PANGS
The *p* of death......................Ps 18:4
labors with birth *p* .... Rom 8:22

PARABLE(S)
do You speak this *p*.......Luke 12:41
rest it is given in *p*...........Luke 8:10

PARADISE
will be with Me in *P*......Luke 23:43
in the midst of the *P* ....Rev 2:7

PARDON
He will abundantly *p*............Is 55:7
p all their iniquities............. Jer 33:8

PARDONING
is a God like You, *p* .... Mic 7:18

PARENTS
will rise up against *p* .....Matt 10:21
has left house or *p*.........Luke 18:29
disobedient to *p*............... Rom 1:30

PART
chosen that good *p*........Luke 10:42
you, you have no *p* ....John 13:8
For we know in *p* ....1 Cor 13:9
shall take away his *p*.......Rev 22:19

PARTAKER
in hope should be *p* .... 1 Cor 9:10
Christ, and also a *p*........... 1 Pet 5:1

PARTAKERS
Gentiles have been *p* ..... Rom 15:27
know that as you are *p* ... 2 Cor 1:7
qualified us to be *p* ....Col 1:12

PARTIALITY
that God shows no *p*......Acts 10:34
doing nothing with *p* ......1 Tim 5:21
good fruits, without *p*....James 3:17

PASS
I will *p* over you ....Ex 12:13
When you *p* through the.......Is 43:2
and earth will *p*...............Matt 24:35

PASSED
forbearance God had *p* ... Rom 3:25
High Priest who has *p*.......Heb 4:14
know that we have *p*.... 1 John 3:14

PASSES
of Christ which *p*...............Eph 3:19

PASSION(S)
uncleanness, *p* ....Col 3:5
gave them up to vile *p*... Rom 1:26

PASSOVER
It is the LORD's *P*................Ex 12:11
I will keep the *P*............Matt 26:18

indeed Christ, our *P*.......... 1 Cor 5:7
By faith he kept the *P*......Heb 11:28

PASTORS
and some *p* and ....Eph 4:11

PASTURE(S)
the sheep of Your *p* ....Ps 74:1
in and out and find *p*........John 10:9
to lie down in green *p* ....Ps 23:2

PATH
You will show me the *p* .....Ps 16:11

PATHS
He leads me in the *p*............Ps 23:3
Make His *p* straight..........Matt 3:3
and make straight *p*........Heb 12:13

PATIENCE
'Master, have *p* ....Matt 18:26
and bear fruit with *p*.......Luke 8:15
labor of love, and *p* ...... 1 Thess 1:3
faith, love, *p* ....1 Tim 6:11
your faith produces *p* ......James 1:3
p have its perfect.............James 1:4
in the kingdom and *p* .... Rev 1:9

PATIENT
rejoicing in hope, *p*........ Rom 12:12
the weak, be *p*.............. 1 Thess 5:14

PATRIARCHS
begot the twelve *p*.............Acts 7:8

PATTERN
p which you were...............Ex 26:30
as you have us for a *p* ......Phil 3:17
p shown you on the ....Heb 8:5

PEACE
you, And give you *p* .... Num 6:26
both lie down in *p*...................Ps 4:8
p have those who...........Ps 119:165
I am for *p*...........................Ps 120:7
war, And a time of *p*....... Eccl 3:8
Father, Prince of *P*..................Is 9:6
keep him in perfect *p* ....Is 26:3
p they have not.....................Is 59:8
slightly, Saying, '*P*............. Jer 6:14
place I will give *p*...............Hag 2:9
is worthy, let your *p* ....Matt 10:13
that I came to bring *p*....Matt 10:34
And on earth *p* ....Luke 2:14
if a son of *p* is there..........Luke 10:6
that make for your *p* ......Luke 19:42
leave with you, My *p* ..... John 14:27
Me you may have *p* ....John 16:33
Grace to you and *p* ....Rom 1:7
by faith, we have *p* ....Rom 5:1
God has called us to *p*... 1 Cor 7:15
p will be with you .... 2 Cor 13:11
Spirit is love, joy, *p*.............Gal 5:22
He Himself is our *p*............Eph 2:14
and the *p* of God.................Phil 4:7
And let the *p* of God ....Col 3:15
faith, love, *p* ....2 Tim 2:22
meaning "king of *p*,"...........Heb 7:2

PEACEABLE
is first pure, then *p*........James 3:17

PEACEABLY
on you, live *p* .... Rom 12:18

PEACEMAKERS
Blessed are the *p* ....Matt 5:9

PEARL
had found one *p* ....Matt 13:46

PEARLS
nor cast your *p* ....Matt 7:6
gates were twelve *p*........Rev 21:21

PENTECOST
P had fully come ....Acts 2:1

PEOPLE
will take you as My *p* ....Ex 6:7
p shall be my *p* .... Ruth 1:16
p who know the joyful ....Ps 89:15
We are His *p* and the...........Ps 100:3
"Blessed is Egypt My *p* ......Is 19:25
to make ready a *p* ....Luke 1:17
take out of them a *p*.......Acts 15:14
who were not My *p*.......... Rom 9:25

they shall be My *p* .... 2 Cor 6:16
Lord will judge His *p* ...... Heb 10:30
but are now the *p* .... 1 Pet 2:10
tribe and tongue and *p* .... Rev 5:9
they shall be His *p* .... Rev 21:3

PERCEIVE
seeing, but do not *p* .... Is 6:9
may see and not *p* .... Mark 4:12

PERDITION
except the son of *p* .... John 17:12
revealed, the son of *p* ... 2 Thess 2:3
who draw back to *p* .... Heb 10:39

PERFECT
Noah was a just man, *p* ...... Gen 6:9
Father in heaven is *p* .... Matt 5:48
they may be made *p* ...... John 17:23
and *p* will of God.............. Rom 12:2
when that which is *p* .... 1 Cor 13:10
present every man *p* .... Col 1:28
good gift and every *p* ... James 1:17
in word, he is a *p* .... James 3:2
p love casts out fear ...... 1 John 4:18

PERFECTED
third day I shall be *p* .... Luke 13:32
or am already *p* .... Phil 3:12
Son who has been *p* .... Heb 7:28

PERFECTION
let us go on to *p* .... Heb 6:1

PERISH
so that we may not *p* .... Jon 1:6
little ones should *p* .... Matt 18:14
in Him should not *p* .... John 3:16
they shall never *p* .... John 10:28
among those who *p* ... 2 Thess 2:10
that any should *p* .... 2 Pet 3:9

PERISHABLE
do it to obtain a *p* .... 1 Cor 9:25

PERISHED
Truth has *p* and has........... Jer 7:28

PERISHING
We are *p* .... Matt 8:25

PERMITTED
p no one to do them.......... Ps 105:14
we are *p* .... 2 Cor 4:8

PERSECUTE
when they revile and *p* ..... Matt 5:11

PERSECUTED
If they *p* Me.................... John 15:20
p, but not forsaken........... 2 Cor 4:9

PERSECUTION
p arises because of.......... Matt 13:21
At that time a great *p* .... Acts 8:1
do I still suffer *p* .... Gal 5:11

PERSECUTOR
a blasphemer, a *p*............ 1 Tim 1:13

PERSEVERANCE
tribulation produces *p* .... Rom 5:3

PERSON
do not regard the *p* .... Matt 22:16
express image of His *p*........ Heb 1:3

PERSUADE
"You almost *p* me .... Acts 26:28

PERSUADED
neither will they be *p*..... Luke 16:31
p that He is able .... 2 Tim 1:12

PERVERSE
your way is *p* .... Num 22:32
p man sows strife .... Prov 16:28
from this *p* generation...... Acts 2:40

PERVERT
"You shall not *p*.............. Deut 16:19
p the gospel of Christ .... Gal 1:7

PESTILENCE(S)
from the perilous *p* .... Ps 91:3
Before Him went *p*.............. Hab 3:5
will be famines, *p*.............. Matt 24:7

PHARISEE
to pray, one a *P* .... Luke 18:10

PHILOSOPHERS
p encountered him.......... Acts 17:18

PHILOSOPHY
cheat you through *p* .... Col 2:8

PHYSICIAN(S)
have no need of a *p* .... Matt 9:12
her livelihood on *p*........... Luke 8:43

PIECES
they took the thirty *p*....... Matt 27:9

PIERCE
a sword will *p* .... Luke 2:35

PIERCED
p My hands and My feet.... Ps 22:16
whom they have *p* .... Zech 12:10
of the soldiers *p* .... John 19:34
p themselves through..... 1 Tim 6:10
and they also who *p* .... Rev 1:7

PILGRIMS
we are aliens and *p*...... 1 Chr 29:15
were strangers and *p*...... Heb 11:13

PILLAR
and she became a *p* .... Gen 19:26
and by night in a *p*............ Ex 13:21
the living God, the *p* .... 1 Tim 3:15

PILLARS
break their sacred *p*........... Ex 34:13
Blood and fire and *p*......... Joel 2:30
and his feet like *p*............. Rev 10:1

PIT
who go down to the *p*........... Ps 28:1
a harlot is a deep *p* .... Prov 23:27
my life in the *p*.............. Lam 3:53
up my life from the *p*......... Jon 2:6
into the bottomless *p* .... Rev 20:3

PITY
for someone to take *p*......... Ps 69:20
p He redeemed them .... Is 63:9
just as I had *p* .... Matt 18:33

PLACE
Come, see the *p* .... Matt 28:6
My word has no *p* .... John 8:37
I go to prepare a *p* .... John 14:2
might go to his own *p*...... Acts 1:25

PLACES
And the rough *p* .... Is 40:4
They love the best *p* .... Matt 23:6
in the heavenly *p*.................. Eph 1:3

PLAGUE(S)
bring yet one more *p* .... Ex 11:1
p that are written .... Rev 22:18

PLANK
First remove the *p*.............. Matt 7:5

PLANS
He makes the *p* of the .... Ps 33:10
that devises wicked *p* .... Prov 6:18

PLANT
A time to *p*............................. Eccl 3:2
Him as a tender *p*................. Is 53:2
p of an alien vine................ Jer 2:21
p which My heavenly ..... Matt 15:13

PLANTED
shall be like a tree *p* .... Ps 1:3
by the roots and be *p*....... Luke 17:6
I *p*, Apollos watered .... 1 Cor 3:6

PLEASANT
food, that it was *p* .... Gen 3:6
how good and how *p*....... Ps 133:1

PLEASE
in the flesh cannot *p* .... Rom 8:8
p his neighbor for his...... Rom 15:2
he may *p* the Lord........... 1 Cor 7:32
is impossible to *p* Him....... Heb 11:6

PLEASED
Then You shall be *p* .... Ps 51:19
in whom I am well *p*....... Matt 3:17

God was not well *p*......... 1 Cor 10:5
testimony, that he *p*........... Heb 11:5

PLEASING
sacrifice, well *p*.................. Phil 4:18
for this is well *p*....................Col 3:20
in you what is well *p* .... Heb 13:21

PLEASURE
Do good in Your good *p* ....Ps 51:18
p will be a poor man...... Prov 21:17
shall perform all My *p*........ Is 44:28
your Father's good *p* ....Luke 12:32
to the good *p* of His .... Eph 1:5
for sin You had no *p*.......... Heb 10:6
My soul has no *p*............ Heb 10:38
p that war in your .... James 4:1

PLEASURES
Your right hand are *p* .... Ps 16:11
cares, riches, and *p*.......... Luke 8:14
to enjoy the passing *p* .....Heb 11:25

PLOW
put his hand to the *p*........ Luke 9:62

PLUCK
p the heads of grain........ Mark 2:23

PLUCKED
cheeks to those who *p*........... Is 50:6
And His disciples *p*......... Luke 6:1
you would have *p*................ Gal 4:15

PLUNDER
p the Egyptians.................... Ex 3:22
The *p* of the poor is................ Is 3:14
house and *p* his goods....Matt 12:29

PLUNDERED
a people robbed and *p*......... Is 42:22
"And when you are *p* ..... Jer 4:30

PLUNDERING
me Because of the *p*.............. Is 22:4
accepted the *p* of your.....Heb 10:34

POISONED
p by bitterness .... Acts 8:23

POMPOUS
and a mouth speaking *p* .... Dan 7:8

PONDER
P the path of your .... Prov 4:26

PONDERED
p them in her heart.......... Luke 2:19

PONDERS
p all his paths.................... Prov 5:21

POOR
p will never cease.......... Deut 15:11
So the *p* have hope .... Job 5:16
I delivered the *p*............... Job 29:12
p shall eat and be............... Ps 22:26
But I am *p* and needy .... Ps 40:17
Let the *p* and needy........... Ps 74:21
He raises the *p*.................. Ps 113:7
slack hand becomes *p*...... Prov 10:4
p man is hated even....... Prov 14:20
has mercy on the *p* .... Prov 14:21
who oppresses the *p* ...... Prov 14:31
p reproaches his............... Prov 17:5
Do not rob the *p* .... Prov 22:22
that same *p* man............... Eccl 9:15
The alien or the *p*............. Zech 7:10
"Blessed are the *p* .... Matt 5:3
p have the gospel .... Matt 11:5
"For you have the *p* .... Matt 26:11
sakes He became *p*.......... 2 Cor 8:9
should remember the *p*......Gal 2:10
God not chosen the *p*.....James 2:5
wretched, miserable, *p*......Rev 3:17

PORTION
O Lord, You, are the *p* ....Ps 16:5
heart and my *p* forever ..... Ps 73:26
You are my *p* ....Ps 119:57
I will divide Him a *p* ....Is 53:12
rejoice in their *p* ....Is 61:7
The *P* of Jacob is not....... Jer 10:16
"The Lord is my *p* ....Lam 3:24
and appoint him the *p* ....Matt 24:51
to give them their *p*.......Luke 12:42
give me the *p* ....Luke 15:12

POSSESS
descendants shall p.........Gen 22:17
p the land which..............Josh 1:11
"By your patience p ......Luke 21:19
p his own vessel .... 1 Thess 4:4

POSSESSION(S)
as an everlasting p............Gen 17:8
and an enduring p............Heb 10:34
and sold their p.................Acts 2:45

POSSIBLE
God all things are p ....Matt 19:26
p that the blood ....Heb 10:4

POUR
p My Spirit on your ....Is 44:3
P out Your fury................. Jer 10:25
That I will p out My...........Joel 2:28
"And I will p...................Zech 12:10
angels, "Go and p..............Rev 16:1

POURED
I am p out like water ....Ps 22:14
grace is p upon Your............Ps 45:2
strong, Because He p..........Is 53:12
and My fury will be p........ Jer 7:20
broke the flask and p ..... Mark 14:3
I am already being p.........2 Tim 4:6
whom He p out on us .... Titus 3:6

POVERTY
leads only to p .... Prov 14:23
p put in all the...................Luke 21:4
and their deep p .... 2 Cor 8:2
p might become rich........ 2 Cor 8:9
tribulation, and p..............Rev 2:9

POWER
that I may show My p ....Ex 9:16
him who is without p...........Job 26:2
p who can understand.....Job 26:14
p belongs to God ....Ps 62:11
p Your enemies shall...........Ps 66:3
gives strength and p ....Ps 68:35
a king is, there is p............Eccl 8:4
No one has p over the ....Eccl 8:8
'Not by might nor by p......Zech 4:6
the kingdom and the p.....Matt 6:13
the Son of Man has p ....Matt 9:6
Scriptures nor the p.......Matt 22:29
p went out from Him.......Luke 6:19
are endued with p ....Luke 24:49
I have p to lay it ....John 10:18
"You could have no p....John 19:11
you shall receive p...........Acts 1:8
though by our own p......Acts 3:12
man is the great p ....Acts 8:10
"Give me this p ....Acts 8:19
for it is the p....................Rom 1:16
saved it is the p............ 1 Cor 1:18
Greeks, Christ the p..... 1 Cor 1:24
that the p of Christ........ 2 Cor 12:9
greatness of His p ....Eph 1:19
the Lord and in the p......Eph 6:10
to His glorious p.............Col 1:11
the glory of His p .... 2 Thess 1:9
of fear, but of p................2 Tim 1:7
by the word of His p ....Heb 1:3
p of death, that ....Heb 2:14
as His divine p .... 2 Pet 1:3
Dominion and p ....Jude 25
to him I will give p ....Rev 2:26
honor and glory and p ......Rev 5:13

POWERFUL
of the LORD is p ....Ps 29:4
of God is living and p......Heb 4:12

POWERS
principalities and p ....Col 2:15
word of God and the p........Heb 6:5

PRAISE
p shall be of You in............Ps 22:25
the people shall p ....Ps 45:17
P is awaiting You.................Ps 65:1
Let all the peoples p ....Ps 67:3
p shall be continually.........Ps 71:6
And the heavens will p ....Ps 89:5
Seven times a day I p.....Ps 119:164
that has breath p.............Ps 150:6
Let another man p ....Prov 27:2
let her own works p....... Prov 31:31

And your gates P ....Is 60:18
He makes Jerusalem a p.......Is 62:7
For You are my p.............. Jer 17:14
Me a name of joy, a p...... Jer 33:9
give you fame and p ....Zeph 3:20
You have perfected p .....Matt 21:16
men more than the p ......John 12:43
p is not from men but..... Rom 2:29
Then each one's p .... 1 Cor 4:5
should be to the p..............Eph 1:12
to the glory and p.............Phil 1:11
I will sing p to You ....Heb 2:12
the sacrifice of p..............Heb 13:15
and for the p of those ... 1 Pet 2:14
saying, "P our God............Rev 19:5

PRAISED
daily He shall be p ....Ps 72:15
LORD's name is to be p......Ps 113:3
and greatly to be p ....Ps 145:3
the Most High and p ...... Dan 4:34

PRAISES
it is good to sing p...............Ps 147:1
and he p .... Prov 31:28

PRAISEWORTHY
if there is anything p ....Phil 4:8

PRAISING
They will still be p ....Ps 84:4
of the heavenly host p....Luke 2:13
in the temple p................Luke 24:53

PRAY
at noon I will p ....Ps 55:17
who hate you, and p.........Matt 5:44
"And when you p ....Matt 6:5
manner, therefore, p............Matt 6:9
"Watch and p ....Matt 26:41
"Lord, teach us to p ....Luke 11:1
"And I will p....................John 14:16
I do not p for the ....John 17:9
"I do not p for ....John 17:20
p without ceasing........ 1 Thess 5:17
Brethren, p for us....... 1 Thess 5:25
Let him p ....James 5:13
to one another, and p ...James 5:16
say that he should p ..... 1 John 5:16

PRAYED
p more earnestly ....Luke 22:44
p earnestly that it ....James 5:17

PRAYER
p made in this place........2 Chr 7:15
And my p is pure................Job 16:17
A p to the God of my ....Ps 42:8
P also will be made.............Ps 72:15
He shall regard the p......Ps 102:17
to the LORD, But the p......Prov 15:8
go out except by p.........Matt 17:21
all night in p to God........Luke 6:12
continually to p...................Acts 6:4
where p was.....................Acts 16:13
steadfastly in p .... Rom 12:12
to fasting and p.............. 1 Cor 7:5
always with all p..............Eph 6:18
but in everything by p......Phil 4:6
the word of God and p....1 Tim 4:5
And the p of faith..........James 5:15

PRAYERS
though You make many p....Is 1:15
pretense make long p......Matt 23:14
fervently for you in p........Col 4:12
p may not be hindered ...... 1 Pet 3:7
which are the p...................Rev 5:8

PREACH
time Jesus began to p......Matt 4:17
you hear in the ear, p .....Matt 10:27
P the gospel to the ....Luke 4:18
And how shall they p ...... Rom 10:15
p Christ crucified .... 1 Cor 1:23
I or they, so we p............ 1 Cor 15:11
P the word......................2 Tim 4:2

PREACHED
p that people ....Mark 6:12
out and p........................Mark 16:20
of sins should be p.........Luke 24:47
p Christ to them ....Acts 8:5
lest, when I have p .... 1 Cor 9:27
than what we have p ....Gal 1:8

the gospel was p...................Heb 4:2
also He went and p .... 1 Pet 3:19

PREACHES
the Jesus whom
Paul p ....Acts 19:13
p another Jesus ....2 Cor 11:4
p any other gospel ....Gal 1:9
p the faith which he...........Gal 1:23

PREACHING
p Jesus as the......................Acts 5:42
not risen, then our p ..... 1 Cor 15:14

PRECEPTS
all His p are sure ....Ps 111:7
how I love Your p ....Ps 119:159

PRECIOUS
P in the sight of the..........Ps 116:15
She is more p than...........Prov 3:15
p things shall not..................Is 44:9
if you take out the p....... Jer 15:19
farmer waits for the p ....James 5:7
more p than gold............... 1 Pet 1:7
who believe, He is p......... 1 Pet 2:7
p in the sight of.................. 1 Pet 3:4

PREDESTINED
foreknew, He also p......... Rom 8:29
having p us to ....Eph 1:5
inheritance, being p..........Eph 1:11

PREEMINENCE
He may have the p.............Col 1:18
loves to have the p .... 3 John 9

PREPARE
p a table before me in..........Ps 23:5
P the way of the LORD ...... Mark 1:3
p a place for you .... John 14:2

PREPARED
for whom it is p ....Matt 20:23
Which You have p ....Luke 2:31
mercy, which He had p... Rom 9:23
things which God has p ... 1 Cor 2:9
Now He who has p .... 2 Cor 5:5
p beforehand that we ....Eph 2:10
God, for He has p.............Heb 11:16

PRESENCE
themselves from the p.........Gen 3:8
went out from the p.........Gen 4:16
P will go with you ....Ex 33:14
afraid in any man's p ...... Deut 1:17
p is fullness of joy ....Ps 16:11
shall dwell in Your p.......Ps 140:13
not tremble at My p .... Jer 5:22
shall shake at My p.......Ezek 38:20
and drank in Your p......Luke 13:26
full of joy in Your p ....Acts 2:28
but his bodily p .... 2 Cor 10:10
obeyed, not as in my p......Phil 2:12

PRESENT
we are all p before ....Acts 10:33
evil is p with me .... Rom 7:21
p your bodies a living...... Rom 12:1
or death, or things p........ 1 Cor 3:22
absent in body but p......... 1 Cor 5:3
that He might p ....Eph 5:27
p you faultless....................Jude 24

PRESERVE
He shall p your soul.............Ps 121:7
The LORD shall p..................Ps 121:8
loses his life will p........Luke 17:33
every evil work and p ....2 Tim 4:18

PRESERVES
For the LORD p the...............Ps 31:23
p the souls of His................Ps 97:10
who keeps his way p ..... Prov 16:17

PRICE
one pearl of great p ....Matt 13:46
were bought at a p.......... 1 Cor 6:20

PRIDE
p serves as...........................Ps 73:6
By p comes nothing....... Prov 13:10
P goes before .... Prov 16:18
her daughter had p.......Ezek 16:49
was hardened in p............ Dan 5:20
For the p of the ....Zech 11:3

evil eye, blasphemy, *p*.... Mark 7:22
p he fall into the .... 1 John 3:6
eyes, and the *p*................ 1 John 2:16

PRIEST
he was the *p* of God........Gen 14:18
p forever According............Ps 110:4
So He shall be a *p* ....Zech 6:13
and faithful High *P* ....Heb 2:17
we have a great High *P*.....Heb 4:14
p forever according ....Heb 5:6
Christ came as High *P*......Heb 9:11

PRIESTHOOD
p being changed................Heb 7:12
has an unchangeable *p* .....Heb 7:24
generation, a royal *p* .... 1 Pet 2:9

PRINCE
is the house of the *p*..........Job 21:28
Everlasting Father, *P*...........Is 9:6
Until Messiah the *P* ...... Dan 9:25
days without king or *p* ....Hos 3:4
p asks for gifts ....Mic 7:3
"and killed the *P*................Acts 3:15
His right hand to be *P*......Acts 5:31
the *p* of the power..............Eph 2:2

PRISON
and put him into the *p*.....Gen 39:20
Bring my soul out of *p* ....Ps 142:7
in darkness from the *p*..........Is 42:7
the opening of the *p*............Is 61:1
John had heard in *p*..........Matt 11:2
I was in *p* and you ....Matt 25:36

PRIZE
the goal for the *p*...............Phil 3:14

PROCEEDS
by every word that *p* .... Deut 8:3
by every word that *p*.........Matt 4:4
Spirit of truth who *p*......John 15:26

PROCLAIM
began to *p* it freely..........Mark 1:45
knowing, Him I *p* ....Acts 17:23
drink this cup, you *p*..... 1 Cor 11:26

PROCLAIMED
p the good news ....Ps 40:9
he went his way and *p*...Luke 8:39

PROCLAIMS
good news, Who *p* ....Is 52:7

PROFANE
and priest are *p* .... Jer 23:11
tried to *p* the temple ....Acts 24:6
But reject *p* and old ....1 Tim 4:7

PROFANED
and *p* My Sabbaths.........Ezek 22:8

PROFESS
They *p* to know God........Titus 1:16

PROFIT
For what *p* is it to...........Matt 16:26
"For what will it *p* ....Mark 8:36
"For what is it to ....Luke 9:25
her masters much *p*........Acts 16:16
brought no small *p*........Acts 19:24
what is the *p* of...................Rom 3:1
seeking my own *p* ...... 1 Cor 10:33
Christ will *p* you...................Gal 5:2
about words to no *p*.......2 Tim 2:14
them, but He for our *p*....Heb 12:10
What does it *p*................James 2:14
sell, and make a *p*.........James 4:13

PROFITABLE
It is doubtless not *p*........2 Cor 12:1
of God, and is *p* ....2 Tim 3:16

PROFITS
have not love, it *p*............. 1 Cor 13:3

PROMISE
"Behold, I send the *P*.....Luke 24:49
but to wait for the *P*...........Acts 1:4
"For the *p* is to you ....Acts 2:39
for the hope of the *p*........Acts 26:6
p might be sure.................. Rom 4:16
Therefore, since a *p* ....Heb 4:1
to the heirs of *p* ....Heb 6:17
did not receive the *p*........Heb 11:39

PROMISES
For all the *p* of God........2 Cor 1:20
his Seed were the *p*.............Gal 3:16
having received the *p*......Heb 11:13
great and precious *p*..........2 Pet 1:4

PROPERLY
Let us walk *p* .... Rom 13:13

PROPHECY
to another *p*...................... 1 Cor 12:10
for *p* never came by........2 Pet 1:21
is the spirit of *p*..................Rev 19:10
of the book of this *p*.........Rev 22:19

PROPHESIED
Lord, have we not *p*.........Matt 7:22
and the law *p* ....Matt 11:13

PROPHESIES
p edifies the church .... 1 Cor 14:4

PROPHESY
prophets, "Do not *p*.............Is 30:10
The prophets *p* falsely........ Jer 5:31
your daughters shall *p*.....Joel 2:28
Who can but *p* ....Amos 3:8
saying, "*P* to us................Matt 26:68
your daughters shall *p*.....Acts 2:17
in part and we *p* .... 1 Cor 13:9

PROPHET
raise up for you a *P* ...... Deut 18:15
"I alone am left a *p*...... 1 Kin 18:22
I ordained you a *p*..................Jer 1:5
The *p* is a fool ....Hos 9:7
Nor was I a son of a *p*......Amos 7:14
send you Elijah the *p*..........Mal 4:5
p shall receive a...............Matt 10:41
p is not without honor......Matt 13:57
by Daniel the *p* ....Mark 13:14
is not a greater *p*..............Luke 7:28
it cannot be that a *p*......Luke 13:33
who was a *P*.....................Luke 24:19
"Are you the *P* ....John 1:21
"This is truly the *P* ....John 6:14
with him the false *p*.........Rev 19:20

PROPHETIC
p word confirmed..............2 Pet 1:19

PROPHETS
the Law or the *P*................Matt 5:17
is the Law and the *P*........Matt 7:12
or one of the *p* ....Matt 16:14
the tombs of the *p* ....Matt 23:29
indeed, I send you........Matt 23:34
one who kills the *p*.........Matt 23:37
Then many false *p*.........Matt 24:11
Moses and the *p*.............Luke 16:29
are sons of the *p*...............Acts 3:25
p did your fathers not.......Acts 7:52
"To Him all the *p*............Acts 10:43
do you believe the *p*........Acts 26:27
by the Law and the *P* ......Rom 3:21
have killed Your *p* ....Rom 11:3
to be apostles, some *p*......Eph 4:11
this salvation the *p*.......... 1 Pet 1:10
because many false *p* ..... 1 John 4:1
found the blood of *p*........Rev 18:24

PROPITIATION
set forth as a *p* .... Rom 3:25
to God, to make *p*..............Heb 2:17
He Himself is the *p* .... 1 John 2:2
His Son to be the *p* .... 1 John 4:10

PROSPER
they *p* who love you ....Ps 122:6
of the LORD shall *p* ....Is 53:10
against you shall *p*..............Is 54:17
up as he may *p* .... 1 Cor 16:2
I pray that you may *p*........ 3 John 2

PROSPERITY
p all your days.................. Deut 23:6
p the destroyer...................Job 15:21
Now in my *p* I said ....Ps 30:6
has pleasure in the *p*........Ps 35:27
When I saw the *p* ....Ps 73:3
I pray, send now *p*..........Ps 118:25
that we have our *p*........Acts 19:25

PROSPEROUS
will make your way *p*........Josh 1:8

PROUD
tongue that speaks *p* ....Ps 12:3
And fully repays the *p*......Ps 31:23
does not respect the *p* ....Ps 40:4
a haughty look and a *p*.....Ps 101:5
p He knows from afar........Ps 138:6
Everyone *p* ....Prov 16:5
by wine, He is a *p*...............Hab 2:5
He has scattered the *p*.....Luke 1:51
"God resists the *p*............... 1 Pet 5:5

PROVERB(S)
of a drunkard Is a *p*.........Prov 26:9
one shall take up a *p* .... Mic 2:4
to the true *p*.......................2 Pet 2:22
three thousand *p* .... 1 Kin 4:32
in order many *p*................. Eccl 12:9

PROVIDE
"My son, God will *p* ....Gen 22:8
"*P* neither gold nor ....Matt 10:9
if anyone does not *p* ....1 Tim 5:8

PROVOKE
"Do they *p* Me to .... Jer 7:19
you, fathers, do not *p* ....Eph 6:4

PROVOKED
p the Most High...................Ps 78:56
his spirit was *p* ....Acts 17:16
seek its own, is not *p* ...... 1 Cor 13:5

PRUDENCE
To give *p* to the...................Prov 1:4
wisdom, dwell with *p* ....Prov 8:12
us in all wisdom and *p*........Eph 1:8

PRUDENT
p man covers shame...... Prov 12:16
A *p* man conceals........... Prov 12:23
The wisdom of the *p*.........Prov 14:8
p considers well.............. Prov 14:15
heart will be called *p* ...... Prov 16:21
p man foresees evil..........Prov 22:3
Therefore the *p*................Amos 5:13
from the wise and *p*........Matt 11:25

PRUNES
that bears fruit He *p* .... John 15:2

PSALM(S)
each of you has a *p*....... 1 Cor 14:26
to one another in *p*............Eph 5:19
Let him sing *p*................James 5:13

PUNISH
p the righteous is........... Prov 17:26
Shall I not *p* them for ....Jer 5:9

PUNISHED
p them often in every .....Acts 26:11
These shall be *p*............. 2 Thess 1:9

PUNISHMENT
p is greater than I...............Gen 4:13
you do in the day of *p* ....Is 10:3
p they shall perish........... Jer 10:15
not turn away its *p*..........Amos 1:3
into everlasting *p* ....Matt 25:46
p which was inflicted .... 2 Cor 2:6
Of how much worse *p*.....Heb 10:29
sent by him for the *p* .... 1 Pet 2:14
the unjust under *p*..............2 Pet 2:9

PURE
a mercy seat of *p* gold.....Ex 25:17
'My doctrine is *p* ....Job 11:4
that he could be *p*.............Job 15:14
of the LORD are *p* ....Ps 12:6
ways of a man are *p* ....Prov 16:2
a generation that is *p*..... Prov 30:12
things indeed are *p*........ Rom 14:20
whatever things are *p*........Phil 4:8
keep yourself *p* ....1 Tim 5:22
p all things are *p* ....Titus 1:15
above is first *p* ....James 3:17
babes, desire the *p* .... 1 Pet 2:2
just as He is *p*................. 1 John 3:3

PURGED
away, And your sin *p* ....Is 6:7

PURIFIED
all things are *p*...................Heb 9:22
Since you have *p*............... 1 Pet 1:22

PURIFIES
hope in Him *p* himself.... 1 John 3:3
PURIFY
and *p* your hearts.............James 4:8
PURIFYING
p their hearts by...............Acts 15:9
sanctifies for the *p* ....Heb 9:13
PURIM
called these days *P* ....Esth 9:26
PURITY
spirit, in faith, in *p* ....1 Tim 4:12
PURPOSE
A time for every *p*..............Eccl 3:1
But for this *p* I came......John 12:27
by the determined *p*.......Acts 2:23
to fulfill His *p*...................Rev 17:17
PURSUE
p righteousness................ Rom 9:30
P love.............................. 1 Cor 14:1

Q

QUAIL
and it brought *q*.............Num 11:31
QUARRELSOME
but gentle, not *q* ....1 Tim 3:3
QUENCH
Many waters cannot *q* ......Song 8:7
flax He will not *q* ....Matt 12:20
q all the fiery.....................Eph 6:16
Do not *q* the Spirit ..... 1 Thess 5:19
QUICKLY
with your adversary *q*......Matt 5:25
"Surely I am coming *q* ....Rev 22:20
QUIET
aspire to lead a *q*......... 1 Thess 4:11
a gentle and *q* spirit........... 1 Pet 3:4
QUIETNESS
a handful with *q* ....Eccl 4:6
In *q* and confidence ....Is 30:15
of righteousness, *q*.............Is 32:17
that they work
  in *q*............................. 2 Thess 3:12

R

RABBI
be called by men, 'R ....Matt 23:7
RACA
to his brother, 'R ....Matt 5:22
RACE
man to run its *r*....................Ps 19:5
r is not to the swift........... Eccl 9:11
I have finished the *r*.........2 Tim 4:7
with endurance the *r*.......Heb 12:1
RAIN
had not caused it to *r*..........Gen 2:5
And the *r* was on the........Gen 7:12
I will *r* down on him ..... Ezek 38:22
given you the former *r*.......Joel 2:23
the good, and sends *r*.......Matt 5:45
"and the *r* descended.......Matt 7:25
r that often comes ....Heb 6:7
that it would not *r*.........James 5:17
RAINBOW
"I set My *r* in the.................Gen 9:13
and there was a *r* ....Rev 4:3
RAISE
third day He will *r*..............Hos 6:2
in three days I will *r* ....John 2:19
and I will *r* him up at......John 6:40
and the Lord will *r*........James 5:15
RAISED
be killed, and be *r* ....Matt 16:21
Just as Christ was *r*..........Rom 6:4
Spirit of Him who *r*.......... Rom 8:11
"How are the dead *r* .... 1 Cor 15:35
the dead will be *r* .... 1 Cor 15:52
and *r* us up together ....Eph 2:6

RAISES
"For as the Father *r*.........John 5:21
but in God who *r*...............2 Cor 1:9
RANSOM
to give His life a *r*.........Mark 10:45
who gave Himself a *r*.......1 Tim 2:6
RANSOMED
And the *r* of the LORD ....Is 35:10
redeemed Jacob, And *r*.... Jer 31:11
RASHLY
and do nothing *r*.............Acts 19:36
RAVENS
"Consider the *r* ....Luke 12:24
READ
day, and stood up to *r* .....Luke 4:16
hearts, known and *r* .... 2 Cor 3:2
READY
and those who were *r*.....Matt 25:10
"Lord, I am *r* ....Luke 22:33
Be *r* in season and out......2 Tim 4:2
and always be *r* .... 1 Pet 3:15
REAP
they neither sow nor *r*......Matt 6:26
you knew that I *r*............Matt 25:26
REAPED
You have *r* iniquity.........Hos 10:13
REAPING
r what I did not..............Luke 19:22
REAPS
sows and another *r* .... John 4:37
REASON
"Come now, and let us *r* ....Is 1:18
who asks you a *r*............. 1 Pet 3:15
REBEL
if you refuse and *r*..................Is 1:20
REBELLING
more against Him By *r*.......Ps 78:17
REBELLION
hearts as in the *r* ....Heb 3:8
REBELLIOUS
day long to a *r* people...........Is 65:2
REBUKE
Turn at my *r*......................Prov 1:23
R a wise man ....Prov 9:8
r is better Than love ....Prov 27:5
R the oppressor ....Is 1:17
sins against you, *r*...........Luke 17:3
Do not *r* an older man......1 Tim 5:1
who are sinning *r*...........1 Tim 5:20
"The Lord *r* you......................Jude 9
"As many as I love, I *r*.......Rev 3:19
REBUKED
r the winds and the..........Matt 8:26
r their unbelief.............. Mark 16:14
but he was *r* for his.........2 Pet 2:16
RECEIVE
believing, you will *r*.......Matt 21:22
and His own did not *r*...... John 1:11
will come again and *r*...... John 14:3
the world cannot *r*.........John 14:17
Ask, and you will *r* ....John 16:24
"*R* the Holy Spirit...........John 20:22
"Lord Jesus, *r*...................Acts 7:59
r the Holy Spirit...............Acts 19:2
R one who is weak............ Rom 14:1
r the Spirit by the.................Gal 3:2
suppose that he will *r*......James 1:7
RECEIVED
But as many as *r* ....John 1:12
for God has *r* him............. Rom 14:3
For I *r* from the Lord .... 1 Cor 11:23
r Christ....................................Col 2:6
R up in glory ....1 Tim 3:16
RECEIVES
r you *r* Me.......................Matt 10:40
and whoever *r* Me.......... Mark 9:37

RECONCILE
and that He might *r* ....Eph 2:16
RECONCILED
First be *r* to your ....Matt 5:24
we were *r*........................... Rom 5:10
Christ's behalf, be *r* ......2 Cor 5:20
RECONCILIATION
now received the *r* .... Rom 5:11
to us the word of *r*..........2 Cor 5:19
RECONCILING
cast away is the *r* .... Rom 11:15
God was in Christ........2 Cor 5:19
REDEEM
But God will *r* my soul.......Ps 49:15
r their life from ....Ps 72:14
was going to *r* Israel......Luke 24:21
r those who were..................Gal 4:5
us, that He might *r*..........Titus 2:14
REDEEMED
Let the *r* of the LORD ....Ps 107:2
r shall walk there ....Is 35:9
sea a road For the *r*............Is 51:10
And you shall be *r*................Is 52:3
and *r* His people.............Luke 1:68
Christ has *r* us from...........Gal 3:13
that you were not *r* .... 1 Pet 1:18
were slain, And have *r*......Rev 5:9
REDEEMER
For I know that my *R* ......Job 19:25
Our *R* from Everlasting.......Is 63:16
REDEEMING
r the time ....Eph 5:16
REDEMPTION
those who looked
  for *r*...............................Luke 2:38
your *r* draws near ....Luke 21:28
grace through the *r*.......... Rom 3:24
the adoption, the *r*........... Rom 8:23
sanctification and *r*........ 1 Cor 1:30
In Him we have *r* ....Eph 1:7
for the day of *r*...................Eph 4:30
obtained eternal *r*.............Heb 9:12
REFINED
us as silver is *r*...................Ps 66:10
REFINER
He will sit as a *r*.................. Mal 3:3
REFRESHED
his spirit has been *r* ....2 Cor 7:13
for he often *r*....................2 Tim 1:16
REFRESHING
r may come from the........Acts 3:19
REFUGE
eternal God is your *r* ..... Deut 33:27
God is our *r* and ....Ps 46:1
who have fled for *r* ....Heb 6:18
REGENERATION
to you, that in the *r*.........Matt 19:28
the washing of *r* ....Titus 3:5
REGULATIONS
yourselves to *r*....................Col 2:20
REIGN
"And He will *r*...................Luke 1:33
righteousness will *r*.......... Rom 5:17
so grace might *r* .... Rom 5:21
do not let sin *r*.................. Rom 6:12
For He must *r* till He.... 1 Cor 15:25
of Christ, and shall *r*.........Rev 20:6
REIGNED
so that as sin *r* .... Rom 5:21
You have *r* as kings.......... 1 Cor 4:8
And they lived and *r*........Rev 20:4
REIGNS
to Zion, "Your God *r*............Is 52:7
Lord God Omnipotent *r*....Rev 19:6
REJECT
"All too well you *r*............ Mark 7:9
R a divisive man...............Titus 3:10

REJECTED
He is despised and r ....Is 53:3
r Has become the ....Matt 21:42
many things and be r ......Luke 17:25
Moses whom they r ....Acts 7:35
to a living stone, r .... 1 Pet 2:4

REJECTS
he who r Me r ....Luke 10:16

REJOICE
R in the LORD.........................Ps 33:1
of Your wings I will r ....Ps 63:7
Let them r before God..........Ps 68:3
Let the heavens r................Ps 96:11
Let the earth r.......................Ps 97:1
We will r and be glad ....Ps 118:24
She shall r in time to ..... Prov 31:25
R, O young man .... Eccl 11:9
your heart shall r................Is 66:14
Do not r over me .... Mic 7:8
do not r...............................Luke 10:20
you would r ....John 14:28
but the world will r........John 16:20
and your heart will r......John 16:22
R with those who .... Rom 12:15
and in this I r ....Phil 1:18
faith, I am glad and r.........Phil 2:17
R in the Lord always ....Phil 4:4
R always .... 1 Thess 5:16
yet believing, you r .... 1 Pet 1:8

REJOICED
And my spirit has r..........Luke 1:47
In that hour Jesus r........Luke 10:21
Abraham r........................ John 8:56

REJOICES
glad, and my glory r.............Ps 16:9
but r in the truth.............. 1 Cor 13:6

REJOICING
come again with r ....Ps 126:6
he went on his way r......Acts 8:39
confidence and the r............Heb 3:6

RELIGION
in self-imposed r.................Col 2:23
and undefiled r ....James 1:27

RELIGIOUS
things you are very r......Acts 17:22

REMAIN
that My joy may r ....John 15:11
your fruit should r.........John 15:16
"If I will that he r...........John 21:22
the greater part r............ 1 Cor 15:6
are alive and r............... 1 Thess 4:15
the things which r ....Rev 3:2

REMAINS
"While the earth r ....Gen 8:22
Therefore your sin r........John 9:41
There r therefore a..............Heb 4:9

REMEMBER
"R the Sabbath day.............Ex 20:8
But we will r the name.........Ps 20:7
r Your name in the............Ps 119:55
R now your Creator.......... Eccl 12:1
r the former things..............Is 43:18
and their sin I will r ....Jer 31:34
In wrath r mercy ....Hab 3:2
And to r His holy.............Luke 1:72
"R Lot's wife...................Luke 17:32
r the words of the..........Acts 20:35
R that Jesus Christ............2 Tim 2:8
R those who rule ....Heb 13:7

REMEMBERED
Then God r Noah ....Gen 8:1
r His covenant with .... Ex 2:24
r His covenant forever ......Ps 105:8
yea, we wept When we r....Ps 137:1
And Peter r the word......Matt 26:75
r the word of the Lord....Acts 11:16

REMEMBRANCE
r my song in the night..........Ps 77:6
Put Me in r.........................Is 43:26
do this in r of Me............Luke 22:19
do this in r of Me ...... 1 Cor 11:24

REMISSION
for the r...............................Mark 1:4
Jesus Christ for the r........Acts 2:38
where there is r ....Heb 10:18

REMNANT
The r will return ....Is 10:21
time there is a r .... Rom 11:5

REMOVE
r this cup from Me ....Luke 22:42
r your lampstand.................Rev 2:5

REMOVED
Though the earth be r ....Ps 46:2
And the hills be r.................Is 54:10
this mountain, 'Be r........Matt 21:21

RENDER
What shall I r to the..........Ps 116:12
"R therefore to Caesar....Matt 22:21

RENEW
r a steadfast........................Ps 51:10
on the LORD Shall r ....Is 40:31

RENEWED
that your youth is r.............Ps 103:5
inward man is being r ....2 Cor 4:16
and be r in the spirit ....Eph 4:23

RENEWING
transformed by the r........ Rom 12:2

REPAID
Shall evil be r....................Jer 18:20

REPAY
again, I will r.................Luke 10:35
they cannot r..................Luke 14:14
R no one evil for evil ..... Rom 12:17
is Mine, I will r.............. Rom 12:19
r their parents...................1 Tim 5:4

REPENT
I abhor myself, And r.........Job 42:6
"R, for the kingdom ....Matt 3:2
you r you will all ....Luke 13:3
said to them, "R.............Acts 2:38
men everywhere to r......Acts 17:30
be zealous and r ....Rev 3:19

REPENTANCE
you with water unto r.......Matt 3:11
a baptism of r for the........Mark 1:4
persons who need no r....Luke 15:7
renew them again to r.........Heb 6:6
found no place for r..........Heb 12:17
all should come to r ....2 Pet 3:9

REPENTED
it, because they r...........Matt 12:41

REPROACH
R has broken my heart ......Ps 69:20
with dishonor comes r......Prov 18:3
not remember the r...............Is 54:4
Because I bore the r..........Jer 15:15
these things You r..........Luke 11:45
lest he fall into r ....1 Tim 3:7
esteeming the r................Heb 11:26
and without r ....James 1:5

REPROACHED
If you are r for the............ 1 Pet 4:14

REPROOF
for doctrine, for r.............2 Tim 3:16

REPUTATION
seven men of good r ....Acts 6:3
made Himself of no r..........Phil 2:7

REQUESTS
r be made known .... Phil 4:6

REQUIRE
offering You did not r ....Ps 40:6
what does the LORD r ...... Mic 6:8

REQUIRED
your soul will be r..........Luke 12:20
him much will be r........Luke 12:48

RESERVED
"I have r for Myself.......... Rom 11:4
r in heaven for you .... 1 Pet 1:4
habitation, He has r ....Jude 6

RESIST
r an evil person..................Matt 5:39
r the Holy Spirit................Acts 7:51
R the devil and he ....James 4:7

RESISTED
For who has r His will..... Rom 9:19
for he has greatly r ....2 Tim 4:15
You have not yet r ....Heb 12:4

RESISTS
"God r the proud ....James 4:6
for "God r the proud .... 1 Pet 5:5

REST
is the Sabbath of r............. Ex 31:15
to build a house of r .... 1 Chr 28:2
R in the LORD.......................Ps 37:7
fly away and be at r.............Ps 55:6
"This is the r.........................Is 28:12
is the place of My r............Is 66:1
and I will give you r.......Matt 11:28
shall not enter My r..........Heb 3:11
remains therefore a r...........Heb 4:9
that they should r...............Rev 6:11
"that they may r ....Rev 14:13
But the r of the dead.........Rev 20:5

RESTED
He had done, and He r.......Gen 2:2
"And God r on the...............Heb 4:4

RESTORE
R to me the joy ....Ps 51:12
"So I will r to you ....Joel 2:25
and will r all things........Matt 17:11
You at this time r ....Acts 1:6
who are spiritual r ....Gal 6:1

RESTORES
He r my soul.........................Ps 23:3

RESTS
r quietly in the heart...... Prov 14:33

RESURRECTION
to her, "I am the r...........John 11:25
them Jesus and the r ......Acts 17:18
the likeness of His r...........Rom 6:5
say that there is no r.... 1 Cor 15:12
and the power of His r......Phil 3:10
obtain a better r...............Heb 11:35
This is the first r ....Rev 20:5

RETURN
womb, naked shall he r.... Eccl 5:15
Let him r to the LORD...........Is 55:7
me, and I will r .... Jer 31:18
"R to Me............................Zech 1:3
he says, 'I will r ....Matt 12:44

RETURNED
astray, but have now r .... 1 Pet 2:25

RETURNING
r evil for evil or.................. 1 Pet 3:9

RETURNS
As a dog r to his own .... Prov 26:11
"A dog r to his own..........2 Pet 2:22

REVEAL
the Son wills to r Him ....Matt 11:27
r His Son in me...................Gal 1:16

REVEALED
things which are r.......... Deut 29:29
righteousness to be r...........Is 56:1
the Son of Man is r ......Luke 17:30
the wrath of God is r ...... Rom 1:18
glory which shall be r....... Rom 8:18
the Lord Jesus is r........... 2 Thess 1:7
lawless one will be r..... 2 Thess 2:8
ready to be r in the .... 1 Pet 1:5
when His glory is r .... 1 Pet 4:13
r what we shall be.......... 1 John 3:2

REVELATION
Where there is no r........ Prov 29:18
it came through the r...........Gal 1:12
spirit of wisdom and r......Eph 1:17
r He made known to...........Eph 3:3
and glory at the r .... 1 Pet 1:7

REVERENCE
and r My sanctuary ....Lev 19:30
God acceptably with r.....Heb 12:28

REVERENT
man who is always *r* ..... Prov 28:14
their wives must be *r*.....1 Tim 3:11

REVILE
are you when they *r*.........Matt 5:11
r God's high priest ....Acts 23:4

REVILED
crucified with Him *r* ..... Mark 15:32
who, when He was *r*........ 1 Pet 2:23

REVIVAL
give us a measure of *r*........Ezra 9:8

REVIVE
Will You not *r* us...................Ps 85:6
two days He will *r*.................Hos 6:2

REWARD
exceedingly great *r*............Gen 15:1
look, And see the *r*................Ps 91:8
Behold, His *r* is with ....Is 40:10
for great is your *r*..............Matt 5:12
you, they have their *r*........Matt 6:2
no means lose his *r*........Matt 10:42
we receive the due *r*......Luke 23:41
will receive his own *r* ..... 1 Cor 3:8
cheat you of your *r* ....Col 2:18
for he looked to the *r*........Heb 11:26
quickly, and My *r*.............Rev 22:12

REWARDS
Whoever *r* evil for........ Prov 17:13
And follows after *r*................Is 1:23

RICH
Abram was very *r*............Gen 13:2
The *r* and the poor...........Prov 22:2
r rules over the poor.........Prov 22:7
r man is wise in his...... Prov 28:11
Do not curse the *r* .... Eccl 10:20
it is hard for a *r* ....Matt 19:23
to you who are *r*............Luke 6:24
the *r* man's table...........Luke 16:21
for he was very *r* ....Luke 18:23
You are already *r*............... 1 Cor 4:8
though He was *r*............. 2 Cor 8:9
who desire to be *r* ....1 Tim 6:9
of this world to be *r*.........James 2:5
you say, 'I am *r*...................Rev 3:17

RICHES
R and honor are ....Prov 8:18
R do not profit ....Prov 11:4
in his *r* will fall .... Prov 11:28
of the wise is their *r* .... Prov 14:24
and *r* are an.................... Prov 19:14
of the LORD Are *r*.........Prov 22:4
r are not forever .... Prov 27:24
do you despise the *r*...........Rom 2:4
make known the *r*............ Rom 9:23
what are the *r*..................Eph 1:18
show the exceeding *r*.......Eph 2:7
the unsearchable *r* ....Eph 3:8
r than the treasures..........Heb 11:26
To receive power
and *r* ....Rev 5:12

RICHLY
Christ dwell in you *r*..........Col 3:16
God, who gives us *r*........1 Tim 6:17

RIGHT
the *r* of the firstborn ..... Deut 21:17
"Is your heart *r* .... 2 Kin 10:15
Lord, "Sit at My *r*...............Ps 110:1
a way which seems *r*...... Prov 14:12
clothed and in his *r*...... Mark 5:15
to them He gave the *r*.......John 1:12
your heart is not *r*..............Acts 8:21
seven stars in His *r*...........Rev 2:1

RIGHTEOUS
also destroy the *r*..............Gen 18:23
and they justify the *r*....... Deut 25:1
that he could be *r*..............Job 15:14
"The *r* see it and.............Job 22:19
r shows mercy and..............Ps 37:21
I have not seen the *r*..........Ps 37:25
The LORD loves the *r*..........Ps 146:8
r is a well of life............ Prov 10:11
r will be gladness ..... Prov 10:28
r will be delivered .... Prov 11:21
r will be recompensed... Prov 11:31

the prayer of the *r*.......... Prov 15:29
r are bold as a lion.................Prov 28:1
r considers the cause........Prov 29:7
Do not be overly *r*........... Eccl 7:16
event happens to the *r*........ Eccl 9:2
with My *r* right hand........Is 41:10
By His knowledge My *r*......Is 53:11
The *r* perishes...........................Is 57:1
they sell the *r*.......................Amos 2:6
not come to call the *r*........Matt 9:13
r men desired to see.........Matt 13:17
r will shine forth as........Matt 13:43
that they were *r*................Luke 18:9
this was a *r*....................Luke 23:47
"There is none *r*................. Rom 3:10
r man will one die............Rom 5:7
Jesus Christ the *r* .... 1 John 2:1

RIGHTEOUSLY
should live soberly, *r*.......Titus 2:12
to Him who judges *r*........1 Pet 2:23

RIGHTEOUSNESS
it to him for *r*......................Gen 15:6
I put on *r*............................Job 29:14
I call, O God of my *r*...............Ps 4:1
from the LORD, And *r*.........Ps 24:5
shall speak of Your *r*.........Ps 35:28
the good news of *r*................Ps 40:9
heavens declare His *r*..........Ps 50:6
R and peace have..............Ps 85:10
R will go before Him..........Ps 85:13
r endures forever................Ps 111:3
r delivers from death........Prov 10:2
The *r* of the blameless......Prov 11:5
the way of *r* is life .... Prov 12:28
R exalts a nation .... Prov 14:34
He who follows *r*............ Prov 21:21
R lodged in it..........................Is 1:21
in the LORD I have *r*...........Is 45:24
r will be forever......................Is 51:8
I will declare your *r* ....Is 57:12
r as a breastplate.................Is 59:17
r goes forth as.........................Is 62:1
THE LORD OUR *R*....... Jer 23:6
to David A Branch
of *r*.................................... Jer 33:15
The *r* of the righteous......Ezek 18:20
who turn many to *r*........... Dan 12:3
to fulfill all *r*......................Matt 3:15
exceeds the *r* of the..........Matt 5:20
to you in the way of *r*........Matt 21:32
For in it the *r*........................Rom 1:17
even the *r* of God.............. Rom 3:22
accounted to him for *r*...... Rom 4:22
r will reign in life............. Rom 5:17
might reign through *r*....... Rom 5:21
ignorant of God's *r*............ Rom 10:3
might become the *r*........... 2 Cor 5:21
the breastplate of *r*............Eph 6:14
not having my own *r*...........Phil 3:9
r which we have ....Titus 3:5
not produce the *r*............James 1:20
a preacher of *r*................... 2 Pet 2:5
a new earth in which *r*... 2 Pet 3:13
who practices *r*.............. 1 John 2:29
He who practices *r*.......... 1 John 3:7

RIGHTLY
wise uses knowledge *r*.....Prov 15:2
r dividing the word.........2 Tim 2:15

RISE
for He makes His sun *r*....Matt 5:45
third day He will *r*............Matt 20:19
third day He will *r*..........Luke 18:33
be the first to *r*...............Acts 26:23
in Christ will *r*.............. 1 Thess 4:16

RISEN
there has not *r*...............Matt 11:11
disciples that He is *r*.......Matt 28:7
"The Lord is *r*...................Luke 24:34
then Christ is not *r*........ 1 Cor 15:13
if Christ is not *r* .... 1 Cor 15:17
But now Christ is *r*........ 1 Cor 15:20

RIVER(S)
peace to her like a *r*...........Is 66:12
he showed me a pure *r*.....Rev 22:1
By the *r* of Babylon............Ps 137:1
All the *r* run into the........... Eccl 1:7
his heart will flow *r*.........John 7:38

ROARING
and the waves *r*.............Luke 21:25
walks about like a *r*........... 1 Pet 5:8

ROARS
"The LORD *r* from..............Amos 1:2
as when a lion *r*.................Rev 10:3

ROBBER
is a thief and a *r* ....John 10:1
Barabbas was a *r* ....John 18:40

ROBBERS
also crucified two *r*...... Mark 15:27
Me are thieves and *r*........John 10:8

ROBBERY
did not consider it *r* ....Phil 2:6

ROBE
'Bring out the best *r*.......Luke 15:22
on Him a purple *r*.............John 19:2
Then a white *r* was ....Rev 6:11

ROBES
have stained all My *r*............Is 63:3
go around in long *r*........Luke 20:46
clothed with white *r*............Rev 7:9

ROCK
you shall strike the *r*...........Ex 17:6
and struck the *r*.............. Num 20:11
For their *r* is not .... Deut 32:31
"The LORD is my *r*.........2 Sam 22:2
And who is a *r*..................2 Sam 22:32
Blessed be my *R*............2 Sam 22:47
For You are my *r*.................Ps 31:3
r that is higher than............Ps 61:2
been mindful of the *R*........Is 17:10
shadow of a great *r*...........Is 32:2
his house on the *r*............Matt 7:24
r I will build My.............Matt 16:18
stumbling stone and *r*...... Rom 9:33
R that followed them...... 1 Cor 10:4

ROD
Your *r* and Your staff..........Ps 23:4
shall come forth a *R* ....Is 11:1
rule them with a *r* .... Rev 2:27

ROOM
you a large upper *r* .... Mark 14:15
no *r* for them in the...........Luke 2:7
into the upper *r*...............Acts 1:13

ROOT
day there shall be a *R*.........Is 11:10
because they had no *r*......Matt 13:6
of money is a *r*.................1 Tim 6:10
lest any *r* of ....Heb 12:15
I am the *R* and the ....Rev 22:16

ROOTED
r and built up in Him............Col 2:7

ROSE
end Christ died and *r*...... Rom 14:9
buried, and that He *r* ...... 1 Cor 15:4
Jesus died and *r* ..... 1 Thess 4:14

RULE
And he shall *r*.....................Gen 3:16
puts an end to all *r*........ 1 Cor 15:24
let the peace of God .... Col 3:15
Let the elders who *r*........1 Tim 5:17
Remember those
who *r*.............................Heb 13:7

RULER
to Me The One to be *r* .... Mic 5:2
by Beelzebub, the *r*........Matt 12:24
the *r* of this world ....John 12:31
'Who made you a *r* ....Acts 7:27

RULERS
And the *r* take counsel...........Ps 2:2
"You know that the *r*.......Matt 20:25
which none of the *r*.......... 1 Cor 2:8
powers, against the *r*........Eph 6:12

RULES
That the Most High *r*....... Dan 4:17
that the Most High *r* .... Dan 4:32
r his own house well........1 Tim 3:4

RUN
r and not be weary...............Is 40:31
us, and let us *r* ....Heb 12:1

S

SABAOTH
S had left us a .... Rom 9:29
ears of the Lord of *S*........James 5:4

SABBATH(S)
"Remember the *S* .... Ex 20:8
S was made for man....... Mark 2:27
S you shall keep .... Ex 31:13

SACRIFICE
to the LORD than *s* ....Prov 21:3
For the LORD has a *s* ....Is 34:6
of My offerings they *s* ....Hos 8:13
LORD has prepared a *s* ......Zeph 1:7
desire mercy and not *s*....Matt 9:13
an offering and a *s*...............Eph 5:2
put away sin by the *s*.........Heb 9:26
no longer remains a *s*.....Heb 10:26
offer the *s* of praise.........Heb 13:15

SACRIFICED
s their sons And their.......Ps 106:37

SACRIFICES
The *s* of God are a ....Ps 51:17
multitude of your *s*..............Is 1:11
priests, to offer up *s* ....Heb 7:27
s God is well pleased......Heb 13:16

SAINTS
s who are on the earth ....Ps 16:3
does not forsake His *s*......Ps 37:28
Is the death of His *s*.........Ps 116:15
war against the *s*............... Dan 7:21
Jesus, called to be *s* .... 1 Cor 1:2
the least of all the *s*..............Eph 3:8
be glorified in His *s*..... 2 Thess 1:10
all delivered to the *s* ....Jude 3
shed the blood of *s*............Rev 16:6

SALT
shall season with *s*............ Lev 2:13
"You are the *s*...................Matt 5:13
s loses its flavor.............. Mark 9:50

SALVATION
still, and see the *s*...............Ex 14:13
S belongs to the LORD............Ps 3:8
is my light and my *s* ....Ps 27:1
God is the God of *s*.........Ps 68:20
joy in the God of my *s*.... Hab 3:18
raised up a horn of *s*.......Luke 1:69
"Nor is there *s*................Acts 4:12
the power of God to *s*..... Rom 1:16
now is the day of *s*........... 2 Cor 6:2
work out your own *s* ....Phil 2:12
chose you for *s* .... 2 Thess 2:13
neglect so great a *s* ....Heb 2:3

SAMARITAN
a drink from me, a *S*.........John 4:9

SANCTIFICATION
will of God, your *s* .... 1 Thess 4:3

SANCTIFIED
they also may be *s* ....John 17:19
but you were *s* .... 1 Cor 6:11
for it is *s* by the.................1 Tim 4:5

SANCTIFIES
For both He who *s* ....Heb 2:11

SANCTIFY
s My great name ....Ezek 36:23
"*S* them by Your............John 17:17
that He might *s* ....Eph 5:26

SANCTUARY
let them make Me a *s* ....Ex 25:8
and the earthly *s* ....Heb 9:1

SAND
descendants as the *s*..... Gen 32:12
innumerable as the *s* ....Heb 11:12

SAT
into heaven, and *s*......... Mark 16:19
And He who *s* there was..... Rev 4:3

SATAN
before the LORD, and *S* ....Job 1:6
"Away with you, *S*...........Matt 4:10
"Get behind Me, *S*...........Matt 16:23
"How can *S* cast out .... Mark 3:23

S has asked for you ....Luke 22:31
to the working of *S* .... 2 Thess 2:9
known the depths of *S* ...... Rev 2:24
years have expired, *S*........ Rev 20:7

SATIATED
s the weary soul .... Jer 31:25
that are never *s*............... Prov 30:15
of His soul, and be *s* ....Is 53:11

SATISFIED
I shall be *s* when I..............Ps 17:15

SATISFIES
s the longing soul...............Ps 107:9

SATISFY
s us early with Your ....Ps 90:14
long life I will *s*.................Ps 91:16
for what does not *s* ....Is 55:2

SAVE
Oh, *s* me for Your ....Ps 6:4
s the children of the..............Ps 72:4
s the souls of the ....Ps 72:13
That it cannot *s*.......................Is 59:1
s you And deliver you ...... Jer 15:20
other, That he may *s*.........Hos 13:10
JESUS, for He will *s*............Matt 1:21
s his life will....................Matt 16:25
s that which was ....Matt 18:11
let Him *s* Himself if........Luke 23:35
but to *s* the world ....John 12:47
the world to *s* sinners.....1 Tim 1:15

SAVED
"He *s* others.......................Matt 27:42
That we should be *s*........Luke 1:71
"Your faith has *s* ....Luke 7:50
might be *s* ....John 3:17
them, saying, "Be *s* ....Acts 2:40
what must I do to be *s*.....Acts 16:30
which also you are *s*....... 1 Cor 15:2
grace you have been *s*.........Eph 2:8
to His mercy He *s*............. Titus 3:5
of those who are *s*............ Rev 21:24

SAVIOR
I, the LORD, am your *S*......Is 60:16
rejoiced in God my *S*......Luke 1:47
the city of David a *S*.......Luke 2:11
up for Israel a *S* ....Acts 13:23
God, who is the *S*............. 1 Tim 4:10
and *S* Jesus Christ ....Titus 2:13

SCALES
on it had a pair of *s*............ Rev 6:5

SCARLET
your sins are like *s*................Is 1:18

SCATTERED
"Israel is like *s* sheep........ Jer 50:17
the sheep will be *s*......... Mark 14:27

SCOFFER(S)
"He who corrects a *s* ....Prov 9:7
s is an abomination...........Prov 24:9

SCORPIONS
on serpents and *s* ....Luke 10:19
They had tails like *s*...........Rev 9:10

SCOURGE
will mock Him, and *s* ... Mark 10:34

SCOURGES
s every son whom ....Heb 12:6

SCRIBES
"Beware of the *s* .... Mark 12:38

SCRIPTURE(S)
S cannot be broken........John 10:35
All *S* is given by ....2 Tim 3:16
S must be fulfilled........ Mark 14:49

SCROLL
eat this *s*...............................Ezek 3:1
the sky receded as a *s* .....Rev 6:14

SEA
drowned in the Red *S*..........Ex 15:4
who go down to the *s* ....Ps 107:23
and the *s* obey Him...........Matt 8:27
throne there was a *s* ....Rev 4:6
there was no more *s* ....Rev 21:1

SEAL
stands, having this *s* ....2 Tim 2:19

SEALED
by whom you were *s* ....Eph 4:30

SÉANCE
"Please conduct a *s* ....1 Sam 28:8

SEARCH
glory of kings is to *s* ....Prov 25:2
s the Scriptures................. John 5:39

SEARCHED
s the Scriptures...............Acts 17:11

SEARCHES
For the Spirit *s*................. 1 Cor 2:10

SEASON
Be ready in *s* and out ......2 Tim 4:2

SEASONS
the times and the *s*........ 1 Thess 5:1

SEAT
shall make a mercy *s*.........Ex 25:17
before the judgment *s*..... 2 Cor 5:10

SECRET
s things belong .... Deut 29:29
In the *s* place of His..............Ps 27:5
Father who is in the *s*.........Matt 6:6

SECRETLY
He lies in wait *s*.....................Ps 10:9

SECRETS
For He knows the *s*.............Ps 44:21
God will judge the *s*......... Rom 2:16

SECURELY
nation that dwells *s*........... Jer 49:31

SEDUCED
flattering lips she *s*............Prov 7:21

SEE
in my flesh I shall *s*..........Job 19:26
For they shall *s* God ....Matt 5:8
seeing they do not *s*........Matt 13:13
rejoiced to *s* My day ....John 8:56
They shall *s* His face .... Rev 22:4

SEED(S)
He shall see His *s* ....Is 53:10
S were the promises ....Gal 3:16
you are Abraham's *s* ....Gal 3:29
the good *s* are the...........Matt 13:38

SEEK
pray and *s* My face ....2 Chr 7:14
S the LORD while He...........Is 55:6
s, and you will find ....Matt 7:7
of Man has come to *s* .....Luke 19:10
"You will *s* Me and ....John 7:34
For all *s* their own..............Phil 2:21
s those things which ....Col 3:1

SEEKING
like a roaring lion, *s*........... 1 Pet 5:8

SEEKS
There is none who *s* .... Rom 3:11

SEEMS
is a way which *s*............. Prov 14:12

SEEN
s God face to face.............Gen 32:30
No one has *s* God at .... John 1:18
s Me has *s* the ....John 14:9
things which are not *s* ....2 Cor 4:18

SELF-CONTROL
gentleness, *s*.................Gal 5:23
to knowledge *s* ....2 Pet 1:6

SELF-SEEKING
envy and *s* exist..............James 3:16

SEND
"Behold, I *s* you out ....Matt 10:16
has sent Me, I also *s* ...... John 20:21

SENSUAL
but is earthly, *s*................James 3:15

SENT
unless they are *s*............. Rom 10:15

SEPARATES
who repeats a matter s.....Prov 17:9

SEPARATION
the middle wall of s ....Eph 2:14

SERAPHIM
Above it stood s.......................Is 6:2

SERIOUS
therefore be s and .... 1 Pet 4:7

SERPENT
s was more cunning............Gen 3:1
"Make a fiery s ....Num 21:8
Moses lifted up the s........ John 3:14

SERVANT(S)
s will rule over a son ....Prov 17:2
good and faithful s.......Matt 25:21
are unprofitable s..........Luke 17:10

SERVE(S)
to be served, but to s ......Matt 20:28
but through love s..............Gal 5:13
"If anyone s Me ....John 12:26

SERVICE
is your reasonable s......... Rom 12:1
with good will doing s........Eph 6:7

SERVING
fervent in spirit, s .... Rom 12:11

SETTLED
O LORD,Your word is s ....Ps 119:89

SEVENTY
"S weeks are .... Dan 9:24

SEVERE
not to be too s .... 2 Cor 2:5

SHADOW
In the s of His hand ....Is 49:2
the law, having a s...........Heb 10:1

SHAKE
s the earth...............................Is 2:19
I will s all nations................Hag 2:7

SHAKEN
not to be soon s .... 2 Thess 2:2

SHAME
never be put to s...............Joel 2:26
to put to s the wise..........1 Cor 1:27
glory is in their s ....Phil 3:19

SHAMEFUL
For it is s even to...............Eph 5:12

SHARE
to do good and to s ....Heb 13:16

SHARING
for your liberal s.............. 2 Cor 9:13

SHARP
S as a two-edged sword .....Prov 5:4

SHARPEN
s their tongue like a..............Ps 64:3

SHARPNESS
I should use s .... 2 Cor 13:10

SHEATH
your sword into the s ....John 18:11

SHEAVES
Bringing his s......................Ps 126:6
gather them like s .... Mic 4:12

SHED
which is s for many ....Matt 26:28

SHEDDING
blood, and without s.........Heb 9:22

SHEEP
s will be scattered ....Zech 13:7
having a hundred s ....Luke 15:4
and I know My s ....John 10:14
"He was led as a s ....Acts 8:32

SHEET
object like a great s.........Acts 10:11

SHELTER(S)
the LORD will be a s.........Joel 3:16
s him all the day long.... Deut 33:12

SHEOL
not leave my soul in S........Ps 16:10
the belly of S I cried ....Jon 2:2

SHEPHERD(S)
The LORD is my S...................Ps 23:1
His flock like a s ....Is 40:11
'I will strike the S............Matt 26:31
"I am the good s ....John 10:11
the dead, that great S ....Heb 13:20
S the flock of God .... 1 Pet 5:2
when the Chief S................ 1 Pet 5:4
"And I will give you s......... Jer 3:15
s have led them astray ...... Jer 50:6

SHIELD
I am your s ....Gen 15:1
truth shall be your s.............Ps 91:4
all, taking the s ....Eph 6:16

SHINE
LORD make His face s ..... Num 6:25
among whom you s ....Phil 2:15

SHINED
them a light has s ....Is 9:2

SHINES
heed as a light that s.........2 Pet 1:19

SHINING
light is already s .... 1 John 2:8

SHIPWRECK
faith have suffered s ....1 Tim 1:19

SHOOT
They s out the lip ....Ps 22:7

SHORT
have sinned and fall s ..... Rom 3:23

SHORTENED
those days were s............Matt 24:22

SHOUT
heaven with a s............. 1 Thess 4:16

SHOW
a land that I will s ....Gen 12:1
s Him greater works........John 5:20

SHOWBREAD
s which was not lawful ....Matt 12:4

SHOWERS
make it soft with s.............Ps 65:10

SHREWDLY
because he had dealt s ....Luke 16:8

SHRINES
who made silver s ....Acts 19:24

SHRIVELED
You have s me up ....Job 16:8

SHUFFLES
with his eyes, He s ....Prov 6:13

SHUNNED
feared God and s evil ....Job 1:1

SHUT(S)
For you s up the ....Matt 23:13
s his eyes from seeing........Is 33:15
who opens and no one s ..... Rev 3:7

SICK
I was s and you..............Matt 25:36
faith will save the s........James 5:15

SICKLE
"Thrust in Your s ....Rev 14:15

SICKNESS
will sustain him in s....... Prov 18:14
"This s is not unto ....John 11:4

SICKNESSES
And bore our s...................Matt 8:17

SIDE
The LORD is on my s.........Ps 118:6

SIFT
s the nations with the ....Is 30:28

SIGH
our years like a s..................Ps 90:9

SIGHING
For my s comes before......Job 3:24

SIGHT
and see this great s .... Ex 3:3
by faith, not by s .... 2 Cor 5:7

SIGN(S)
will give you a s....................Is 7:14
seeks after a s ....Matt 12:39
For Jews request a s ...... 1 Cor 1:22
and let them be for s.........Gen 1:14
cannot discern the s..........Matt 16:3
did many other s ....John 20:30

SILENCE
That You may s.....................Ps 8:2
seal, there was s ....Rev 8:1

SILENT
season, and am not s...........Ps 22:2

SILK
covered you with s.........Ezek 16:10

SILLY
They are s children............. Jer 4:22

SILVER
may buy the poor for s.....Amos 8:6
him thirty pieces of s.......Matt 26:15

SIMILITUDE
been made in the s...........James 3:9

SIMPLE
making wise the s ....Ps 19:7

SIN
and be sure your s .... Num 32:23
Be angry, and do not s ....Ps 4:4
s is always before me..........Ps 51:3
soul an offering for s ....Is 53:10
And He bore the s ....Is 53:12
who takes away the s.......John 1:29
"He who is without s ....John 8:7
convict the world of s........John 16:8
s entered the world......... Rom 5:12
s is not imputed .... Rom 5:13
s shall not have................. Rom 6:14
Shall we s because we...... Rom 6:15
Him who knew no s .... 2 Cor 5:21
man of s is revealed...... 2 Thess 2:3
we are, yet without s ....Heb 4:15
do it, to him it is s..........James 4:17
say that we have no s.... 1 John 1:8
and he cannot s .... 1 John 3:9

SINCERE
and from s faith.................1 Tim 1:5

SINCERITY
simplicity and godly s ....2 Cor 1:12

SINFUL
from me, for I am a s........Luke 5:8
become exceedingly s ... Rom 7:13

SING
Let him s psalms ....James 5:13

SINGERS
The s went before ....Ps 68:25

SINGING
His presence with s.............Ps 100:3
and spiritual songs, s........Eph 5:19

SINK
I s in deep mire....................Ps 69:2
to s he cried out..............Matt 14:30

SINNED
You only, have I s ....Ps 51:4
"Father, I have s ....Luke 15:18
for all have s and .... Rom 3:23
that we have not s .... 1 John 1:10

SINNER(S)
s who repents than ....Luke 15:7
the ungodly and the s...... 1 Pet 4:18
in the path of s......................Ps 1:1

the righteous, but s ....Matt 9:13
while we were still s ....Rom 5:8
many were made s........... Rom 5:19
the world to save s...........1 Tim 1:15
such hostility from s ....Heb 12:3

SINS
from presumptuous s..........Ps 19:13
You, Our secret s..................Ps 90:8
The soul who s shall........Ezek 18:4
if your brother s ....Matt 18:15
s according to the........... 1 Cor 15:3
the forgiveness of s..............Eph 1:7
If we confess our s .... 1 John 1:9
propitiation for our s ...... 1 John 2:2

SIT(S)
but to s on My right........Matt 20:23
"S at My right hand ....Heb 1:13
I will grant to s ....Rev 3:21
It is He who s above ....Is 40:22
so that he s as God....... 2 Thess 2:4

SKIN
God made tunics of s.........Gen 3:21
LORD and said, "S ....Job 2:4
Ethiopian change his s......Jer 13:23

SKULL
to say, Place of a S..........Matt 27:33

SLACK
The Lord is not s.................2 Pet 3:9

SLAIN
is the Lamb who was s......Rev 5:12

SLANDER
whoever spreads s ....Prov 10:18

SLANDERERS
be reverent, not s ....1 Tim 3:11

SLAUGHTER
led as a lamb to the s.............Is 53:7
as sheep for the s .... Rom 8:36

SLAVE
commits sin is a s.............John 8:34
should no longer be s ....Rom 6:6

SLAY
s the righteous ....Gen 18:25

SLEEP
God caused a deep s.........Gen 2:21
neither slumber nor s.........Ps 121:4
He gives His beloved s.......Ps 127:2
and many s...................... 1 Cor 11:30
We shall not all s............. 1 Cor 15:51

SLEEPLESSNESS
in labors, in s .... 2 Cor 6:5

SLEEPS
"Our friend Lazarus s....John 11:11

SLEPT
I lay down and s.....................Ps 3:5

SLING
he had, and his s ....1 Sam 17:40

SLIP
Their foot shall s .... Deut 32:35

SLIPPERY
set them in s places............Ps 73:18

SLOW
hear, s to speak, s..........James 1:19

SLUGGARD
will you slumber, O s...........Prov 6:9

SLUMBERING
upon men, While s............Job 33:15

SMALL
And I saw the dead, s......Rev 20:12

SMELL(S)
and he smelled the s........Gen 27:27
s the battle from afar........Job 39:25

SMITTEN
Him stricken, S.....................Is 53:4

SMOOTH
And the rough places s ....Is 40:4

SMOOTH-SKINNED
man, and I am a s............Gen 27:11

SNARE
is a fowler's s ....Hos 9:8
it will come as a s..........Luke 21:35
and escape the s ....2 Tim 2:26

SNARED
All of them are s..................Is 42:22

SNARES
who seek my life lay s........Ps 38:12

SNATCH
neither shall anyone s ...John 10:28

SNATCHES
s away what was.............Matt 13:19

SNEER
And you s at it ....Mal 1:13

SNIFFED
They s at the wind .... Jer 14:6

SNOW
shall be whiter than s...........Ps 51:7
shall be as white as s.............Is 1:18

SOAKED
Their land shall be s ....Is 34:7

SOBER
the older men be s............. Titus 2:2

SOBERLY
think, but to think s .... Rom 12:3

SODOMITES
nor homosexuals, nor s.... 1 Cor 6:9

SOJOURNER(S)
no s had to lodge...............Job 31:32
are strangers and s .... Lev 25:23

SOLD
s his birthright ....Gen 25:33
s all that he had..............Matt 13:46
but I am carnal, s .... Rom 7:14

SOLDIER(S)
hardship as a good s.........2 Tim 2:3
s twisted a crown ....John 19:2

SOLITARY
God sets the s in...................Ps 68:6

SOMETHING
thinks himself to be s ....Gal 6:3

SON
Me, 'You are My S..................Ps 2:7
is born, Unto us a S..............Is 9:6
fourth is like the S............. Dan 3:25
will bring forth a S.............Matt 1:21
"This is My beloved S.......Matt 3:17
Jesus,You S of God............Matt 8:29
are the Christ, the S.......Matt 16:16
Whose S is He ....Matt 22:42
of the S of Man ....Matt 24:37
'I am the S of God..........Matt 27:43
of Jesus Christ, the S........ Mark 1:1
out, the only s ....Luke 7:12
The only begotten S.........John 1:18
that this is the S................John 1:34
of the only begotten S .....John 3:18
S can do nothing ....John 5:19
s abides forever ....John 8:35
you believe in the S ....John 9:35
I said, 'I am the S ....John 10:36
behold your s ....John 19:26
Jesus Christ is the S..........Acts 8:37
by sending His own S........Rom 8:3
not spare His own S .... Rom 8:32
live by faith in the S ....Gal 2:20
God sent forth His S............Gal 4:4
the knowledge of the S .....Eph 4:13
"You are My S......................Heb 1:5
though He was a S..............Heb 5:8
but made like the S..............Heb 7:3
"This is My beloved S......2 Pet 1:17
denies the S................... 1 John 2:23
One like the S of Man ......Rev 1:13

SONG(S)
Sing to Him a new s ....Ps 33:3
He has put a new s ....Ps 40:3

I will sing a new s ....Ps 144:9
they sang a new s .... Rev 5:9
my Maker, Who gives s....Job 35:10
and spiritual s ....Eph 5:19

SONS
s shall come from afar ....Is 60:4
He will purify the s ....Mal 3:3
you may become s ....John 12:36
who are of faith are s ....Gal 3:7
the adoption as s ....Gal 4:5
in bringing many s............Heb 2:10
speaks to you as to s.........Heb 12:5

SOON
For it is s cut off ....Ps 90:10

SORCERESS
shall not permit a s ....Ex 22:18

SORCERY
idolatry, s.............................Gal 5:20

SORES
and putrefying s ....Is 1:6

SORROW
multiply your s ....Gen 3:16
s is continually.....................Ps 38:17
And He adds no s........... Prov 10:22
Your s is incurable........... Jer 30:15
them sleeping from s.......Luke 22:45
s will be turned...............John 16:20
s produces
  repentance...................2 Cor 7:10
s as others who........... 1 Thess 4:13
no more death, nor s ....Rev 21:4

SORROWFUL
But I am poor and s ....Ps 69:29
he went away s...............Matt 19:22
soul is exceedingly s.......Matt 26:38
and I may be less s ....Phil 2:28

SORROWS
s shall be multiplied.............Ps 16:4
by men, A Man of s ....Is 53:3
are the beginning of s......Matt 24:8

SORRY
s that He had made
  man...............................Gen 6:6
For you were made s........2 Cor 7:9

SOUGHT
I s the LORD.........................Ps 34:4
s what was lost ....Ezek 34:4

SOUL
with all your s .... Deut 6:5
"My s loathes my life.........Job 10:1
s draws near the Pit........Job 33:22
will not leave my s ....Ps 16:10
converting the s ....Ps 19:7
He restores my s ....Ps 23:3
you cast down, O my s.......Ps 42:5
Let my s thrive...............Ps 119:175
No one cares for my s ......Ps 142:4
me wrongs his own s.........Prov 8:36
When You make His s.......Is 53:10
s delight itself.......................Is 55:2
The s of the father As.....Ezek 18:4
able to destroy both s ....Matt 10:28
and loses his own s..........Matt 16:26
with all your s ....Matt 22:37
your whole spirit, s ..... 1 Thess 5:23
to the saving of the s ......Heb 10:39
his way will save a s.....James 5:20
health, just as your s........3 John 2

SOULS
And will save the s.............Ps 72:13
And he who wins s ...... Prov 11:30
unsettling your s..............Acts 15:24
is able to save your s .....James 1:21

SOUND
voice was like the s..........Ezek 43:2
do not s a trumpet..............Matt 6:2
s words which you...........2 Tim 1:13

SOUNDNESS
him this perfect s..............Acts 3:16

SOUNDS
a distinction in the s ..... 1 Cor 14:7

SOW
s trouble reap..........................Job 4:8
Those who s in tears...........Ps 126:5
Blessed are you who s...........Is 32:20
"They s the wind ....Hos 8:7
s is not made alive .... 1 Cor 15:36

SOWER
"Behold, a s went ....Matt 13:3

SOWN
s spiritual things............. 1 Cor 9:11
of righteousness is s ......James 3:18

SOWS
s the good seed is the .....Matt 13:37
'One s and another...............Matt 13:25
for whatever a man s ....Gal 6:7

SPARE
He who did not s ...... Rom 8:32
if God did not s..................2 Pet 2:4

SPARES
s his rod hates his .... Prov 13:24

SPARKLES
it is red, When it s.......... Prov 23:31

SPARKS
to trouble, As the s...............Job 5:7

SPARROW(S)
s has found a home..............Ps 84:3
than many s ....Matt 10:31

SPAT
Then they s on Him ....Matt 27:30

SPEAK
only the word that I s ....Num 22:35
oh, that God would s ....Job 11:5
And a time to s ....Eccl 3:7
s anymore in His name...... Jer 20:9
or what you should s .....Matt 10:19
to you when all men s .....Luke 6:26
s what I have seen ....John 8:38
He hears He will s..........John 16:13
Spirit and began to s ....Acts 2:4

SPEAKING
envy, and all evil s .... 1 Pet 2:1

SPEAKS
to face, as a man s ....Ex 33:11
God has sent s ....John 3:34
When he s a lie.................John 8:44
he being dead still s...........Heb 11:4
of sprinkling that s..........Heb 12:24

SPEAR(S)
His side with a s ....John 19:34
And their s into.........................Is 2:4

SPECK
do you look at the s ....Matt 7:3

SPECTACLE
you were made a s ....Heb 10:33

SPEECH
one language and one s ....Gen 11:1
his s contemptible ....2 Cor 10:10
s always be with grace.........Col 4:6

SPEEDILY
I call, answer me s ....Ps 102:2

SPEND
you s money for ....Is 55:2
amiss, that you may s ......James 4:3

SPEW
nor hot, I will s ....Rev 3:16

SPIES
men who had been s.........Josh 6:23

SPIN
neither toil nor s ....Matt 6:28

SPINDLE
her hand holds the s ...... Prov 31:19

SPIRIT
And the S of God was ....Gen 1:2
S shall not strive.................Gen 6:3
S that is upon you .... Num 11:17
portion of your s.................2 Kin 2:9

Then a s passed..................Job 4:15
hand I commit my s...........Ps 31:5
The s of a man is the ..... Prov 20:27
s will return to God............Eccl 12:7
S has gathered them...........Is 34:16
I have put My S ....Is 42:1
"The S of the Lord ....Is 61:1
S entered me when He......Ezek 2:2
and a new s ....Ezek 18:31
"I will put My S ....Ezek 36:27
walk in a false s................. Mic 2:11
and He saw the S ....Matt 3:16
I will put My S ....Matt 12:18
S descending upon........... Mark 1:10
s indeed is willing .... Mark 14:38
go before Him in the s........Luke 1:17
manner of s you are of....Luke 9:55
hands I commit My s.....Luke 23:46
they had seen a s...........Luke 24:37
"God is S..........................John 4:24
I speak to you are s...........John 6:63
"the S of truth ....John 14:17
but if a s or an angel.........Acts 23:9
the flesh but in the S...........Rom 8:9
does not have the S...........Rom 8:9
s that we are children...... Rom 8:16
what the mind of the S.... Rom 8:27
to us through His S...... 1 Cor 2:10
gifts, but the same S .... 1 Cor 12:4
but the S gives life ....2 Cor 3:6
Now the Lord is the S ...2 Cor 3:17
Having begun in the S.........Gal 3:3
has sent forth the S...........Gal 4:6
with the Holy S..................Eph 1:13
the unity of the S.................Eph 4:3
stand fast in one s.............Phil 1:27
S expressly says that.......1 Tim 4:1
S who dwells in us...........James 4:5
made alive by the S .... 1 Pet 3:18
do not believe every s ... 1 John 4:1
you know the S............... 1 John 4:2
has given us of His S... 1 John 4:13
S who bears witness...... 1 John 5:6
not having the S ....Jude 19
I was in the S on the.........Rev 1:10
him hear what the S ....Rev 2:7
And the S and the ....Rev 22:17

SPIRITS
Who makes His angels s ...Ps 104:4
heed to deceiving s ....1 Tim 4:1

SPIRITUAL
s judges all things .... 1 Cor 2:15
However, the s is not.... 1 Cor 15:46
s restore such a one.............Gal 6:1

SPIRITUALLY
s minded is life ....Rom 8:6

SPITEFULLY
for those who s...............Matt 5:44

SPITTING
face from shame and s..........Is 50:6

SPOKE
"No man ever s................John 7:46
I was a child, I s.............. 1 Cor 13:11
in various ways s ....Num 12:8
s as they were moved......2 Pet 1:21

SPONGE
them ran and took a s ....Matt 27:48

SPOT(S)
church, not having s ....Eph 5:27
Himself without s ....Heb 9:14
These are s in your ....Jude 12

SPRING
Truth shall s out of..............Ps 85:11
s send forth fresh ....James 3:11

SPRINGING
a fountain of water s .... John 4:14

SPRINKLED
having our hearts s ....Heb 10:22

SPRINKLING
s that speaks ....Heb 12:24

SPROUT
and the seed should s ..... Mark 4:27

STAFF
this Jordan with my s......Gen 32:10
Your rod and Your s ....Ps 23:4
on the top of his s............Heb 11:21

STAMMERING
s tongue that you..................Is 33:19

STAMPING
At the noise of the s........... Jer 47:3

STAND
one shall be able to s .... Deut 7:24
lives, And He shall s.........Job 19:25
ungodly shall not s.................Ps 1:5
not lack a man to s .... Jer 35:19
And who can s when He.... Mal 3:2
that kingdom cannot s ... Mark 3:24
he will be made to s.......... Rom 14:4
Watch, s fast in the........ 1 Cor 16:13
for by faith you s .... 2 Cor 1:24
having done all, to s ....Eph 6:13
S therefore......................Eph 6:14
of God in which you s ... 1 Pet 5:12
"Behold, I s at the.............Rev 3:20

STANDING
they love to pray s ....Matt 6:5
and the Son of Man s ....Acts 7:56

STANDS
him who thinks he s ..... 1 Cor 10:12

STAR(S)
He made the s also............Gen 1:16
For we have seen His s ......Matt 2:2
born as many as the s ......Heb 11:12
Bright and Morning S ...Rev 22:16

STATE
learned in whatever s........Phil 4:11

STATURE
in wisdom and s ....Luke 2:52

STATUTE(S)
shall be a perpetual s......... Lev 3:17
the s of the LORD are ....Ps 19:8
Teach me Your s...........Ps 119:12

STAY
S here and watch ....Matt 26:38

STEADFAST
brethren, be s................. 1 Cor 15:58
soul, both sure and s.........Heb 6:19
Resist him, s in the............ 1 Pet 5:9

STEADFASTLY
s set His face to go..........Luke 9:51
And they continued s ....Acts 2:42

STEADFASTNESS
good order and the s ....Col 2:5

STEADILY
could not look s .... 2 Cor 3:13

STEADY
and his hands were s.........Ex 17:12

STEAL
"You shall not s ....Ex 20:15
thieves break in and s ......Matt 6:19
night and s Him away ....Matt 27:64

STEM
forth a Rod from the s...........Is 11:1

STENCH
there will be a s ....Is 3:24
this time there is a s.......John 11:39

STEP
s has turned from the ....Job 31:7

STEPS
The s of a good man...........Ps 37:23
And established my s...........Ps 40:2
the LORD directs his s.......Prov 16:9
should follow His s .... 1 Pet 2:21

STEWARD
be blameless, as a s ....Titus 1:7

STEWARDS
of Christ and s .... 1 Cor 4:1

STEWARDSHIP
entrusted with a s............ 1 Cor 9:17

STICK
'For Joseph, the s .... Ezek 37:16

STICKS
a man gathering s .... Num 15:32

STIFF
rebellion and your s....... Deut 31:27

STIFF-NECKED
"You s and......................... Acts 7:51

STILL
When I awake, I am s ......Ps 139:18
sea, "Peace, be s .... Mark 4:39

STILLBORN
burial, I say that a s .... Eccl 6:3

STINGS
like a serpent, And s...... Prov 23:32

STIR
I remind you to s ....2 Tim 1:6

STIRRED
So the LORD s up the.........Hag 1:14

STIRS
It s up the dead for.................Is 14:9

STOCKS
s that were in the .... Jer 20:2

STOIC
and S philosophers ....Acts 17:18

STOMACH
Foods for the s .... 1 Cor 6:13

STOMACH'S
little wine for your s ....1 Tim 5:23

STONE
him, a pillar of s ....Gen 35:14
s shall be a witness........Josh 24:27
s which the builders..........Ps 118:22
I lay in Zion a s ....Is 28:16
take the heart of s ....Ezek 36:26
will give him a s ....Matt 7:9
s will be broken...............Matt 21:44
s which the builders........Luke 20:17
those works do you s......John 10:32
Him as to a living s .... 1 Pet 2:4

STONED
s Stephen as he was ....Acts 7:59
They were s.......................Heb 11:37

STONES
Abraham from these s ......Matt 3:9
command that these s ....Matt 4:3

STONY
fell on s ground .... Mark 4:5

STOOPED
And again He s down........ John 8:8

STORM
He calms the s ....Ps 107:29
for a shelter from s ....Is 4:6

STRAIGHT
Make s in the desert A ....Is 40:3
and make s paths for........Heb 12:13

STRANGE
s thing happened.............. 1 Pet 4:12

STRANGER(S)
and loves the s.................. Deut 10:18
I was a s and you ....Matt 25:35
know the voice of s.........John 10:5
you are no longer s ....Eph 2:19

STRAP
than I, whose sandal s...... Mark 1:7

STRAW
stones, wood, hay, s........1 Cor 3:12

STRAYED
Yet I have not s ....Ps 119:110
some have s.....................1 Tim 6:10

STREET(S)
In the middle of its s......Rev 22:2
You taught in our s.......Luke 13:26

STRENGTH
s no man shall...................1 Sam 2:9
The LORD is the s ....Ps 27:1
is our refuge and s ....Ps 46:1
They go from s to.................Ps 84:7
S and honor are her....... Prov 31:25
might He increases s ....Is 40:29
O LORD, my s and my ...... Jer 16:19
were still without s.............Rom 5:6
s is made perfect ....2 Cor 12:9

STRENGTHEN
And He said s ....Ps 27:14
S the weak hands................Is 35:3
s your brethren...............Luke 22:32
s the things ....Rev 3:2

STRENGTHENED
unbelief, but was s .... Rom 4:20
stood with me and s........2 Tim 4:17

STRENGTHENING
s the souls of the ....Acts 14:22

STRENGTHENS
through Christ who s.........Phil 4:13

STRETCHED
I have s out my hands.........Ps 88:9
"All day long I have s.... Rom 10:21

STRETCHES
For he s out his hand.......Job 15:25

STRICKEN
of My people He was s.........Is 53:8

STRIFE
man stirs up s .... Prov 15:18
even from envy and s.......Phil 1:15
which come envy, s ....1 Tim 6:4

STRIKE
The sun shall not s..............Ps 121:6
"S the Shepherd ....Zech 13:7
'I will s the Shepherd......Matt 26:31

STRIPES
s we are healed...................Is 53:5
s you were healed .... 1 Pet 2:24

STRIVE
"My Spirit shall not s..........Gen 6:3
"S to enter through ....Luke 13:24
the Lord not to s..............2 Tim 2:14

STRONG
The LORD s and mighty ....Ps 24:8
S is Your hand....................Ps 89:13
"When a s man..............Luke 11:21
We then who are s .... Rom 15:1
weak, then I am s..........2 Cor 12:10
my brethren, be s............Eph 6:10
were made s.....................Heb 11:34

STRONGHOLD
of my salvation, my s ....Ps 18:2

STRUCK
s the rock twice .... Num 20:11
the hand of God has s ......Job 19:21
Behold, He s the rock.........Ps 78:20
in My wrath I s ....Is 60:10
s the head from the.......... Hab 3:13
took the reed and s ....Matt 27:30

STUBBORN-HEARTED
"Listen to Me, you s........Is 46:12

STUBBORNNESS
do not look on the s.........Deut 9:27

STUDIED
having never s .... John 7:15

STUMBLE
have caused many to s.......Mal 2:8
you will be made to s .....Matt 26:31
immediately they s.......... Mark 4:17
who believe in Me to s .... Mark 9:42
For we all s in many........James 3:2

STUMBLING
the deaf, nor put a s........ Lev 19:14

But a stone of s ....Is 8:14
Behold, I will lay s .... Jer 6:21
I lay in Zion a s .... Rom 9:33
this, not to put a s.......... Rom 14:13
of yours become a s.......... 1 Cor 8:9
and "A stone of s................ 1 Pet 2:8
to keep you from s.............Jude 24

STUPID
hates correction is s..........Prov 12:1

SUBDUE
s all things to.....................Phil 3:21

SUBJECT
for it is not s ....Rom 8:7
Let every soul be s .... Rom 13:1
all their lifetime s ....Heb 2:15

SUBJECTION
put all things in s..................Heb 2:8

SUBMISSION
his children in s ....1 Tim 3:4

SUBMISSIVE
Yes, all of you be s............. 1 Pet 5:5

SUBMIT
Therefore s to God..........James 4:7
s yourselves to every .... 1 Pet 2:13

SUBSTANCE
Bless his s .... Deut 33:11

SUCCESS
please give me s ....Gen 24:12
But wisdom brings s....... Eccl 10:10

SUCCESSFUL
Joseph, and he was a s......Gen 39:2

SUDDENLY
s there was with the.........Luke 2:13

SUE
s you and take away........Matt 5:40

SUFFER
for the Christ to s ....Luke 24:46
Christ, if indeed we s....... Rom 8:17
in Him, but also to s...........Phil 1:29

SUFFERED
s these things and to......Luke 24:26
for whom I have s...........Phil 3:8
after you have s .... 1 Pet 5:10

SUFFERING(S)
anyone among you s .....James 5:13
I consider that the s .... Rom 8:18
perfect through s...............Heb 2:10

SUFFERS
Love s long and is........... 1 Cor 13:4

SUFFICIENCY
but our s is from God .... 2 Cor 3:5

SUFFICIENT
S for the day is Its............Matt 6:34

SUM
How great is the s ....Ps 139:17

SUMPTUOUSLY
fine linen and fared s.....Luke 16:19

SUN
So the s stood still..........Josh 10:13
s shall not strike you........Ps 121:6
s returned ten degrees......Is 38:8
The s and moon grow .....Joel 2:10
s shall go down on the.... Mic 3:6
for He makes His s ....Matt 5:45
the s was darkened........Luke 23:45
do not let the s ....Eph 4:26
s became black as..............Rev 6:12
had no need of the s ....Rev 21:23

SUPPER
to eat the Lord's S........ 1 Cor 11:20
took the cup after s .... 1 Cor 11:25
together for the s..............Rev 19:17

SUPPLICATION
by prayer and s ....Phil 4:6

SUPPLIES
by what every joint s ....Eph 4:16

SUPPLY
And my God shall s ....Phil 4:19

SUPPORT
this, that you must s ....Acts 20:35

SURE
s your sin will find .... Num 32:23
call and election s ....2 Pet 1:10

SURETY
Be s for Your servant ....Ps 119:122
Jesus has become a s ....Heb 7:22

SURROUND
LORD, mercy shall s ....Ps 32:10

SURROUNDED
also, since we are s ....Heb 12:1

SUSPICIONS
reviling, evil s ....1 Tim 6:4

SUSTAIN
S me with cakes of............Song 2:5

SWADDLING
Him in s cloths..................Luke 2:7

SWALLOW
a gnat and s a camel.....Matt 23:24

SWEAR
'You shall not s..................Matt 5:33
began to curse and s......Matt 26:74

SWEARING
By s and lying......................Hos 4:2

SWEARS
but whoever s by the......Matt 23:18

SWEAT
His s became like ....Luke 22:44

SWEET
s are Your words............Ps 119:103
but it will be as s ....Rev 10:9

SWEETNESS
mouth like honey in s........Ezek 3:3

SWELLING
they speak great s............2 Pet 2:18

SWIFT
let every man be s..........James 1:19

SWIM
night I make my bed s............Ps 6:6

SWOON
As they s like the..............Lam 2:12

SWORD
s which turned every........Gen 3:24
The s of the LORD is...............Is 34:6
'A s is sharpened.............Ezek 21:9
Bow and s of battle I........Hos 2:18
to bring peace but a s.....Matt 10:34
for all who take the s......Matt 26:52
the s of the Spirit...............Eph 6:17
than any two-edged s......Heb 4:12
mouth goes a sharp s ......Rev 19:15

SWORDS
shall beat their s......................Is 2:4

SWORE
So I s in My wrath ....Heb 3:11

SWORN
"By Myself I have s..........Gen 22:16
"The LORD has s.................Heb 7:21

SYMBOLIC
which things are s...............Gal 4:24

SYMPATHIZE
Priest who cannot s ....Heb 4:15

SYMPATHY
My s is stirred....................Hos 11:8

SYNAGOGUE
but are a s of Satan.............Rev 2:9

T

TABERNACLE
t He shall hide me................Ps 27:5
I will abide in Your t ....Ps 61:4
And will rebuild the t.....Acts 15:16
and more perfect t ....Heb 9:11

TABERNACLES
Feast of T was at hand......John 7:2

TABLE(S)
prepare a t before me..........Ps 23:5
dogs under the t .... Mark 7:28
of the Lord's t ....1 Cor 10:21
and overturned the t.......Matt 21:12

TABLET
is engraved On the t ....Jer 17:1

TAKE
t Your Holy Spirit...............Ps 51:11
"T My yoke upon ....Matt 11:29
and t up his cross........... Mark 8:34
My life that I may t........John 10:17

TAKEN
He was t from prison ....Is 53:8
one will be t and the......Matt 24:40
until He is t out of........ 2 Thess 2:7

TALEBEARER
t reveals secrets.............. Prov 11:13

TALENT
went and hid your t........Matt 25:25

TALK
shall t of them when......... Deut 6:7

TALKED
within us while He t ......Luke 24:32

TALKERS
both idle t and ....Titus 1:10

TARES
the t also appeared.........Matt 13:26

TARGET
You set me as Your t.........Job 7:20

TARRY
come and will not t..........Heb 10:37

TASTE
Oh, t and see that the..........Ps 34:8
might t death for.................Heb 2:9

TASTED
t the heavenly gift...............Heb 6:4

TAUGHT
as His counselor has t.........Is 40:13
from man, nor was I t ....Gal 1:12

TAXES
t to whom t ....Rom 13:7

TEACH
"Can anyone t...................Job 21:22
T me Your paths ....Ps 25:4
t you the fear of the...........Ps 34:11
t transgressors Your..........Ps 51:13
So t us to number our ....Ps 90:12
t you again the first ....Heb 5:12

TEACHER
for One is your T...............Matt 23:8
know that You are a t.......John 3:2
named Gamaliel, a t...........Acts 5:34
a t of the Gentiles in........1 Tim 2:7

TEACHERS
than all my t ....Ps 119:99
prophets, third t ....1 Cor 12:28
and some pastors and t.....Eph 4:11
desiring to be t ....1 Tim 1:7
there will be false t ....2 Pet 2:1

TEACHES
the Holy Spirit t .... 1 Cor 2:13
the same anointing t..... 1 John 2:27

TEACHING
"t them to observe all.....Matt 28:20
t every man in all................Col 1:28

TEAR(S)
I, even I, will t.....................Hos 5:14
will wipe away every t......Rev 21:4
my couch with my t..............Ps 6:6
mindful of your t...............2 Tim 1:4
it diligently with t ....Heb 12:17

TELL
"Who can t if God.................Jon 3:9
t him his fault ....Matt 18:15
whatever they t ....Matt 23:3
He comes, He will t ....John 4:25

TEMPERATE
prize is t in all...................1 Cor 9:25
husband of one wife, t .....1 Tim 3:2

TEMPEST
And suddenly a great t ....Matt 8:24

TEMPLE(S)
So Solomon built the t... 1 Kin 6:14
LORD is in His holy t ....Ps 11:4
One greater than the t.......Matt 12:6
"Destroy this t ....John 2:19
your body is the t...........1 Cor 6:19
grows into a holy t............Eph 2:21
sits as God in the t........ 2 Thess 2:4
and the Lamb are its t.....Rev 21:22
t made with hands...........Acts 7:48

TEMPORARY
which are seen are t.......2 Cor 4:18

TEMPT
t the LORD your God..........Matt 4:7
does He Himself t ....James 1:13

TEMPTATION
do not lead us into t..........Matt 6:13
man who endures t.......James 1:12

TEMPTED
forty days, t by Satan..... Mark 1:13
lest you also be t ....Gal 6:1
in all points t......................Heb 4:15

TEMPTER
Now when the t came.......Matt 4:3

TENDER
your heart was t............2 Kin 22:19

TENDERHEARTED
to one another, t.................Eph 4:32

TENT
earthly house, this t..........2 Cor 5:1

TENTS
Than dwell in the t ....Ps 84:10

TERRESTRIAL
bodies and t bodies....... 1 Cor 15:40

TERRIBLE
is great and very t..............Joel 2:11

TERRIFY
me with dreams And t ....Job 7:14

TERRIFYING
t was the sight ....Heb 12:21

TERROR
are nothing, You see t........Job 6:21
not be afraid of the t............Ps 91:5

TERRORS
consumed with t..................Ps 73:19

TEST
said, "Why do you t........Matt 22:18
T all things .... 1 Thess 5:21
but t the spirits ....1 John 4:1

TESTED
God t Abraham ....Gen 22:1
Where your fathers t........Heb 3:9
though it is t by fire........... 1 Pet 1:7

TESTIFIED
who has seen has t ....John 19:35
which He has t ....1 John 5:9

TESTIFY
t what We have................John 3:11
t that the Father ....1 John 4:14

TESTIFYING
was righteous, God *t* ....Heb 11:4

TESTIMONIES
those who keep His *t*.........Ps 119:2
t are my meditation.........Ps 119:99

TESTIMONY
two tablets of the *T* ....Ex 31:18
under your feet as a *t*.... Mark 6:11
no one receives His *t*........John 3:32
not believed the *t* .... 1 John 5:10
For the *t* of Jesus is.........Rev 19:10

TESTING
came to Him, *t* Him ....Matt 19:3

TESTS
men, but God who *t* ...... 1 Thess 2:4

THANK
"I *t* You, Father................Matt 11:25
t You that I am not ....Luke 18:11

THANKFUL
as God, nor were *t* .... Rom 1:21

THANKS
the cup, and gave *t* ....Matt 26:27
T be to God for His.........2 Cor 9:15

THANKSGIVING
His presence with *t*............Ps 95:2
into His gates with *t* ....Ps 100:4
supplication. with *t*.............Phil 4:6

THIEF
do not despise a *t*.............Prov 6:30
because he was a *t*..........John 12:6
Lord will come as a *t*.......2 Pet 3:10

THINGS
in heaven give good *t*.....Matt 7:11
kept all these *t* ....Luke 2:51
share in all good *t*................Gal 6:6

THINK(S)
t you have eternal...........John 5:39
not to *t* of himself .... Rom 12:3
Yet the LORD *t* upon
  me ....Ps 40:17
For as he *t* in his ....Prov 23:7
t he stands take heed ... 1 Cor 10:12

THIRST
those who hunger and *t*.....Matt 5:6
in Me shall never *t* ....John 6:35
anymore nor *t* anymore....Rev 7:16

THIRSTS
My soul *t* for God.................Ps 42:2
saying, "If anyone *t* ....John 7:37
freely to him who *t* ....Rev 21:6

THIRSTY
I was *t* and you gave .....Matt 25:35

THORN
a *t* in the flesh..........2 Cor 12:7

THORNS
Both *t* and thistles it.........Gen 3:18
some fell among *t* ....Matt 13:7
wearing the crown of *t*....John 19:5

THOUGHT(S)
You understand my *t* ....Ps 139:2
I *t* as a child .... 1 Cor 13:11
The LORD knows the *t*.........Ps 94:11
unrighteous man his *t*..........Is 55:7
"For My *t* are not your.........Is 55:8
Jesus, knowing their *t*........Matt 9:4
heart proceed evil *t*........Matt 15:19
The LORD knows the *t*... 1 Cor 3:20

THREAT
shall flee at the *t*..................Is 30:17

THREATEN
suffered, He did not *t* ...... 1 Pet 2:23

THREE
hope, love, these *t* .... 1 Cor 13:13

THROAT
t is an open tomb .... Rom 3:13

THRONE(S)
Your *t*, O God, is..................Ps 45:6
Lord sitting on a *t*.....................Is 6:1
"Heaven is My *t*....................Is 66:1
for it is God's *t*....................Matt 5:34
will give Him the *t* ....Luke 1:32
"Your *t*, O God, is ....Heb 1:8
come boldly to the *t*..........Heb 4:16
My Father on His *t* ....Rev 3:21
I saw a great white *t*........Rev 20:11

THROW
t Yourself down ....Matt 4:6

THROWN
neck, and he were *t* .... Mark 9:42

THRUST
and rose up and *t*............Luke 4:29

THUNDER
The voice of Your *t*............Ps 77:18
the voice of loud *t* ....Rev 14:2

THUNDERED
"The LORD *t* from.........2 Sam 22:14

THUNDERINGS
the sound of mighty *t*........Rev 19:6

THUNDERS
The God of glory *t* ....Ps 29:3

TIDINGS
I bring you good *t*............Luke 2:10

TILL
no man to *t* the ground.......Gen 2:5

TILLER
but Cain was a *t* ....Gen 4:2

TIME
pray to You In a *t* ....Ps 32:6
for the *t* is near....................Rev 1:3

TIMES
the signs of the *t*................Matt 16:3
not for you to know *t* ....Acts 1:7
last days perilous *t*............2 Tim 3:1

TITHE(S)
And he gave him a *t*........Gen 14:20
For you pay *t* of mint .....Matt 23:23
and to bring the *t*............ Neh 10:37
Bring all the *t*.....................Mal 3:10

TITHING
the year of *t*....................Deut 26:12

TITTLE
away, one jot or one *t*......Matt 5:18

TODAY
T I have begotten You............Ps 2:7
t you will be with Me ....Luke 23:43
"T, if you will hear...............Heb 3:7

TOMB(S)
in the garden a new *t* .... John 19:41
like whitewashed *t*.........Matt 23:27

TOMORROW
drink, for *t* we die ....Is 22:13
do not worry about *t* ....Matt 6:34
what will happen *t*.........James 4:14

TONGUE
remember you, Let my *t*....Ps 137:6
forever, But a lying *t* ..... Prov 12:19
t breaks a bone............. Prov 25:15
t should confess that ....Phil 2:11
does not bridle his *t*......James 1:26
no man can tame the *t*,,,,James 3:8
every nation, tribe, *t* ....Rev 14:6

TONGUES
From the strife of *t*............Ps 31:20
speak with new *t* .... Mark 16:17
divided *t*, as of fire............Acts 2:3
I speak with the *t* .... 1 Cor 13:1

TOOTH
eye for an eye and a *t* ......Matt 5:38

TOPHET
the high places of *T* .... Jer 7:31

TORCH
and like a fiery *t*...............Zech 12:6

TORCHES
When he had set the *t*.... Judg 15:5
come with flaming *t* .... Nah 2:3

TORMENT
You come here to *t* ....Matt 8:29
t ascends forever.............Rev 14:11

TORMENTED
And they will be *t* ....Rev 20:10

TORMENTS
"And being in *t*...............Luke 16:23

TORN
of the temple was *t* ....Matt 27:51

TOSSED
t to and fro and ....Eph 4:14

TOWER
t whose top is in the ....Gen 11:4
a watchman in the *t*..............Is 21:5

TRADITION
transgress the *t*..................Matt 15:2
according to the *t*.................Col 2:8

TRAIN
T up a child in the.............Prov 22:6

TRAINING
bring them up in the *t* ....Eph 6:4

TRAITOR(S)
also became a *t*.................Luke 6:16
t, headstrong.....................2 Tim 3:4

TRAMPLE
serpent you shall *t* ....Ps 91:13
swine, lest they *t* ....Matt 7:6

TRAMPLED
t the Son of God...............Heb 10:29
the winepress was *t*.........Rev 14:20

TRANCE
t I saw a vision ....Acts 11:5

TRANSFIGURED
and was *t* before them .....Matt 17:2

TRANSFORMED
this world, but be *t*.......... Rom 12:2

TRANSGRESSED
"Yes, all Israel has *t*......... Dan 9:11
t your commandment....Luke 15:29

TRANSGRESSES
Whoever *t* and does
  not.....................................2 John 9

TRANSGRESSION(S)
no law there is no *t*.......... Rom 4:15
deceived, fell into *t* ....1 Tim 2:14
mercies, Blot out my *t*........Ps 51:1
For I acknowledge my *t*......Ps 51:3
was wounded for our *t*.........Is 53:5
For the *t* of My people ....Is 53:8

TRANSGRESSOR(S)
I make myself a *t* ....Gal 2:18
Then I will teach *t*..............Ps 51:13
numbered with the *t*...........Is 53:12

TRAP(S)
of Israel, As a *t*.....................Is 8:14
for me, And from the *t*.......Ps 141:9

TREACHEROUSLY
"This man dealt *t* ....Acts 7:19

TREAD(S)
You shall *t* upon the...........Ps 91:13
an ox while it *t* ....1 Tim 5:18
t the winepress.................Rev 19:15

TREASURE
and you will have *t*........Matt 19:21
he who lays up *t*.............Luke 12:21
But we have this *t* .... 2 Cor 4:7

TREASURED
t the words of His ....Job 23:12

TREASURES
it more than hidden *t* ....Job 3:21
I will give you the *t*...............Is 45:3
for yourselves *t* ....Matt 6:19
are hidden all the *t* ....Col 2:3
riches than the *t* ....Heb 11:26

TREATY
Now Solomon made a *t*... 1 Kin 3:1

TREE
you eaten from the *t*.........Gen 3:11
t Planted by the ....Ps 1:3
like a native green *t*............Ps 37:35
t bears good fruit ....Matt 7:17
His own body on the *t*..... 1 Pet 2:24
the river, was the *t*............Rev 22:2

TREES
late autumn *t* without..........Jude 12
the sea, or the *t*....................Rev 7:3

TREMBLE
That the nations may *t*..........Is 64:2
they shall fear and *t* .... Jer 33:9

TREMBLING
in fear, and in much *t*....... 1 Cor 2:3
t you received..................2 Cor 7:15
flesh, with fear and *t*..........Eph 6:5

TRENCH
and he made a *t* .... 1 Kin 18:32

TRESPASSES
forgive men their *t*...........Matt 6:14
not imputing their *t* ....2 Cor 5:19
who were dead in *t*............Eph 2:1

TRIAL
concerning the fiery *t*...... 1 Pet 4:12

TRIBE(S)
the Lion of the *t*...................Rev 5:5
blood Out of every *t* .... Rev 5:9
t which are scattered......James 1:1

TRIBULATION
there will be great *t* ....Matt 24:21
world you will have *t* ....John 16:33
with her into great *t* ....Rev 2:22
out of the great *t* ....Rev 7:14

TRIBULATIONS
t enter the kingdom........Acts 14:22
but we also glory in *t*........Rom 5:3
t that you endure .... 2 Thess 1:4

TRIED
A *t* stone, a precious............Is 28:16

TRIMMED
and *t* their lamps...............Matt 25:7

TRIUMPH
always leads us in *t* ....2 Cor 2:14

TRIUMPHED
the Lord, For He has *t*........Ex 15:1

TRODDEN
t the winepress alone ....Is 63:3

TROUBLE
few days and full of *t* ....Job 14:1
t He shall hide me.................Ps 27:5
not in *t* as other men...........Ps 73:5
will be with him in *t*.........Ps 91:15
Savior in time of *t*............... Jer 14:8
there are some who *t* ....Gal 1:7

TROUBLED
worried and *t*.................Luke 10:41
shaken in mind or *t* ...... 2 Thess 2:2

TROUBLES
Out of all their *t*...............Ps 25:22
will be famines and *t*..... Mark 13:8
him out of all his *t*............Acts 7:10

TROUBLING
wicked cease from *t* ....Job 3:17

TRUE
He who sent Me is *t*........ John 7:28
Indeed, let God be *t*...........Rom 3:4
whatever things are *t*........Phil 4:8

Him who is *t* .... 1 John 5:20
for these words are *t*......... Rev 21:5

TRUMPET
deed, do not sound a *t*........Matt 6:2
t makes an uncertain ..... 1 Cor 14:8
For the *t* will sound ..... 1 Cor 15:52

TRUST
T in the Lord.......................Ps 37:3
T in the Lord with all ....Prov 3:5
Do not *t* in a friend............. Mic 7:5
who *t* in riches.............. Mark 10:24

TRUSTED
"He *t* in the Lord..................Ps 22:8
"He *t* in God....................Matt 27:43

TRUSTS
But he who *t* in the.............Ps 32:10

TRUTH
led me in the way of *t* ....Gen 24:48
Behold, You desire *t*..............Ps 51:6
t shall be your shield.....Ps 91:4
And Your law is *t*.........Ps 119:142
t is fallen in the ....Is 59:14
called the City of *T* ....Zech 8:3
you shall know the *t*.......John 8:32
"I am the way, the *t* ....John 14:6
He, the Spirit of *t* ....John 16:13
to Him. "What is *t*.........John 18:38
who suppress the *t* .... Rom 1:18
but, speaking the *t*.............Eph 4:15
your waist with *t*...............Eph 6:14
I am speaking the *t*...........1 Tim 2:7
they may know the *t* ......2 Tim 2:25
the knowledge of the *t*....2 Tim 3:7
that we are of the *t* ...... 1 John 3:19
the Spirit is *t* .... 1 John 5:6

TUNIC(S)
Also he made him a *t*........Gen 37:3
the Lord God made *t*.......Gen 3:21

TURN
you shall not *t*................. Deut 17:11
"Repent, *t* away from......Ezek 14:6
on your right cheek, *t*......Matt 5:39
t them from darkness.....Acts 26:18

TURNING
marvel that you are *t*...........Gal 1:6
or shadow of *t* ....James 1:17

TURNS
A soft answer *t*..................Prov 15:1
that he who *t*....................James 5:20

TUTOR
the law was our *t* ....Gal 3:24

TWO
T are better than one.......... Eccl 4:9
t shall become one...........Matt 19:5
new man from the *t*...........Eph 2:15

TYPE
of Adam, who is a *t* .... Rom 5:14

U

UNAFRAID
Do you want to be *u* .... Rom 13:3

UNBELIEF
because of their *u*...........Matt 13:58
help my *u*.........................Mark 9:24
did it ignorantly in *u*.......1 Tim 1:13
enter in because of *u* ....Heb 3:19

UNBELIEVERS
yoked together with *u* ....2 Cor 6:14

UNBELIEVING
Do not be *u*......................John 20:27
u nothing is pure ....Titus 1:15
"But the cowardly, *u*..........Rev 21:8

UNCIRCUMCISED
not the physically *u* .... Rom 2:27

UNCLEAN
I am a man of *u* lips.................Is 6:5
man common or *u*............Acts 10:28
there is nothing *u*........... Rom 14:14
that no fornicator, *u*............Eph 5:5

UNCLEANNESS
men's bones and all *u*.....Matt 23:27
flesh in the lust of *u*.........2 Pet 2:10

UNDEFILED
incorruptible and *u* .... 1 Pet 1:4

UNDERSTAND
if there are any who *u*..........Ps 14:2
hearing, but do not *u*...............Is 6:9
"Why do you not *u*.........John 8:43
lest they should *u*...........Acts 28:27
some things hard to *u*.....2 Pet 3:16

UNDERSTANDING
His *u* is infinite ....Ps 147:5
lean not on your own *u*......Prov 3:5
u will find good ....Prov 19:8
His *u* is unsearchable ....Is 40:28
also still without *u*..........Matt 15:16
also pray with the *u*...... 1 Cor 14:15
the Lord give you *u*.........2 Tim 2:7
Who is wise and *u*.........James 3:13

UNDERSTANDS
There is none who *u* .... Rom 3:11

UNDERSTOOD
Then I *u* their end ....Ps 73:17
clearly seen, being *u*....... Rom 1:20

UNDIGNIFIED
I will be even more *u*.....2 Sam 6:22

UNDISCERNING
u, untrustworthy.............. Rom 1:31

UNEDUCATED
that they were *u* ....Acts 4:13

UNFAITHFUL
way of the *u* is hard....... Prov 13:15

UNFORGIVING
unloving, *u* .... Rom 1:31

UNFRUITFUL
and it becomes *u* .... Mark 4:19

UNGODLINESS
heaven against all *u*......... Rom 1:18

UNGODLY
u shall not stand....................Ps 1:5
Christ died for the *u* ....Rom 5:6

UNHOLY
the holy and *u*.................Ezek 22:26

UNINTENTIONALLY
kills his neighbor *u* .... Deut 4:42

UNITE
U my heart to fear ....Ps 86:11

UNITY
to dwell together in *u* ....Ps 133:1
to keep the *u* of the.............Eph 4:3

UNJUST
commended the *u*.............Luke 16:8
of the just and the *u*........Acts 24:15
For God is not *u*..................Heb 6:10

UNKNOWN
To The *U* God.................Acts 17:23

UNLEAVENED
the Feast of *U* Bread.........Ex 12:17

UNLOVING
untrustworthy, *u*.............. Rom 1:31

UNMERCIFUL
unforgiving, *u* .... Rom 1:31

UNPROFITABLE
'We are *u* servants ....Luke 17:10
for that would be *u* ....Heb 13:17

UNPUNISHED
wicked will not go *u* ...... Prov 11:21

UNQUENCHABLE
up the chaff with *u*............Matt 3:12

UNRIGHTEOUS
u man his thoughts ....Is 55:7
u will not inherit the......... 1 Cor 6:9

UNRIGHTEOUSNESS
all ungodliness and u ...... Rom 1:18
cleanse us from all u....... 1 John 1:9
All u is sin...................... 1 John 5:17

UNSEARCHABLE
u are His judgments....... Rom 11:33

UNSPOTTED
to keep oneself u ....James 1:27

UNTRUSTWORTHY
undiscerning, u................. Rom 1:31

UNWISE
Therefore do not be u........Eph 5:17

UNWORTHY
u manner will be .... 1 Cor 11:27

UPHOLD
U me according to...........Ps 119:116

UPHOLDS
LORD u all who fall ....Ps 145:14

UPPER
show you a large u........ Mark 14:15

UPRIGHT
u is His delight..................Prov 15:8

UPRIGHTNESS
princes for their u .... Prov 17:26

UPROOT
u the wheat with.............Matt 13:29

URIM
Thummim and Your U.... Deut 33:8

US
"God with u........................Matt 1:23
If God is for u.................... Rom 8:31
of them were of u.......... 1 John 2:19

USE
who spitefully u you ....Matt 5:44
u liberty as an.....................Gal 5:13

USELESS
one's religion is u...........James 1:26

USING
u liberty as a .... 1 Pet 2:16

USURY
'Take no u or....................Lev 25:36

UTTERANCE
the Spirit gave them u........Acts 2:4

UTTERED
which cannot be u........... Rom 8:26

UTTERMOST
u those who come ....Heb 7:25

UTTERS
Day unto day u speech.........Ps 19:2

V

VAGABOND
v you shall be on the ....Gen 4:12

VAIN
the people plot a v...................Ps 2:1
you believed in v .... 1 Cor 15:2

VALIANT
They are not v for the...........Jer 9:3

VALIANTLY
God we will do v ....Ps 60:12

VALOR
a mighty man of v.......1 Sam 10:18

VALUE
of more v than they ....Matt 6:26

VALUED
It cannot be v in the.........Job 28:16

VANISH
knowledge, it will v.... 1 Cor 13:8

VANISHED
and He v from their ......Luke 24:31

VANITY
of vanities, all is v .... Eccl 1:2

VAPOR
best state is but v..................Ps 39:5
It is even a v that............James 4:14

VARIATION
whom there is no v ....James 1:17

VEGETABLES
and let them give us v ...... Dan 1:12
is weak eats only v.......... Rom 14:2

VEHEMENT
of fire, A most v.................Song 8:6

VEIL
v of the temple was.........Matt 27:51
Presence behind the v ....Heb 6:19

VENGEANCE
V is Mine .... Deut 32:35

VENOM
It becomes cobra v............Job 20:14

VESSEL(S)
like a potter's v ....Ps 2:9
for he is a chosen v...........Acts 9:15
treasure in earthen v .... 2 Cor 4:7

VEXED
grieved, and I was v............Ps 73:21

VICE
as a cloak for v .... 1 Pet 2:16

VICTIM
And plucked the v.............Job 29:17

VICTORY
v that has overcome .... 1 John 5:4

VIEW
"Go, v the land....................Josh 2:1

VIGILANT
Be sober, be v .... 1 Pet 5:8

VIGOR
nor his natural v.............. Deut 34:7

VILE
them up to v passions...... Rom 1:26

VINDICATED
know that I shall be v.......Job 13:18

VINDICATION
Let my v come from ....Ps 17:2

VINE
"I am the true v.................John 15:1

VINEDRESSER
and My Father is the v ....John 15:1

VINEGAR
As v to the teeth and...... Prov 10:26

VINES
foxes that spoil the v ....Song 2:15

VINEYARD
Who plants a v and........... 1 Cor 9:7

VIOLENCE
was filled with v ....Gen 6:11
of heaven suffers v..........Matt 11:12

VIOLENT
haters of God, v................ Rom 1:30

VIPER(S)
And stings like a v .... Prov 23:32
to them, "Brood of v ...   Matt 3:7

VIRGIN
v shall conceive ....Is 7:14
"Behold, the v shall...........Matt 1:23

VIRGINS
who took their lamps ....Matt 25:1

VIRTUE
to your faith v .... 2 Pet 1:5

VISAGE
was marred more than........Is 52:14

VISIBLE
that are on earth, v ....Col 1:16

VISION
in a trance I saw a v ....Acts 11:5
to the heavenly v.............Acts 26:19

VISIONS
young men shall see v.......Joel 2:28

VISIT
orphans and....................James 1:27

VISITATION
God in the day of v .... 1 Pet 2:12

VISITED
Israel, for He has v...........Luke 1:68

VISITING
v the iniquity of the............ Ex 20:5

VISITOR
am a foreigner and a v......Gen 23:4

VITALITY
v was turned into the...........Ps 32:4

VOICE(S)
fire a still small v........... 1 Kin 19:12
if you will hear His v..........Ps 95:7
"The v of one crying ....Matt 3:3
And suddenly a v ....Matt 3:17
for they know his v..........John 10:4
the truth hears My v......John 18:37
If anyone hears My v......Rev 3:20
And there were loud v.....Rev 11:15

VOID
they are a nation v......... Deut 32:28
heirs, faith is made v .... Rom 4:14

VOLUME
In the v of the book...........Heb 10:7

VOLUNTEERS
Your people shall be v ....Ps 110:3

VOMIT
returns to his own v.........2 Pet 2:22

VOW
for he had taken a v........Acts 18:18

VOWS
to reconsider his v.......... Prov 20:25

W

WAGE(S)
w the good warfare.........1 Tim 1:18
For the w of sin is .... Rom 6:23
Indeed the w of the.........James 5:4

WAILING
There will be w................Matt 13:42

WAIT
w patiently for Him ....Ps 37:7
those who w on the............Is 40:31
To those who eagerly w.....Heb 9:28

WAITED
w patiently for the.................Ps 40:1
Divine longsuffering w ... 1 Pet 3:20

WAITING
ourselves, eagerly w .... Rom 8:23
from that time w..............Heb 10:13

WAITS
the creation eagerly w.... Rom 8:19

WALK
w before Me and be.......Gen 17:1
Yea, though I w...................Ps 23:4
W prudently when you ...... Eccl 5:1
"This is the way, w..............Is 30:21
be weary, they shall w ....Is 40:31
w humbly with your God.... Mic 6:8
W while you have the ... John 12:35
so we also should w..........Rom 6:4
For we w by faith .... 2 Cor 5:7
W in the Spirit....................Gal 5:16
And w in love......................Eph 5:2
that you may w worthy......Col 1:10
and they shall w .... Rev 3:4

WALKED
Methuselah, Enoch *w*........Gen 5:22
The people who *w*...................Is 9:2
in which you once *w*...........Eph 2:2

WALKS
the LORD your God *w*.... Deut 23:14
is the man Who *w*......................Ps 1:1
he who *w* in darkness ... John 12:35
adversary the devil *w*........ 1 Pet 5:8

WALL(S)
then the *w* of the city.........Josh 6:5
you whitewashed *w*.........Acts 23:3
a window in the *w* ....2 Cor 11:33
Now the *w* of the city ......Rev 21:14
By faith the *w* of..............Heb 11:30

WANDERED
They *w* in deserts and.....Heb 11:38

WANDERERS
And they shall be *w*..........Hos 9:17

WANT
I shall not *w* ....Ps 23:1

WANTING
balances, and found *w* ..... Dan 5:27

WANTON
have begun to grow *w*....1 Tim 5:11

WAR
"There is a noise of *w*........Ex 32:17
w may rise against...............Ps 27:3
shall they learn *w*....................Is 2:4
going to make *w*..........Luke 14:31
You fight and *w*.................James 4:2
fleshly lusts which *w*...... 1 Pet 2:11
judges and makes *w*........Rev 19:11

WARFARE
to her, That her *w* ....Is 40:2
w entangles.........................2 Tim 2:4

WARN
w those who are......... 1 Thess 5:14

WARNED
Then, being divinely *w*.....Matt 2:12
Who *w* you to flee..............Matt 3:7

WARNING
w every man and ....Col 1:28

WARPED
such a person is *w* ....Titus 3:11

WARRING
w against the law of .... Rom 7:23

WARRIOR
He runs at me like a *w* .....Job 16:14

WARS
you will hear of *w*............Matt 24:6
Where do *w* and fights....James 4:1

WASH
w myself with snow...........Job 9:30
W me thoroughly.................Ps 51:2
w His feet with her ....Luke 7:38
said to him, "Go, *w*.........John 9:7
w the disciples'................John 13:5
w away your sins ....Acts 22:16

WASHED
w his hands before.........Matt 27:24
But you were *w* .... 1 Cor 6:11
Him who loved us and *w*....Rev 1:5

WASHING
us, through the *w* ....Titus 3:5

WASTE
the cities are laid *w*...............Is 6:11
"Why this *w* ....Matt 26:8

WASTED
this fragrant oil *w* ....Mark 14:4

WATCH
is past, And like a *w*..........Ps 90:4
"*W* therefore ....Matt 24:42

WATCHES
Blessed is he who *w* ....Rev 16:15

WATCHFUL
But you be *w* in all............2 Tim 4:5

WATCHING
he comes, will find *w*.....Luke 12:37

WATER
Eden to *w* the garden........Gen 2:10
I am poured out like *w*.......Ps 22:14
For I will pour *w*....................Is 44:3
given you living *w*...........John 4:10
rivers of living *w* ....John 7:38
can yield both salt *w*......James 3:12
the Spirit, the *w*.............. 1 John 5:8
are clouds without *w*..........Jude 12
let him take the *w* ....Rev 22:17

WATERED
I planted, Apollos *w*.......... 1 Cor 3:6

WATERS
me beside the still *w*...........Ps 23:2
Though its *w* roar and..........Ps 46:3
your bread upon the *w*..... Eccl 11:1
thirsts, Come to the *w* ....Is 55:1
fountain of living *w* .... Jer 2:13
living fountains of *w*..........Rev 7:17

WAVERING
of our hope without *w*...Heb 10:23

WAY(S)
As for God, His *w* ....2 Sam 22:31
the LORD knows the *w* ....Ps 1:6
Teach me Your *w*...................Ps 27:11
in the *w* everlasting ....Ps 139:24
w that seems right .... Prov 14:12
The *w* of the just is ....Is 26:7
wicked forsake his *w*............Is 55:7
And pervert the *w*..............Amos 2:7
he will prepare the *w*..........Mal 3:1
and broad is the *w*............Matt 7:13
will prepare Your *w*........Matt 11:10
to him, "I am the *w* ....John 14:6
to him the *w*....................Acts 18:26
to have known the *w*.....2 Pet 2:21
For all His *w* are...............Deut 32:4
transgressors Your *w*.........Ps 51:13
w please the LORD ....Prov 16:7
"Stand in the *w*...................Jer 6:16
and owns all your *w*.........Dan 5:23
w are everlasting.................Hab 3:6
unstable in all his *w*.........James 1:8
and true are Your *w* ....Rev 15:3

WEAK
gives power to the *w* ....Is 40:29
knee will be as *w*............Ezek 7:17
but the flesh is *w*............Matt 26:41
Receive one who is *w*...... Rom 14:1
God has chosen the *w*... 1 Cor 1:27
We are *w* ....1 Cor 4:10
w I became as *w* .... 1 Cor 9:22
For when I am *w* ....2 Cor 12:10

WEAKER
the wife, as to the *w*........... 1 Pet 3:7

WEAKNESS(ES)
w were made strong..........Heb 11:34
also helps in our *w*........... Rom 8:26

WEALTH
W gained by....................... Prov 13:11

WEALTHY
rich, have become *w*..........Rev 3:17

WEAR
'What shall we *w*...............Matt 6:31

WEARIED
You have *w* Me with ....Is 43:24
therefore, being *w*.............. John 4:6

WEARINESS
say, 'Oh, what a *w* ....Mal 1:13

WEARISOME
and much study is *w*........ Eccl 12:12

WEARY
shall run and not be *w* ....Is 40:31
And let us not grow *w*.........Gal 6:9
do not grow *w* in......... 2 Thess 3:13

WEATHER
'It will be fair *w* ....Matt 16:2

WEDDING
day there was a *w* ....John 2:1

WEEK(S)
the first day of the *w* ....Matt 28:1
w are determined............. Dan 9:24

WEEP
A time to *w*.......................... Eccl 3:4
You shall *w* no more ....Is 30:19
are you who *w*.................Luke 6:21
do not *w* ....Luke 23:28
w with those who *w*....... Rom 12:15

WEEPING
the noise of the *w*.............Ezra 3:13
They shall come
with *w* .... Jer 31:9
There will be *w*...............Matt 8:12
by the tomb *w*.................John 20:11

WEIGH
O Most Upright, You *w*..........Is 26:7

WEIGHED
You have been *w* .... Dan 5:27

WEIGHS
eyes, But the LORD *w* ......Prov 16:2

WEIGHT
us lay aside every *w* ....Heb 12:1

WEIGHTIER
have neglected the *w*......Matt 23:23

WELFARE
does not seek the *w* .... Jer 38:4

WELL
have done *w*.................... Prov 31:29
wheel broken at the *w*...... Eccl 12:6
"Those who are *w*.............Matt 9:12
said to him, 'W done ......Matt 25:21

WELLS
These are *w* without........2 Pet 2:17

WENT
They *w* out from us ...... 1 John 2:19

WEPT
out and *w* bitterly............Matt 26:75
saw the city and *w*........Luke 19:41
Jesus *w*............................John 11:35

WET
his body was *w* with......... Dan 4:33

WHEAT
w falls into the................John 12:24

WHISPERINGS
backbitings, *w*................2 Cor 12:20

WHITE
clothed in *w* garments........ Rev 3:5
behold, a *w* horse................Rev 6:2
and made them *w* ....Rev 7:14

WHOLE
w body were an eye...... 1 Cor 12:17

WHOLESOME
not consent to *w* words....1 Tim 6:3

WHOLLY
w followed the LORD .... Deut 1:36

WICKED
w shall be silent................1 Sam 2:9
w shall be no more ....Ps 37:10
if there is any *w*.................Ps 139:24
w forsake his way................Is 55:7
And desperately *w*............. Jer 17:9
the sway of the *w*......... 1 John 5:19

WICKEDNESS
LORD saw that the *w*............Gen 6:5
in the tents of *w*................Ps 84:10
man repented of
his *w* ....Jer 8:6
is full of greed and *w*....... Luke 11:39
sexual immorality, *w*....... Rom 1:29
and overflow of *w*..........James 1:21

WIDE
open your hand *w* .... Deut 15:8
w is the gate and .... Matt 7:13
to you, our heart is *w* ..... 2 Cor 6:11

WIDOW
the fatherless and *w* .... Ps 146:9
How like a *w* is she .... Lam 1:1
Then one poor *w* .... Mark 12:42
w has children or .... 1 Tim 5:4

WIDOWS
w were neglected .... Acts 6:1
visit orphans and *w* .... James 1:27

WIFE
and be joined to his *w* ...... Gen 2:24
w finds a good thing ...... Prov 18:22
But a prudent *w* .... Prov 19:14
"Go, take yourself a *w* ...... Hos 1:2
divorces his *w* .... Mark 10:11
'I have married a *w* .... Luke 14:20
"Remember Lot's *w* ...... Luke 17:32
so love his own *w* .... Eph 5:33
the husband of one *w* ...... Titus 1:6
bride, the Lamb's *w* .... Rev 21:9

WILDERNESS
I will make the *w* .... Is 41:18
of one crying in the *w* .... Matt 3:3
the serpent in the *w* .... John 3:14

WILES
to stand against the *w* ...... Eph 6:11

WILL
w be done On earth as .... Matt 6:10
but he who does the *w* ..... Matt 7:21
not My *w* .... Luke 22:42
flesh, nor of the *w* .... John 1:13
not to do My own *w* .... John 6:38
w is present with me .... Rom 7:18
and perfect *w* of God .... Rom 12:2
works in you both to *w* ..... Phil 2:13
according to His own *w* ..... Heb 2:4
work to do His *w* .... Heb 13:21

WILLFULLY
For if we sin *w* .... Heb 10:26
For this they *w* .... 2 Pet 3:5

WILLING
If you are *w* and .... Is 1:19
The spirit indeed is *w* ... Matt 26:41
w that any should .... 2 Pet 3:9

WILLS
to whom the Son *w* .... Matt 11:27
it is not of him who *w* ..... Rom 9:16
say, "If the Lord *w* .... James 4:15

WIND
the chaff which the *w* .... Ps 1:4
reed shaken by the *w* ...... Matt 11:7
"The *w* blows where .... John 3:8
of a rushing mighty *w* ...... Acts 2:2

WINDS
be, that even the *w* .... Matt 8:27

WINE
W is a mocker .... Prov 20:1
love is better than *w* ...... Song 1:2
Yes, come, buy *w* .... Is 55:1
they gave Him sour *w* .... Matt 27:34
do not be drunk with *w* ..... Eph 5:18
not given to much *w* .... Titus 2:3

WINEPRESS
"I have trodden the *w* .... Is 63:3
into the great *w* .... Rev 14:19
Himself treads the *w* .... Rev 19:15

WINESKINS
new wine into old *w* .... Matt 9:17

WING(S)
One *w* of the cherub ...... 1 Kin 6:24
the shadow of Your *w* .... Ps 36:7
With healing in His *w* .... Mal 4:2

WINS
w souls is wise .... Prov 11:30

WIPE
w away every tear .... Rev 21:4

WISDOM
for this is your *w* .... Deut 4:6
man who finds *w* .... Prov 3:13
Get *w* .... Prov 4:5
is the beginning of *w* .... Prov 9:10
w is justified by her .... Matt 11:19
Jesus increased in *w* ...... Luke 2:52
riches both of the *w* .... Rom 11:33
the gospel, not with *w* .... 1 Cor 1:17
w of this world .... 1 Cor 3:19
not with fleshly *w* .... 2 Cor 1:12
all the treasures of *w* .... Col 2:3
If any of you lacks *w* ...... James 1:5
power and riches and *w* ... Rev 5:12

WISE
Do not be *w* in your .... Prov 3:7
who wins souls is *w* ...... Prov 11:30
Therefore be *w* as .... Matt 10:16
five of them were *w* .... Matt 25:2
to God, alone *w* .... Rom 16:27
Where is the *w* .... 1 Cor 1:20
not as fools but as *w* .... Eph 5:15
able to make you *w* .... 2 Tim 3:15

WISER
he was *w* than all men ... 1 Kin 4:31
of God is *w* than men ..... 1 Cor 1:25

WITCHCRAFT
is as the sin of *w* .... 1 Sam 15:23

WITHER(S)
also shall not *w* .... Ps 1:3
The grass *w* .... Is 40:7
The grass *w* .... 1 Pet 1:24

WITHHOLD
good thing will He *w* .... Ps 84:11

WITHOUT
pray *w* ceasing .... 1 Thess 5:17
w works is dead .... James 2:26

WITHSTAND
you may be able to *w* .... Eph 6:13

WITNESS
all the world as a *w* .... Matt 24:14
This man came for a *w* ..... John 1:7
do not receive Our *w* ...... John 3:11
Christ, the faithful *w* .... Rev 1:5
beheaded for their *w* .... Rev 20:4

WITNESSES
"You are My *w* .... Is 43:10
presence of many *w* .... 1 Tim 6:12
so great a cloud of *w* .... Heb 12:1

WIVES
Husbands, love your *w* ..... Eph 5:25
w must be reverent .... 1 Tim 3:11

WOMAN
She shall be called *W* ...... Gen 2:23
whoever looks at a *w* ...... Matt 5:28
Then the *w* of Samaria .... John 4:9
"W, behold your .... John 19:26
natural use of the *w* .... Rom 1:27
His Son, born of a *w* .... Gal 4:4
w being deceived .... 1 Tim 2:14
w clothed with the sun .... Rev 12:1

WOMB
in the *w* I knew you .... Jer 1:5
is the fruit of your *w* .... Luke 1:42

WOMEN
O fairest among *w* .... Song 1:8
w will be grinding .... Matt 24:41
are you among *w* .... Luke 1:28
admonish the young *w* .... Titus 2:4
times, the holy *w* .... 1 Pet 3:5

WONDER
marvelous work and a *w* ... Is 29:14

WONDERFUL
name will be called *W* .... Is 9:6

WONDERFULLY
fearfully and *w* made ...... Ps 139:14

WONDERS
signs, and lying *w* .... 2 Thess 2:9

WONDROUS
w works declare that .... Ps 75:1

WONDROUSLY
God, Who has dealt *w* ...... Joel 2:26

WOOL
They shall be as *w* .... Is 1:18
hair were white like *w* ...... Rev 1:14

WORD
w is very near you .... Deut 30:14
w I have hidden .... Ps 119:11
w is a lamp to my feet .... Ps 119:105
Every *w* of God is pure .... Prov 30:5
the *w* of our God .... Is 40:8
for every idle *w* .... Matt 12:36
The seed is the *w* .... Luke 8:11
beginning was the *W* .... John 1:1
W became flesh and .... John 1:14
Your *w* is truth .... John 17:17
Let the *w* of Christ .... Col 3:16
to you in *w* only .... 1 Thess 1:5
by the *w* of His power .... Heb 1:3
For the *w* of God is .... Heb 4:12
does not stumble in *w* ..... James 3:2
through the *w* of God ...... 1 John 1:23
let us not love in *w* .... 1 John 3:18
name is called The *W* ..... Rev 19:13

WORDS
Let the *w* of my mouth ...... Ps 19:14
The *w* of the wise are ..... Eccl 12:11
pass away, but My *w* .... Matt 24:35
You have the *w* of .... John 6:68
not with wisdom of *w* ..... 1 Cor 1:17
those who hear the *w* .... Rev 1:3

WORK
day God ended His *w* .... Gen 2:2
the *w* of Your fingers .... Ps 8:3
w is honorable and .... Ps 111:3
will bring every *w* .... Eccl 12:14
"This is the *w* of God ...... John 6:29
"I must *w* the works .... John 9:4
know that all things *w* ..... Rom 8:28
Do not destroy the *w* ..... Rom 14:20
abounding in the *w* ..... 1 Cor 15:58
If anyone will not *w* .... 2 Thess 3:10
but a doer of the *w* .... James 1:25

WORKER(S)
w is worthy of his .... Matt 10:10
w who does not need ...... 2 Tim 2:15
we are God's fellow *w* ...... 1 Cor 3:9

WORKMANSHIP
For we are His *w* .... Eph 2:10

WORKS
are Your wonderful *w* .... Ps 40:5
And let her own *w* .... Prov 31:31
"For I know their *w* .... Is 66:18
show Him greater *w* .... John 5:20
w that I do he will do .... John 14:12
might stand, not of *w* ...... Rom 9:11
same God who *w* .... 1 Cor 12:6
not justified by the *w* .... Gal 2:16
Now the *w* of the flesh .... Gal 5:19
not of *w*, lest anyone .... Eph 2:9
for it is God who *w* .... Phil 2:13
but does not have *w* ...... James 2:14
also justified by *w* .... James 2:25
"I know your *w* .... Rev 2:2
their *w* follow them .... Rev 14:13
according to their *w* .... Rev 20:12

WORLD(S)
"The field is the *w* .... Matt 13:38
He was in the *w* .... John 1:10
God so loved the *w* .... John 3:16
His Son into the *w* .... John 3:17
w cannot hate you .... John 7:7
You are of this *w* .... John 8:23
overcome the *w* .... John 16:33
w may become guilty ...... Rom 3:19
be conformed to
this *w* .... Rom 12:2
loved this present *w* ...... 2 Tim 4:10
Do not love the *w* .... 1 John 2:15
w is passing away .... 1 John 2:17
also He made the *w* .... Heb 1:2

WORM

But I am a w............................Ps 22:6
w does not die.................. Mark 9:44

WORRY

to you, do not w.................Matt 6:25

WORRYING

w can add one....................Matt 6:27

WORSHIP

come to w Him ....Matt 2:2
w what you do not ....John 4:22
the angels of God w.............Heb 1:6

WORSHIPED

on their faces and w ....Rev 11:16

WORSHIPER

if anyone is a w .... John 9:31

WORTHLESS

Indeed they are all w...........Is 41:29

WORTHLESSNESS

long will you love w ....Ps 4:2

WORTHY

present time are not w .... Rom 8:18
to walk w ....Eph 4:1
the world was not w........Heb 11:38
"W is the Lamb who..........Rev 5:12

WOUND

And my w incurable........ Jer 15:18
and his deadly w .... Rev 13:3

WOUNDED

But He was w for our ....Is 53:5

WOUNDS

Faithful are the w..............Prov 27:6

WRATH

speak to them in His w ....Ps 2:5
Surely the w of man ....Ps 76:10
So I swore in My w ....Ps 95:11
W is cruel and anger a.....Prov 27:4
in My w I struck you ....Is 60:10
w remember mercy.............Hab 3:2
For the w of God is .... Rom 1:18
up for yourself w................Rom 2:5
nature children of w ....Eph 2:3

sun go down on your w ....Eph 4:26
Let all bitterness, w ....Eph 4:31
holy hands, without w......1 Tim 2:8
So I swore in My w............Heb 3:11
not fearing the w.............Heb 11:27
for the w of man..............James 1:20
of the wine of the w..........Rev 14:8
for in them the w................Rev 15:1
fierceness of His w...........Rev 16:19

WRESTLE

For we do not w ....Eph 6:12

WRETCHED

w man that I am............... Rom 7:24
know that you are w..........Rev 3:17

WRETCHEDNESS

let me see my w..............Num 11:15

WRINKLE

not having spot or w..........Eph 5:27

WRITE

w them on their hearts.....Heb 8:10

WRITING(S)

the w was the w.................Ex 32:16
do not believe his w..........John 5:47

WRITTEN

tablets of stone, w.............Ex 31:18
your names are w ....Luke 10:20
"What I have w...............John 19:22

WRONG

done nothing w...............Luke 23:41
But he who does w ....Col 3:25

WRONGED

We have w no one ....2 Cor 7:2

WRONGS

me w his own soul ....Prov 8:36

WROUGHT

And skillfully w.................Ps 139:15

Y

YEAR(S)

the acceptable y.....................Is 61:2
of sins every y.....................Heb 10:3

and for days and y.............Gen 1:14
lives are seventy y...............Ps 90:10
when He was twelve y ....Luke 2:42
with Him a thousand y......Rev 20:6

YES

let your 'Y' be 'Y,' ....Matt 5:37

YESTERDAY

For we were born y...............Job 8:9

YOKE

"Take My y upon you.....Matt 11:29

YOKED

Do not be unequally y....2 Cor 6:14

YOUNG

I have been y.......................Ps 37:25
she may lay her y..................Ps 84:3
I write to you, y .... 1 John 2:13

YOUNGER

Likewise you y people....... 1 Pet 5:5

YOURS

the battle is not y...........2 Chr 20:15
Y is the kingdom...............Matt 6:13
all Mine are Y.................John 17:10
for I do not seek y........2 Cor 12:14

YOUTH

the sins of my y ....Ps 25:7
and y are vanity............... Eccl 11:10
I have kept from
  my y...............................Matt 19:20

YOUTHFUL

Flee also y lusts ....2 Tim 2:22

YOUTHS

y shall faint and be ....Is 40:30

Z

ZEAL

The z of the LORD
  of................................. 2 Kin 19:31
"Z for Your house has.....John 2:17
that they have a z............. Rom 10:2

ZEALOUS

z for good works.............Titus 2:14

WORLD OF THE PATRIARCHS

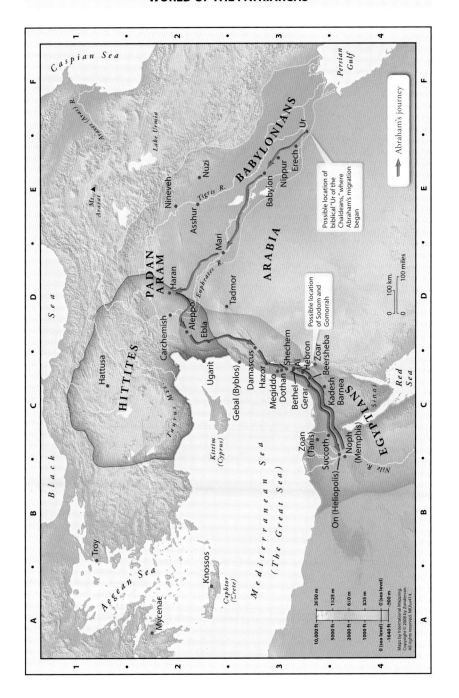

EXODUS AND CONQUEST OF CANAAN

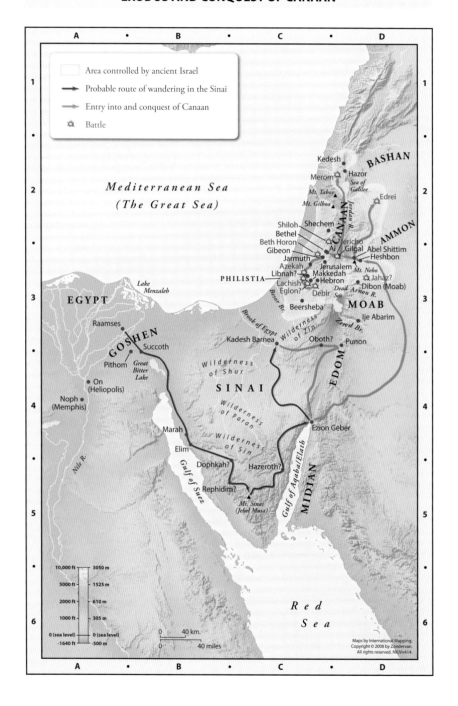

Area controlled by ancient Israel
Probable route of wandering in the Sinai
Entry into and conquest of Canaan
Battle

Mediterranean Sea
(The Great Sea)

BASHAN
Kedesh
Merom
Hazor
Mt. Tabor
Sea of Galilee
Edrei
Mt. Gilboa
CANAAN
Jordan R.
AMMON
Shiloh
Shechem
Bethel
Beth Horon
Jericho
Gibeon
Ai
Gilgal
Abel Shittim
Jarmuth
Heshbon
Azekah
Makkedah
Jerusalem
Mt. Nebo
Libnah?
PHILISTIA
Hebron
Jahaz?
Lachish
Dibon (Moab)
Eglon?
Debir
Dead Sea
Arnon R.
Beersheba
MOAB
Ije Abarim
EGYPT
Lake Menzaleh
Zered Br.
Brook of Egypt
Wilderness of Zin
Oboth?
Punon
Raamses
GOSHEN
Kadesh Barnea
Succoth
Pithom
Great Bitter Lake
Wilderness of Shur
EDOM
On (Heliopolis)
SINAI
Noph (Memphis)
Wilderness of Paran
Marah
Ezion Geber
Elim
Wilderness of Sin
Dophkah?
Hazeroth?
Gulf of Suez
Rephidim?
Gulf of Aqaba/Elath
MIDIAN
Mt. Sinai (Jebel Musa)
Nile R.

Red
Sea

10,000 ft — 3050 m
5000 ft — 1525 m
2000 ft — 610 m
1000 ft — 305 m
0 (sea level) — 0 (sea level)
-1640 ft — -500 m

0   40 km.
0   40 miles

LAND OF THE TWELVE TRIBES

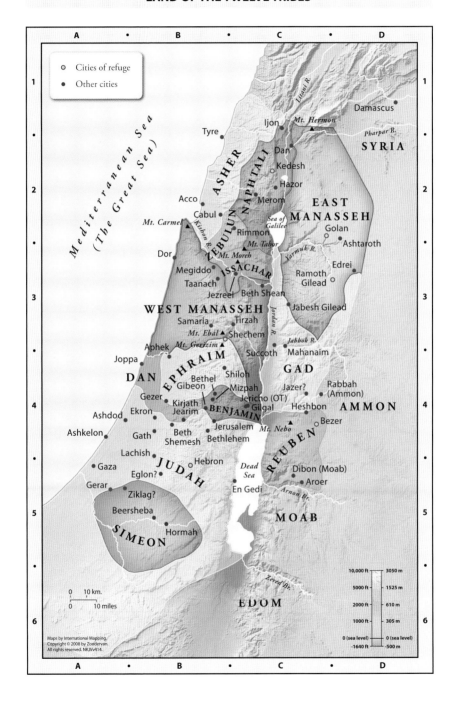

Maps by International Mapping.
Copyright © 2008 by Zondervan.
All rights reserved. NKJVv414.

KINGDOM OF DAVID AND SOLOMON

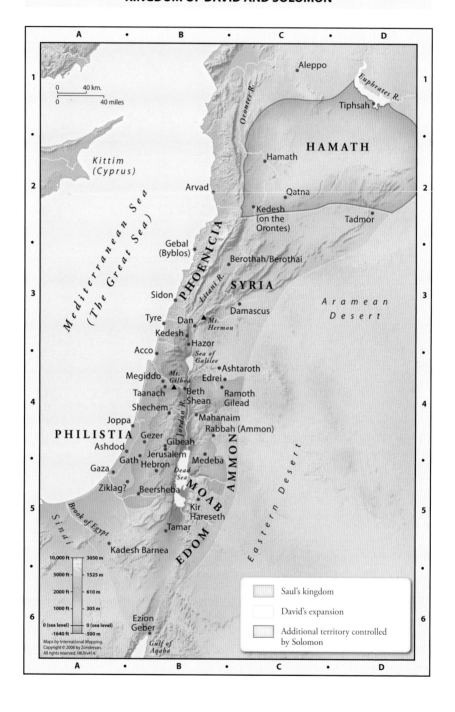

Aleppo
Euphrates R.
Tiphsah

Oronte R.

HAMATH

Kittim
(Cyprus)

Hamath

Mediterranean Sea

Arvad
Qatna

Kedesh
(on the
Orontes)
Tadmor

Gebal
(Byblos)
Berothah/Berothai

PHOENICIA

Litani R.

SYRIA

Aramean
Desert

Sidon

Tyre
Dan
Mt.
Hermon
Damascus

Kedesh

Acco
Hazor

Sea of
Galilee
Ashtaroth

Megiddo
Mt.
Gilboa
Edrei

Taanach
Beth
Shean
Ramoth
Gilead

Shechem

Joppa
Jordan R.
Mahanaim

PHILISTIA
Gezer
Gibeah
Rabbah (Ammon)

Ashdod

Gath
Jerusalem
Medeba

Gaza
Hebron
Dead
Sea

Ziklag?
Beersheba
MOAB

AMMON

Kir
Hareseth

Tamar
EDOM
Eastern Desert

Kadesh Barnea

Sinai

Brook of Egypt

10,000 ft — 3050 m
5000 ft — 1525 m
2000 ft — 610 m
1000 ft — 305 m
0 (sea level) — 0 (sea level)
-1640 ft — -500 m

Ezion
Geber

Gulf of
Aqaba

Saul's kingdom

David's expansion

Additional territory controlled
by Solomon

Maps by International Mapping.
Copyright © 2008 by Zondervan.
All rights reserved. NKJV414.

0   40 km.
0   40 miles

JESUS' MINISTRY

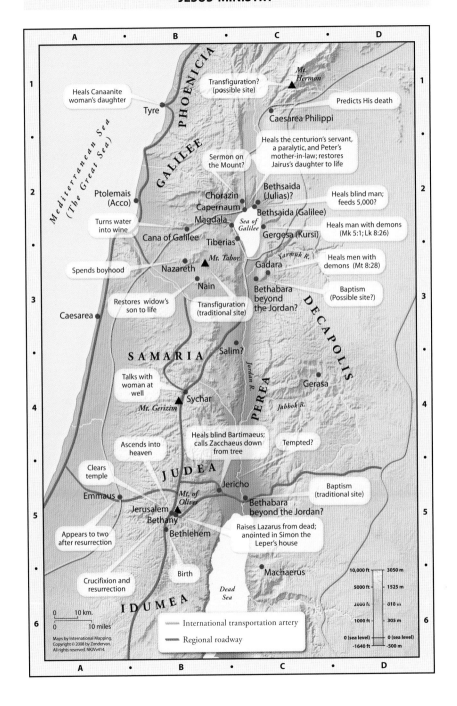

Heals Canaanite woman's daughter

Transfiguration? (possible site)

Mt. Hermon

Predicts His death

Tyre

PHOENICIA

Caesarea Philippi

GALILEE

Heals the centurion's servant, a paralytic, and Peter's mother-in-law; restores Jairus's daughter to life

Sermon on the Mount?

Mediterranean Sea (The Great Sea)

Ptolemais (Acco)

Chorazin

Bethsaida (Julias)?

Heals blind man; feeds 5,000?

Capernaum

Bethsaida (Galilee)

Turns water into wine

Magdala

Sea of Galilee

Heals man with demons (Mk 5:1; Lk 8:26)

Cana of Galilee

Tiberias

Gergesa (Kursi)

Yarmuk R.

Spends boyhood

Mt. Tabor

Gadara

Heals men with demons (Mt 8:28)

Nazareth

DECAPOLIS

Caesarea

Nain

Bethabara beyond the Jordan?

Baptism (Possible site?)

Restores widow's son to life

Transfiguration (traditional site)

SAMARIA

Salim?

Talks with woman at well

Jordan R.

Gerasa

Sychar

PEREA

Jabbok R.

Mt. Gerizim

Ascends into heaven

Heals blind Bartimaeus; calls Zacchaeus down from tree

Tempted?

Clears temple

JUDEA

Jericho

Emmaus

Mt. of Olives

Baptism (traditional site)

Jerusalem

Bethabara beyond the Jordan?

Appears to two after resurrection

Bethany

Raises Lazarus from dead; anointed in Simon the Leper's house

Bethlehem

Crucifixion and resurrection

Birth

Machaerus

10,000 ft — 3050 m

Dead Sea

5000 ft — 1525 m

IDUMEA

2000 ft — 610 m

0   10 km.

1000 ft — 305 m

0   10 miles

.... International transportation artery

0 (sea level) — 0 (sea level)

Maps by International Mapping.
Copyright © 2008 by Zondervan.
All rights reserved. NKJVv414.

—— Regional roadway

-1640 ft — -500 m

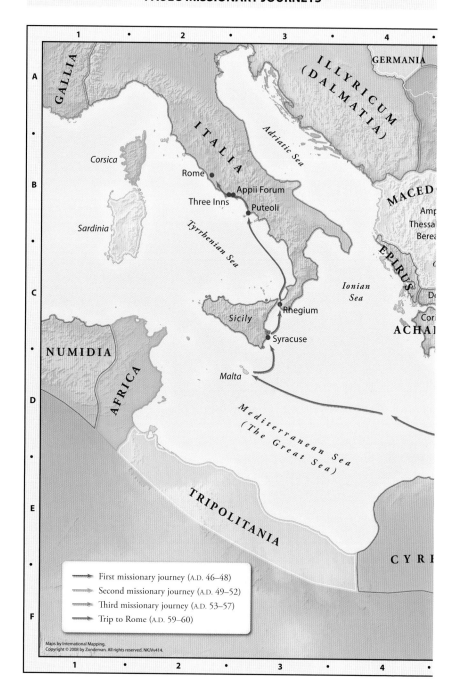

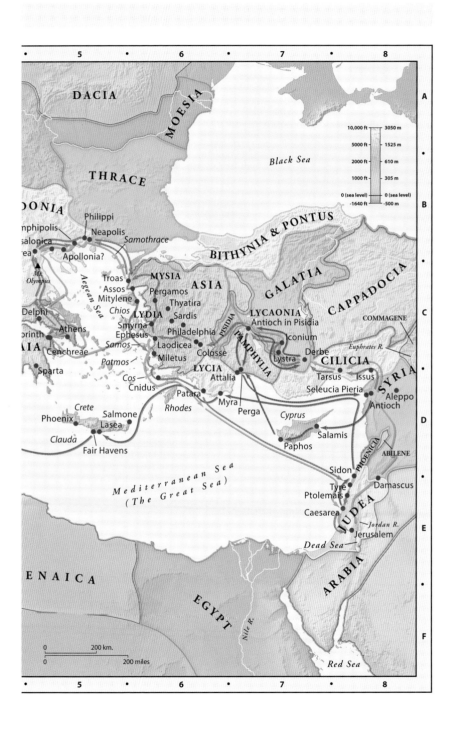

JERUSALEM IN THE TIME OF JESUS

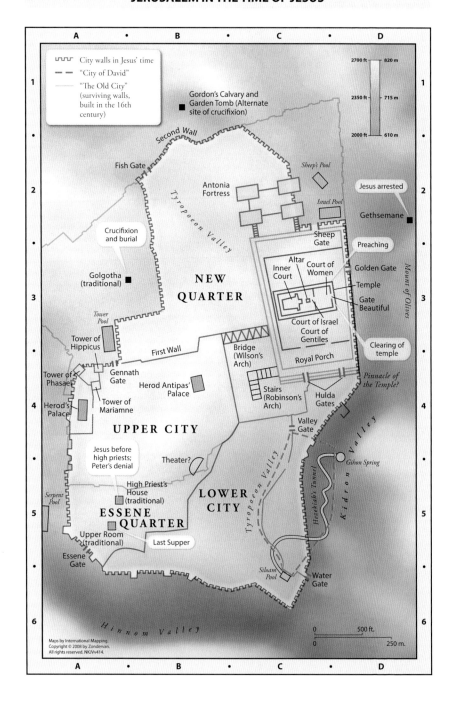

City walls in Jesus' time
"City of David"
"The Old City" (surviving walls, built in the 16th century)

2700 ft — 820 m
2350 ft — 715 m
2000 ft — 610 m

Gordon's Calvary and Garden Tomb (Alternate site of crucifixion)

Second Wall

Fish Gate

Tyropoeon Valley

Antonia Fortress

Sheep's Pool

Israel Pool

Jesus arrested

Gethsemane

Crucifixion and burial

Sheep Gate

Preaching

Altar
Inner Court
Court of Women

Golden Gate

Temple

Gate Beautiful

Golgotha (traditional)

NEW QUARTER

Court of Israel
Court of Gentiles

Mount of Olives

Clearing of temple

Tower Pool

Tower of Hippicus

First Wall

Bridge (Wilson's Arch)

Royal Porch

Pinnacle of the Temple?

Tower of Phasael

Gennath Gate

Herod Antipas' Palace

Stairs (Robinson's Arch)

Hulda Gates

Tower of Mariamne

Herod's Palace

UPPER CITY

Valley Gate

Tyropoeon Valley

Kidron Valley

Gihon Spring

Jesus before high priests; Peter's denial

Theater?

Serpent Pool

High Priest's House (traditional)

LOWER CITY

Hezekiah's Tunnel

ESSENE QUARTER

Upper Room (traditional)

Last Supper

Essene Gate

Siloam Pool

Water Gate

Hinnom Valley

0   500 ft.
0   250 m.

Maps by International Mapping.
Copyright © 2008 by Zondervan.
All rights reserved. NKJVv414.

she didn't approve of, stealing her place. I shouldn't have said anything to her. If I'd kept my mouth shut she might not have taken the action she did. Even now, she won't admit to it. *Prove* it, she says, and names Soames as the culprit because Victoria jilted him. *Soames* put the ricin in her dinner that night . . ."

The noise persisted.

He peered over my shoulder. "That will be Trehearn searching for us. We had best go."

They were all assembled in the dining room, each face registering surprise when David and I arrived together. Immediately detaching myself from his arm, I went to stand by Lianne.

The major chatted with Lady Hartley and I noticed her eyes kept flickering to the door, as though she expected—or feared—someone unpleasant to enter. To me, the major merely inclined his head, his quick eyes scanning my outfit.

To my surprise, the evening turned out quite enjoyable, just the five of us, and repairing to the courtyard for tea and cake, Lady Hartley ordered more bottles of champagne.

WARRIORS

SUPER EDITIONS

Firestar's Quest

Bluestar's Prophecy

SkyClan's Destiny

Crookedstar's Promise

Yellowfang's Secret

Tallstar's Revenge

Bramblestar's Storm

Moth Flight's Vision

Hawkwing's Journey

Tigerheart's Shadow

Crowfeather's Trial

Squirrelflight's Hope

Graystripe's Vow

"What are we celebrating, my lady?" the major asked, jovial, not showing the least surprise when Mrs. Trehearn crept up to whisper in her ladyship's ear.

"A caller! Whoever can be calling at *this* hour?" Lady Hartley's demand echoed through the house. "Sir Edward, you say! And he wants to see *me.*"

"Yes, my lady. And Lord David."

"Show him here, then."

Returning to her guests, Lady Hartley shrugged. "I shall have to speak to Sir Edward about his gross sense of decorum. One does not call at this hour. Whatever can he want?"

Sir Edward arrived, two policemen behind him.

"Forgive my intrusion, my lady, but I've come with a warrant."

"A warrant!" Lady Hartley shouted. "For who, pray? On what grounds?"

"For you, Lady Hartley. On the grounds of *circumstantial evidence* in the murder of Victoria Bastion."

"Evidence," she cried. "What evidence? If you need to arrest someone, arrest Soames. We all know there was something odd between him and Victoria. *Imagine.* The cook's girlfriend lands the lord of the house! How that must rile the man's pride and he's plenty of it—you only have to ask at the village."

"But Mr. Soames was in London at the time—"

"He *planted* it beforehand. He's a cook and he prepared all of Victoria's meals, probably slipped the solution taking up her morning tea. Oh, yes, he took tea to her sometimes, and I say on that last day he decided to avenge himself or, more accurately, his pride."

I glanced up at Lord David. He stood there, watching her, his eyes growing larger by the minute. "Mother, *please*."

"I will not be accused of anything for I am innocent. Of course, I didn't *like* the girl— she wasn't good enough for my son—but I certainly did not poison her."

"Ah!" Sir Edward tapped his brow. "There is only one murderer in this room and it is you, my lady."

"Preposterous! How do you suppose I killed her? What proof do you have?"

"Proof of the poison ricin found in a perfume bottle you yourself gave to Victoria Bastion. Proof of Victoria's own words in

445

her diary naming you as the giver of the gift and, more important, her fear of you. Fear that she would die. Fear that she would never become Lady Hartley because *you* didn't want her to be!"

I'd never seen Lady Hartley silenced before.

"I suggest, my lady," Sir Edward said, calm, but firm, "that you come with me now."

Staring at her empty champagne glass, she smiled. "The perfume bottle . . ."

Her tone sounded odd, whimsical.

"The perfume bottle," she murmured again.

"Traces of ricin were found inside that bottle," Sir Edward reiterated. "Who do you suppose put it there if not you, my lady?"

Bewildered, she looked at Lianne, me, and David. I could see her mind ticking, wondering who had found the perfume bottle. Lianne? Me? David? Trehearn? Annie? Betsy? Who had thought to turn it into the police?

Her gaze arrested me. She knew I'd done it. Her great spidery eyes stayed focused on me as she slowly left her chair and followed Sir Edward out of the door, keeping every ounce of her royal hauteur intact.

Lord David, pacing in the courtyard during Sir Edward's spiel, looked solemn, shocked, and pensive. Perhaps he, like the rest of us, thought Lady Hartley invincible and above the law.

Rubbing her eyes, Lianne went to David. "Where are they taking her?"

David drew Lianne to him. He said nothing, and she didn't ask again but instead looked at me. She knew I'd taken the perfume puffer, as I had given Sir Edward the diary.

She feared the future, as many in the district would, without Lady Hartley's rule.

"Don't worry," David said, "she'll be back."

CHAPTER THIRTY-FIVE

"Who are you, anyway? Clearly not just a major."

Grinning across at me in the car, Major Browning changed the gears. "Because you gave the perfume puffer to me, I'll let you in on a little secret. I work undercover, for Scotland Yard. 'When not at sea . . .'"

"You?!"

Now everything began to make sense. His coming to the area, his interest in the case, and his involvement in all of its details.

"The knights of justice thought Sir Edward needed a little help," he went on, amused at my continuing disbelief.

I recalled the possibility of another investigator looking into the case.

"I am still a *major,*" he enforced.

"And a gentleman, no doubt. I suppose there is no 'uncle,' is there?"

"No," he laughed, "but if anyone's asking, George Filligan will say he is. I am, quite truthfully, staying at his humble abode by the sea."

I turned to him as we drove through the open gates of Padthaway. "You planned it, didn't you? You and Sir Edward."

He stopped the car and turned to me. "I am going to do something I never do."

"Which is?"

"Trust a woman."

He switched off the engine.

"Oh," I said.

"On a case."

"And I am the exception?"

"You are, Miss du Maurier. Without you, Lady Hartley would never have come with us."

"You still can't convict her, can you?"

"The fact will occur to her in the morning,

and no, you are not completely right. We still might be able to convict her without a confession."

"If you're hoping she will give one, she will not."

"We will see."

He sounded mysterious. "You have a strategy in mind to catch her out, don't you?"

"How astute you are." He started up the engine again. "You had better be getting to bed, Miss du Maurier. Seen out in a parked car with a man of my reputation cannot be good, even though I know you *love* driving with me."

He laughed at my ashen face.

"Or is our erstwhile Lord David your favorite?"

My chat with David rose afresh in my mind.

"The man could not protect his own fiancée from his mother. He's weak."

"He is *not* weak," I defended. "He didn't know . . ."

"But he suspected. Is that what he told you? I know he's spoken to you. I can read your face like a book."

I sighed as we reached the village and

he turned the lights down low on the car. "Yes, he told me everything."

"As he should if he is to start courting a new wife."

I glared at him. "How could you be so callous?"

"Because it's the truth, isn't it? He's kissed you, hasn't he?"

"No . . ."

"Word of advice. Don't lie. Your face is redder than Ewe's red roses."

Drat him. He was far too shrewd for my liking.

"What did he say? Your loverboy?"

"He is *not* my loverboy and I am far more interested in the mystery than men, thank you very much. How shallow do you think I am? If I wanted to protect him and his family, why would I have bothered to hand in the perfume puffer? The diary? The beads?"

"What beads? Did you find beads as well? What other evidence are you keeping from us?"

I realized then only Lianne, Ewe, and I knew about the beads. "'To V, Love MSR,' it said. I asked everyone if they know who MSR is but nobody seems to know."

"MSR," he repeated. "How about Mostyn Summerville Ridgeway, also known as Soames, Ridgeway Soames."

"Cousins . . . yes," I said. Now her words began to make sense. Her fear of Soames alluded to a greater connection than a soured love affair. She feared his jealousy, his need to avenge his pride or, perhaps, her reversal of their "plan." The plan for her to marry Lord David, give birth to an heir, and steal Padthaway . . . "Cousins . . . it explains how Victoria got the job, and the picture in the paper—the likeness between the younger Bastion boy and Soames . . . I was right."

The major was amused. "You should work for us. You have a great mind, if a little . . . imaginative. We've interviewed Soames many times. Victoria always promised to marry him, since they were children. They kept their relationship secret because of his affair with Lady Hartley."

"They can't have been lovers. She said she kept herself for Lord David in the diary."

"Yes, I know. I read that entry, too."

"What does Soames say?"

"He says they had a romance but it never

went beyond kissing. Victoria lost interest and both cousins wanted something better."

"You mean richer?"

"Exactly so. So one planned for Lady Hartley and the other—"

"Lord David," I whispered. "So Lady Hartley was correct—correct about Victoria. She was an adventuress. Yet her diary paints a very different picture."

"She may have had that original plan," the major concluded. "To marry a rich man, never expecting to fall in love with Lord David and that he would marry her. In saying as much, he wouldn't have married her without the baby."

"No, I don't think he would have either."

"Braving the mother's disapproval, Victoria knew she'd have to fight for her reputation. Everything was against her, unfortunately, and she made some unwise choices, choices that led to her death."

"What unwise choices? Do you mean the secret London visits? Whatever she was keeping from Lord David?"

He nodded. "One shouldn't keep secrets from one's fiancé. Not a good start to any marriage."

"I think someone was bribing her and she feared losing David over it—a man in her past, perhaps?"

He smiled. "I *do* think I'll recommend you for the service. She was very cautious in her London visits for I cannot track her beyond a hotel."

"Does 'Crow' or 'Crowleys' mean anything to you?"

"Crowleys? Yes, yes it does. It's a club, not a club for reputable ladies."

"Reputable," I murmured. "The last time I heard that word was from Bruce Cameron's lips at the wake. He said he saw Victoria at such a place. He must have meant Crowleys, too."

Amazed, he looked across at me. "Where did you hear of Crowleys?"

"From Connan Bastion," I said, proud.

"The devil . . ."

"Some people prefer talking to a woman. Perhaps I asked Connan the right questions."

"Perhaps I can learn a thing or two from you," the major conceded, and I left him feeling good.

A note arrived in the morning.
Ewe placed it under my door.
It was from the major.

Going to London today.
Meet me at the crossroads at
nine.

I glanced at the time. Eight-thirty. I had half an hour to dress and reach the gate.

Abandoning any thought of breakfast, I readied myself, Ewe watching me with oversized owl eyes.

"Sir Edward did it! He really took her and she went with them? I thought they'd have to drag her out."

Lady Hartley being dragged anywhere did not fit into the scope of the probable. "They'll hold her for questions until she confesses."

"She won't confess," Ewe huffed. "Ain't the evidence enough?"

"The only fingerprints on the bottle belong to Victoria."

"She were clever then. I bet Trehearn mixed it up."

"So do I," I said. "But they won't speak. It's the wall of silence."

"No point protecting her now. They've got her."

Relieved to have achieved the near impossible, leaving Ewe who talked and talked and followed me halfway up the lane, I waited at the crossroads and at a quarter past nine, Major Browning's motorcar came speeding to a halt. Climbing in, I said, "Ewe thinks Mrs. Trehearn prepared the poison."

"Good morning to you, too," the major laughed, perusing my dismal morning outfit. "No time to dress? When I made such an effort?"

He had, too, shining there, newly shaven and smelling of cologne, his hair perfect and attired in a smart silver gray suit.

"What? Too formal?"

"Are we going to dine with the Queen?" Groaning at my ordinary day pants and black sweater, I started to smooth back my hair.

"No point. The wind'll blow it."

He was right, curse him. The only saving grace I possessed was the foresight to have brought along a comb in my handbag. And an umbrella. I'd been caught too many times in the rain recently.

"Mrs. Trehearn is the strangest creature I have ever encountered," the major began, grinning at the passing countryside. "Oh, Cornwall. Beautiful, isn't it?"

"We could have caught the train."

"Too rattly and there's nothing better than a *long* drive when such enchanting company is to be had."

He smiled across at me and I suggested he watch the road. "Mrs. Trehearn?"

"I tried my hardest to wrest a smile from her. A frown, *anything,* but she has what I never thought I'd find. A genuine stone face."

"Therefore she'd make a perfect liar. If the poison can't be traced and you have no fingerprints, Lady Hartley's lawyers will dismiss it."

"Victoria's diary is our greatest weapon, along with the housemaids' testimony. They all knew Victoria received the perfume from Lady Hartley."

"What is Lady Hartley saying?"

"Nothing. She refuses to speak to us without the presence of her lawyer, who, I

457

understand, will be traveling down to Cornwall today from London as we are driving up."

I expected as much from Lady Hartley. "Why did she go so calmly last night?"

"There's a reason for it," the major replied elusively.

He refused to say more and, struggling to hold hair out of my mouth, I intercepted his little smirk. He loved to inspire defiance in me as much as he loved to drive fast, exhibiting his prowess at every bend and hill.

"You were very secretive about the diary, Daphne. Are you keeping abbey secrets from me, too? Or have you lost interest there?"

"The Victoria mystery is better. We have to find out who she met that day—the Wednesday she went to London—and if he's the same man she planned to meet the following week."

"The man of the diary?"

"'Saw him. Went better than expected.' What do you suppose that means?"

"I don't know," the major replied, "but we will soon find out."

Skillfully navigating through the city traffic, he turned down several streets before parking the motorcar at the base of an old gray building boasting long glazed windows, green shutters, and antique balconies.

"It's a place where many clandestine events transpire. No place for a lady like you," he said, getting out the car.

"No place for a true gentleman either, I suspect."

"I never said I was a gentleman," he replied.

The club existed on the fifth floor, up a flight of narrow, winding stairs so steep I wondered how the inhabitants managed to climb down after their indulgences. A red carpet guided the last flight, leading up to a pair of double wooden doors bearing great lion-head handles and a stern-faced guardian. "Not open till twelve . . ."

The major slipped him a card and the white-suited man stood aside.

"Welcome to Crowley's," the major invited. "Try the barman. My attempts have failed so it's up to you."

I entered the club to the sound of a record playing, an Italian operetta, the cleaners looking up at our unexpected approach.

Spying the barman sprucing crystal glasses, a wizened old man well acquainted with life and its foibles, I sat down on a bar stool, a timid, lost smile on my face. "Hello, I know you're not open yet, but I'm wondering if you can help me. A lady used to come here . . . a tall, beautiful girl, dark hair, violet eyes—"

"Victoria Bastion. The murdered girl."

The curt directness put me off guard. "Why, y-yes . . . I am a friend of hers . . . she used to meet somebody here and I need to contact him. It's very important."

The wily old fellow smirked, his keen gaze monitoring a whistling Major Browning's casual forage about the room. Recognition sparked and caution set in, reflected by sharpening eyes and a gruff sneer.

"Oh, please, sir." I tried my damsel in distress appeal. "It's urgent I find this man. I have something of Victoria's to give to him."

My act must have succeeded for his eyes softened a little.

"The fellow you're after usually comes here at three . . . for his whiskey. Want to wait?" He pointed to a curved lounge area.

"No, but we'll be back. Thank you so very

much." I patted his hand. "You're a very kind man."

"Well done." The major whistled once outside the door. "Your tactics do have their charm."

He was treating me as one would treat a partner. I liked the treatment, for it opened a new world for me, a world of research I could use in my writing.

"Have you thought of where to stay for the night yet?" Starting up the engine, he drove out of the building with a grin. "You can always stay with me."

"I'll stay with my family."

"What's your excuse for rushing to London for one night?"

"To collect my typewriter," I said. "My father bought me a new one."

He nodded, pleased. "Good. You can tell me what you plan to do with this typewriter on the way to lunch."

"Lunch!"

"Naturally, one has to eat."

CHAPTER THIRTY-SIX

The scarlet letters of Crowley's loomed before me.

Tucking a wisp of hair behind my ear, I paused on the landing and imagined Victoria's entrance to the infamous club.

Unlike my plodding arrival, I fancied I heard her quick, light step running up the stairs full of purpose and gaiety. On the landing, she stood still, her poise perfect, her figure a dream in her little red suit, a diamond-shaped feather hat and string of lavender beads gracing her beauty. Dancing off her wrist was a lady's purse, red and beaded, with a mirror and a tube of lipstick inside.

The doors to Crowley's swung open, the rigid-faced guardian charmed by her, all eyes drawn to this mysterious beauty traversing through the dimly lit private lounges. She drifted past the bar, bestowing a gracious smile to one admirer, and sailed toward the far back where a man waited under the shade of a greenish lamp.

I headed toward that lamp, alongside the major, toward a man of my father's age relaxing upon the armchair, his combed black hair splintered with gray, his facial structure of fantastic proportion, Roman almost, purple eyes dark, intense, changeable, eyes I'd seen before . . .

"Let me do this," the major hissed under his breath.

No formal greeting or introduction ensued. Commandeering the seat opposite the man, the major casually crossed his legs and ordered a drink. Opting for the end of the settee facing the two of them, I struggled to manage my nerves. Here was the man, the unknown tormentor Victoria feared.

Searching his face, I had my answer. "You're her real father, aren't you?"

The halting whisper left my lips before I could stop it.

I dared not look at Major Browning.

Robbed of his anonymity before he chose to publicize it, Victoria's father smiled, an elusive smile of wary caution. "How'd ye know?"

"The eyes . . . I found her on the beach."

"I thought Miss Hartley found her."

"We found her together," I explained, undaunted, ignoring any silent reprimand from the major. Despite his theory, I felt this was the way to proceed. Natural, open, unmilitary.

"And you're the girl from the papers— Miss du Maurier, isn't it? Allow me to introduce myself. Elias Wynne."

His accent sounded faintly Welsh but I wasn't sure.

"I follow everything Lord David does," Elias said as he winked at me, "ever since me daughter become engaged to the man."

I thought of Victoria's unrelenting search for her true father, her need to find him. Once she succeeded, how did she feel?

Elias chuckled, reinforcing the instinct of distrust creeping up my arm. A vulnerable Victoria, at last finding her father, wanting desperately to recapture the love and affection she'd missed throughout her life, now understanding why she always seemed merely tolerated at home. She must have opened her heart to the man sitting before me, and invited him to share her new life. Her new life with Lord David, as Lady Victoria Hartley, mistress of Padthaway.

Oh yes, it all became so clear to me. Elias's selfish gratification upon discovering he had a beautiful daughter, a gratification that transformed to opportunistic gloating when she announced her wedding plans, and his shock at her death, came into warped view.

"You're trying to blackmail Lord David now, aren't you, Elias? Just as you did your daughter."

Swilling his glass of whiskey, the major ordered another round of drinks.

"I fancied gettin' to know me daughter a bit. What's wrong with that? Besides, she wanted me round for *safety* reasons. Were plannin' to meet me here after her weddin'. Proves she were murdered."

I bristled at the horrific vision of this creature showing up at Padthaway, plundering through the house, demanding to see her ladyship and Lord David. Had Victoria seen Elias this way, as he truly was? I had to find out. "Mr. Wynne, did your daughter invite you to her wedding?"

Now the truth emerged. He couldn't hide the fact.

"No, she didn't, did she? She didn't want you in her life. And when the blackmail attempt failed upon your daughter's death, you decided to blackmail Lord David. Were you successful?"

"Were I successful?" he barked, laughing. "I'd say *more* than successful, for he paid a pretty penny for me to keep me mouth shut. For *I* know."

"What do you know, Elias?" The major refilled the man's beer.

"I know she were murdered, pure and simple. I seen it with me own eyes."

"Liar. You're too drunk to ever find your way to Padthaway."

He shrugged. "Maybe so, but I've got a letter. A letter from me Vicky. In it, she wrote it might be awhile till she can next see her dad and give him a bit of money. I didn't like that note so I, Elias the drunk, if ye please, gets on a train and goes down to Cornwall to see me girl, see me girl get wed, was me plan."

"When did you arrive?"

"On the night of her murder. For on me way to this grand place . . . it were late, I stopped by the pub first, got directions, then went along the sea to the place. Didn't expect to see me girl out there on the cliffs, did I?"

The major and I exchanged an incredulous glance. "You saw her? On the night? Did she see you?"

"Nope, she did not, for she had company."

I didn't like the way he said "company." "Do you mean a man?"

"I mean," his eyes narrowed, "her murderers."

"Murderers?" the major and I echoed, astonished.

"That's what I said and what I saw, me, Elias, with me own two eyes . . . *two* of 'em, yep, two. One, me future son-in-law."

"And the other person you saw was a girl, wasn't it, Elias? Did you see them kill her?"

The major asked the questions now, for I felt too ill to do so. I kept seeing David's face. No, I could not believe it.

"They must of, for she were dead on the beach the next day, weren't she?"

"If Victoria was in trouble, why didn't you go to help her? What happened, Elias?"

Elias now grew quiet, his reddened face betraying his embarrassment. "I tried to get to me Vicky. I tried. But I'd drunk too much beer and threw up. I must have passed out for I remember nothin' till the morning."

"Did you see Victoria dead?"

He nodded, his face grim. "I saw her shoes. And then I looked over . . ."

"And saw the dead body," the major finished. "Why did you scally away then, Elias? Why didn't you report it? I think I know why. You thought you'd turn Victoria's death to your advantage. You thought you'd blackmail Lord David instead and make more than a pretty penny. You gave yourself away before, Elias, when you mentioned he'd been paying you. Paying you to stay quiet! A *chief* witness in your own daughter's murder."

Elias didn't like the denunciation. "What

were I to do, then? She was dead so why not make a buck out of it?"

"Elias, you're going nowhere until you make a full statement, here and now. I hope at some stage of your life you regret your actions for they lack all common decency."

"The shoes are important," I said on the road back to Cornwall the next morning.

"Lord David is the next target," the major replied, "and I leave him to you, Miss Daphne du Maurier. If he trusts you, he'll confess to you."

I doubted his theory, as much as I doubted my own ability to face the family now, after hearing Elias's story.

I went, though; I had no choice as Lianne had called for me.

"Where'd you go?"

Fresh from her bath, Lianne tugged the robe of her dressing gown.

"You were gone *all* day. Ewe says you went to London."

"Yes, I went to get a typewriter."

"I can't believe you went to London without me!"

Sighing, I shook my head, and sat down on the bed. "I fear you're going to be very angry with me. I went with the major. He asked me to go . . . to see if we could discover any more about the man Victoria went to meet in her diary."

"So you didn't go to get a typewriter. You went off to find out who this person is. Well, did you succeed?"

I nodded.

"Who is it?"

"Victoria's father."

"Her father . . ."

The word sounded foreign on her lips. "Funny. I never thought Victoria had a father."

"He wasn't a nice one. He was blackmailing her. I have to speak with your brother."

"What do you need to speak to me about?" Lord David entered Lianne's bedchamber, carrying her ribbon in his hand. "I found this on the terrace."

"Oh, thank you! It's my *favorite* ribbon. Daphne's been busy, Davie. She went to London. Met Victoria's father."

"Did she?"

Lord David's eyes turned suddenly dangerous.

"Y-yes," I stammered. "Elias is a nasty person. Wouldn't surprise me if *he* murdered Victoria."

I hoped to allay the growing suspicion in his face, but it didn't work.

"There's a painting I want to show you, Daphne. Lianne, you stay here for the moment."

"All right." She smiled her merry smile, whistling, quite oblivious to my fear.

We reached the top of the stairs. Searching for any sight of Annie, Betsy, or even Mrs. Trehearn, I attempted to appear calm.

"This way," Lord David gestured down.

"Where are we going?" I said in a small voice.

He did not reply, and I prayed for Annie or Betsy to turn a corner and find me, to save me from this madman.

I soon found myself staring up at the *Beneficent Bride*.

"The lost bride," he murmured. "You have developed a very singular interest in what happened to my lost bride, haven't you, Daphne?"

I felt numb. The voice didn't sound like Lord David's. It sounded like a stranger's.

"Why did you not come to me with the diary?"

"You said your mother did it," I breathed, afraid to look into his eyes. "Has she confessed?"

"Confessed?" He laughed.

"Yes, for she went with Sir Edward willingly. I thought . . ."

"She has no need of confession, for *I* killed Victoria. Why else do you suppose she went to jail? To protect *me*."

I stopped to peruse his face. "You believed she was meeting a man in London, didn't you? A lover? You also thought she and Soames planned to plant a bastard on you. Is that why you chose to get rid of her by poison?"

A flicker of amusement crossed his face. "I am innately curious how you deduced all of this. What did Elias really say?"

"He was blackmailing you because he saw you and Lianne with Victoria on the cliffs that night. Which one of you did it? What happened? Lianne hid the shoes, didn't she? Victoria's shoes."

Heaving a deep sigh, one verging on

regret, he stared up at the painting. "I will finish the story I began in front of this painting. For you, Daphne, for you. I am a man and I will not allow my mother to suffer for a crime I committed."

"You followed Victoria to London a few times, didn't you? You watched her go into the club, thinking she met a lover there, the father of her child."

"Yes." Silently, he touched the face of the bride in the painting with his finger. "She was beautiful, like a doll. But I couldn't trust her. She had not told me about Soames, and I found out. Her necklace fell off one day—the clasp opened. She swore Soames and she had never been lovers but I didn't believe her."

"She was a virgin when she came to you. She said so herself in her diary."

"Was she," he whispered, a haunting pallor creeping into his face. "I couldn't tell; we'd drunk too much that first time."

"She *was* innocent," I maintained. "But she should have trusted you. She tried to handle everything herself—Soames, Connan, her father—but she only served to feed your doubts."

He nodded, a faint smile appearing on

his lips. "You do care for me, don't you, Daphne? You justify things for me."

"I can't justify murder, David. That's why you've written your confession, haven't you? To release your mother?"

He nodded again. "When I saw her sacrifice herself for me so willingly, I knew the truth would come out. Besides, I am tired of people bleeding me. Elias is only one. Death or jail for me is a release, a haven."

"What happened? You bought the poison or did Mrs. Trehearn mix it for you?"

"A friend of mine gave me the poison."

"Bruce Cameron?"

"We were at the club, drinking. I started talking and by the end of the night, the poison ended up in my pocket. I took it home. I saw the perfume bottle on her dresser and simply slipped it inside. That was after the argument when she taunted me about the baby. We made up before dinner though, and I went to her room to get the bottle, but it had disappeared . . ."

"You were too late. She'd sprayed herself with the poison, its lethal inhalation worsening through dinner."

"Yes."

"Then she fled to her room, not knowing the reason for her sickness, maybe thinking it had to do with the baby and emotional distress, and decided to go for a walk. She felt heated, maybe. She collected her shoes and walked out to the cliffs. Why did you follow her? You knew she was going to die, didn't you?"

"I was hoping to save her, but she ran so crazily. When I caught up to her she just stood there, her black hair blowing in the wind, and laughed at me. 'You poor fool, David,' she said. 'Can't you see I want to be alone?' She ordered me to go and stood on the edge of the cliff, peering over. 'Why do I feel so ill?' she kept saying, and I asked her if she'd used the perfume spray. She looked at me then, a queer kind of look. I saw the notion of poison occurring in her eyes and it surprised her so much she stumbled and fell. Fell straight down to the sea, and to this day I don't know if she meant to do it or whether it was an accident."

"She died thinking it was your mother who had poisoned her. Not you."

"That's why I won't allow my mother to suffer for the crime. If I were truly callous,

I'd leave her to her fate. Better she returns, though, and better I hang since I cannot escape my destiny."

"What destiny is that?"

"Madness. Just like my father. Go now, Daphne. Go now before I hurt you. Break the news to my mother . . . if you would."

"I will," I promised, and hastened out of the house.

CHAPTER THIRTY-SEVEN

"The house of death," Ewe chorused, long silent after the dramatic turn of events.

"I hear Lady Hartley has reinstalled herself supreme back at Padthaway," Miss Perony said. "I heard she fired Soames *and* Mrs. Trehearn."

"Wants a fresh start. Changes servants like linen," Ewe muttered.

"She will mourn the loss of her son," Miss Perony whispered. "I still can't believe Lord David could do that. Every time I saw him, he always appeared so charming and circumspect. Will he really hang for murder, Major?"

"It depends on the jury."

"I heard you delivered the news to Mrs. Bastion," Miss Perony went on.

I thought of the beads, the beads I'd dropped into Mrs. Bastion's lap. She thanked me when the major and I left, the major elaborate in his praise of my help during the case.

I did not return to the abbey. Upon hearing the news of Lord David's arrest, I had been summoned home, and coming home with this tale contented me more than discovering ancient scrolls.

The mood at Padthaway was of a house in mourning.

Lady Hartley, Jenny, Betsy, Annie, and Lianne commiserated in the courtyard. I imagined they had all stood outside to watch Lord David being taken away, never to return.

Lady Hartley was furious with me. She blamed me for the loss of her son.

"*You*. You did it all. When we did nothing but *befriend* you, you turned out to be a viper in the bosom."

In her grief, Lady Hartley had turned on everyone, hence Soames and Mrs. Trehearn's prompt dismissal.

I walked past Mrs. Trehearn's study on my way out, eager to catch a glimpse of the room where the strange woman had spent most of her days. To my disappointment, the room shone new and clean, but for the housekeeping journal left on the table. I knew I shouldn't have taken it, but curiosity overcame me.

"What have ye there?" Ewe spotted me when I returned to the cottage, book under my arm. "Get a lashin' from her ladyship?"

"Yes," I smiled, "and I've borrowed Mrs. Trehearn's housekeeping journal. I'm going to my room to read it."

Mrs. Trehearn's housekeeping journal I discovered to be a meticulous notation of household affairs, extending back twenty years, amazingly detailed. Records on everything from the price of eggs to new linen.

Flicking through the early dates, I stumbled upon one circled entry:

October 21 £300 Dr. Castlemaine, Penzance

This was a peculiar entry, for that was a great deal of money back then for a doctor's visit. Was the appointment for Mrs.

Trehearn or for some other staff member? It must be for some household affair or it wouldn't have been featured in this book.

The circle emphasized its importance. Other amounts weren't circled, only this one.

Penzance and Dr. Castlemaine . . . another country drive in order, Major Browning?

He thought I was mad.

"I might be," I sighed, "but I have two days left and what else am I to do? I can't rest now that I've got a taste for mystery."

He lifted an amused brow at the delivery of my logic. "I've learned to trust your instincts. I'll take you then. Are you ready now?"

Seeing me enter the car with the book on my lap, the major gave me a surreptitious glance. "So, what have you pinched there, Sherlock?"

"It's Mrs. Trehearn's housekeeping journal." Opening the book in my lap, I perused the entries. "Two pounds for sugar . . . six for meat . . ."

"Fascinating reading."

"It's this one—'October 21 £300 Dr. Castlemaine, Penzance.' Twenty-odd years ago."

"I fail to see the significance."

So intent in my further examination of the journal, I failed to hear him.

"Where do you think to find this Dr. Castlemaine?"

"I don't know." Listening to the putting engine, a sound I found oddly soothing, I prepared for the long journey. Pity I hadn't thought to bring coffee and biscuits. Alerted to hunger, my stomach rumbled in protest and mortified, I twisted my head away.

"Ah, hunger breeds irritability, and we can't have Sherlock's mind working bald. I suggest we make a stop at a charming seaside village."

A break sounded wonderful.

"If that suits you and your schedule, Sherlock."

I no longer bothered to roll my eyes at the Sherlock quips. He seemed determined to use it, it amused him, and one must amuse one's driver. I did, however, send him a sweet smile. "It suits me perfectly, *Thomas*."

To my chagrin, he grinned. "I like the way

'Thomas' sounds on your lips . . . want to take the wheel later?"

He did enjoy vexing me, didn't he?

"Unless, of course, you *can't* drive."

"I can so!"

"Excellent. I knew I was correct in that assumption."

I endured thirty more minutes of his assumptions regarding my character. By the time we reached the village, I was ravenous. Promising the best Cornish pasties and strong coffee, the major guided me inside the humble wayside inn, conveniently isolated, I noticed on arrival.

"Don't worry," he smirked. "If I planned a rakish abduction, I'd have chosen a better location to conduct the affair. I do have singular knowledge in that department, you know."

"I'm sure you do." While we waited for breakfast, served by a gracious, plump farmer's wife, I upbraided him for sending me into Padthaway alone. "I am lucky. Lord David could have killed me, too."

"That's unlikely." He refused to look even slightly remorseful. "Besides, you're a resourceful girl. You would have found a way to escape."

"You are no gentleman," I retorted.

The rain started two minutes after we climbed back into the car and arrived at the next crossroad.

"Cornwall," the major chuckled, "and its changeable weather."

Cornwall and its changeable weather. Padthaway, the house of a thousand mysteries, its changeable seasons.

"Dreaming up another story?"

"Just a headache. Are we nearly there yet?"

"Almost."

As we entered the thriving city, a bustling town once alive with pirates, thieves, and smugglers, the rain began to subside. The air outside the car was cool and I shivered.

Taking off the sweater under his jacket, the major wrapped it firmly around my shoulders and drew me into the nearest pub, where an open fire called my querulous, shaky limbs.

"You sit down. I'll make the inquiries," the major directed.

I smiled my thanks, attuned to the plethora of noise surrounding me.

"Aw, ye're in luck today, Mister. Mister

Brown, was it? Casper, I am, and used to live right above that fancy doctor. He had rooms—all private ones. I had to use the back steps."

"Do you remember the street name, Casper?"

"Aw, call me Casp. Me friends do and I'll take ye there if ye like. It's only a few blocks away."

Walking down seemingly endless lanes of slimy, treacherous cobbles, we arrived at the site of a building.

A demolished building.

Casper cursed. "I don't believe me eyes! It's gone . . ."

Detecting a black-caped man strolling across the street, the major left us to gape at the dirt mound.

"No joy there," he called back, betraying a little glumness. "Any ideas, Daphne? Casper?"

Wracking his half head of hair, Casper's foul breath exploded. "I know! Mrs. Tremayne! If ever a snoop. She knows everybody's business. Been here for centuries."

It was only a mild exaggeration. Mrs. Martine Tremayne lived across the street, at number fifty-nine. Sprightly for a seventy-two-year-old, and sharper than a thistle, the wizened eyes made a quick summary of our likely trio. Gripping her broom like a weapon, she listened to the reason for our call.

"Castlemaine, eh? Ye'd best come in . . . No, not you, Casper Polwarren. Get ye back to the pub."

Casper Polwarren, suddenly the proud owner of a five-pound note slipped to him by the major, was more than happy to comply.

Mrs. Tremayne's ground floor, mercifully, failed to exhibit that old smell. The other usual relics existed, several tiny tables, dusted lace curtains, photo frames, last decade's cushions, worn but well tended furniture.

Invited to sit down, she sped off to fetch a newspaper clipping of some sort. The major and I shared a look of amusement. Ewe Sinclaire had a soul mate.

"Here, read this."

Huddled together on Mrs. Tremayne's couch, we examined the black-and-white face of a European man, bald and slim, and the title below it.

DOCTOR EXPOSED

Since the burning down of his building, further details have emerged regarding the doctor's *secret* clients . . .

"He'd take them in," Mrs. Tremayne huffed. "Fancy types wantin' to get rid of their babes. They paid well, ye see. We plain folk with our sniveling noses don't even tinkle to the likes of him . . . snooty pig he were."

"Look here"—I showed the major—"they've printed his entire appointment book, listing all the names."

"That's why I kept the clippin'," a proud Mrs. Tremayne declared. "Ye don't throw away things like that. A copper found it on the street, half burn out it were, but still readable. He got greedy. Sold it to the papers and lost his job, but I'm sure he got a goodly sum for it."

I'm sure he did, too, recognizing one or two of the names. Some were skillful abbreviations or alterations to conceal identities, but the shrewd Dr. Castlemaine had noted the true names in a small column to the side, directly under the monetary amount.

Balking at the exorbitant sums, the major lifted a brow. "I am obviously in the wrong industry."

A lucrative clinic of scandalous proportions. "Whatever happened to the doctor?"

"Ha! Lost his mind, he did, and there were never a more fittin' punishment for the likes of him. Thinkin' himself so smart. You'll find him at Doreen's nursin' home up yonder, but it's really a nuthouse for droolin' nutters."

Drooling nutters. Smiling at the colloquial phrase, I ran my finger down the names and dates until a name flashed before me, a curious name. "Hearn!"

Hearn for Trehearn? I quickly looked to the side notation. *300 pounds, Jenny Pollock, took dead child.*

I must have half choked for the major thumped my back.

"Know her, do ye?" Mrs. Tremayne sniggered.

"Yes, she's a nurse in a household where I've stayed."

"Humph! She won't have been the first. Caught the eye of the lord, did she? Sent off here to squash the scandal?"

The clipping fell to my lap. Jenny Pollock, the pretty nursery maid with the children . . . Jenny and Lord Hartley. Like a diamond shower, everything sprinkled into place. I suddenly remembered her defense of him: *He weren't mad, or if he were, it was she that sent him that way.*

What had Lady Hartley said of their discreet arrangement? She had her affairs and her husband had his, extending among the household staff, as was often the case in large households. She must have turned a blind eye to it until Jenny became pregnant!

A pregnant nursery maid must have been a source of irritation to the lady of the house, especially if her husband loved Jenny. Was that a possibility?

"A simple carte blanche, of sorts," the major decreed, dismissing my theory. "The problem solved with the hasty removal of the goods."

I sent him a look of reproach.

"Well, it's true." He failed to display adequate repentance. "You can't have the illegitimate playing with the legitimate, can you?"

A good point, a point I found very disturbing. "We have to get back to Padthaway."

488

CHAPTER THIRTY-EIGHT

The long, winding drive to Padthaway, the silent mansion, filled me with a sense of dread.

Shaken of now another secret, a secret the house wished to reveal to me, I absorbed the warnings of the gusty wind, the naked branches strewn of their leaves, their skeletal fingers encroaching upon the drive.

Then a burst of beauty. Padthaway, gracing the grassland. *My* Padthaway, standing proud, ready to receive me.

"Do you want me to drop you here?" the major asked.

"Yes, I must talk to Jenny alone. You keep Lianne occupied."

He grinned. "A pleasant occupation . . . are you sure you can handle this?"

"Oh, please." I exited the car with a huff and hurried up to the house.

Going around the back way, I spotted Annie in the hallway and asked for Jenny's whereabouts.

"Oh, Miss D, she's in her garden last time I saw her."

"Thank you, Annie."

Watching her go, I thought it would take the servants a long time to grow used to the place without Lord David.

None more so than Jenny.

I feared her reaction.

Putting aside her garden spade, she wiped her hands on her apron. "Different now Trehearn's not here. Lady Muck's in- terviewin' butlers now. Got a new cook, too. Mrs. Lockley. We all like her."

"That's good," I said, drawing out one of her garden chairs. Heeding the major's warning, I acted normal on arrival, chatting, mentioning my recent drive with the major.

"Oh, where'd ye go?"

"Penzance."

She dropped the spade. "Oh, and what were ye reason for going there?"

She was nervous.

"Jenny, don't be afraid. I know about the baby, *your* baby. The one Dr. Castlemaine took from you."

Turning red at the name, she drifted to the chair opposite me.

"Please talk to me," I implored. "I'm your friend. I'm here to listen to you and *your side* of the story."

"Does the major know about it?"

I couldn't lie to her. "Yes, he does. I asked him if I could see you first."

She nodded, grimly accepting she now had to divulge the story she'd kept hidden for so many years.

"I were thirteen when I came to his house," she began, "young, full of silly dreams. I came to nurse little baby David." A fond smile tempered her lips. "What a sweet thing he were . . . he took to me and I to him. We were two little happy peas, livin' in our own world. Oh, I had to answer to the head nurse and all, but most of the time, me and baby David were alone. The mother didn't want 'im. She'd only poke her head in every now and then, hear the progress report, and go back to her parties. She never wanted to hold him."

"But the baby didn't suffer," I said softly. "You gave him plenty of love."

Her face softened. "Aye, I did. Me whole heart."

"I can see you both," I smiled, "little David, perfect, and you, Jenny, pretty Jenny with the golden hair and blue eyes. I can see why Lord Hartley fell in love with you."

Her eyes froze at the mention of his name.

"Tell me about him, Jenny. Did he treat you kindly?"

Silently walking further down that closed tunnel, she eventually responded. "He were a strange one, his lordship, but he loved visitin' the nursery. *He'd* pick up the child, nurse 'im, and the babe adored him. He were unhappy . . . unhappy with *her.* Outside, he were different, but in the nursery, he were meek as a lamb."

"He started to come more regularly," I proceeded, "you and he . . . in the secret garden . . . a happy little family."

A capricious smile touched her lips. "Aye, it were like that, I s'pose. A play family for him."

"But you didn't mind. You loved him and he was good to you."

She nodded. "Passionate lover he were, but gentle, ever so gentle. Never once did he lay a finger on me or speak nasty."

"But outside he behaved differently."

Forced to nod again, she succumbed to the beauty of her memories, the love, the kindness, the happiness.

"When did Lady Hartley find out, Jenny?"

Startled out of her trance, she shivered. "We hid it from her. Terry said we must be careful of her and we were . . . for years. Mrs. T and the head nurse, they knew. Went to Mrs. T for me herbs . . ."

"But then you fell pregnant, even *on* Mrs. T's herbs."

"Aye. When her ladyship carried Miss Lianne, I found out I were expectin', too, to me horror. After all these years . . ."

"How did Terry react?"

"*She* said he had to give me up. She'd not have his *bastard* in the house. But Terry didn't want to give me up. He started to go a little crazy. He always did when he were confused. He *hurt* people."

"But never you, Jenny. Never you."

A tear rolled down her face. "I never got

to say good-bye to him. They drove him to shoot himself. I just wish they'd let me say good-bye . . ."

"But they didn't. Just as they didn't let you keep your child. They packed you off to Penzance."

The horror of the locked memory opened with force. "I did it . . . to keep me job. And if it weren't for Lee Lee, bless her heart, *madam* would've sent me packin'. But she couldn't stomach the screamin' child. Nobody could. She were left to me . . . I calmed her. Only me."

Which explained her deep bond with Lianne. "What happened to your baby, Jenny? The baby you took from Dr. Castlemaine's?"

Crazed eyes greeted me again, followed by a curiously slow smile, ominous in nature, eerie, unlike the Jenny I knew. "I wanted to keep her. I tried to, but it were too late. *He* killed her and I took my little girl with me. I placed her in a safe place. . . ." Her gaze slowly turned to the herb garden.

I shuddered. "It must have been very hard. How you must have hated Mrs. T and Lady H for what they'd done to you . . .

you had David and Lianne, but you couldn't forget what they'd done, could you, Jenny?"

"No!" Flying out of her chair, Jenny's hands seized my neck. "Just as I can't forgive you for hurtin' my Davie boy. He'll die, die, die, because of you!"

Her crazed eyes obstructing my vision, I desperately tried to loosen her grip on my throat. I couldn't breathe . . . and felt nauseous, faint . . . dizzy . . .

Then relief. The major's strong arms enclosing me, Lianne restraining the frenzied Jenny.

"It's all right, Jenny," Lianne soothed. "Daphne did the right thing. You always told me to do the right thing, and it was Davie that gave himself up. You lost your baby, but you have me. *Your* Lee Lee, always."

Jenny nodded, and as I watched Lianne hold and rock her, I came to appreciate the close bond they shared and the full reason for Lianne's nightmares. Seeing her father shoot himself and die before her eyes, and later, to see David, the brother she adored, the brother she would do anything to protect, convicted of murder.

"Forgive me." Jenny gazed at me, getting

up, a little embarrassed over her behavior. "I don't usually . . ."

"I know." I pressed her hand.

She nodded and disappeared inside for a moment or two.

Upon her return, she dangled something before the major. "I s'pose I don't need to hide these now, do I?"

Clutched in her hand were the sandy bottoms of a pair of shoes.

Victoria's shoes.

CHAPTER THIRTY-NINE

"Jenny knew. Lianne had seen David do it. She had followed her brother out to the cliffs that night. Jenny protected them both by hiding the shoes in her room."

"A fitting end," Ewe declared. "I always knew one of 'em Hartleys did it. Just didn't know which one."

"We have Miss du Maurier to thank for Jenny and the clue of the shoes," the major said, tipping his hat to me. "Nobody would think twice about it, but our Miss Sleuth remembered the shoes . . . and that conversation on the cliff whilst picnicking with Jenny and Lianne."

"She's a bright lass." Ewe smiled at me fondly. "Even if she does scuttle off when she's supposed to stay with me!"

"And the other clues," I prompted the major. "Admit it, you and Sir Edward were lost. You needed me."

"We did."

It was a simple and genuine praise, without mocking, and I confess I felt rather proud, too.

LONDON HOUSE, *SOME MONTHS LATER*

The gloomy pathway beckoned. She paid no attention to its dilapidated state, neither seeing nor hearing the windstorm brewing around her. Such was her state of mind as she progressed toward her destination, knowing this was the last time—

"Daphne!"

Jostled out of my chair, I typed the last sentence. My finger still poised on the full stop, I ripped out the page and gleefully reviewed those last beaming words.

"Daphne! Are you ready? We're late."

Jeanne and Angela were groaning in the

498

hallway. Unconcerned with their panicky prompting, I dressed, taking one last look at the bleakness of the day outside. Hamstead in London failed to compare with my beloved Cornwall. I missed seeing the water, feeling the fresh sea air on my face. I missed the boats gracing the harbor and most of all, I missed those frightful days at Padthaway.

"You *cannot* wear that to a luncheon with Winston Churchill."

I smiled at Angela's deadpan face. "I certainly can and I will. In any case, nobody shall notice me."

"Doing the usual, are we? Sitting in a dark corner, taking notes about everybody."

"At least she does it *mentally* these days," Jeanne cried behind her, ever cheerful. "Here's your hat, Daph."

Our parents waited for us outside. Father, presenting his usual dashing image, and Mother, graceful, conscious of the time, and frowning over my hasty appearance.

"Daphne, dearest, you ought to take more care. I know there are no obscure Lord Davids to tempt you at political luncheons."

"You never know," Angela grinned, delighted at the thought of making new influential connections. "Perhaps your Major

Browning will show up. He seems to have friends in high places."

"Oh, I believe he's away at sea," my mother echoed, lowering her voice to a modest whisper, "and after that one call in Fowey, we never heard from him, did we, Daphne dearest?"

I wished she would stop preempting the major's lack of interest. That one call, a mere friendly follow-up one, obligatory after those horror-filled days at Padthaway, had spurred her to think of him as a possible future husband for me.

"Better watch out," Angela warned. "I might take an interest in the dashing major if you don't."

"The major's promised to take me sailing when he comes back," Jeanne piped in, full of faith.

"When he comes back?" my mother lamented. "When*ever* will that be?"

My father rolled his eyes. "You women, always ready to spear a man. Paint on a smile now because we're here."

The luncheon party commenced.

Spotting a willowy tree outside Sir Winston's mansion, I slipped the notebook out of my reticule. I had two letters to write.

One to Ewe, and one to Lianne. I'd not forget Lianne needed a friend now, especially as it appeared likely her brother would hang for murdering Victoria Bastion.

"Hello, old girl."

I smiled up to see J. M. Barrie usurp a seat beside me. "Are we in camouflage? I hope so. I simply can't abide political mumbo jumbo, can you?"

I watched him try to hide, albeit unsuccessfully, behind a palm leaf, and laughed. I loved Uncle Jack for his eccentricity and penchant for Brussels sprouts. I said I didn't spy any of his favorite vegetables on the table fare this day and he gave me a woebegone look. "Woebegone, dismal . . . I found a new word the other day, Uncle Jack. Lugubrious . . . for a gloomy, cheerless character, and I know exactly the person who fits it. Mrs. Trehearn, except I'll have to call her something else, won't I?"

"How about Danvers?" he reflected behind his palm branch, his fingers splaying across in horror. "Oh, hide me, there's the chancellor and he's after a signing. Trouble is, I can never get away. . . ."

So we camped out, the two of us, for a good hour or so until Father found us and roused us back to normal land. Mother was most put out, but, of course, she sent Uncle Jack a charming smile.

I was grateful to go home to Cornwall.

To the house at Ferryside, to my room overlooking the river, my writing desk, the boats in the harbor . . .

Putting aside Ewe's letter, where she recounted all of the local Windemere news, including Lianne doing well and taking up Jenny's love of monograms, I gazed out the window.

I thought of Padthaway. I thought of all the people, the faces, the long, winding drive up to the gracious mansion, a white-faced Mrs. Trehearn waiting at the door, the corridors leading to the west wing and that magnificent room, crazy old Ben snipping at his hedges in the garden . . . and an idea for a novel burned within me, deep and irrepressible.

I sat down to write.

A boat in the harbor drifted toward me, its name elusive but for the first letter.

A monogram . . . large, scrawling, distinctive.

A monogram . . . beginning with *R*.